THE BLOOD OF THE EARTH

High Lord Elena stooped to the EarthBlood. Covenant's cry did not penetrate her exultation. She took one steady sip and swallowed it.

At once, she leaped to her feet as if she were possessed. The fire of the Staff ran down the wood to her hands. Instantly, her whole form burst into flame. For one fierce moment she stood motionless, trapped in conflagration. Then she spoke as if uttering words of flame.

"Come! I have tasted EarthBlood. You must obey my will. The walls of death do not prevail. Son of Loric, come!"

No! howled Covenant. *Don't.* But even his inner cry was swamped by a great voice which shivered in the air so hugely that he seemed to hear it with the whole surface of his body.

"Fool!" Waves of anguish poured from the voice. "Desist!"

"An intricately crafted fantasy that presents a most unusual and memorable anti-hero in Thomas Covenant. But it is the spellbinding tapestry of the Land through which he journeys that will linger on in the reader's imagination long after the last page is turned. It will be turned all too quickly."

—Terry Brooks, author of
The Sword of Shannara

The Chronicles of Thomas

Covenant the Unbeliever

"The *War and Peace* of fantasy literature."
—*Kansas City Star*

"The books are filled with wondrous beings. There is a special warmth in Donaldson's feeling for the Land, and for the power and life inherent to it. Because his eye for detail is good and his feeling for the Land authentic, the Land is as real and substantial as the more prosaic ground we walk upon."
—*Chicago Tribune Book World*

"Here is classical fantasy with just enough of the modern to give it an added dimension. The background is carefully built, the writing has a sweep of grandeur, the imaginative factors display a depth that is seldom seen."
—Clifford D. Simak

"Stephen R. Donaldson meets the novelist's major challenge—fashioning a whole new fantasy world of his own to share with readers who esteem creative imagination."
—Robert Bloch

By Stephen R. Donaldson
Published by Ballantine Books:

THE CHRONICLES OF THOMAS COVENANT

Book One: Lord Foul's Bane

Book Two: The Illearth War

Book Three: The Power That Preserves

THE SECOND CHRONICLES OF THOMAS COVENANT

Book One: The Wounded Land

Book Two: The One Tree

The Chronicles of Thomas Covenant the Unbeliever

The Illearth War

STEPHEN R. DONALDSON

A Del Rey Book

BALLANTINE BOOKS • NEW YORK

A Del Rey Book
Published by Ballantine Books

Library of Congress Catalog Card Number: 77-8621

ISBN 0-345-31029-2

Published in hardcover by Holt, Rinehart and Winston

Manufactured in the United States of America

First Ballantine Books Edition: September 1978
Fourteenth Printing: February 1983

Cover art by Darrell K. Sweet

For James R. Donaldson, M.D.,
whose life expressed compassion and commitment
more eloquently than any words.

Contents

What Has Gone Before

THOMAS COVENANT is a happy and successful author until an unfelt infection leads to the amputation of two fingers. Then his doctor tells him he has leprosy. The disease is arrested at a leprosarium, but he returns home to find himself an outcast. His wife has divorced him and ignorant fear makes all his neighbors shun him. He becomes a lonely, bitter pariah.

In rebellion, he goes to town. There, just after he meets a strange beggar, he stumbles in front of a police car. Disorientation overcomes him. He revives in a strange world where the evil voice of Lord Foul gives him a mocking message of doom to the Lords of the Land. When Foul leaves, a young girl named Lena takes him to her home. There he is treated as a legendary hero, Berek Halfhand. He finds that his white gold wedding ring is a talisman of great power in the Land.

Lena treats him with a mud called hurtloam, which seems to cure his leprosy. The sensations of healing are more than he can handle, and losing control of himself, he rapes Lena. Despite this, her mother Atiaran agrees to guide him to Revelstone; his message is more important than her hatred of him. She tells him of the ancient war between the Old Lords and Foul, which resulted in millennia of desecration for the Land.

Covenant cannot accept the Land, where there is too much beauty and where stone and wood are subject to the power of magic. He becomes the Unbeliever, because he dares not relax the watchful discipline which a leper needs to survive. To him, the Land is an escape from reality by his injured and perhaps delirious mind.

At the Soulsease River, a friendly Giant takes Covenant by boat to Revelstone, where the Lords meet. There the Lords accept him as one of themselves, calling him the ur-Lord. But his message from Lord Foul dismays them. If Drool Rockworm— an evil Cavewight—holds the supremely powerful Staff of Law, their position is perilous indeed. They no longer have even the powers of the Old Lords, whom Foul overcame. Of Old Lord Kevin's Seven Wards of lore they have only the first, which they partly understand.

They determine to seek the Staff, held by Drool in caverns under Mount Thunder. Covenant goes with them as they flee through the attacks of Lord Foul's minions. They go south, to the Plains of Ra, where the Ramen serve the Ranyhyn, the great free horses. There the Ranyhyn bow to the power of Covenant's ring. As some recompense to Lena for what he did, he orders that one horse shall go to do her will each year.

Then the Lords ride to Mount Thunder. There, after many encounters with evil creatures and dark magic, they face Drool. High Lord Prothall wrests the Staff from Drool. They escape from the catacombs when Covenant manages to use the power of his ring —but without understanding how.

As the Lords escape, Covenant is beginning to fade away. He finds himself in a hospital bed a few hours after his accident. His leprosy has returned, suggesting it was all delusion. Yet he cannot quite accept any reality now. He is not seriously injured, however, and he is discharged from the hospital. He returns home.

This is a brief summary of *Lord Foul's Bane,* the first Chronicle of Thomas Covenant, the Unbeliever.

That beauty and truth should pass utterly

THE LAND

Outer Earth

North Plains

Grimmerdhore
Forest

Westron
Mountains

Revelstone

Guards
Gap

Trothgard

Maeri R.

White R.

Gray R.

Soulsease R.

Llurallln R.

Rill R.

Revelwood

Andelainian
Hills

Last Hills

Center Plains

Garroting Deep

Black River

Melenkurion
Skyweir

South Plains

Mithil R.

Kevin's
Watch

Rivenrock

Doom's
Retreat

Mithil
Stonedown

N

Cravenhaw

Doriendor
Corishev

Southron Wastes

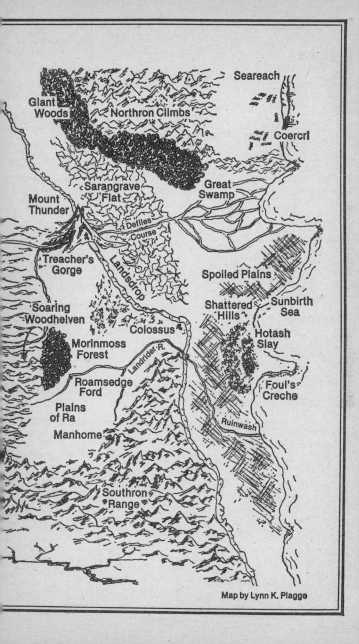

Map by Lynn K. Plagge

PART I

Revelstone

ONE: "The Dreams of Men"

BY the time Thomas Covenant reached his house the burden of what had happened to him had already become intolerable.

When he opened the door, he found himself once more in the charted neatness of his living room. Everything was just where he had left it—just as if nothing had happened, as if he had not spent the past four hours in a coma or in another world where his disease had been abrogated despite the fact that such a thing was impossible, impossible. His fingers and toes were numb and cold; their nerves were dead. That could never be changed. His living room—all his rooms—were organized and carpeted and padded so that he could at least try to feel safe from the hazard of bumps, cuts, burns, bruises which could damage him mortally because he was unable to feel them, know that they had happened. There, lying on the coffee table in front of the sofa, was the book he had been reading the previous day. He had been reading it while he was trying to make up his mind to risk a walk into town. It was still open to a page which had had an entirely different meaning to him just four hours ago. It said, ". . . modeling the incoherent and vertiginous matter of which dreams are composed was the most difficult task a man could undertake. . . ." And on another page it said, ". . . the dreams of men belong to God. . . ."

He could not bear it.

He was as weary as if the Quest for the Staff of Law had actually happened—as if he had just survived an ordeal in the catacombs and on the moun-

3

tainside, and had played his involuntary part in wresting the Staff from Lord Foul's mad servant. But it was suicide for him to believe that such things had happened, that such things could happen. They were impossible, like the nerve-health he had felt while the events had been transpiring around him or within him. His survival depended on his refusal to accept the impossible.

Because he was weary and had no other defense, he went to bed and slept like the dead, dreamless and alone.

Then for two weeks he shambled through his life from day to day in a kind of somnolence. He could not have said how often his phone rang, how often anonymous people called to threaten or berate or vilify him for having dared to walk into town. He wrapped blankness about himself like a bandage, and did nothing, thought nothing, recognized nothing. He forgot his medication, and neglected his VSE (his Visual Surveillance of Extremities—the discipline of constant self-inspection on which the doctors had taught him his life depended). He spent most of his time in bed. When he was not in bed, he was still essentially asleep. As he moved through his rooms, he repeatedly rubbed his fingers against table edges, doorframes, chair backs, fixtures, so that he had the appearance of trying to wipe something off his hands.

It was as if he had gone into hiding—emotional hibernation or panic. But the vulture wings of his personal dilemma beat the air in search of him ceaselessly. The phone calls became angrier and more frustrated; his mute irresponsiveness goaded the callers, denied them any effective release for their hostility. And deep in the core of his slumber something began to change. More and more often, he awoke with the dull conviction that he had dreamed something which he could not remember, did not dare remember.

After those two weeks, his situation suddenly reasserted its hold on him. He saw his dream for the first time. It was a small fire—a few flames without location or context, but somehow pure and absolute. As he gazed at them, they grew into a blaze, a conflagration. And he was feeding the fire with paper—the pages of his writings, both the published best-seller and the new novel he had been working on when his illness was discovered.

This was true; he had burned both works. After he had learned that he was a leper—after his wife, Joan, had divorced him and taken his young son, Roger, out of the state—after he had spent six months in the leprosarium—his books had seemed to him so blind and complacent, so destructive of himself, that he had burned them and given up writing.

But now, watching that fire in dreams, he felt for the first time the grief and outrage of seeing his handiwork destroyed. He jerked awake wide-eyed and sweating—and found that he could still hear the crackling hunger of the flames.

Joan's stables were on fire. He had not been to the place where she had formerly kept her horses for months, but he knew they contained nothing which could have started this blaze spontaneously. This was vandalism, revenge; this was what lay behind all those threatening phone calls.

The dry wood burned furiously, hurling itself up into the dark abyss of the night. And in it he saw Soaring Woodhelven in flames. He could smell in memory the smoldering dead of the tree village. He could feel himself killing Cavewights, incinerating them with an impossible power which seemed to rage out of the white gold of his wedding band.

Impossible!

He fled the fire, dashed back into his house and turned on the lights as if mere electric bulbs were his only shield against insanity and darkness.

Pacing there miserably around the safety of his living room, he remembered what had happened to him.

He had walked—leper outcast unclean!—into town from Haven Farm where he lived, to pay his phone bill, to pay it in person as an assertion of his common humanity against the hostility and revulsion and black charity of his fellow citizens. In the process, he had fallen down in front of a police car—

And had found himself in another world. A place which could not possibly exist, and to which he could not possibly have traveled if it did exist: a place where lepers recovered their health.

That place had called itself "the Land." And it had treated him like a hero because of his resemblance to Berek Halfhand, the legendary Lord-Fatherer—and because of his white gold ring. But he was not a hero. He had lost the last two fingers of his right hand, not in combat, but in surgery; they had been amputated because of the gangrene which had come with the onset of his disease. And the ring had been given to him by a woman who had divorced him because he was a leper. Nothing could have been less true than the Land's belief in him. And because he was in a false position, he had behaved with a subtle infidelity which now made him squirm.

Certainly none of those people had deserved his irrectitude. Not the Lords, the guardians of the health and beauty of the Land; not Saltheart Foamfollower, the Giant who had befriended him; not Atiaran Trellmate, who had guided him safely toward Revelstone, the mountain city where the Lords lived; and not, oh, not her daughter Lena, whom he had raped.

Lena! he cried involuntarily, beating his numb fingers against his sides as he paced. How could I do that to you?

But he knew how it had happened. The health which the Land gave him had taken him by surprise. After months of impotence and repressed fury, he had not been prepared for the sudden rush of his vitality. And that vitality had other consequences, as well. It had seduced him into a conditional cooperation with the Land, though he knew that what was happening to him was impossible, a dream. Because of that health, he had taken to the Lords at Revelstone a message of doom given to him by the Land's great enemy, Lord Foul the Despiser. And he had gone with the Lords on their Quest for the Staff of Law, Berek's rune staff which had been lost by High Lord Kevin, last of the Old Lords, in his battle against the Despiser. This weapon the new Lords considered to be

their only hope against their enemy; and he had unwillingly, faithlessly, helped them to regain it.

Then almost without transition he had found himself in a bed in the town's hospital. Only four hours
had passed since his accident with the police car. His
leprosy was unchanged. Because he appeared essentially uninjured, the doctor sent him back to his house
on Haven Farm.

And now he had been roused from somnolence, and
was pacing his lighted house as if it were an eyot of
sanity in a night of darkness and chaos. Delusion! He
had been deluded. The very idea of the Land sickened him. Health was impossible to lepers; that was
the law on which his life depended. Nerves do not
regenerate, and without a sense of touch there is no
defense against injury and infection and dismemberment and death—no defense except the exigent law
which he had learned in the leprosarium. The doctors
there had taught him that his illness was the definitive
fact of his existence, and that if he did not devote himself wholly, heart and mind and soul, to his own protection, he would ineluctably become crippled and
putrescent before his ugly end.

That law had a logic which now seemed more in-
fallible than ever. He had been seduced, however con-
ditionally, by a delusion; and the results were deadly.

For two weeks now he had completely lost his grasp
on survival, had not taken his medication, had not
performed one VSE or any other drill, had not even
shaved.

A dizzy nausea twisted in him. As he checked himself over, he was trembling uncontrollably.

But somehow he appeared to have escaped harm.
His flesh showed no scrapes, burns, contusions, none
of the fatal purple spots of resurgent leprosy.

Panting as if he had just survived an immersion in
horror, he set about trying to regain his hold on his
life.

Quickly, urgently, he took a large dose of his medication—DDS, diamino-dephenyl-sulfone. Then he
went into the white fluorescence of his bathroom,

stropped his old straight razor, and set the long sharp blade to his throat.

Shaving this way, with the blade clutched in the two fingers and thumb of his right hand, was a personal ritual which he had taught himself in order to discipline and mortify his unwieldy imagination. It steadied him almost in spite of himself. The danger of that keen metal so insecurely held helped him to concentrate, helped to rid him of false dreams and hopes, the alluring and suicidal progeny of his mind. The consequences of a slip were acid-etched in his brain. He could not ignore the law of his leprosy when he was so close to hurting himself, giving himself an injury which might reawaken the dormant rot of his nerves, cause infection and blindness, gnaw the flesh off his face until he was too loathsome to be beheld.

When he had shaved off two weeks of beard, he studied himself for a moment in the mirror. He saw a gray, gaunt man with leprosy riding the background of his eyes like a plague ship in a cold sea. And the sight gave him an explanation for his delusion. It was the doing of his subconscious mind—the blind despairwork or cowardice of a brain that had been bereft of everything which had formerly given it meaning. The revulsion of his fellow human beings taught him to be revolted at himself, and this self-despite had taken him over while he had been helpless after his accident with the police car. He knew its name: it was a death wish. It worked in him subconsciously because his conscious mind was so grimly devoted to survival, to avoiding the outcome of his illness.

But he was not helpless now. He was awake and afraid.

When morning finally came, he called his lawyer, Megan Roman—a woman who handled his contracts and financial business—and told her what had happened to Joan's stables.

He could hear her discomfort clearly through the connection. "What do you want me to do, Mr. Covenant?"

"Get the police to investigate. Find out who did it. Make sure it doesn't happen again."

She was silent for a long, uncomfortable moment. Then she said, "The police won't do it. You're in Sheriff Lytton's territory, and he won't do a thing for you. He's one of the people who thinks you should be run out of the county. He's been sheriff here a long time, and he gets pretty protective about 'his' county. He thinks you're a threat. Just between you and me, I don't think he has any more humanity than he absolutely needs to get reelected every two years."

She was talking rapidly as if to keep him from saying anything, offering to do anything. "But I think I can make him do something for you. If I threaten him —tell him you're going to come into town to press charges—I can make him make sure nothing like this happens again. He knows this county. You can bet he already knows who burned your stables."

Joan's stables, Covenant answered silently. I don't like horses.

"He can keep those people from doing anything else. And he'll do it—if I scare him right."

Covenant accepted this. He seemed to have no choice.

"Incidentally, some of the people around here have been trying to find some legal way to make you move. They're upset about that visit of yours. I've been telling them it's impossible—or at least more trouble than it's worth. So far, I think most of them believe me."

He hung up with a shudder. He gave himself a thorough VSE, checking his body from head to foot for danger signs. Then he went about the task of trying to recover all his self-protective habits.

For a week or so, he made progress. He paced through the charted neatness of his house like a robot curiously aware of the machinery inside him, searching despite the limited functions of his programming for one good answer to death. And when he left the house, walked out the driveway to pick up his groceries, or hiked for hours through the woods along Righters Creek in back of Haven Farm, he moved with an extreme caution, testing every rock and branch and breeze as if he suspected it of concealing malice.

But gradually he began to look about him, and as he did so some of his determination faltered. April was on the woods—the first signs of a spring which should have appeared beautiful to him. But at unexpected moments his sight seemed to go suddenly dim with sorrow as he remembered the spring of the Land. Compared to that, where the very health of the sap and buds was visible, palpable, discernible by touch and scent and sound, the woods he now walked looked sadly superficial. The trees and grass and hills had no savor, no depth of beauty. They could only remind him of Andelain and the taste of *aliantha*.

Then other memories began to disturb him. For several days, he could not get the woman who had died for him at the battle of Soaring Woodhelven out of his thoughts. He had never even known her name, never even asked her why she had devoted herself to him. She was like Atiaran and Foamfollower and Lena; she assumed that he had a right to such sacrifices.

Like Lena, about whom he could rarely bear to think, she made him ashamed; and with shame came anger—the old familiar leper's rage on which so much of his endurance depended. By hell! he fumed. They had no right. They had no right! But then the uselessness of his passion rebounded against him, and he was forced to recite to himself as if he were reading the catechism of his illness, Futility is the defining characteristic of life. Pain is the proof of existence. In the extremity of his moral solitude, he had no other answers.

At times like that, he found bitter consolation in psychological studies where a subject was sealed off from all sensory input, made blind, deaf, silent, and immobile, and as a result began to experience the most horrendous hallucinations. If conscious normal men and women could be placed so much at the mercy of their own inner chaos, surely one abject leper in a coma could have a dream that was worse than chaos —a dream specifically self-designed to drive him mad. At least what had happened to him did not altogether surpass comprehension.

Thus in one way or another he survived the days for nearly three weeks after the fire. At times he was almost aware that the unresolved stress within him was building toward a crisis; but repeatedly he repressed the knowledge, drove the idea down with anger. He did not believe he could endure another ordeal; he had handled the first one so badly.

But even the concentrated vitriol of his anger was not potent enough to protect him indefinitely. One Thursday morning, when he faced himself in the mirror to shave, the crisis abruptly surged up in him, and his hand began to shake so severely that he had to drop the razor in the sink in order to avoid cutting his jugular.

Events in the Land were not complete. By regaining the Staff of Law, the Lords had done exactly what Lord Foul wanted them to do. That was just the first step in Foul's plotting—machinations which had begun when he had summoned Covenant's white gold ring to the Land. He would not be done until he had gained the power of life and death over that entire Earth. And to do that, Foul needed the wild magic of the white gold.

Covenant stared desperately at himself in the mirror, trying to retain a grip on his own actuality. But he saw nothing in his own eyes capable of defending him.

He had been deluded once.

It could happen again.

Again? he cried, in a voice so forlorn that it sounded like the wail of an abandoned child. Again? He could not master what had happened to him in his first delusion; how could he so much as live through a second?

He was on the verge of calling the doctors at the leprosarium—calling them to beg!—when he recovered some of his leper's intransigence. He would not have survived this long if he had not possessed some kind of fundamental capacity to refuse defeat if not despair, and that capacity stopped him now. What could I tell them that they would believe? he rasped. I don't believe it myself.

The people of the Land had called him the Unbeliever. Now he found that he would have to earn
that title whether the Land actually existed or not.

And for the next two days he strove to earn it with
a grimness which was as close as he could come to
courage. He only made one compromise: since his
hands shook so badly, he shaved with an electric razor, pushing it roughly at his face as if he were trying
to remold his features. Beyond that, he acknowledged
nothing. At night, his heart quivered so tangibly in his
chest that he could not sleep; but he clenched his teeth
and did without sleep. Between himself and delusion
he placed a wall of DDS and VSEs; and whenever
delusion threatened to breach his defense, he drove it
back with curses.

But Saturday morning came, and still he could not
silence the dread which made his hands shake.

Then at last he decided to risk going among his
fellow human beings once more. He needed their actuality, their affirmation of the reality he understood,
even their revulsion toward his illness. He knew of no
other antidote to delusion; he could no longer face his
dilemma alone.

TWO: Halfhand

BUT that decision itself was full of fear, and he
did not act on it until evening. He spent most of the
day cleaning his house as if he did not expect to return to it. Then, late in the afternoon, he shaved with
the electric razor and showered meticulously. For the
sake of prudence, he put on a tough pair of jeans, and
laced his feet into heavy boots; but over his T-shirt
he wore a dress shirt, tie, and sports coat, so that the

informality of his jeans and boots would not be held against him. His wallet—generally so useless to him that he did not carry it—he placed in his coat pocket. And into a pocket of his trousers he stuffed a small, sharp penknife—a knife which he habitually took with him in case he lost control of his defensive concentration, and needed something dangerous to help him refocus himself. Finally, as the sun was setting, he walked down his long driveway to the road, where he extended his thumb to hitch a ride away from town.

The next place down the road was ten miles from Haven Farm, and it was bigger than the town where he had had his accident. He headed for it because he was less likely to be recognized there. But his first problem was to find a safe ride. If any of the local motorists spotted him, he was in trouble from the beginning.

In the first few minutes, three cars went by without stopping. The occupants stared at him in passing as if he were some kind of minor freak, but none of the drivers slowed down. Then, as the last sunlight faded into dusk, a large truck came toward him. He waved his thumb, and the truck rode to a halt just past him on the loud hissing of air brakes. He climbed up to the door, and was gestured into the cab by the driver.

The man was chewing over a black stubby cigar, and the air in the cab was thick with smoke. But through the dull haze, Covenant could see that he was big and burly, with a distended paunch, and one heavy arm that moved over the steering wheel like a piston, turning the truck easily. He had only that one arm; his right sleeve was empty, and pinned to his shoulder. Covenant understood dismemberment, and he felt a pang of sympathy for the driver.

"Where to, buddy?" the big man asked comfortably.

Covenant told him.

"No problem," he responded to a tentative inflection in Covenant's tone. "I'm going right through there." As the automatic transmission whined upward through its gears, he spat his cigar out the window, then let go of the wheel to unwrap and light a new smoke. While his hand was busy, he braced the wheel with his belly. The green light of the instrument panel

did not reach his face, but the glow of the cigar coal
illuminated massive features whenever he inhaled. In
the surging red, his face looked like a pile of boulders.

With his new smoke going, he rested his arm on the
wheel like a sphinx, and abruptly began talking. He
had something on his mind.

"You live around here?"

Covenant said noncommittally, "Yes."

"How long? You know the people?"

"After a fashion."

"You know this leper—this Thomas something-or-
other—Thomas Covenant?"

Covenant flinched in the gloom of the cab. To disguise his distress, he shifted his position on the seat.
Awkwardly, he asked, "What's your interest?"

"Me? I got no interest. Just passing through—haul-
ing my ass where they give me a load to go. I never
even been around here before. But where I et at back
in town I heard talk about this guy. So I ask the
broad at the counter, and she damn near yaks my ear
off. One question—and I get instant mouth with everything I eat. You know what a leper is?"

Covenant squirmed. "After a fashion."

"Well, it's a mess, let me tell you. My old lady reads
about this stuff all the time in the Bible. Dirty beggars.
Unclean. I didn't know there was creeps like that in
America. But that's what we're coming to. You know
what I think?"

"What do you think?" Covenant asked dimly.

"I think them lepers ought to leave decent folks
alone. Like that broad at the counter. She's okay,
even with that motor mouth, but there she is, juiced
to the gills on account of some sick bastard. That
Covenant guy ought to stop thinking of hisself. Other
folks don't need that aggravation. He ought to go
away with every other leper and stick to hisself, leave
decent folks alone. It's just selfishness, expecting ordinary guys like you and me to put up with that. You
know what I mean?"

The cigar smoke in the cab was as thick as in-
cense, and it made Covenant feel light-headed. He
kept shifting his weight, as if the falseness of his po-

sition gave him an uncomfortable seat. But the talk and his vague vertigo made him feel vengeful. For a moment, he forgot his sympathy. He turned his wedding ring forcefully around his finger. As they neared the city limits, he said, "I'm going to a nightclub— just up the road here. How about joining me for a drink?"

Without hesitation, the trucker said, "Buddy, you're on. I never pass up a free drink."

But they were still several stoplights from the club. To fill the silence, and satisfy his curiosity, Covenant asked the driver what had happened to his arm.

"Lost it in the war." He brought the truck to a stop at a light while adjusting his cigar in his lips and steering with his paunch. "We was on patrol, and walked right into one of them antipersonnel mines. Blew the squad to hell. I had to crawl back to camp. Took me two days—I sort of got unhinged, you know what I mean? Didn't always know what I was doing. Time I got to the doc, it was too late to save the arm.

"What the hell, I don't need it. Least my old lady says I don't—and she ought to know by now." He chuckled. "Don't need no two arms for that."

Ingenuously, Covenant asked, "Did you have any trouble getting a license to drive this rig?"

"You kidding? I can handle this baby better with my gut than you can with four arms and sober." He grinned around his cigar, relishing his own humor.

The man's geniality touched Covenant. Already he regretted his duplicity. But shame always made him angry, stubborn—a leper's conditioned reflex. When the truck was parked behind the nightclub, he pushed open the door of the cab and jumped to the ground as if he were in a hurry to get away from his companion.

Riding in the darkness, he had forgotten how far off the ground he was. An instant of vertigo caught him. He landed awkwardly, almost fell. His feet felt nothing, but the jolt gave an added throb to the ache of his ankles.

Over his moment of dizziness, he heard the driver

say, "You know, I figured you got a head start on the booze."

To avoid meeting the man's stony, speculative stare, Covenant went ahead of him around toward the front of the nightclub.

As he rounded the corner, Covenant nearly collided with a battered old man wearing dark glasses. The old man stood with his back to the building, extending a bruised tin cup toward the passersby, and following their movements with his ears. He held his head high, but it trembled slightly on his thin neck; and he was singing "Blessed Assurance" as if it were a dirge. Under one arm he carried a white-tipped cane. When Covenant veered away from him, he waved his cup vaguely in that direction.

Covenant was leery of beggars. He remembered the tattered fanatic who had accosted him like an introduction or preparation just before the onset of his delusion. The memory made him alert to a sudden tension in the night. He stepped close to the blind man and peered into his face.

The beggar's song did not change inflection, but he turned an ear toward Covenant, and poked his cup at Covenant's chest.

The truck driver stopped behind Covenant. "Hell," he growled, "they're swarming. It's like a disease. Come on. You promised me a drink."

In the light of the streetlamp, Covenant could see that this was not that other beggar, the fanatic. But still the man's blindness affected him. His sympathy for the maimed rushed up in him. Pulling his wallet out of his jacket, he took twenty dollars and stuffed them in the tin cup.

"Twenty bucks!" ejaculated the driver. "Are you simple, or what? You don't need no drink, buddy. You need a keeper."

Without a break in his song, the blind man put out a gnarled hand, crumpled the bills, and hid them away somewhere in his rags. Then he turned and went tapping dispassionately away down the sidewalk, secure in the private mysticism of the blind—singing as he moved about "a foretaste of glory divine."

Covenant watched his back fade into the night, then swung around toward his companion. The driver was a head taller than Covenant, and carried his bulk solidly on thick legs. His cigar gleamed like one of Drool Rockworm's eyes.

Drool, Covenant remembered, Lord Foul's mad, Cavewightish servant or pawn. Drool had found the Staff of Law, and had been destroyed by it or because of it. His death had released Covenant from the Land.

Covenant poked a numb finger at the trucker's chest, trying vainly to touch him, taste his actuality. "Listen," he said, "I'm serious about that drink. But I should tell you"—he swallowed, then forced himself to say it—"I'm Thomas Covenant. That leper."

The driver snorted around his cigar. "Sure, buddy. And I'm Jesus Christ. If you blew your wad, say so. But don't give me that leper crap. You're just simple, is all."

Covenant scowled up at the man for a moment longer. Then he said resolutely, "Well, in any case, I'm not broke. Not yet. Come on."

Together, they went on to the entrance of the nightclub. It was called The Door. In keeping with its name, the place had a wide iron gate like a portal into Hades. The gate was lit in a sick green, but spotlighted whitely at its center was a large poster which bore the words:

Positively the last night
America's newest singing sensation
SUSIE THURSTON

Included was a photograph which tried to make Susie Thurston look alluring. But the flashy gloss of the print had aged to an ambiguous gray.

Covenant gave himself a perfunctory VSE, adjured his courage, and walked into the nightclub, holding his breath as if he were entering the first circle of hell.

Inside, the club was crowded; Susie Thurston's farewell performance was well attended. Covenant and his companion took the only seats they could find—at a small table near the stage. The table was already occupied by a middle-aged man in a tired suit. Something about the way he held his glass suggested that he had been drinking for some time. When Covenant asked to join him, he did not appear to notice. He stared in the direction of the stage with round eyes, looking as solemn as a bird.

The driver discounted him with a brusque gesture. He turned a chair around, and straddled it as if bracing the burden of his belly against the chair back. Covenant took the remaining seat and tucked himself close to the table, to reduce the risk of being struck by anyone passing between the tables.

The unaccustomed press of people afflicted him with anxiety. He sat still, huddling into himself. A fear of exposure beat on his pulse, and he gripped himself hard, breathing deeply as if resisting an attack of vertigo; surrounded by people who took no notice of him, he felt vulnerable. He was taking too big a chance. But they were people, superficially like himself. He repulsed the urge to flee. Gradually, he realized that his companion was waiting for him to order.

Feeling vaguely ill and defenseless, he raised his arm and attracted the waiter's attention. The driver ordered a double Scotch on the rocks. Apprehension momentarily paralyzed Covenant's voice, but then he forced himself to request a gin and tonic. He regretted the order at once; gin and tonic had been Joan's drink. But he did not change it. He could hardly help sighing with relief when the waiter moved away.

Through the clutch of his tension, he felt that the order came with almost miraculous promptitude. Swirling around the table, the waiter deposited three drinks, including a glass of something that looked like raw alcohol for the middle-aged man. Raising his glass, the driver downed half his drink, grimaced, and muttered, "Sugar water." The solemn man poured his alcohol past his jumping Adam's apple in one movement.

A part of Covenant's mind wondered if he were going to end up paying for all three of them.

Reluctantly, he tasted his gin and tonic, and almost gagged in sudden anger. The lime in the drink reminded him intensely of *aliantha*. Pathetic! he snarled at himself. For punishment, he drank off the rest of the gin, and signaled to the waiter for more. Abruptly he determined to get drunk.

When the second round came, the waiter again brought three drinks. Covenant looked stiffly at his companions. Then the three of them drank as if they had tacitly engaged each other in a contest.

Wiping his mouth with the back of his hand, the driver leaned forward and said, "Buddy, I got to warn you. It's your dough. I can drink you under the table."

To give the third man an opening, Covenant replied, "I think our friend here is going to last longer than both of us."

"What, a little guy like him?" There was humor in the trucker's tone, an offer of comradeship. "No way. No way at all."

But the solemn man did not recognize the driver's existence with even a flick of his eyes. He kept staring into the stage as if it were an abyss.

For a while, his gloom presided over the table. Covenant ordered again, and a few minutes later the waiter brought out a third round—three more drinks. This time, the trucker stopped him. In a jocose way as if he were assuming responsibility for Covenant, he jerked his thumb at the middle-aged man and said, "I hope you know we ain't payin' for *him*."

"Sure." The waiter was bored. "He has a standing order. Pays in advance." Disdain seemed to tighten his face, pulling it together like the closing of a fist around his nose. "Comes here every night just to watch her and drink himself blind." Then someone else signaled to him, and he was gone.

For a moment, the third man said nothing. Slowly, the houselights went down, and an expectant hush dropped like a shroud over the packed club. Then into the silence the man croaked quietly, "My wife."

A spotlight centered on the stage, and the club MC came out of the wings. Behind him, musicians took their places—a small combo, casually dressed.

The MC flashed out a smile, started his spiel. "It makes me personally sad to introduce our little lady tonight, because this is the last time she'll be with us—

for a while, at least. She's going on from here to the
places where famous people get famouser. We at The
Door won't soon forget her. Remember, you heard her
here first. Ladies and gentlemen, Miss Susie Thurston!"

The spotlight picked up the singer as she came out,
carrying a hand microphone. She wore a leather outfit
—a skirt that left most of her legs bare and a sleeveless
vest with a fringe across her breasts, emphasizing their
movement. Her blond hair was bobbed short, and her
eyes were dark, surrounded by deep hollow circles like
bruises. She had a full and welcoming figure, but her
face denied it; she wore the look of an abandoned
waif. In a pure, frail voice that would have been good
for supplication, she sang a set of love ballads defiantly, as if they were protest songs. The applause
after each number was thunderous, and Covenant
quaked at the sound. When the set was over and Susie
Thurston retired for a break, he was sweating coldly.

The gin seemed to be having no effect on him. But
he needed some kind of help. With an aspect of desperation, he signaled for another round. To his relief,
the waiter brought the drinks soon.

After he had downed his Scotch, the driver hunched
forward purposefully, and said, "I think I got this bastard figured out."

The solemn man was oblivious to his tablemates.
Painfully, he croaked again, "My wife."

Covenant wanted to keep the driver from talking
about the third man so openly, but before he could
distract him, his guest went on, "He's doing it out of
spite, that's what."

"Spite?" echoed Covenant helplessly. He missed the
connection. As far as he could tell, their companion—
no doubt happily or at least doggedly married, no
doubt childless—had somehow conceived a hopeless
passion for the waif-woman behind the microphone
Such things happened. Torn between his now-grim
fidelity and his obdurate need, he could do nothing but
torment himself in search of release, drink himself into
stupefaction staring at the thing he wanted and both
could not and should not have.

With such ideas about their tablemate, Covenant

was left momentarily at sea by the driver's comment. But the big man went on almost at once. "Course. What'd you think, being a leper is fun? He's thinking he'll just sort of share it around. Why be the only one, you know what I mean? That's what this bastard thinks. Take my word, buddy. I got him figured out." As he spoke, his cobbled face loomed before Covenant like a pile of thetic rubble. "What he does, he goes around where he ain't known, and he hides it, like, so nobody knows he's sick. That way he spreads it; nobody knows so they don't take care, and all of a sudden we got us an epidemic. Which makes Covenant laugh hisself crazy. Spite, like I tell you. You take my word. Don't go shaking hands when you don't know the guy you're shaking with."

Dully, the third man groaned, "My wife."

Gripping his wedding band as if it had the power to protect him, Covenant said intently, "Maybe that isn't it. Maybe he just needs people. Do you ever get lonely —driving that rig all alone, hour after hour? Maybe this Thomas Covenant just can't stand to go on living without seeing other faces once in a while. Did you think about that?"

"So let him stick to lepers. What call is he got to bother decent folks? Use your head."

Use my head? Covenant almost shouted. Hellfire! What do you think I'm doing? Do you think I like doing this, being here? A grimace that he could not control clutched his face, Fuming, he waved for more drinks. The alcohol seemed to be working in reverse, tightening his tension rather than loosening it. But he was too angry to know whether or not he was getting drunk. The air swarmed with the noise of The Door's patrons. He was conscious of the people behind him as if they lurked there like ur-viles.

When the drinks came, he leaned forward to refute the driver's arguments. But he was stopped by the dimming of the lights for Susie Thurston's second set.

Bleakly, their tablemate groaned, "My wife." His voice was starting to blur around the edges; whatever he was drinking was finally affecting him.

In the moment of darkness before the MC came on,

the driver responded, "You mean that broad's your wife?"

At that, the man moaned as though in anguish.

After a quick introduction, Susie Thurston reseated herself within the spotlight. Over a querulous accompaniment from her combo, she put some sting into her voice, and sang about the infidelities of men. After two numbers, there were slow tears running from the dark wounds of her eyes.

The sound of her angry laments made Covenant's throat hurt. He regretted fiercely that he was not drunk. He would have liked to forget people and vulnerability and stubborn survival—forget and weep.

But her next song burned him. With her head back so that her white throat gleamed in the light, she sang a song that ended,

> Let go my heart—
> Your love makes me look small to myself.
> Now, I don't want to give you any hurt,
> But what I feel is part of myself:
> What you want turns what I've got to dirt—
> So let go of my heart.

Applause leaped on the heels of her last note, as if the audience were perversely hungry for her pain. Covenant could not endure any more. Buffeted by the noise, he threw dollars—did not count them—on the table, and shoved back his chair to escape.

But when he moved around the table, he passed within five feet of the singer. Suddenly she saw him. Spreading her arms, she exclaimed joyfully, "Berek!"

Covenant froze, stunned and terrified. No!

Susie Thurston was transported. "Hey!" she called, waving her arms to silence the applause, "Get a spot out here! On him! Berek! Berek, honey!"

From over the stage, a hot white light spiked down at Covenant. Impaled in the glare, he turned to face the singer, blinking rapidly and aching with fear and rage.

No!

"Ladies and gentlemen, kind people, I want you to

meet an old friend of mine, a dear man." Susie Thurston was excited and eager. "He taught me half the songs I know. Folks, this is Berek." She began clapping for him as she said, "Maybe he'll sing for us." Good-naturedly, the audience joined her applause.

Covenant's hands limped about him, searching for support. In spite of his efforts to control himself, he stared at his betrayer with a face full of pain. The applause reverberated in his ears, made him dizzy.

No!

For a long moment, he cowered under Susie Thurston's look. Then, like a wash of revelation, all the houselights came on. Over the bewildered murmurs and rustlings of the audience, a commanding voice snapped, "Covenant."

Covenant spun as if to ward off an attack. In the doorway, he saw two men. They both wore black hats and khaki uniforms, pistols in black holsters, silver badges; but one of them towered over the other. Sheriff Lytton. He stood with his fists on his hips. As Covenant gaped at him, he beckoned with two fingers. "You, Covenant. Come here."

"Covenant?" the trucker yelped. "You're really Covenant?"

Covenant heeled around awkwardly, as if under tattered canvas, to meet this fresh assault. As he focused his eyes on the driver, he saw that the big man's face was flushed with vehemence. He met the red glare as bravely as he could. "I told you I was."

"Now I'm going to get it!" the driver grated. "We're all going to get it! What the hell's the matter with you?"

The patrons of The Door were thrusting to their feet to watch what was happening. Over their heads, the sheriff shouted, "Don't touch him!" and began wading through the crowd.

Covenant lost his balance in the confusion. He tripped, caught something like a thumb or the corner of a chair in his eye, and sprawled under a table.

People yelled and milled around. The sheriff roared orders through the din. Then with one heave of his arm, he knocked away the table over Covenant.

Covenant looked gauntly up from the floor. His bruised eye watered thickly, distorting everything over him. With the back of his hand, he pushed away the tears. Blinking and concentrating fiercely, he made out two men standing above him—the sheriff and his former tablemate.

Swaying slightly on locked knees, the solemn man looked dispassionately down at Covenant. In a smudged and expended voice, he delivered his verdict. "My wife is the finest woman in the world."

The sheriff pushed the man away, then bent over Covenant, brandishing a face full of teeth. "That's enough. I'm just looking for something to charge you with, so don't give me any trouble. You hear me? Get up."

Covenant felt too weak to move, and he could not see clearly. But he did not want the kind of help the sheriff might give him. He rolled over and pushed himself up from the floor.

He reached his feet, listing badly to one side; but the sheriff made no move to support him. He braced himself on the back of a chair, and looked defiantly around the hushed spectators. At last, the gin seemed to be affecting him. He pulled himself erect, adjusted his tie with a show of dignity.

"Get going," the sheriff commanded from his superior height.

But for one more moment Covenant did not move. Though he could not be sure of anything he saw, he stood where he was and gave himself a VSE.

"Get going," Lytton repeated evenly.

"Don't touch me." When his VSE was done, Covenant turned and stalked grayly out of the nightclub.

Out in the cool April night, he breathed deeply, steadying himself. The sheriff and his deputy herded him toward a squad car. Its red warning lights flashed balefully. When he was locked into the back seat behind the protective steel grating, the two officers climbed into the front. While the deputy drove away in the direction of Haven Farm, the sheriff spoke through the grating.

"Took us too long to find you, Covenant. The

Millers reported you were trying to hitch a ride, and we figured you were going to try your tricks somewhere. Just couldn't tell where. But it's still my county, and you're walking trouble. There's no law against you—I can't arrest you for what you've done. But it sure was mean. Listen, you. Taking care of this county is my business, and don't you forget it. I don't want to hunt around like this for you. You pull this stunt again, and I'll throw you in the can for disturbing the peace, disorderly conduct, and everything else I can think of. You got that?"

Shame and rage struggled in Covenant, but he could find no way to let them out. He wanted to yell through the grate, It isn't catching! It's not my fault! But his throat was too constricted; he could not release the wail. At last, he could only mumble, "Let me out. I'll walk."

Sheriff Lytton regarded him closely, then said to the deputy, "All right. We'll let him walk. Maybe he'll have an accident." Already they were well out of town.

The deputy drove to a halt on the berm, and the sheriff let Covenant out. For a moment, they stood together in the night. The sheriff glared at him as if trying to measure his capacity to do harm. Then Lytton said, "Go home. Stay home." He got back into the car. It made a loud squealing turn and fled back toward town. An instant later, Covenant sprang into the road and cried after the taillights, "Leper outcast unclean!" They looked as red as blood in the darkness.

His shout did not seem to dent the silence. Before long, he turned back toward Haven Farm, feeling as small as if the few stars in the dense black sky were deriding him. He had ten miles to walk.

The road was deserted. He moved in empty stillness like a hiatus in his surroundings; though he was retreating into open countryside, he could hear no sounds, no night talk of birds or insects. The silence made him feel deaf and alone, vulnerable to the hurrying vultures at his back.

It was a delusion! He raised his protest like a defiance; but even to his ears, it had the hollow ring of despair, composed equally of defeat and stubbornness. Through it, he could hear the girl shouting *Berek!* like the siren of a nightmare.

Then the road went through a stand of trees which cut out the dim light of the stars. He could not feel the pavement with his feet; he was in danger of missing his way, of falling into a ditch or injuring himself against a tree. He tried to keep up his pace, but the risk was too great, and finally he was reduced to waving his arms before him and testing his footing like a blind man. Until he reached the end of the woods, he moved as if he were wandering lost in a dream, damp with sweat, and cold.

After that, he set a hard pace for himself. He was spurred on by the cries that rushed after him, *Berek! Berek!* When at last, long miles later, he reached the driveway into Haven Farm, he was almost running.

In the sanctuary of his house, he turned on all the lights and locked the doors. The organized chastity of his living space surrounded him with its unconsoling dogma. A glance at the kitchen clock told him that the time was just past midnight. A new day, Sunday —a day when other people worshiped. He started some coffee, threw off his jacket, tie, and dress shirt, then carried his steaming cup into the living room. There he took a position on the sofa, adjusted Joan's picture on the coffee table so that it looked straight at him, and braced himself to weather the crisis.

He needed an answer. His resources were spent, and he could not go on the way he was.

Berek!

The girl's shout, and the raw applause of her audience, and the trucker's outrage, reverberated in him like muffled earth tremors. Suicide loomed in all directions. He was trapped between mad delusion and the oppressive weight of his fellow human beings.

Leper outcast unclean!

He gripped his shoulders and hugged himself to try to still the gasping of his heart.

I can't stand it! Somebody help me!

Suddenly, the phone rang—cut through him as stridently as a curse. Disjointedly, like a loose collection of broken bones, he jumped to his feet. But then he did not move. He lacked the courage to face more hostility, indemnification.

The phone shrilled again.

His breath shuddered in his lungs. Joan seemed to reproach him from behind the glass of the picture frame.

Another ring, as insistent as a fist.

He lurched toward the phone. Snatching up the receiver, he pressed it to his ear to hold it steady.

"Tom?" a faint, sad voice sighed. "Tom—it's Joan. Tom? I hope I didn't wake you. I know it's late, but I had to call. Tom?"

Covenant stood straight and stiff, at attention, with his knees locked to keep him from falling. His jaw worked, but he made no sound. His throat felt swollen shut, clogged with emotions, and his lungs began to hurt for air.

"Tom? Are you there? Hello? Tom? Please say something. I need to talk to you. I've been so lonely. I —I miss you." He could hear the effort in her voice.

His chest heaved fiercely, as if he were choking. Abruptly he broke through the block in his throat, and took a deep breath that sounded as if he were between sobs. But still he could not force up words.

"Tom! Please! What's happening to you?"

His voice seemed to be caught in a death grip. Desperate to shatter the hold, to answer Joan, cling to her voice, keep her on the line, he picked up the phone and started back toward the sofa—hoping that movement would ease the spasm that clenched him, help him regain control of his muscles.

But he turned the wrong way, wrapping the phone cord around his ankle. As he jerked forward, he tripped and pitched headlong toward the coffee table. His forehead struck the edge of the table squarely. When he hit the floor, he seemed to feel himself bounce.

Instantly, his sight went blank. But he still had the

receiver clutched to his ear. During a moment of white stillness, he heard Joan's voice clearly. She was becoming upset, angry.

"Tom, I'm serious. Don't make this any harder for me than it already is. Don't you understand? I want to talk to you. I need you. Say something. Tom. Tom! Damn you, say something!"

Then a wide roaring in his ears washed out her voice. No! he cried. No! But he was helpless. The rush of sound came over him like a dark tide, and carried him away.

THREE: The Summoning

THE wide roar modulated slowly, changing the void of his sight. On the surge of the sound, a swath of gray-green spread upward until it covered him like a winding sheet. The hue of the green was noxious to him, and he felt himself smothering in its close, sweet, fetid reek—the smell of attar. But the note which filled his ears grew more focused, scaled up in pitch. Droplets of gold bled into view through the green. Then the sound turned softer and more plaintive, higher still in pitch, so that it became a low human wail. The gold forced back the green. Soon a warm, familiar glow filled his eyes.

As the sound turned more and more into a woman's song, the gold spread and deepened—cradled him as if it were carrying him gently along the flood of the voice. The melody wove the light, gave it texture and shape, solidity. Helpless to do otherwise, he clung to the sound, concentrated on it with his mouth stretched open in protest.

Slowly, the singing throat opened. Its harmonic pattern became sterner, more demanding. Covenant felt

himself pulled forward now, hurried down the tide of
the song. Arching with supplication, it took on words.

> Be true, Unbeliever—
> Answer the call.
> Life is the Giver:
> Death ends all.
> The promise is truth,
> And banes disperse
> With promise kept:
> But soul's deep curse
> On broken faith
> And faithless thrall,
> For doom of darkness
> Covers all.
> Be true, Unbeliever—
> Answer the call.
> Be true.

The song seemed to reach back into him, stirring
memories, calling up people he had once, in one fey
mood, thought had the right to make demands of him.
But he resisted it. He kept silent, held himself in.

The melody drew him on into the warm gold.

At last, the light took on definition. He could locate
its shape before him now; it washed out his vision as
if he were staring into the sun. But on the last words
of the song, the light dimmed, lost its brilliance. As the
voice sang, "Be true," it was seconded by many
throats: "Be true!" That adjuration stretched him like
the tightening of a string to its final pitch.

Then the source of the light fell into scale, and he
could see beyond it.

He recognized the place. He was in the Close, the
council chamber of the Lords in the heart of Revelstone. Its tiers of seats reached above him on all sides
toward the granite ceiling of the hall.

He was surprised to find himself standing erect on
the bottom of the Close. The stance confused his sense
of balance, and he stumbled forward toward the pit
of graveling, the source of the gold light. The fire-

stones burned there before him without consumption, filling the air with the smell of newly broken earth.

Strong hands caught him by either arm. As his fall was halted, drops of blood spattered onto the stone floor at the edge of the graveling pit.

Regaining his feet, he cried hoarsely, "Don't touch me!"

He was dizzy with confusion and rage, but he braced himself while he put a hand to his forehead. His fingers came away covered with blood. He had cut himself badly on the edge of the table. For a moment, he gaped at his red hand.

Through his dismay, a quiet, firm voice said, "Be welcome in the Land, ur-Lord Thomas Covenant, Unbeliever and Ringthane. I have called you to us. Our need for your aid is great."

"You called me?" he croaked.

"I am Elena," the voice replied, "High Lord by the choice of the Council, and holder of the Staff of Law. I have called you."

"You called me?" Slowly, he raised his eyes. Thick wetness ran from the sockets as if he were weeping blood. "You called me?" He felt a crumbling inside him like rocks breaking, and his hold over himself cracked. In a voice of low anguish, he said, "I was talking to Joan."

He saw the woman dimly through the blood in his eyes. She stood behind the stone table on the level above him, holding a long staff in her right hand. There were other people around the table, and behind them the gallery of the Close held many more. They were all watching him.

"To Joan, do you understand? I was talking to Joan. *She* called me. After all this time. When I needed—needed. You have no right." He gathered force like a storm wind. "You've got no right! I was talking to *Joan!*" He shouted with all his might, but it was not enough. His voice could not do justice to his emotion. "To Joan! to Joan! do you hear me? She was my *wife!*"

A man who had been standing near the High Lord hurried around the broad open *C* of the table, and came down to Covenant on the lower level. Covenant recognized the man's lean face, with its rudder nose mediating between crooked, humane lips and acute, gold flecked, dangerous eyes. He was Lord Mhoram.

He placed a hand on Covenant's arm, and said softly, "My friend. What has happened to you?"

Savagely, Covenant threw off the Lord's hand. "Don't touch me!" he raged in Mhoram's face. "Are you deaf as well as blind?! I was talking to Joan! On the phone!" His hand jerked convulsively, struggling to produce the receiver out of the empty air. "She needed"—abruptly his throat clenched, and he swallowed roughly—"she said she needed me. Me!" But his voice was helpless to convey the crying of his heart. He slapped at the blood on his forehead, trying to clear his eyes.

The next instant, he grabbed the front of Mhoram's sky-blue robe in his fists, hissed, "Send me back! There's still time! If I can get back fast enough!"

Above them, the woman spoke carefully. "Ur-Lord Covenant, it grieves me to hear that our summoning has done you harm. Lord Mhoram has told us all he could of your pain, and we do not willingly increase it. But it is our doom that we must. Unbeliever, our need is great. The devastation of the Land is nearly upon us."

Pushing away from Mhoram to confront her, Covenant fumed, "I don't give a bloody damn about the Land!" His words came in such a panting rush that he could not shout them. "I don't care what you need. You can drop dead for all I care. You're a delusion! A sickness in my mind. You don't exist! Send me back! You've got to send me back. While there's still time!"

"Thomas Covenant." Mhoram spoke in a tone of authority that pulled Covenant around. "Unbeliever. Listen to me."

Then Covenant saw that Mhoram had changed. His face was still the same—the gentleness of his mouth still balanced the promise of peril in his gold-concentrated irises—but he was older, old enough now to be Covenant's father. There were lines of use around his eyes and mouth, and his hair was salted with white. When he spoke, his lips twisted with self-deprecation, and the depths of his eyes stirred uneasily. But he met the fire of Covenant's glare without flinching.

"My friend, if the choice were mine, I would return you at once to your world. The decision to summon you was painfully made, and I would willingly undo it. The Land has no need of service which is not glad and free. But, ur-Lord"—he gripped Covenant's arm again to steady him—"my friend, we cannot return you."

"Cannot?" Covenant groaned on a rising, half-hysterical note.

"We have no lore for the releasing of burdens. I know not how it is in your world—you appear unchanged to my eyes—but forty years have passed since we stood together on the slopes of Mount Thunder, and you freed the Staff of Law for our hands. For long years we have striven—"

"Cannot?" Covenant repeated more fiercely.

"We have striven with power which we fail to master, and Lore which we have been unable to penetrate. It has taken forty years to bring us here, so that we may ask for your aid. We have reached the limit of what we can do."

"No!" He turned away because he could not bear the honesty he saw in Mhoram's face, and yelled up at the woman with the Staff, "Send me back!"

For a moment, she looked at him squarely, measuring the extremity of his demand. Then she said, "I entreat you to understand. Hear the truth of our words. Lord Mhoram has spoken openly. I hear the hurt we have done you. I am not unmoved." She was twenty or thirty feet away from him, beyond the pit of graveling and behind the stone table, but her voice carried to him clearly through the crystal acoustics of the Close. "But I cannot undo your summoning. Had I the power, still the Land's need would deny me. Lord Foul the Despiser—"

Head back, arms thrown wide, Covenant howled, "I don't care!"

Stung into sharpness, the High Lord said, "Then return yourself. You have the power. You wield the white gold."

With a cry, Covenant tried to charge at her. But before he could take a step, he was caught from behind. Wrestling around, he found himself in the grasp of Bannor, the unsleeping Bloodguard who had warded him during his previous delusion.

"We are the Bloodguard," Bannor said in his toneless alien inflection. "The care of the Lords is in our hands. We do not permit any offer of harm to the High Lord."

"Bannor," Covenant pleaded, "she was my wife."

But Bannor only gazed at him with unblinking dispassion.

Throwing his weight wildly, he managed to turn in the Bloodguard's powerful grip until he was facing Elena again. Blood scattered from his forehead as he jerked around. "She was my wife!"

"Enough," Elena commanded.

"Send me back!"

"Enough!" She stamped the iron heel of the Staff of Law on the floor, and at once blue fire burst from its length. The flame roared vividly, like a rent in the fabric of the gold light, letting concealed power shine through; and the force of the flame drove Covenant back into Bannor's arms. But her hand where she held the Staff was untouched. "I am the High Lord," she said sternly. "This is Revelstone— Lord's Keep, not Foul's Creche. We have sworn the Oath of Peace."

At a nod from her, Bannor released Covenant, and he stumbled backward, falling in a heap beside the graveling. He lay on the stone for a moment, gasping harshly. Then he pried himself into a sitting position. His head seemed to droop with defeat. "You'll get Peace," he groaned. "He's going to destroy you all. Did you say forty years? You've only got nine left. Or have you forgotten his prophecy?"

"We know," Mhoram said quietly. "We do not forget." With a crooked smile, he bent to examine Covenant's wound.

While Mhoram did this, High Lord Elena quenched the blaze of the Staff, and said to a person Covenant could not see, "We must deal with this matter now, if we are to have any hope of the white gold. Have the captive brought here."

Lord Mhoram mopped Covenant's forehead gently, peered at the cut, then stood and moved away to consult with someone. Left alone, with most of the blood out of his eyes, Covenant brought his throbbing gaze into focus to take stock of where he was. Some still-uncowed instinct for self-preservation made him try to measure the hazards around him. He was on the lowest level of the tiered chamber, and its high vaulted and groined ceiling arched over him, lit by the gold glow of the graveling, and by four large smokeless *lillianrill* torches set into the walls. Around the center of the Close, on the next level, was the three-quarters-round stone council table of the Lords, and above and behind the table were the ranked seats of the gallery. Two Bloodguard stood at the high massive doors, made by Giants to be large enough for Giants, of the main entryway, above and opposite the High Lord's seat.

The gallery was diversely filled with warriors of the Warward of Lord's Keep, Lorewardens from the Loresraat, several Hirebrands and Gravelingases dressed respectively in their traditional cloaks and tunics, and a few more Bloodguard. High up behind the High Lord sat two people Covenant thought he recognized—the Gravelingas Tohrm, a Hearthrall of Lord's Keep; and Quaan, the Warhaft who had accompanied the Quest for the Staff of Law. With them were two others—one a Hirebrand, judging by his Woodhelvennin cloak and the circlet of leaves about his head, probably the other Hearthrall; and one the First Mark of the Bloodguard. Vaguely, Covenant wondered who had taken that position after the loss of Tuvor in the catacombs under Mount Thunder.

His gaze roamed on around the Close. Standing at the table were seven Lords, not counting the High Lord and Mhoram. Covenant recognized none of them. They must all have passed the tests and joined the Council in the last forty years. Forty years? he asked dimly. Mhoram had aged, but he did not look forty years older. And Tohrm, who had been hardly more than a laughing boy when Covenant had known him, now seemed far too young for middle age. The Bloodguard were not changed at all. Of course, Covenant groaned to himself, remembering how old they were said to be. Only Quaan showed a believable age: white thinning hair gave the former Warhaft the look of sixty or sixty-five summers. But his square commanding shoulders did not stoop. And the openness of his countenance had not changed; he frowned down on the Unbeliever with exactly the frank disapproval that Covenant remembered.

He did not see Prothall anywhere. Prothall had been the High Lord during the Quest, and Covenant knew that he had survived the final battle on the slopes of Mount Thunder. But he also knew that Prothall had been old enough to die naturally in forty years. In spite of his pain, he found himself hoping that the former High Lord had died as he deserved, in peace and honor.

With a sour mental shrug, he moved his survey to the one man at the Lords' table who was not standing. This individual was dressed like a warrior, with high, soft-soled boots over black leggings, a black sleeveless shirt under a breastplate molded of a yellow metal, and a yellow headband; but on his breastplate were the double black diagonal marks which distinguished him as the Warmark, the commander of the Warward, the Lords' army. He was not looking at anyone. He sat back in his stone chair, with his head down and his eyes covered with one hand, as if he were asleep.

Covenant turned away, let his gaze trudge at random around the Close. High Lord Elena was conferring in low tones with the Lords nearest her. Mhoram stood waiting near the broad stairs leading up to the main doors. The acoustics of the chamber carried the commingled voices of the gallery to Covenant, so that the air was murmurous about his head. He wiped the gathering blood from his brows, and thought about dying.

It would be worth it, he mused. After all it would be worth it to escape. He was not tough enough to persevere when even his dreams turned against him. He should leave living to the people who were potent for it.

Ah, hellfire, he sighed. Hellfire.

Distantly, he heard the great doors of the Close swing open. The murmuring in the air stopped at once; everyone turned and looked toward the doors. Forcing himself to spend some of his waning strength, Covenant twisted around to see who was coming.

The sight struck him cruelly, seemed to take the last rigor out of his bones.

He watched with bloodied eyes as two Bloodguard came down the stairs, holding upright between them a green-gray creature that oozed with fear. Though they were not handling it roughly, the creature trembled in terror and revulsion. Its hairless skin was slick with sweat. It had a generally human outline, but its torso was unusually long, and its limbs were short, all equal in length, as if it naturally ran on four legs through low caves. But its limbs were bent and useless—contorted as if they had been broken many times and not reset. And the rest of its body showed signs of worse damage.

Its head was its least human feature. Its bald skull had no eyes. Above the ragged slit of its mouth, in the center of its face, were two wide, wet nostrils that quivered fearfully around the edges as the creature smelled its situation. Its small pointed ears perched high on its skull. And the whole back of its head was gone. Over the gap was a green membrane like a scar, pulsing against the remaining fragment of a brain.

Covenant knew immediately what it was. He had seen a creature like it once before—whole in body, but dead, lying on the floor of its Waymeet with an iron spike through its heart.

It was a Waynhim. A Demondim-spawn, like the ur-viles. But unlike their black roynish kindred, the Waynhim had devoted their lore to the services of the Land.

This Waynhim had been lavishly tortured.

The Bloodguard brought the creature down to the bottom of the Close, and held it opposite Covenant. Despite his deep weakness, he forced himself to his feet, and kept himself up by leaning against the wall of the next level. Already, he seemed to be regaining some of the added dimension of sight which characterized the Land. He could see into the Waynhim, could feel with his eyes what had been done to it. He saw torment and extravagant pain—saw the healthy body of the Waynhim caught in a fist of malice, and crushed gleefully into this crippled shape. The sight made his eyes hurt. He had to lock his knees to brace himself up. A cold mist of hebetude and despair filled his head, and he was glad for the blood which clogged his eyes; it preserved him from seeing the Waynhim.

Through his fog, he heard Elena say, "Ur-Lord Covenant, it is necessary to burden you with this sight. We must convince you of our need. Please forgive such a welcome to the Land. The duress of our plight leaves us little choice.

"Ur-Lord, this poor creature brought us to the decision of your summoning. For years we have known that the Despiser prepares his strength to march against the Land—that the time appointed in his prophecy grows short for us. You delivered that prophecy unto us, and the Lords of Revelstone have not been idle. From the day in which Lord Mhoram brought to Lord's Keep the Staff of Law and the Second Ward of Kevin's Lore, we have striven to meet this doom. We have multiplied the Warward, studied our defenses, trained ourselves in all our skills and strengths. We have learned some of the uses of the Staff. The Loresraat has explored with all its wisdom and devotion the Second Ward. But in forty years, we have gained no clear knowledge of Lord Foul's intent. After the wresting of the Staff from Drool Rockworm, the Despiser's presence left Kiril Threndor in Mount Thunder, and soon reseated itself in the great throne-hall of Ridjeck Thome, Foul's Creche, the Gray Slayer's ancient home. And since that time, our scouts have been unable to penetrate Lord Foul's demesne.

Power has been at work there—power and ill—but we could learn nothing of it, though Lord Mhoram himself assayed the task. He could not breach the Despiser's forbidding might.

"But there have been dim and dark foreboding movements throughout the Land. *Kresh* from the east and ur-viles from Mount Thunder, *griffins* and other dire creatures from Sarangrave Flat, Cavewights, little-known denizens of Lifeswallower, the Great Swamp—we have heard them all wending toward the Spoiled Plains and Foul's Creche. They disappear beyond the Shattered Hills, and do not return. We need no great wisdom to teach us that the Despiser prepares his army. But still we have lacked clear knowledge. Then at last knowledge came to us. During the summer, our scouts captured this creature, this broken remnant of a Waynhim, on the western edges of Grimmerdhore Forest. It was brought here so that we might try to gain tidings from it."

"So you tortured it to find out what it knows." Covenant's eyes were sticky with blood, and he kept them shut, giving himself up to useless rage and mist.

"Do you believe that of us?" The High Lord sounded hurt. "No. We are not Despisers. We would not so betray the Land. We have treated the Waynhim as gently as we could without releasing it. It has told us willingly all that we would know. Now it begs us to kill it. Unbeliever, hear me. This is Lord Foul's handiwork. He possesses the Illearth Stone. This is the work of that bane."

Through the grayness in his mind, Covenant heard the doors open again. Someone came down the stairs and whispered with Lord Mhoram. Then Mhoram said, "High Lord, hurtloam has been brought for the Unbeliever. I fear that his wound extends far beyond this simple cut. There is other ill at work in him. He must be tended without delay."

"Yes, at once," High Lord Elena responded promptly. "We must do all that we can to heal him."

With a steady stride, Mhoram came toward Covenant.

At the thought of hurtloam, Covenant pushed himself away from the wall, rubbed the caked blood out of his eyes. He saw Mhoram holding a small stoneware bowl containing a light mud spangled with gold gleams that seemed to throb in the glow of the Close.

"Keep that stuff away from me," he whispered.

Mhoram was taken aback. "This is hurtloam, ur-Lord. It is the healing soil of the Earth. You will be renewed by it."

"I know what it does!" Covenant's voice was raw from all the shouting he had done, and it sounded spectral and empty, like the creaking of a derelict. "I've had it before. You put that stuff on my head, and before you know it the feeling comes back into my fingers and toes, and I go around ra—" He barely caught himself. "Hurting people."

He heard Elena say softly, "I know," but he disregarded her.

"That's the real lie," he snarled at the bowl, "that stuff there. That's what makes me feel so healthy I can't stand it." He took a long breath, then said fervidly, "I don't want it."

Mhoram held Covenant in a gaze intense with questions. And when Covenant did not waver, the Lord asked in a low voice, a tone of amazement, "My friend, do you wish to die?"

"Use it on that poor devil over there," Covenant replied dully. "It's got a right to it."

Without bending the straitness of his look, Mhoram said, "We have made the attempt. You have known us, Unbeliever. You know that we could not refuse the plea of such distress. But the Waynhim is beyond all our succor. Our Healers cannot approach its inner wound. And it nearly died at the touch of hurtloam."

Still Covenant did not relent.

Behind him, High Lord Elena continued what Mhoram had been saying. "Even the Staff of Law cannot match the power which has warped this Waynhim. Such is our plight, ur-Lord. The Illearth Stone surpasses us.

"This Waynhim has told us much. Much that was obscure is now clear. Its name was *dharmakshetra,* which in the Waynhim tongue means, 'to brave the enemy.' Now it calls itself *dukkha*—'victim.' Because its people desired knowledge of the Despiser's plotting, it went to Foul's Creche. There it was captured, and—and wronged—and then set free—as a warning to its people, I think. It has told us much.

"Unbeliever, we know that when you first delivered the Despiser's prophecy to High Lord Prothall son of Dwillian and the Council of Lords forty years ago, many things were not understood concerning the Gray Slayer's intent. Why did he warn the Lords that Drool Rockworm had found the Staff of Law under Mount Thunder? Why did he seek to prepare us for our fate? Why did he aid Drool's quest for dark might, and then betray the Cavewight? These questions are now answered. Drool possessed the Staff, and with it unearthed the buried bane, the Illearth Stone. By reason of these powers, the Despiser was at Drool's mercy while the Cavewight lived.

"But with Lord Mhoram and High Lord Prothall, you retrieved the Staff and brought the threat of Drool Rockworm to an end. Thus the Stone fell into Lord Foul's hands. He knew that the Stone, joined with his own lore and power, is a greater strength than the Staff of Law. And he knew that we are no masters for even that little might which we possess.

"In forty years, we have not rested. We have spoken to all the people of the Land. The Loresraat has grown greatly, giving us warriors and Lorewardens and Lords to meet our need. The *rhadhamaerl* and *lillianrill* have labored to the utmost. And all have given themselves to the study of the Two Wards, and of the Staff. Gains have been made. Trothgard, where the Lords swore their promise of healing to the Land, has flowered, and we have made there works undreamed by our forefathers. The Staff meets many needs. But the heart of our failure remains.

"For all our lore, all our knowledge of the Staff and the Earthpower, comes to us from Kevin, High Lord of the Old Lords. And he was defeated—yes, and worse than defeated. Now we face the same foe, made greatly stronger by the Illearth Stone. And we have recovered only Two of the Seven Wards in which

Kevin left his Lore. And at their core these Two are beyond us. Some weakness of wisdom or incapacity of spirit prevents our grasp of their mystery. Yet without mastery of the Two we cannot gain the rest, for Kevin, wise to the hazards of unready knowledge and power, hid his Wards each in its turn, so that the comprehension of one would lead to the discovery of the next.

"For forty years, this failure has clung to us. And now we have learned that Lord Foul, too, has not been idle. We have learned from this Waynhim. The Land's enemy has grown power and armies until the region beyond the Shattered Hills teems with warped life— myriads of poor bent creatures like *dukkha,* held by the power of the Stone in soul chattelry to Lord Foul. He has built for himself a force more ill than any the Land has known, more fell than any we can hope to conquer. He has gathered his three Ravers, the servants of his right hand, to command his armies. It may be that his hordes are already afoot against us.

"So it is that we have called you, ur-Lord Covenant, Unbeliever and white gold wielder. You are our hope at the last. We summoned you, though we knew it might carry a cost hard for you to bear. We have sworn our service to the Land, and could not do otherwise. Thomas Covenant! Will you not help us?"

During her speech, her voice had grown in power and eloquence until she was almost singing. Covenant could not refuse to listen. Her tone reached into him, and made vivid all his memories of the Land's beauty. He recalled the bewitching Dance of the Celebration of Spring, and the lush, heart-soothing health of the Andelainian Hills, the uneasy eldritch gleaming of Morinmoss, the stern swift Plains of Ra and the rampant Ranyhyn, the great horses. And he remembered what it was like to feel, to have lively nerves in his fingers, capable of touching grass and stone. The poignancy of it made his heart ache.

"Your hope misleads you," he groaned into the stillness after Elena's appeal. "I don't know anything about power. It has something to do with life, and I'm as good as dead. Or what do you think life is? Life is feeling. I've lost that. I'm a leper."

He might have started to rage again, but a new voice cut sharply through his protest. "Then why don't you throw away your ring?"

He turned, and found himself confronting the warrior who had been sitting at the end of the Lords' table. The man had come down to the bottom of the Close, where he faced Covenant with his hands on his hips. To Covenant's surprise, the man's eyes were covered with dark, wraparound sunglasses. Behind the glasses, his head moved alertly, as if he were studying everything. He seemed to possess a secret. Without the support of his eyes, the slight smile on his lips looked private and unfathomable, like an utterance in an alien tongue.

Covenant grasped the inconsistency of the sunglasses—they were oddly out of place in the Close—but he was too stung by the speaker's question to stop for discrepancies. Stiffly, he answered, "It's my wedding ring."

The man shrugged away this reply. "You talk about your wife in the past tense. You're separated—or divorced. You can't have your life both ways now. Either get rid of the ring and stick to whatever it is you seem to think is real, or get rid of her and do your duty here."

"My duty?" The affront of the man's judgment gave Covenant the energy to object. "How do you know what my duty is?"

"My name is Hile Troy." The man gave a slight bow. "I'm the Warmark of the Warward of Lord's Keep. My job is to figure out how to meet Foul's army."

"Hile Troy," added Elena slowly, almost hesitantly, "comes from your world, Unbeliever."

What?

The High Lord's assertion seemed to snatch the ground from under Covenant. The enervation in his bones suddenly swamped him. Vertigo came over him as if he were on the edge of a cliff, and he stumbled.

Mhoram caught him as he dropped heavily to his knees.

His movement distracted the Bloodguard holding *dukkha*. Before they could react, the Waynhim broke away from them and sprang at Covenant, screaming with fury.

To save Covenant, Mhoram spun and blocked *dukkha*'s charge with his staff. The next instant, the Bloodguard recaptured the Waynhim. But Covenant did not see it. When Mhoram turned away from him, he fell on his face beside the graveling pit. He felt weak, overburdened with despair, as if he were bleeding to death. For a few moments, he lost consciousness.

He awoke to the touch of cool relief on his forehead. His head was in Mhoram's lap, and the Lord was gently spreading hurtloam over his cut brow.

He could already feel the effect of the mud. A soothing caress spread from his forehead into the muscles of his face, relaxing the tension which gripped his features. Drowsiness welled up in him as the healing earth unfettered him, anodyned the restless bondage of his spirit. Though his weariness, he saw the trap of his delusion winding about him. With as much supplication as he could put into his voice, he said to Mhoram, "Get me out of here."

The Lord seemed to understand. He nodded firmly, then got to his feet, lifting Covenant with him. Without a word to the Council, he turned his back and went up the stairs, half carrying Covenant out of the Close.

FOUR: "May Be Lost"

COVENANT hardly heard the shutting of the great doors behind him; he was hardly conscious of his surroundings at all. His attention was focused inward on the hurtloam's progress. It seemed to spread around his skull and down his flesh, soothing as it radiated within him. It made his skin tingle, and the sensation soon covered his face and neck. He scrutinized it as if it were a poison he had taken to end his life.

When the touch of the loam reached past the base of his throat into his chest, he stumbled, and could not recover. Bannor took his other arm. The Lord and the Bloodguard carried him on through the stone city, working generally upward through the interlocking levels of Lord's Keep. At last, they brought him to a spacious suite of living quarters. Gently, they bore him into the bedroom, laid him on the bed, and undressed him enough to make him comfortable.

Then Mhoram bent close to him and said reassuringly, "This is the power of the hurtloam. When it works upon a dire wound, it brings a deep sleep to speed healing. You will rest well now. You have done without rest too long." He and Bannor turned to go.

But Covenant could feel the cool, tingling touch near his heart. Weakly, he called Mhoram back. He was full of dread; he could not bear to be alone. Without caring what he said—seeking only to keep Mhoram near him—he asked, "Why did that—*dukkha* attack me?"

Again, Lord Mhoram appeared to understand. He brought a wooden stool near the head of the bed, and seated himself there. In a quiet, steady voice, he said,

44

"That is a searching question, my friend. *Dukkha* has been tormented out of all recognition, and I can only guess at the sore impulses which drive it. But you must remember that it is a Waynhim. For many generations after the Desecration, when the new Lords began their work at Revelstone, the Waynhim served the Land—not out of allegiance to the Lords, but rather out of their desire to expiate to the Land for the dangerous works and dark lore of the ur-viles. Such a creature still lives, somewhere far within *dukkha*. Despite what has been done to it—even if its soul has been enslaved by the power of the Stone, so that now it serves the Despiser—it still remembers what it was, and hates what it is. That is Lord Foul's way in all things—to force his foes to become that which they most hate, and to destroy that which they most love.

"My friend, this is not pleasant to say. But it is in my heart that *dukkha* attacked you because you refuse to aid the Land. The Waynhim knows the might you possess—it is of the Demondim, and in all likelihood comprehends more of the uses and power of white gold than any Lord. Now it is in pain too great to allow it to understand you. The last remnant of itself saw dimly that you—that you refuse. For a moment, it became its former self enough to act.

"Ah, ur-Lord. You have said that the Land is a dream for you—and that you fear to be made mad. But madness is not the only danger in dreams. There is also the danger that something may be lost which can never be regained."

Covenant sighed. The Lord had given him an explanation he could grasp. But when Mhoram's steady voice stopped, he felt how much he needed it—how close he was to the brink of some precipice which appalled him. He reached a hand outward, into the void around him, and felt his fingers clasped firmly in Mhoram's. He tried once more to make himself understood.

"She was my wife," he breathed. "She needed me. She—she'll never forgive me for doing this to her."

He was so exhausted that he could no longer see

Mhoram's face. But as he ran out of consciousness, he felt the Lord's unfaltering hold on his hand. Mhoram's care comforted him, and he slept.

Then he hung under a broad sky of dreams, measurable only by the strides of stars. Out of the dim heavens, a succession of dark shapes seemed to hover and strike. Like carrion, he was helpless to fend them off. But always a hand gripped his and consoled him. It anchored him until he returned to consciousness.

Without opening his eyes, he lay still and probed himself tentatively, as if he were testing buboes. He was enfolded from his chest down in soft clean sheets. And he could feel the fabric with his toes. The cold numbness of dead nerves was gone from them, warmed away by a healing glow which reached into the marrow of his bones.

The change in his fingers was even more obvious. His right fist was knotted in the sheets. When he moved his fingers, he could feel the texture of the cloth with their tips. The grip on his left hand was so hard that he could feel the pulse in his knuckles.

But nerves do not regenerate—cannot—

Damnation! he groaned. The sensation of touch prodded his heart like fear. Involuntarily, he whispered, "No. No." But his tone was full of futility.

"Ah, my friend," Mhoram sighed, "your dreams have been full of such refusals. But I do not understand them. I hear in your breathing that you have resisted your own healing. And the outcome is obscure to me. I cannot tell whether your denials have brought you to good or ill."

Covenant looked up into Mhoram's sympathetic face. The Lord still sat beside the bed; his iron-shod staff leaned against the wall within easy reach of his hand. But now there were no torches in the room. Sunlight poured through a large oriel beside the bed.

Mhoram's gaze made Covenant acutely conscious of their clasped hands. Carefully, he extricated his fingers. Then he propped himself up on his elbows, and asked how long he had been asleep. His rest after the shouting he had done in the Close made his voice rattle harshly in his throat.

"It is now early afternoon," Mhoram replied. "The summoning was performed in the evening yesterday."

"Have you been here—all that time?"

The Lord smiled. "No. During the night— How shall I say it? I was called away. High Lord Elena sat with you in my absence." After a moment, he added, "She will speak with you this evening, if you are willing."

Covenant did not respond. The mention of Elena reawakened his outrage and fear at the act which had compelled him into the Land. He thought of the summoning as her doing; it was her voice which had snatched him away from Joan. Joan! he wailed. To cover his distress, he climbed out of bed, gathered up his clothes, and went in search of a place to wash himself.

In the next room, he found a stone basin and tub connected to a series of balanced stone valves which allowed him to run water where he wanted it. He filled the basin. When he put his hands into the water, its sharp chill thrilled the new vitality of his nerves. Angrily, he thrust his head down into the water, and did not raise it until the cold began to make the bones of his skull hurt. Then he went and stood dripping over a warm pot of graveling near the tub.

While the glow of the fire-stones dried him, he silenced the aching of his heart. He was a leper, and knew down to the core of his skeleton the vital importance of recognizing facts. Joan was lost to him; that was a fact, like his disease, beyond any possibility of change. She would become angry when he did not speak to her, and would hang up, thinking that he had deliberately rebuffed her appeal, her proud, brave effort to bridge the loneliness between them. And he could do nothing about it. He was trapped in his delusion again. If he meant to survive, he could not afford the luxury of grieving over lost hopes. He was a leper; all his hopes were false. They were his enemies. They could kill him by blinding him to the lethal power of facts.

It was a fact that the Land was a delusion. It was a fact that he was trapped, caught in the web of his own weakness. His leprosy was a fact. He insisted on these things while he protested weakly to himself, No! I can't stand it! But the cold water dried from his skin, and was replaced by the kind, earthy warmth of the graveling. Sensations ran excitedly up his limbs from his fingers and toes. With a wild, stubborn look as if he were battering his head against a wall, he gave himself a VSE.

Then he located a mirror of polished stone, and used it to inspect his forehead. No mark was there— the hurtloam had erased his injury completely.

He called out, "Mhoram!" But his voice had an unwanted beseeching tone. To counter it, he began shoving himself into his clothes. When the Lord appeared in the doorway, Covenant did not meet his eyes. He pulled on his T-shirt and jeans, laced up his boots, then moved away to the third room of his suite.

There he found a door opening onto a balcony. With Mhoram behind him, he stepped out into the open air. At once, perspectives opened, and a spasm of vertigo clutched at him. The balcony hung halfway up the southern face of Revelstone—more than a thousand feet straight above the foothills which rested against the base of the mountain. The depth of the fall seemed to gape unexpectedly under his feet. His fear of heights whirred in his ears; he flung his arms around the stone railing, clung to it, clutched it to his chest.

In a moment, the worst of the spasm passed. Mhoram asked him what was wrong, but he did not explain. Breathing deeply, he pushed himself erect, and stood with his back pressed against the reassuring stone of the Keep. From there, he took in the view.

As he remembered it, Revelstone filled a long wedge of the mountains which stood immediately to the west. It had been carved out of the mountain promontory by the Giants many centuries ago, in the time of Old Lord Damelon Giantfriend. Above the Keep was a plateau which went beyond it west and north, past Furl Falls for a distance of a league or two before rising up into the rugged Westron Mountains. The Falls were too far away to be seen, but in the distance

the White River angled away south and slightly east
from its head in the pool of Furl Falls.

Beyond the river to the southwest, Covenant
made out the open plains and hills that led toward
Trothgard. In that direction, he saw no sign of culti-
vation or habitation; but eastward from him were ripe
fields, stands of trees, streams, villages—all glowing
under the sun as if they were smiling with health.
Looking over them, he sensed that the season was
early autumn. The sun stood in the southern sky, the
air was not as warm as it seemed, and the breeze
which blew gently up the face of Revelstone was
flavored with the loamy lushness of fall.

The Land's season—so different from the spring
weather from which he had been wrenched away—
gave him a renewed sense of discrepancy, of stark
and impossible translation. It reminded him of many
things, but he forced himself to begin with the previous evening. Stiffly, he said, "Has it occurred to you
that Foul probably let that poor Waynhim go just to
get you to call me here?"

"Of course," Mhoram replied. "That is the Despiser's way. He intends you to be the means of our
destruction."

"Then why did you do it? Hellfire! You know how
I feel about this—I told you often enough. I don't
want—I'm not going to be responsible for what happens to you."

Lord Mhoram shrugged. "That is the paradox of
white gold. Hope and despair run together for us.
How could we refuse the risk? Without every aid
which we can find or make for ourselves, we cannot
meet Lord Foul's might. We trust that at the last you
will not turn your back on the Land."

"You've had forty years to think about it. You
ought to know by now how little I deserve or even
want your trust."

"Perhaps. Warmark Hile Troy argues much that
way—though there is much about you that he does
not know. He feels that faith in one who is so unwilling is folly. And he is not convinced that we will lose
this war. He makes bold plans. But I have heard the

Despiser laughing. For better or worse, I am seer and oracle for this Council. I hear—I approve the High Lord's decision of summoning. For many reasons.

"Thomas Covenant, we have not spent our years in seclusion here, dreaming sweet dreams of peace while Lord Foul grows and moves against us. From your last moment in the Land to this day, we have striven to prepare our defense. Scouts and Lords have ridden the Land from end to end, drawing the people together, warning them, building what lore we have. I have braved the Shattered Hills, and fought on the marge of Hotash Slay—but of that I do not speak. I brought back knowledge of the Ravers. *Dukkha* alone did not move us to summon you."

Even in the direct beam of the sun, the word *Ravers* gave Covenant a chill he could not suppress. Remembering the other Waynhim he had seen, dead with an iron spike through its heart—killed by a Raver—he asked, "What about them? What did you learn?"

"Much or little," Mhoram sighed, "according to the uses of the knowledge. The importance of this lore cannot be mistaken—and yet its value eludes us.

"While you were last in the Land, we learned that the Ravers were still aboard—that like their master they had not been undone by the Ritual of Desecration, which Kevin Landwaster wreaked in his despair. Some knowledge of these beings had come to us through the old legends, the Lore of the First Ward, and the teachings of the Giants. We knew that they were named Sheol, Jehannum, and Herem, and that they lived without bodies, feeding upon the souls of others. When the Despiser was powerful enough to give them strength, they enslaved creatures or people by entering into their bodies, subduing their wills, and using the captured flesh to enact their master's purposes. Disguised in forms not their own, they were well hidden, and so could gain trust among their foes. By that means, many brave defenders of the Land were lured to their deaths in the age of the Old Lords.

"But I have learned more. There near Foul's Creche, I was beaten—badly overmastered. I fled through the Shattered Hills with only the staff of Variol my father between me and death, and could not prevent my foe from laying hands upon me. I had thought that I was in battle with a supreme loremaster of the ur-viles. But I learned—I learned otherwise."

Lord Mhoram stared unseeing into the depths of the sky, remembering with grim, concentrated eyes what had happened to him. After a moment, he continued: "It was a Raver I fought—a Raver in the flesh of an ur-vile. The touch of its hand taught me much. In the oldest time—beyond the reach of our most hoary legends, even before the dim time of the coming of men to the Land, and the cruel felling of the One Forest—the Colossus of the Fall had both power and purpose. It stood on Landsdrop like a forbidding fist over the Lower Land, and with the might of the Forest denied a dark evil from the Upper Land."

Abruptly, he broke into a slow song like a lament, a quiet declining hymn which told the story of the Colossus as the Lords had formerly known it, before the son of Variol had gained his new knowledge. In restrained sorrow over lost glory, the song described the Colossus of the Fall—the huge stone monolith, upraised in the semblance of a fist, which stood beside the waterfall where the River Landrider of the Plains of Ra became the Ruinwash of the Spoiled Plains.

Since a time that was ancient before Berek Lord-Fatherer lost half his hand, the Colossus had stood in lone somber guard above the cliff of Landsdrop; and the oldest hinted legends of the Old Lords told of a time, during the ages of the One Forest's dominion in the Land, when that towering fist had held the power to forbid the shadow of Despite—held it, and did not wane until the felling of the Forest by that unsuspected enemy, man, had cut too deeply to be halted. But then, outraged and weakened by the slaughter of the trees, the Colossus had unclasped its interdict, and let the shadow free. From that time, from the moment of that offended capitulation, the Earth had slowly lost the power or the will or the chance to defend itself. So the burden of resisting the Despiser had fallen to a race which had brought the shadow upon itself, and the Earth lay under the outcome.

"But it was not Despite which the Colossus resisted," Mhoram resumed when his song was done. "Despite was the bane of men. It came with them into the Land from the cold anguish of the north, and from the hungry kingdom of the south. No, the Colossus of the Fall forbade another foe—three tree- and soil-hating brothers who were old in the Spoiled Plains before Lord Foul first cast his shadow there. They were triplets, the spawn of one birth from the womb of their long-forgotten mother, and their names were *samadhi, moksha,* and *turiya.* They hated the Earth and all its growing things, just as Lord Foul hates all life and love. When the Colossus eased its interdict, they came to the Upper Land, and in their lust for ravage and dismay fell swiftly under the mastery of the Despiser. From that time, they have been his highest servants. They have performed treachery for him when he could not show his hand, and have fought for him when he would not lead his armies.

"It was *samadhi,* now named Sheol, who mastered the heart of Berek's liege—Sheol who slaughtered the champions of the Land, and drove Berek, half-unhanded and alone, to his extremity on the slopes of Mount Thunder. It was *turiya* and *moksha,* Herem and Jehannum, who lured the powerful and austere Demondim to their breeding dens, and to the spawning of the ur-viles. Now the three are united with Lord Foul again—united, and clamoring for the decimation of the Land. But alas—alas for my ignorance and weakness. I cannot foresee what they will do. I can hear their voices, loud with lust for the ripping of trees and the scorching of soil, but their intent eludes me. The Land is in such peril because its servants are weak."

The rough eloquence of Mhoram's tone carried Covenant along, and under its spell the brilliant sunlight seemed to darken in his eyes. Grimly, unwillingly, he caught a sense of the looming and cruel ill which crept up behind the Land's spirit, defying its inadequate defenders. And when he looked at himself, he

saw nothing but omens of futility. Other people who
had protested their weakness to him had suffered terribly at the hands of his own irreducible and immedicable impotence. Harshly—more harshly than he
intended—he asked, "Why?"

Mhoram turned away from his private visions, and
cocked an inquiring eyebrow at Covenant.

"Why are you weak?"

The Lord met this with a wry smile. "Ah, my friend
—I had forgotten that you ask such questions. You
lead me into long speeches. I think that if I could reply to you briefly, I would not need you so." But Covenant did not relent, and after a pause Mhoram said,
"Well, I cannot refuse to answer. But come—there is
food waiting. Let us eat. Then I will make what answer I can."

Covenant refused. Despite his hunger, he was unwilling to make any more concessions to the Land until he knew better where he stood.

Mhoram considered him for a moment, then replied
in a measured tone, "If what you say is true—if Land
and Earth and all are nothing more than a dream, a
threat of madness for you—then still you must eat.
Hunger is hunger, and need is need. How else—?"

"No." Covenant dismissed the idea heavily.

At that, the gold flecks in Mhoram's eyes flared, as
if they reflected the passion of the sun, and he said
levelly, "Then answer that question yourself. Answer
it, and save us. If we are helpless and unfriended, it is
your doing. Only you can penetrate the mysteries
which surround us."

"No," Covenant repeated. He recognized what
Mhoram was saying, and refused to tolerate it. No, he
responded to the heat of Mhoram's look. That's too
much like blaming me for being a leper. It's not my
fault. "You go too far."

"Ur-Lord," Mhoram replied, articulating each word
distinctly, "there is peril upon the Land. Distance will
not restrain me."

"That isn't what I meant. I meant you're taking
what I said too far. I'm not the—the shaper. I'm not

in control. I'm just another victim. All I know is what you tell me.

"What I want to know is why you keep trying to make me responsible. What makes you any weaker than I am? You've got the Staff of Law. You've got the *rhadhamaerl* and *lillianrill*. What makes you so bloody weak?"

The heat slowly faded from the Lord's gaze. Folding his arms so that his staff was clasped across his chest, he smiled crookedly. "Your question grows with each asking. If I require you to ask again, I fear that nothing less than a Giant's tale will suffice for answer. Forgive me, my friend. I know that our peril cannot be laid on your head. Dream or no—there is no difference for us. We must serve the Land.

"Now, I must first remind you that the *rhadhamaerl* and *lillianrill* are another question, separate from the weakness of the Lords. The stone-lore of the *rhadhamaerl,* and the wood-lore of the *lillianrill,* have been preserved from past ages by the people of Stonedown and Woodhelven. In their exile after the Ritual of Desecration, the people of the Land lost much of the richness of their lives. They were sorely bereft, and could cling only to that lore which enabled them to endure. Thus, when they returned to the Land, they brought with them those whose work in exile was to preserve and use the lore—Gravelingases of the *rhadhamaerl,* and Hirebrands of the *lillianrill.* It is the work of Hirebrand and Gravelingas to make the lives of the villages bounteous—warm in winter and plentiful in summer, true to the song of the Land.

"The Lore of High Lord Kevin Landwaster is another matter. That knowledge is the concern of the Loresraat and the Lords.

"The age of the Old Lords, before Lord Foul broke into open war with Kevin son of Loric, was among the bravest and gladdest and strongest of all the times of the Land. Kevin's Lore was mighty with Earthpower, and pure with Landservice. Health and gaiety flowered in the Land, and the bright Earth jewel of Andelain bedizened the Land's heart with precious woods and stones. That was a time—

"Yet it came to an end. Despair darkened Kevin, and in the Ritual of Desecration he destroyed that which he loved, intending to destroy the Despiser as well. But before the end, he was touched with prophecy or foresight, and found means to save much of power and beauty. He warned the Giants and the Ranyhyn, so that they might flee. He ordered the Bloodguard into safety. And he left his Lore for later ages—hid it in Seven Wards so that it would not fall into wrong or unready hands. The First Ward he gave to the Giants, and when the exile was ended they gave it to the first of the new Lords, the forebearers of this Council. In turn, these Lords conceived the Oath of Peace and carried it to all the people of the Land—an Oath to guard against Kevin's destroying passion. And these Lords, our forebearers, swore themselves and their followers in fealty and service to the Land and the Earthpower.

"Now, my friend, you know we have found the Second Ward. The Two contain much knowledge and much power, and when they are mastered they will lead us to the Third Ward. In this way, mastery will guide us until all Kevin's Lore is ours. But we fail—we fail to penetrate. How can I say it? We translate the speech of the Old Lords. We learn the skills and rites and songs of the Lore. We study Peace, and devote ourselves to the life of the Land. And yet something lacks. In some way, we miscomprehend—we do not suffice. Only a part of the power of this knowledge answers to our touch. We can learn nothing of the other Wards—and little of the Seven Words which evoke the Earthpower. Something—ur-Lord, it is something in us which fails. I feel it in my heart. We lack. We have not the stature of mastery."

The Lord fell silent, musing with his head down and his cheek pressed against his staff. Covenant watched him for a time. The warmth of the sun and the cool breeze seemed to underscore Mhoram's stern self-judgment. Revelstone itself dwarfed the people who inhabited it.

Yet the Lord's influence or example strengthened Covenant. At last, he found the courage to ask his most important question. "Then why am I here? Why did he let you summon me? Doesn't he want the white gold?"

Without raising his head, Mhoram said, "Lord Foul is not yet ready to defeat you. The wild magic still surpasses him. Instead, he strives to make you destroy yourself. I have seen it."

"Seen it?" Covenant echoed softly, painfully.

"In gray visions I have caught glimpses of the Despiser's heart. In this matter, I speak from sure comprehension. Even now, Lord Foul believes that his might is not equal to the wild magic. He is not yet ready to battle you.

"Remember that forty years ago Drool Rockworm held both Staff and Stone. Desiring still more power—desiring all power—he exerted himself against you in ways which the Despiser would not have chosen—ways which were wasteful or foolish. Drool was mad. And Lord Foul had no wish to teach him wisdom.

"Matters are otherwise now. Lord Foul wastes no power, takes no risks which do not gain his ends. He seeks indirectly to make you do his bidding. If it comes to the last, and you are still unmastered, he will fight you—but only when he is sure of victory. Until that time, he will strive to bend your will so that you will choose to strike against the Land—or to withhold your hand from our defense, so that he will be free to destroy us.

"But he will make no open move against you now. He fears the wild magic. White gold is not bound by the law of Time, and he must prevent its use until he can know that it will not be used against him."

Covenant heard the truth of Mhoram's words. The Despiser had told him much the same thing, high on Kevin's Watch, when he had first appeared in the Land. He shivered under the livid memory of Lord Foul's contempt—shivered and felt cold, as if behind the clean sunlight over Revelstone blew the dank mist of Despite, dampening his soul with the smell of attar, filling his ears on a level just beyond hearing with the rumble of an avalanche. Looking into Mhoram's eyes, he knew that he had to speak truly as well, reply as honestly as he could.

"I don't have any choice." Even this made him want to duck his head in shame, but he forced himself to hold the Lord's gaze. "I'll have to do it that way. Even if that's not the one good answer—even if madness is not the only danger in dreams. Even if I believed in this wild magic. I haven't got one idea how to use it."

With an effort, Mhoram smiled gently. But the somberness of his glance overshadowed his smile. He met Covenant's eyes unwaveringly, and when he spoke, his voice was sad. "Ah, my friend, what will you do?"

The uncritical softness of the question caught Covenant by the throat. He was not prepared for such sympathy. With difficulty, he answered, "I'll survive."

Mhoram nodded slowly, and a moment later he turned away, back toward the room. As he reached the door, he said, "I am late. The Council waits for me. I must go."

But before the Lord could leave, Covenant called after him, "Why aren't you the High Lord?" He was trying to find some way to thank Mhoram. "Don't they appreciate you around here?"

Over his shoulder, Mhoram replied simply, "My time has not yet come." Then he left the room, closing the door carefully behind him.

FIVE: Dukkha

COVENANT turned back to the southward view from Revelstone. He had many things to think about, and no easy way to grasp them. But already his senses seemed to be swinging into consonance with the Land. He could smell the crops in the fields east of him— they were nearly ready for harvesting—and see the

inner ripeness of the distant trees. He found autumn
in the way the sunlight stroked his face. Such sensations accented the excitement in his veins, but they
confused his efforts to deal clearly with his situation.
No leper, he thought painfully, no leper should be
asked to live in such a healthy world.

Yet he could not deny it; he was moved by
Mhoram's account of the dilemmas of the Lords. He
was moved by the Land, and by the people who
served it—though they made him look so small to
himself. Sourly, he left the balcony, and scanned the
tray of food which had been set for him on a stone
table in the center of his sitting room. The soup and
stew still steamed, reminding him how hungry he was.

No. He could not afford to make any more concessions. Hunger was like nerve-health—illusion,
deception, dream. He could not—

A knock at the door interrupted him. For a
moment, he stood still, irresolute. He did not want to
talk to anyone until he had had more time to think.
But at the same time he did not want to be alone. The
threat of madness was always at its worst when he
was alone.

Keep moving, don't look back, he muttered bitterly
to himself, echoing a formula which had served him
ambiguously at best.

He went to open the door.

Standing in the outer hallway was Hile Troy.

He was dressed as Covenant had seen him before,
with his sunglasses firmly in place; and again the slight
smile on his lips looked vaguely mysterious and apolo-
getic. A sharp pang of anxiety joined the tingling of
Covenant's blood. He had been trying not to think
about this man.

"Come on," Troy said. His tone was full of the
power of command. "The Lords are doing something
you ought to see."

Covenant shrugged to disguise a tremor in his
shoulders. Troy was an adversary—Covenant could
sense it. But he had made his decision when he had
opened the door. Defiantly, he strode out into the hall.

In the hallway, he found Bannor standing watch by his door.

Hile Troy started away with a swift, confident stride, but Covenant turned toward the Bloodguard. Bannor met his look with a nod; for a moment they held each other's eyes. Bannor's flat, brown, unreadable face had not changed a whit, not aged a day that Covenant could discern. As he stood relaxed and ready, the Bloodguard radiated a physical solidity, a palpable competence, which intimidated or belittled Covenant; and yet Covenant sensed something extreme and sad in Bannor's timeless impenetrability.

The Bloodguard were said to be two thousand years old. They were clenched into immutability by a strait and consuming Vow of service to the Lords, while all the people they had ever known—including the long-lived Giants, and High Lord Kevin, who had inspired them to their Vow—fell into dust.

Looking now at Bannor, with his alien countenance and his bare feet and his short brown tunic, Covenant received a sudden intuitive impression, as if a previous subliminal perception had crystallized. How many times had Bannor saved his life? For an instant, he could not remember. He felt unexpectedly sure that the Bloodguard could tell him what he needed to know, that from the extravagance of his two-thousand-year perspective, bereft by the unforeseen power of his Vow of home and sleep and death, of everyone he had ever loved, he had gained the knowledge Covenant needed.

"Bannor—" he began.

"Ur-Lord." The Bloodguard's voice was as passionless as time.

But Covenant did not know how to ask; he could not put his need into words which would not sound like an attack on the Bloodguard's impossible fidelity. Instead, he murmured, "So we're back to this."

"The High Lord has chosen me to keep watch over you."

"Come on," called Troy peremptorily. "You should see this."

Covenant disregarded him for a moment longer. To

Bannor, he said, "I hope—I hope it works out better than the last time." Then he turned and moved down the hall after Troy. He knew that Bannor came be-' hind him, though the Bloodguard walked without a sound.

Impatiently, Hile Troy guided Covenant inward through the levels of the Keep. They passed briskly across high vaulted halls, along connecting corridors, and down stairs until they reached a place that Covenant recognized: the long circular passage around the sacred enclosure, where the inhabitants of Revelstone worshipped.

He followed Troy in through one of the many doors onto a balcony which hung in the great cavern. The cavity was cylindrical in shape, with seven balconies cut into the walls, a flat floor with a dais on one side, and a domed ceiling too high above the balconies to be seen clearly. The enclosure was dim; the only illumination came from four large *lillianrill* torches set around the dais. Bannor closed the door, shutting out the light from the outer hallway; and in the gloom Covenant clung to the railing for security against the depth of the cavity. He was several hundred feet above the dais.

The balconies were nearly empty. Clearly, whatever ceremony was about to be enacted was not intended for the general population of Revelstone.

The nine Lords were already on the dais. They stood in a circle facing each other. With their backs to the torches, their faces were shadowed, and Covenant could not make out their features.

"This is your doing," said Troy in an intent whisper. "They have tried everything else. You shamed them into this."

Two Bloodguard bearing some figure between them moved toward the dais. With a start, Covenant identified the injured Waynhim. *Dukkha* was struggling feebly, but it could not prevent the Bloodguard from placing it within the circle of the Lords.

"They're going to try to break the hold of the Illearth Stone," Troy continued. "This is risky. If they fail, it could spread to one of them. They'll be too exhausted to fight it."

Clutching the railing with both hands, Covenant watched the scene below him. The two Bloodguard left *dukkha* cowering in the circle, and retreated to the wall of the enclosure. For a long moment, the Lords stood in silent concentration, preparing themselves. Then they lifted their heads, planted their staffs firmly before them on the stone, and began to sing. Their hymn echoed in the enclosure as if the domed gloom itself were resonating. They appeared small in the immense chamber, but their song stood up boldly, filling the air with authority and purpose.

As the echoes died, Troy whispered in Covenant's ear, "If something goes wrong here, you're going to pay for it."

I know, Covenant said like a prophet. I'm going to have to pay for everything.

When silence at last refilled the enclosure, High Lord Elena said in a clear voice, "*Dharmakshetra* Waynhim, if you can hear us through the wrong which has been done to you, listen. We seek to drive the power of the Illearth Stone from you. Please aid us. Resist the Despiser. *Dukkha,* hear! Remember health and hope, and resist this ill!"

Together, the Lords raised their staffs.

Troy's fingers reached out of the darkness and gripped Covenant's arm above the elbow.

Crying in one voice, "*Melenkurion abatha!*" the Lords struck their staffs on the stone. The metal rang through the sacred enclosure like a clashing of shields, and blue Lords-fire burst from the upheld end of each staff. The incandescent flames burned hotly, outshining the light of the torches. But the Staff of Law dazzled them all, flaring like a tongue of lightning. And the fire of the staffs made a low sound like the rush of distant storm winds.

Slowly, one of the lesser staffs bent toward the head of *dukkha.* It descended, then stopped with its flame well above the Waynhim's head, as if at that point the fire met resistance. When the wielding Lord pressed down, the air between *dukkha*'s skull and the staff

ignited; the whole space burned. But the fire there
was as green as cold emerald, and it devoured the
Lords' blue power.

Troy's fingers dug like claws into the flesh of Covenant's arm. But Covenant hardly felt them.

To meet the green flame, the Lords broke into a
stern antiphonal chant, using words that Covenant
could not understand. Their voices pounded against
the green, and the rushing wind of their power
mounted. Yet through it could be heard the voice of
dukkha Waynhim, gibbering.

One by one, the Lords added their fires to the
struggle over *dukkha*'s head, until only the Staff of
Law remained uncommitted. As each new power
touched the green, a sound of hunger and the crushing of bones multiplied in the air, and the baleful emerald fire blazed up more mightily, expanding like an
inferno of cruel ice to combat the Lords' strength.

Abruptly, the *lillianrill* torches went out, as if extinguished by a high wind.

Troy's fingers tightened.

Then High Lord Elena's voice sprang out over the
song of the Lords. *"Melenkurion abatha! Duroc minas
mill khabaal!"* With a sweeping stroke, she swung the
Staff of Law into the fray.

For an instant, the force of her attack drove the
conflicting fires together. Blue and green became one,
and raged up over the circle of the Lords, ravening
and roaring like a holocaust. But the next moment,
dukkha shrieked as if its soul were torn in two. The
towering flame ruptured like a thunderhead.

The detonation blew out all the fire in the enclosure. At once a darkness as complete as a grave
closed over the Lords.

Then two small torches appeared in the hands of
the Bloodguard. The dim light showed *dukkha* lying
on the stone beside two prostrate Lords. The others
stood in their places, leaning on their staffs as if
stunned by their exertion.

Seeing the fallen Lords, Troy drew a breath that
hissed fiercely through his teeth. His fingers seemed to

be trying to bare Covenant's bone. But Covenant bore the pain, watched the Lords.

Swiftly, the Bloodguard relit the four torches around the dais. At the touch of the warm light, one of the Lords—Covenant recognized Mhoram—shook off his numbness, and went to kneel beside his collapsed comrades. He examined them for a moment with his hands, using his sense of touch to explore the damage done to them; then he turned and bent over *dukkha*. Around him vibrated a silence of hushed fear.

At last he climbed to his feet, bracing himself with his staff. He spoke in a low voice, but his words carried throughout the enclosure. "The Lords Trevor and Amatin are well. They have only lost consciousness." Then he bowed his head, and sighed. "The Waynhim *dukkha* is dead. May its soul at last find peace."

"And forgive us," High Lord Elena responded, "for we have failed."

Breathing in his deep relief, Troy released Covenant. Covenant felt sudden stabs of pain in his upper arm. The throbbing made him aware that his own hands hurt. The intensity of his hold on the railing had cramped them until they felt crippled. The pain was sharp, but he welcomed it. He could see death in the broken limbs of the Waynhim. The bruises on his arms, the aching stiffness in his palms, were proof of life.

Dully, he said, "They killed it."

"What did you want them to do?" Troy retorted with ready indignation. "Keep it captive, alive and in torment? Let it go, and disclaim responsibility? Kill it in cold blood?"

"No."

"Then this is your only choice. This was the only thing left to try."

"No. You don't understand." Covenant tried to find the words to explain, but he could go no further. "You don't understand what Foul is doing to them." He pulled his cramped fingers away from the railing, and left the enclosure.

When he regained his rooms, he was still shaken.

He did not think to close the door behind him, and the Warmark strode after him into the suite without bothering to ask admittance. But Covenant paid no attention to his visitor. He went straight to the tray of food, picked up the flask which stood beside the still-steaming bowls, and drank deeply, as if he were try-ing to quench the heat of his blood. The springwine in the flask had a light, fresh, beery taste; it washed into him, clearing the dust from his internal passages. He emptied the flask, then remained still for a mo-ment with his eyes shut, experiencing the sensation of the draft. When its clear light had eased some of the constriction in his chest, he seated himself at the table and began to eat.

"That can wait," Troy said gruffly. "I've got to talk to you."

"So talk," Covenant said around a mouthful of stew. In spite of his visitor's insistent impatience, he kept on eating. He ate rapidly, acting on his decision before doubt could make him regret it.

Troy paced the room stiffly for a moment, then brought himself to take a seat opposite Covenant. He sat as he stood—with unbending uprightness. His gleaming, impenetrable, black sunglasses emphasized the tightness of the muscles in his cheeks and fore-head. Carefully, he said, "You're determined to make this hard, aren't you? You're determined to make it hard for everyone."

Covenant shrugged. As the springwine unfurled within him, he began to recover from what he had seen in the sacred enclosure. At the same time, he re-membered his distrust of Troy. He ate with increasing wariness, watched the Warmark from under his eye-brows.

"Well, I'm trying to understand," Troy went on in a constrained tone. "God knows I've got a better chance than anyone else here."

Covenant put down the wooden fork and looked squarely at Troy.

"The same thing happened to us both." To the ob-vious disbelief in Covenant's face, he responded, "Oh, it's all clear enough. A white gold wedding ring.

Boots, jeans, and a T-shirt. You were talking on the phone with your wife. And the time before that— have I got this right?—you were hit by a car of some kind."

"A police car," Covenant murmured, staring at the Warmark.

"You see? I can recognize every detail. And you could do the same for my story. We both came here from the same place, the same world, Covenant. The real world."

No, Covenant breathed thickly. None of this is happening.

"I've even heard of you," Troy went on as if this argument would be incontrovertible. "I've read—your book was read to me. It made an impression on me."

Covenant snorted. But he was disturbed. He had burned that book too late; it continued to haunt him.

"No, hold on. Your damn book was a best-seller. Hundreds of thousands of people read it. It was made into a movie. Just because I know about it doesn't mean I'm a figment of your imagination. In fact, my presence here is proof that you are not going crazy. Two independent minds perceiving the same phenomenon."

He said this with confident plausibility, but Covenant was not swayed. "Proof?" he muttered. "I would be amused to hear what else you call proof."

"Do you want to hear how I came here?"

"No!" Covenant was suddenly vehement. "I want to hear why you don't want to go back."

For a moment, Troy sat still, facing Covenant with his sunglasses. Then he snapped to his feet, and started to pace again. Swinging tightly around on his heel at one end of the room, he said, "Two reasons. First, I like it here. I'm useful to something worth being useful to. The issues at stake in this war are the only ones I've ever seen worth fighting for. The life of the Land is beautiful. It deserves preservation. For once, I can do some good. Instead of spending my time on troop deployment, first- and second-strike capabilities, superready status, demoralization parameters, nuclear induction of lethal genetic events," he recited bitterly, "I can help defend against a genuine evil. The world we came from—the 'real' world—hasn't got such clear colors, no blue and black and green and red, 'ebon ichor incarnadine viridian.' Gray is the color of 'reality.'

"Actually"—he dropped back into his chair, and his voice took on a more conversational tone—"I didn't even know what gray was until I came here. That's my second reason."

He reached up with both hands and removed his sunglasses.

"I'm blind."

His sockets were empty, orbless, lacking even lids and lashes. Blank skin grew in the holes where his eyes should have been.

"I was born this way," the Warmark said, as if he could see Covenant's astonishment. "A genetic freak. But my parents saw fit to keep me alive, and by the time they died I had learned various ways to function on my own. I got myself into special schools, got special help. It took a few extra years because I had to have most things read to me, but eventually I got through high school and college. After which my only real skill was keeping track of spatial relationships in my head. For instance, I could play chess without a board. And if someone described a room to me, I could walk through it without bumping into anything. Basically I was good at that because it was how I kept myself alive.

"So I finally got a job in a think tank with the Department of Defense. They wanted people who could understand situations without being able to see them—people who could use language to deal with physical facts. I was the expert on war games, computer hypotheticals, that sort of thing. All I needed was accurate verbal information on topography, troop strength, hardware and deployment, support capabilities—then leave the game to me. I always won. So what did it all amount to? Nothing. I was the freak of the group, that's all.

"I took care of myself as well as I could. But for a place to live, I was pretty much at the mercy of what

I could get. So I lived in this apartment house on the ninth floor, and one night it burned down. That is, I assume it burned down. The fire company still hadn't come when my apartment caught. There was nothing I could do. The fire backed me to the wall, and finally I climbed out the window. I hung from the window-sill while the heat blistered my knuckles. I was determined not to let go because I had a very clear idea of how far above the ground nine floors is. Made no difference. After a while, my fingers couldn't hold on anymore.

"The next thing I knew, I was lying on something that felt like grass. There was a cool breeze—but with enough warmth behind it to make me think it must be daylight. The only thing wrong was a smell of burned flesh. I assumed it was me. Then I heard voices—urgent, people hurrying to try to prevent something. They found me.

"Later, I learned what had happened. A young student at the Loresraat had an inspiration about a piece of the Second Ward he was working on. All this was about five years ago. He thought he had figured out how to get help for the Land—how to summon you, actually. He wanted to try it, but the Lorewardens refused to let him. Too dangerous. They took his idea to study, and sent to Revelstone for a Lord to help them decide how to test his theory.

"Well, he didn't want to wait. He left the Loresraat and climbed a few miles up into the western hills of Trothgard until he thought he was far enough away to work in peace. Then he started the ritual. Somehow, the Lorewardens felt the power he was using, and went after him. But they were too late. He succeeded—in a manner of speaking. When he was done, I was lying there on the grass, and he— He had burned himself to death. Some of the Lorewardens think he caught the fire that should have killed me. As they said, it was too dangerous.

"The Lorewardens took me in, cared for me, put hurtloam on my hands—even on my eyesockets. Before long, I began having visions. Colors and shapes started to jump at me out of the—out of whatever it was I was used to. This round, white-orange circle passed over me every day—but I didn't know what it was. I didn't even know it was 'round.' I had no visual concept of 'round.' But the visions kept getting stronger. Finally, Elena—she was the Lord who came down from Revelstone, only she wasn't High Lord then—she told me that I was learning to see with my mind—as if my brain were actually starting to see through my forehead. I didn't believe it, but she showed me. She demonstrated how my sense of spatial relationships fitted what I was 'seeing,' and how my sense of touch matched the shapes around me."

He paused for a moment, remembering. Then he said strongly, "I'll tell you—I never think about going back. How can I? I'm here, and I can see. The Land's given me a gift I could never repay in a dozen lifetimes. I've got too big a debt— The first time I stood on the top of Revelwood and looked over the valley where the Rill and Llurallin rivers come together— the first time in my life that I had ever seen—the first time, Covenant, I had ever even known that such sights existed—I swore I was going to win this war for the Land. Lacking missiles and bombs, there are other ways to fight. It took me a little while to convince the Lords—just long enough for me to outsmart all the best tacticians in the Warward. Then they made me their Warmark. Now I'm just about ready. A difficult strategic problem—we're too far from the best line of defense, Landsdrop. And I haven't heard from my scouts. I don't know which way Foul is going to try to get at us. But I can beat him in a fair fight. I'm looking forward to it.

"Go back? No. Never."

Hile Troy had been speaking in a level tone, as if he did not want to expose his emotions to his auditor. But Covenant could hear an undercurrent of enthusiasm in the words—a timbre of passion too unruly to be concealed.

Now Troy leaned toward Covenant intently, and his ready indignation came back into his voice. "In fact, I can't understand you at all. Do you know that this whole place"—he indicated Revelstone with a brusque gesture—"revolves around you? White gold. The wild magic that destroys peace. The Unbeliever who found the Second Ward and saved the Staff of Law—unwillingly, I hear. For forty years, the Loresraat and the Lords have worked for a way to get you back. Don't get me wrong—they've done everything humanly possible to try to find other ways to defend the Land. They've built up the Warward, racked their brains over the Lore, risked their necks on things like Mhoram's trip to Foul's Creche. And they're scrupulous. They insist that they accept your ambivalent position. They insist that they don't expect you to save them. All they want is to make it possible for the wild magic to aid the Land, so they won't have to reproach themselves for neglecting a possible hope. But I tell you—they don't believe there is any hope but you.

"You know Lord Mhoram. You should have some idea of just how tough that man is. He's got backbone he hasn't even touched yet. Listen. He screams in his sleep. His dreams are that bad. I heard him once. He— I asked him the next morning what possessed him. In that quiet, kind voice of his, he told me that the Land would die if you didn't save it.

"Well, I don't believe that—Mhoram or no Mhoram. But he isn't the only one. High Lord Elena eats, drinks, and sleeps Unbeliever. Wild magic and white gold, Covenant Ringthane. Sometimes I think she's obsessed. She—"

But Covenant could not remain silent any longer. He could not stand to be held responsible for so much commitment. Roughly, he cut in, "Why?"

"I don't know. She doesn't even know you."

"No. I mean, why is she High Lord—instead of Mhoram?"

"What does it matter?" said Troy irritably. "The Council chose her. A couple of years ago—when Osondrea, the old High Lord, died. They put their minds together—you must have noticed when you were here before how the Lords can pool their thoughts, think together—and she was elected." As he spoke, the irritation faded from his tone. "They said she has some special quality, some inner mettle

that makes her the best leader for this war. Maybe I
don't know what they mean—but I know she's got
something. She's impossible to refuse. I would fight
with stew forks and soup spoons against Foul—

"So I don't understand you. You may be the last
man alive who's seen the Celebration of Spring. And
there she stands, looking like all the allure of the Land
put together—practically begging you. And you!"
Troy struck the table with his hand, brandished his
empty sockets at Covenant. "You refuse."

Abruptly, he slapped his sunglasses back on, and
flung away from the table to pace the room again, as
if he could not sit still in the face of Covenant's per-
versity.

Covenant watched him, seething at the freedom of
Troy's judgment—the trust he placed in his own
rectitude. But Covenant had heard something else in
Troy's voice, a different explanation. Probing bluntly,
he asked, "Is Mhoram in love with her, too?"

At that, Troy spun, pointed a finger rigid with accusation at the Unbeliever. "You know what I think?
You're too cynical to see the beauty here. You're too
cheap. You've got it made in your 'real' world, with
all those royalties rolling in. So what if you're sick?
That doesn't stop you from getting rich. Coming here
just gets in the way of hacking out more best-sellers.
Why should you fight the Despiser? You're just like
him yourself."

Before the Warmark could go on, Covenant rasped
thickly, "Get out. Shut up and get out."

"Forget it. I'm not going to leave until you give me
one—"

"Get out."

"—one good reason for the way you're acting. I'm
not going to walk away and let you destroy the Land
just because the Lords are too scrupulous to lean on
you."

"That's enough!" Covenant was on his feet. His
hurt blazed up before he could catch hold of himself.
"Don't you even know what a leper is?"

"What difference does that make? It's no worse
than not having any eyes. Aren't you healthy here?"

Mustering all the force of his injury, his furious grief, Covenant averred, "No!" He waved his hands. "Do you call this health? It's a lie!"

That cry visibly stunned Troy. The black assertion of his sunglasses faltered; the inner aura of his spirit was confused by doubt. For the first time, he looked like a blind man.

"I don't understand," he said softly.

He faced the onslaught of Covenant's glare for a moment longer. Then he turned and left the room, moving quietly, as if he had been humbled.

SIX: The High Lord

WHEN evening came, Thomas Covenant sat on his balcony to watch the sun set behind the Westron Mountains. Though summer was hardly past, there was a gleam of white snow on many of the peaks. As the sun dropped behind them, the western sky shone with a sharing of cold and fire. White silver reflected from the snow across the bottom of a glorious sky, an orange-gold gallant display sailing with full canvas over the horizon.

Covenant watched it bleakly. A scowl knotted his forehead like a fist. He had spent the afternoon in useless rage, but after a time his anger at Troy had died down among the embers of his protest against being summoned to the Land. Now he felt cold at heart, desolate and alone. The resolve he had expressed to Mhoram, his determination to survive, seemed pretentious—fey and anile. And the frown clenched his forehead as if the flesh over his skull refused to admit that it had been healed.

He was thinking of jumping from the balcony. To quell his fear of heights, he would have to wait until the darkness of the night was complete, and he could no longer see the ground. But considered in that way, the idea both attracted and repelled him. It offended his leper's training, heaped ridicule on everything he had already endured to cling to life. It spoke of a defeat that was as bitter as starkest gall to him. But he yearned for relief from his dilemma. He felt as dry as a wasteland, and rationalizations came easily. Chiefest of these was the argument that since the Land was not real it could not kill him; a death here would only force him back into the reality that was the only thing in which he could believe. In his aloneness, he could not tell whether that argument expressed courage or cowardice.

Slowly, the last of the sun fell behind the mountains, and its emblazonry faded from the sky. Gloaming spread out of the shadow of the peaks, dimming the plains below Covenant until he could only discern them as uneasy, recumbent shapes under the heavens. The stars came out and grew gradually brighter, as if to clarify trackless space; but the voids between them were too great, and the map they made was unreadable. In his dusty, unfertile gaze, they seemed to twinkle unconsolably.

When he heard the polite knock at his door, his need for privacy groaned at the intrusion. But he had other needs as well. He pushed himself to go answer the knock.

The stone door swung open easily on noiseless hinges, and light streamed into the room from the bright-lit hall, dazzling him so that for a moment he did not recognize either of the men outside. Then one of them said, "Ur-Lord Covenant, we bid you welcome," in a voice that seemed to bubble with good humor. Covenant identified Tohrm.

"Welcome and true," said Tohrm's companion carefully, as if he were afraid he would make a mistake. "We are the Hearthralls of Lord's Keep. Please accept welcome and comfort."

As Covenant's eyes adjusted, he considered the two men. Tohrm's companion wore a gray-green Woodhelvennin cloak, and had a small wreath in his hair—

the mark of a Hirebrand. In his hands he carried several smooth wooden rods for torches. Both the Hearthralls were clean-shaven, but the Hirebrand was taller and slimmer than his partner. Tohrm had the stocky, muscular frame of a Stonedownor, and he wore a loam-colored tunic with soft trousers. His companion's cloak was bordered in Lords' blue; he had blue epaulets woven into the shoulders of his tunic. Cupped in each of his hands was a small, covered, stone bowl.

Covenant scrutinized Tohrm's face. The Hearthrall's nimble eyes and swift smile were soberer than Covenant remembered them, but still essentially unchanged. Like Mhoram, he did not show enough years to account for the full forty.

"I am Borillar," Tohrm's companion recited, "Hirebrand of the *lillianrill* and Hearthrall of Lord's Keep. This is Tohrm, Gravelingas of the *rhadhamaerl* and likewise Hearthrall of Lord's Keep. Darkness withers the heart. We have brought you light."

But as Borillar spoke, a look of concern touched Tohrm's face, and he said, "Ur-Lord, are you well?"

"Well?" Covenant murmured vaguely.

"There is a storm on your brow, and it gives you pain. Shall I call a Healer?"

"What?"

"Ur-Lord Covenant, I am in your debt. I am told that at the hazard of your life you rescued my old friend Birinair from beyond the forbidding fire under Mount Thunder. That was bravely done—though it came too late to save his life. Do not hesitate to ask of me. For Birinair's sake, I will do all in my power for you."

Covenant shook his head. He knew he should correct Tohrm, tell him that he had braved that fire in an effort to immolate himself, not to save Birinair. But he lacked the courage. Dumbly, he stepped aside and let the Hearthralls into his rooms.

Borillar immediately set about lighting his torches; he moved studiously to the wall sockets as if he were trying to create a good, grave impression. Covenant watched him for a moment, and Tohrm said with a covered smile, "Good Borillar is in awe of you, ur-Lord. He has heard the legends of the Unbeliever from his cradle. And he has not been Hearthrall long. His former master in the *lillianrill* lore resigned this post to oversee the completion of the Gildenlode keels and rudders which they have been devising for the Giants —as High Lord Loric Vilesilencer promised. Borillar feels himself untimely thrust into responsibility. My old friend Birinair would have called him a whelp."

"He's young," Covenant said dully. Then he turned to Tohrm, forced himself to ask the question which most concerned him. "But you—you're too young. You should be older. Forty years."

"Ur-Lord, I have seen fifty-nine summers. Forty-one have passed since you came to Revelstone with the Giant, Saltheart Foamfollower."

"But you're not old enough. You don't look more than forty now."

"Ah," said Tohrm, grinning broadly, "the service of our lore, and of Revelstone, keeps us young. Without us, these brave Giant-wrought halls would be dark, and in winter—to speak truly—they would be cold. Who could grow old on the joy of such work?"

Happily, he moved off, set one of his pots on the table in the sitting room, and another in the bedroom by the bed. When he uncovered the pots, the warm glow of the graveling joined the light of the torches, and gave the illumination in the suite a richer and somehow kinder cast.

Tohrm breathed the graveling's aroma of newly broken earth with a glad smile. He finished while his companion was lighting the last of his torches in the bedroom. Before Borillar could return to the sitting room, the older Hearthrall stepped close to Covenant and whispered, "Ur-Lord, say a word to good Borillar. He will cherish it."

A moment later, Borillar walked across the room to stand stiffly by the door. He looked like a resolute acolyte, determined not to fail a high duty. Finally his young intentness, and Tohrm's appeal, moved Covenant to say, awkwardly, "Thank you, Hirebrand."

At once, pleasure transformed Borillar's face. He

tried to maintain his gravity, to control his grin, but the man of legends, Unbeliever and Ringthane, had spoken to him, and he blurted out, "Be welcome, ur-Lord Covenant. You will save the Land."

Tohrm cocked an amused eyebrow at his fellow Hearthrall, gave Covenant a gay, grateful bow, and ushered the Hirebrand from the room. As they departed, Tohrm started to close the door, then stopped, nodded to someone in the hall, and went away leaving the door open.

Bannor stepped into the room. He met Covenant's gaze with eyes that never slept—that only rarely blinked—and said, "The High Lord would speak with you now."

"Oh, hell," Covenant groaned. He looked back with something like regret at his balcony and the night beyond. Then he went with the Bloodguard.

Walking down the hall, he gave himself a quick VSE. It was a pointless exercise, but he needed the habit of it, if for no other reason than to remind himself of who he was, what the central fact of his life was. He did it deliberately, as a matter of conscious choice. But it did not hold his attention. As he moved, Revelstone exerted its old influence over him again.

The high, intricate ways of the Keep had a strange power of suasion, an ability to carry conviction. They had been delved into the mountain promontory by Saltheart Foamfollower's laughing, story-loving ancestors; and like the Giants they had an air of bluff and inviolable strength. Now Bannor was taking Covenant deeper down into Revelstone than he had ever been before. With his awakening perceptions, he could feel the massive gut-rock standing over him; it was as if he were in palpable contact with absolute weight itself. And on a pitch of hearing that was not quite audible, or not quite hearing, he could sense the groups of people who slept or worked in places beyond the walls from him. Almost he seemed to hear the great Keep breathe. And yet all those myriad, uncountable tons of stone were not fearsome. Revelstone gave him an impression of unimpeachable security; the mountain refused to let him fear that it would fall.

Then he and Bannor reached a dim hall sentried by two Bloodguard standing with characteristic relaxed alacrity on either side of the entrance. There were no torches or other lights in the hall, but a strong glow illuminated it from its far end. With a nod to his comrades, Bannor led Covenant inward.

At the end of the hall, they entered a wide, round courtyard under a high cavern, with a stone floor as smooth as if it had been meticulously polished for ages. The bright, pale-yellow light came from this floor; the stone shone as if a piece of the sun had gone into its making.

The courtyard held no other lights. But though it was not blinding at the level of the floor, the glow cast out all darkness. Covenant could survey the cave clearly from bottom to top. At intervals up the walls were railed coigns with doors behind them which provided access to the open space above the court.

Bannor paused for a moment to allow Covenant to look around. Then he walked barefoot out onto the shining floor. Tentatively, Covenant followed, fearing that his feet would be burned. But he felt nothing through his boots except a quiet resonance of power. It set up a tingling vibration in his nerves.

Only after he became accustomed to the touch of the floor did he notice that there were doors widely spaced around the courtyard. He counted fifteen. Bloodguard sentries stood at nine of them, and several feet into the shining floor from each of these nine was a wooden tripod. Three of these tripods held Lords' staffs—and one of the staffs was the Staff of Law. It was distinguished from the smooth wood of the other staffs by its greater thickness, and by the complex runes carved into it between its iron heels.

Bannor took Covenant to the door behind the Staff. The Bloodguard there stepped forward to meet them, greeted Bannor with a nod.

Bannor said, "I have brought ur-Lord Covenant to the High Lord."

"She awaits him." Then the sentry leveled the impassive threat of his gaze at Covenant. "We are the Bloodguard. The care of the Lords is in our hands. I am Morin, First Mark of the Bloodguard since the passing of Tuvor. The High Lord will speak with you alone. Think no harm against her, Unbeliever. We will not permit it." Without waiting for an answer, Morin stepped aside to let him approach the door.

Covenant was about to ask what harm he could possibly do the High Lord, but Bannor forestalled him. "In this place," the Bloodguard explained, "the Lords set aside their burdens. Their staffs they leave here, and within these doors they rest, forgetting the cares of the Land. The High Lord honors you greatly in speaking to you here. Without Staff or guard, she greets you as a friend in her sole private place. Ur-Lord, you are not a foe of the Land. But you give little respect. Respect this."

He held Covenant's gaze for a moment as if to enforce his words. Then he went and knocked at the door.

When the High Lord opened her door, Covenant saw her clearly for the first time. She had put aside her blue Lord's robe, and instead wore a long, light brown Stonedownor shift with a white pattern woven into the shoulders. A white cord knotted at her waist emphasized her figure, and her thick hair, a rich brown with flashes of pale honey, fell to her shoulders, disguising the pattern there. She appeared younger than he had expected—he would have said that she was in her early thirties at most—but her face was strong, and the white skin of her forehead and throat knew much about sternness and discipline, though she smiled almost shyly when she saw Covenant.

But behind the experience of responsibility and commitment in her features was something strangely evocative. She seemed distantly familiar, as if in the background of her face she resembled someone he had once known. This impression was both heightened and denied by her eyes. They were gray like his own; but though they met him squarely they had an elsewhere cast, a disunion of focus, as if she were watching something else—as if some other, more essential eyes, the eyes of her mind, were looking somewhere else. Her gaze touched parts of him which had not responded for a long time.

"Please enter," she said in a voice like a clear spring.

Moving woodenly, Covenant went past her into her rooms, and she shut the door behind him, closing out the light from the courtyard. Her antechamber was illumined simply by a pot of graveling in each corner. Covenant stopped in the center of the room, and looked about him. The space was bare and unadorned, containing nothing but the graveling, a few stone chairs, and a table on which stood a white carving; but still the room seemed quiet and comfortable. The light gave this effect, he decided. The warm graveling glow made even flat stone companionable, enhanced the essential security of Revelstone. It was like being cradled—wrapped in the arms of the rock and cared for.

High Lord Elena gestured toward one of the chairs. "Will you sit? There is much of which I would speak with you."

He remained standing, looking away from her. Despite the room's ambience, he felt intensely uncomfortable. Elena was his summoner, and he distrusted her. But when he found his voice, he half surprised himself by expressing one of his most private concerns. Shaking his head, he muttered, "Bannor knows more than he's telling."

He caught her off guard. "More?" she echoed, groping. "What has he said that leaves more concealed?"

But he had already said more than he intended. He kept silent, watching her out of the corner of his sight.

"The Bloodguard know doubt," she went on unsurely. "Since Kevin Landwaster preserved them from the Desecration and his own end, they have felt a distrust of their own fidelity—though none would dare to raise any accusation against them. Do you speak of this?"

He did not want to reply, but her direct attention compelled him. "They've already lived too long. Bannor knows it." Then, to escape the subject, he went over to the table to look at the carving. The white statuette stood on an ebony base. It was a rearing Ranyhyn mare made of a material that looked like bone. The work was blunt of detail, but through some secret of its art it expressed the power of the great muscles, the intelligence of the eyes, the oriflamme of the fluttering mane.

Without approaching him, Elena said, "That is my craft—marrowmeld. Does it please you? It is Myrha, the Ranyhyn that bears me."

Something stirred in Covenant. He did not want to think about the Ranyhyn, but he thought that he had found a discrepancy. "Foamfollower told me that the marrowmeld craft had been lost."

"So it was. I alone in the Land practice this Ramen craft. *Anundivian yajña,* also named marrowmeld or bone-sculpting, was lost to the Ramen during their exile in the Southron Range—during the Ritual of Desecration. I do not speak in pride—I have been blessed in many things. When I was a child, a Ranyhyn bore me into the mountains. For three days we did not return, so that my mother thought me dead. But the Ranyhyn taught me much—much— In my learning, I recovered the ancient craft. The lore to reshape dry bones came to my hands. Now I practice it here, when the work of the Lords wearies me."

Covenant kept his back to her, but he was not studying her sculpture. He was listening to her voice as if he expected it to change at any moment into the voice of someone he knew. Her tone resonated with implicit meanings. But he could not make them out. Abruptly, he turned to meet her eyes. Again, though she faced him, she seemed to be looking at or thinking about something else, something beyond him. Her elsewhere glance disturbed him. Studying her, his frown deepened until he wore the healing of his forehead like a crown of thorns.

"What do you want?" he demanded.

"Will you sit?" she said quietly. "There is much I would speak of with you."

"Like what?"

The hardness of his tone did not make her flinch,

but she spoke more quietly still. "I hope to find a way to win your help against the Despiser."

Thinking self-contemptuous thoughts, he retorted, "How far are you willing to go?"

For an instant, the other focus of her eyes came close to him, touched him like a lick of fire. Blood rushed to his face, and he almost recoiled a step—so strongly did he feel for that instant that she had the capacity to go far beyond anything he could imagine. But the glimpse passed before he could guess at what it was. She turned unhurriedly away, went briefly into one of her other rooms. When she returned, she bore in her hands a wooden casket bound with old iron.

Holding the casket as if it contained something precious, she said, "The Council has been much concerned in this matter. Some said, 'Such a gift is too great for anyone. Let it be kept and safe for as long as we may be able to endure.' And others said, 'It will fail of its purpose, for he will believe that we seek to buy his aid with gifts. He will be angered against us, and will refuse.' So spoke Lord Mhoram, whose knowledge of the Unbeliever is more than any other's. But I said, 'He is not our foe. He gives us no aid because he cannot give aid. Though he holds the white gold, its use is beyond him or forbidden him. Here is a weapon which surpasses us. It may be that he will be able to master it, and that with such a weapon he will help us, though he cannot use the white gold.'

"After much thought and concern, my voice prevailed. Therefore the Council asks to give you this gift, so that its power will not lie idle, but will turn against the Despiser.

"Ur-Lord Covenant, this is no light offering. Forty years ago, it was not in the possession of the Council. But the Staff of Law opened doors deep in Revelstone —doors which had been closed since the Desecration. The Lords hoped that these chambers contained other Wards of Kevin's Lore—but no Wards were there. Yet among many things of forgotten use or little power this was found—this which we offer to you."

She pressed curiously on the sides of the casket, and the lid swung open, revealing a cushioned velvet interior, on which lay a short silver sword. It was a two-edged blade, with straight guards and a ribbed hilt; and it was forged around a clear white gem, which occupied the junction of the blade, guards, and hilt. This gem looked strangely lifeless; it reflected no light from the graveling, as if it were impervious or dead to any ordinary flame.

With awe in her low voice, Elena said, "This is the *krill* of Loric Vilesilencer son of Damelon son of Berek. With this he slew the Demondim guise of *moksha* Raver, and delivered the Land from the first great peril of the ur-viles. Ur-Lord Covenant, Unbeliever and Ringthane, will you accept it?"

Slowly, full of a leper's fascinated dread of things that cut, Covenant lifted the *krill* from its velvet rest. Hefting it, he found that its balance pleased his hand, though his two fingers and thumb could not grip it well. Cautiously, he tested its edges with his thumb. They were as dull as if they had never been honed— as dull as the white gem. For a moment, he stood still, thinking that a knife did not need to be sharp to harm him.

"Mhoram was right," he said out of the dry, lonely hebetude of his heart. "I don't want any gifts. I've had more gifts than I can bear."

Gifts! It seemed to him that everyone he had ever known in the Land had tried to give him gifts—Foamfollower, the Ranyhyn, Lord Mhoram, even Atiaran. The Land itself gave him an impossible nerve-health. But the gift of Lena Atiaran-daughter was more terrible than all the others. He had raped her, raped! And afterward, she had gone into hiding so that her people would not learn what had happened to her and punish him. She had acted with an extravagant forbearance so that he could go free—free to deliver Lord Foul's prophecy of doom to the Lords. Beside that self-abnegation, even Atiaran's sacrifices paled.

Lena! he cried. A violence of grief and self-recrimination blazed up in him. "I don't want any more." Thunder blackened his face. He grasped the *krill* in both fists, its blade pointing downward. With a convulsive movement, he stabbed the sword at the heart of the table, trying to break its blunt blade on the stone.

A sudden flash of white blinded him like an instant of lightning. The *krill* wrenched out of his hands. But he did not try to see what had happened to it. He spun instantly back to face Elena. Through the white dazzle that confused his sight, he panted, "No more *gifts!* I can't afford them!"

But she was not looking at him, not listening to him. She held her hands to her mouth as she stared past him at the table. "By the Seven!" she whispered. "What have you done?"

What—?

He whirled to look.

The blade of the *krill* had pierced the stone; it was embedded halfway to its guards in the table.

Its white gem burned like a star.

Dimly, he became conscious of a throbbing ache in his wedding finger. His ring felt hot and heavy, almost molten. But he ignored it; he was afraid of it. Trembling, he reached out to touch the *krill*.

Power burned his fingers.

Hellfire!

He snatched his hand away. The fierce pain made him clasp his fingers under his other arm, and groan.

At once, Elena turned to him. "Are you harmed?" she asked anxiously. "What has happened to you?"

"Don't touch me!" he gasped.

She recoiled in confusion, then stood watching him, torn between her concern for him and her astonishment at the blazing gem. After a moment, she shook herself as if throwing off incomprehension, and said softly, "Unbeliever—you have brought the *krill* to life."

Covenant made an effort to match her, but his voice quavered as he said, "It won't make any difference. It won't do you any good. Foul's got all the power that counts."

"He does not possess the white gold."

"To hell with the white gold!"

"No!" she retorted vehemently. "Do not say such a thing. I have not lived my life for nothing. My mother, and her mother before her, have not lived for nothing!"

He did not understand her, but her sudden passion silenced him. He felt trapped between her and the *krill;* he did not know what to say or do. Helpless, he stared at the High Lord as her own emotions grew into speech.

"You say that this makes no difference—that it does no good. Are you a prophet? And if you are, what do you say that we should do? Surrender?" For an instant, her self-possession wavered, and she exclaimed furiously, "Never!" He thought that he heard hatred in her words. But then she lowered her voice, and the sound of loathing faded. "No! There is no one in the Land who could endure to stand aside and allow the Despiser to work his will. If we must suffer and die without hope, then we will do so. But we will not despair, though it is the Unbeliever himself who says that we must."

Useless emotions writhed across his face, but he could not answer. His own conviction or energy had fallen into dust. Even the pain in his hand was almost gone. He looked away from her, then winced at the sharp sight of the *krill.* Slowly, as if he had aged in the past few moments, he lowered himself into a chair. "I wish," he murmured blankly, emptily, "I wish I knew what to do."

At the edge of his attention, he was aware that Elena had left the room. But he did not raise his head until she returned and stood before him. In her hands she held a flask of springwine which she offered to him.

He could see a concern he did not deserve in the complex otherness of her gaze.

He accepted the flask and drank deeply, searching for a balm to ease the splitting ache in his forehead—and for some way to support his failing courage. He dreaded the High Lord's intentions, whatever they were. She was too sympathetic, too tolerant of his violence; she allowed him too much leeway without setting him free. Despite the solidity of Revelstone under his sensitive feet, he was on unsteady ground.

When after a short silence she spoke again, she had an air of bringing herself to the point of some difficult honesty; but there was nothing candid in the unexplained disfocus of her eyes. "I am lost in this matter," she said. "There is much that I must tell you, if I am to be open and blameless. I do not wish to be reproached with any lack of knowledge in you—the Land will not be served by any concealment which might later be called by another name. Yet my courage fails me, and I know not what words to use. Mhoram offered to take this matter from me, and I refused, believing that the burden is mine. Yet now I am lost, and cannot begin."

Covenant bent his frown toward her, refusing with the pain in his forehead to give her any aid.

"You have spoken with Hile Troy," she said tentatively, unsure of this approach. "Did he describe his coming to the Land?"

Covenant nodded without relenting. "An accident. Some misbegotten kid—a young student, he says—was trying to get me."

Elena moved as if she meant to pursue that idea, but then she stopped herself, reconsidered, and took a different tack. "I do not know your world—but the Warmark tells me that such things do not happen there. Have you observed Lord Mhoram? Or Hiltmark Quaan? Or perhaps Hearthrall Tohrm? Any of those you knew forty years ago? Does it appear to you that—that they are young?"

"I've noticed." Her question agitated him. He had been clinging to the question of age, trying to establish it as a discrepancy, a breakdown in the continuity of his delusion. "It doesn't fit. Mhoram and Tohrm are too young. It's impossible. They are not forty years older."

"I also am young," she said intently, as if she were trying to help him guess a secret. But at the sight of his glowering incomprehension, she retreated from the plunge. To answer him, she said, "This has been true for as long as there has been such lore in the Land. The Old Lords lived to great age. They were not long-lived as the Giants are—because that is the

natural span of their people. No, it was the service of
the Earthpower which preserved them, secured them
from age long past their normal years. High Lord
Kevin lived centuries as people live decades.

"So, too, it is in this present time, though in a lesser
way. We do not bring out all the potency of the Lore.
And the Warlore does not preserve its followers, so
Quaan and his warriors alone of your former comrades carry their full burden of years. But those of
the *rhadhamaerl* and the *lillianrill,* and the Lords who
follow Kevin's Lore, age more slowly than others.
This is a great boon, for it extends our strength. But
also it causes grief—"

She fell silent for a moment, sighed quietly to herself as if she were remembering an old injury. But
when she spoke again, her voice was clear and steady.
"So it has always been. Lord Mhoram has seen ten
times seven summers—yet he hardly carries fifty of
them. And—" Once again, she stopped herself and
changed directions. With a look that searched Covenant, she said, "Does it surprise you to hear that I
rode a Ranyhyn as a child? There is no other in the
Land who has had such good fortune."

He finished his springwine, and got to his feet to
pace the room in front of her. The tone in which she
recurred to the Ranyhyn was full of suggestions; he
sensed wide possibilities of distress in it. More in anxiety than in irritation, he growled at her, "Hellfire.
Get on with it."

She tensed as if in preparation for a struggle, and
said, "Warmark Hile Troy's account of his summoning
to the Land may not have been altogether accurate. I
have heard him tell his tale, and he confuses something which I—we—have not thought it well to correct. We have kept this matter secret between us.

"Ur-Lord Covenant." She paused, steadying herself, then said carefully, "Hile Troy was summoned
by no young student, ignorant of the perils of power.
The summoner was one whom you have known."

Triock! Covenant almost missed his footing. Triock
son of Thuler, of Mithil Stonedown, had reason to
hate the Unbeliever. He had loved Lena— But Cove-

nant could not bear to say that name aloud. Squirm-
ing at his cowardice, he avoided Triock by saying,
"Pietten. That poor kid—from Soaring Woodhelven.
The ur-viles did something to him. Was it him?" He
did not dare to meet the High Lord's eyes.

"No, Thomas Covenant," she said gently. "It was
no man. You knew her well. She was Atiaran Trell-
mate—she who guided you from Mithil Stonedown
to your meeting with Saltheart Foamfollower at the
Soulsease River."

"Hellfire!" he groaned. At the sound of her name,
he saw in his mind Atiaran's spacious eyes, saw the
courage with which she had denied her passion
against him in order to serve the Land. And he caught
a quick visionary image of her face as she incinerated
herself trying to summon him—entranced, bitter, livid
with the conflagration of all the inner truces which he
had so severely harmed. "Ah, hell," he breathed.
"Why? She needed—she needed to forget."

"She could not. Atiaran Trell-mate returned to the
Loresraat in her old age for many reasons, but two
were uppermost. She desired to bring—no, desire is
too small a word. She hungered for you. She could not
forget. But whether she wanted you for the Land, or
for herself, I do not know. She was a torn woman,
and it is in my heart that both hungers warred in her
to the last. How otherwise? She said that you permitted the ravage of the Celebration of Spring, though
my mother taught me a different tale."

No! moaned Covenant, pacing bent as if borne
down by the weight of the darkness on his forehead.
Oh, Atiaran!

"Her second reason touches on the grief of long
years and extended strength. For her husband was
Trell, Gravelingas of the *rhadhamaerl*. Their marriage
was brave and glad in the memory of Mithil Stonedown, for though she had surpassed her strength during her youth in the Loresraat, and had left in
weakness, yet was she strong enough to stand with
Trell her husband.

"But her weakness, her self-distrust, remained. The
grave test of her life came and passed, and she grew

old. And to the pain you gave her was added another; she aged, and Trell Atiaran-mate did not. His lore sustained him beyond his years. So after so much hurt she began to lose her husband as well, though his love was steadfast. She was his wife, yet she became old enough to be his mother.

"So she returned to the Loresraat, in grief and pain—and in devotion, for though she doubted herself, her love for the Land did not waver. Yet at the last ill came upon her. Fleeing the restraint of the Lorewardens, she wrought death upon herself. In that way, she broke her Oath of Peace, and ended her life in despair."

No! he protested. But he remembered Atiaran's anguish, and the price she had paid to repress it, and the wrong he had done her. He feared that Elena was right.

In a sterner voice that did not appear to match her words, the High Lord continued, "After her death, Trell came to Revelstone. He is one of the mightiest of all the *rhadhamaerl,* and he remains here, giving his skill and lore to the defense of the Land. But he knows bitterness, and I fear that his Oath rests uneasily upon him. For all his gentleness, he has been too much made helpless. It is in my heart that he does not forgive. There was no aid he could give Atiaran —or my mother."

Through the ache of his memories, Covenant wanted to protest that Trell, with his broad shoulders and his strange power, knew nothing about the true nature of helplessness. But this objection was choked off by the grip of Elena's voice as she said, *my mother.* He stood still, bent as if he were about to capsize, and waited for the last unutterable blackness to fall on him.

"So you must understand why I rode a Ranyhyn as a child. Every year at the last full moon before the middle night of spring, a Ranyhyn came to Mithil Stonedown. My mother understood at once that this was a gift from you. And she shared it with me. It was so easy for her to forget that you had hurt her. Did I not tell you that I also am young? I am Elena daughter

of Lena daughter of Atiaran Trell-mate. Lena my
mother remains in Mithil Stonedown, for she insists
that you will return to her."

For one more moment, he stood still, staring at the
pattern woven into the shoulders of her shift. Then a
flood of revelations crashed through him, and he understood. He stumbled, dropped into a chair as suddenly as if his spine had broken. His stomach churned,
and he gagged, trying to heave up his emptiness.

"I'm sorry." The words burst between his teeth as
if torn out of his chest by a hard fist of contrition.
They were as inadequate as stillborns, too dead to
express what he felt. But he could do nothing else.
"Oh, Lena! I'm sorry." He wanted to weep, but he
was a leper, and had forgotten how.

"I was impotent." He forced the jagged confession
through his sore throat. "I forgot what it's like. Then
we were alone. And I felt like a man again, but I
knew it wasn't true, it was false, I was dreaming, had
to be, it couldn't happen any other way. It was too
much. I couldn't stand it."

"Do not speak to me of impotence," she returned
tightly. "I am the High Lord. I must defeat the Despiser using arrows and swords." Her tone was harsh;
he could hear other words running through it, as if
she were saying, Do you think that mere explanation
or apology is sufficient reparation? And without the
diseased numbness which justified him, he could not
argue.

"No," he said in a shaking voice. "Nothing suffices."

Slowly, heavily, he raised his head and looked at
her. Now he could see in her the sixteen-year-old child
he had known, her mother. That was her hidden fa-
miliarity. She had her mother's hair, her mother's figure. Behind her discipline, her face was much like her
mother's. And she wore the same white leaf-pattern
woven into the cloth at her shoulders which Lena had
worn—the pattern of Trell's and Atiaran's family.

When he met her eyes, he saw that they, too, were
like Lena's. They glowed with something that was
neither anger nor condemnation; they seemed to contradict the judgment he had heard a moment earlier.

"What are you going to do now?" he said weakly. "Atiaran wanted—wanted the Lords to punish me."

Abruptly, she left her seat, moved around behind him. She put her hands tenderly on his clenched brow and began to rub it, seeking to stroke away the knots and furrows. "Ah, Thomas Covenant," she sighed, with something like yearning in her voice. "I am the High Lord. I bear the Staff of Law. I fight for the Land, and will not quail though the beauty may die, or I may die, or the world may die. But there is much of Lena my mother in me. Do not frown at me so. I cannot bear it."

Her soft, cool, consoling touch seemed to burn his forehead. Mhoram had said that she had sat with him during his ordeal the previous night—sat, and watched over him, and held his hand. Trembling, he got to his feet. Now he knew why she had summoned him. There was a world of implications in the air between them; her whole life was on his head, for good or ill. But it was too much; he was too staggered and drained to grasp it all, deal with it. His stiff face was only capable of grimaces. Mutely, he left her, and Bannor guided him back to his rooms.

In his suite, he extinguished the torches, covered the graveling pots. Then he went out onto his balcony.

The moon was rising over Revelstone. It was still new, and it came in silver over the horizon, tinting the plains with unviolated luminescence. He breathed the autumn air, and leaned on the railing, immune for the moment from vertigo. Even that had been drained out of him.

He did not think about jumping. He thought about how difficult Elena was to refuse.

SEVEN: Korik's Mission

SOMETIME before dawn, an insistent pounding at his door woke him. He had been dreaming about the Quest for the Staff of Law—about his friend, Saltheart Foamfollower, whom the company of the Quest had left behind to guard their rear before they had entered the catacombs of Mount Thunder. Covenant had not seen him again, did not know whether the Giant had survived that perilous duty. When he awoke, his heart was laboring as if the clamor at the door were the beating of his dread.

Numbly, dazed with sleep, he uncovered a graveling pot, then shambled into the sitting room to answer the door.

He found a man standing in the brightness of the hall. His blue robe belted in black and his long staff identified him as a Lord.

"Ur-Lord Covenant," the man began at once. "I must apologize profusely for disturbing your rest. Of all the Lords, I am the one who most regrets such an intrusion. I have a deep love for rest. Rest and food, ur-Lord—sleep and sustenance. They are exquisite. Although there are some who would say that I have tasted so much sustenance that I should no longer require rest. No doubt some such argument caused me to be chosen for this arduous and altogether unsavory journey." Without asking for permission, he bustled past Covenant into the room. He was grinning.

Covenant blinked his bleary gaze into focus, and took a close look at the man.

He was short and corpulent, with a round, beatific face, but the serenity of his countenance was punctured by his gleeful eyes, so that he looked like a misbegotten cherub. His expression was constantly roiled; fleet smiles, smirks, frowns, grimaces chased each other across the surface of his essential good humor. Now he was regarding Covenant with a look of appraisal, as if he were trying to gauge the Unbeliever's responsiveness to jesting.

"I am Hyrim son of Hoole," he said fluidly, "a Lord of the Council, as you see, and a lover of all good cheer, as you have perhaps not failed to notice." His eyes gleamed impishly. "I would tell you of my parentage and history, so that you might know me better—but my time is short. There are consequences to this riding of Ranyhyn, but when I offered myself to their choice I did not know that the honor could be so burdensome. Perhaps you will consent to accompany me?"

Mutely, Covenant's lips formed the word, Accompany?

"To the courtyard, at least—if I can persuade you no farther. I will explain while you ready yourself."

Covenant felt too groggy to understand what was being asked of him. The Lord wanted him to get dressed and go somewhere. Was that all? After a moment, he found his voice, and asked, "Why?"

With an effort, Hyrim pulled an expression of seriousness onto his face. He studied Covenant gravely, then said, "Ur-Lord, there are some things which are difficult to say to you. Both Lord Mhoram and High Lord Elena might have spoken. They do not desire that this knowledge should be withheld from you. But brother Mhoram is reluctant to describe his own pain. And the High Lord—it is in my heart that she fears to send you into peril."

He grinned ruefully. "But I am not so selfless. You will agree that there is much of me to consider—and every part is tender. Courage is for the lean. I am wiser. Wisdom is no more and no less deep than the skin—and mine is very deep. Of course, it is said that trial and hardship refine the spirit. But I have heard the Giants reply that there is time enough to refine the spirit when the body has no other choice."

Covenant had heard that, too; Foamfollower had

said it to him. He shook his head to clear away the painful memory. "I don't understand."

"You have cause," said the Lord. "I have not yet uttered anything of substance. Ah, Hyrim," he sighed to himself, "brevity is such a simple thing—and yet it surpasses you. Ur-Lord, will you not dress? I must tell you news of the Giants which will not please you."

A pang of anxiety stiffened Covenant. He was no longer sleepy. "Tell me."

"While you dress."

Cursing silently, Covenant hurried into the bedroom and began to put on his clothes.

Lord Hyrim spoke from the other room. His tone was careful, as if he were making a deliberate effort to be concise. "Ur-Lord, you know of the Giants. Saltheart Foamfollower himself brought you to Revelstone. You were present in the Close when he spoke to the Council of Lords, telling them that the omens which High Lord Damelon had foreseen for the Giants' hope of Home had come to pass."

Covenant knew; he remembered it vividly. Back in the age of the Old Lords, the Giants had been wanderers of the sea who had lost their way. For that reason, they called themselves the Unhomed. They had roamed for decades in search of their lost homeland, but had not found it. At last, they had come to the shores of the Land in the region known as Seareach, and there—welcomed and befriended by Damelon—they had made a place for themselves to live until they rediscovered their ancient Home.

Since that time, three thousand years ago, their search had been fruitless. But Damelon Giantfriend had prophesied for them; he had foreseen an end to their exile.

After, and perhaps because, they had lost their Home, the Giants had begun to decline. Though they dearly loved children, few children were born; their seed did not replenish itself. For many centuries, their numbers had been slowly shrinking.

Damelon had foretold that this would change, that their seed would regain its vitality. That was his omen, his sign that the exile was about to end, for good or ill.

In his turn, Damelon's son, Loric, had made a promise to support and affirm that prophecy. He had said that, when Damelon's omens were fulfilled, the Lords would provide the Giants with potent Gildenlode keels and rudders for the building of new ships for their homeward journey.

So it was that Foamfollower had reported to the Council that Wavenhair Haleall, the wife of Sparlimb Keelsetter, had given birth to triplets, three sons—an event unprecedented in Seareach. And at the same time, scouting ships had returned to say that they had found a way which might lead the Giants Home. Foamfollower had come to Revelstone to claim High Lord Loric's promise.

"For forty years," Lord Hyrim went on, "the *lillianrill* of Lord's Keep have striven to meet that promise. The seven keels and rudders are now nearly complete. But time hurries on our heels, driving us dangerously. When this war begins, we will be unable to transport the Gildenlode to Seareach. And we will need the help of the Giants to fight Lord Foul. Yet it may be that all such helps or hopes will fail. It may be—"

"Foamfollower," Covenant interrupted. He fumbled at the laces of his boots. A keen concern made him impatient, urgent. "What about him? Is he—? What happened to him—after the Quest?"

The Lord's tone became still more careful. "When the Quest for the Staff of Law made its way homeward, it found that Saltheart Foamfollower was alive and unharmed. He had gained the safety of Andelain, and so had escaped the Fire-Lions. He returned to his people, and since that time he has come twice to Revelstone to help in the shaping of the Gildenlode and to share knowledge. Many Giants came and went, full of hope.

"But now, ur-Lord—" Hyrim stopped. There was sorrow and grimness in his voice. "Ah, now."

Covenant strode back into the sitting room, faced the Lord. "Now?" His own voice was unsteady.

"Now for three years a silence has lain over Seareach. No Giant has come to Revelstone—no

Giant has set foot on the Upper Land." To answer
the sudden flaring of Covenant's gaze, he continued,
"Oh, we have not been idle. For a year we did nothing—Seareach is near to four hundred leagues distant,
and a silence of a year is not unusual. But after a year,
we became concerned. Then for a year we sent mes-
sengers. None have ever returned. During the spring,
we sent an entire Eoman. Twenty warriors and their
Warhaft did not return.

"Therefore the Council decided to risk no more
warriors. In the summer, Lord Callindrill and Lord
Amatin rode eastward with their Bloodguard, seeking
passage. They were thrown back by a dark and
nameless power in Sarangrave Flat. Sister Amatin
would have died when her horse fell, but the Ranyhyn
of Callindrill bore them both to safety. Thus a shadow
has come between us and our ancient Rockbrothers,
and the fate of the Giants is unknown."

Covenant groaned inwardly. Foamfollower had
been his friend—and yet he had not even said good-
bye to the Giant when they had parted. He felt an
acute regret. He wanted to see Foamfollower again,
wanted to apologize.

But at the same time he was conscious of Hyrim's
gaze on him. The Lord's naturally gay eyes held a look
of painful somberness. Clearly, he had some reason
for awakening Covenant before dawn like this. With
a jerk of his shoulders, Covenant pushed down his
regret, and said, "I still don't understand."

At first Lord Hyrim did not falter. "Then I will
speak plainly. During the night after your summoning,
Lord Mhoram was called from your side by a vision.
The hand of his power came upon him, and he saw
sights which turned his blood to dread in his veins. He
saw—" Then abruptly he turned away. "Ah, Hyrim,"
he sighed, "you are a fat, thistle-brained fool. What
business had you to dream of Lords and Lore, of
Giants and bold undertakings? When such thoughts
first entered your childish head, you should have been
severely punished and sent to tend sheep. Your thick,
inept self does scant honor to Hoole Gren-mate your
father, who trusted that your foolish fancies would

not lead you astray." Over his shoulder, he said softly, "Lord Mhoram saw the death of the Giants marching toward them. He could not make out the face of that death. But he saw that if they are not aided soon— soon, perhaps in a score of days!—they will surely be destroyed."

Destroyed? Covenant echoed silently. Destroyed? Then he went a step further. Is that my fault, too? "Why," he began, then swallowed roughly. "Why are you telling me? What do you expect me to do?"

"Because of brother Mhoram's vision, the Council has decided that it must send a mission to Seareach at once—now. Because of the war, we cannot spare much of our strength—but Mhoram says that speed is needed more than strength. Therefore High Lord Elena has chosen two Lords—two Lords who have been accepted by the Ranyhyn—Shetra Verement-mate, whose knowledge of Sarangrave Flat is greater than any other's, and Hyrim son of Hoole, who has a passing acquaintance with the lore of the Giants. To accompany us, First Mark Morin has chosen fifteen Bloodguard led by Korik, Cerrin, and Sill. The High Lord has given the mission to them as well as to us, so that if we fall they will go on to the Giants' aid.

"Korik is among the most senior of the Blood-guard." The Lord seemed to be digressing, avoiding something that he hesitated to say. "With Tuvor, Morin, Bannor, and Terrel, he commanded the original *Haruchai* army which marched against the Land —marched, and met High Lord Kevin, with the Ranyhyn and the Giants, and was moved by love and wonder and gratitude to swear the Vow of service which began the Bloodguard. Sill is the Bloodguard who holds me in his especial care, just as Cerrin holds Lord Shetra. I will require them to hold us well," Hyrim growled with a return to humor. "I do not wish to lose all this flesh which I have so joyfully gained."

In frustration, Covenant repeated sharply, "What do you expect me to do?"

Slowly, Hyrim turned to face him squarely. "You have known Saltheart Foamfollower," he said. "I wish you to come with us."

Covenant gaped at the Lord in astonishment. He felt suddenly faint. From a distance, he heard himself asking weakly, "Does the High Lord know about this?"

Hyrim grinned. "Her anger will blister the skin of my face when she hears what I have said to you." But a moment later, he was sober again. "Ur-Lord, I do not say that you should accompany us. Perhaps I am greatly wrong in my asking. There is much that we do not know concerning the Despiser's intent for this war—and of these one of the greatest is our ignorance of the direction from which he will attack. Will he move south of Andelain as he has in past ages, and then strike northward through the Center Plains, or will he march north along Landsdrop to approach us from the east? This ignorance paralyzes our defense. The Warward cannot move until we know the answer. Warmark Troy is much concerned. But if Lord Foul chooses to assail us from the east, then our mission to Seareach will ride straight into his strength. For that reason, it would be unsurpassable folly for the white gold to accompany us.

"No, if it were wise for you to ride with us, Lord Mhoram would have spoken of it with you. Nevertheless I ask. I love the Giants deeply, ur-Lord. They are precious to all the Land. I would brave even High Lord Elena's wrath to give them any aid."

The simple sincerity of the Lord's appeal touched Covenant. Though he had just met the man, he found that he liked Hyrim son of Hoole—liked him and wanted to help him. And the Giants were a powerful argument. He could not bear to think that Foamfollower, so full of life and laughter and comprehension, might be killed if he were not given aid. But that argument reminded Covenant bitterly that he was less capable of help than anyone in the Land. And Elena's influence was still strong on him. He did not want to do anything to anger her, anything that would give her additional cause to hate him. He was torn; he could not answer the candid question in Hyrim's gaze.

Abruptly, the Lord's eyes filled with tears. He looked away, blinking rapidly. "I have given you pain, ur-Lord," he said softly. "Forgive me." Covenant expected to hear irony, criticism, in the words, but Hyrim's tone expressed only an uncomplex sorrow. When he faced Covenant again, his lips wore a lame smile. "Well, then. Will you not at least come with me to the courtyard? The mission will soon meet there to depart. Your presence will say to all Revelstone that you act from choice rather than from ignorance."

That Covenant could not refuse; he was too ashamed of his essential impotence, too angry. Kicking himself vehemently into motion, he strode out of his suite.

At once, he found Bannor at his elbow. Between the Bloodguard and the Lord, he stalked downward through the halls and passages toward the gates of Revelstone.

There was only one entrance to Lord's Keep, and the Giants had designed it well to defend the city. At the wedge tip of the plateau, they had hollowed out the stone to form a courtyard between the main Keep and the watchtower which protected the outer gates. Those gates—huge, interlocking stone slabs which could close inward to seal the entrance completely— led to a tunnel under the tower. The tunnel opened into the courtyard, and the entrance from the courtyard to the Keep was defended by another set of gates as massive and solid as the first. The main Keep was joined to the tower by a series of wooden crosswalks suspended at intervals above the court, but the only ground-level access to the tower was through two small doors on either side of the tunnel. Thus any enemy who accomplished the almost impossible task of breaking the outer gates would then have to attempt the same feat at the inner gates while under attack from the battlements of both the watchtower and the main Keep.

The courtyard was paved with flagstones except in the center, where an old Gilden tree grew, nourished by springs of fresh water. Lord Hyrim, Bannor, and Covenant found the rest of the mission there beside the tree, under the waning darkness of the sky. Dawn had begun.

Shivering in the crisp air, Covenant looked around the court. In the light which reflected from within the Keep, he could see that all the people near the tree were Bloodguard except for one Lord, a tall woman. She stood facing into Revelstone; Covenant could see her clearly. She had stiff, iron-gray hair that she wore cropped short; and her face was like the face of a hawk—keen of nose and eye, lean of cheek. Her eyes held a sharp gleam like the hunting stare of a hawk. But behind the gleam, Covenant discerned something that looked like an ache of desire, a yearning which she could neither satisfy nor repress.

Lord Hyrim greeted her companionably, but she ignored him, stared back into the Keep as if she could not bear to leave it.

Behind her, the Bloodguard were busy distributing burdens, packing their supplies into bundles with *clingor* thongs. These they tied to their backs so that their movements would not be hampered. Soon one of them—Covenant recognized Korik—stepped forward and announced to Lord Hyrim that he was ready.

"Ready, friend Korik?" Hyrim's voice had a jaunty sound. "Ah, would that I could say the same. But, by the Seven! I am not a man suited for great dangers— I am better made to applaud victories than to perform them. Yes, that is where my skills lie. Were you to bring me a victory, I could drink a pledge to it which would astound you. But this—riding at speed across the Land, into the teeth of who knows what ravenous perils—! Can you tell us of these perils, Korik?"

"Lord?"

"I have given this matter thought, friend Korik— you may imagine how difficult it was for me. But I see that the High Lord gave this mission into your hands for good reason. Hear what I have thought—efforts like mine should not be wasted. Consider this. Of all the people of Revelstone, only the Bloodguard have known the Land before the Desecration. You have known Kevin himself. Surely you know far more of him than do we. And surely, also, you know far more of the Despiser. Perhaps you know how he wages war. Perhaps you know more than Lord Callindrill could tell us of the dangers which lie between us and Seareach."

Korik shrugged slightly.

"It is in my heart," Hyrim went on, "that you can measure the dangers ahead better than any Lord. You should speak of them, so that we may prepare. It may be that we should not risk Grimmerdhore or the Sarangrave, but should rather ride north and around, despite the added length of days."

"The Bloodguard do not know the future." Korik's tone was impassive, yet Covenant heard a faint stress on the word *know*. Korik seemed to use that word in a different sense than Hyrim did, a larger or more prophetic sense.

And the Lord was unsatisfied. "Perhaps not. But you did not share Kevin's reign and learn nothing. Do you fear we cannot endure the knowledge you bear?"

"Hyrim, you forget yourself," Lord Shetra cut in abruptly. "Is this your respect for the keepers of the Vow?"

"Ah, sister Shetra, you misunderstand. My respect for the Bloodguard is unbounded. How could I feel otherwise about men sworn beyond any human oath to keep me alive? Now if they were to promise me good food, I would be totally in their debt. But surely you see where we stand. The High Lord has given this mission into their hands. If the peril we ride to meet so blithely forces them to the choice, the Bloodguard will pursue the mission rather than defend us."

For a moment, Lord Shetra fixed Hyrim with a hard glance like an expression of contempt. But when she spoke, her voice did not impugn him. "Lord Hyrim, you are not blithe. You believe that the survival of the Giants rides on this mission, and you seek to conceal your fear for them."

"*Melenkurion* Skyweir!" Hyrim growled to keep himself from laughing. "I seek only to preserve my fine and hard-won flesh from inconsiderate assault. It would become you to share such a worthy desire."

"Peace, Lord. I have no heart for jesting," sighed

Shetra, and turned away to resume her study of Revelstone.

Lord Hyrim considered her in silence briefly, then said to Korik, "Well, she has less body to preserve than I have. It may be that fine spirit is reserved for neglected flesh. I must speak of this with the Giants— if we reach them."

"We are the Bloodguard," answered Korik flatly. "We will gain Seareach."

Hyrim glanced up at the night sky, and said in a soft, musing tone, "Summon or succor. Would that there were more of us. The Giants are vast, and if they are in need the need will be vast."

"They are the Giants. Are they not equal to any need?"

The Lord flashed a look at Korik, but did not reply. Soon he moved to Shetra's side, and said quietly, "Come, sister. The journey calls. The way is long, and if we hope to end we must first begin."

"Wait!" she cried softly, like the distant scream of a bird.

Hyrim studied her for another moment. Then he came back to Covenant. In a whisper so low that Covenant could hardly hear it, the Lord said, "She desires to see Lord Verement her husband before we go. Theirs is a sad tale, ur-Lord. Their marriage is troubled. Both are proud— Together they made the journey to the Plains of Ra to offer themselves to the Ranyhyn. And the Ranyhyn—ah, the Ranyhyn chose her, but refused him.

"Well, they choose in their own way, and even the Ramen cannot explain them. But it has made a difference between these two. Brother Verement is a worthy man—yet now he has reason to believe himself unworthy. And sister Shetra can neither accept nor deny his self-judgment. And now this mission— Verement should rightly go in my place, but the mission requires the speed and endurance of the Ranyhyn. For her sake alone, I would wish that you might go in her stead."

"I don't ride Ranyhyn," Covenant replied unsteadily.

"They would come to your call," answered Hyrim.

Again Covenant could not respond; he feared that this was true. The Ranyhyn had pledged themselves to him, and he had not released them. But he could not ride one of the great horses. They had reared to him out of fear and loathing. Again he had nothing to offer Hyrim but the look of his silent indecision.

Moments later, he heard movement in the throat of the Keep behind him. Turning, he saw two Lords striding out toward the courtyard—High Lord Elena and a man he had not met.

Elena's arrival made him quail; at once, the air seemed to be full of wings, vulturine implications. But the man at her side also compelled his attention. He knew immediately that this was Lord Verement. The man resembled Shetra too much to be anyone else. He had the same short stiff hair, the same hawklike features, the same bitter taste in his mouth. He moved toward her as if he meant to throw himself at her.

But he stopped ten feet away. His eyes winced away from her sharp gaze; he could not bring himself to look at her directly. In a low voice, he said, "Will you go?"

"You know that I must."

They fell silent. Heedless of the fact that they were being observed, they stood apart from each other. Some test of will that needed no utterance hung between them. For a time, they remained still, as if refusing to make any gestures which might be interpreted as compromise or abdication.

"He did not wish to come," Hyrim whispered to Covenant, "but the High Lord brought him. He is ashamed."

Then Lord Verement moved. Abruptly, he tossed his staff upright toward Shetra. She caught it, and threw her own staff to him. He caught it in turn. "Stay well, wife," he said bleakly.

"Stay well, husband," she replied.

"Nothing will be well for me until you return."

"And for me also, my husband," she breathed intensely.

Without another word, he turned on his heel and hastened back into Revelstone.

For a moment, she watched him go. Then she turned also, moved stiffly out of the courtyard into the tunnel. Korik and the other Bloodguard followed her. Shortly, Covenant was left alone with Hyrim and Elena.

"Well, Hyrim," the High Lord said gently, "your ordeal must begin. I regret that it will be so arduous for you."

"High Lord—" Hyrim began.

"But you are capable of it," she went on. "You have not begun to take the measure of your true strength."

"High Lord," Hyrim said, "I have asked ur-Lord Covenant to accompany us."

She stiffened. Covenant felt a surge of tension radiate from her; she seemed suddenly to emanate a palpable tightness. "Lord Hyrim," she said in a low voice, "you tread dangerous ground." Her tone was hard, but Covenant could hear that she was not warning Hyrim, threatening him. She respected what he had done. And she was afraid.

Then she turned to Covenant. Carefully, as if she feared to express her own acute desire, she asked, "Will you go?"

The light from Revelstone was at her back, and he could not see her face. He was glad of this; he did not want to know whether or not her strange gaze was focused on him. He tried to answer her, but for a moment his throat was so dry that he could not make a sound.

"No," he said at last. "No." For Hyrim's sake, he made an effort to tell the truth. "There's nothing I can do for them." But as he said it, he knew that that was not the whole truth. He refused to go because Elena daughter of Lena wanted him to stay.

Her relief was as tangible in the gloom as her tension had been. "Very well, ur-Lord." For a long moment, she and Hyrim faced each other, and Covenant sensed the current of their silent communication, their mental melding. Then Hyrim stepped close to her and kissed her on the forehead. She hugged him, released him. He bowed to Covenant, and walked away into the tunnel.

In turn, she moved away from Covenant, entered the tower through one of the small doors beside the mouth of the tunnel. Covenant was left alone. He breathed deeply, trying to steady himself as if he had just come through an interrogation. Despite the coolness of the dawn, he was sweating. For a moment, he remained in the courtyard, uncertain of what to do. But then he heard whistling from outside the Keep—shrill piercing cries that echoed off the wall of Revelstone. Korik's mission was calling the Ranyhyn.

At once, Covenant hurried into the tunnel.

Outside the shadowed court, the sky was lighter. In the east, the first rim of the sun had broken the horizon. Morning streamed westward, and in it fifteen Bloodguard and two Lords raised their call again. And again. While the echoes of the third cry faded, the air filled with the thunder of mighty hooves.

For a long moment, the earth rumbled to the beat of the Ranyhyn, and the air pulsed deeply. Then a shadow swept up through the foothills. Seventeen strong, clean-limbed horses came surging and proud to Revelstone. Their white forehead stars looked like froth on a wave as they galloped toward the riders they had chosen to serve. With keen whinnying and the flash of hooves, they slowed their pace.

In response, the Bloodguard and the two Lords bowed, and Korik shouted, "Hail, Ranyhyn! Land-riders and proud-bearers! Sun-flesh and sky-mane, we are glad that you have heard our call. Evil and war are upon the Land! Peril and fatigue await the foes of Fangthane. Will you bear us?"

The great horses nodded and nickered as they came forward the last few steps to nuzzle their riders, urging them to mount. Instantly, all the Bloodguard leaped onto the backs of their Ranyhyn. They used no saddles or reins; the Ranyhyn bore their riders willingly, and replied to the pressure of a knee or the touch of a hand—even to the command of a thought. The same strange power of hearing which made it

possible for them to answer their riders at once, anywhere in the Land—allowed them to sense the call
tens or scores of days before it was actually uttered,
and to run from the Plains of Ra to answer as if mere
moments, not three or four hundred leagues, separated the southeast corner of the Land from any
other region—also enabled them to act as one with
their riders, a perfect meeting of mind and bone.

The Lords Shetra and Hyrim mounted more slowly,
and Covenant watched them with a thickness in his
throat, as if they were accepting a challenge which
rightly belonged to him. Foamfollower, please— he
thought. Please— But he could not articulate the
words, forgive me.

Then he heard a shout behind and above him.
Turning back toward Revelstone, he saw a small, slim
figure standing with arms raised atop the watchtower
—the High Lord. As the mounted company swung
around to face her, she flourished the Staff of Law,
drew from its tip an intense blue blaze that flared
and coruscated against the deep sky—a paean of
power which in her hands burned with a core of inter-
fused blue and white turning to purest azure along
the flame. Three times she waved the Staff, and its
blaze was so bright that its path seemed to linger
against the heavens. Then she cried, "Hail!" and
thrust the Staff upward. For an instant the whole
length of it flashed, so that an immense incandescent
burst of Lords-fire sprang toward the sky. For that
instant, she cast so much light over the feet of Revelstone that the dawn itself was effaced—as if to show
the assembled company that she was strong enough
to erase the fate written in the morning.

The Lords answered, wielding their own power and
returning the vibrant cry, "Hail!" And the Bloodguard
shouted together as one, "Fist and faith! Hail, High
Lord!"

For a moment, all the staffs were upraised in fire.
Then all the Lords silenced their flames. On that signal, the company of the mission wheeled in a smooth
turn and galloped away into the sunrise.

EIGHT: "Lord Kevin's Lament"

THE departure of the mission—and his meeting with High Lord Elena the previous evening—left Covenant deeply disturbed. He seemed to be losing what little independence or authenticity he possessed. Instead of determining for himself what his position should be, and then acting according to that standard, he was allowing himself to be swayed, seduced even more fundamentally than he had been during his first experience with the Land. Already, he had acknowledged Elena's claim on him, and only that claim had prevented him from acknowledging the Giants as well.

He could not go on in this fashion. If he did, he would soon come to resemble Hile Troy—a man so overwhelmed by the power of sight that he could not perceive the blindness of his desire to assume responsibility for the Land. That would be suicide for a leper. If he failed, he would die. And if he succeeded, he would never again be able to bear the numbness of his real life, his leprosy. He knew lepers who had died that way, but for them the death was never quick, never clean. Their ends lay beyond a fetid ugliness so abominable that he felt nauseated whenever he remembered that such putrefaction existed.

And that was not the only argument. This seduction of responsibility was Foul's doing. It was the means by which Lord Foul attempted to ensure the destruction of the Land. When inadequate men assumed huge burdens, the outcome could only serve Despite. Covenant had no doubt that Troy was inadequate. Had he not been summoned to the Land by Atiaran in her despair? And as for himself—he, Thomas Covenant,

105

was as incapable of power as if such a thing did not
exist. For him it could not. If he pretended otherwise,
then the whole Land would become just another leper
in Lord Foul's hands.

By the time he reached his rooms, he knew that he
would have to do something, take some action to establish the terms on which he had to stand. He would
have to find or make some discrepancy, some incontrovertible proof that the Land was a delusion. He
could not trust his emotions; he needed logic, an argument as inescapable as the law of leprosy.

He paced the suite for a time as if he were searching the stone floor for an answer. Then, on an impulse,
he jerked open the door and looked out into the hallway. Bannor was there, standing watch as imperturba-
bly as if the meaning of his life were beyond question.
Stiffly, Covenant asked him into the sitting room.

When Bannor stood before him, Covenant reviewed
quickly what he knew about the Bloodguard. They
came from a race, the *Haruchai,* who lived high in the
Westron Mountains beyond Trothgard and the Land.
They were a warlike and prolific people, so it was perhaps inevitable that at some time in their history they
would send an army east into the Land. This they had
done during the early years of Kevin's High Lordship.
On foot and weaponless—the *Haruchai* did not use
weapons, just as they did not use lore; they relied
wholly on their own physical competence—they had
marched to Revelstone and challenged the Council of
Lords.

But Kevin had refused to fight. Instead, he had per-
suaded the *Haruchai* to friendship.

In return, they had gone far beyond his intent. Apparently, the Ranyhyn, and the Giants, and Revelstone itself—as mountain dwellers, the *Haruchai* had
an intense love of stone and bounty—had moved
them more deeply than anything in their history. To
answer Kevin's friendship, they had sworn a Vow of
service to the Lords; and something extravagant in
their commitment or language had invoked the Earthpower, binding them to their Vow in defiance of time
and death and choice. Five hundred of their army had

become the Bloodguard. The rest had returned home.

Now there were still nearly five hundred. For every Bloodguard who died in battle was sent on his Rany-hyn up through Guards Gap into the Westron Mountains, and another *Haruchai* came to take his place. Only those whose bodies could not be recovered, such as Tuvor, the former First Mark, were not replaced.

Thus the great anomaly of the Bloodguard's history was the fact that they had survived the Ritual of Desecration intact even though Kevin and his Council and all his works had been destroyed. They had trusted him. When he had ordered them all into the mountains without explaining his intent, they had obeyed. But afterward they had seen reason to doubt that their service was truly faithful. They had sworn the Vow; they should have died with Kevin in Kiril Threndor under Mount Thunder—or prevented him from meeting Lord Foul there in his despair, prevented him from uttering the Ritual which brought the age of the Old Lords to its destruction. They were faithful to an extreme that defied their own mortality, and yet they had failed in their promise to preserve the Lords at any cost to themselves.

Covenant wanted to ask Bannor what would happen to the Bloodguard if they ever came to believe that their extravagant fidelity was false, that in their Vow they had betrayed both Kevin and themselves. But he could not put such a question into words. Bannor deserved better treatment than that from him. And Bannor, too, had lost his wife— She had been dead for two thousand years.

Instead, Covenant concentrated on his search for a discrepancy.

But he soon knew he would not find one by questioning Bannor. In his flat, alien voice, the Bloodguard gave brief answers that told Covenant what he both wanted and did not want to hear concerning the survivors of the Quest for the Staff of Law. He had already learned what had happened to Foamfollower and Lord Mhoram. Now Bannor told him that High Lord Prothall, who had led the Quest, had resigned his Lordship even before his company had returned to

Revelstone. He had not been able to forget that the old Hearthrall Birinair had died in his place. And he had felt that in regaining the Staff he had fulfilled his fate, done all that was in him. He had committed the Staff and the Second Ward to Lord Mhoram's care, and had ridden away to his home in the Northron Climbs. The inhabitants of Lord's Keep never saw him again.

So upon Mhoram's return Osondrea had assumed the High Lordship. Until her death, she had used her power to rebuild the Council, expand the Warward, and grow Revelwood, the new home of the Loresraat.

After returning to Revelstone, Quaan—the Warhaft of the Eoman that had accompanied Prothall and Mhoram—had also tried to resign. He had been ashamed to bring only half of his warriors back alive. But High Lord Osondrea, knowing his worth, had refused to release him, and soon he had returned to his duties. Now he was the Hiltmark of the Warward, Hile Troy's second-in-command. Though his hair was white and thin—though his gaze seemed rubbed smooth by age and use—still he was the same strong, honest man he had always been. The Lords respected him. In Troy's absence they would willingly have trusted Quaan to lead the Warward.

Covenant sighed sourly, and let Bannor go. Such information did not meet his need. Clearly, he was not going to find any easy solutions to his dilemma. If he wanted proof of delusion, he would have to make it for himself.

He faced the prospect with trepidation. Anything he might do would take a long time to bear fruit. It would not become proof, brookless and unblinkable, until his delusion ended—until he had returned to his real life. In the meantime, it would do little to sustain him. But he had no choice; his need was urgent.

He had available three easy ways to create a definitive discontinuity: he could destroy his clothes, throw away his penknife—the only thing he had in his pockets—or grow a beard. Then, when he awakened, and found himself clothed, or still possessed of his penknife, or clean-shaven, he would have his proof.

The obvious discrepancy of his healed forehead he

did not trust. Past experience made him fear that he would be reinjured shortly before this delusion ended. But he could not bring himself to act on his first two alternatives. The thought of destroying his tough, familiar apparel made him feel too vulnerable, and the expedient of discarding his penknife was too uncertain. Cursing at the way his plight forced him to abandon all the strict habits upon which his survival depended, he decided to give up shaving.

When at last he summoned the courage to leave his rooms and go into the Keep in search of breakfast, he brandished the stubble on his cheeks as if it were a declaration of defiance.

Bannor guided him to one of the great refectories of Revelstone, then left him alone to eat. But before he was done, the Bloodguard came striding back to his table. There was an extra alertness in the spring of Bannor's steps—a tightness that looked oddly like excitement. But when he addressed Covenant, his flat, shrouded eyes expressed nothing, and the repressed lilt of his voice was as inflectionless as ever.

"Ur-Lord, the Council asks that you come to the Close. A stranger has entered Revelstone. The Lords will soon meet with him."

Because of Bannor's heightened alertness, Covenant asked cautiously, "What kind of stranger?"

"Ur-Lord?"

"Is it—is it someone like me? or Troy?"

"No."

In his confusion, Covenant did not immediately perceive the certitude of Bannor's reply. But as he followed the Bloodguard out of the refectory and down through Revelstone, he began to hear something extra in the denial, something more than Bannor's usual confidence. That *No* resembled Bannor's stride; it was tenser in some way. Covenant could not fathom it. As they descended a broad, curved stair through several levels of the Keep, he forced himself to ask, "What's so urgent about this stranger? What do you know about him?"

Bannor ignored the question.

When they reached the Close, they found that High

Lord Elena, Lord Verement, and four other Lords had already preceded them. The High Lord was at her place at the head of the curved table, and the Staff of Law lay on the stone before her. To her right sat two men, then two women. Verement was on her left beyond two empty seats. Eight Bloodguard sat behind them in the first row of the gallery, but the rest of the Close was empty. Only First Mark Morin and the Hearthralls Tohrm and Borillar occupied their positions in back of the High Lord.

An expectant hush hung over the chamber. For an instant, Covenant half expected Elena to announce the start of the war.

Bannor guided him to a seat at the Lords' table one place down from Lord Verement. The Unbeliever settled himself in the stone chair, rubbing the stubble of his new beard with one hand as if he expected the Council to know what it meant. The eyes of the Lords were on him, and their gaze made him uncomfortable. He felt strangely ashamed of the fact that his fingertips were alive to the touch of his whiskers.

"Ur-Lord Covenant," the High Lord said after a moment, "while we await Lord Mhoram and Warmark Troy, we should make introduction. We have been remiss in our hospitality. Let me present to you those of the Council whom you do not know."

Covenant nodded, glad of anything that would turn her disturbing eyes away from him, and she began on her left. "Here is Lord Verement Shetra-mate, whom you have seen." Verement glowered at his hands, did not glance at Covenant.

Elena turned to her right. The man next to her was tall and broad; he had a wide forehead, a watchful face draped with a warm blond beard, and an expression of habitual gentleness. "Here is Lord Callindrill Faer-mate. Faer his wife is a rare master of the ancient *suru-pa-maerl* craft." Lord Callindrill smiled half shyly at Covenant, and bowed his head.

"At his side," the High Lord went on, "are the Lords Trevor and Loerya." Lord Trevor was a thin man with an air of uncertainty, as if he were not sure that he belonged at the Lords' table; but Lord Loerya his wife looked solid and matronly, conscious that she contained power. "They have three daughters who gladden all our hearts." Both Lords replied with smiles, but where his was both surprised and proud, hers was calm, confident.

Elena concluded, "Beyond them is Lord Amatin daughter of Matin. Only a year ago she passed the tests of the Sword and Staff at the Loresraat, and joined the Council. Now her work is with the schools of Revelstone—the teaching of the children." In her turn, Lord Amatin bowed gravely. She was slight, serious, and hazel-eyed, and she watched Covenant as if she were studying him.

After a pause, the High Lord began the ritual ceremonies of welcoming the Unbeliever to Lord's Keep, but she stopped short when Lord Mhoram entered the Close. He came through one of the private doors behind the Lords' table. There was weariness in his step and febrile concentration in his eyes, as if he had spent all night wrestling with darkness. In his fatigue, he needed his staff to hold himself steady as he took his seat at Elena's left.

All the Lords watched him as he sat there, breathing vacantly, and a wave of support flowed from their minds to his. Slowly, their silent help strengthened him. The hot glitter faded from his gaze, and he began to see the faces around him.

"Have you met success?" Elena asked softly. "Can you withdraw the *krill?*"

"No." Mhoram's lips formed the word, but he made no sound.

"Dear Mhoram," she sighed, "you must take greater care of yourself. The Despiser marches against us. We will need all your strength for the coming war."

Through his weariness, Mhoram smiled his crooked, humane smile. But he did not speak.

Before Covenant could muster the resolve to ask Mhoram what he hoped to accomplish with the *krill,* the main doors of the Close opened, and Warmark Troy strode down the stairs to the table. Hiltmark Quaan came behind him. While Troy went to sit opposite Covenant, Quaan made his way to join Morin,

Tohrm, and Borillar. Apparently, Troy and Quaan had just come from the Warward. They had not taken the time to set aside their swords, and their scabbards clashed dully against the stone as they seated themselves.

As soon as they were in their places, High Lord Elena began. She spoke softly, but her clear voice carried perfectly throughout the Close. "We are gathered thus without forewarning because a stranger has come to us. Crowl, the stranger is in your care. Tell us of him."

Crowl was one of the Bloodguard. He arose from his seat near the broad stairs of the chamber, and faced the High Lord impassively to make his report. "He passed us. A short time ago, he appeared at the gate of Revelstone. No scout or sentry saw his approach. He asked if the Lords were within. When he was answered, he replied that the High Lord wished to question him. He is not as other men. But he bears no weapon, and intends no ill. We chose to admit him. He awaits you."

In a sharp voice like the barking of a hawk, Lord Verement asked, "Why did the scouts and sentries fail?"

"The stranger was hidden from our eyes," Crowl replied levelly. "Our watch did not falter." His unfluctuating tone seemed to assert that the alertness of the Bloodguard was beyond question.

"That is well," said Verement. "Perhaps one day the whole army of the Despiser will appear unnoticed at our gates, and we will still be sleeping when Revelstone falls."

He was about to say more, but Elena interposed firmly, "Bring the stranger now."

As the Bloodguard at the top of the stairs swung open the high wooden doors, Amatin asked the High Lord, "Does this stranger come at your request?"

"No. But I do now wish to question him."

Covenant watched as two more Bloodguard came into the Close with the stranger between them. He was slim, simply clad in a cream-colored robe, and his movements were light, buoyant. Though he was nearly as tall as Covenant, he seemed hardly old enough to have his full growth. There was a sense of boyish laughter in the way his curly hair bounced as he came down the steps, as if he were amused by the precautions taken against him. But Covenant was not amused. With the new dimension of his sight, he could see why Crowl had said that the boy was "not as other men." Within his young, fresh flesh were bones that seemed to radiate oldness—not age—they were not weak or infirm—but rather antiquity. His skeleton carried this oldness, this aura of time, as if he were merely a vessel for it. He existed for it rather than in spite of it. The sight baffled Covenant's perceptions, made his eyes ache with conflicting impressions of dread and glory as he strained to comprehend.

When the boy reached the floor of the Close, he stepped near to the graveling pit, and made a cheerful obeisance. In a high, young voice, he exclaimed, "Hail, High Lord!"

Elena stood and replied gravely, "Stranger, be welcome in the Land—welcome and true. We are the Lords of Revelstone, and I am Elena daughter of Lena, High Lord by the choice of the Council, and holder of the Staff of Law. How may we honor you?"

"Courtesy is like a drink at a mountain stream. I am honored already."

"Then will you honor us in turn with your name?"

With a laughing glance, the boy said, "It may well come to pass that I will tell you who I am."

"Do not game with us," Verement cut in. "What is your name?"

"Among those who do not know me, I am named Amok."

Elena controlled Verement with a swift look, then said to the youth, "And how are you named among those who know you?"

"Those who know me have no need of my name."

"Stranger, we do not know you." An edge came into her quiet voice. "These are times of great peril in the Land, and we can spend neither time nor delicacy with you. We require to know who you are."

"Ah, then I fear I cannot help you," replied Amok with an impervious gaiety in his eyes.

For a moment, the Lords met his gaze with stiff silence. Verement's thin lips whitened; Callindrill frowned thoughtfully; and Elena faced the boy with low anger flushing her cheeks, though her eyes did not lose their odd, dislocated focus. Then Lord Amatin straightened her shoulders and said, "Amok, where is your home? Who are your parents? What is your past?"

Lightly, Amok turned and gave her an unexpected bow. "My home is Revelstone. I have no parents. And my past is both wide and narrow, for I have wandered everywhere, waiting."

A surge ran through the Council, but no one interrupted Amatin. Studying the boy, she said, "Your home is Revelstone? How can that be? We have no knowledge of you."

"Lord, I have been away. I have feasted with the *Elohim,* and ridden Sandgorgons. I have danced with the Dancers of the Sea, and teased brave *Kelenbhrabanal* in his grave, and traded apothegms with the Gray Desert. I have waited."

Several of the Lords stirred, and a gleam came into Loerya's eyes, as if she recognized something potent in Amok's words. They all watched him closely as Amatin said, "Yet everything that lives has ancestry, forebearers of its own kind. Amok, what of your parentage?"

"Do I live?"

"It appears not," Verement growled. "Nothing mortal would try our patience so."

"Peace, Verement," said Loerya. "There is grave import here." Without taking her eyes off Amok, she asked, "Are you alive?"

"Perhaps. While I have purpose, I move and speak. My eyes behold. Is this life?"

His answer confused Lord Amatin. Thinly, as if her uncertainty pained her, she said, "Amok, who made you?"

Without hesitation, Amok replied, "High Lord

Kevin son of Loric son of Damelon son of Berek Heartthew the Lord-Fatherer."

A silent clap of surprise echoed in the Close. Around the table, the Lords gaped in astonishment. Then Verement smacked the stone with the flat of his hand, and barked, "By the Seven! This whelp mocks us."

"I think not," answered Elena.

Lord Mhoram nodded wearily, and sighed his agreement. "Our ignorance mocks us."

Quickly, Trevor asked, "Mhoram, do you know Amok? Have you seen him?"

Lord Loerya seconded the question, but before Mhoram could gather his strength to respond, Lord Callindrill leaned forward to ask, "Amok, why were you made? What purpose do you serve?"

"I wait," said the boy. "And I answer."

Callindrill accepted this with a glum nod, as if it proved an unfortunate point, and said nothing more. After a pause, the High Lord said to Amok, "You bear knowledge, and release it in response to the proper questions. Have I understood you aright?"

In answer, Amok bowed, shaking his head so that his gay hair danced like laughter about his head.

"What knowledge is this?" she inquired.

"Whatever knowledge you can ask for, and receive answer."

At this, Elena glanced ruefully around the table. "Well, that at least was not the proper question," she sighed. "I think we will need to know Amok's knowledge before we can ask the proper questions."

Mhoram looked at her and nodded.

"Excellent!" Verement's retort was full of suppressed ferocity. "So ignorance increases ignorance, and knowledge makes itself unnecessary."

Covenant felt the force of Verement's sarcasm. But Lord Amatin ignored it. Instead, she asked the youth, "Why have you come to us now?"

"I felt the sign of readiness. The *krill* of Loric came to life. That is the appointed word. I answer as I was made to do."

As he mentioned the *krill*, Amok's inner cradled

glory and dread seemed to become more visible. The sight gave Covenant a pang. Is this my fault, too? he groaned. What have I gotten myself into now? But the glimpse was mercifully brief; Amok's boyish good humor soon veiled it again.

When it was past, Lord Mhoram climbed slowly to his feet, supporting himself on his staff like an old man. Standing beside the High Lord as if he were speaking for her, he said, "Then you have— Amok, hear me. I am seer and oracle for this Council. I speak words of vision. I have not seen you. You have come too soon. We did not give life to the *krill*. That was not our doing. We lack the lore for such work."

Amok's face became suddenly grave, almost frightened, showing for the first time some of the antiquity of his skull. "Lack the lore? Then I have erred. I have misserved my purpose. I must depart; I will do great harm else."

Quickly, he turned, slipped with deceptive speed between the Bloodguard, and darted up the stairs.

When he was halfway to the doors, everyone in the Close lost sight of him. He vanished as if they had all taken their eyes off him for an instant, allowing him to hide. The Lords jumped to their feet in amazement. On the stairs, the pursuing Bloodguard halted, looked rapidly about them, and gave up the chase.

"Swiftly!" Elena commanded. "Search for him! Find him!"

"What is the need?" Crowl replied flatly. "He is gone."

"That I see! But where has he gone? Perhaps he is still in Revelstone."

But Crowl only repeated, "He is gone." Something in his certitude reminded Covenant of Bannor's subdued, unusual excitement. Are they in this together? he asked himself. *My purpose?* The words repeated dimly in his mind. *My purpose?*

Through his mystification, he almost did not hear Troy whisper, "I thought—for a minute—I thought I saw him."

High Lord Elena paid no attention to the Warmark. The attitude of the Bloodguard seemed to baffle her, and she sat down to consider the situation. Slowly, she spread about her the melding of the Council, one by one bringing the minds of the other Lords into communion with her own. Callindrill shut his eyes, letting a look of peace spread over his face, and Trevor and Loerya held hands. Verement shook his head two or three times, then acquiesced when Mhoram touched him gently on the shoulder.

When they all were woven together, the High Lord said, "Each of us must study this matter. War is near at hand, and we must not be taken unaware by such mysteries. But to you, Lord Amatin, I give the chief study of Amok and his secret knowledge. If it can be done, we must seek him out and learn his answers."

Lord Amatin nodded with determination in her small face.

Then, like an unclasping of mental hands, the melding ended, and an intensity which Covenant could sense but not join faded from the air. In silence, the Lords took up their staffs, and began to leave.

"Is that it?" Covenant muttered in surprise. "Is that all you're going to do?"

"Watch it, Covenant," Troy warned softly.

Covenant shot a glare at the Warmark, but his black sunglasses seemed to make him impervious. Covenant turned toward the High Lord. "Is that all?" he insisted. "Don't you even want to know what's going on here?"

Elena faced him levelly. "Do you know?"

"No. Of course not." He wanted to add, to protest, But Bannor does. But that was something else he could not say. He had no right to make the Bloodguard responsible. Stiffly, he remained silent.

"Then do not be too quick to judge," Elena replied. "There is much here that requires explanation, and we must seek answers in our own way if we hope to be prepared."

Prepared for what? he wanted to ask. But he lacked the resolution to challenge the High Lord; he was afraid of her eyes. To escape the situation, he brushed past Bannor and hurried out of the Close ahead of the Lords and Troy.

But back in his rooms he found no relief for his

frustration. And in the days that followed, nothing happened to give him any relief. Elena, Mhoram, and Troy were as absent from his life as if they were deliberately avoiding him. Bannor answered his aimless questions courteously, curtly, but the answers shed no light. His beard grew until it was thick and full, and made him look to himself like an unraveled fanatic; but it proved nothing, solved nothing. The full of the moon came and went, but the war did not begin; there arrived no word from the scouts, no signs, no insights. Around him, Revelstone palpably trembled in the clench of its readiness; everywhere he went, he heard whispers of tension, haste, urgency, but no action was taken. Nothing. He roamed for leagues in Lord's Keep as if he were treading a maze. He drank inordinate quantities of springwine, and slept the sleep of the dead as if he hoped that he would never be resurrected. At times he was even reduced to standing on the northern battlements of the city to watch Troy and Quaan drill the Warward. But nothing happened.

His only oasis in this static and frustrated wilderland was given to him by Lord Callindrill and his wife, Faer. One day, Callindrill took the Unbeliever to his private quarters beyond the floor-lit courtyard, and there Faer provided him with a meal which almost made him forget his plight. She was a hale Stonedownor woman with a true gift for hospitality. Perhaps he would have been able to forget—but she studied the old *suru-pa-maerl* craft, as Lena had done, and that evoked too many painful memories in him. He did not visit long with Faer and her husband.

Yet before he left, Callindrill had explained to him some of the oddness of his current position in Revelstone. The High Lord had summoned him, Callindrill said, when the Council had agreed that the war could begin at any moment, when any further postponement of the call might prove fatal. But Warmark Troy's battle plans could not be launched until he knew which of two possible assault routes Lord Foul's army would take. Until the Warmark received clear word from his scouts, he could not afford to commit his Eowards. If he risked a guess, and guessed wrong, disaster would result. So Covenant had been urgently summoned, and yet now was left to himself, with no demands upon him.

In addition, the Lord went on, there was another reason why he had been summoned at a time which now appeared to have been premature. Warmark Troy had argued urgently for the summons. This surprised Covenant until Callindrill explained Troy's reasoning. The Warmark had believed that Lord Foul would be able to detect the summons. So by means of Covenant's call Troy had hoped to put pressure on the Despiser, force him, because of his fear of the wild magic, to launch his attack before he was ready. Time favored Lord Foul because his war resources far surpassed those of the Council, and if he prepared long enough he might well field an army that no Warward could defeat. Troy hoped that the ploy of summoning Covenant would make the Despiser cut his preparations short.

Lastly, Callindrill explained in a gentle voice, High Lord Elena and Lord Mhoram were in fact evading the Unbeliever. Covenant had not asked that question, but Callindrill seemed to divine some of the causes of his frustration. Elena and Mhoram, each in their separate ways, felt so involved in Covenant's dilemma that they stayed away from him in order to avoid aggravating his distress. They sensed, said Callindrill, that he found their personal appeals more painful than any other. The possibility that he might go to Seareach had jolted Elena. And Mhoram was consumed by his work on the *krill*. Until the war bereft them of choice, they refrained as much as possible from imposing upon him.

Well, Troy warned me, Covenant muttered to himself as he left Callindrill and Faer. He said that they're scrupulous. After a moment, he added sourly, I would be better off if all these people would stop trying to do me favors.

Yet he was grateful to Faer and her husband. Their companionly gestures helped him to get through the next few days, helped him to keep the vertiginous darkness at bay. He felt that he was rotting inside, but he was not going mad.

But he knew that he could not stand it much longer. The ambience of Revelstone was as tight as a string about to snap. Pressure was building inside him, rising toward desperation. When Bannor knocked at his door one afternoon, he was so startled that he almost cried out.

However, Bannor had not come to announce the start of the war. In his flat voice, he asked Covenant if the Unbeliever would like to go hear a song.

A song, he echoed numbly. For a moment, he was too confused to respond. He had not expected such a question, certainly not from the Bloodguard. But then he shrugged jerkily. "Why not?" He did not stop to ask what had prompted Bannor's unusual initiative. With a scowl, he followed the Bloodguard out of his suite.

Bannor took him up through the levels of the Keep until they were higher in the mountain than he had ever been before. Then the wide passage they followed rounded a corner, and came unexpectedly into open sunlight. They entered a broad, roofless amphitheater. Rows of stone benches curved downward to form a bowl around a flat center stage; and behind the topmost row the stone wall rose straight for twenty or thirty feet, ending in the flat of the plateau, where the mountain met the sky. The afternoon sun shone into the amphitheater, drenching the dull white stone of the stage and benches and wall with warmth and light.

The seats were starting to fill when Bannor and Covenant arrived. People from all the occupations of the Keep, including farmers and cooks and warriors, and the Lords Trevor and Loerya with their daughters, came through several openings in the wall to take seats around the bowl. But the Bloodguard formed the largest single group. Covenant estimated roughly that there were a hundred of them on the benches. This vaguely surprised him. He had never seen more than a score of the *Haruchai* in one place before. After looking around for a while, he asked Bannor, "What song is this, anyway?"

"Lord Kevin's Lament," Bannor replied dispassionately.

Then Covenant felt that he understood. Kevin, he nodded to himself. Of course the Bloodguard wanted to hear this song. How could they be less than keenly interested in anything which might help them to comprehend Kevin Landwaster?

For it was Kevin who had summoned Lord Foul to Kiril Threndor to utter the Ritual of Desecration. The legends said that when Kevin had seen that he could not defeat the Despiser, his heart had turned black with despair. He had loved the Land too intensely to let it fall to Lord Foul. And yet he had failed; he could not preserve it. Torn by his impossible dilemma, he had been driven to dare that Ritual. He had known that the unleashing of that fell power would destroy the Lords and all their works, and ravage the Land from end to end; make it barren for generations. He had known that he would die. But he had hoped that Lord Foul would also die, that when at last life returned to the Land it would be life free of Despite. He chose to take that risk rather than permit Lord Foul's victory. Thus he dared the Despiser to join him in Kiril Threndor. He and Lord Foul spoke the Ritual, and High Lord Kevin Landwaster destroyed the Land which he loved.

And Lord Foul had not died. He had been reduced for a time, but he had survived, preserved by the law of Time which emprisoned him upon the Earth— so the legends said. So now all the Land and the new Lords lay under the consequences of Kevin's despair.

It was not surprising that the Bloodguard wanted to hear this song—or that Bannor had asked Covenant to come hear it also.

As he mused, Covenant caught a glimpse of blue from across the amphitheater. Looking up, he saw High Lord Elena standing near one of the entrances. She, too, wanted to hear this song.

With her was Warmark Troy.

Covenant felt an urge to go join them, but before

he could make up his mind to move, the singer entered the amphitheater. She was a tall, resplendent woman, simply clad in a crimson robe, with golden hair that flew like sparks about her head. As she moved down the steps to the stage, her audience rose to its feet and silently gave her the salute of welcome. She did not return it. Her face bore a look of concentration, as if she were already feeling her song.

When she reached the stage, she did not speak, said nothing to introduce or explain or identify her song. Instead, she took her stance in the center of the stage, composed herself for a moment as the song came over her, then lifted her face to the sun and opened her throat.

At first, her melody was restrained, arid and angular —only hinting at buried pangs and poignancies.

I stood on the pinnacle of the Earth:
Mount Thunder,
its Lions in full flaming mane,
raised its crest no higher
than the horizons that my gaze commanded;
the Ranyhyn,
hooves unfettered since the Age began,
galloped gladly to my will;
iron-thewed Giants
from beyond the sun's birth in the sea
came to me in ships as mighty as castles,
and cleft my castle from the
raw Earth rock
and gave it to me out of pure friendship—
a handmark of allegiance and fealty
in the eternal stone of Time;
the Lords under my Watch labored
to find and make manifest
the true purpose of the Earth's Creator,
barred from His creation by the very
power of that purpose—
power graven into the flesh and bone of the Land
by the immutable Law of its creation:
how could I stand so,
so much glory and dominion comprehended

by the outstretch of my arms—
stand thus,
eye to eye with the Despiser,
and not be dismayed?

But then the song changed, as if the singer opened
inner chambers to give her voice more resonance. In
high, arching spans of song, she gave out her threnody
—highlighted it and underscored it with so many
implied harmonies, so many suggestions of other accompanying voices, that she seemed to have a whole
choir within her, using her one throat for utterance.

Where is the Power that protects
beauty from the decay of life?
preserves truth pure of falsehood?
secures fealty from that slow stain of chaos
which corrupts?
How are we so rendered small by Despite?
Why will the very rocks not erupt
for their own cleansing,
or crumble into dust for shame?
Creator!
When You desecrated this temple,
rid Yourself of this contempt by
inflicting it upon the Land,
did You intend
that beauty and truth should pass utterly from the
Earth?
Have You shaped my fate into the Law of life?
Am I effectless?
Must I preside over,
sanction,
acknowledge with the bitter face of treachery,
approve
the falling of the world?

Her music ached in the air like a wound of song.
And as she finished, the people came to their feet with
a rush. Together they sang into the fathomless
heavens:

Ah, Creator!
Timelord and Landsire!
Did You intend
that beauty and truth should pass utterly
from the Earth?

Bannor stood, though he did not join the song. But
Covenant kept his seat, feeling small and useless beside the community of Revelstone. Their emotion cli-
maxed in the refrain, expending sharp grief and then
filling the amphitheater with a wash of peace which
cleansed and healed the song's despair, as if the united
power of the singing alone were answer enough to
Kevin's outcry. By making music out of despair, the
people resisted it. But Covenant felt otherwise. He
was beginning to understand the danger that threatened the Land.

So he was still sitting, gripping his beard and staring
blankly before him, when the people filed out of the
amphitheater, left him alone with the hot brightness of
the sun. He remained there, muttering grimly to himself, until he became aware that Hile Troy had come
over to him.

When he looked up, the Warmark said, "I didn't
expect to see you here."

Gruffly, Covenant responded, "I didn't expect to
see *you*." But he was only obliquely thinking about
Troy. He was still trying to grapple with Kevin.

As if he could hear Covenant's thoughts, the
Warmark said, "It all comes back to Kevin. He's the
one who made the Seven Wards. He's the one who
inspired the Bloodguard. He's the one who did the
Ritual of Desecration. And it wasn't necessary—or
it wasn't inevitable. He wouldn't have been driven
that far if he hadn't already made his big mistake."

"His big mistake," Covenant murmured.

"He admitted Foul to the Council, made him a
Lord. He didn't see through Foul's disguise. After that
it was too late. By the time Foul declared himself and
broke into open war, he'd had time for so much subtle
treachery that he was unbeatable.

"In situations like that, I guess most ordinary men

kill themselves. But Kevin was no ordinary man—he had too much power for that, even though it seemed useless. He killed the Land instead. All that survived were the people who had time to escape into exile.

"They say that Kevin understood what he'd done— just before he died. Foul was laughing at him. He died howling.

"Anyway, that's why the Oath of Peace is so important now. Everyone takes it—it's as fundamental as the Lords' oath of service to the Land. Together they all swear that somehow they'll resist the destructive emotions—like Kevin's despair. They—"

"I know," Covenant sighed. "I know all about it." He was remembering Triock, the man who had loved Lena in Mithil Stonedown forty years ago. Triock had wanted to kill Covenant, but Atiaran had prevented him on the strength of the Oath of Peace. "Please don't say any more. I'm having a hard enough time as it is."

"Covenant," Troy continued as if he were still on the same subject, "I don't see why you aren't ecstatic about being here. How can the 'real' world be any more important than this?"

"It's the only world there is." Covenant climbed heavily to his feet. "Let's get out of here. This heat is making me giddy."

Moving slowly, they left the amphitheater. The air in Revelstone welcomed them back with its cool, dim pleasance, and Covenant breathed it deeply, trying to steady himself.

He wanted to get away from Troy, evade the questions he knew Troy would ask him. But the Warmark had a look of determination. After a few moments, he said, "Listen, Covenant. I'm trying to understand. Since the last time we talked, I've spent half my time trying. Somebody has got to have some idea what to expect from you. But I just don't see it. Back there, you're a leper. Isn't this better?"

Dully, answering as briefly as possible, Covenant said, "It isn't real. I don't believe it." Half to himself, he added, "Lepers who pay too much attention to their own dreams or whatever don't live very long."

"Jesus," Troy muttered. "You make it sound as if leprosy is all there is." He thought for a moment, then demanded, "How can you be so sure this isn't real?"

"Because life isn't like this. Lepers don't get well. People with no eyes don't suddenly start seeing. Such things don't happen. Somehow, we're being betrayed. Our own—our own needs for something that we don't have—are seducing us into this. It's crazy. Look at you. Come on—think about what happened to you. There you were, trapped between a nine-story fall and a raging fire—blind and helpless and about to die. Is it so strange to think that you cracked up?

"That is," he went on mordantly, "assuming you exist at all. I've got an idea about you. I must've made you up subconsciously so that I would have someone to argue with. Someone to tell me I'm wrong."

"Damn it!" Troy cried. Turning swiftly, he snatched up Covenant's right hand and gripped it at eye level between them. With his head thrust defiantly forward, he said intensely, "Look at me. Feel my grip. I'm here. It's a fact. It's real."

For a moment, Covenant considered Troy's hand. Then he said, "I feel you. And I see you. I even hear you. But that only proves my point. I don't believe it. Now let go of me."

"Why?!"

Troy's sunglasses loomed at him darkly, but Covenant glared back into them until they turned away. Gradually, the Warmark released the pressure of his grip. Covenant yanked his hand away, and walked on with a quiver in his breathing. After a few strides, he said, "Because I *can* feel it. And I can't afford it. Now listen to me. Listen hard. I'm going to try to explain this so you can understand.

"Just forget that you know there's no possible way you could have come here. It's impossible— But just forget that for a while. Listen. I'm a leper. Leprosy is not a directly fatal disease, but it can kill indirectly. I can only—any leper can only stay alive by concentrating all the time every minute to keep himself from getting hurt—and to take care of his hurts as soon as they happen. The one thing— Listen to me. The one thing no leper can afford is to let his mind wander. If he wants to stay alive. As soon as he stops concentrating, and starts thinking about how he's going to make a better life for himself, or starts dreaming about how his life was before he got sick, or about what he would do if he only got cured, or even if people simply stopped abhorring lepers"—he threw the words at Troy's head like chunks of stone—"then he is as good as dead.

"This—Land—is suicide to me. It's an escape, and I can't afford even thinking about escapes, much less actually falling into one. Maybe a blind man can stand the risk, but a leper can't. If I give in here, I won't last a month where it really counts. Because I'll have to go back. Am I getting through to you?"

"Yes," Troy said. "Yes. I'm not stupid. But think about it for a minute. If it should happen—if it should somehow be true that the Land is real—then you're denying your only hope. And that's—"

"I know."

"—that's not all. There's something you're not taking into account. The one thing that doesn't fit this delusion theory of yours is power—your power. White gold. Wild magic. That damn ring of yours changes everything. You're not a victim here. This isn't being done to you. You're responsible."

"No," Covenant groaned.

"Wait a minute! You can't just deny this. You're responsible for your dreams, Covenant. Just like anybody else."

No! Nobody can control dreams. Covenant tried to fill himself with icy confidence, but his heart was chilled by another cold entirely.

Troy pressed his argument. "There's been plenty of evidence that white gold is just exactly what the Lords say it is. How were the defenses of the Second Ward broken? How did the Fire-Lions of Mount Thunder get called down to save you? White gold, that's how. You've already got the key to the whole thing."

"No." Covenant struggled to give his refusal some force. "No. It isn't like that. What white gold does in the Land has nothing to do with me. It isn't me. I can't touch it, make it work, influence it. It's just another thing that's happened to me. I've got no power. For all I know or can do about it, this wild magic could turn on tomorrow or five seconds from now and blast us all. It could crown Foul king of the universe whether I want it to or not. It has nothing to do with me."

"Is that a fact?" Troy said sourly. "And since you don't have any power, no one can hold you to blame."

Troy's tone gave Covenant something on which to focus his anger. "That's right!" he flared. "Let me tell you something. The only person in life who's free at all, ever, is a person who's impotent. Like me. Or what do you think freedom is? Unlimited potential? Unrestricted possibilities? Hellfire! Impotence is freedom. When you're incapable of anything, no one can expect anything from you. Power has its own limits— even ultimate power. Only the impotent are free.

"No!" he snapped to stop Troy's protest. "I'll tell you something else. What you're really asking me to do is learn how to use this wild magic so I can go around butchering the poor, miserable creatures in Foul's army. Well, I'm not going to do it. I'm not going to do any more killing—and certainly not in the name of something that isn't even real!"

"Hooray," muttered Troy in tight sarcasm. "Sweet Jesus. Whatever happened to people who used to believe in things?"

"They got leprosy and died. Weren't you listening to that song?"

Before Troy could reply, they rounded a corner, and entered an intersection where several halls came together. Bannor stood in the junction as if he were waiting for them. He blocked the hall Covenant had intended to take. "Choose another way," he said expressionlessly. "Turn aside. Now."

Troy did not hesitate; he swung away to his right. While he moved, he asked quickly, "Why? What's going on?"

But Covenant did not follow. The crest of his anger, his bone-deep frustration, still held him up. He stopped where he was and glared at the Bloodguard.

"Turn aside," Bannor repeated. "The High Lord desires that you should not meet."

From the next hallway, Troy called, "Covenant! Come on!"

For a moment, Covenant maintained his defiance. But Bannor's impervious gaze deflated him. The Bloodguard looked as immune to affront or doubt as a stone wall. Muttering uselessly under his breath, Covenant started after Troy.

But he had delayed too long. Before he was hidden in the next hallway, a man came into the intersection from the passage behind Bannor. He was as tall, thick, and solid as a pillar; his deep chest easily supported his broad massive shoulders and brawny arms. He walked with his head down, so that his heavy, red-gray beard rested like a burden on his breast; and his face had a look of ruddy strength gone ominously rancid, curdled by some admixture of gall.

Woven into the shoulders of his brown Stonedownor tunic was a pattern of white leaves.

Covenant froze; a spasm of suspense and fear gripped his guts. He recognized the Stonedownor. In the still place at the center of the spasm, he felt sorrow and remorse for this man whose life he had ruined as if he were incapable of regret.

Striding back into the intersection, Troy said, "I don't understand. Why shouldn't we meet this man? He's one of the *rhadhamaerl*. Covenant, this is—"

Covenant cut Troy off. "I know him."

Trell's eyes held Covenant redly, as if after years of pressure they were charged with too much blood. "And I know you, Thomas Covenant." His voice came out stiffly; it sounded disused, cramped, as if he had kept it fettered for a long time, fearing that it would betray him. "Are you not satisfied? Have you come to do more harm?"

Through a roar of pounding blood in his ears, Covenant heard himself saying for the second time, "I'm sorry."

"Sorry?" Trell almost choked on the word. "Is that enough? Does it raise the dead?" For a moment, he shuddered as if he were about to break apart. His breath came in deep, hoarse gasps. Then, convulsively, he threw his strong arms wide like a man breaking bonds. Jumping forward, he caught Covenant around the chest, lifted him off the floor. With a fierce snarl, he hugged Covenant, striving to crush his ribs.

Covenant wanted to cry out, howl his pain, but he could make no sound. The vise of Trell's arms drove the air from his lungs, stunned his heart. He felt himself collapsing inwardly, destroying himself with his own pressure.

Dimly, he saw Bannor at Trell's back. Twice Bannor punched at Trell's neck. But the Gravelingas only increased his grip, growling savagely.

Someone, Troy, shouted, "Trell! Trell!"

Bannor turned and stepped away. For one frantic instant, Covenant feared that the Bloodguard was abandoning him. But Bannor only needed space for his next attack. He leaped high in the air, and as he dropped toward Trell, he chopped the Gravelingas across the base of his neck with one elbow. Trell staggered; his grip loosened. Continuing the same motion, Bannor caught Trell under the chin with his other arm. The sharp backward jerk pulled Trell off balance. As he toppled, he lost his hold on Covenant.

Covenant landed heavily on his side, retching for air. Through his dizzy gasps, he heard Troy shouting, heard the warning in Troy's voice. He looked up in time to see Trell charge toward him again. But Bannor was swifter. As Trell lunged, Bannor met him head-on, butted him with such force that he reeled backward, crashed against the wall, fell to his hands and knees.

The impact stunned him. His massive frame writhed in pain, and his fingers gouged involuntarily at the stone, as if he were digging for breath.

They clenched into the floor as if it were only stiff clay. In a moment, both his fists were knotted in the rock.

Then he drew a deep shuddering breath, and snatched his hands out of the floor. He stared at the holes he had made; he was appalled to see that he had damaged stone. When he raised his head, he was panting hugely, so that his broad chest strained at the fabric of his tunic.

Bannor and Troy stood between him and Covenant. The Warmark held his sword poised. "Remember your Oath!" he commanded sharply. "Remember what you swore. Don't betray your own life."

Tears started running soundlessly from Trell's eyes as he stared past the Warmark at Covenant. "My Oath?" he rasped. "He brings me to this. What Oath does he take?" With a sudden exertion, he heaved himself to his feet. Bannor stepped slightly ahead of Troy to defend against another attack, but Trell did not look at Covenant again. Breathing strenuously, as if there were not enough air for him in the Keep, he turned and shambled away down one of the corridors.

Hugging his bruised chest, Covenant moved over to sit with his back against the wall. The pain made him cough thickly. Troy stood nearby, tight-lipped and intense. But Bannor appeared completely unruffled; nothing surprised his comprehensive dispassion.

"Jesus! Covenant," Troy said at last. "What has he got against you?"

Covenant waited until he found a clear space between coughs. Then he answered, "I raped his daughter."

"You're joking!"

"No." He kept his head down, but he was avoiding Bannor's eyes rather than Troy's.

"No wonder they call you the Unbeliever." Troy spoke in a low voice to keep his rage under control. "No wonder your wife divorced you. You must have been unsufferable."

No! Covenant panted. I was never unfaithful to her. Never. But he did not raise his head, made no effort to meet the injustice of Troy's accusation.

"Damn you, Covenant." Troy's voice was soft, fervid. He sounded too furious to shout. As if he could no longer bear the sight of the Unbeliever, he turned on his heel and strode away. But as he moved he could no longer contain his rage. "Good God!" he yelled. "I don't know why you don't drop him in some dungeon and throw away the key! We've got enough trouble as it is!" Soon he was out of view down one of the halls, but his voice echoed after him like an anathema.

Sometime later, Covenant climbed to his feet, hugging the pain in his chest. His voice was weak from the effort of speaking around his hurt. "Bannor."

"Ur-Lord?"

"Tell the High Lord about this. Tell her everything—about Trell and me—and Troy."

"Yes."

"And, Bannor—"

The Bloodguard waited impassively.

"I wouldn't do it again—attack a girl like that. I would take it back if I could." He said it as if it were a promise that he owed Bannor for saving his life.

But Bannor gave no sign that he understood or cared what the Unbeliever was saying.

After a while, Covenant went on, "Bannor, you're practically the only person around here who hasn't at least tried to forgive me for anything."

"The Bloodguard do not forgive."

"I know. I remember. I should count my blessings." With his arms wrapped around his chest to hold the pieces of himself together, he went back to his rooms.

NINE: Glimmermere

ANOTHER evening and night passed without any word or sign of Lord Foul's army—no glimmer of the fire warnings which the Lords had prepared across the Center and North Plains, no returning scouts, no omens. Nevertheless Covenant felt an increase in the tension of Revelstone; as the suspense mounted, the ambient air almost audibly quivered with strain, and Lord's Keep breathed with a sharper intake, a more cautious release. Even the walls of his room expressed a mood of imminence. So he spent the evening on his balcony, drinking springwine to soothe the ache in his chest, and watching the vague shapes of the twilight as if they were incipient armies, rising out of the very ground to thrust bloodshed upon him. After a few flasks of the fine, clear beverage, he began to feel that only the tactile sensation of beard under his fingertips stood between him and actions—war and killing—which he could not stomach.

When he slept that night, he had dreams of blood—wounds glutted with death in a vindictive and profligate expenditure which horrified him because he knew so vividly that only a few drops from an untended scratch were enough; there was no need or use for this hacking and slaughtering of flesh. But his dreams went on, agitating his sleep until at last he threw himself out of bed and went to stand on his balcony in the dawn, groaning over his bruised ribs.

Wrapped in the Keep's suspense, he tried to compose himself to continue his private durance—waiting in mixed anxiety and defiance for a peremptory summons from the High Lord. He did not expect her to take his encounter with her grandfather calmly, and he had kept to his rooms since the previous afternoon so that she would know where to find him. Still, when it came, the knock at his door made his heart jump. His fingers and toes tingled—he could feel his pulse in them—and he found himself breathing hard again, in spite of the pain in his chest. He had to swallow down a quick sour taste before he could master his voice enough to answer the knock.

The door opened, and Bannor entered the room. "The High Lord wishes to speak with you," he said without inflection. "Will you come?"

Yes, Covenant muttered grimly to himself. Of course. Do I have a choice? Holding his chest to keep himself from wincing, he strode out of his suite and down the hall.

He started in the direction of the Close. He expected that Elena would want to make her anger at him public—to make him writhe before the assembled disapproval of Revelstone. He could have avoided Trell; it would have cost him nothing more than one instant of simple trust or considerateness. But Bannor soon steered him into other corridors. They passed through a small, heavy door hidden behind a curtain in one of the meeting halls, and went down a long, twisting stairwell into a deep part of the Keep unfamiliar to Covenant. The stair ended in a series of passages so irregular and dim that they confused him until he knew nothing about where he was except that he was deep in the gut-rock of Revelstone—deeper than the private quarters of the Lords.

But before long Bannor halted, facing a blank wall of stone. In the dim light of one torch, he spread his arms to the wall as if he were invoking it, and spoke three words in a language that came awkwardly to his tongue. When he lowered his arms, a door became visible. It swung inward, admitting the Bloodguard and Covenant to a high, brilliant cavern.

The makers of Revelstone had done little to shape or work this spacious cave. They had given it a smooth floor, but had left untouched the raw rough stone of its walls and ceiling; and they had not altered the huge rude columns which stood thickly through it like massive tree trunks, reaching up from the floor to take the burden of the ceiling upon their shoulders. However, the whole cavern was lit by large urns of graveling placed between the columns so that all the surfaces of the walls and columns were clearly illumined.

Displayed on these surfaces everywhere were works of art. Paintings and tapestries hung on the walls; large sculptures and carvings rested on stands between the columns and urns; smaller pieces, carvings and statuettes and stoneware and *suru-pa-maerl* works, sat on wooden shelves cunningly attached to the columns.

In his fascination, Covenant forgot why he had been brought here. He began moving around the hall, looking avidly. The smaller works caught his attention first. Many of them appeared in some way charged with action, imminent heat, as if they had been captured in a moment of incarnation; but the differences in materials and emotions were enormous. Where an oaken figure of a woman cradling a baby wept protectively over the griefs and hurts of children, a similar granite subject radiated confident generative power; where a polished Gildenlode flame seemed to yearn upward, a *suru-pa-maerl* blaze expressed comfort and practical warmth. Studies of children and Ranyhyn and Giants abounded; but scattered among them were darker subjects—roynish ur-viles, strong, simpleminded Cavewights, and mad, valorous Kevin, reft of judgment and foresight but not courage or compassion by sheer despair. There was little copying of nature among them; the materials used were not congenial to mirroring or literalism. Instead, they revealed the comprehending hearts of their makers. Covenant was entranced.

Bannor followed him as he moved around the columns, and after a while the Bloodguard said, "This is the Hall of Gifts. All these were made by the people of the Land, and given to the Lords. Or to Revelstone." He gazed about him with unmoved eyes. "They were given for honor or love. Or to be seen. But the Lords do not desire such gifts. They say that no one can possess such things. The treasure comes from the Land, and belongs to the Land. So all gifts given to the Lords are placed here, so that any who wish it may behold them."

Yet Covenant heard something deeper in Bannor's voice. Despite its monotone, it seemed to articulate a glimpse of the hidden and unanswerable passion which bound the Bloodguard to the Lords. But Covenant did not pursue it, did not intrude on it.

From among the first columns, he was drawn to a large, thick arras hanging on one of the walls. He recognized it. It was the same work he had once tried to destroy. He had thrown it out of his room in the watchtower in a fit of outrage at the fable of Berek's life—and at the blindness which saw himself as Berek reborn. He could not be mistaken. The arras was tattered around the edges, and had a carefully repaired rent down its center halfway through the striving, irenic figure of Berek Halfhand. In scenes around the central figure, it showed the hero's soul-journey to his despair on Mount Thunder, and to his discovery of the Earthpower. From it, Berek gazed out at the Unbeliever with portents in his eyes.

Roughly, Covenant turned away, and a moment later he saw High Lord Elena walking toward him from the opposite side of the hall. He remained where he was, watched her. The Staff of Law in her right hand increased the stateliness and authority of her step, but her left hand was open in welcome. Her robe covered her without disguising either the suppleness or the strength of her movements. Her hair hung loosely about her shoulders, and her sandals made a whispering noise on the stone.

Quietly, she said, "Thomas Covenant, be welcome to the Hall of Gifts. I thank you for coming."

She was smiling as if she were glad to see him.

That smile contradicted his expectations, and he distrusted it. He studied her face, trying to discern her true feelings. Her eyes invited study. Even while they regarded him, they seemed to look beyond him or into him or through him, as if the space he occupied were shared by something entirely different. He thought fleetingly that perhaps she did not actually, concretely, see him at all.

As she approached, she said, "Do you like the Hall? The people of the Land are fine artists, are they not?" But when she neared him, she stopped short with a look of concern, and asked, "Thomas Covenant, are you in pain?"

He found that he was breathing rapidly again. The air in the Hall seemed too rarefied for him. When he shrugged his shoulders, he could not keep the ache of the movement off his face.

Elena reached her hand toward his chest. He half winced, thinking that she meant to strike him. But she only touched his bruised ribs gently with her palm for a moment, then turned away toward Bannor. "Bloodguard," she said sharply, "the ur-Lord has been hurt. Why was he not taken to a Healer?"

"He did not ask," Bannor replied stolidly.

"Ask? Should help wait for asking?"

Bannor met her gaze flatly and said nothing, as if he considered his rectitude to be self-evident. But the reproach in her tone gave Covenant an unexpected pang. In Bannor's defense, he said, "I don't need—didn't need it. He kept me alive."

She sighed without taking her eyes off the Bloodguard. "Well, that may be. But I do not like to see you harmed." Then, relenting, she said, "Bannor, the ur-Lord and I will go upland. Send for us at once if there is any need."

Bannor nodded, bowed slightly, and left the Hall.

When the hidden door was closed behind him, Elena turned back to Covenant. He tensed instinctively. *Now*, he muttered to himself. *Now she'll do it.* But to all appearances her irritation was gone. And she made no reference to the arras; she seemed unaware of the connection between him and that work. With nothing but innocence in her face, she said, "Well, Thomas Covenant. Do you like the Hall? You have not told me."

He hardly heard her. Despite her pleasant expression, he could not believe that she did not intend to task him for his encounter with Trell. But then he saw concern mounting in her cheeks again, and he hurried to cover himself.

"What? Oh, the Hall. I like it fine. But isn't it a little out of the way? What good is a museum if people can't get to it?"

"All Revelstone knows the way. Now we are alone, but in times of peace—or in times when war is more distant—there are always people here. And the children in the schools spend much time here, learning of the crafts of the Land. Craftmasters come from all the Land to share and increase their skills. The Hall of Gifts is thus deep and concealed because the Giants who wrought the Keep deemed such a place fitting—and because if ever Revelstone is whelmed the Hall may be hidden and preserved, in hope of the future."

For an instant, the focus of her gaze seemed to swing closer to him, and her vision tensed as if she meant to burn her way through his skull to find out what he was thinking. But then she turned away with a gentle smile, and walked toward another wall of the cavern. "Let me show you another work," she said. "It is by one of our rarest Craftmasters, Ahanna daughter of Hanna. Here."

He followed, and stopped with her before a large picture in a burnished ebony frame. It was a dark work, but glowing bravely near its center was a figure that he recognized immediately: Lord Mhoram. The Lord stood alone in a hollow tightly surrounded by black fiendish shapes which were about to fall on him like a flood, deluge him utterly. His only weapon was his staff, but he wielded it defiantly; and in his eyes was a hot, potent look of extremity and triumph, as if he had discovered within himself some capacity for peril that made him unconquerable.

Elena said respectfully, "Ahanna names this 'Lord Mhoram's Victory.' She is a prophet, I think."

The sight of Mhoram in such straits hurt Covenant, and he took it as a reproach. "Listen," he said. "Stop playing around with me like this. If you've got something to say, say it. Or take Troy's advice, and lock me up. But don't do this to me."

"Playing around? I do not understand."

"Hellfire! Stop looking so innocent. You got me down here to let me have it for that run-in with Trell. Well, get it over with. I can't stand the suspense."

The High Lord met his glare with such openness that he turned away, muttering under his breath to steady himself.

"Ur-Lord." She placed an appealing hand on his arm. "Thomas Covenant. How can you believe such thoughts? How can you understand us so little? Look at me. Look at me!" She pulled his arm until he turned back to her, faced the sincerity she expressed with every line of her face. "I did not ask you here to torment you. I wished to share my last hour in the Hall of Gifts with you. This war is near—near—and I will not soon stand here again. As for the Warmark —I do not take counsel from him concerning you. If there is any blame in your meeting with Trell, it is mine. I did not give you clear warning of my fears. And I did not see the extent of the danger—else I would have told all the Bloodguard to prevent your meeting.

"No, ur-Lord. I have no hard words to speak to you. You should reproach me. I have endangered your life, and cost Trell Atiaran-mate my grandfather his last self-respect. He was helpless to heal his daughter and his wife. Now he will believe that he is helpless to heal himself."

Looking at her, Covenant's distrust fell into dust. He took a deep breath to clean stale air from his lungs. But the movement hurt his ribs. The pain made him fear that she would reach toward him, and he mumbled quickly, "Don't touch me."

For an instant, she misunderstood him. Her fingers leaped from his arm, and the otherness of her vision flicked across him with a virulence that made him flinch, amazed and baffled. But what she saw corrected her misapprehension. The focus of her gaze left him; she extended her hand slowly to place her palm on his chest.

"I hear you," she said. "But I must touch you. You have been my hope for too long. I cannot give you up."

He took her wrist with the two fingers and thumb of his right hand, but he hesitated a moment before he removed her palm. Then he said, "What happens to Trell now? He broke his Oath. Is anything done to him?"

"Alas, there is little we can do. It lies with him. We will try to teach him that an Oath which has been broken may still be kept. But it was not his intent to harm you—he did not plan his attack. I know him, and am sure of this. He has known of your presence in Revelstone, yet he made no effort to seek you out. No, he was overcome by his hurt. I do not know how he will recover."

As she spoke, he saw that once again he had failed to comprehend. He had been thinking about punishment rather than healing. Hugging his sore ribs, he said, "You're too gentle. You've got every right to hate me."

She gave him a look of mild exasperation. "Neither

Lena my mother nor I have ever hated you. It is impossible for us. And what would be the good? Without you, I would not be. It may be that Lena would have married Triock, and given birth to a daughter—but that daughter would be another person. I would not be who I am." A moment later, she smiled. "Thomas Covenant, there are few children in all the history of the Land who have ridden a Ranyhyn."

"Well, at least that part of it worked out." He shrugged aside her questioning glance. He did not feel equal to explaining the bargain he had tried to make with the Ranyhyn—or the way in which that bargain had failed him.

A mood of constraint came between them. Elena turned away from it to look again at "Lord Mhoram's Victory."

"This picture disturbs me," she said. "Where am I? If Mhoram is thus sorely beset, why am I not at his side? How have I fallen, that he is so alone?" She touched the picture lightly, brushed her fingertips over Mhoram's lone, beleaguered, invincible stance. "It is in my heart that this war will go beyond me."

The thought stung her. Suddenly she stepped back from the painting, stood tall with the Staff of Law planted on the stone before her. She shook her head so that her brown-and-honey hair snapped as if a wind blew about her shoulders, and breathed intensely, "No! I will see it ended! Ended!"

As she repeated *Ended,* she struck the floor with the Staff's iron heel. An instant of bright blue fire ignited in the air. The stone lurched under Covenant's feet, and he nearly fell. But she quenched her power almost at once; it passed like a momentary intrusion of nightmare. Before he could regain his balance, she caught his arm and steadied him.

"Ah, you must pardon me," she said with a look like laughter. "I forgot myself."

He braced his feet, tried to determine whether or not he could still trust the floor. The stone felt secure. "Give me fair warning next time," he muttered, "so I can sit down."

The High Lord broke into clear laughter, then subdued herself abruptly. "Your pardon again, Thomas Covenant. But your expression is so fierce and foolish."

"Forget it," he replied. He found that he liked the sound of her laugh. "Ridicule may be the only good answer."

"Is that a proverb from your world? Or are you a prophet?"

"A little of both."

"You are strange. You transpose wisdom and jest —you reverse their meanings."

"Is that a fact?"

"Yes, ur-Lord Covenant," she said lightly, humorously. "That is a fact." Then she appeared to remember something. "But we must go. I think we are expected. And you have never seen the upland. Will you come with me?"

He shrugged. She smiled at him, and he followed her toward the door of the Hall.

"Who's expecting us?" he asked casually.

She opened the door and preceded him through it. When it was closed behind them, she answered, "I would like to surprise you. But perhaps that would not be fair warning. There is a man—a man who studies dreams—to find the truth in them. One of the Unfettered."

His heart jumped again, and he wrapped his arms protectively around his sore chest. Hellfire, he groaned to himself. An interpreter of dreams. Just what I need. An Unfettered One had saved him and Atiaran from the ur-viles at the Celebration of Spring. By a perverse trick of recollection, he heard the Unfettered One's death cry in the wake of Elena's clear voice. And he remembered Atiaran's grim insistence that it was the responsibility of the living to make meaningful the sacrifices of the dead. With a brusque gesture, he motioned for Elena to lead the way, then walked after her, muttering, Hellfire. Hellfire.

She guided him back up through the levels of Revelstone until he began to recognize his surroundings. Then they moved westward, still climbing, and after a while they joined a high, wide passage like a road along the length of the Keep, rising slowly. Soon the decreasing weight of the stone around him, and the growing autumnal tang of the air, told him that they were approaching the level of the plateau which topped the Keep. After two sharp switchbacks, the passage ended, and he found himself out in the open, standing on thick grass under the roofless heavens. A league or two west of him were the mountains.

A cool breeze hinting a fall crispness touched him through the late morning sunlight—a low blowing as full of ripe earth and harvests as if it were clairvoyant, foretelling bundled crops and full fruit and seeds ready for rest. But the trees on the plateau and the upland hills were predominantly evergreens, feathery mimosas and tall pines and wide cedars with no turning of leaves. And the hardy grass made no concessions to the changing season.

The hills of the upland were Revelstone's secret strength. They were protected by sheer cliffs on the east and south, by mountains on the north and west; and so they were virtually inaccessible except through Lord's Keep itself. Here the people of the city could get food and water to withstand a siege. Therefore Revelstone could endure as long as its walls and gates remained impregnable.

"So you see," said Elena, "that the Giants wrought well for the Land in all ways. While Revelstone stands, there remains one bastion of hope. In its own way, the Keep is as impervious to defeat as Foul's Creche is said to be—in the old legends. This is vital, for the legends also say that the shadow of Despite will never be wholly driven from the Land while Ridjeck Thome, Lord Foul's dire demesne, endures. So our debt to the Giants is far greater than for unfaltering friendship. It is greater than anything we can repay."

Her tone was grateful, but her mention of the Giants cast a gloom over her and Covenant. She turned away from it, and led him northward along the curve of the upland.

In this direction, the plateau rose into rumpled hills; and soon, on their left, away from the cliff, they began to pass herds of grazing cattle. Cattleherds saluted the High Lord ceremoniously, and she responded with quiet bows. Later, she and Covenant crossed a hilltop from which they could see westward across the width of the upland. There, beyond the swift river that ran south toward the head of Furl Falls, were fields where crops of wheat and maize rippled in the breeze. And a league behind the grazeland and the river and the fields stood the mountains, rising rugged and grand out of the hills. The peaks were snow-clad, and their white be-mantling made them look hoary and aloof—sheer, wild, and irreproachable. The *Haruchai* lived west and south in this same range.

Covenant and the High Lord continued northward, slowly winding away from the cliffs and toward the river as Elena chose an easy path among the hills. She seemed content with the silence between them, so they both moved without speaking. Covenant walked as if he were drinking in the upland with his eyes and ears. The sturdy health of the grass, the clean, hale soil and the inviolate rock, the ripeness of the wheat and maize—all were vivid to his sight. The singing and soaring of the birds sounded like joy in the air. And when he passed close to a particularly tall, magisterial pine, he felt that he could almost hear the climbing of its sap. For a league, he forgot himself in his enjoyment of the Land's late summer.

Then he began to wonder vaguely how far Elena meant to take him. But before he became willing to interrupt the quietness with a question, they crossed the rise of a high hill, and she announced that they had arrived. "Ah," she said with a sigh of gladness, "Glimmermere! Lakespring and riverhead—hail, clean pool! It pleases my heart to see you again."

They were looking down on a mountain lake, the headwater of the river which ran to Furl Falls. For all the swiftness of the current rushing from it, it was a still pool, with no inflowing streams; all its water came from springs within it. And its surface was as flat, clear, and reflective as polished glass. It echoed the mountains and the sky with flawless fidelity, imaging the world in every detail.

"Come," Elena said suddenly. "The Unfettered One will ask us to bathe in Glimmermere." Throwing a quick smile at him, she ran lightly down the hill. He followed her at a walk, but the springy grass seemed to urge him forward until he was trotting. On the edge of the lake, she dropped the Staff as if she were discarding it, tightened the sash of her robe, and with a last wave toward him dove into the water.

When he reached Glimmermere, he was momentarily appalled to find that she had vanished. From this range, the reflection was transparent, and behind it he could see the rocky bottom of the lake. Except for a darkness like a deep shadow at its center, he could see the whole bottom in clear detail, as if the pool were only a few feet deep. But he could not see Elena. She seemed to have dived out of existence.

He leaned over the water to peer into it, then stepped back sharply as he noticed that Glimmermere did not reflect his image. The noon sun was repeated through him as if he were invisible.

The next instant, Elena broke water twenty yards out in the lake. She shook her head clear, and called for him to join her. When she saw the wide gape of his astonishment, she laughed gaily. "Does Glimmermere surprise you?"

He stared at her. He could see nothing of her below the plane where she broke the water. Her physical substance seemed to terminate at the waterline. Above the surface, she bobbed as if she were treading water; below, the bottom of the pool was clearly visible through the space she should have occupied. With an effort, he pulled his mouth shut, then called to her, "I told you to give me fair warning!"

"Come!" she replied. "Do not be concerned. There is no harm." When he did not move, she continued, "This is water, like any other—but stronger. There is Earthpower here. Our flesh is too unsolid for Glimmermere. It does not see us. Come!"

Tentatively, he stooped and dipped his hand in the water. His fingers vanished as soon as they passed below the surface. But when he snatched them back, they were whole and wet, tingling with cold.

Impelled by a sense of surprise and discovery, he

pulled off his boots and socks, rolled up his pant legs, and stepped into the pool.

At once, he plunged in over his head. Even at its edges, the lake was deep; the clarity with which he could see the bottom had misled him. But the cold, tangy water buoyed him up, and he popped quickly back to the surface. Treading water and sputtering, he looked around until he located Elena. "Fair warning!" He tried to sound angry despite Glimmermere's fresh, exuberant chill. "I'll teach you fair warning!" He reached her in a few swift strokes, and shoved her head down.

She reappeared immediately, laughing almost before she lifted her head above water. He lunged at her, but she slipped past him, and pushed him under instead. He grappled for her ankles and missed. When he came up, she was out of sight.

He felt her tugging at his feet. Grabbing a deep breath, he upended himself and plunged after her. For the first time, he opened his eyes underwater, and found that he could see well. Elena swam near him, grinning. He reached her in a moment, and caught her by the waist.

Instead of trying to pull away, she turned, put her arms around his neck, and kissed him on the mouth.

Abruptly, all the air burst from his lungs as if she had kicked his sore ribs. He thrust away from her, scrambled back to the surface. Coughing and gasping, he thrashed over to the edge of the pool where he had left his boots, and climbed out to collapse on the grass.

His chest hurt as if he had reinjured his ribs, but he knew he had not. The first touch of Glimmermere's potent water had effaced his bruises, simply washed them away, and they did not ache now. This was another pain; in his exertions underwater he seemed to have wrenched his heart.

He lay panting face down on the grass, and after a while, his breathing relaxed. He became aware of other sensations. The cold, tart touch of the water left his whole body excited; he felt cleaner than he had at any time since he had learned of his leprosy. The sun was warm on his back, and his fingertips tingled vividly. And his heart ached when Elena joined him on the grass.

He could feel her eyes on him before she asked quietly, "Are you happy in your world?"

Clenching himself, he rolled over, and found that she sat close to him, regarding him softly. Unable to resist the sensation, he touched a strand of her wet hair, rubbed it between his fingers. Then he lifted his gray, gaunt eyes to meet her gaze. The way he held himself made his voice unintentionally harsh. "Happiness has got nothing to do with it. I don't think about happiness. I think about staying alive."

"Could you be happy here?"

"That's not fair. What would you say if I asked you that?"

"I would say yes." But a moment later she saw what he meant, and drew herself up. "I would say that happiness lies in serving the Land. And I would say that there is no happiness in times of war."

He lay back on the grass so that he would not have to look at her. Bleakly, he murmured, "Where I come from, there is no 'Land.' Just 'ground.' Dead. And there's always war."

After a short pause, she said with a smile in her voice, "If I have heard rightly, it is such talk as this which makes Hiltmark Quaan angry with you."

"I can't help it. It's the simple fact."

"You have a great respect for facts."

He breathed carefully around his sore heart before answering. "No. I hate them. They're all I've got."

A gentle silence came over them. Elena reclined beside him, and they lay still to let the sunlight dry them. The warmth, the smell of the grass, seemed to offer him a sense of well-being; but when he tried to relax and flow with it, his pulse throbbed uncomfortably in his chest. He was too conscious of Elena's presence. But gradually he became aware that a larger silence covered Glimmermere. All the birds and even the breeze had become quiet, hushed. For a time, he kept his breathing shallow and explored the ambience of the air with his ears.

Shortly, Elena said, "He comes," and went to retrieve the Staff. Covenant sat up and looked around. Then he heard it—a soft, clean sound like a flute, spreading over Glimmermere from one source that he could see, as if the air itself were singing. The tune moved, came closer. Soon he could follow the words.

> Free
> Unfettered
> Shriven
> Free—
> Dream that what is dreamed will be:
> Hold eyes clasped shut until they see,
> And sing the silent prophecy—
> And be
> Unfettered
> Shriven
> Free.

> Lone
> Unfriended
> Bondless
> Lone—
> Drink of loss 'til it is done,
> 'Til solitude has come and gone,
> And silence is communion—
> And yet
> Unfriended
> Bondless
> Lone.

> Deep
> Unbottomed
> Endless
> Deep—
> Touch the true mysterious Keep
> Where halls of fealty laugh and weep;
> While treachers through the dooming creep
> In blood

Unbottomed
Endless
Deep.

"Stand to meet him," the High Lord said quietly. "He is One of the Unfettered. He has gone beyond the knowledge of the Loresraat, in pursuance of a private vision open to him alone."

Covenant arose, still listening to the song. It had an entrancing quality which silenced his questions and doubts. He stood erect, with his head up as if he were eager. And soon the Unfettered One came into sight over the hills north of Glimmermere.

He stopped singing when he saw Covenant and Elena, but his appearance sustained his influence over them. He wore a long flowing robe that seemed to have no color of its own; instead it caught the shades around it, so that it was grass-green below his waist, azure on his shoulders, and the rock and snow of the mountains flickered on his right side. His unkempt hair flared, reflecting the sun.

He came directly toward Covenant and Elena, and soon Covenant could make out his face—soft androgynous features thickly bearded, deep eyes. When he stopped before them, he and the High Lord exchanged no rituals or greetings. He said to her simply, "Leave us," in a high, fluted voice like a woman's. His tone expressed neither rejection nor command, but rather something that sounded like necessity, and she bowed to it without question.

But before she left, she put her hand again on Covenant's arm, looked searchingly into his face. "Thomas Covenant," she said with a low quaver in her voice as if she were afraid of him or for him. "Ur-Lord. When I must leave for this war—will you accompany me?"

He did not look at her. He stood as if his toes were rooted in the grass, and gazed into the Unfettered One's eyes. When after a time he failed to reply, she bowed her head, squeezed his arm, then moved away toward Revelstone. She did not look back. Soon she was out of sight beyond the hill.

"Come," said the Unfettered One in the same tone of necessity. Without waiting for a response, he started to return the way he had come.

Covenant took two uncertain steps forward, then stopped as a spasm of anxiety clenched his features. He tore his eyes off the Unfettered One's back, looked urgently around him. When he located his socks and boots, he hurried toward them, dropped to the grass and pulled them onto his feet. With a febrile deliberateness, as if he were resisting the tug of some current or compulsion, he laced his boots and tied them securely.

When his feet were safe from the grass, he sprang up and ran after the interpreter of dreams.

TEN: Seer and Oracle

LATE the next evening, Lord Mhoram answered a knock at the door of his private quarters, and found Thomas Covenant standing outside, silhouetted darkly like a figure of distress against the light of the glowing floor. He had an aspect of privation and fatigue, as if he had tasted neither food nor rest since he had gone upland. Mhoram admitted him without question to the bare room, and closed the door while he went to stand before the stone table in the center of the chamber—the table Mhoram had brought from the High Lord's rooms, with the *krill* of Loric still embedded and burning in it.

Looking at the bunched muscles of Covenant's back, Mhoram offered him food or drink or a bed, but Covenant shrugged them away brusquely, despite his inanition. In a flat and strangely closed tone, he said, "You've been beating your brains out on this thing ever since—since it started. Don't you ever rest?

I thought you Lords rested down here—in this place."

Mhoram crossed the room, and stood opposite his guest. The *krill* flamed whitely between them. He was uncertain of his ground; he could see the trouble in Covenant's face, but its causes and implications were confused, obscure. Carefully, the Lord said, "Why should I rest? I have no wife, no children. My father and mother were both Lords, and Kevin's Lore is the only craft I have known. And it is difficult to rest from such work."

"And you're driven. You're the seer and oracle around here. You're the one who gets glimpses of the future whether you want them or not, whether they make you scream in your sleep or not, whether you can stand them or not." Covenant's voice choked for a moment, and he shook his head fiercely until he could speak again. "No wonder you can't rest. I'm surprised you can stand to sleep at all."

"I am not a Bloodguard," Mhoram returned calmly. "I need sleep like other men."

"What have you figured out? Do you know what this thing is good for? What was that Amok business about?"

Mhoram gazed at Covenant across the *krill,* then smiled softly. "Will you sit down, my friend? You will hear long answers more comfortably if you ease your weariness."

"I'm not tired," the Unbeliever said with obvious falseness. The next moment, he dropped straight into a chair. Mhoram took a seat, and when he sat down he found that Covenant had positioned himself directly across the table, so that the *krill* stood between their faces. This arrangement disturbed Mhoram, but he could think of no other way to help Covenant than to listen and talk, so he stayed where he was, and focused his other senses to search for what was blocked from his sight by the gem of the *krill.*

"No, I do not comprehend Loric's sword—and I cannot draw it from the table. I might free it by breaking the stone, but that would serve no purpose. We would gain no knowledge—only a weapon we could not touch. If the *krill* were free, it would not help us. It is a power altogether new to us. We do not know its uses. And we do not like to break wood or stone, for any purpose.

"As to Amok—that is an open question. Lord Amatin could answer better."

"I'm asking you."

"It is possible," Mhoram said steadily, "that he was created by Kevin to defend against the *krill* itself. Perhaps the power here is so perilous that in unwise hands, or ignorant hands, it would do great harm. If that is true, then it may be that Amok's purpose is to warn us from any unready use of this power, and to guide our learning."

"You shouldn't sound so plausible when you say things like that. That isn't right. Didn't you hear what he said? 'I have misserved my purpose.' "

"Perhaps he knows that if we are too weak to bring the *krill* to life, we are powerless to use it in any way, for good or ill."

"All right. Forget it. Just forget that this is something else I did to you without any idea what in hell I was doing. Let it stand. What makes you think that good old Kevin Landwaster who started all this anyway is lurking in back of everything that happens to you like some kind of patriarch, making sure you don't do the wrong thing and blow yourselves to bits? No, forget it. I know better than that, even if I have spent only a few weeks going crazy over this and not forty years like the rest of you. Tell me this. What's so special about Kevin's Lore? Why are you so hot to follow it? If you need power, why don't you go out and find it for yourselves, instead of wasting whole generations of perfectly decent people on a bunch of incomprehensible Wards? In the name of sanity, Mhoram, if not for the sake of mere pragmatic usefulness."

"Ur-Lord, you surpass me. I hear you, and yet I am left as if I were deaf or blind."

"I don't care about that. Tell me why."

"It is not difficult—the matter is clear. The Earthpower is here, regardless of our mastery or use. The Land is here. And the banes and the evil—the Illearth

Stone, the Despiser—are here, whether or not we can defend against them.

"Ah, how shall I speak of it? At times, my friend, the most simple, clear matters are the most difficult to utter." He paused for a moment to think. But through the silence he felt an upsurge of agitation from Covenant, as if the Unbeliever were clinging to the words between them, and could not bear to have them withdrawn. Mhoram began to speak again, though he did not have his answer framed to his satisfaction.

"Consider it in this way. The study of Kevin's knowledge is the only choice we can accept. Surely you will understand that we cannot expect the Earth to speak to us, as it did to Berek Halfhand. Such things do not happen twice. No matter how great our courage, or how imposing our need, the Land will not be saved that way again. Yet the Earthpower remains, to be used in Landservice—if we are able. But that Power—all power—is dreadful. It does not preserve itself from harm, from wrong use. As you say, we might strive to master the Earthpower in our own way. But the risk forbids.

"Ur-Lord, we have sworn an Oath of Peace which brooks no compromise. Consider—forgive me, my friend, but I must give you a clear example—consider the fate of Atiaran Trell-mate. She dared powers which were beyond her, and was destroyed. Yet the result could have been far worse. She might have destroyed others, or hurt the Land. How could we, the Lords— we who have sworn to uphold all health and beauty— how could we justify such hazards?

"No, we must work in other ways. If we are to gain the power to defend the Earth, and yet not endanger the Land itself, we must be the masters of what we do. And it was for this purpose that Lord Kevin created his Wards—so that those who came after him could hold power wisely."

"Oh, right!" Covenant snapped. "Look at the good it did him. Hellfire! Even supposing you're going to have the luck or the brains or even the chance to find all Seven Wards and figure them out, what—bloody damnation!—what's going to happen when dear, old, dead Kevin finally lets you have the secret of the Ritual of Desecration? And it's your last chance to stop Foul in a war—again! How're you going to rationalize that to the people who'll have to start from scratch a thousand years from now because you just couldn't get out of repeating history? Or do you think that when the crisis comes you're somehow going to do a better job than Kevin did?"

He spoke coldly, rapidly, but a smudged undercurrent in his voice told Mhoram that he was not talking about what was uppermost in his mind. He seemed to be putting the Lord through a ritual of questions, testing him. Mhoram responded carefully, hoping for Covenant's sake that he would not make a mistake.

"We know the peril now. We have known it since the Giants returned the First Ward to us. Therefore we have sworn the Oath of Peace—and will keep it— so that never again will life and Land be harmed by despair. If we are brought to the point where we must desecrate or be defeated, then we will fight until we are defeated. The fate of the Earth will be in other hands."

"Which I'm doing nothing but make difficult for you. Just having this white gold raises prospects of eradication that never occurred to you before—not to mention the fact that it's useless. Before this there wasn't enough power around to make it even worth your while to worry about despair, since you couldn't damage the Land if you wanted to. But now Foul might get my ring—or I might use it against you—but it'll never save you."

Covenant's hands twitched on the table as if he were fumbling for something. His fingers knotted together, tensed, then sprang apart to grope separately, aimlessly. "All right. Forget that, too. I'm coming to that. How in the name of all the gods are you going to fight a war—a war, Mhoram, not just fencing around with a bunch of Cavewights and ur-viles!— when everyone you've got who's tall enough to hold a sword has sworn this Oath of Peace? Or are there special dispensations like fine print in your contracts exempting wars from moral strictures or even the simple horror of blood?"

It was in Mhoram's heart to tell Covenant that he went too far. But the fumbling, graspless jerks of his hands—one maimed, the other carrying his ring like a fetter—told Mhoram that the affront of the Unbeliever's language was directed inward at himself, not at the Lords or the Land. This perception increased Mhoram's concern, and again he replied with steady dignity.

"My friend, killing is always to be abhorred. It is a measure of our littleness that we cannot evade it. But I must remind you of a few matters. You have heard Berek's Code—it is part of our Oath. It commands us:

Do not hurt where holding is enough;
do not wound where hurting is enough;
do not maim where wounding is enough;
and kill not where maiming is enough;
the greatest warrior is he who does not need to kill.

And you have heard High Lord Prothall say that the Land would not be served by angry bloodshed. There he touched upon the heart of the Oath. We will do all that might or mastery permits to defend the Land from Despite. But we will do nothing—to the Land, to our foes, to each other—which is commanded to us by our hearts' black passions or pain or lust for death. Is this not clear to you, ur-Lord? If we must fight and, yes, kill, then our only defense and vindication is to fight so that we do not become like our Enemy. Here Kevin Landwaster failed—he was weakened by that despair which is the Despiser's strength.

"No, we must fight—if only to preserve ourselves from watching the evil, as Kevin watched and was undone. But if we harm each other, or the Land, or hate our foes—ah, there will be no dawn to the night of that failure."

"That's sophistry."

"Sophistry? I do not know this word."

"Clever arguments to finance what you've already decided to do. Rationalizations. War in the name of

Peace. As if when you poke your sword into a foe you aren't slicing up ordinary flesh and blood that has as much right to go on living as you do."

"Then do you truly believe that there is no difference between fighting to destroy the Land and fighting to preserve it?"

"Difference? What has that got to do with it? It's still killing. But never mind. Forget that, too. You're doing too good a job. If I can't pick holes in your answers any better than this, I'm going to end up—" His hands began to shake violently, and he snatched them out of sight, shoved them below the table. "I'll end up freezing to death, that's what."

Slumped back in his chair, Covenant fell into an aching silence. Mhoram felt the pressure between them build, and decided that the time had come to ask questions of his own. Breathing to himself the Seven Words, he said kindly, "You are troubled, my friend. The High Lord is difficult to refuse, is she not?"

"So?" Covenant snapped. But a moment later, he groaned, "Yes. Yes, she is. But that isn't it. The whole Land is difficult to refuse. I've felt that way from the beginning. That isn't it." After a tense pause, he went on: "Do you know what she did to me yesterday? She took me upland to see that Unfettered One —the man who claims to understand dreams. I was there for a day or more— But you're the seer and oracle—I don't have to tell you about him. You've probably gone up there yourself more than anyone else, couldn't help it, if only because mere ordinary human ears can only stand to hear so much contempt and laughter and no more, regardless of whether you're asleep or not. So you know what it's like. You know how he latches onto you with those eyes, and holds you down, and dissects— But you're the seer and oracle. You probably even know what he said to me."

"No," Mhoram replied quietly.

"He said— Hellfire!" He shook his head as if he were dashing water from his eyes. "He said that I dream the truth. He said that I am very fortunate. He said that people with such dreams are the true enemies of Despite—it isn't Law, the Staff of Law wasn't made to fight Foul with—no, it's wild magic and dreams that are the opposite of Despite." For an instant, the air around him quivered with indignation. "He also said that I don't believe it. That was a big help. I just wish I knew whether I am a hero or a coward.

"No, don't answer that. It isn't up to you."

Lord Mhoram smiled to reassure Covenant, but the Unbeliever was already continuing, "Anyway, I've got a belief—for what it's worth. It just isn't exactly the one you people want me to have."

Probing again, Mhoram said, "That may be. But I do not see it. You do not show us belief, but Unbelief. If this is believing, then it is not belief for, but rather belief against."

Covenant jumped to his feet as if he had been stung. "I deny that! Just because I don't affirm the Land or whatever, carry on like some unraveled fanatic and foam at the mouth for a chance to fight like Troy does, doesn't mean— Assuming that there's some kind of justice in the labels and titles which you people spoon around—assuming you can put a name at all to this gut-broken whatever that I can't even articulate much less prove to myself. That is not what Unbelief means."

"What does it mean?"

"It means—" For a moment, Covenant stopped, choking on the words as if his heart suffered some blockage. Then he reached forward and shaded the gem of the *krill* with his hands so that it did not shine in his eyes. In a voice suddenly and terribly suffused with the impossibility of any tears which would have eased him, he shouted, "It means I've got to withhold —to discount—to keep something for myself! Because I don't know why!" The next instant, he dropped back into his chair and bowed his head, hiding it in his arms as if he were ashamed.

" 'Why'?" Mhoram said softly. "That is not so hard a matter here, thus distant from 'how.' Some of our legends hint at one answer. They tell of the beginning of the Earth, in a time soon after the birth of Time, when the Earth's Creator found that his brother and Enemy, the Despiser, had marred his creation by placing banes of surpassing evil deep within it. In outrage and pain, the Creator cast his Enemy down—out of the universal heavens onto the Earth—and emprisoned him here within the arch of Time. Thus, as the legends tell it, Lord Foul came to the Land."

As he spoke, he felt that he was not replying to Covenant's question—that the question had a direction he could not see. But he continued, offering Covenant the only answer he possessed.

"It is clear now that Lord Foul lusts to strike back at his brother, the Creator. And at last, after ages of bootless wars carried on out of malice, out of a desire to harm the creation because he could not touch the Creator, Lord Foul has found a way to achieve his end, to destroy the arch of Time, unbind his exile, and return to his forbidden home, for spite and woe. When the Staff of Law, lost by Kevin at the Desecration, came within his influence, he gained a chance to bridge the gap between worlds—a chance to bring white gold into the Land.

"I tell you simply: it is Lord Foul's purpose to master the wild magic—'the anchor of the arch of life that spans and masters Time'—and with it bring Time to an end, so that he may escape his bondage and carry his lust throughout the universe. To do this, he must defeat you, must wrest the white gold from you. Then all the Land and all the Earth will surely fall."

Covenant raised his head, and Mhoram tried to anticipate his next question. "But how?—how does the Despiser mean to accomplish this purpose? Ah, my friend, that I do not know. He will choose ways which resemble our own desires so closely that we will not resist. We will not be able to distinguish between his service and our own until we are bereft of all aids but you, whether you choose to help us or no."

"But why?" Covenant repeated. "Why me?"

Again, Mhoram felt that his answer did not lie in the direction of Covenant's question. But still he offered it, humbly, knowing that it was all he had to give his tormented visitor.

"My friend, it is in my heart that you were chosen by the Creator. That is our hope. Lord Foul taught Drool to do the summoning because he desired white gold. But Drool's hands were on the Staff, not Lord Foul's. The Despiser could not control who was summoned. So if you were chosen, you were chosen by the Creator.

"Consider. He is the Creator, the maker of the Earth. How can he stand careless and see his making destroyed? Yet he cannot reach his hand to help us here. That is the law of Time. If he breaks the arch to touch the Land with his power, Time will end, and the Despiser will be free. So he must resist Lord Foul elsewhere. With you, my friend."

"Damnation," Covenant mumbled.

"Yet even this you must understand. He cannot touch you here, to teach or help you, for the same reason that he cannot help us. Nor can he touch or teach or help you in your own world. If he does, you will not be free. You will become his tool, and your presence will break the arch of Time, unbinding Despite. So you were chosen. The Creator believes that your uncoerced volition and strength will save us in the end. If he is wrong, he has put the weapon of his own destruction into Lord Foul's hands."

After a long silence, Covenant muttered, "A hell of a risk."

"Ah, but he is the Creator. How could he do otherwise?"

"He could burn the place down, and try again. But I guess you don't think gods are that humble. Or do you call it arrogance—to burn—? Never mind. I seem to remember that not all the Lords believe in this Creator as you do."

"That is true. But you came to me. I answer as I can."

"I know. Don't mind me. But tell me this. What would you do in my place?"

"No," said Mhoram. At last he moved his chair to one side, so that he could see Covenant's face. Gazing into the Unbeliever's unsteady features, he replied, "That I will not answer. Who can declare? Power is a dreadful thing. I cannot judge you with an answer. I have not yet judged myself."

The instability of Covenant's expression momentarily resolved into seeking. But he did not speak, and after a time Mhoram decided to risk another question. "Thomas Covenant, why do you take this so? Why are you so hurt? You say that the Land is a dream— a delusion—that we have no real life. Then do not be concerned. Accept the dream, and laugh. When you awaken, you will be free."

"No," Covenant said. "I recognized something in what you said—I'm starting to understand this. Listen. This whole crisis here is a struggle inside me. By hell, I've been a leper so long, I'm starting to think that the way people treat lepers is justified. So I'm becoming my own enemy, my own Despiser—working against myself when I try to stay alive by agreeing with the people who make it so hard. That's why I'm dreaming this. Catharsis. Work out the dilemma subconsciously, so that when I wake up I'll be able to cope."

He stood up suddenly, and began to pace Mhoram's ascetic chamber with a voracious gleam in his eyes. "Sure. That's it. Why didn't I think of it before? I've been telling myself all the time that this is escapism, suicide. But that's not it—that's not it at all. Just forget that I'm losing every one of the habits that keep me alive. This is dream therapy."

But abruptly a grimace of pain clutched his face. "Hellfire!" he rasped intensely. "That sounds like a story I should have burned—back when I was burning stories—when I still had stories to burn."

Mhoram heard the anguished change, the turning to dust, in Covenant's tone, and he stood to reach out toward his visitor. But he did not need to move; Covenant came almost aimlessly in his direction, as if within the four walls of the chamber he had lost his way. He stopped at the table near Mhoram, and gazed miserably at the *krill*. His voice shook.

"I don't believe it. That's just another easy way to die. I already know too many of them."

He seemed to stumble, though he was standing still. He lurched forward, and caught himself on Mhoram's shoulder. For a moment, he clung there, pressing his forehead into Mhoram's robe. Then Mhoram lowered him into a chair.

"Ah, my friend, how can I help you? I do not understand."

Covenant's lips trembled, but with a visible effort he regained control of his voice. "Just tired. I haven't eaten since yesterday. That Unfettered One—drained me. Some food would be very nice."

The opportunity to do something for Covenant gave Mhoram a feeling of relief. Moving promptly, he brought his guest a flask of springwine. Covenant drank as if he were trying to break an inner drought, and Mhoram went to his back rooms to find some food.

While he was placing bread and cheese and grapes on a tray, he heard a sharp, distant shout; a voice cried his name with an urgency that smote his heart. He set the tray down, hastened to throw open the door of his chambers.

In the sudden wash of light from the courtyard, he saw a warrior standing in one of the coigns high above him. The warrior was a young man—too young for war meat, Mhoram thought grimly—who had lost command of himself. "Lord Mhoram!" he blurted. "Come! Now! The Close!"

"Stop." The authority in Mhoram's tone caught the young man like a bit. He winced, stiffened, forced down a chaotic tumult of words. Then he recovered his self-possession. Seeing this, the Lord said more gently, "I hear you. Speak."

"The High Lord asks that you come to the Close at once. A messenger has come from the Plains of Ra. The Gray Slayer is marching."

"War?" Mhoram spoke softly to conceal a sharp prevision of blood.

"Yes, Lord Mhoram."

"Please say to the High Lord that—that I have heard you."

Bearing himself carefully, Mhoram turned back toward Covenant. The Unbeliever met his gaze with a hot, oddly focused look, as if his skull were splitting between his eyes. Mhoram asked simply, "Will you come?"

Covenant gripped the Lord's gaze, and said, "Tell me something, Mhoram. How did you get away—when that Raver caught you—near Foul's Creche?"

Mhoram answered with a conscious serenity, a refusal of dismay, which looked like danger in his gold-flecked eyes. "The Bloodguard with me were slain. But when *samadhi* Raver touched me, he knew me as I knew him. He was daunted."

For a moment, Covenant did not move. Then he dropped his glance. Wearily, he set the stoneware flask on the table, pushed it over so that it clicked against the *krill*. He tugged momentarily at his beard, then pulled himself to his feet. To Mhoram's gaze, he looked like a thin candle clogged with spilth—guttering, frail, and portionless.

"Yes," he said. "Elena asked me the same thing. For all the good it'll do any of us. I'm coming."

Awkwardly, he shambled out onto the burning floor.

PART II

The Warmark

ELEVEN: War Council

HILE Troy was sure of one thing; despite whatever Covenant said, the Land was no dream. He perceived this with an acuteness which made his heart ache.

In the "real" world, he had not been simply blind, he had been eyeless from birth. He lacked even the organs of sight which could have given him a conception of what vision was. Until the mysterious event which had snatched him from between opposing deaths, and had dropped him on the sunlit grass of Trothgard, light and dark had been equally incomprehensible to him. He had not known that he lived in immitigable midnight. The tools with which he had handled his physical surroundings had been hearing and touch and language. His sense of ambience, his sensitivity to the auras of objects and the resonances of space, was translated by words until it became his sole measure of the concrete world. He had been a good strategist precisely because his perceptions of space and interacting force were pure, undistracted by any knowledge of day or night or color or brilliance or illusion.

Therefore he could not be imagining the Land. His former mind had not contained the raw materials out of which such dreams were made. When he appeared in the Land—when Lord Elena taught him that the rush of sensations which confused him was sight— the experience was altogether new. It did not restore to him something that he had lost. It opened in front of him like an oracle.

He knew that the Land was real.

And he knew that its future hung by the thread of

165

his strategy in this war. If he made a mistake, then more brightness and color than he could ever take into account were doomed.

So when Ruel, the Bloodguard assigned to watch over him, came to him in his quarters and informed him that a Ramen Manethrall had arrived from the Plains of Ra, bringing word of Lord Foul's army, Troy felt an instant of panic. It had begun—the test of all his training, planning, hopes. If he had believed Mhoram's tales of a Creator, he would have dropped to his knees to pray—

But he had never learned to rely on anyone but himself. The Warward and the strategy were his; he was in command. He paused just long enough to strap the traditional ebony sword of the Warmark to his waist and don his headband. Then he followed Ruel toward the Close.

As he moved, he was grateful for the brightness of the torches in the hallways. Even with their help, his sight was dim. In daylight, he could see clearly, with more grasp of detail and more distance than the far-eyed Giants. The sun brought distant things close to him; at times, he felt that he possessed more of the Land than anyone else. But night restored his blindness like an insistent reminder of where he had come from. While the sun was down, he was lost without torches or fires. Starlight did not touch his private darkness, and even a full moon cast no more than a gray smudge across his mind.

Sometimes in the middle of the night, his sightlessness scared him like a repudiation of sunlight and vision.

By force of habit, he adjusted his sunglasses. He had worn them for so long, out of consideration for the people with eyes who had to look at him, that they felt like a part of his face. But he never saw them; they had no effect on his vision. Nothing that came within six inches of his orbless sockets blocked his mental sight at all.

To control his tension, he strode toward the Close without hurrying. At one point, a group of Hafts, the commanders of Eoward, saluted him and then jogged

ahead with their swords clattering; and later Lord
Verement came hawklike down a broad staircase and
rushed past him. But he did not vary his step until he
reached the high doors of the council chamber. There
he found Quaan waiting for him.

The sight of the old stalwart Hiltmark gave him a
pang. In this dim light, Quaan's thin white hair made
him look frail. But he saluted Troy briskly, and reported that all fifty Hafts were now in the Close.

Fifty. Troy recited the numbers to himself as if he
were repeating a rite of command: Fifty Eoward, one
thousand Eoman; a total of twenty-one thousand fifty
warriors; First Haft Amorine, Hiltmark Quaan, and
himself. He nodded as if to assure Quaan that they
would be enough. Then he marched down into the
Close to take his seat at the Lords' table.

Around him, the chamber was almost filled, and
most of the leaders were in their chairs. The space
was so well-lit that now he could see clearly. The
High Lord sat with quiet intensity at the head of the
table; and between her and him were Callindrill,
Trevor, Loerya, and Amatin, each keeping a private
silence. But Troy knew them, and could guess something of their thoughts. Lord Loerya hoped despite
the demands of her Lordship that she and Trevor
would not be chosen to leave Revelstone and her
daughters. And her husband seemed to be remembering that he had fallen under the strain of fighting the
ill in *dukkha* Waynhim—remembering, and wondering if he had the strength for this war.

About Elena, Troy did not speculate. Her beauty
confused him; he did not want to think that something
might happen to her in this war. Deliberately, he kept
his gaze away from her.

On her left beyond Mhoram's empty chair was
Lord Verement and two more unoccupied seats—
places for the Lords Shetra and Hyrim. For a moment,
Troy paused to wonder how Korik's mission was doing. Four days after their departure, word had been
brought to Revelstone by some of the scouts that they
had passed into Grimmerdhore Forest. But after that,
of course, Troy knew he could not expect to hear any

more news until long days after the mission was over, for good or ill. In the privacy of his heart, he dreamed that sometime during the course of this war he would have the joy of seeing Giants march to his aid, led by Hyrim and Shetra. He missed them all, Shetra as much as Korik, Hyrim as much as the Giants. He feared that he would need them.

Above and behind the High Lord, the Hearthralls Tohrm and Borillar sat in their places with Hiltmark Quaan and First Mark Morin. And behind the Lords, spaced around the first rows of seats in the gallery, were other Bloodguard: Morril, Bann, Howor, Koral, and Ruel on Troy's side; Terrel, Thomin, and Bannor opposite him.

Most of the remaining people in the Close were his Hafts. As a group they were restless, tense. Most of them had no experience of war, and they had been training rigorously under his demanding gaze. He found himself hoping that what they saw and heard at this Council would galvanize their courage, turn their tightness into fortitude. They had such an ordeal ahead of them—

The few Lorewardens visiting Revelstone were all present, as were the most skilled of the Keep's *rhadhamaerl* and *lillianrill*. But Troy noticed that the Gravelingas Trell was not among them. He felt vaguely relieved—more for Trell's sake than for Covenant's.

Shortly, Lord Mhoram entered the Close, bringing the Unbeliever with him. Covenant was tired—his hunger and weakness were plainly visible in the gaunt pallor of his face—but Troy could see that he had suffered no real harm. And his reliance upon Mhoram's support expressed how little he was a threat to the Lords at this moment. Troy frowned behind his sunglasses, tried not to let his indignation at Covenant surge back up again. As Mhoram seated Covenant, and then walked around to take his own place at Elena's left, Troy turned his attention to the High Lord.

She was ready to begin now; and as always her every movement, her every inflection, fascinated him.

Slowly, she looked around the table, meeting the eyes of each of the Lords. Then in a clear, stately voice, she said, "My friends, Lords and Lorewardens and servers of the Land, our time has come. For good or ill, weal or woe, the trial is upon us. The word of war is here. In our hands now is the fate of the Land, to keep or to lose, as our strength permits. The time of preparation is ended. No longer do we build or plan against the future. Now we go to war. If our might is not potent to preserve the Land, then we fall, and whatever world is to come will be of the Despiser's making, not ours.

"Hear me, my friends. I do not speak to darken your hearts, but to warn against false hope and wishful dreams, which could unbind the thews of purpose. We are the chance of the Land. We have striven for worth. Now our worthiness meets its test. Harken, and make no mistake. This is the test which determines." For a moment, she paused to gaze over all the attentive faces in the Close. When she had seen the resolution in their eyes, she gave a smile of approval, and said quietly, "I am not afraid."

Troy nodded to himself. If his warriors felt as he did, she had nothing to fear.

"Now," said High Lord Elena, "let us hear the bearer of these tidings. Admit the Manethrall."

At her command, two Bloodguard opened the doors, and made way for the Ramen.

The woman wore a deep brown shift which left her arms and legs free, and her long black hair was knotted at her neck by a cord. This cord, and the small woven garland of yellow flowers around her neck, sadly wilted now after long days of wear, marked her as a Manethrall—a member of the highest rank of her people. She was escorted by an honor guard of four Bloodguard, but she moved ahead of them down the stairs, bearing the fatigue of her great journey proudly. Yet despite her brave spirit, Troy saw that she could barely stand. The slim grace of her movements was dull, blunted. She was not young. Her eyes, long familiar with open sky and distance, nested in fine wrinkles of age, and the weariness of several hundred leagues lay like lead in the marrow of her bones, giving a pallid underhue to the dark suntan of her limbs.

With a sudden rush of anxiety, Troy hoped that she had not come too late.

As she descended to the lowest level of the Close, and stopped before the graveling pit, High Lord Elena rose to greet her. "Hail, Manethrall, highest of the Ramen, the selfless tenders of the Ranyhyn! Be welcome in Lord's Keep—welcome and true. Be welcome whole or hurt, in boon or bane—ask or give. To any requiring name we will not fail while we have life or power to meet the need. I am High Lord Elena. I speak in the presence of Revelstone itself."

Troy recognized the ritual greeting of friends, but the Manethrall gazed up at Elena darkly, as if unwilling to respond. Then she turned to her right, and said in a low, bitter voice unlike the usual nickering tones of the Ramen, "I know you, Lord Mhoram." Without waiting for a response, she moved on. "And I know you, Covenant Ringthane." As she looked at him, the quality of her bitterness changed markedly. Now it was not weariness and defeat and old Ramen resentment of the Lords for presuming to ride the Ranyhyn, but something else. "You demanded the Ranyhyn at night, when no mortal may demand them at all. Yet they answered—one hundred proud Manes, more than most Ramen have ever seen in one place. They reared to you, in homage to the Ringthane. And you did not ride." Her voice made clear her respect for such an act, her awe at the honor which the Ranyhyn had done this man. "Covenant Ringthane, do you know me?"

Covenant stared at her intensely, with a look of pain as if his forehead were splitting. Several moments passed before he said thickly, "Gay. You're—you were Winhome Gay. You waited on—you were at Manhome."

The Manethrall returned his stare. "Yes. But you have not changed. Forty-one summers have ridden past me since you visited the Plains of Ra and Manhome, and would not eat the food I brought to you. But you are changeless. I was a child then, a Winhome then, barely near my Cording—and now I am a tired old woman, far from home, and you are young. Ah, Covenant Ringthane, you treated me roughly."

He faced her with a bruised expression; the memories she called up were sore in him. After another moment, she raised her hands until her palms were turned outward level with her head, and bowed to him in the traditional Ramen gesture of greeting. "Covenant Ringthane, I know you. But you do not know me. I am not Winhome Gay, who passed her Cording and studied the Ranyhyn in the days when Manhome was full of tales of your Quest—when Manethrall Lithe returned from the dark underground, and from seeing the Fire-Lions of Mount Thunder. And I am not Cord Gay, who became a Manethrall, and later heard the word of the Lords asking for Ramen scouts to search the Spoiled Plains between Landsdrop and the Shattered Hills. This requesting word was heard, though these same Lords knew that all the life of the Ramen is on the Plains of Ra, in the tending of the Ranyhyn—yes, heard, and accepted by Manethrall Gay, with the Cords in her watch. She undertook the task of scouting because she hated Fangthane the Render, and because she admired Manethrall Lithe, who dared to leave sunlight for the sake of the Lords, and because she honored Covenant Ringthane, the bearer of white gold, who did not ride when the Ranyhyn reared to him. Now that Manethrall Gay is no more."

As she said this, her fingers hooked into claws, and her exhausted legs bent into the semblance of a fighting crouch. "I am Manethrall Rue—old bearer of the flesh of her who was named Gay. I have seen Fangthane marching, and all the Cords in my watch are dead." Then she sagged, and her proud head dropped low. "And I have come here—I, who should never have left the Plains of home. I have come here, to the Lords who are said to be the friends of the Ranyhyn, in no other name but grief."

While she spoke, the Lords kept silence, and all the Close watched her in anxious suspense, torn between respect for her fatigue and desire to hear what she had to say. But Troy heard dangerous vibrations in her voice. Her tone carried a pitch of recrimination which she had not yet articulated clearly. He was familiar with the grim, suppressed outrage that filled all the Ramen when any human had the insolence, the almost blasphemous audacity, to ride a Ranyhyn. But he did not understand it. And he was impatient for the Manethrall's news.

Rue seemed to sense the increasing tension around her. She stepped warily away from Covenant, and addressed all her audience for the first time. "Yes, it is said that the Lords are our friends. It is said. But I do not know it. You come to the Plains of Ra and give us tasks without thought for the pain we feel on hills which are not our home. You come to the Plains of Ra, and offer yourselves to the generosity of the Ranyhyn as if you were an honor for some Mane to accept. And when you are accepted, as the Bloodguard are accepted—five hundred Manes thralled like chattel to purposes not their own—you call the Ranyhyn away from us into danger, where none can protect, where the flesh is rent and the blood spilt, with no *amanibhavam* to stem the pain or forestall death. Ah, Ranyhyn!

"Do not flex your distrust at me. I know you all."

In a soft, careful voice, containing neither protest nor apology, the High Lord said, "Yet you have come."

"Yes," Manethrall Rue returned in tired bitterness, "I have come. I have fled, and endured, and come. I know we are united against Fangthane, though you have betrayed us."

Lord Verement stiffened angrily, but Elena controlled him with a glance, and said, still softly and carefully, to Rue, "In what way betrayed?"

"Ah, the Ramen do not forget. In tales preserved in Manhome from the age of mighty *Kelenbhrabanal,* we know Fangthane, and the wars of the Old Lords. Always, when Fangthane built his armies in the Lower Land, the Old Lords came to the ancient battleground north of the Plains of Ra and the Roamsedge River, and fought at Landsdrop, to forbid Fangthane from the Upper Land. So the Ranyhyn were preserved, for the enemy could not turn his teeth to the Plains of Ra while fighting the Lords. And in recognition, the Ramen left their hills to fight with the Lords.

"But you—! Fangthane marches, and your army is here. The Plains of Ra are left without defense or help."

"That was my idea." His impatience made Troy sound sharper than he intended.

"For what reason?" A dangerous challenge pulsed in her quiet tone.

"I think they were good reasons," he responded. Impelled by an inner need to reassure himself that he had not been wrong, he spoke swiftly. "Think about it. You're right—every time in the past that Foul has built up an army, the Lords have gone to fight him at Landsdrop. And every time, they've lost. They've been pushed back. There are too many different ways up from the Lower Land. And the Lords have been too far from their supplies and support. Sure, they put up a good fight—and that takes some of the pressure off the Plains of Ra because Foul is occupied elsewhere. But the Lords lose. Whole Eoward get hacked to pieces, and the Warward has to retreat on the run just to stay alive long enough to regroup and fight the same fight all over again, farther west—closer to Revelstone.

"And that's not all. This time, Foul might be building his army farther north—in Sarangrave Flat north of the Defiles Course. He's never done that before. But back then the Giants always kept the north Sarangrave clear. This time"—he winced at the thought of the Giants—"this time it's different. If we marched an army down to you while Foul was on his way north of Mount Thunder toward Revelstone, we'd be helpless to stop him from attacking the Keep. Revelstone might fall. So I made the decision. We wait here.

"Don't get me wrong—we're not abandoning you. The fact is, I don't think you're in that much danger. Look, suppose Foul has an army of fifty thousand— or even a hundred thousand. How long is it going to take him to conquer the Plains of Ra?"

"He will not," Rue breathed between her teeth.

The Warmark nodded. "And even if he does, it'll take him years. You're too good at hunting—he can't beat you on your own ground. You and the Ranyhyn will run circles around his troops, and every time they turn their backs, you'll throttle a few score of them. Even if he outnumbers you fifty to one, you'll just send the Ranyhyn into the mountains, and keep chipping away at him for God knows how long. He'll need years to do it. Even assuming we are not attacking his rear. No, until he's got the Lords beaten, he can't afford to tackle you. That's why I've been thinking all along that he would come north."

He stopped, and faced Rue squarely with his argument. The recital of his reasoning calmed him; he knew that his logic was sound. And the Manethrall was forced to acknowledge it. After considering his explanation for a time, she sighed, "Ah, very well. I see your reasons. But I do not like such ideas. You juggle risk for the Ranyhyn too freely."

Tiredly, she turned back toward Elena. "Hear me, High Lord," she said in a gray, empty voice. "I will speak my message, for I am weary and must rest, come what may.

"I have journeyed here from the Shattered Hills which surround and defend Foul's Creche. I left that maimed place when I saw a great army issuing from the Hills. It marched as straight as the eye sees toward Landsdrop and the Fall of the River Landrider. It was an army dire and numberless—I could not guess its size, and did not wait to count. With the four Cords in my watch, I fled so that I might keep my word to the Lords."

The south way, Troy breathed to himself. At once, his brain took hold of the information; concrete images of the Spoiled Plains and Landsdrop filled his mind. He began to calculate Lord Foul's progress.

"But some enemy knew my purpose. We were pursued. A black wind came upon us, and from it fearsome, abominable creatures fell like birds of prey. My Cords were lost so that I might escape—yet I was driven far from my way, north into the marge of the Sarangrave.

"I knew that the peril was great. Yet I knew that there was no waiting army of friends or Lords on the Upper Land to help the Ranyhyn. A shadow came over my heart. Almost I turned aside from my purpose, and left the Lords to a fate of their own devising. But I contended with the Sarangrave, so that the lives of my Cords would not have been lost in vain.

"Over the ancient battleground, through the rich joy of Andelain, then across a stern plain south of a great forest like unto Morinmoss, but darker and more slumberous—thus I made my way, so that your idea might have its chance. That is my message. Ask what questions you will, and then release me, for I must rest."

With quiet dignity, the High Lord arose, holding the Staff of Law before her. "Manethrall Rue, the Land is measureless in your debt. You have paid a grim price to bring your word to us, and we will do our uttermost to honor that cost. Please hear me. We could not turn away from the Ranyhyn and their Ramen. To do so, we would cease to be what we are. Only one belief has kept us from your side. It is in our hearts that this is the final war against Fangthane. If we fall, there will be none left to fight again. And we have not the strength of the Old Lords. What force we have we must use cunningly. Please do not harden your heart against us. We will pay many prices to match your own." Holding the Staff at the level of her eyes, she bent forward in a Ramen bow.

A faint smile flickered across Rue's lips—amusement at Elena's approximation of the fluid Ramen salute—and she returned it to show how it should be done. "It is also said among the Ramen that the Lords are courteous. Now I know it. Ask your questions. I will answer as I can."

The High Lord reseated herself. Troy was eager to speak, but she did not give him permission. To Manethrall Rue she said, "One question is first in my heart. What of Andelain? Our scouts report no evil there, but they have not your eyes. Are the Hills free of wrong?"

A surge of frustration bunched the muscles of

Troy's shoulders. He was eager, urgent, to begin probing the Manethrall. But he recognized the tact of
Elena's inquiry. The Andelainian Hills rode through
Ramen legend like an image of paradise; it would
ease Rue's heart to speak of them.

In response, her grim bitterness relaxed for a moment. Her eyes filled with tears that ran down over
the slight smile on her lips. "The Hills are free," she
said simply.

A glad murmur ran through the Close, and several
of the Lords nodded in satisfaction. This was not
something about which a Manethrall could be mistaken. The High Lord sighed her gratitude. When she
freed the Warmark to begin his questions, she did so
with a look that urged him to be gentle.

"All right," Troy said, rising to his feet. His heart
labored with anxiety, but he ignored it. "I understand
that you don't know the size of Foul's army. I accept
that. But I've got to know how much head start he
has. Exactly how many days ago did you see his army
leave the Shattered Hills?"

The Manethrall did not need to count back. She
replied promptly, "Twenty days."

For an instant, the Warmark regarded her eyelessly
from behind his sunglasses, stunned into silence. Then
he whispered, "Twenty days?" His brain reeled.
"Twenty?" With a violence that wrenched his heart,
his image of the Despiser's army surged forward
thirty-five leagues—five days. He had counted on receiving word of Lord Foul's movements in fifteen
days. He had studied the Ramen; he knew to a league
how far a Manethrall could travel in a day. "Oh, my
God." Rue should have been able to reach Revelstone
in fifteen days.

He was five days short. Five days less in which to
march over three hundred leagues—! And Lord Foul's
army would be in the Center Plains ten days from
now.

Without knowing how he had reached that position,
he found himself sitting with his face in his hands as
if he could not bear to look at the ruin of all his fine
strategy. Numbly, as if it were a matter of no con-

sequence, he realized that he had been right about one thing: Covenant's summons coincided with the start of Lord Foul's army. That ploy had triggered the Despiser's attack. Or did it work the other way around? Had Lord Foul somehow anticipated the call?

"How—?" For a moment, he could not find what he wanted to ask, and he repeated stupidly, "How—?"

"Ask!" Rue demanded softly.

He heard the warning in her voice, the danger of offending her pride after an exhausting ordeal. It made him raise his head, look at her. She was glaring at him, and her hands twitched as if they yearned to snatch the fighting cord from her hair. But he had to ask the question, had to be sure—"What happened to you? Why did it take so long?" His voice sounded small and lorn to himself.

"I was driven from my way," she said through her teeth, "north into the marge of the Sarangrave."

"Dear God," Troy breathed weakly. He felt the way Rue looked at him, felt all the eyes in the Close on him. But he could not think; his brain was inert. Lord Foul was only a three-day march from Morinmoss.

The Manethrall snorted disdainfully, and turned away toward the High Lord. "Is this the man who leads your warriors?" she asked sourly.

"Please pardon him," Elena replied. "He is young in the Land, and in some matters does not see clearly. But he has been chosen by the Ranyhyn. In time he will show his true value."

Rue shrugged. "Do you have other questions?" she said wearily. "I would end this."

"You have told us much. We have no more doubt of Lord Foul's movements, and can guess his speed. Only one question remains. It concerns the composition of Fangthane's army. What manner of beings comprise it?"

Bitterness stiffened Rue's stance, and she said harshly, "I have spoken of the wind, and the evil in the air which felled my Cords. In the army I saw ur-viles, Cavewights, a mighty host of *kresh*, great lion-like beasts with wings which both ran and flew, and many other ill creatures. They wore shapes like dogs or horses or men, yet they were not what they seemed. They shone with great wrong. To my heart, they appeared as the people and beasts of the Land made evil by Fangthane."

"That is the work of the Illearth Stone," the High Lord murmured.

But Manethrall Rue was not done. "One other thing I saw. I could not be mistaken, for it marched near the forefront, commanding the movements of the horde. It controlled the creatures with a baleful green light, and called itself Fleshharrower. It was a Giant."

For an instant, a silence like a thunderclap broke over the Close. It snatched Troy's attention erect, lit a fire of dread in his chest. The Giants! Had Lord Foul conquered them? Already?

Then First Mark Morin came to his feet and said in a voice flat with certainty, "Impossible. Rockbrother is another name for fealty and faith. Do you rave?"

At once, the chamber clamored in protest against the very idea that a Giant could join the Despiser. The thought was too shocking to be admitted; it cast fundamental beliefs into hysteria. The Hafts burst out lividly, and several of them shouted through the general uproar that Rue was lying. Two Lorewardens took up Morin's question and made it an accusation: Rue was in the grip of a Raver. Confusion overcame even the Lords. Trevor and Loerya paled with fear; Verement barked at Mhoram; Elena and Callindrill were staggered; and Amatin burst into tears.

The noise aggravated swiftly in the clear acoustics of the Close, exacerbated itself, forced each voice to become rawer and wilder. There was panic in the din. If the Giants could be made to serve Despite, then nothing was safe, sure; betrayal lurked everywhere. Even the Bloodguard had an aspect of dismay in their flat faces.

Yet under the protesting and the abuse, Manethrall Rue stood firmly, holding up her head with a blaze of pride and fury in her eyes.

The next moment, Covenant reached her side.

Shaking his fists at the assembly, he howled, "Hellfire! Can't you see that she's telling the truth?"

His voice had no effect. But something in his yell penetrated Hiltmark Quaan. The old veteran knew the Ramen well; he had known Rue during her youth. He jumped to his feet and shouted, "Order!!"

Caught in their trained military reactions, the Hafts sprang to attention.

Then High Lord Elena seemed to realize what was happening around her. She reasserted her control with a blast of blue fire from the Staff, and one hot cry:

"I am ashamed!"

A stung silence, writhing with fear and indignation, burned in answer to her shout. But she met it passionately, sternly, as if something precious were in danger. *"Melenkurion abatha!* Have we come to this? Does fear so belittle us? Look! Look at her. If you have not heard the truth in her voice, then look at her now. Remember your Oath of Peace, and look at her. By the Seven! What evil do you see? No—I will hear no protestations that ill can be disguised. We are in the Close of Revelstone. This is the Council of Lords. No Raver could utter falsehood and betrayal here. If there were any wrong in the Manethrall, you would have known it."

When she saw that she had mastered the assembly, she continued more quietly. "My friends, we are more than this. I do not know the meaning of Manethrall Rue's tidings. Perhaps the Despiser has captured and broken a Giant through the power of the Illearth Stone. Perhaps he can create ill wights in any semblance he desires, and showed a false Giant to Rue, knowing how the tale of a betraying Rockbrother would harm us. We must gain answers to these questions. But here stands Manethrall Rue of the Ramen, exhausted in the accomplishment of a help which we can neither match nor repay. Cleanse your hearts of all thought against her. We must not do such injustice."

"Right." Troy heaved himself to his feet. His brain was working again. He was ashamed of his weakness —and, by extension, ashamed of his Hafts as well. Belatedly, he remembered that the Lords Callindrill and Amatin had been unable to breach Sarangrave Flat—and yet Rue had survived it, so that she could come to warn Revelstone. And he did not like to think that Covenant had behaved better than he. "You're right." He faced the Ramen squarely. "Manethrall, my Hafts and I owe you an apology. You deserve better—especially from us." He put acid in his tone for the ears of the Hafts. "War puts burdens on people without caring whether they're ready for them or not."

He did not wait for any reply. Turning toward Quaan, he said, "Hiltmark—my thanks for keeping your head. Let's make sure that nothing like this happens again." Then he sat down and withdrew behind his sunglasses to try to think of some way to salvage his battle plans.

Quaan commanded, "Rest!" The Hafts reseated themselves, looking abashed—and yet in some way more determined than before. That seemed to mark the end of an ugliness. Manethrall Rue and ur-Lord Covenant sagged, leaned tiredly toward each other as if for support. The High Lord started to speak, but Rue interrupted her in a low voice. "I want no more apologies. Release me. I must rest."

Elena nodded sadly. "Manethrall Rue, go in Peace. All the hospitality Revelstone can provide is yours for as long as you choose to stay. We do not take the service you have done us lightly. But please hear me. We have never taken the Ramen lightly. And the value of the Ranyhyn to all the Land is beyond any measure. We do not forget. Hail, Manethrall! May the bloom of *amanibhavam* never fail. Hail, Ramen! May the Plains of Ra be forever swift under your feet. Hail, Ranyhyn! Tail of the Sky, Mane of the World." Once again, she bowed to Rue in the Ramen fashion.

Manethrall Rue returned the gesture, and added the traditional salute of farewell; touching the heels of her hands to her forehead, she bent forward and spread her arms wide as if baring her heart. Together, the Lords answered her bow. Then she turned and started up toward the high doors. Covenant went with her, walking at her side awkwardly, as if he wanted and feared to take her arm.

At the top of the stairs, they stopped and faced each other. Covenant looked at her with emotions that seemed to make the bone between his eyes bulge. He had to strain to speak. "What can I—is there anything I can do—to make you Gay again?"

"You are young and I am old. This journey has taken much from me. I have few summers left. There is nothing."

"My time has a different speed. Don't covet my life."

"You are Covenant Ringthane. You have power. How should I not covet?"

He ducked away from her gaze; and after a short pause she added, "The Ranyhyn still await your command. Nothing is ended. They served you at Mount Thunder, and will serve you again—until you release them." When she passed through the doors away from him, he was left staring down at his hands as if their emptiness pained him.

But after a moment he pulled himself up, and came back down the stairs to take his seat again.

For a time, there was silence in the Close. The gathered people watched the Lords, and the Lords sat still, bending their minds in toward each other to meld their purpose and strength. This had a calming effect on the assembly. It was part of the mystery of being a Lord, and all the people of the Land, Stonedownor and Woodhelvennin, trusted the Lords. As long as the Council was capable of melding and leadership, Revelstone would not be without hope. Even Warmark Troy gained a glimpse of encouragement from this communion he could not share.

At last, the contact broke with an almost audible snap from Lord Verement, and the High Lord raised her head to the assembly. "My friends, warriors, servants of the Land," she said, "now is the time of decision. Deliberation and preparation are at an end. War marches toward us, and we must meet it. In this matter, the chief choice of action is upon Warmark Hile Troy. He will command the Warward, and

we will support it with our best strength, as the need
of the Land demands.

"But one matter compels us first—this Giant named
Fleshharrower. The question of this must be answered."

Roughly, Verement said, "The Stone does not explain. It is not enough. The Giants are strong—yes,
strong and wise. They would resist the Stone or evade
it."

"I agree," said Loerya. "The Seareach Giants
understand the peril of the Illearth Stone. It is easier
to believe that they have left the Land in search of
their lost Home."

"Without the Gildenlode?" Trevor countered uncomfortably. "That is unlikely. And it is not—it is not
what Mhoram saw."

The other Lords turned to Mhoram, and after a
moment he said, "No, it is not what I have seen. Let
us pray that I have seen wrongly—or wrongly understood what I have seen. But for good or ill, this
matter is beyond us at present. We know that Korik
and the Lords Hyrim and Shetra will do their uttermost for the Giants. And we cannot send more of
our strength to Seareach now, to ask how a Giant has
been made to lead Lord Foul's army. It is in my heart
that we will learn that answer sooner than any of us
would wish."

"Very well," the High Lord sighed. "I hear you.
Then let us now divide among ourselves the burdens
of this war." She looked around the Council, measuring each member against the responsibilities which
lay ahead. Then she said, "Lord Trevor—Lord
Loerya—to you I commit the keeping of Revelstone.
It will be your task to care for the people made
homeless by this war—to lay up stores and strengthen
defenses against any siege that may come—to fight
the last battle of the Land if we fail. My friends, hear
me. It is a grim burden I give you. Those who remain
here may in the end require more strength than all
others—for if we fall, then you must fight to the last
without surrender or despair. You will be in a strait
place like that which drove High Lord Kevin to his

Desecration. I trust you to resist. The Land must not be doomed in that way again."

Troy nodded to himself; her choice was a good one. Lord Loerya would fight extravagantly, and yet would never take any action that would imperil her daughters. And Lord Trevor would work far beyond his strength in the conviction that he did not do as much as others could. They accepted the High Lord's charge quietly, and she went on to other matters.

"After the defense of Revelstone, our concern must be for the Loresraat and Trothgard. The Loresraat must be preserved. And Trothgard must be held for as long as may be—as a sanctuary for the homeless, men or beasts—and as a sign that in no way do we bow to the Despiser. Within the Valley of Two Rivers, Trothgard is defensible, though it will not be easy. Lord Callindrill—Lord Amatin—this burden I place upon your shoulders. Preserve Trothgard, so that the ancient name of Kurash Plenethor, Stricken Stone, will not become the new name of our promise to the Land."

"Just a minute," Warmark Troy interrupted hesitantly. "That leaves just you, Mhoram, and Verement to go with me. I think I'm going to need more than that."

Elena considered for a moment. Then she said, "Lord Amatin, will you accept the burden of Trothgard alone? Trevor and Loerya will give you all possible aid."

"We fight a war," Amatin replied simply. "It is bootless to protest that I do not suffice. I must learn to suffice. The Lorewardens will support me."

"You will be enough," responded the High Lord with a smile. "Very well. Those Lords who remain— Callindrill, Verement, Mhoram, and myself—will march with the Warward. Two other matters, and then the Warmark will speak. First Mark Morin."

"High Lord." Morin stood to receive her requests.

"Morin, you are the First Mark. You will command the Bloodguard as your Vow requires. Please assign to Warmark Troy every Bloodguard who can be spared from the defense of Revelstone."

"Yes, High Lord. Two hundred will join the War-mark's command."

"That is well. Now I have another task for you. Rid-ers must be sent to every Stonedown and Woodhelven in the Center and South Plains, and in the hills be-yond. All the people who may live in the Despiser's path must be warned, and offered sanctuary at Troth-gard if they choose to leave their homes. And all who dwell along the southward march of the War-ward must be asked for aid—food for the warriors, so that they may march more easily, carrying less. *Aliantha* alone will not suffice for so many."

"It will be done. The Bloodguard will depart be-fore moonset."

Elena nodded her approval. "No thanks can repay the Bloodguard. You give a new name to unflawed service. While people endure in the Land, you will be remembered for faithfulness."

Bowing slightly, the First Mark sat down.

The High Lord set the Staff of Law on the table before her, took her seat, and signed to Warmark Troy. He took a deep breath, then got stiffly to his feet. He was still groping, juggling. But he had re-gained a grip on his situation; he was thinking clearly again. Even as he started to speak, new ideas were coming into focus.

"I'm not going to waste time apologizing for this mess I've gotten us into. I built my strategy on the idea that we would get word of where Foul was marching in fifteen days. Now we're five days short. That's all there is to it.

"Most of you know generally what I had in mind. As far as I can learn, the Old Lords had two prob-lems fighting Foul—the simple attrition of doing battle all the way from Landsdrop, and the terrain. The Center Plains favor whichever army is fresher and larger. My idea was to let Foul get halfway here on his own, and meet him at the west end of the Mithil valley, where the Mithil River forms the south border of Andelain. Then we would retreat southwest, luring Foul after us across to Doom's Retreat. In all the legends, that's the place armies run to when they're routed. But in fact it's a hell of a place to take on armies that are bigger and faster than you are. The terrain—that bottleneck between the mountains—gives a tremendous advantage to the side that gets there first—if it gets there in time to dig in before the enemy arrives.

"Well, it was a nice idea. Now we're in a different war. We're five days short. Foul will be through the Mithil valley ten days from now. And he'll turn north, forcing us to fight him wherever he wants in the Center Plains. If we have to retreat at all, we'll end up in Trothgard."

He paused for a moment, half expecting groans of dismay. But most of the people simply watched him closely, and several of the Lords had confidence in their eyes. Their trust touched him. He had to swallow down a sudden lump in his throat before he could continue.

"There's one way we can still do it. It's going to be hell—but it's just about possible."

Then for an instant he faltered. *Hell* was a mild word for what his warriors would have to endure. How could he ask them to do it, when he was to blame for the miscalculation which made it necessary? How—?

But Elena was watching him steadily. From the beginning, she had supported his desire to command the Warward. And now he was the Warmark. He, Hile Troy. In a tone of anger at the extremity of what he was asking, he said, "Here it is. First. We have nine days. I absolutely guarantee that Foul will hit the western end of the Mithil valley by the end of the ninth day from now. That's one of the things not having any eyes is good for. I can measure things like this. All right? Nine days. We've got to get there before that and block the valley.

"Morin, your two hundred Bloodguard have got to leave tonight. Callindrill, you go with them. On Ranyhyn you can get there in seven days. You've got to stop Foul right there.

"Borillar, how many of those big rafts have you got in the lake?"

Surprised, Hearthrall Borillar answered, "Three, Warmark."

"How many warriors and horses can they carry?"

Borillar glanced helplessly over at Quaan. The Hiltmark replied, "Each raft will carry two Eoman and their Warhafts—forty-two warriors and horses. But the crowding will be dangerous."

"If you ride a raft as far as Andelain, how fast can you get those Eoman to the Mithil valley?"

"If there is no mishap—in ten days. Four days may be saved through the use of rafts."

"All right. We have twelve horse-mounted Eoward —two hundred forty Eoman. Borillar, I need one hundred twenty of those rafts. Quaan, you're in command of this. You've got to get all twelve mounted Eoward— and Verement—down to the Mithil valley as fast as possible—to help Callindrill and the Bloodguard keep Foul from coming through. You've got to buy us the time we need. Get on it."

Hiltmark Quaan spoke a word to the Hafts, and twelve of them jumped up to form ranks behind him as he hastened out of the Close. Borillar looked at the High Lord with an expression of indecision, but she nodded to him. Rubbing his hands nervously as if to warm them, he left the chamber, taking all the *lillianrill* with him.

"Second," Troy said. "The rest of the Warward will march straight south from here to Doom's Retreat. That's something less than three hundred leagues." He called the remaining Hafts to their feet, and addressed them directly. "I think you should explain this to your commands. We've got to get to Doom's Retreat in twenty-eight days. And that's only enough if the Hiltmark can do everything I've got in mind for him. Tell your Eoward—ten leagues a day. That's going to be the easy part of this war."

In the back of his mind, he was thinking, Ten leagues a day for twenty-eight days. Good God! Half of them will be dead before we reach the South Plains.

For a moment, he studied the Hafts, trying to judge their mettle. Then he said, "First Haft Amorine."

The First Haft stepped forward, and responded,

"Warmark." She was a short, broad, dour woman with blunt features which appeared to have been molded in a clay too hard and dry for detailed handiwork. But she was a seasoned veteran of the Warward—one of the few survivors of the Eoman which Quaan had commanded on the Quest for the Staff of Law.

"Ready the Warward. We march at dawn. Pay special attention to the packs. Make them as light as possible. Use all the rest of the horses for cartage if you have to. If we don't make it to Doom's Retreat in time, Revelstone won't have any use for the last few hundred horses. Get started."

First Haft Amorine gave a stern command to the Hafts. Saluting the Lords together, they moved out of the Close behind her.

Troy watched until they were gone, and the doors were shut after them. Then he turned to the High Lord. With an effort, he forced himself to say, "You know I've never commanded a war before. In fact, I've never commanded anything. All I know is theory— just mental exercises. You're putting a lot of faith in me."

If she felt the importance of what he said, she gave no sign. "Do not fear, Warmark," she replied firmly. "We see your value to the Land. You have given us no cause to doubt the rightness of your command."

A rush of gratitude took Troy's voice away from him. He saluted her, then sat down and braced his arms on the table to keep himself from trembling.

A moment later, High Lord Elena said to the remaining assembly, "Ah, my friends, there is much to be done, and the night will be all too short for our need. This is not the time for long talk or exhortation. Let us all go about our work at once. I will speak to the Keep, and to the Warward, at dawn.

"Hearthrall Tohrm."

"High Lord," Tohrm responded with alacrity.

"I think that there are ways in which you may make the rafts more stable, safer for horses. Please do so. And send any of your people who may be spared to assist Hearthrall Borillar in the building.

"My friends, this war is upon us. Give your best

strength to the Land now. If mortal flesh may do it, we must prevail." She drew herself erect, and flourished the Staff. "Be of good heart. I am Elena daughter of Lena, High Lord by the choice of the Council, and wielder of the Staff of Law. My will commands. I speak in the presence of Revelstone itself." Bowing to the assembly, she swept from the Close through one of the private doors, followed variously by the other Lords.

The chamber emptied rapidly as the people hurried away to their tasks. Troy stood and started toward the stairs. But on the way, Covenant accosted him. "Actually," Covenant said as if he were telling Troy a secret, "it isn't you they've got faith in at all. Just as they don't have faith in me. It's the student who summoned you. That's whom they've staked their faith on."

"I'm busy," Troy said stiffly. "I've got things to do. Let me go."

"Listen!" Covenant demanded. "I'm trying to warn you. If you could hear it. It's going to happen to you, too. One of these days, you're going to run out of people who'll march their hearts out to make your ideas work. And then you'll see that you put them through all that for nothing. Three-hundred-league marches—blocked valleys—your ideas. Paid for and wasted. All your fine tactics won't be worth a rusty damn.

"Ah, Troy," he sighed wearily. "All this responsibility is going to make another Kevin Landwaster out of you." Instead of meeting Troy's taut stare, he turned away and wandered out of the Close as if he hardly knew or cared where he was going.

TWELVE: Forth to War

JUST before dawn, Troy rode away from the gates of Revelstone in the direction of the lake at the foot of Furl Falls. The predawn dimness obscured his sight, blinded him like a mist in his mind. He could not see where he was going, could hardly discern the ears of his mount. But he was in no danger; he was riding Mehryl, the Ranyhyn that had chosen to bear him.

Yet as he trotted westward under the high south wall of the Keep, he had a precarious aspect, like a man trying to balance himself on a tree limb that was too small. He had spent a good part of the night reviewing the decisions he had made in the war council, and they scared him. He had committed the Lords and the Warward to a path as narrow and fatal as a swaying tightrope.

But he had no choice. He had either to go ahead or to abandon his command, leave the war in Quaan's worthy but unimaginative hands. So in spite of his anxiety he did not hesitate. He intended to show all the Land that he was the Warmark for good reason.

Time was urgent. The Warward had to begin its southward march as soon as possible. So he trusted Mehryl to carry him through his inward fog. Letting the Ranyhyn pick their way, he hastened toward the blue lake where the rafts were being built.

Before he rounded the last wide foothill, he moved among scattered ranks of warriors holding horses. Men and women saluted him as he passed, but he could recognize none of them. He held up his right hand in blank acknowledgment, and rode down the

189

thronged road without speaking. If his strategy failed, these warriors—and the two hundred Bloodguard who had already followed Lord Callindrill toward the Mithil valley—would be the first to pay for his mistake.

He found the edge of the lake by the roar of the Falls and the working sounds of the raft builders, and slipped immediately off Mehryl's back. The first shadowy figure that came near him he sent in search of Hiltmark Quaan. Moments later, Quaan's solid form appeared out of the fog, accompanied by a lean man carrying a staff—Lord Verement. Troy spoke directly to the Hiltmark. He felt uneasy about giving orders to a Lord.

"How many rafts are ready?"

"Three and twenty are now in the water," Quaan replied. "Five yet lack the *rhadhamaerl* rudders, but that task will be accomplished by sunrise."

"And the rest?"

"Hearthrall Borillar and the raft builders promise that all one hundred twenty will be complete by dawn tomorrow."

"Damn! Another day gone. Well, you can't wait for them. Lord Callindrill is going to need help faster than that." He calculated swiftly, then went on: "Send the rafts downriver in groups of twenty—two Eoman at a time. If there's any trouble, I want them to be able to defend themselves. You go first. And—Lord Verement, will you go with Quaan?"

Verement answered with a sharp nod.

"Good. Now, Quaan. Get your group going right away. Put whomever you want in command of the other Eoward—tell them to follow you in turn just as soon as another twenty rafts are ready to go. Have the warriors who are going last try to help the raft builders—speed this job up."

His private fog was clearing now as the sun started to rise. Quaan's age-lined bulwark of a face drifted into better focus, and Troy fell silent for a moment, half dismayed by what he was asking his friend to do. Then he shook his head roughly, forced himself to continue.

"Quaan, you've got the worst job in this whole damn business. You and those Bloodguard with Callindrill. You have got to make this plan of mine work."

"If it can be done, we will do it." Quaan spoke steadily, almost easily, but his experience with grim, desperate undertakings gave his statement conviction.

Troy went on hurriedly, "You've got to hold Foul's army in that valley. Even after you get your whole force there, you're going to be outnumbered ten to one. You've got to hold Foul back, and still keep enough of your force alive to lead him down to Doom's Retreat."

"I understand."

"No, you don't. I haven't told you the worst of it yet. You have got to hold Foul back for eight days."

"Eight?" Verement snapped. "You jest!"

Controlling himself sternly, Troy said, "Figure it out for yourself. We've got to march all the way to Doom's Retreat. We need that much time just to get there. Eight days will hardly give us time to get in position."

"You ask much," Quaan said slowly.

"You're the man who can do it," Troy replied. "And the truth is, the warriors'll follow you better in a situation like that than they would me. You'll have two Lords working with you, plus all the Bloodguard Callindrill has left. There's nobody who can take your place."

Quaan met this in silence. Despite the square set of his shoulders, he appeared to be hesitating. Troy leaned close to him, whispered intently through the noise of Furl Falls, "Hiltmark, if you accomplish what I ask, I swear that I will win this war."

"Swear?" Verement cut in again. "Does the Despiser know that you bind him with your oaths?"

Troy ignored the Lord. "I mean it. If you get that chance for me, I won't waste it."

A low, war-ready grin touched Quaan's lips. "I hear you," he said. "I felt the dour hand of your skill when you won the command of the Warward from me.

Warmark, you will be given your eight days if they lie within the reach of human thew and will."

"Good!" Quaan's promise gave Troy an obscure feeling of relief, as if he were no longer alone on his narrow limb. "Now. When you engage Foul in the Mithil valley, what you've got to do is force him southward. Push him down into the southern hills—the farther the better. Hold the valley closed until he has enough of his army in the hills to attack you from that side. Then run like hell straight toward Doom's Retreat."

"That will be costly."

"Not as costly as letting that army go north when we're in the south." Quaan nodded grimly, and Troy went on, "And not as costly as letting Foul get to the Retreat ahead of us. Whatever else happens, we've got to avoid that. If you can't hold him back eight days' worth, you'll have to figure out where we are, and lead him to us instead of to the Retreat. We'll try to pull him the last way south ourselves."

Quaan nodded again, and the lines of his face clenched. To relax him, Troy said dryly, "Of course, it would be better if you just defeated him yourself, and saved us the trouble."

The Hiltmark started to reply, but Lord Verement interrupted him. "If that is your desire, you should choose someone other than an old warrior and a Ranyhyn-less Lord to do your bidding."

Troy was about to respond when he heard hooves coming toward him from the direction of Revelstone. Now the sun had started to rise—light danced on the blue water pouring over the top of the Falls—and the fog over his vision had begun to fade. When he turned, he made out the Bloodguard Ruel riding toward him.

Ruel stopped his Ranyhyn with a touch of his hand, and said without dismounting, "Warmark, the War-ward is ready. High Lord Elena awaits you."

"On my way," Troy answered, and swung back to Quaan. For a moment, the Hiltmark's gaze replied firmly to his. Torn between affection and resolve, he

muttered, "By God, I will earn what you do for me."
Springing onto Mehryl's back, he started away.

He moved so suddenly that he almost ran into
Manethrall Rue. She had been standing a short distance away, regarding Mehryl as if she expected to
find that Troy had injured the Ranyhyn. Unintentionally he urged his mount straight toward her. But she
stepped aside just as he halted the Ranyhyn.

Her presence surprised him. He acknowledged her,
then waited for her to speak. He felt that she deserved
any courtesy he could give her.

While she stroked Mehryl's nose with loving hands,
she said as if she were explaining something, "I have
done my part in your war. I will do no more. I am
old, and need rest. I will ride your rafts to Andelain,
and from there make my own way homeward."

"Very well." He could not deny her permission to
ride a raft, but he sensed that this was only a preparation for what she meant to say.

After a heavy pause, she went on: "I will have no
further use for this." With a brusque movement, she
twitched the fighting cord from her hair, hesitated,
then handed it to Troy. Softly, she said, "Let there
be peace between us."

Because he could think of no fit response, he accepted the cord. But it gave him a pang, as if he
were not worthy of it. He tucked it into his belt, and
with his hands free, he gave the Manethrall his best
approximation of a Ramen bow.

She bowed in turn, gestured for him to move on.
But as he started away, she called after him, "Tell
Covenant Ringthane that he must defeat Fangthane.
The Ranyhyn have reared to him. They require him.
He must not let them fall." Then she was gone, out of
sight in the mist.

The thought of Covenant gave him a bitter taste in
his mouth, but he forced it down. With Ruel at his
side, he left Quaan shouting orders, and urged Mehryl
into a brisk trot up the road toward the gate of
Revelstone. As he moved, the sunrise began to burn
away the last dimness of his vision. The great wrought
wall of the Keep became visible; it shone in the new

light with a vivid glory that made him feel at once both small and resolute. In it, he caught a glimpse of the true depth of his willingness to sacrifice himself for the Land. Now he could only hope that what he had to offer would be enough.

There was only one thing for which he could not forgive Covenant. That was the Unbeliever's refusal to fight.

Then he topped the last rise, and found the Lords assembled before the gates, above the long, ranked massing of the Warward.

The sight of the Warward gave him a surge of pride. This army was his—a tool of his own shaping, a weapon which he had sharpened himself and knew how to wield. Each warrior stood in place in an Eoman; each Eoman held its position around the fluttering standard of its Eoward; and the thirty-eight Eoward spread out around the foot of Lord's Keep like a human mantle. More than fifteen thousand metal breastplates caught the rising fire of the sun.

All the warriors were on foot except the Hafts and a third of the Warhafts. These officers were mounted to bear the standards and the marching drums, and to carry messages and commands through the Warward. Troy was acutely aware that the one thing his army lacked was some instantaneous means of communication. Without such a resource, he felt more vulnerable than he liked to admit. To make up for it, he had developed a network of riders who could shuttle from place to place in battle. And he had trained his officers in complex codes of signals and flares and banners, so that under at least some circumstances messages could be communicated by sight. But he was not satisfied. Thousands upon thousands of lives were in his hands. As he gazed out over his command, his tree limb seemed to be shaking in the wind.

He swung away from the Warward, and scanned the mounted gathering before the gates. Only Trevor and Loerya were absent. The Lords Amatin and Mhoram were there, with twenty Bloodguard, a handful of Hirebrands and Gravelingases, all the visiting Lorewardens, and First Haft Amorine. Covenant sat on a *clingor* saddle astride one of the Revelstone mustangs. And at his side was the High Lord. Myrha, her golden Ranyhyn mare, made her look more than ever like a concentrated heroine, a noble figure like that legended Queen for whom Berek had fought his great war.

She was leaning toward Covenant, listening to him with interest—almost with deference—in every line of her form.

The sight galled Troy.

His own feelings for the High Lord were confused: he could not fit them into any easy categories. She was the Lord who had taught him the meaning of sight. And as he had learned to see, she had taught him the Land, introduced him to it with such gentle delight that he always thought of her and the Land together, as if she herself summarized it. When he came to understand the peril of the Land—when he began to search for a way to serve what he saw—she was the one who breathed life into his ideas. She recognized the potential value of his tactical skill, put faith in it; she gave his voice the power of command. Because of her, he was now giving orders of great risk, and leading the Warward in a cause for which he would not be ashamed to die.

Yet Covenant appeared insensitive to her, immune to her. He wore an aura of weary bitterness. His beard darkened his whole face, as if to assert that he had not one jot or tittle of belief to his name. He looked like an Unbeliever, an infidel. And his presence seemed to demean the High Lord, sully her Landlike beauty.

Various sour thoughts crossed Troy's mind, but one was uppermost. There was still something he had to say to Covenant—not because Covenant would or could profit from it, but because he, Troy, wanted to leave no doubt in Covenant's mind.

The Warmark waited until Elena had turned away to speak with Mhoram. Then he pulled Mehryl up to Covenant's side. Without preamble, he said bluntly, "There's something I've got to tell you before we leave. I want you to know that I spoke against you to the

Council. I told them what you did to Trell's daughter."

Covenant cocked an eyebrow. After a pause, he said, "And then you found out that they already knew all about it."

"Yes." For an instant, he wondered how Covenant had known this. Then he went on: "So I demanded to know why they put up with you. I told them they can't afford to waste their time and strength rehabilitating people like you when they've got Foul to worry about."

"What did they say?"

"They made excuses for you. They told me that not all crimes are committed by evil people. They told me that sometimes a good man does ill because of the pain in his soul. Like Trell. And Mhoram told me that the blade of your Unbelief cuts both ways."

"And that surprises you?"

"Yes! I told them—"

"You should have expected it. Or what did you think this Oath of Peace is about? It's a commitment to the forgiving of lepers—of Kevin and Trell. As if forgiveness weren't the one thing no leper or criminal either could ever have any use for."

Troy stared into Covenant's gray, gaunt face. Covenant's tone confused him. The words seemed to be bitter, even cynical, but behind them was a timbre of pain, a hint of self-judgment, which he had not expected to hear. Once again, he was torn between anger at the folly of the Unbeliever's stubbornness and amazement at the extent of Covenant's injury. An obscure shame made him feel that he should apologize. But he could not force himself to go that far. Instead, he gave a relenting sigh, and said, "Mhoram also suggested that I should be patient with you. Patience. I wish I had some. But the fact is—"

"I know," Covenant murmured. "The fact is that you're starting to find out just how terrible all this responsibility is. Let me know when you start to feel like a failure. We'll commiserate together."

That stung Troy. "I'm not going to fail!" he snapped.

Covenant grimaced ambiguously. "Then let me know when you succeed, and I'll congratulate you."

With an effort, Troy swallowed his anger. He was in no mood to be tolerant of Covenant, but for his own sake—and Elena's—rather than for the Unbeliever's, he said, "Covenant, I really don't understand what your trouble is. But if there's ever anything I can do for you, I'll do it."

Covenant did not meet his gaze. Self-sarcastically, the Unbeliever muttered, "I'll probably need it."

Troy shrugged. He leaned his weight to send Mehryl toward First Haft Amorine. But then he saw Hearthrall Tohrm striding briskly toward them from the gate of the Keep. He held Mehryl back, and waited for the Gravelingas.

When Tohrm stepped between their mounts, he saluted them both, then turned to Covenant. The usual playfulness of his expression was cloaked in sobriety as he said, "Ur-Lord, may I speak?"

Covenant glowered at him from under his eyebrows, but did not refuse.

After a brief pause, Tohrm said, "You will soon depart from Revelstone, and it may be that yet another forty years will pass before you return again. Perhaps I will live forty years more—but the chance is uncertain. And I am still in your debt. Ur-Lord Covenant, may I give you a gift?"

Reaching into his robe, he pulled out and held up a smooth, lopsided stone no larger than his palm. Its appearance struck the Warmark. It gave the impression of being transparent, but he could not see through it; it seemed to open into unglimpsed depths like a hole in the visible fabric of Tohrm's hand and the air and the ground.

Startled, Covenant asked, "What is it?"

"It is *orcrest,* a rare piece of the One Rock which is the heart of the Earth. The Earthpower is abundant in it, and it may serve you in many ways. Will you accept it?"

Covenant stared at the *orcrest* as if there were something cruel in Tohrm's offer. "I don't want it."

"I do not offer it for any want," said Tohrm. "You have the white gold, and need no gifts of mine. No, I offer it out of respect for my old friend Birinair, whom you released from the fire which consumed him. I offer it in gratitude for a brave deed."

"Brave?" Covenant muttered thickly. "I didn't do it for him. Don't you know that?"

"The deed was done by your hand. No one in the Land could do such a thing. Will you accept it?"

Slowly, Covenant reached out and took the stone. As his left hand closed around it, it changed color, took on an argent gleam from his wedding ring. Seeing this, he quickly shoved it into the pocket of his pants. Then he cleared his throat, and said, "If I ever—if I ever get a chance—I'll give it back to you."

Tohrm grinned. "Courtesy is like a drink at a mountain stream. Ur-Lord, it is in my heart that behind the thunder of your brow you are a strangely courteous man."

"Now you're making fun of me," Covenant replied glumly.

The Hearthrall laughed at this as if it were a high jest. With a sprightly step, he moved away to reenter the Keep.

Warmark Troy frowned. Everyone in Revelstone seemed to see something in Covenant that he himself could not perceive. To escape that thought, he sent Mehryl trotting from Covenant's side toward his army.

First Haft Amorine joined him a short way down the hill, and together they spent a brief time speaking with the mounted Warhafts who carried the drums. Troy counted out the pace he wanted them to set, and made sure that they knew it by heart. It was faster than the beat he had trained into them, and he did not want the army to lag. In the back of his mind, he chafed at the delay which kept the march from starting. The sun was well up now; the Warward had already lost the dawn.

He was discussing the terrain ahead with his First Haft when a murmur ran through the army. All the warriors turned toward the great Keep. The Lords Trevor and Loerya had finally arrived.

They stood atop the tower which guarded Revelstone's gates. Between them they held a bundle of blue cloth.

As the Lords took their places, the inhabitants of the Keep began to appear at the south wall. In a rush, they thronged the balconies and ramparts, filled the windows, crowded out onto the edge of the plateau. Their voices rolled expectantly.

Leaving Amorine with the army, Warmark Hile Troy rode back up the hill to take his place with the Lords while Trevor and Loerya busied themselves around the tall flagpole atop the tower. His blood suddenly stirred with eagerness, and he wanted to shout some kind of war cry, hurl some fierce defiance at the Despiser.

When Trevor and Loerya were ready, they waved to High Lord Elena. At their signal, she clapped Myrha with her heels, and galloped away from her mounted companions. A short distance away, between the wall of the Keep and the main body of the Warward, she halted. Swinging Myrha in a tight circle with the Staff of Law raised high over her head, she shouted to the warriors and the inhabitants of Revelstone, "Hail!" Her clear cry echoed off the cliff like a tantara, and was answered at once by one thrilling shout from a myriad of voices:

"Hail!!"

"My friends, people of the Land!" she called out to them, "the time has come. War is upon us, and we march to meet it. Hear me, all! I am the High Lord, holder of the Staff of Law—sworn and dedicate to the services of the Land. At my will, we march to do battle with the Gray Slayer—to pit our strength against him for the sake of the Earth. Hear me! It is I, Elena daughter of Lena, who say it: do not fear! Be of strong heart and bold hand. If it lies within our power, we will prevail!"

As she held high the Staff, she caught the early sunlight. Her hair shone about her like an anadem, and the golden Ranyhyn bore her up like an offering to the wide day. For a moment, she had a look of immolation, and Troy almost choked on the fear of losing her. But there was nothing sacrificial in the upright peal of her voice as she addressed the people of Revel-stone.

"Do not mistake. This peril is severe—the gravest danger of our age. It may be that all we have ever seen or heard or felt will be lost. If we are to live—if the Land is to live—we must wrest life from the De-spiser. It is a task that surpassed the Old Lords who came before us.

"But I say to you, do not fear! The coming battle is our great test, our soul measure. It is our opportunity to repudiate utterly the Desecration which destroys what it loves. It is our opportunity to shape courage and service and faith out of the very rock of doom. Even if we fall, we will not despair.

"Yet I do not believe that we shall fall." Taking the Staff in one hand, she thrust it straight toward the heavens, and a bright flame burst from its end. "Hear me, all!" she cried. "Hear the Dedication in Time of War!" Then she opened her throat and began to sing a song that pulsed like the stalking of drums.

> Friends! comrades!
> Proud people of the Land!
> There is war upon us;
> blood and pain and killing are at hand.
> Together we confront the test of death.

> Friends and comrades,
> remember Peace!
> Repeat the Oath with every breath.
> Until the end and Time's release,
> we bring no fury or despair,
> no passion of hatred, spite, or slaughter,
> no Desecration to the service of the Land.
> We fight to mend, anneal, repair—
> to free the Earth of detestation;
> for health and home and wood and stone,
> for beauty's fragrant bloom and gleam,
> and rivers clear and fair
> we strike;
> nor will we cease,

let fall our heads to ash and dust,
lose faith and heart and hope and bone.

We strike
until the Land is clean of wrong and pain,
and we have kept our trust.
Let no great whelm of evil wreak despair!
Remember Peace:
brave death!
We are the proud preservers of the Land!

As she finished, she turned Myrha, faced the watch-tower. From the Staff of Law, she sent crackling into the sky a great, branched lightning tree. At this sign, Lord Loerya threw her bundle into the air, and Lord Trevor pulled strongly on the lines of the flag-pole. The defiant war-flag of Revelstone sprang open and snapped in the mountain wind. It was a huge ori-flamme, twice as tall as the Lords who raised it, and it was clear blue, the color of High Lord's Furl, with one stark black streak across it. As it flapped and fluttered, a mighty cheer rose up from the Warward, and was repeated on the thronged wall of Revelstone.

For a moment, High Lord Elena kept the Staff blazing. Then she silenced her display of power. As the shouting subsided, she looked at the group of rid-ers, and called firmly, "Warmark Hile Troy! Let us begin!"

At once, Troy sent Mehryl prancing toward the Warward. When he was alone in front of the riders, he saluted his second-in-command, and said quietly, to control his excitement, "First Haft Amorine, you may begin."

She returned his salute, swung her mount toward the army.

"Warward!" she shouted. "Order!"

With a wide surge, the warriors came to attention. "Drummers ready!"

The pace-beaters raised their sticks. When she thrust her right fist into the air, they began their beat, pounding out together the rhythm Troy had taught them.

"Warriors, march!"

As she gave the command, she pulled down her fist. Nearly sixteen thousand warriors started forward to the cadence of the drums.

Troy watched their precision with a lump of pride in his throat. At Amorine's side, he moved with his army down the road toward the river.

The rest of the riders followed close behind him. Together, they kept pace with the Warward as it marched westward under the high south wall of Revelstone.

THIRTEEN: The Rock Gardens of the Maerl

TOGETHER, the riders and the marching Warward passed down the road to the wide stone bridge which crossed the White River a short distance south of the lake. As they mounted the bridge, they received a chorus of encouraging shouts from the horsemen and raft builders at the lake; but Warmark Troy did not look that way. From the top of the span, he gazed downriver: there he could see the last rafts of Hiltmark Quaan's first two Eoward moving around a curve and out of sight. They were only a small portion of Troy's army, but they were crucial. They were risking their lives in accordance with his commands, and the fate of the Land went with them. In pride and trepidation, he watched until they were gone, on their way to receive the measure of bloodshed he had assigned to them. Then he rode on precariously across the bridge.

Beyond it, the road turned southward, and began winding down away from the Keep's plateau toward the rough grasslands which lay between Revelstone and Trothgard. As he moved through the foothills,

Troy counted the accompanying Hirebrands and Gravelingases, to be sure that the Warward had its full complement of support from the *lillianrill* and *rhadhamaerl*. In the process, he caught a glimpse of an extra Gravelingas mounted and traveling behind the group of riders.

Trell.

The powerful Gravelingas kept to the back of the group, but he made no attempt to hide his face or his presence. The sight of him gave Troy a twinge of anxiety. He stopped and waited for the High Lord. Motioning the other riders past him, he said to Elena in a low voice, "Did you know that he's coming with us. Is it all right with you?" High Lord Elena met him with a questioning look which he answered by nodding toward Trell.

Covenant had stopped with Elena, and at Troy's nod he turned to look behind him. When he saw the Gravelingas, he groaned.

Most of the riders were past Elena, Troy, and Covenant now, and Trell could clearly see the three watching him. He halted where he was—still twenty-five yards away—and returned Covenant's gaze with a raw, bruised stare.

For a moment, they all held their positions, regarded each other intently. Then Covenant cursed under his breath, gripped the reins of his horse, and moved up the road toward Trell.

Bannor started after the Unbeliever, but High Lord Elena stopped him with a quick gesture. "He needs no protection," she said quietly. "Do not affront Trell with your doubt."

Covenant faced Trell, and the two men glared at each other. Then Covenant said something. Troy could not hear what he said, but the Gravelingas answered it with a red-rimmed stare. Under his tunic, his broad chest heaved as if he were panting. His reply was inaudible also.

There was violence in Trell's limbs, struggling for action; Troy could see it. He did not understand Elena's assertion that Covenant was safe. As he watched, he whispered to her, "What did Covenant say?"

Elena responded as if she could not be wrong, "The ur-Lord promises that he will not harm me."

This surprised Troy. He wanted to know why Covenant would try to reassure Trell in that way, but he could not think of a way to ask Elena what the connection was between her and Trell. Instead, he asked, "What's Trell's answer?"

"Trell does not believe the promise."

Silently, Troy congratulated Trell's common sense.

A moment later, Covenant jerked his horse into motion, and came trotting back down the road. His free hand pulled insistently at his beard. Without looking at Elena, he shrugged his shoulders defensively as he said, "Well, he has a good point." Then he urged his mount into a canter to catch up with the rest of the riders.

Troy wanted to wait for Trell, but the High Lord firmly took him with her as she followed Covenant. Out of respect for the Gravelingas, Troy did not look back.

But when the Warward broke march at midday for food and rest, Troy saw Trell eating with the other *rhadhamaerl*.

By that time, the army had wound out of the foothills into the more relaxed grasslands west of the White River. Troy gauged the distance they had covered, and used it as a preliminary measure of the pace he had set for the march. So far, the pace seemed right. But many factors influenced a day's march. The Warmark spent part of the afternoon with First Haft Amorine, discussing how to match the frequency and duration of rest halts with such variables as the terrain, the distance already traversed, and the state of the supplies. He wanted to prepare her for his absences.

He was glad to talk about his battle plan; he felt proud of it, as if it were a work of objective beauty. Traditionally, beaten people fled to Doom's Retreat, but he meant to remake it into a place of victory. His plan was the kind of daring strategic stroke that only a blind man could create. But after a time Amorine responded by gesturing over the Warward and saying dourly, "One day of such a pace is no great matter. Even five days may give no distress to a good warrior. But twenty days, or thirty— In that time, this pace may kill."

"I know," Troy replied carefully. His trepidation returned in a rush. "But we haven't got any choice. Even at this pace, too many warriors and Bloodguard are going to get killed buying us the time we need."

"I hear you," Amorine grated. "We will keep the pace."

When the army stopped for the night, Mhoram, Elena, and Amatin moved among the bright campfires, singing songs and telling gleeful Giantish stories to buttress the hearts of the warriors. As he watched them, Troy felt a keen regret that long days would pass before the Lords could again help Amorine maintain the Warward's spirit.

But the separation was necessary. High Lord Elena had several reasons for visiting the Loresraat. But Revelwood was out of the way; the added distance was prohibitive for the marching warriors. So the Lords and the Warward parted company the next afternoon. The three Lords, accompanied by Covenant and Troy, the twenty Bloodguard, and the Lorewardens, turned with the road southwest toward Trothgard and Revelwood. And First Haft Amorine led the Warward, with its mounted Hirebrands and Gravelingases, almost due south in a direct line toward Doom's Retreat.

Troy had business of his own at the Loresraat, and he was forced to leave Amorine alone in command of his army. That afternoon, the autumn sky turned dim as rainclouds moved heavily eastward. When he gave the First Haft his final instructions, his vision was blurred; he had to peer through an ominous haze. "Keep the pace," he said curtly. "Push it even faster when you reach easier ground past the Gray River. If you can gain a little time, we won't have to drive so hard around the Last Hills. If those Bloodguard the High Lord sent out were able to do their jobs, there should be plenty of supplies along the way. We'll catch up to you in the Center Plains." His voice was stiff with awareness of the difficulties she faced.

Amorine responded with a nod that expressed her seasoned resolve. A light rain started to fall. Troy's vision became so clouded that he could no longer make out individual figures in the massed Warward. He gave the First Haft a tight salute, and she turned to lead the warriors angling away from the road.

The Lords and Lorewardens gave a shout of encouragement, but Troy did not join it. He took Mehryl to the top of a bare knoll, and stood there with his ebony sword raised against the drizzle while the whole length of his army passed by like a shadow in the fog below him. He told himself that the Warward was not going into battle without him—that his warriors would only march until he rejoined them. But the thought did not ease him. The Warward was his tool, his means of serving the Land; and when he returned to the other riders he felt awkward, disjointed, almost dismembered, as if only the skill of the Ranyhyn kept him on balance. He rode on through the rest of the day wrapped in the familiar loneliness of the blind.

The drizzle continued throughout the remainder of the afternoon, all that night, and most of the next day. Despite the piled thickness of the clouds, the rain did not come down hard; but it kept out the sunlight, tormented Troy by obscuring his vision. In the middle of the night, sleeping in wet blankets that seemed to cling to him like winding sheets, he was snatched awake by a wild, inchoate conviction that the weather would be overcast when he went into battle at Doom's Retreat. He needed sunlight, clarity. If he could not see—!

He arose depressed, and did not recover his usual confidence until the rainclouds finally blew away to the east, letting the sun return to him.

Before midmorning the next day, the company of the Lords came in sight of the Maerl River. They had been traveling faster since they had left the Warward, and when they reached the river, the northern boundary of Trothgard, they were halfway to Revelwood. The Maerl flowed out of high places in the Westron Mountains, and ran first northeast, then southeast, until it joined the Gray, became part of the Gray, and went eastward to the Soulsease. Beyond the Maerl was the region where the Lords concentrated their efforts to heal the ravages of Desecration and war.

Trothgard had borne the name Kurash Plenethor, Stricken Stone, from the last years of Kevin Landwaster until it was rechristened when the new Lords first swore their oath of service after the Desecration. At that time, the region had been completely blasted and barren. The last great battle between the Lords and the Despiser had taken place there, and had left it burned, ruined, soaked in scorched blood, almost soilless. Some of the old tales said that Kurash Plenethor had smoked and groaned for a hundred years after that last battle. And forty years ago the Maerl River had still run thick with eroded and unfertile mud.

But now there was only a trace of silt left in the current. For all the limitations of their comprehension, the Lords had learned much about the nurturing of damaged earth from the Second Ward, and on this day the Maerl carried only a slight haze of impurity. Because of centuries of past erosion, it lay in a ravine like a crack across the land. But the sides of the ravine were gentle with deep-rooted grasses and shrubs, and healthy trees lifted their boughs high out of the gully.

The Maerl was a vital river again.

Looking down into it from the edge of the ravine, the company paused for a moment of gladness. Together, Elena, Mhoram, and Amatin sang softly part of the Lords' oath. Then they galloped down the slope and across the road ford, so that the hooves of the Ranyhyn and the horses made a gay, loud splashing as they passed into Trothgard.

This region lay between the Westron Mountains and the Maerl, Gray, and Rill rivers. Within these borders, the effects of the Lords' care were everywhere, in everything. Generations of Lords had made Stricken Stone into a hale woodland, a wide hilly country of forests and glades and dales. Whole grassy hillsides were vivid with small blue and yellow flowers. For scores of leagues south and west of the riders, profuse *aliantha* and deep grass were full of gold-leaved Gilden and other trees, cherry and apple and white linden, prodigious oaks and elms and maples anademed in autumn glory. And air that for decades after the battle had still echoed with the blasts and shrieks of war was now so clear and clean that it seemed to glisten with birdcalls.

This was what Troy had first seen when his vision began; this was what Elena had used to teach him the meaning of sight.

Riding now on Mehryl's back under brilliant sun in Trothgard's luminous ambience, he felt more free of care than he had for a long time.

As the company of the Lords moved through the early part of the afternoon, the country around them changed. Piles of tumbled rock began to appear among the trees and through the greensward; rugged boulders several times taller than the riders thrust their heads out of the ground, and smaller stones overgrown with moss and lichen lay everywhere. Soon the company seemed to be riding within the ancient rubble of a shattered mountain, a tall, incongruous peak which had risen out of the hills of Kurash Plenethor until some immense force had blasted it to bits.

They were approaching the rock gardens of the Maerl.

Troy had never taken the time to study the gardens, but he knew that they were said to be the place where the best *suru-pa-maerl* Craftmasters of the *rhadhamaerl* did their boldest work. Though in the past few years he had ridden along this road through the bristling rocks many times, he could not say where the gardens themselves began. Except for a steady increase in the amount of rubble lying on or sticking through the grass, he could locate no specific changes or boundaries until the company crested a hill above a wide valley. Then at least he was sure that he was in one of the gardens.

Most of the long, high hillside facing the valley was thickly covered with stones, as if it had once been the heart of the ancient shattered peak. The rocks clus-

tered and bulged on all sides, raising themselves
up in huge piles or massive single boulders, so that
virtually the only clear ground on the steep slope was
the roadway.

None of these rocks and boulders was polished or
chipped or shaped in any way, though scattered individual stones and clusters of stones appeared to have
had their moss and lichen cleaned away. And they all
seemed to have been chosen for their natural gro-
tesquerie. Instead of sitting or resting on the ground,
they jutted and splintered and scowled and squatted
and gaped, reared and cowered and blustered like a
mad, packed throng of troglodytes terrified or ecstatic
to be breathing open air. On its way to the valley, the
road wandered among the weird shapes as if it were
lost in a garish forest, so that as they moved downward the riders were constantly in the shadow of one
tormented form or another.

Troy knew that the jumbled amazement of that hillside was not natural; it had been made by men for
some reason which he did not grasp.

On past journeys, he had never been interested
enough in it to ask about its significance. But now he
did not object when High Lord Elena suggested that
the company go to look at the work from a distance.
Across the grassy bottom of the valley was another
hill, even steeper and higher than the one it faced. The
road turned left, and went away along the bottom of
the valley, ignoring the plainer hill. Elena suggested
that the riders climb this hill to look back at the gardens.

She spoke to her companions generally, but her
gaze was on Covenant. When he acquiesced with a
vague shrug, she responded as if he had expressed the
willingness of all the riders.

The front of the hill was too steep for the horses, so
they turned right and cantered up the valley until
they found a place where they could swing around
and mount the hill from behind. As they rode, Troy
began to feel mildly expectant. The High Lord's
eagerness to show the view to Covenant invested it
with interest. He remembered other surprises—like

the Hall of Gifts, which had not interested him until Mhoram had practically dragged him to it.

At the top, the hill bulged into a bare knoll. The riders left their mounts behind, and climbed the last distance on foot. They moved quickly, sharing Elena's mood, and soon reached the crest.

Across the valley, the rock garden lay open below them, displayed like a bas-relief. From this distance, they could easily see that all its jumbled rock formed a single pattern.

Out of tortured stone, the makers of the garden had designed a wide face—a broad countenance with lumped gnarled and twisted features. The unevenness of the rock made the face appear bruised and contorted; its eyes were as ragged as deep wounds, and the roadway cut through it like an aimless scar. But despite all this, the face was stretched with a grin of immense cheerfulness. The unexpectedness of it startled Troy into a low, glad burst of laughter.

Though the Lords and Lorewardens were obviously familiar with the garden, all their faces shared a look of joy, as if the displayed hilarious grin were contagious. High Lord Elena clasped her hands together to contain a surge of happiness, and Lord Mhoram's eyes glittered with keen pleasure. Only Covenant did not smile or nod, or show any other sign of gladness. His face was as gaunt as a shipwreck. His eyes held a restless, haggard look of their own, and his right hand fumbled at his ring in a way that emphasized his two missing fingers. After a moment, he muttered through the company's murmuring, "Well, the Giants certainly must be proud of you."

His tone was ambiguous, as if he were trying to say two contradictory things at once. But his reference to the Giants overshadowed anything else he might have meant. Lord Amatin's smile faltered, and a sudden scrutinizing gleam sprang from under Mhoram's brows. Elena moved toward him, intending to speak, but before she could begin, he went on, "I knew a woman like that once." He was striving to sound casual, but his voice was awkward. "At the leprosarium."

Troy groaned inwardly, but held himself still.

"She was beau— Of course, I didn't know her then. And she didn't have any pictures of herself, or if she did she didn't show them. I don't think she could even stand to look in the mirror anymore. But the doctors told me that she used to be beautiful. She had a smile— Even when I knew her, she could still smile. It looked just like that." He nodded in the direction of the rock garden, but he did not look at it. He was concentrating on his memory.

"She was a classic case." As he continued, his tone became harsher and more bitter. He articulated each word distinctly, as if it had jagged edges. "She was exposed to leprosy as a kid in the Philippines or somewhere—her parents were stationed there in the military, I suppose—and it caught up with her right after she got married. Her toes went numb. She should have gone to a doctor right then, but she didn't. She was one of those people whom you can't interrupt. She couldn't take time away from her husband and friends to worry about cold toes.

"So she lost her toes. She finally went to a doctor when her feet began to cramp so badly that she could hardly walk, and eventually he figured out what was wrong with her, and sent her to the leprosarium, and the doctors there had to amputate. That gave her some trouble—it's hard to walk when you don't have any toes—but she was irrepressible. Before long she was back with her husband.

"But she couldn't have any kids. It's just criminal folly for lepers who know better to have any kids. Her husband understood that—but he still wanted children, and so in due course he divorced her. That hurt her, but she survived it. Before long, she had a job and new friends and a new life. And she was back in the leprosarium. She was just too full of vitality and optimism to take care of herself. This time, two of her fingers were numb.

"That cost her her job. She was a secretary, and needed her fingers. And of course her boss didn't want any lepers working for him. But once her disease was arrested again, she learned how to type without using those dead fingers. Then she moved to a new area, got another job, more new friends, and went right on living as if absolutely nothing had happened.

"At about this time—or so they told me—she conceived a passion for folk dancing. She'd learned something about it in her travels as a kid, and now it became her hobby, her way of making new friends and telling them that she loved them. With her bright clothes and her smile, she was—"

He faltered, then went on almost at once: "But she was back in the leprosarium two years later. She didn't have very good footing, and she took too many falls. And not enough medication. This time she lost her right leg below the knee. Her sight was starting to blur, and her right hand was pretty much crippled. Lumps were growing in her face, and her hair was falling out.

"As soon as she learned how to hobble around on her artificial limb, she started folk-dancing lessons for the lepers.

"The doctors kept her a long time, but finally she convinced them to let her out. She swore she was going to take better care of herself this time. She'd learned her lesson, she said, and she wasn't ever coming back.

"For a long time, she didn't come back. But it wasn't because she didn't need to. Bit by bit, she was whittling herself away. When I met her, she was back at the leprosarium because a nursing home had thrown her out. She didn't have anything left except her smile.

"I spent a lot of time in her room, watching her lie there in bed—listening to her talk. I was trying to get used to the stench. Her face looked as if the doctors hit her with clubs every morning, but she still had that smile. Of course, most of her teeth were gone—but her smile hadn't changed.

"She tried to teach me to dance. She'd make me stand where she could see me, and then she'd tell me where to put my feet, when to jump, how to move my legs." Again he faltered. "And in between she used to take hours telling me what a full life she'd had.

"She must've been all of forty years old."

Abruptly, he stooped to the ground, snatched up a stone, and hurled it with all his strength at the grinning face of the rock garden. His throw fell far short, but he did not stop to watch the stone roll into the valley. Turning away from it, he rasped thickly, "If I ever get my hands on her husband, I'll wring his bloody neck." Then he strode down off the knoll toward the horses. In a moment, he was astride his mount and galloping away to rejoin the road. Bannor was close behind him.

Troy took a deep breath, trying to shake off the effect of Covenant's tale, but he could think of nothing to say. When he looked over at Elena, he saw that she was melding with Mhoram and Amatin as if she needed their support to bear what she had heard. After a moment, Mhoram said aloud, "Ur-Lord Covenant is a prophet."

"Does he foretell the fate of the Land?" Amatin asked painfully.

"No!" Elena's denial was fierce, and Mhoram breathed also, "No." But Troy could hear that Mhoram meant something different.

Then the melding ended, and the Lords returned to their mounts. Soon the company was back on the road, riding after Covenant in the direction of Revelwood.

For the rest of the afternoon, Troy was too disturbed by the Lords' reaction to Covenant to relax and enjoy the journey. But the next day, he found a way to soothe his vague distress. He envisioned in detail the separate progresses of the Warward—the Bloodguard riding with Lord Callindrill, the mounted Eoward rafting and galloping, the warriors marching behind Amorine. On his mental map of the Land, these various thrusts had a deliberate symmetry that pleased him in some fundamental way. Before long, he began to feel better.

And Trothgard helped him, also. South of the rock gardens, the land's mantle of soil became thicker and more fertile, so that the hills through which the company rode had no bare stone jutting up among the grass and flowers. Instead, copses and broad swaths of woodland grew everywhere, punctuating the slopes and unfurling oratorically across the vales and valleys. Under the bright sky and the autumn balm of Troth-gard, Troy put his uncertainty about Covenant behind him like a bad dream.

At that point, even the problem of communications did not bother him. Ordinarily, he was even more concerned by his inability to convey messages to Quaan than by his ignorance of what was happening to Korik's mission. But he was on his way to Revel-wood. High Lord Elena had promised him that the Loresraat was working on his problem. He looked forward hopefully to the chance that the students of the Staff had found a solution for him.

That evening, he enjoyed the singing and talk of the Lords around the campfire. Mhoram was with-drawn and silent, with a strange look of foreboding in his eyes, and Covenant glowered glum and taciturn into the coals of the fire. But High Lord Elena was in vibrant good spirits. With Amatin, she spread a mood of humor and gaiety over the company until even the somberest of the Lorewardens seemed to effervesce. Troy thought that she had never looked more lovely.

Yet he went to the blindness of his bed with an ache in his heart. He could not help knowing that Elena exerted her brilliance for Covenant's sake, not for his.

He fell at once into sleep as if to escape his sightless-ness. But in the darkest part of the moonless night, sharp voices and the stamping of hooves roused him. Through the obscure illumination of the fire embers, he saw a Bloodguard on a Ranyhyn standing in the center of the camp. The Ranyhyn steamed in the cold air; it had galloped hotly to reach the Lords.

First Mark Morin and Lord Mhoram already stood by the Ranyhyn, and the High Lord was hurrying from her blankets with Lord Amatin behind her. Troy threw an armful of kindling on the fire. The sudden blaze gave him a better view of the Blood-guard.

The grime of hard fighting streaked his face, and among the rents there were patches of dried blood on his robe. He dismounted slowly, as if he were tired or reluctant.

Troy felt his balance suddenly waver, as if the tree limb of his efforts for the Land had jumped under his feet. He recognized the Bloodguard. He was Runnik, one of the members of Korik's mission to Seareach.

FOURTEEN: Runnik's Tale

FOR a moment, Troy groped around him, trying to regain his balance. Runnik should not be here; it was too soon. Only twenty-three days had passed since the departure of Korik's mission. Even the mightiest Ranyhyn could not gallop to Seareach and back in that time. So Runnik's arrival here meant— meant— Even before the High Lord could speak, Troy found himself demanding in a constricted voice, "What happened? What happened?"

But Elena stopped him with a sharp word. He could see that the implications of Runnik's presence were not lost on her. She stood with the Staff of Law planted firmly on the ground, and her face was full of fire.

At her side, Covenant had a look of nausea, as if he were already sickened by what he expected to hear. He had the aspect of a man who wanted to know whether or not he had a terminal illness as he rasped at the Bloodguard, "Are they dead?"

Runnik ignored both Covenant and Troy. He nodded to First Mark Morin, then bowed slightly to the High Lord. Despite its flatness, his countenance had a reluctant cast, an angle of unwillingness, that made Troy groan in anticipation.

"Speak, Runnik," Elena said sternly. "What word

have you brought to us?" And after her Morin said, "Speak so that the Lords may hear you."

Yet Runnik did not begin. Barely visible in the background of his unblinking gaze, there was an ache —a pang that Troy had never expected to see in any Bloodguard. "Sweet Jesus," he breathed. "How bad *is* it?"

Then Lord Mhoram spoke. "Runnik," he said softly, "the mission to Seareach was given into the hands of the Bloodguard. This is a difficult burden, for you are Vowed to the preservation of the Lords above all things. There is no blame for you if your Vow and the mission have come into conflict, requiring that one or the other must be set aside. There can be no doubt of the Bloodguard, whatever the doom that brings you to us thus battle-rent at the dark of the moon."

For a moment longer, Runnik hesitated. Then he said, "High Lord, I have come from the depths of Sarangrave Flat—from the Defiles Course and the mission to Seareach. To me, and to Pren and Porib with me, Korik said, 'Return to the High Lord. Tell her all —all the words of Warhaft Hoerkin, all the struggles of the Ranyhyn, all the attacks of the lurker. Tell her of the fall of Lord Shetra.'" Amatin moaned in her throat, and Mhoram stiffened. But Elena held Runnik with the intensity of her face. "'She will know how to hear this tale of Giants and Ravers. Tell her that the mission will not fail.'

"'Fist and faith,' we three responded. 'We will not fail.'

"But for four days we strove with the Sarangrave, and Pren fell to the lurker that has awakened. Then we won our way to the west of the Flat, and there regained our Ranyhyn. With our best speed we rode toward Revelstone. But when we entered Grimmerdhore, we were beset by wolves and ur-viles, though we saw no sign of them when we passed eastward. Porib and his Ranyhyn fell so that I might escape, and I rode onward.

"Then on the west of Grimmerdhore, I met with scouts of the Warward, and learned that Corruption was marching, and that the High Lord had ridden toward Revelwood. So I turned aside from Revelstone and came in pursuit to find you here.

"High Lord, there is much that I must say."

"We will hear you," Elena said. "Come." Turning, she moved to the campfire. There she seated herself with Mhoram and Amatin beside her. At a sign from her, Runnik sat down opposite her, and allowed one of the Lorewardens who had skill as a Healer to clean his cuts. Troy piled wood on the fire so that he could see better, then positioned himself near the Lords on the far side from Covenant. In a moment, Runnik began to speak.

At first, his narration was brief and awkward. The Bloodguard lacked the Giants' gift for storytelling; he skimmed crucial subjects, and ignored things his hearers needed to know. But the Lords questioned him carefully. And Covenant repeatedly insisted on details. At times, he seemed to be trying to stall the narrative, postpone the moment when he would have to hear its outcome. Gradually, the events of the mission began to emerge in a coherent form.

Troy listened intensely. He could see nothing beyond the immediate light of the campfire; nothing distracted his attention. Despite the flatness of Runnik's tone, the Warmark seemed to see what he was hearing as if the mission were taking place in the air before him.

The mission had made its way eastward through Grimmerdhore, and then for three days had ridden in rain. But no rain could halt the Ranyhyn, and this was no great storm. On the eighth day of the mission, when the clouds broke and let sunlight return to the earth, Korik and his party were within sight of Mount Thunder.

It grew steadily against the sky as they rode through the sunshine. They passed twenty-five leagues to the north of it, and reached the great cliff of Landsdrop late that afternoon. They were at one of its highest points, and could look out over the Lower Land from a vantage of more than four thousand feet. Here Landsdrop was as sheer as if the Lower Land had been cut away with an ax. And below it beyond a hilly strip of grassland less than five leagues wide lay Sarangrave Flat.

It was a wet land, latticed with waterways like exposed veins in the flesh of the ground, overgrown with fervid luxuriance, and full of subtle dangers—strange, treacherous, water-bred, and man-shy animals; cunning, old, half-rotten willows and cypresses that sang quiet songs which could bind the unwary; stagnant, poisonous pools, so covered with slime and mud and shallow plants that they looked like solid ground; lush flowers, beautifully bedewed with clear liquids that could drive humans mad; deceptive stretches of dry ground that turned suddenly to quicksand. All this was familiar to the Bloodguard. However ominous to human eyes, or unsuited to human life, Sarangrave Flat was not naturally evil. Rather, because of the darknesses which slumbered beneath it, it was simply dangerous—a wild haven for the misborn of the Land, the warped fruit of evils long past. The Giants, who knew how to be wary, had always been able to travel freely through the Flat, and they had kept paths open for others, so that the crossing of the Sarangrave was not normally a great risk.

But now something else met the gaze of the mission. Slumbering evil stirred; the hand of Corruption was at work, awakening old wrongs.

The peril was severe, and Lord Hyrim was dismayed. But neither the Lords nor the Bloodguard were surprised. The Lords Callindrill and Amatin—the Bloodguard Morril and Koral—had spoken of this danger. And though he was dismayed, Lord Hyrim did not propose that the mission should evade the danger by riding north and around Sarangrave Flat, a hundred leagues from their way. Therefore in the dawn of the ninth day the mission descended Landsdrop, using a horse trail which the Old Lords had made in the great cliff, and rode eastward across the grassland foothills toward the main Giantway through the Sarangrave.

The air was noticeably warmer and thicker than it had been above Landsdrop. It breathed as if it were clogged with invisible, damp fibers, and it seemed to leave something behind in the lungs when it was exhaled.

Then shrubs and low, twisted bushes began to appear through the grass. And the grass itself grew longer, wetter. At odd intervals, stray, hidden puddles of water splashed under the hooves of the Ranyhyn. Soon gnarled, lichenous trees appeared, spread out moss-draped limbs. They grew thicker and taller as the mission passed into the Sarangrave. In moments, the riders entered a grassy avenue that lay between two unrippling pools and angled away just north of eastward into a jungle which already appeared impenetrable. The Ranyhyn slowed to a more cautious pace. Abruptly, they found themselves plunging through chest-deep elephant grass.

When the riders looked behind them, they could see no trace of the Giantway. The Flat had closed like jaws.

But the Bloodguard knew that that was the way of the Sarangrave. Only the path ahead was visible. The Ranyhyn moved on, thrusting their broad chests through the grass.

As the jungle tightened, the Giantway narrowed until they could ride no more than three abreast— each of the Lords flanked by Bloodguard. But the elephant grass receded, allowing them to move with better speed.

Their progress was loud. They disturbed the Flat, and as they traveled they set waves and wakes and noise on both sides. Birds and monkeys gibbered at them; small, furry animals that yipped like hyenas broke out of the grass in front of them and scurried away; and when the jungle gave way on either side for dark, rancid pools or sluggish streams, waterfowl with iridescent plumage clattered fearfully into the air. Sudden splashes echoed across still ponds; pale, vaguely human forms darted away under the ripples.

Throughout the morning, the mission followed the winding trail which careful Giants had made in times long past. No danger threatened, but still the Ranyhyn grew tense. When the riders stopped beside a shallow lake to rest and eat, their mounts became increasingly restive. Several of them made low, blowing noises; their ears were up and alert, shifting directions in sharp jerks, almost quivering. One of them—the youngest stallion, bearing the Bloodguard Tull—stamped a hoof irrhythmically. The Lords and the Bloodguard increased their caution, and rode on down the Giantway.

They had covered only two more leagues when Sill called the Bloodguard to observe Lord Hyrim.

The Lord's face was flushed as if he had a high fever. Sweat rolled down his cheeks, and he was panting hoarsely, almost gasping for breath. His eyes glittered. But he was not alone. Lord Shetra, too, was flushed and panting.

Then even the Bloodguard found that they were having trouble breathing. The air felt turgid. It resisted being drawn into their lungs, and once within them it clung there with miry fingers, like the grasp of quicksand.

The sensation grew rapidly worse.

Suddenly, all the noise of the Flat ceased.

It was as Lord Callindrill had said.

But the Lord Amatin's mount had not been a Ranyhyn. Trusting to the great horses, the mission continued on its way.

The riders moved slowly. The Ranyhyn walked with their heads straining forward, ears cocked, nostrils flared. They were sweating, though the air was not warm.

They covered a few hundred yards this way—forcing passage through the stubborn, mucky air and the silence. After that, the jungle fell away on both sides. The Giantway lay along a grassy ridge like a dam between two still pools. One of them was blue and bright, reflecting the sky and the afternoon sunlight, but the other was dark and rank.

The mission was halfway down the ridge when the sound began.

It started low, wet, and weak, like the groan of a dying man. But it seemed to come from the dark pool. It transfixed the riders. As they listened to it, it slowly swelled.

It scaled upward in pitch and volume—became a ragged scream—echoed across the pools. Higher and louder it went on. Through it, the Lords shouted together, *"Melenkurion abatha! Duroc minas mill khabaal!"* But they could hardly make themselves heard.

Then the young Ranyhyn bearing Tull lost control. It whinnied in fear, whirled and sprang toward the blue pool. As it leaped, Tull threw himself to the safety of the grass.

The Ranyhyn crashed into the chest-deep water. At once, it gave a squeal of pain that almost matched the screaming in the air. Plunging frantically, it heaved itself out of the pool, and fled westward, back down the Giantway.

The howling mounted eagerly higher.

The other Ranyhyn broke and bolted. They reared, spun, pounded away after their fleeing brother. The jerk of their start unhorsed Lord Hyrim, and he only saved himself from the dark pool by a thrust of his staff. Immediately, Lord Shetra dropped off her mount to join him. Sill, Cerrin, and Korik also dismounted. As he jumped, Korik ordered the other Bloodguard to protect the Ranyhyn.

Runnik and his comrades clung to their horses. The Ranyhyn followed the injured stallion. As they raced, the howling behind them faded, and the air began to thin. But for some distance, the Bloodguard could not regain control of their mounts. The Ranyhyn plunged along a wide path which was unfamiliar; the Bloodguard knew that they had missed the Giantway.

Then the leading Ranyhyn crested a knoll, and blundered without warning into a quagmire. But the rest of the great horses were able to stop safely. The Bloodguard dismounted, and took *clingor* lines from their packs. By the time Korik, Cerrin, Sill, Tull, and the Lords reached them, the free Ranyhyn were busy pulling their trapped kindred from the quagmire.

Seeing that the other Ranyhyn were uninjured, the Lords turned to the stallion which had jumped into the pool. It stood to one side, champed its teeth and jerked its head from side to side in agony. Under its coat all the flesh of its limbs and belly was covered with blisters and boils. Blood streamed from its sores. Through some of them, the bone was visible. Despite the determination in its eyes, it whimpered at the pain.

The Lords were deeply moved. There were tears in Hyrim's eyes, and Shetra cursed bitterly. But they could do nothing. They were not Ramen. And they could find no *amanibhavam,* that potent, yellow-flowered grass which could heal horses but which drove humans mad. They could only close their ears to the stallion's pain, and try to consider what course the mission should take.

Soon all the other Ranyhyn were safe on solid ground. They shed the mud of the quagmire easily but they could not rid themselves of the shame of their panic. Their eyes showed that they felt they had disgraced themselves.

But when they heard the whimpering of their injured brother, they pricked up their ears. They shuffled their feet and nudged each other. Slowly, their eldest went to face Tull's mount. For a moment, the two spoke together, nose to nose. Several times the younger Ranyhyn nodded its head.

Then the old Ranyhyn reared; he stretched high in the ancient Ranyhyn expression of homage. When he descended, he struck the head of his injured brother powerfully with both fore hooves. The younger horse shuddered once under the force of the blow, and fell dead.

The rest of the Ranyhyn watched in silence. When their eldest turned away from the fallen horse, they nickered their approval and sorrow softly.

In their own way, the Bloodguard were not unmoved. But High Lord Elena had given the need of the Giants into their hands. To the Lords, Korik said, "We must go. The mission waits. Tull may ride with Doar."

"No!" Lord Shetra cried. "We will take the Ranyhyn no deeper into Sarangrave Flat." And Lord Hyrim said, "Friend Korik, surely you know as much as we of this force which forbids us to cross the Flat. Surely you know that to stop us this force must first see us. It must perceive us, and know where we are."

Korik nodded.

"Then you must also know that it is no easy matter to sense the presence of human beings. We are mere ordinary life amid the multitudes of the Sarangrave. But the Ranyhyn are unordinary. They are stronger than we—the power of life burns more brightly in them. Their presence here is more easily seen than ours. It may be that the force against us is attuned to them. The Despiser is wise enough for such strategy. For this reason, we must travel without the Ranyhyn."

"The mission requires their speed," Korik said. "We lack the time to walk."

"I know," Hyrim sighed. "Without mishap, we would spend at least one full cycle of the moon at that journey. But to ride around the Sarangrave will take too long also."

"Therefore we must ride through. We must fight."

"Ride through, forsooth," Shetra snapped. "We do not know how to fight such a thing—or we would have given it battle already. I tell you plainly, Korik—if we encounter that forbidding again, we will lose more than Ranyhyn. No! We must go another way."

"What way?"

For a moment, the Lords gazed into each other. Then Lord Shetra said, "We will build a raft, and ride the Defiles Course."

The Bloodguard were surprised. Even the boat-loving Giants chose to walk Sarangrave Flat rather than to put themselves in the hands of that river. Korik said, "Can it be done?"

"We will do it," Shetra replied.

Seeing the strength of her purpose, the Bloodguard responded to themselves, "We will do it." And Korik said, "Then we must make great haste while the Ranyhyn are yet with us."

So began the great run of the Ranyhyn, in which the horses of Ra redeemed their shame. When all the riders had remounted, they moved cautiously back to the true path of the Giantway. But then the Ranyhyn cast all but the simplest caution to the wind. First at a canter, then galloping, they ran westward out of the peril of the Sarangrave.

This was no gait for distance, no easy, strength-conserving pace. It was a gallop to surpass the best fleetness of ordinary horses. And it did not slow or falter. At full stretch, the Ranyhyn came out of Sarangrave Flat under the eaves of Landsdrop before moonrise. Then they veered away just east of southward along the line of the cliff.

On the open ground, their running became harder. The rough foothills of Landsdrop cut across their way like rumpled folds in the earth, forced them to plummet down and then labor up uncertain slopes twenty times a league. And southward the terrain worsened. The grass slowly failed from the hillsides, so that the Ranyhyn pounded over bare rock and shale and scree.

The moon was nearly full, and in its light Mount Thunder, ancient Gravin Threndor, was visible against the sky. Already it dominated the southern horizon, and as the mission traveled, it lifted its crown higher and higher.

Under its shadow, the Ranyhyn mastered both the night and the foothills. Breathing hoarsely, blowing foam, sweating and straining extremely, but never faltering, they struck daylight no more than five leagues from the Defiles Course. Now they began to stumble and slip on the hillsides, scattering froth from their lips, tearing the skin of their knees. Yet they refused to fail.

In the middle of the morning on the tenth day, they lumbered over the crest of one ankle and dropped down into the narrow valley between Mount Thunder's legs—the valley of the Defiles Course.

To their right at the base of the mountain was the head of the river. There rank black water erupted roaring from under a sheer cliff. This was the Soulsease River of Andelain transformed. That fair river entered Mount Thunder through Treacher's Gorge, then plunged into the depths of the earth, where it ran through abandoned Wightwarrens and Demondim breeding dens, Cavewightish slag and refuse pits, charnels and offal grounds and lakes of acid, the excreta of the buried banes. When it broke out thick, oily, and fetid at the base of Gravin Threndor, it carried the sewage of the catacombs, the pollution of ages of filthy use.

From Mount Thunder to Lifeswallower, the Great Swamp, nothing lived along the banks of the Defiles Course except Sarangrave Flat, which grew thickest on either side of the Course, flourishing on the black water. But high in the sides of the valley were two or three thin streams of clean water, which nourished grass and shrubs and some trees, so that only the bottom of the valley was barren. There the Ranyhyn rested at last. Quivering and blowing, they put their noses in a stream to drink.

The Lords disregarded their own weariness, went immediately in search of *amanibhavam*. Shortly Shetra returned with a double handful of the horse-healing grass. With it she tended the Ranyhyn while Hyrim brought more of it to her. Only when all the great horses had eaten some of the *amanibhavam* did the Lords allow themselves to rest.

Then the Bloodguard turned their attention to the task of building a raft. The only trees hardy enough to grow in the valley were teaks, and in one stand nearby three of the tallest were dead. Their ironwood trunks showed what had happened to them; when they had grown above a certain size, their roots had reached down deep enough to touch soil soaked by the river, and so they had died.

Using hatchets and *clingor* ropes, the Bloodguard were able to bring down these three trees. Each they sectioned into four logs of roughly equal length. When they had rolled the logs down to the dead bank of the Course, they began lashing them together with *clingor* thongs.

The task was slow because of the size and weight of the ironwood logs, and the Bloodguard worked carefully to make sure that the raft was secure. But they were fifteen, and made steady progress. Shortly after noon, the raft was complete. After they had prepared several steering poles, they were ready to continue on their way.

The Lords readied themselves also. After a moment of melding, they bid ceremonious farewell to the

Ranyhyn. Then they came down to the banks of the Defiles Course and bid Korik launch the raft.

Two of the Bloodguard fastened ropes to the raft while the others positioned themselves along its sides. Together, they lifted the massive ironwood logs, heaved the raft into the river. It bucked in the stiff current, but the two ropes secured it. Cerrin and Sill leaped out onto it to see how it held together. When they gave their approval, Korik signed for the Lords to precede him.

Lord Shetra sprang down to the raft, and at once set about wedging her staff between the center logs so that she could use its power for a rudder. Lord Hyrim followed her, as did the other Bloodguard, until only the two who held the ropes remained on the bank. Lord Shetra began to sing quietly, calling up the Earthpower through her staff. When she was ready, she nodded to Korik.

At his command, the last two Bloodguard sprang for the raft as the current ripped it away.

The raft plunged, swirled; the boiling water spun it out into the middle of the river.

But then Lord Shetra caught her balance. The power of her staff took hold like a Gildenlode rudder in the hands of a Giant. The raft resisted her, but slowly it became steady. She piloted it down the torrent of the stream, and in moments the mission rushed out of the valley back into the grasp of Sarangrave Flat.

Free of the constriction of the valley, the Defiles Course gradually widened, slowed. Then it began to wind and spill out into the waterways of the Sarangrave, and the worst of the current was past.

For the rest of the afternoon, Lord Shetra remained in the stern of the raft, guided it along the black water. The riverbed bent and twisted as the Defiles Course became more and more woven into the fabric of Sarangrave Flat. Side currents ran into and away from the main stream, and rocky eyots topped with tufts of jungle began to dot the river. When the pace of the Course grew sluggish, she used her staff to propel the raft; she needed headway to navigate the channels. By evening she was greatly weary.

Then four of the Bloodguard took up the poles and began thrusting the raft through twilight into night, where only their dark-familiar eyes could see well enough to keep the raft moving safely. Lord Shetra ate the meal Hyrim prepared for her over a small *lillianrill* fire, then dropped into slumber despite the stink and spreading dampness of the river.

But at dawn she returned to work, plying the Defiles Course with her staff.

However, Lord Hyrin soon came to her aid. Alternately they propelled the raft throughout the day, and at night they rested while the Bloodguard used their poles. In this way, the mission traveled down the Defiles Course until the evening of the twelfth day. During the days, the sky was clear, and the sunlight was full of butterflies. The raft made good progress.

But that night dark clouds hid the moon, and rain soaked the Lords, damaging their sleep. When Korik called to them in the last blackness before dawn, they both threw off their blankets at once and came to their feet.

Korik pointed into the night. In the darkness of a jungled islet ahead of the raft, there was a faint light. It flickered and waned like a weak fire on wet wood, but revealed nothing.

As the raft approached the eyot, the Lords stared at it. Then Shetra whispered, "That is a made light. It is not natural to the Sarangrave."

The Bloodguard agreed. None of the Flat's light-bearing animals or insects were abroad in the rain.

"Pull in to the islet," Shetra breathed. "We must see the maker of this light."

Korik gave the orders. The Bloodguard at the poles moved the raft so that it floated toward the head of the islet. When it was within ten yards of the edge, Doar and Pren slipped into the water. They swam to the eyot, then faded up into the underbrush. The steersmen swung the raft so that it floated downstream within jumping distance of the bank.

The islet was long and narrow. As the mission

floated by almost within reach of the low-hanging branches, the light came into clearer view. It was a thin flame—a weak flickering like the burn of a torch. But it revealed nothing around it except the tree shadows which passed between it and the raft.

When the raft was some distance past it, the light went out. Both the Lords started, raised their staffs, but they said nothing. The steering Bloodguard leaned on their poles until one side of the raft nudged the bank. Almost at once, Doar and Pren leaped out onto the logs, bearing between them the battered form of a man.

Immediately, the steersmen sent the raft swinging out into the main channel. Lord Hyrim bent to light a *lillianrill* rod.

In the rain the torch shone dimly, but it revealed the man. His face and limbs were streaked with dirt and grime, clotted with the blood of numerous small wounds, cuts, and scratches. Surrounded by dirt and blood, the whites of his eyes glistened. His clothes, like the wounds and mud on him, spoke of a long struggle to survive the Flat. The remains of a uniform hung about him in shreds.

Only one piece of his apparel was intact. He wore a scarred metal breastplate, yellow under the filth, with one black diagonal insignia across it.

"By the Seven!" Lord Shetra said. "A Warhaft!" She caught hold of the man's shoulders. But then she recoiled as if the man had burned her. *"Melenkurion!* Warhaft," she cried, "what has been done to you? Your flesh is ice!"

The man gave no sign that he heard her. He stood where Doar and Pren had placed him, and his head hung to one side. His breathing was shallow. He did not move in any way, except to blink his eyes at long intervals.

But Shetra did not wait for answers. "Hyrim," she said, "this man is freezing!" She snatched up her blanket, threw it over him. Lord Hyrim built his torch into a fire. There he boiled a stoneware pot of water until it was clean, while Shetra seated the man by the fire. She took hold of his head to force some spring-wine between his lips.

The cold of his flesh blistered her fingers.

She and Hyrim wrapped their hands in blankets for protection, then laid the man down by the fire and stripped him of his rags. They washed him with boiling water. When he was clean, Lord Shetra drew a stone vial of hurtloam from her robe, and spread some of the healing mud over the worst of his wounds.

Dawn came through the rain. In the light, the Bloodguard saw the result of the Lords' work. The man's skin looked like the flesh of a corpse. On his wounds, the hurtloam lay impotent. The cold in him was uneased.

Yet he breathed and blinked. When the Lords covered him and lifted him into a sitting posture, he squeezed his eyes, and water began to run from them like tears. It spread out over his cheeks and formed beads of ice in his beard.

"By the Seven. By the Seven!" Lord Shetra moaned. "He is dead, and yet he lives. What has been done to him?"

Lord Hyrim made no answer.

After a time, Korik spoke for the Bloodguard. "He is Hoerkin, a Warhaft of the Warward. He commanded the First Eoman of the Tenth Eoward. The High Lord sent his command to seek out the Giants in Seareach."

"Yes," Hyrim murmured. "I remember. When his Eoman did not return, the High Lord sent Callindrill and Amatin to attempt the Sarangrave. Twenty-one warriors—Warhaft Hoerkin and his command—all lost. Callindrill and Amatin found no trace."

Lord Shetra addressed herself to the man. "Hoerkin. Warhaft Hoerkin. Do you hear me? Speak! I am Shetra Verement-mate, Lord of the Council of Revelstone. I adjure you to speak."

At first, Hoerkin did not respond. Then his jaw moved, and a low noise came from his mouth.

"I am *ahamkara*, the Door. I am sent—"

His voice trailed off into the flow of his tears.

"Sent? Door?" Shetra said. "Hoerkin, speak!"

230 THE WARMARK

The Warhaft did not seem to hear. He sat in silence,
while his tears formed clusters of ice in his beard.

Then Lord Hyrim commanded, *"Ahamkara,* answer!"

Hoerkin swallowed, and spoke.

"I am *ahamkara,* the Door. I am sent to bear witness to—to—"

He faltered, but resumed a moment later.

"I am sent to bear witness to the downfall of Giants."

For all the Bloodguard, Korik said, "You lie!" And
Lord Shetra sprang on Hoerkin. Regardless of the
pain, she gripped his face between her hands, and
shouted, "Despiser!"

He gave a cry and tore himself from her grasp.
Huddling with his face against the logs of the raft, he
sobbed like a child.

Appalled, Shetra backed away from him. At Lord
Hyrim's side, she stopped and waited. Long moments
passed before Hoerkin moved. Then he pushed himself
up into his former posture. Still his tears ran down into
his beard.

"—the downfall of Giants. There were three, brothers of one birth. Omen of the end. They serve
Satansheart Soulcrusher."

He stopped again.

After a moment, Korik said, "This cannot be. It is
impossible. The Giants of Seareach are the Rockbrothers of the Land."

Hoerkin did not respond. Staring at the logs of the
raft, he sat like dead clay. But soon he spoke again.

"—crusher. They are named Fleshharrower, Satansfist—and one other not to be named."

He swallowed once more.

"They are the three Ravers."

For a time, all the mission was silent. Then both
Hyrim and Shetra strove to compel Hoerkin to say
more. But he remained beyond their reach, unspeak-
ing.

At last, Lord Shetra said to Hyrim, "How do you
hear his words? What meaning do you see?"

"I hear truth," Lord Hyrim said. "Omen of the end."

Korik said, "No. By the Vow, it is impossible."

Quickly Lord Hyrim said, "Do not swear by your Vow here."

His reproof was just. The Bloodguard were not ignorant of his meaning. Korik did not speak again. But Lord Shetra said, "I agree with Korik. It surpasses belief to think that a Raver could master any Giant. If the Despiser's power extended so far, why did he not enslave Giants in the past?"

Lord Hyrim answered her, "That is true. The Ravers do not suffice. They do not explain. But now Lord Foul has possession of the Illearth Stone. That was not so in the age of the Old Lords. Perhaps the Ravers and the Stone together—"

"Hyrim, we are speaking of the Giants! If such an ill had come upon them, they would have sent word to us."

"Yes," Lord Hyrim said. "How was it done?"

"Done?"

"How were they prevented? What has been done to them?"

"To them?" said Lord Shetra. "Ask a more immediate question. What has been done to Hoerkin? What has been done to us?"

"It is the Despiser's way. In the battle of Soaring Woodhelven—we are told—he damaged the Heer Llaura and the child Pietten so that they would help destroy what they loved."

"They were used to bait a trap. Hyrim, we are baited!"

She did not wait for an answer. She sprang to the rear of the raft, jammed her staff between the logs, began her song. Strength ran through the ironwood; the raft moved forward through the rain. "Join me!" she called to Lord Hyrim. "We must flee this place!"

Lord Hyrim climbed wearily to his feet. "At Soaring Woodhelven, the trap was complete without Llaura and Pietten. They were an arrogance—a taunt —unnecessary." As he spoke, his breath began to labor in his chest. The muscles of his neck corded with the strain of inhaling.

The Bloodguard, too, could not breathe easily.

In moments, Hyrim fell to his knees, clutching at his chest. Lord Shetra gasped at the effort of each breath.

The rain falling on the river seemed to make no sound.

Then Warhaft Hoerkin leaped to his feet. From between his lips came a low moan of pain. The sound was terrible. His head bent back, and his cry rose until it became a scream.

It was the same scream which had caused the Ranyhyn to panic.

Korik was the first of the Bloodguard to recover his strength. At once, he knocked the Warhaft from the raft.

Hoerkin sank like a stone. The voice was immediately silent.

Yet the thickness of the air only increased. It tightened around the mission like a fist.

Lord Hyrim struggled to his feet. To Doar, he panted, "Did you put out his fire? Hoerkin's fire?"

"No," Doar said. "It fell when we laid hands upon him."

"By the Seven!" Hyrim said. "It was you! The Bloodguard! Not the Ranyhyn. This ill force listens to you!—to the power of the Vow!"

The Bloodguard had no answer. The Vow was not something which could be concealed or denied.

But Lord Shetra was surprised. Her strength dropped away from the raft.

At Korik's command, the four steersmen took up their poles, and thrust the raft toward the north bank of the Course. He wished to meet the attack on land, if he could. He made the steersmen responsible for the raft, then called the other Bloodguard to the defense of the Lords.

In that instant, the river erupted. Silently, water blasted upward, hurling the raft into the air, overturning it.

Behind the burst, a black tentacle flicked out of the water. It twisted, coiled, caught Lord Shetra.

Most of the Bloodguard dove clear of the fall of the raft. But Sill and Lord Hyrim were directly under it.

With Pren and Tull, Korik swam for the place where Lord Shetra had been taken. But the dark water blinded them; they could see nothing, find nothing. The river seemed to have no bottom.

Korik made his decision. The mission to Seareach was in his hands. In a tone that allowed no refusal, he ordered the Bloodguard out of the Course.

Soon he stood on the north bank in the fringe of the jungle. Most of the other Bloodguard were with him. Sill and Lord Hyrim had preceded them. The Lord was uninjured; Sill had protected him from the raft.

Downriver, two of the steersmen were tying up the raft, while the other two dove for the company's supplies.

There was no sign of Cerrin and Lord Shetra.

Hyrim was coughing severely—he had swallowed some of the rank water—but he struggled to his feet, and gasped, "Save her!"

But the Bloodguard made no move to obey. The mission to Seareach was in their hands. And they knew that Cerrin was still alive. He could call to them if their aid would be worth the cost.

"I tried," Hyrim panted. "But I cannot swim. Oh, worthless!" A convulsion came over him. He threw his arms wide, and cried out into the rain, "Shetra!" A bolt of power struck from his staff down through the water toward the river bottom. Then he collapsed into Sill's arms.

His blast seemed to have an effect. The river around the point of Lord Shetra's disappearance started to boil. A turmoil in the water sent up gouts of blood and hunks of black flesh. Steam arose from the current. Deep down in the Defiles Course, a flash of blue was briefly visible.

Then a noise like a thunderclap shook the ground. The river hissed like a torment. And the thickness of the air broke. It was swept away as if it had been washed off the Sarangrave.

The Bloodguard knew that Cerrin was dead.

Only one sign came back from Lord Shetra's struggle. Porib saw it first, dove into the river to retrieve it.

Silently, he put it into Lord Hyrim's hands—Lord Shetra's staff.

Between its metal-shod ends, it was completely burned and brittle. It snapped like kindling in Hyrim's grasp.

The Lord pulled away from Sill, and seated himself against a tree. With tears running openly down his cheeks, he hugged the pieces of Shetra's staff to his chest.

But the peril was not ended. For the sake of his Vow, Korik said to the Lord, "The lurker is not dead. It has only been cut back here. We must go on."

"Go?" Hyrim said. "Go on? Shetra is dead. How can I go on? I feared from the first that your Vow was a voice which the evil in the Sarangrave could hear. But I said nothing." There was bitterness in him. "I believed that you would speak of it if my fear were justified."

Again the Bloodguard had no answer. They had not known beyond doubt or possibility of error that the lurker was alert to their presence. And so many manifestations of power were not what they appeared to be. In respect for the Lord's grief, the Bloodguard left him alone while they readied the raft to go on their way.

The steersmen had been able to salvage the poles and food, most of the *clingor* and the *lillianrill* rods, but none of the clothes or blankets. The raft itself was intact.

Then Korik spoke to Runnik, Pren, and Porib, charged them to bear word of the mission to High Lord Elena. The three accepted without question, but waited for the mission's departure before starting their westward trek.

When all things were prepared, Korik and Sill lifted Lord Hyrim between them, and guided him like a child down the bank onto the raft. He appeared to be unwell. Perhaps the river water he had swallowed was sickening him. As the steersmen thrust the raft out into the center of the Defiles Course, he murmured to himself, "This is not the end. There will be pain and death to humble this. Hyrim son of Hoole, you are a coward." Then the mission was gone. Together, Runnik,

Pren, and Porib started into the jungle of Sarangrave Flat.

The fire had died down to coals, and without its light Troy could see nothing—nothing to counteract the images of death and grief in his mind. He knew that there were questions he should ask Runnik, but in the darkness they did not seem important. He was dismayed to think that Shetra's fall had taken place ten days ago; it felt too immediate for such a lapse of time.

The Lords beside him sat still, as if they were stunned or melding; and Covenant was silent—too moved for speech. But after a time Elena said with a shudder of emotion in her voice, "Ah, Verement! How will you bear it?" Her eyes were only visible as embers. In the darkness they had an aspect of focus and unendurable virulence.

Softly, Lord Mhoram sang:

> Death is passing on—
> the making way of life and time for life.
> Hate dying and killing, not death.
> Be still, heart:
> make no expostulation.
> Hold peace and grief,
> and be still.

FIFTEEN: Revelwood

THE High Lord's company reached the Loresraat by nightfall of the sixth day. During the last leagues, the road worked gradually down into the lowlands of Trothgard; and just as the sun started to dip

into the Westron Mountains, the riders entered the
wide Valley of Two Rivers.

There the Rill and Llurallin came together in a
broad *V,* joined each other in the narrow end of the
valley, to the left of the riders. The Llurallin River,
which flowed almost due east below them, arose from
clear springs high in the raw rock of the mountains beyond Guards Gap, and had a power of purity that had
rendered it inviolate to all the blood and hacked flesh
and blasted earth which had ruined Kurash Plenethor.
Now, generations after the Desecration, it ran with the
same crystal taintlessness which had given it its ancient
name—the Llurallin.

Across the valley was the Rill River, the southern
boundary of Trothgard. Like the Maerl, the Rill had
been greatly improved by the long work of the Lords,
and the water which flowed from the Valley of Two
Rivers no longer deserved the name Gray.

In the center of the valley, within the broad middle
of the river *V,* was Revelwood, the tree city of the
Loresraat.

It was an immense and expansive banyan. Invoked
and strengthened by the new knowledge of the Second
Ward, and by the Staff of Law, it grew to the height of
a mighty oak, sent down roots as thick as hawsers from
boughs as broad as walkways—roots which formed
new trunks with new boughs and new roots—and
spread out in the valley until the central core of the
first tree was surrounded by six others, all intergrown,
part of each other, the fruit of one seed.

Once these seven trunks were established, the
shapers of the tree prevented any more of the hanging roots from reaching the ground, and instead wove
the thick bundles into chambers and rooms—homes
and places of study for the students and teachers of
the Loresraat. Three of the outer trees had been similarly woven before their roots found the soil, and so
now their trunks contained cavities large enough for
meeting halls and libraries. On the sheltered acres of
ground beneath the trees were gardens and practice
fields, training areas for the students of both Staff and
Sword. And above the main massive limbs of the

trees, the lesser branches had been trained and shaped for leaf-roofed dwellings and open platforms.

Revelwood was a thriving city, amply supplied by the fertile lowlands of Trothgard; and the Loresraat was busier now than at any other time in its history. The Lorewardens and apprentices of the Sword and Staff did all the work of the city—all the cooking, farming, herding, cleaning—but they were not its only inhabitants. A band of *lillianrill* lived there to care for the tree itself. Visitors came from all over the Land. Villages sent emissaries to seek knowledge from the Lorewardens; Hirebrands came to study the Tree; and Gravelingases used Revelwood as a dwelling from which to visit the rock gardens. And the Lords worked there to keep their promises to the Land.

As the riders looked down at it, its broad, glossy leaves caught the orange-red fire of the sun, so that it appeared to burn proudly above the shadows spreading down the valley. The company responded to the sight with a glad hail. Clapping their heels to their mounts, they galloped down the slope toward the ford of the Llurallin.

In the time when Revelwood was being grown, the Lords had been mindful of its defense. They had made only two fords for the valley, one across each river. And the ford beds were submerged; they had to be raised before they could be used. All the High Lord's company except Covenant had the necessary knowledge and skill, so Troy was vaguely surprised when Elena halted on the riverbank, and gravely asked Trell to open the ford. Troy understood that she was doing the Gravelingas an honor, but he did not know why. Her gesture deepened the mystery of Trell.

Without meeting her gaze, Trell dismounted, and walked to the Llurallin's edge. At first, he did not appear to know the ford's secret. Troy had learned a few quick words in a strange language and two gestures to raise the bed, but Trell used none of them. He stood on the bank as if he were presenting himself to the deep current, and began to sing a rumbling, cryptic song. The rest of the company watched him in hushed stillness. Troy could not grasp the words of the song, but he felt their effect. They had an old, buried, cavernous sound, as if they were being sung by the bedrock of the valley. For a moment, they made him want to weep.

But soon Trell's singing stopped. In silence, he lifted his arms—and the flat rock of the ford stood up out of the river bottom. It broke water in sections with channels between them so that it did not dam the current. By the time it was ready for crossing, it was as dry as if it had never been submerged.

With his head bowed, Trell walked back to his mount.

When the last horse had crossed the river, and all the company was within the valley, the ford closed itself without any of the usual signals.

Troy was impressed. Remembering Trell's attack on Covenant, he thought that the Unbeliever was lucky to be alive. And he began to feel that he would be well advised to solve the riddle of Trell before he left Trothgard.

But he could do nothing immediately. The last twilight was ebbing out of the valley as if the river currents carried the light away, and he had to concentrate to keep a grip on his own location. The Lorewardens lit torches, but torchlight could not take the place of the sun. Focusing himself sternly, he rode between Lord Mhoram and Ruel across the valley toward Revelwood.

The High Lord's company was met on the ground near the Tree by a welcoming group of Lorewardens. They greeted the Lords with solemn dignity, and embraced their comrades who returned from visiting Lord's Keep. To Warmark Troy, whom they knew well, they gave a special welcome. But when they caught sight of Covenant, they all turned toward him. Squaring their shoulders as if to meet an inspection, they saluted him, and said together, "Hail, white gold wielder!—you who are named ur-Lord Thomas Covenant, Unbeliever and Ringthane. Be welcome in Revelwood! You are the crux and pivot of our age in the Land—the keeper of the wild magic which destroys peace. Honor us by accepting our hospitality."

Troy expected some discomforting sarcasm from Covenant. But the Unbeliever replied in a gruff, embarrassed voice, "Your hospitality honors me."

The Lorewardens bowed in answer, and their leader stepped forward. He was an old, wrinkled man with hooded eyes and a stooped posture—the result of decades of back-bending study. His voice had a slight tremor of age. "I am Corimini," he said, "the Eldest of the Loresraat. I speak for all the seekers of the Lore, both Sword and Staff. The accepting of a gift returns honor to the giver. Be welcome." As he spoke, he held out his hand to help Covenant dismount.

But Covenant either misunderstood the gesture or went beyond it intuitively. Instead of swinging off his mount, he brusquely pulled his wedding band from his left hand and dropped it into Corimini's extended palm.

The Eldest caught his breath; a look of astonishment widened his eyes. Almost at once, he turned to show the ring to the other Lorewardens. With muted awed murmurings of invocation like low snatches of prayer, they crowded around Corimini to gaze at the white gold, and to handle it with fingers that trembled.

But their touches were brief. Shortly Corimini returned to Covenant. The Eldest's eyes were damp with emotion, and his hand shook as he passed the ring back up to the Unbeliever. "Ur-Lord Covenant," he said with a pronounced quaver, "you exceed us. We will need many generations to repay this honor. Command us, so that we may serve you."

"I don't need service," Covenant replied bluntly. "I need an alternative. Find some way to save the Land without me."

"I do not wholly understand you," said Corimini. "All our strength is bent toward the preservation of the Land. If that may aid you also, we will be pleased." Facing the company of the Lords more generally, he went on, "Will you now enter Revelwood with us? We have prepared food and pleasure for you."

High Lord Elena made a gracious answer, and dropped lightly from Myrha's back. The rest of the

riders promptly dismounted. At once, a group of students hurried out of the shadows of the Tree to take
charge of the horses. Then the company was escorted
through the ring of trunks toward the central tree.
Many lights had appeared throughout Revelwood, and
their combined illumination ameliorated the dimness
of Troy's sight. He was able to walk confidently with
the Lords, and to look up with fondness into the
branches of the familiar city. In some ways, he felt
more at home here than in Lord's Keep. In Revelwood
he had learned to see.

And he felt that Revelwood also suited the High
Lord. The two were inextricably linked for him. He
was gratified by her just preeminence, her glow of
gentle authority, and her easy grace as she swung up
the wide ladder of the central trunk. Under her influence, he found the fortitude to give Covenant a word
of encouragement when the Unbeliever balked at
climbing into the Tree.

"You don't understand," Covenant responded
vaguely. "I'm afraid of heights." With a look of rigid
trepidation, he forced his hands to the rungs of the
ladder.

Bannor took a position close behind Covenant,
making himself responsible for the ur-Lord's safety.
Soon they had climbed to the level of the first
branches.

Troy moved easily up into the Tree after them. The
smooth, strong wood of the rungs made him feel that
he could not miss his grip; it almost seemed to lift
him upward, as if Revelwood were eager for him. In
moments, he was high up the trunk, stepping away
from the ladder onto one of the main boughs of the
city. The shapers of Revelwood had grown the banyan so that the upper surfaces of the branches were
flat, and the level stretch down which Troy walked
was wide enough for three or four people to stand
safely abreast. As he moved, he waved greetings to
the people he knew—most of the Sword Lorewardens,
and a few students whose families lived in Lord's
Keep.

The procession of the Lords crossed an intersection

where several limbs came together, and passed beyond it toward one of the outer trunks. Formed in this trunk was a large hall, and when Troy entered it he found that the room had been set for a banquet. The chamber was brilliant with *lillianrill* torches; long tables with carpets of moss between them covered the floor; and students of all ages bustled around, carrying trays laden with steaming bowls and flagons.

There Troy was joined by Drinishok, Sword-Elder of the Lorewardens, and the Warmark's first battle-teacher. Except for his grizzled eyebrows, Drinishok did not look like a warrior; his thin, spidery limbs and fingers did not seem sturdy enough to handle either a sword or a bow. But three Lords and three-quarters of Troy's Warward had trained under the old Sword-Elder; and his tanned forearms were laced with many white battle scars. Troy greeted his mentor warmly, and after standing together in the Land's customary thanks for food, they sat down to the feast.

The fare of Revelwood was simple but excellent— it made up in convivial gusto what it lacked in complexity—and all the Lords and Lorewardens were bountifully supplied with meats, rice, cheeses, bread, fruit, and springwine. Warmed by the glow of Revelwood's welcome, the High Lord's company ate with enthusiasm, talking and joking all the while with their hosts and the busy students. Then, when the eating was done, High Lord Elena presided over an entertainment which the students had prepared. Champions of the Sword gave demonstrations of gymnastics and blade work, and the apprentices of the Staff told an intricate tale which they had distilled from the ancient Giantish story of Bahgoon the Unbearable and Thelma Twofist who tamed him. Troy had never heard it before, and it delighted him.

He was reluctant to lose this pleased and comfortable mood, so when the Lords left the hall with the Lorewardens to speak with them concerning the tidings which Runnik had brought from Sarangrave Flat, Troy did not accompany them. Instead, he accepted Drinishok's invitation, and went to spend the night in the old Sword-Elder's home.

High in one of the outer trees, in a chamber woven of leaves and branches, he and Drinishok sat up for a long time, drinking springwine and discussing the war. Drinishok was excited by the prospect of the battle, and he avowed that only Revelwood's need for a strong defense kept him from marching with the Warward. As always, he showed a swift grasp of Troy's ideas, and when the Warmark finally went to bed the only immediate blot on his private satisfaction was the mystery of Trell.

The breeze in the branches lulled him into a fine sleep, and he awoke early the next morning feeling eager for the new day. He was amused but not surprised to find that his host was up and away before him; he knew the rigorous schedule of the Loresraat. He bathed and dressed, pulled his high boots over his black leggings, and carefully adjusted his headband and his sunglasses. After a quick breakfast, he spent a few moments polishing his breastplate and his gleaming ebony sword. When he was properly appareled as the Warmark of the Lords' Warward, he left Drinishok's chambers, moved to the central tree, and started up it toward the lookout of Revelwood.

On a small platform in the uppermost branches of the Tree, he joined the two students on watch duty. While he exchanged pleasantries with them, he breathed the crisp autumn air and studied the whole length and breadth of the Valley of Two Rivers. In the west, he could see the snow crests of the mountains. He was not being cautious, looking for danger. He loved the fertile hills of Trothgard, and he wanted to fix them in his mind so that he would never forget them. If something were to strike him down during the coming war, he wanted to be sure to the very end, death or blindness, that he had in fact seen this place.

He was still in the lookout when he heard the signal for the gathering of the Loresraat.

At once, he took leave of the two students, and started down the Tree. Shortly, he reached the wide, roofless bowl of the gathering place. High in the city, on a frame of four heavy boughs radiating from the central trunk, the shapers of Revelwood had woven

an immense net of banyan roots and hung it around
the central trunk. It formed a wide basin supported
by the four boughs and anchored by the roots themselves in each of the six outer trees. The result was
the *viancome,* a meeting place large enough for half
the population of the city. People sat on the roots and
dangled their feet through the gaps of the net.

These gaps were rarely larger than a foot square,
but they made the *viancome* an uneasy experience
for novices. However, the people of Revelwood
moved and even ran lightly over the net. Warmark
Troy, with a blind man's alert, careful feet, was able
to walk confidently away from the central trunk to
join Drinishok and the other Sword Lorewardens
where they stood partway up one side of the bowl.

Lord Amatin was already there, talking intently
with a cluster of Staff Lorewardens and advanced students. Most of the Bloodguard were stationed around
the edge of the net, and past them came a steady flow
of Revelwood's inhabitants. As Troy joined Drinishok,
he caught sight of Lord Mhoram moving across the
bowl toward Amatin. If the *viancome* caused Mhoram
any anxiety, he did not show it; he strode boldly from
root to root with his staff held in the crook of his arm.

Soon High Lord Elena arrived in the company of
the Staff-Elder, Asuraka. Troy was taken slightly
aback; he had expected her to be with Corimini, the
Eldest of the Loresraat. But when Corimini entered
the bowl, he brought with him ur-Lord Covenant.
Troy saw what had happened. The Loresraat ranked
Covenant above Elena, and so the highest honor of
Revelwood's hospitality, the invitation of the Eldest,
had gone to the Unbeliever. This nettled Troy; he did
not like to see the High Lord slighted in favor of
Covenant. But he consoled himself by watching the
sick look with which Covenant regarded the net and
fall below it.

Shortly all the Lorewardens were in their places.
The sides of the *viancome,* and the branches overhead, thronged with the people of Revelwood. Covenant clung to a root over one of the supporting
boughs, and Bannor crouched protectively near him.

The Lords and Warmark Troy sat in a fanned group with the Elder Lorewardens, facing south, and Corimini stood before them, looking out over the assembly with a dignified mien. When all the people were still, hushed and expectant, he began the ceremonies of the meeting.

He and the High Lord exchanged traditional salutations, and sang to each other the ritual invocations which they considered appropriate to the purpose of the meeting. Their stately alternation spun a mood of reverent seriousness over the *viancome,* wrapped all the people together as if it were weaving them into the grim and wondrous history of the Land. Under the influence of the ceremonies, Troy was almost able to forget that half of what was said and sung was intended to honor the white gold wielder.

But Covenant did not look as if he were being honored. He sat with an awkward stiffness, as if the point of a knife were pressed against his spine.

After the last song was done, Corimini gazed at Covenant in silence, giving the Unbeliever a chance to speak. But the glare which Covenant returned almost made the Eldest wince. He turned away, and said, "High Lord Elena, Lord Mhoram, Lord Amatin, Warmark Troy, be welcome in the *viancome* of Revelwood. We are the Loresraat, the seekers and servants of Kevin's Lore. We gather to honor you—and to offer you the help of all our knowledge in the name of the approaching war. The preservation of Land and Lore is in your hands, as the mystery of Land and Lore is in ours. If there is any way in which we may aid you, only speak of it, and we will put forth all our strength to meet the need."

With a deep bow, High Lord Elena replied formally, "The gathering of the Loresraat honors us, and I am honored to speak before the people of Revelwood." Troy thought that he had rarely seen her look more radiant. "Eldest, Elders, Lorewardens, students of the Sword and Staff, friends of the Land— my friends, in the name of all the Lords, I thank you. We will never be defeated while such faithfulness is alive in the Land.

"My friends, there are matters of which I would speak. I do not speak of the danger that war brings to Revelwood. The Lore of the Sword will not neglect your defense. And Lord Amatin will remain with you, to do all that a Lord may do to preserve the Valley of Two Rivers."

A cheer started up on the edges of the bowl, but she stopped it with a commanding glance, and went on, "More, I do not speak of Stonedowns and Woodhelvens which will be destroyed by war—or of people made homeless. I know that the dispossessed of this war will find here all comfort and relief and restitution that human hearts may ask or give. This is sure, and requires no urging.

"More, I do not speak of any need for mastery of Kevin's Lore. You have given your best strength, and have achieved much. You will give and achieve more. All these matters are secure in your fidelity.

"But there are two questions of which I must speak." A change in the cadence of her voice showed that she was approaching the heart of her reasons for coming to Revelwood. "The second concerns a stranger who has visited Lord's Keep. But the first is one which was presented to you a year ago—at the request of Warmark Hile Troy." She offered Troy a chance to speak, but he declined with a shake of his head, and she continued, "It is our hope that the Loresraat has discovered a way to speak and hear messages across distances. The Warmark believes that such a way will be of great value in this war."

Cormini's look of satisfaction revealed his answer before he spoke it. "High Lord, we have learned a way." Troy's heart surged at the news, and he gripped the handle of his sword. His battle plan appeared suddenly flawless. He was grinning broadly as the Eldest went on, "Several of our best students and Lorewardens have devoted themselves to this need. And they were aided by Hirebrands of the *lillianrill*. With the Hirebrands and two students, Staff-Elder Asuraka learned that messages may be spoken and heard through *lomillialor*, the High Wood of the *lillianrill*. The task is difficult, and requires strength—

but it will not surpass any Lord accustomed to the
Earthpower." Nodding at the Staff-Elder, he said,
"Asuraka will teach the knowledge to you. We have
prepared three *lomillialor* rods for this purpose. More
we could not do, for the High Wood is very rare."

Lomillialor. Troy had heard of it. It was the
lillianrill parallel to *orcrest*—a potent white wood
descended from the One Tree from which Berek
Halfhand had formed the Staff of Law. The Hirebrands used it—as the Gravelingases used *orcrest*—to
give the test of truth. *Lomillialor* was said to be a sure
test of fidelity—if the one tested did not far surpass
the strength of the tester. Some of the old tales of
Covenant's first visit to the Land said that the Unbeliever had passed a test of truth given to him at
Soaring Woodhelven.

And Soaring Woodhelven had later been destroyed.

As Troy got up to join Elena in thanking the
Loresraat for what it had achieved, he looked over
to see how Covenant took Corimini's news.

For some reason, the Unbeliever was on his feet.
Swaying uncertainly, afraid of falling, he muttered,
"*Lomillialor*. The test of truth. Are you going to trust
that?"

A hot retort leaped into Troy's mouth, but something about Covenant's appearance silenced it. Troy
blocked his sight with his hand, adjusted his sunglasses, then looked again. The strangeness was still
there.

Covenant's chest seemed to ripple like roiled water.
He was solid, but something disturbed the center of
his chest, making it waver like a mirage.

Troy had seen an effect like this once before. He
glanced quickly away toward the High Lord. She
regarded him with a question in her face. Nothing
distorted her. The rippling touched no one else in the
viancome. And even Covenant seemed unaware of it.
But the Bloodguard around the bowl stood as if at
attention, and Bannor held himself at Covenant's side
with a coiled poise that belied his blank expression.

Then Troy saw the area of distortion detach itself
from Covenant and float lazily toward the High Lord.

The other time he had seen it, it had appeared so briefly, with such evanescence, that he had finally disregarded it as a trick of his vision, a misconception. But now he knew what it was.

He bowed deliberately to Corimini. "Forgive the interruption. I forget what I was going to say." Without waiting for an answer, he addressed Elena. He hoped that she would understand him through the careful nonchalance of his tone. "Why don't you go ahead? There was something else you wanted to talk to the Loresraat about." While he spoke, he took a few steps in her direction, as if this were a natural expression of deference. On the edges of his sight, he watched the mirage float toward her.

He turned to get closer to it.

He faced Covenant in a way that allowed him to take two more steps, and remarked pointedly, "You know, it just might turn out that that white gold of yours has been good for something after all." Some of his excitement forced its way into his tone.

The next instant, he sprang into motion. He took three rapid strides, and threw himself at the roiling distortion in the air.

It tried to evade him, but he caught it in time. He hit it with a jarring impact, and toppled to the net with it in his arms.

It struggled—he could feel invisible arms and legs —but he kept his grip. He tightened his hold until the form stopped resisting and lay still. When he heaved himself to his feet, he lifted the light, limp weight easily in his arms.

"All right, my friend," he gritted at it. "Show yourself. Or shall I ask the High Lord to tickle your ribs with the Staff of Law?"

Covenant was staring at Troy as if the Warmark had lost his mind. But Lord Amatin watched him avidly, and the High Lord moved forward as if to support his threat.

A peal of high, young laughter rang out. "Ah, very well," said a bodiless voice bubbling with gaiety. "I am captured. You have surprising vision. Release me —I will not escape."

The air swirled suddenly, and Amok became visible in Troy's grasp. He was the same incongruously ancient youth who had appeared before the Council of Lords in Revelstone.

"Hail, High Lord!" he said cheerfully. When Troy let go of him, he bowed humorously to her, then turned and repeated his bow to his captor. "Hail, Warmark! You are perceptive—but rough. Is this the hospitality of Revelwood?" Glee filled his voice, effaced any reproof in his words. "Your strength was not needed. I am here."

"By hell," Covenant muttered. "By hell."

"Indeed?" said Amok with a boyish grin that seemed to light up the laughing curls of his hair. "Well, that is not for me to say. But I am well made. You bear the white gold. It is for your sake that I have returned."

All the people of Revelwood had surged to their feet when Amok appeared, and the Lorewardens now stood in a ready circle around the Warmark and his captive. Both Corimini and Asuraka were confusedly questioning the High Lord. But Elena deferred to Lord Amatin. Stepping into the circle, Amatin asked Amok, "How so?"

Amok replied, "Lord, the white gold surpasses my purpose. I felt the sign of readiness when the *krill* of Loric came to life. I went to Revelstone. There I learned that the *krill* was not awakened by the Lords of Kevin's Lore. I feared that I had erred. But now I have traveled the Land, and seen the peril. And I have learned of the white gold, which awakened Loric's *krill*. This shows the wisdom of my creation. Though the conditions of my life are not met, I see the need, and I appear."

"Are you changed?" said Amatin. "Will you give us your knowledge now?"

"I am who I am. I respect the white gold, but I am unchanged."

"Who is he?" Corimini insisted.

By answering the Eldest, High Lord Elena provided Amatin with a moment in which to prepare herself. "He is Amok, the waiting bearer of knowledge.

He was made by High Lord Kevin to—to answer certain questions. It was Kevin's thought that when those who came after him had mastered the *krill,* they would be ready for Amok's knowledge. But we have not mastered the *krill.* We do not know the questions."

At this, a breath of astonishment blew through the Loresraat. But Troy could see that the Lorewardens immediately understood the situation better than he did. Their eyes gleamed with possibilities he did not comprehend.

At a nod from Corimini, the two Elders, Asuraka and Drinishok, entered the circle and stood on either side of Lord Amatin, placing their knowledge at her service. She acknowledged them, then raised her studious face to Amok and said, "Stranger, who are you?"

"Lord, I am what you see," Amok responded cryptically. "Those who know me have no need for my name."

"Who made you?"

"High Lord Kevin son of Loric son of Damelon son of Berek Heartthew the Lord-Fatherer."

"Why were you made?"

"I wait. And I answer." The boy's open grin seemed to mock the incorrectness of Amatin's questions.

Irritated by Amok's riddling, Drinishok interposed, "Boy, do you bear knowledge that belongs to the Warlore?"

Amok laughed. "Old man, I was old when the grandsire of your grandsire's grandsire was a babe. Do I appear to be a warrior?"

"I care nothing for age," the Sword-Elder snapped. "You behave as a child."

"I am what I am. I behave as I was made to behave."

When Lord Amatin spoke again, she emphasized her words intently. "Amok, what are you?"

Without hesitation, Amok replied, "I am the Seventh Ward of High Lord Kevin's Lore."

His answer threw a stunned silence over the whole gathering. Both Elders gasped, and Corimini had to

brace himself on Elena's shoulder. A burst of wild
emotion shot across Elena's face. Mhoram's eyes
crackled with sudden visionary fire. And Lord Amatin
gaped—amazed or appalled at what she had uncovered. Even Troy, who had not devoted his whole life
to the mysteries of the Wards, felt abruptly unbalanced, as if his precarious perch had been jolted by
something inscrutable. Then a ragged cheer sprang up
among the students. The Lorewardens pressed eagerly
forward, as if they wanted to verify Amok's existence
by touching him. And through the clamor, Troy heard
High Lord Elena exclaim, "By the Seven! We are
saved!"

Covenant also heard her. "Saved?" he rasped across
the din. "You don't even know what the Seventh Ward
is!"

Elena ignored him. She beamed grateful congratulations to Lord Amatin, then raised her arms to quiet
the assembly. When some degree of order had returned to the *viancome,* she said, "Amok, you are indeed well made. You chose wisely in returning to us.
Now the Despiser does not overpower us as much as
he may think."

With an effort, old Corimini forced himself to remember his long experience with the unattainability of
the Wards. In a thin voice, he quavered, "But still we
do not know the questions to unlock this knowledge."

"We will find them," Elena responded. Sharp determination thrummed in her voice.

After a pause to steady herself, Lord Amatin returned to her inquiry. "Amok, the Wards which we
have found contain various knowledges on many subjects. It is so with the Seventh Ward?"

Amok seemed to think that this was a penetrating
question. He bowed to her as seriously as his bubbling
spirits permitted, and said, "Lord, the Seventh Ward
has many uses, but I am only one answer."

"What answer are you?"

"I am the way and the door."

"How so?"

"That is my answer."

Lord Amatin looked toward Elena and Mhoram

for suggestions, and Troy took the opportunity to ask, "The way and the door to what?"

With a chuckle, Amok replied, "Those who know me have no need for my name."

"Yes, I remember," Troy growled. "And among those who do not know you, you are named Amok. Why don't you think of something else to say?"

"Think of some other question," the youth retorted gaily.

Troy retreated, baffled, and after a moment Lord Amatin was ready to continue. "Amok, knowledge is the way and door of power. The Earthpower answers those who know its name. How great is the power of the Seventh Ward?"

"It is the pinnacle of Kevin's Lore," said Amok slyly, as if he were making a subtle joke.

"Can it be used to defeat the Despiser?"

"Power is power. Its uses are in the hands of the user."

"Amok," Amatin said, then hesitated. She seemed almost afraid of her next question. But she clenched her resolve, and spoke it. "Does the Seventh Ward contain knowledge of the Ritual of Desecration?"

"Lord, Desecration requires no knowledge. It comes freely to any willing hand."

The Lord sighed, then turned to Asuraka and asked the Staff-Elder for advice. Asuraka referred the question to Drinishok, but he was out of his element, and could offer her nothing. On an impulse, she turned to Corimini. The two conferred in hushed tones for a moment. When Asuraka returned to Amok, she said tentatively, "Amok, the other Wards teach knowledge concerning power. Are you the power of the Seventh Ward?"

"I am the way and the door."

"Do you bear the power itself within you?" she insisted.

For a moment, Amok appeared to study the legitimacy of this question. Then he said simply, "No."

"Are you a teacher?"

"I am the way and——"

Suddenly Lord Amatin grasped a new idea, and interrupted Amok. "You are a guide."

"Yes."

"You were created to teach us the location of some knowledge or power?"

"Ah, that may be as it happens. Much is taught, but few learn."

"Where is this power?"

"Where all such powers should be—hidden."

"What is the power?"

Laughing, the youth replied, "There is a time for all things." Then he added, "Those who know me have no need of my name."

Amatin sagged, and turned away toward the High Lord. Her thin face held a look of strain as she admitted defeat. Around her, the assembly of the Loresraat sighed as the people shared her disappointment. But the High Lord answered Amatin by stepping calmly forward, and planting the Staff of Law in front of Amok. In a voice soft and confident, she said, "Amok, will you guide me?"

With an unexpected seriousness, Amok bowed. "High Lord, yes. If the white gold permits."

"Don't ask me for permission," Covenant said quickly. But no one listened to him. The High Lord smiled and asked, "Where will we go?"

The youth did not speak, but he gave a general nod toward the Westron Mountains.

"And when will we go?"

"Whenever the High Lord desires." Throwing back his head, he began to laugh again as if he were releasing an overflow of high humor. "Think of me, and I will join you."

As he laughed, he flourished his arms intricately, and vanished.

Either his power was stronger than before, or he moved more swiftly; Troy caught no last glimpse of him.

The Warmark found that he regretted Amok's appearance intensely.

Soon after that, the gathering of the Loresraat broke up. The Lorewardens and students of the Staff hurried away to begin analyzing what had happened, and Drinishok ordered all his students and fellow teachers away to the practice fields. Elena, Mhoram, and Amatin went with Corimini and Staff-Elder Asuraka to their main library. In moments, Troy, Covenant, and Bannor were the only people left in the bowl.

Troy felt that he should speak with Covenant; there were things that he needed to understand. But he feared that he would not be able to keep his temper, so he also moved away, leaving Bannor to help Covenant struggle off the net. He wanted to talk to the High Lord, ask her why she had made such a foolhardy offer to Amok. But he was not in command of his emotions. He climbed out of the *viancome,* and strode away along one of the boughs toward Drinishok's quarters.

In the Sword-Elder's larder, he ate a little bread and meat, and drank quantities of springwine in an effort to dissipate the dark sensation of foreboding which Amok had given him. The idea that Elena might wander off somewhere with the youth, hunting for a cryptic and probably useless power when she was desperately needed elsewhere, made him grind his teeth in frustration. His heart groaned with a prescience that told him he was going to lose her. The Land was going to lose her. Searching for balance, he consumed a great deal of springwine. But it did not steady him; his brain reeled as if dangerous winds were buffeting him.

Early in the afternoon, he went in search of the Lords, but one of the Lorewardens soon told him that they were closeted with Asuraka, studying the *lomillialor* communication rods. So he descended to the ground, whistled for Mehryl, and rode away from Revelwood with Ruel at his side. He wanted to visit the grave of the student who had summoned him to the Land.

Covenant had said, *It isn't you they've got faith in at all. It's the student who summoned you.* Troy needed to think about that. He could not simply shrug it away. One reason he distrusted Covenant was because the Unbeliever had first been called by Drool

Rockworm at Lord Foul's behest. Did the nature of the summoner have any connection to the worth of the one summoned?

Furthermore, Covenant had referred to that student strangely, as if he knew something about the young man Troy did not know.

Troy went to the place of his summons hoping that its physical context, its concrete location in Trothgard, would ease his vague fears and forebodings. He needed to regain his self-confidence. He knew he could not challenge Elena's decision to follow Amok if he did not believe in himself.

But when he reached the site of the grave, he found Trell there. The big Gravelingas knelt by the grassy mound as if he were praying. When he heard Troy's approach, he raised his head suddenly, and his face was so swollen with grief that it struck Troy momentarily dumb. He could think of no reason why Trell Gravelingas should be here grieving.

Before Troy could collect his thoughts to ask for an explanation, Trell jumped up and hastened away toward his mount, which he had tethered nearby.

"Trell—!" Troy started to call after him, but Ruel interposed flatly, "Warmark, let him go."

Troy turned in surprise toward the Bloodguard. Ruel's visage was as passionless as ever, but something in the way his eyes followed Trell seemed to express an unwonted sympathy. Carefully Troy said, "Why? I don't understand."

"That you must ask the High Lord," Ruel replied without inflection.

"I'm asking you!" the Warmark snapped before he could control his irritation.

"Nevertheless."

With an effort, Troy mastered himself. Ruel's mien said as plainly as words that he was acting on the High Lord's instructions, and that nothing which did not threaten her life could induce him to disobey her. "All right," Troy said stiffly. "I'll do that." Turning Mehryl, he trotted after Trell's galloping mount back toward Revelwood.

But when he reentered the Valley of Two Rivers

and approached the Tree, he found Drinishok waiting impatiently for him. The Lords had announced
that they would leave Revelwood the next morning,
and the Sword-Elder wanted Troy to discuss the defense of the city with all the Lorewardens and students
of the Sword. This was a responsibility which Troy
could not ignore, so while his private fog turned to
dusk and then to night blindness, he addressed the
assembled discipline of the Sword. He did not even
try to see what he was talking about; he went into the
strategy of the Valley from memory.

But when he was done, he found that he had lost
his chance to talk to the Lords. In the darkness, he
seemed to lack courage as well as vision. After his
lecture, he went to Drinishok's home, and shared a
meal full of indigestible lumps of silence with the
Sword-Elder. Then he went to bed early; he could not
endure any more of the blurred half-sight of torches.
Drinishok respected his mood, and left him alone. In
blind isolation, he stared uselessly into the darkness,
and tried to recover his balance. He felt certain that
he was going to lose Elena.

He ached to talk to her, to dissuade her, cling to
her. But the next morning, when all the riders gathered with their mounts just after dawn on the south
side of the great Tree, he found that he could not
confront the High Lord with his fears. Sitting regally
on Myrha's back in the gleam of day, she had too
much presence, too much personal authority. He
could not deny or challenge her. And while she was
surrounded by so many people, he could not ask her
his questions about Trell. His apprehension was too
personal to be aired so publicly. He strove to occupy
his mind with other things until he got a chance to
talk to someone.

Deliberately, he scanned the company of riders.
Standing by their Ranyhyn behind the Lords were
twenty Bloodguard—First Mark Morin, Terrel, Bannor, Ruel, Runnik, and fifteen others. Obviously,
Koral would remain with Lord Amatin at Revelwood.
In addition to them, the group included only five others: High Lord Elena, Lord Mhoram, Covenant, Troy,

and Trell. When he saw the Gravelingas, Troy again felt a desire to speak to him. The unconcealed wound of Trell's expression was taut with suspense, as if he awaited some decision from Elena with a degree of agony that surprised Troy. But the Warmark refrained, despite his mounting anxiety. The High Lord had begun to address Lord Amatin and Eldest Corimini.

"My friends," she said gravely, "I leave Revelwood in your care. Ward it well! The Tree and the Loresraat are the two great achievements of the new Lords—two symbols of our service. If it may be done, they must be preserved. Remember vigilance, and watch the Center Plains. If war comes upon you, you must not be taken unaware. And remember that if Revelwood cannot be saved, the Lore still must be preserved, and Lord's Keep warned. The Loresraat and the Wards must find safety in Revelstone at need.

"Sister Amatin, these are great burdens. But I place them in your hands without fear. They do not surpass you. And the help of Corimini the Eldest, and of Asuraka and Drinishok the Elders, is beyond price. I do not believe that the Warward will fall in this war. But you must be prepared for all chances, even the worst. You will not fail. This trust becomes you."

Lord Amatin blinked back a moment of tears, and bowed silently to the High Lord. Then Elena lifted her head to Revelwood, and projected her voice so that she could be heard in the Tree.

"Friends! Comrades! Proud people of the Land! There is war upon us. Together we confront the test of death. Now is the time of parting, when all the defenders of the Land must go to their separate tasks. Do not desire to change your lot for another's. All faith and service are equal, alike worthy and perilous, in this time of need. And do not grieve at parting. We go to the greatest glory of our age—we are honored by the chance to give our utmost for the Land. This is the test of death, that at the last we may prove worthy of what we serve.

"Be of good heart. If the needs of this war go beyond your strength, do not despair. Give all your strength, and hold Peace, and do not despair. Hold courage and faith high! It is better to fall and die in Peace than to re-Desecrate the Land.

"My friends, I am honored that I have shared life with you."

High in Revelwood, a strident voice cried, "Hail to the High Lord and the Staff of Law!" And all the people in the Tree and on the ground answered, "Hail! Hail to the High Lord!"

Elena bowed deeply to Revelwood, spreading her arms wide in the traditional gesture of farewell. Then she turned Myrha toward the riders, and spoke to Lord Mhoram.

"Now, Mhoram, my most trusted friend, you must depart. You and Warmark Hile Troy must rejoin the Warward, to guide it into war. I have decided. I will leave you now, and follow Amok to the Seventh Ward of Kevin's Lore."

In spite of himself, Troy groaned, and clutched at Mehryl's mane as if to keep himself from falling. But the High Lord took no notice of him. Instead, she said to Mhoram, "You know that I do not do this to evade the burden of war. But you also know that you are the more experienced and ready in battle. And you know that the outcome of the war may allow us no second opportunity to discover this Ward. Yet the Ward may enable a victory which would otherwise be taken from us. I cannot choose otherwise."

Lord Mhoram gazed at her intently for a time. When he finally spoke, his voice was thick with suppressed appeals. "Beware, High Lord. Even the Seventh Ward is not enough."

Elena met him squarely, but her own gaze appeared unfocused. The other dimension of her sight was so pronounced that she did not seem to see him at all. "Perhaps it was not enough for Kevin Landwaster," she replied softly, "but it will suffice for me."

"No!" Mhoram protested. "The danger is too great. Either this power did not meet Kevin's need in any way, or its peril was so great that he feared to use it. Do not take this risk."

"Have you seen it?" she asked. "Do you speak from vision?"

With an effort, Mhoram forced himself to say, "I have not seen it. But I feel it in my heart. There will be death because of it. People will be slain."

"My friend, you are too careful of all risks but your own. If you held the Staff of Law in my place, you would follow Amok to the ends of the Earth. And people will still be slain. Mhoram, ask your heart—do you truly believe that the future of the Land can be won in war? It was not so for Kevin. I must not lose any chance which may teach me another way to resist the Despiser."

Mhoram bowed his head, too moved to make any answer. In the silence, they melded their thoughts, and after a moment the strain in his face eased. When he looked up again, he directed his gaze explicitly toward Covenant and Troy. Softly, he said, "Then—if you must go—please do not go alone. Take someone with you—someone who may be of service."

For one wild instant, Troy thought that the High Lord was going to ask him to go with her. Despite his responsibilities to the Warward, his lips were already forming his answer—Yes—when she said, "That is my desire. Ur-Lord Covenant, will you accompany me? I wish to share this quest with you."

Awkwardly, as if her request embarrassed him, Covenant said, "Do you really think I'm going to be of service?"

A gentle smile touched Elena's lips. "Nevertheless."

He stared into the expanse of her eyes for a moment. Then, abruptly, he looked away and shrugged. "Yes. I'll come."

Troy hardly heard the things that were said next— the last formal speeches by Elena and Corimini, the Loresraat's brief song of encouragement, the exchange of farewells. When the High Lord said a final word to him, he could barely bring himself to bow in answer. With his Yes frozen on his lips, he watched the end of the ceremonies, and saw Elena and Covenant ride away together westward, accompanied only by Bannor and First Mark Morin. He felt paralyzed in

the act of falling—crying, I'm going to lose you! Lord
Mhoram came close to him, and spoke. But he did not
move until he realized through his distress that Trell
had not followed Covenant and the High Lord.

Suddenly, his restraint broke. He spun urgently toward Trell, turned in time to see the Gravelingas yank
his heavy fists out of his hair, snatch up the reins of his
horse, and start away at a gallop toward the ford of
the Llurallin north of Revelwood.

Troy went after him. Mehryl flashed under the Tree,
and caught up with Trell in the sunlight beyond the
city. Troy ordered the Gravelingas to stop, but Trell
ignored him. At once, the Warmark told Mehryl to halt
Trell's mount. Mehryl gave one short, commanding
whinny, and the horse stopped so sharply that Trell
almost lost his seat.

When the Gravelingas forced his head up to meet
Troy, his eyes ran with tears, and he panted as if he
were being slowly suffocated. But Troy had no more
time to spare for considerateness. "What're you doing?"
he rasped. "Where're you going?"

"Revelstone," croaked Trell. "There is nothing for
me here."

"So? We're going south—don't you know that? You
live in the South Plains, don't you? Don't you want to
help defend your home?" This was not what Troy
wanted to ask, but he had not found the words for his
real question.

"No."

"Why not?"

"I cannot go back. She is there—I cannot bear it.
After this!"

As Trell panted his answer, Lord Mhoram rode up
to them. At once, he started to speak, but Troy cut
him off with a savage gesture. "She?" the Warmark demanded. "Who? Your daughter?" When Trell nodded
dumbly, Troy said, "Wait a minute. Wait a minute."
Things he did not know buffeted him; he had to find
answers. "I don't understand. Why don't you go back
home—to your daughter? She's going to need you."

"*Melenkurion!*" Trell gasped. "I cannot! How could

I look into her face—answer questions—after this? Do not torment me!"

"Warmark!" Mhoram's voice was hard and dangerous—a warning, almost a threat. "Let him be. Nothing that he can say will help you."

"No!" Troy retorted. "I've got to know. Trell, listen to me. I have got to know. Believe me, I understand how you feel about him."

Trell no longer seemed to hear Troy. "She chose!" he panted, "chose!" He heaved the words between his clenched teeth as if they were about to burst him. "She chose him—him!"

"Trell, answer me. What were you doing out there yesterday?—at that grave? Trell!"

The word *grave* penetrated Trell's passion. Abruptly, he wrapped his arms around his chest, hunched forward. Through his tears, he glared at Troy. "You are a fool!" he hissed. "Blind! She wasted her life."

"Wasted?" Troy gaped. "Wasted?" *It's the student who summoned you.* Was Covenant right?

"Perhaps," Lord Mhoram said grimly. This time his tone compelled Troy's attention. Troy stared at Mhoram with a gaze thick with dread. "He has abundant reason to visit that grave," the Lord went on. "Atiaran Trell-mate is buried there. She died in the act which summoned you to the Land. She gave her life in an effort to regain ur-Lord Covenant—but she failed of her purpose. Your presence here is the outcome of her Peace-less grief and her hunger for retribution."

Mhoram's explanation exceeded the limit of Trell's endurance. Pain convulsed his features. He struck his horse a fierce blow with his heels, and it sprang at once into a frightened gallop toward the Llurallin ford. But Troy did not even see him go. The Warmark turned sharply, and found that he could still discern Elena, Covenant, and the two Bloodguard riding westward out of the Valley. Amok was already with them, walking jauntily at the High Lord's side.

Atiaran Trell-mate? *Trell*-mate? She was his wife? He knew of Atiaran—he had heard too much talk about Covenant not to know that she was the woman

who had guided the Unbeliever from Mithil Stonedown to Andelain and the Soulsease River. But he
had not known that Trell was her husband. That had
been kept from him.

Then he went a step further. Covenant had raped
Trell's daughter—*Atiaran's* daughter—the daughter of
the woman who—!

"Covenant! You bastard!" Troy howled. "What
have you done?" But he knew that the travelers could
not hear him across the distance; the noise of the two
rivers obliterated distant shouts. A stiff gust of helplessness knocked down his protest, so that his voice
cracked and stumbled into silence.

It was no wonder that Trell could not return home,
face his daughter. How could he tell her that the High
Lord had chosen friendship rather than retribution
for the man who had raped her? Troy did not understand how she could do such a thing to Trell.

Another moment passed before he grasped the rest
of what Mhoram had said. *She died in the act—*
Atiaran was his summoner, not some young ignorant
or inspired student. That, too, had been kept from
him. He was the result and consequence of her unanswerable pain.

It isn't you— Was Covenant right? Were all his
plans only so much despair work, set in motion by
the extravagance of Atiaran's death?

"Warmark." Lord Mhoram's tone was stern. "That
was not well done. Trell's hurt is great enough."

"I know," Troy gritted over the aching of his heart.
"But why didn't you tell me? You knew about all
this."

"The Council decided together to withhold this
knowledge from you. We saw only harm in the sharing
of it. We wished to spare you pain. And we hoped
that you would learn to trust ur-Lord Covenant."

"You were dreaming," Troy groaned. "That bastard
thinks this whole thing is some kind of mental game.
All that Unbelieving is just a bluff. He thinks he can
get away with anything. You can't trust him." Grimly,
he pushed the argument to its conclusion. "And you
can't trust me—or you would have told me all this

before. She was trying to summon him. As far as you know, I'm just a surrogate." He tried to sound lucid, but his voice shook.

"You misunderstand me," Mhoram said carefully.

"No, I don't misunderstand." He could feel deadly forces at work around him—choosing, manipulating, determining. He had to clench himself to articulate, "Mhoram, something terrible is going to happen to her."

He looked at the Lord, then turned away; he could not bear the compassion in Mhoram's gaze. Patting Mehryl's neck, he sent the Ranyhyn trotting around the east side of Revelwood. He avoided the waiting Lorewardens, avoided having to bid them farewell. Gesturing roughly for the Bloodguard and Lord Mhoram to follow him, he rode straight away from Revelwood toward the south ford.

He was looking forward to this war. He wanted to get to it in a hurry.

SIXTEEN: Forced March

YET even in this mood, he could not cross the ford of the Rill out of Trothgard without regret. He loved the sun-bright beauty of Revelwood, the uncomplex friendship of the Lorewardens; he did not want to lose them. But he did not look back. He could not understand why Elena had repudiated Trell Atiaran-mate's just rage and grief. And he sensed now, in a way more fundamental than he had ever seen it before, that he would have to prove himself in this war. He would have to prove that he was the fruit of hope, not of despair.

He would have to win.

If he did not, then he was more than a failure; he was an active evil—a piece of treachery perpetrated against the Land in defiance of his own love or volition—worse than Covenant, for Covenant at least tried to avoid the lie of being trusted. But he, Hile Troy, had deliberately sought trust, responsibility, command—

No, that thought was intolerable. He had to win, had to win.

When he had passed the crest of the south hill, he slowed Mehryl to a better traveling pace, and allowed Lord Mhoram and the remaining eighteen Bloodguard to catch up with him. Then he said through his teeth, biting down on his voice to avoid accusing Mhoram, "Why is she taking him? He raped Trell's daughter."

Mhoram responded gently, "Warmark Troy, my friend, you must understand that the High Lord has little choice. The way of her duty is narrow, and beset with perils. She must seek out the Seventh Ward. And she must take ur-Lord Covenant with her—because of the white gold. With the Staff of Law, she must ensure that his ring does not fall into Lord Foul's hands. And if he turns against the Land, she must be near him —to fight him."

Troy nodded to himself. That was reasoning he could comprehend. Abruptly, he shook himself, forced down his instinctive protest. With an effort, he unclenched his teeth, and sighed, "I'll tell you something, Mhoram. When I'm done with this war—when I can look back and tell myself that poor Atiaran is satisfied —I'm going to take a vacation for a few years. I'm going to sit down in Andelain and not move a muscle until I get to see the Celebration of Spring. Otherwise I'm never going to be able to forgive that damn Covenant for being luckier than I am." But he meant *luckier* in another way. Though he realized now that no other choice was possible, he ached to think that Elena had chosen Covenant, not him.

If Mhoram understood him, however, the Lord tactfully followed what he had said rather than what he meant. "Ah, if we are victorious"—Mhoram was smiling, but his tone was serious—"you will not be alone. Half the Land will be in Andelain when next the dark of the moon falls on the middle night of spring. Few who yet live have seen the Dance of the Wraiths of Andelain."

"Well, I'm going to get there first," Troy muttered, trying to sustain this conversation. But then he could not keep himself from reverting to the subject of the Unbeliever. "Mhoram, don't you resent him? After what he's done?"

Evenly and openly, Lord Mhoram said, "I have no special virtue to make me resent him. One must have strength in order to judge the weakness of others. I am not so mighty."

This answer surprised Troy. For a moment, he stared at Mhoram, asking silently, Is that true? Do you believe that? But he could see that Mhoram did believe it. Baffled, Troy turned away.

Surrounded by the Bloodguard, he and Lord Mhoram followed a curve through the hills that took them generally east-southeast to intercept the Warward.

As the day passed, Troy was able to turn his thoughts more and more toward his marching army. Questions began to crowd his mind. Were the villages along the march able to provide enough food for the warriors? Was First Haft Amorine able to keep up the pace? Such concerns enabled him to put aside his foreboding, his aching sense of loss. He became another man—less the blind uncertain stranger to the Land, and more the Warmark of the Warward of Lord's Keep.

The change steadied him. He felt more comfortable with this aspect of himself.

He wanted to hurry, but he resisted the temptation because he wanted to make this part of the journey as easy as possible for the Ranyhyn. Still, by the end of that day, the eighth since he had left Revelstone, he, Lord Mhoram, and the Bloodguard had left behind the reblooming health of Trothgard. Even at a pace which covered no more than seventeen leagues in a day, the land through which they rode changed rapidly. East and southeast of them was the more austere

country of the Center Plains. In this wide region the
stern rock of the Earth seemed closer to the surface
of the soil than in Trothgard. The Plains supported
life without encouraging it, sustained people who were
tough, hardy.

Most of the men and women who made up the Warward came from the villages of the Center Plains. This
was traditionally true—and for good reason. In all the
great wars of the Land, the Despiser's armies had
struck through the Center Plains to approach Revelstone. Thus these Plains bore much of the brunt of
Lord Foul's malice. The people of the Plains remembered this, and sent their sons and daughters to the
Loresraat to be trained in the skills of the Sword.

As he made camp that night, Troy was intensely
conscious of how personally his warriors depended on
him. Their homes and families were at the mercy of his
success or failure. At his command they were enduring
the slow hell of this forced march.

And he knew that the war would begin within the
next day. By that time, the vanguard of Lord Foul's
army would reach the western end of the Mithil valley,
and would encounter Hiltmark Quaan and the Lords
Callindrill and Verement. He was sure of it; no later
than the evening of the ninth day. Then men and
women would begin to die—his warriors. Bloodguard
would begin to die. He wanted to be with them, wanted
to keep them alive, but he could not. And the march to
Doom's Retreat would go on and on and on, grinding
down the Warward like the millstone of an unanswerable need. Soon Troy stretched himself out in his
blankets and pressed his face against the earth as if
that were the only way he could keep his balance.

He spent most of the night reviewing every facet of
his battle plan, trying to assure himself that he had not
made any mistakes.

The next morning, he felt full of urgency, and he
found that whenever he forgot himself he began to
hurry Mehryl's pace. So he turned to Mhoram and
asked the Lord to talk to him, distract him.

In response, the Lord slowly dropped into a musing,
half-singing tone, and began to tell Troy about the

various legended or potent parts of the Land which lay between them and Doom's Retreat. In particular, he narrated some of the old tales about the One Forest, the mighty wood which had covered the Land in an age that was ancient before Berek Halfhand's time, with its Forestals and its fierce foes, the Ravers. During the centuries when the trees were still awake, he said, the Forestals had cherished their consciousness and guided their defenses against *turiya, moksha,* and *samadhi.* But now, if the old tales spoke truly, no active remnant or vestige of the One Forest and the Forestals remained in the Land, except the grim woods of Garroting Deep and Caerroil Wildwood. And none who entered Garroting Deep, for good or ill, ever returned.

This dark forest lay near the line of the Warward's march, beyond the Last Hills.

Then Troy talked for a while about himself and his reactions to the Land. He felt close to Mhoram, and this enabled him to discuss the way High Lord Elena personified his sense of the Land. Gradually, he relaxed, regained his ability to say to himself, It doesn't matter who summoned me. I am who I am. I'm going to do it.

So he was not just surprised when he and Mhoram caught up with the struggling march of the warriors by midafternoon. He was shocked.

The Warward was almost half a day's march behind schedule.

The warriors met him with a halting cheer that stumbled into silence as they realized that the High Lord was not with him. But Troy ignored them. Riding straight up to First Haft Amorine, he barked, "You're slow! Speed up the beat! At this rate, we're going to be exactly one and a half days too late!"

The welcome on Amorine's face fell into chagrin, and she whirled away at once toward the drummers. With a wide, sighing groan of pain, the warriors stepped up their pace, hurried to the demand of the drums until they were half running. Then Warmark Troy rode up and down beside their ranks like a flail, enforcing the new rhythm with his angry presence.

When he found one Eoward lagging slightly, he shouted into the young drummer's face, "By God! I'm not going to lose this war because of you!" He clapped his beat by the shamed Warhaft's ear until the drummer copied it exactly.

Only after his dismay had subsided did he observe what nine days of hard marching had done to the Warward. Then he wished that he could recant his harshness. The warriors were suffering severely. Almost all of them limped in some way, pushed themselves unevenly against the nagging pain of cuts and torn muscles and bone bruises. Many were so tired that they had stopped sweating, and the overheated flush of their faces was caked with dust, giving them a yellow and demented look. More than a few bled at the shoulders from sores worn by the friction of their pack straps. Despite their doggedness, they marched raggedly, as if they could hardly remember the ranked order which had been trained into them ninety leagues ago at Revelstone.

And they were behind schedule. They were still one hundred eighty leagues away from Doom's Retreat.

By the time they lurched and gasped their way into camp for the night, Troy was almost frantic for some way to save them. He sensed that bare determination would not be enough.

As soon as the accompanying Hirebrands and Gravelingases had started their campfires, Lord Mhoram went to do what he could for the Warward. He moved from Eoward to Eoward, helping the cooks. In each stewpot, his blue fire worked some effect on the food, enhanced it, increased its health and vitality. And when the meal was done, he walked through all the Warward, spreading the balm of his presence— talking to the warriors, helping them with their bruises and bandages, jesting with any who could muster the strength to laugh.

While the Lord did this, Troy met with his officers, the Hafts and Warhafts. After he had explained High Lord Elena's absence, he turned to the problem of the march. Painfully, he reviewed the circumstances which made this ordeal so imperative, so irretrievably necessary. Then he addressed himself to specific details. He organized a rotation schedule for the leather water jugs, so that they would be passed continuously through the ranks for the sake of the overheated warriors. He made arrangements for the packs of the men and women with bleeding shoulders to be carried by the horses. He ordered all the mounted officers except the drummers to ride double, so that the most exhausted warriors could rest on horseback; and he told these officers to gather *aliantha* for the marchers as they rode. He assigned all scouting and water duties to the Bloodguard, thus freeing more horses to help the warriors. Then he sent the Hafts and Warhafts back to their commands.

When they were gone, First Haft Amorine came over to speak with him. Her blunt, dour face was charged with some grim statement, and he forestalled her quickly. "No, Amorine," he said, "I am not going to put someone else in your place." She tried to protest, and he hurried on more gently, "I know I've made it sound as if I blame you because we're behind schedule. But that's just because I really blame myself. You're the only one for this job. The Warward respects you—just as it respects Quaan. The warriors trust your experience and honesty." Glumly, he concluded, "After all this, I'm not so sure how they feel about me."

At once, her self-doubt vanished. "You are the Warmark. Who has dared to question you?" Her tone implied that anyone who wanted to challenge him would have to deal with her first.

Her loyalty touched him. He was not entirely sure that he deserved it. But he intended to deserve it. Swallowing down his emotion, he replied, "No one is going to question me as long as we keep up the pace. And we are going to keep it up." To himself, he added, I promised Quaan. "We're going to gain back the time we've lost—and we're going to do it here, in the Center Plains. The terrain gets worse south of the Black River."

The First Haft nodded as if she believed him.

After she had left him, he went to his blankets, and

spent the night battering the private darkness of his brain in search of some alternative to his dilemma. But he could conceive nothing to eliminate the need for this forced march. When he slept, he dreamed of warriors shambling into the south as if it were an open grave.

The next morning, when the ranks of the Warward stirred, tensed weakly, lumbered into motion like a long dark groan across the Plains, Warmark Hile Troy marched with them. Eschewing his Ranyhyn, he started the beat of the drums, verified it, and moved to it himself. As he marched, he worked his way up and down among the Eoward, visiting every Eoman, encouraging every Warhaft by name, surprising the warriors out of their numb fatigue with his presence and concern—striving in spite of his own untrained physical condition to set an example that would be of some help to his army. At the end of one day in the ranks, he was so weary that he barely reached the small camp he shared with Lord Mhoram and First Haft Amorine before he mumbled something about dying and pitched into sleep. But the next day he hauled himself up and repeated his performance, hiding his pain behind the commiseration which he carried in one way or another to the warriors of the Warward.

He marched with his army for four days across the Center Plains. After each day at his cruel pace, he felt that he had passed his limit—that the whole forced march was impossible, and he must give it up. But each night Lord Mhoram helped cook the army's food, and then went among the warriors, sharing his courage with them. And twice during those four days the Warward came upon Bloodguard tending large caches of food—supplies prepared by the villagers of the Center Plains. Fresh and abundant food had a surprising efficacy; it restored the fortitude of warriors who no longer believed in their ability to drive themselves forward. At the end of his fourth day on foot—the thirteenth day of the march—Troy finally allowed himself to think that the condition of the Warward had stabilized.

He had walked more than forty leagues.

Fearing to do anything which might damage his army's fragile balance, he planned to continue his own march. Both Mhoram and Amorine urged him to stop—they were concerned about his exhaustion, about his bleeding feet and unsteady gait—but he shrugged their arguments aside. In his heart, he was ashamed to ride when his warriors were suffering afoot.

But the next morning he tasted a worse shame. When the light of dawn woke him, he struggled out of his blankets to find Amorine standing before him. In a grim voice, she reported that the Warward had been attacked during the night.

Sometime after midnight, the Bloodguard scouts had reported that the tethered horses were being stalked by a pack of *kresh*. At once, the alarm spread throughout the camp, but only the mounted Hafts and Warhafts had been able to answer it swiftly. With the Bloodguard, they rushed to the defense of the horses.

They found themselves confronting a huge pack of the great yellow wolves—at least tenscore *kresh*. The Bloodguard on their Ranyhyn met the first brunt of the attack, but they were outnumbered ten to one. And the officers behind them were on foot. The scent of the *kresh* had panicked the horses, so that they could not be mounted, or herded out of danger. One Ranyhyn, five horses, and nearly a dozen Hafts and Warhafts were slain before Amorine and Lord Mhoram were able to mobilize their defense effectively enough to drive back the wolves.

And before the *kresh* were repelled, a score or more of them broke past the officers and charged into a part of the camp where some of the warriors, stunned by exhaustion, were still asleep. Ten of those men and women lay dead or maimed in their blankets after the Bloodguard and Mhoram had destroyed the wolves.

Hearing this, Troy became livid. Brandishing his fists in anger and frustration, he demanded, "Why didn't you wake me?"

Without meeting his gaze, the First Haft said, "I

spoke to you, shook you, shouted in your ear. But I could not rouse you. The need was urgent, so I went to meet it."

After that, Troy did no more marching. He did not intend to be betrayed by his weakness again. Astride Mehryl, he rode with Ruel along the track of the *kresh;* and when he had assured himself that the wolves were not part of a concerted army, he returned to take his place at the head of the Warward. From time to time, he cantered around his army as if he were prepared to defend it single-handed.

The *kresh* attacked again that night, and again the next night. But both times, Warmark Troy was ready for them. Though he was blind in the darkness, unable to fight, he studied the terrain and chose his camp-sites carefully before dusk. He made provision for the protection of the horses, planned his defenses. Then he set ambushes of Bloodguard, archers, fire. Many *kresh* were killed, but his Warward suffered no more losses.

After that third assault, the wolves left him alone. But then he had other things to worry about. During the morning of the march's sixteenth day, a wall of black clouds moved out of the east toward the warriors. Before noon, gusts of wind reached them, ruffling their hair, riling the tall grass of the Plains. The wind stiffened as the outer edges of the storm drew nearer. Soon rain began to flick at them out of the darkening sky.

The intense blackness of the clouds promised a murderous downpour. It effectively blinded Troy. All the Hirebrands and Gravelingases lit their fires, to provide light to hold the Warward together against the force of the torrents. But the main body of the storm did not come that far west; it seemed to focus its center on a point somewhere in the eastern distance, and when it had taken its position it remained stationary.

The warriors marched through the outskirts of the grim weather. The ragged and tormented rain which lashed at them out of the infernal depths of the storm did not harm them much, but their spirits suf-

fered nevertheless. They all felt the ill force which
drove the blast. They did not need Troy to tell them
that it was almost certainly directed at Hiltmark
Quaan's command.

By the time the storm had dissipated itself late the
next day, Troy had lost nearly one Eoman. Somewhere in the darkness and the fear of what assailed
Quaan, almost a score of the least hardy warriors lost
their courage; amid all the slipping and struggling of
the Warward, they simply lay down in the mud and
died.

But they were only eighteen. Close to sixteen thousand men and women survived the storm and marched
on. And for the sake of the living, Warmark Troy
steeled his heart against the dead. Riding Mehryl as
if there were no limit to his courage, he led his army
southward, southward, and did not let his crippling
pace waver.

Then, three days later—the day after the full of
the moon—the Warward had to swim the Black River.

This river formed the boundary between the Center
and South Plains. It flowed northeast out of the
Westron Mountains, and joined the Mithil many
scores of leagues in the direction of Andelain. Old
legends said that when the Black River burst out
from under the great cliff of Rivenrock, the eastward
face of *Melenkurion* Skyweir, its water was as red
as pure heart's-blood. But from Rivenrock the Black
poured into the center of Garroting Deep. Before it
passed through the Last Hills into the Plains, it crossed
the foot of Gallows Howe, the ancient execution
mound of the Forestals. The water which the Warward had to cross was reddish-black, as if it were
thick with a strange silt. In all the history of the
Land, the Black River between the Last Hills and the
Mithil had never tolerated a bridge or ford; it simply
washed away every effort to make a way across it.
The warriors had no choice but to swim.

As they climbed the south bank, they looked
drained, as if some essential stamina or commitment
had been sucked from their bones by the current's
dark hunger.

Still they marched. The Warmark commanded them forward, and they marched. But now they moved like battered empty hulks, driven by a meaningless wind over the trackless sargasso of the South Plains. At times, it seemed that only the solitary fire of Troy's will kept them stumbling, trudging ahead, striving.

And in the South Plains yet another difficulty awaited them. Here the terrain became rougher. In the southwest corner of the Center Plains, only the thick curve of the Last Hills separated Garroting Deep from the Plains. But south of the Black River, these hills became mountains—a canted wedge of rugged peaks with its tip at the river, its eastern corner at the bottleneck of Doom's Retreat, and its western corner at Cravenhaw, where Garroting Deep opened into the Southron Wastes forty leagues southwest of Doom's Retreat. The line of the Warward's march took it deeper and deeper into the rough foothills skirting these mountains.

After two days of struggling with these hills, the warriors looked like reanimated dead. They were not yet lagging very far behind the pace, but clearly it was only a matter of time before they began to drop in their tracks.

As the sun began to set, covering Troy's sight with mist, the Warmark made his decision. The condition of the warriors wrung his heart; he felt his army had reached a kind of crisis. The Warward was still five days from Doom's Retreat, five terrible days. And he did not know where Quaan was. Without some knowledge of the Hiltmark's position and status, some knowledge of Lord Foul's army, Troy could not prepare for what lay ahead. And his army no longer appeared capable of any preparation.

The time had come for him to act.

Though the Warward was still a league away from the end of its scheduled march, he halted it for the night. And while the warriors shambled about the business of making camp, he called Lord Mhoram aside. In the dusk, he could hardly make out the Lord's features, but he concentrated on them with all his determination, strove to convey to Mhoram the intensity of his appeal. "Mhoram," he breathed, "there has got to be something you can do for them. Something—anything to help pull them together. Something you can do with your staff, or sing, or put in the food, something. There has got to be!"

Lord Mhoram studied the Warmark's face closely. "Perhaps," he said after a moment. "There is one aid which may have some effect against the touch of the Black River. But I have been loath to use it, for once it has been done it cannot be done again. We are yet long days from Doom's Retreat—and the need of the warriors for strength in battle will be severe. Should not this aid be kept until that time?"

"No." Troy tried to make Mhoram hear the depth of his conviction. "The time is now. They need strength now—in case they have to fight before they get to the Retreat. Or in case they have to run to get there in time. We don't know what's happening to Quaan. And after tonight you won't get another chance until after the fighting's already started."

"How so?" the Lord asked carefully.

"Because I'm leaving in the morning. I'm going to Kevin's Watch—I want to get a look at Foul's army. I have to know exactly how much time Quaan is giving us. And you're coming with me. You're the one who knows how to use that High Wood communication rod."

Mhoram appeared surprised. "Leave the Warward?" he asked quickly, softly. "Now? Is that wise?"

Troy was sure. "I've got to do it. I've been—ignorant too long. Now I've got to know. From here on we can't afford to let Foul surprise us. And I'm"—he grimaced at the fog—"I'm the only one who can see far enough to tell what Foul's doing." After a moment, he added, "That's why they call it Kevin's Watch. Even he needed to know what he was getting into."

Abruptly, the Lord passed a hand over the strain in his face, and nodded. "Very well. It will be done. Here is the aid which can be given. Each of the Gravelingases bears with him a small quantity of hurtloam. And the Hirebrands have a rare wood dust which they name *rillinlure.* I had hoped to save such aids for use in healing battle wounds. But they will be placed in the food tonight. Pray that they will suffice." Without further question, he turned away to give his instructions to the Hirebrands and Gravelingases.

Soon these men were moving throughout the camp, placing either hurtloam or *rillinlure* in each cooking pot. Each pot received only a pinch; each warrior ate only a minute quantity. But the Hirebrands and Gravelingases knew how to extract the most benefit from the wood dust and loam. With songs and invocations, they made their gift to the warriors strong and efficacious. Shortly after eating, the warriors began to fall asleep; many of them simply dropped to the ground and lost consciousness. For the first time in the long damage of the march, several of them smiled at their dreams.

When Mhoram returned to Warmark Troy after the meal, he was almost smiling himself.

Then Troy began to give First Haft Amorine her instructions for the battle of Doom's Retreat. After they had discussed food and the final stages of the march, they talked about the Retreat itself. In spite of his assurances, she viewed that place with dread. In all the wars of the Land, that was the place to which armies fled when all their hopes had been destroyed. Grim old legends spoke of the ravens which nested high in the sides of the narrow defile, above the piled scree and boulders of the edges—cawing for the flesh of the defeated.

But Troy had never doubted this part of his plan. Doom's Retreat was an ideal place for a small army to fight a large one. The enemy could be lured into the canyon and beaten in segments. "That's the beauty of it," Troy said confidently. "This is one time when we're going to turn Foul's tables on him—we're going to take a curse, and make it into a blessing. Once Quaan arrives, we'll have the upper hand. Foul may not even know we're there until it's too late for him. But even if he does, he'll still have to fight us. He can't afford to turn his back on us. All you have to do," he added, "is keep up the pace for five more days."

Amorine's blunt scowl reminded him just how impossible those five days might be. But in the morning, he felt that he had been justified. Thanks to the roborant of the *rillinlure* and hurtloam, his warriors met the call of dawn with renewed resolution in their eyes and something like strength in their limbs. When he climbed a nearby hill to speak to them, they crowded around him, and gave a cheer that made his chest tight with pride. He wanted to embrace them all.

He faced the Warward with his back to the sunrise, and when he could discern their faces through his mist, he began. "My friends," he shouted, "hear me! I'm going to go to Kevin's Watch to find out what Foul is doing, so this will probably be my last chance to talk to you before the fighting starts. And I want to give you fair warning. We've been taking it pretty easy for the past twenty-two days. But now the soft part is over. We're going to have to start earning our pay."

He risked this bleak joke apprehensively. If the warriors understood him, they might relax a bit, shed some of their pain and care, draw closer to each other. But if they heard derogation in his words, if they were affronted by his grim humor—then they were lost to him.

He felt an immense relief and gratitude when he saw that many of the warriors smiled. A few even laughed aloud. Their response made him feel suddenly and beautifully in harmony with them—in tune with his army, the instrument of his will. At once, he was confident again of his command.

Briskly, he went on, "As you know, we're only five days from Doom's Retreat. We have almost exactly forty-eight leagues left to go. After what you've already done, you should be able to do this in your sleep. But still there are a few things I want to say about it.

"First, you should know that you've already accomplished more than any other army in the history of the Land. No other Warward has ever marched this far this fast. So every one of you is already a hero. I'm not bragging—facts are facts. You are already the best.

"But heroes or not, our job isn't done until we've

won. That's why we're going to Doom's Retreat. It's a perfect place for a trap—once we get there, we can handle an army five times our size. And just getting there—just pulling Foul's army south like this—we've already saved scores of Stonedowns and Woodhelvens in the Center Plains. For most of you, that means we've saved your homes."

He paused, hoping to let his own confidence reach into the hearts of the warriors. Then he said, "But we have got to get to the Retreat in time. That is where Hiltmark Quaan expects to find us. He and his Eoward are fighting like hell to give us these five more days. If we don't reach the Retreat before they do, they will all die.

"It's going to be close. But I can tell you for a fact that the Hiltmark has already bought three of those five days for us. You all saw that storm six days ago. You know what it was—an attack on the Hiltmark's Eoward. That means that six days ago he was still holding Foul's army in the Mithil valley. And you know Hiltmark Quaan. You know he won't let a mere two days get between us and victory.

"It is going to be close. We're not going to get much rest. But once we're in the Retreat, I'm not afraid of the outcome."

At this, the Hafts raised a cheer to answer Troy's bravado, and he stood silently in the ovation with his head bowed, accepting it only because the courage in the shout, the courage of his army, overwhelmed him. When the cheering subsided, and the Warward became silent again, he said thickly into the stillness, "My friends, I'm proud of you all."

Then he turned and almost ran from the hill.

Lord Mhoram followed him as he sprang onto Mehryl's back. Accompanied by Ruel, Terrel, and eight other Bloodguard, the two men galloped away from the Warward. Troy set a hard pace until his army was out of sight in the hills behind him. Then he eased Mehryl back to a gait which would cover the distance to Mithil Stonedown and the base of Kevin's Watch in three days. With Mhoram at his side, he cantered eastward over the rumpled Plains.

After a time, the Lord said quietly, "Warmark Troy, you have moved them."

"You've got it backward," replied Troy in a voice gruff with emotion. "They did it to me."

"No, my friend. They have become very loyal to you."

"They're loyal people. They—all right, yes, I know what you mean. They're loyal to me. If I ever let them down—if I even make any normal human mistakes— they're going to feel betrayed. I know. I've focused too much of their courage and hope on myself, on my plans. But if it gets them to Doom's Retreat in time, the risk'll be worth it."

Lord Mhoram assented with a nod. After a pause, he said, "But you have done your part. My friend, I must tell you this. When I first understood your intention to march toward Doom's Retreat at such a pace, I felt the task to be impossible."

"Then why did you let me do it?" flared Troy. "Why wait until now to say anything?"

"Ah, Warmark," returned the Lord, "everything that passes unattempted is impossible."

At this, Troy turned on Mhoram. But when he met the Lord's probing gaze, he realized that Mhoram would not have raised such a question gratuitously. Forcing himself to relax, he said, "You don't actually expect me to be satisfied with an answer like that."

"No," the Lord replied simply. "I speak only to express my appreciation for what you have done. I trust you. I will follow your lead in this war into any peril."

Abruptly, a rush of gratitude filled Troy's throat, and he had to clench his teeth to keep from grinning foolishly. To meet Mhoram's trust, he whispered, "I won't let you down."

But later, when his emotion had receded, he was disconcerted to remember how many such promises he had made. They seemed to expand with every new development in the march. His speech to the Warward was only one in a series of assertions. Now he felt that he had given his personal guarantee of success to practically the entire Land. He had maneuvered himself into a corner—a place where defeat and betrayal became the same thing.

The simple thought of failure made his pulse labor vertiginously in his head.

If this was the kind of thinking that inspired Covenant's Unbelief, then Troy could see that it made a certain kind of sense. But he had a savage name for it; he called it *cowardice*. He forced the thought down, and turned his attention to the South Plains.

Away from the mountains, the terrain leveled somewhat, and opened into broad stretches of sharp, hardy grass mottled with swaths of gray bracken and heather turning purple in the autumn. It was not a generous land—Troy had been told that there were only five Stonedowns in all the South Plains—but its unprofligate health was vital and strong, like the squat, muscular people who lived with it. Something in its austerity appealed to him, as if the ground itself were appropriate for war. He rode it steadily, keeping a brisk pace while conserving Mehryl's strength for the hard run from Kevin's Watch to Doom's Retreat.

But the second night, his confidence suffered a setback. Soon after moonrise, Lord Mhoram sprang suddenly awake, screaming so vehemently that Troy's blood ran cold. Troy groped toward him through the darkness, but he struck the Warmark down with his staff, and started firing fierce blasts of power into the invulnerable heavens as if they were attacking him. A madness gripped him. He did not stop until Terrel caught his arms, shouted into his face, "Lord! Corruption will see you!"

With an immense effort, Mhoram mastered himself, silenced his power.

Then Troy could see nothing. He had to wait in blind suspense until at last he heard Mhoram breathe, "It is past. I thank you, Terrel." The Lord sounded utterly weary.

Troy thronged with questions, but Mhoram either would not or could not answer them. The force of his vision left him dumb and quivering. He could barely compel his lips to form the few words he spoke to reassure Troy.

The Warmark was not convinced. He demanded a light. But when Ruel built up the campfire, Troy saw the garish heat of torment and danger in Mhoram's eyes. It stilled him, denied his offer of support or consolation. He was forced to leave the Lord alone in his cruel, oracular pain.

For the rest of the night, Troy lay awake, waiting anxiously. But when dawn came and his sight returned, he perceived that Mhoram had weathered the crisis. The fever in his gaze had been replaced by a hard gleam like a warning that it was perilous to challenge him—a gleam that reminded Troy of that picture in the Hall of Gifts entitled "Lord Mhoram's Victory."

The Lord offered no explanation. In silence they rode away into the third day.

On the horizon ahead, Troy could make out the thin, black finger of Kevin's Watch, though the valley of Mithil Stonedown was still twenty-two leagues distant. After the strain of the night, he was under even more pressure than before to climb the Watch and see Lord Foul's army. In that sight he would find the fate of his battle plan. But he did not drive the Ranyhyn beyond their best traveling gait. So the valley was already full of evening shadows when he and Mhoram reached the Mithil River, and followed it upstream into the Southron Range.

Through his personal haze, he caught only one glimpse of Mithil Stonedown. From the top of a heavy stone bridge across the river, he looked southward along the east bank, and dimly made out a dark, round cluster of stone huts. Then the last penetration of his sight faded, and he had to ride into the village on trust.

When Troy and his companions had dismounted within the round, open center of the Stonedown, Lord Mhoram spoke quietly to the people who came out to greet him. Soon the Stonedownors were joined by a group of five, bearing with them a wide bowl of graveling. They placed it on a dais in the center of the circle, where its warm glow and fresh loamy smell spread all around them. The light enabled Troy to see dimly.

The group of five included three women and two men. Four of them were white-haired, aged, and dignified, but one man appeared just past middle age. His thick dark hair was streaked with gray, and over his short, powerful frame he wore a traditional brown Stonedownor tunic, with a curious pattern resembling crossed lightning on his shoulders. He had a permanently twisted bitter expression, as if something had broken in him early in life, turning all the tastes of his experience sour. But despite his bitterness and his relative youth, his companions deferred to him. He spoke first.

"Hail, Mhoram son of Variol, Lord of the Council of Revelstone. Hail, Warmark Hile Troy. Be welcome in Mithil Stonedown. I am Triock son of Thuler, first among the Circle of elders of Mithil Stonedown. It is not our custom to question our guests before hospitality has cleansed the weariness of their way. But these are perilous times. A Bloodguard brought us tidings of war. What need calls you here?"

"Triock, your welcome honors us," replied Lord Mhoram. "And we are honored that you know us. We have not met."

"That is true, Lord. But I studied for a time in the Loresraat. The Lords, and the friends of the Lords"—he nodded to Troy—"were made known to me."

"Then, Triock, elders and people of Mithil Stonedown, I must tell you that there is indeed war upon the Land. The army of the Gray Slayer marches in the South Plains, to do battle with the Warward of Revelstone at Doom's Retreat. We have come so that Warmark Troy may climb Kevin's Watch, and study the movements of the foe."

"He must have brave sight, if he can see so far— though it is said that High Lord Kevin viewed all the Land from his Watch. But that is not our concern. Please accept the welcome of Mithil Stonedown. How may we serve you?"

Smiling, Mhoram answered, "A hot meal would be

a rich welcome. We have eaten camp food for many days."

At this, another of the elders stepped forward. "Lord Mhoram, I am Terass Slen-mate. Our home is large, and Slen my husband is proud of his cooking. Will you eat with us?"

"Gladly, Terass Slen-mate. You honor us."

"Accepting a gift honors the giver," she returned gravely. Accompanied by the other elders, she led Mhoram and Troy out of the center of the Stonedown. Her home was a wide, flat building which had been formed out of one prodigious boulder. Within, it was bright with graveling. After several ceremonious introductions, Troy and Lord Mhoram found themselves seated at a long stone table. The meal that Slen set before them did full justice to his pride.

When all the guests had eaten their fill, and the stoneware dishes and pots had been cleared away, Lord Mhoram offered to answer the questions of the elders. Terass began by asking generally about the war, but before she had gone far Triock interrupted her.

"Lord, what of High Lord Elena? Is she well? Does she fight in this war?"

Something abrupt in Triock's tone irritated Troy, but he left the answers to Mhoram. The Lord replied, "The High Lord is well. She has uncovered knowledge of one of the hidden Wards of Kevin's Lore, and has gone in quest of the Ward itself." He sounded cautious, as if he had some reason to distrust Triock.

"And what of Thomas Covenant the Unbeliever? The Bloodguard said that he has returned to the Land."

"He has returned."

"Ah, yes," said Triock. He seemed aware of Mhoram's caution. "And what of Trell Atiaran-mate? For many years he was the Gravelingas of Mithil Stonedown. How does he meet the need of this war?"

"He is in Revelstone, where his skills serve the defense of the Keep."

At once, Triock's attitude changed. "Trell is not with the High Lord?" he demanded sharply.

"No."

"Why not?"

For a moment, Lord Mhoram searched Triock's face. Then he said as if he were taking a risk, "Ur-Lord Thomas Covenant, Unbeliever and Ringthane, rides with the High Lord."

"With her?" Triock cried, springing to his feet. "Trell permitted this?" He glared bitterly at Mhoram, then spun away and flung out of the house.

His vehemence left an awkward silence in the room, and Terass spoke quietly to ease it. "Please do not be offended, Lord. His life is full of trouble. It may be that you know part of his tale."

Mhoram nodded, assured Terass that he was not offended. But Triock's conduct disturbed Warmark Troy; it reminded him vividly of Trell. "I don't know," he said bluntly. "What business is the High Lord of his?"

"Ah, Warmark," Terass said sadly, "he would not thank me for speaking of it. I—"

A sharp glance from Mhoram silenced her. Troy turned toward Mhoram, but the Lord did not meet his gaze. "Before ur-Lord Covenant's first summoning to the Land," Mhoram said carefully, "Triock was in love with the daughter of Trell and Atiaran."

Troy barely restrained an ejaculation. He wanted to curse Covenant; there seemed to be no end to the damage Covenant had done. But he held himself back for the sake of his hosts. He scarcely heard Mhoram ask, "Is Trell's daughter well? Is there any way in which I may help her?"

"No, Lord," sighed Terass. "The health of her body is strong, but her mind is unsteady. Always she has believed that the Unbeliever will come for her. She has asked the Circle of elders—asked permission to marry him. We can find no Healer able to touch this illness. I fear you would only turn her thoughts more toward him."

Mhoram accepted her judgment morosely. "I am sorry. This failure grieves me. But the Lords know only of one Unfettered Healer with power for such needs—and she left her home, and passed out of knowledge forty years ago, before the battle of Soaring Woodhelven. It humbles us to be of so little use for such needs."

His words left behind a pall of silence in their wake. For a time like a muffled sigh, he stared at his clasped hands. But then, rousing himself from his reverie, he said, "Elders, how will you meet the chance of war? Have you prepared?"

"Yes, Lord," one of the other women replied. "We have little cause to fear the destruction of our homes, so we will hide in the mountains if war comes. We have prepared food stores against that need. From the mountains, we will harass any who assail Mithil Stonedown."

Mhoram nodded, and after a moment Terass said, "Lord, Warmark, will you spend the night with us? We will be honored to provide beds for you. And perhaps you will be able to speak to the gathering of the people?"

"No," said Troy abruptly. Then, hearing his discourtesy, he softened his tone. "Thank you, but no. I need to get up to the Watch—as soon as possible."

"What will you see? The night is dark. You may sleep in comfort here, and still climb to Kevin's Watch before morning."

But Troy was adamant. His anger at Covenant only increased his impatience; he had a strong sense of pressure, of impending crisis. Lord Mhoram's polite, firm support soon satisfied the Stonedownors that this decision was necessary, and in a short time he and Troy were on their way. They accepted a pot of graveling from the elders to light their path, left all the Bloodguard except Terrel and Ruel to care for the Ranyhyn and watch over the valley, then started walking briskly along the Mithil into the night.

Troy could see nothing outside the primary glow of the graveling, but when he was sure he was out of earshot of the Stonedown, he said to Mhoram, "You knew about Triock before tonight. Why didn't you tell me?"

"I did not know the extent of his distress. Why should I burden you? Yet now it is in my heart that I have treated him wrongly. I should have dealt with him openly, and trusted him to bear my words. My caution has only increased his pain."

Troy took a different view. "You wouldn't need to be cautious at all if it weren't for that damned Covenant."

But Mhoram only walked on up the valley in silence.

Together they worked their way south into the foothills of the surrounding mountains, then doubled back northward, up the eastern slopes. On the mountainside, the trail was difficult. Terrel led Lord Mhoram, and Troy followed them with Ruel at his back. As he ascended the path, he could see nothing of his situation—for him, the glow of the graveling was encased in dark fog—but slowly he began to feel a change in the air. The warm autumn night of the South Plains turned cooler, rarer; it made his heart pound. By the time he had climbed a couple thousand feet, he knew that he was moving into mountains which had already received their first winter snows.

Soon after that, he and his companions left the open mountainside and began to work upward through rifts and crevices and hidden valleys. When they reached open space again, they were on a ledge in a cliff face, moving eastward under the huge loom of a peak. This ledge took them to the base of the long, leaning, stone shaft of the Watch. Then, clambering through empty air like solitary dream figures, they went up the exposed stair of the shaft. After another five hundred feet, they found themselves on the parapeted platform of Kevin's Watch.

Troy moved cautiously over the floor of the Watch and seated himself with his back against the surrounding parapet. He knew from descriptions that he was on the tip of the shaft, poised four thousand feet directly above the foothills of a promontory in the Range, and he did not want to give his blindness a chance to betray him. Even sitting with solid stone between his back and the fall, he had an intense impression of abysses. His sense of ambience felt poignantly the absence of any comforting confines or enclosures or limits. This was like being cast adrift in the trackless heavens, and he reacted to it like a blind man—with fear, and a conviction of irremediable isolation. He placed the pot of graveling on the stone before him, so that he could at least vaguely see his three companions. Then he braced both arms against the stone beside him as if to keep himself from falling.

A slight breeze drifted onto the Watch from the towering mountain face south of it, and the air carried a foretaste of winter that made Troy shiver. As midnight passed through the darkness, he began to talk desultorily, as if to warm the vigil by the sound of his voice. His present sense of suspension, of voids, reminded him of his last moments in that world which Covenant insisted on calling "real"—moments during which his apartment had been flame-gutted, forcing him to hang by failing fingers from his windowsill, with the long fall and smash on concrete hovering below him.

He talked erratically about that world until the vividness of the memory eased. Then he said, "Friend Mhoram, remind me—remind me to tell you sometime how grateful I am—for everything." He was embarrassed to say such things aloud, but these feelings were too important to be left unexpressed. "You and Elena and Quaan and Amorine—you're all incredibly precious to me. And the Warward— I think I'd be willing to jump from here if the Warward needed it."

He fell silent again, and time passed. Although he shivered in the chill breeze, his speech had steadied him. He tried to turn his thought to the fighting ahead, but the unknown sight crouched in the coming day dominated his brain, confusing all his anticipations and plans. And around him the blank night remained unchanged, as impenetrable as chaos. He needed to know where he stood. In the distance, he thought he heard dim hoofbeats. But none of his companions reacted to them; he could not be sure he had heard anything.

He needed to distract himself. Half to Mhoram, he growled, "I hate dawns. I can cope with nights. They keep me—they're something I've had experience with, at least. But dawns! I can't stand waiting for what I'm going to see." Then, abruptly, he asked, "Is the sky clear?"

"It is clear," Mhoram said softly.

Troy sighed his relief. For a moment, he was able to relax.

Silence encompassed the Watch again. The waiting went on. Gradually, Troy's shivering became worse. The stone he leaned against remained cold, impervious to his body warmth. He wanted to stand up and pace, but did not dare. Around him, Mhoram, Ruel, and Terrel stood as still as statues. After a while, he could no longer refrain from asking the Lord if he had received any messages from Elena. "Has she tried to contact you? How is she doing?"

"No, Warmark," Mhoram answered. "The High Lord does not bear with her any of the *lomillialor* rods."

"No?" The news dismayed Troy. Until this moment, he had not realized how much trust he had put in Mhoram's power to contact Elena. He wanted to know that she was safe. And as a last resort, he had counted on being able to summon her. But now she was as completely lost to him as if she were already dead. "No?" He felt suddenly so blind that he could not see Mhoram's face, that he had never really seen Mhoram's face. "Why?"

"The High Wood rods were only three. One went to Lord's Keep, and one stayed in Revelwood, so that the Loresraat and Revelstone could act together to defend themselves. One rod remained. It was given into my hands for use in this war."

Troy's voice crackled with protest. "What good is that?"

"At need I will be able to speak to Revelwood and Lord's Keep."

"Oh, you fool." Troy did not know whether he was referring to Mhoram or himself. So many things had been kept from him. And yet he had never thought to ask who had the rods. He had been saving that whole subject until he saw Lord Foul's army, knew what help he would need. "Why didn't you tell me?"

For answer, Mhoram only gazed at him. But through his haze, Troy could not read the Lord's expression. "Why didn't you tell me?" he repeated more bitterly. "How much else is there that you haven't told me?"

Mhoram sighed. "As to the *lomillialor*—I did not speak because you did not ask. The rods are not a tool that you could use. They were made for the Lords, and we used them as we saw fit. It did not occur to us that your desires would be otherwise."

He sounded withdrawn, weary. For the first time, Troy noticed how unresponsive the Lord had been all day. A fit of shivering shook him. That dream Mhoram had had last night—what did it mean? What did the Lord know that made him so unlike his usual self? Troy felt a sudden foretaste of dread. "Mhoram," he began, "Mhoram—"

"Peace, Warmark," the Lord breathed. "Someone comes."

At once, Troy heaved to his feet, and caught at Ruel's shoulder to anchor himself. Though he strained his ears, he could hear nothing but the low breeze. "Who is it?"

For a moment, no one answered. When Ruel spoke, his voice sounded as distant and passionless as the darkness. "It is Tull, who shared the mission of Korik to the Giants of Seareach."

SEVENTEEN: Tull's Tale

TROY's heart lurched, and began to labor heavily. Tull! He could feel his pulse beating in his temples. Korik's mission! After the shock of Runnik's news, he had repressed all thought of the Giants, refused to let himself think of them. He had concentrated on the war, concentrated on something he could do something about. But now his thoughts reeled. The Giants!

Almost instantly he began to calculate. He had been away from Revelstone for twenty-five days. The mission to Seareach had left eighteen days before that. That was almost enough time, almost enough. The Giants could not travel as fast as Bloodguard on Ranyhyn—but surely they would not be far behind. Surely—

Troy could understand how Tull had come here. It made sense. The other Bloodguard would be leading the Giants, and Tull had come ahead to tell the Warward that help was on the way. With war on the Land and Lord Foul marching, the Giants would not go to Revelstone, would not go north at all. They would go south, around Sarangrave Flat if not through it. The Bloodguard knew Troy's battle plan; they would know what to do. They would pick up the trail of Lord Foul's army above Landsdrop south of Mount Thunder, and would follow it—past Morinmoss, through the Mithil valley, then southwest toward Doom's Retreat. They would be hoping to attack Lord Foul's rear during the battle of the Retreat. And Tull, seeking to circumvent Lord Foul's army in search of the Warward, would naturally come south to skirt the Southron Range toward Doom's Retreat. That route would bring him almost to the doorstep of Mithil Stonedown. Surely—!

When Tull topped the stair and stepped onto the Watch, Troy was so eager that he jumped past all preliminary questions. "Where are they?" The words came so rapidly that he could hardly articulate them. "How far behind are they?"

In the dim light of the graveling, he was unable to make out Tull's face. But he could tell that the Bloodguard was not looking at him. "Lord," Tull said, "I was charged by Korik to give my tidings to the High Lord. With Shull and Vale I was charged—" For an instant, his flat voice faltered. "But the Bloodguard in the Stonedown have told me that the High Lord has gone into the Westron Mountains with Amok. I must give my tidings to you. Will you hear?"

Even through his excitement, Troy sensed something strange in Tull's tone, something that sounded like pain. But he could not wait to hear it explained. Before Lord Mhoram could reply, Troy repeated, "Where are they?"

"They?" said the Bloodguard.

"The Giants! How far behind are they?"

Tull turned deliberately away from him to face Lord Mhoram.

"We will hear you," Mhoram said. His voice was tense with dread, but he spoke steadily, without hesitation. "This war is in our hands. Speak, Bloodguard."

"Lord, they—we could not—the Giants—" Suddenly the habitual flatness of Tull's voice was gone. "Lord!" The word vibrated with a grief so keen that the Bloodguard could not master it.

The sound of it stunned Troy. He was accustomed to the characteristic alien lack of inflection of all the Bloodguard. He had long since stopped expecting them to express what they felt—had virtually forgotten that they even had emotions. And he was not braced for grief; his anticipation of good news was so great that he could already taste it.

Instantly, before either he or Lord Mhoram could say anything, react at all, Terrel moved toward Tull. Swinging so swiftly that Troy hardly saw the blow, he struck Tull across the face. The hit resounded heavily in the empty air.

At once, Tull stiffened, came to attention. "Lord," he began again, and now his voice was as expressionless as the night, "with Shull and Vale I was charged to bear tidings to the High Lord. Before the dawn of the twenty-fourth day of the mission—the dawn after the dark of the moon—we left *Coercri* and came south, as Korik charged us, seeking to find the High Lord in battle at Doom's Retreat. But because of the evil which is awake, we were compelled to journey on foot around the Sarangrave, and so twelve days were gone. We came too near to the Shattered Hills, and so Vale and Shull fell to the scouts and defenders of Corruption. But I endured. Borne by the Ranyhyn, I fled to Landsdrop and the Upper Land, following

Corruption's army. Striving to pass around it, I rode
through the hills to the Southron Range, and so came
within hail of Mithil Stonedown—eight days in which
the Ranyhyn has run without rest.

"Lord—" Again he faltered, but at once he con-
trolled himself. "I must tell you of the mission to
Seareach, and of the ill doom which has befallen
The Grieve."

"I hear you," Mhoram said painfully. "But forgive
me—I must sit." Like an old man, he lowered himself down his staff to rest with his back against the
wall of the parapet. "I lack the strength to stand for
such tidings."

Tull seated himself opposite the Lord across the
graveling pot, and Troy sat down also, as if Tull's
movement compelled him. The vestiges of his sight
were locked on the Bloodguard.

After a moment, Mhoram said, "Runnik came to
us in Trothgard. He spoke of Hoerkin and Lord
Shetra, and of the lurker of the Sarangrave. There is
no need to speak of such things again."

"Very well." Tull faced the Lord, but his visage
was shrouded in darkness. Troy could not see his
eyes; he appeared to have no eyes, no mouth, no
features. When he began his tale, his voice seemed
to be the voice of the blind night.

But he told his tale clearly and coherently, as if he
had rehearsed it many times during his journey from
Seareach. And as he spoke, Troy was reminded that
he was the youngest of the Bloodguard—a *Haruchai*
no older than Troy himself. Tull had come to Revelstone to replace one of the Bloodguard who had been
slain during Lord Mhoram's attempt to scout the
Shattered Hills. So he was still new to the Vow.
Perhaps that explained his unexpected emotion, and
his ability to tell a tale in a way that his hearers could
understand.

After the deaths of Lord Shetra and the Bloodguard
Cerrin, there was rain in Sarangrave Flat all that day.
It was cold and merciless, and it harmed the mission,
for Lord Hyrim was sickened by the river water he

had swallowed, and the rain made his sickness worse. And the Bloodguard could give him no ease—neither warmth nor shelter. In the capsizing of the raft, all the blankets had been lost. And the rank water of the Defiles Course did other damage: it spoiled all the food except that which had been kept in tight containers; it ruined the *lillianrill* rods, so that they had no more potency to burn against the rain; it even stained the clothing, so that Lord Hyrim's robe and the raiment of the Bloodguard became black.

Before the end of the day, the Lord was no longer strong enough to propel or steer the raft. Fever filled his eyes, and his lips were blue and trembling with cold. Sitting in the center of the raft, he hugged his staff as if for warmth.

During the night, he began to rant.

In a voice that bubbled through the water running down his face, he spoke to himself as to an adversary and tormentor, alternately cursing and pleading. At times he wept like a child. His delirium was cruel to him, demeaning him as if he were without use or worth. And the Bloodguard could do nothing to succor him.

But at last before dawn the rain broke, and the sky became clear. Then Korik ordered the raft over to one bank. Though it was perilous to stop thus in darkness, he sent half the Bloodguard foraging into the jungle for firewood and *aliantha*.

After Sill fed him a handful of treasure-berries, the Lord rallied enough to call up a flame from his staff. With this, Korik started a fire, built it into a steady blaze near the center of the raft. Then the steersmen pushed the raft out into the night, and the mission continued on its way.

In the course of that day, they slowly passed out of the Sarangrave. Across the leagues, the Defiles Course was now growing constantly wider and shallower, dividing into more channels as islets and mudbanks increased. These channels were treacherous—shallow, barred with mudbanks, full of rotten logs and stumps —and the effort of navigating them slowed the raft still more. And around it, the jungle gradually changed.

The vegetation of the Sarangrave gave way to different kinds of growths: tall, dark trees with limbs that spread out widely above bare trunks, hanging mosses, ferns of all kinds, bushes that clung to naked rock with thin root-fingers and seemed to drink from the river through leaves and branches. Water snakes swam out of the path of the raft. And the stench of the Course slowly faded into a smell of accumulated wet decay and stagnation.

Thus the mission entered Lifeswallower, the Great Swamp.

As they moved, Korik kept the raft in the northern passages. In this way, he was able to begin traveling northeastward—toward Seareach—and to avoid the heart of Lifeswallower.

When night came, they were fortunate that the sky was clear; in that tortuous channel, starless darkness would have halted the mission altogether.

Yet they were still in one of the less difficult regions of Lifeswallower; water still flowed over the deep mud and silt. Eastward, in the heart of the Great Swamp, the water slowly sank into the ground, creating one continuous quagmire for scores of leagues in all directions, where the mud flowed and seethed almost imperceptibly.

But in other things they were not so fortunate. The fever now raged in Lord Hyrim. Though Sill had fed him with *aliantha,* and on water boiled clean, he was failing. Already he looked thinner, and he shook as if there were a palsy in his bones.

And without him—without the power of his staff—the mission could not escape Lifeswallower. The steersmen were forced to keep the raft where the water was deepest because the mud of the Swamp sucked at their poles. If the logs touched that clinging mud, the Bloodguard would be unable to pull the raft free.

Even in the center of the channel, their progress was threatened by the peculiar trees of Lifeswallower. These trees the Giants called marshwaders. Despite their height, and the wide stretch of their limbs, their roots were not anchored in solid ground. Rather they held themselves erect in the mud, and they seemed to

move with the submerged, subtle currents of the
Swamp. Passages that looked open from a distance
were closed when the raft reached them; channels appeared which had been invisible earlier. More than
once trees moved toward each other as the raft passed
between them, as if they sought to capture it.

All these things grew worse as the days passed. The
level of the water in the channel was declining. As the
mission moved north and east, more and more of the
river was swallowed into the mire, and the raft sank
toward the mud.

The Bloodguard could find no escape. Lifeswallower
allowed them no opportunity to work their way northward to solid ground. Although they were always within half a league of the simple marsh which bordered
the Swamp, they could not reach it. They thrust the
raft along, labored tirelessly day and night, paused
only to collect *aliantha* and firewood. But they could
not escape. They needed Lord Hyrim's power—and
he was lost in delirium. His eyes were crusted as if
with dried foam, and only the treasure-berries and
boiled water which Sill forced into him kept him alive.

During the afternoon of the eighteenth day of the
mission, the logs of the raft touched mud. Though thin
water still gleamed among the trees, the raft no
longer floated. The bog held it despite the best efforts
of the steersmen, and drew it eastward deeper into
the Swamp, moving with the slow current of the mire.

Korik could not see any hope. But Sill disagreed.
He insisted that within Lord Hyrim's ill flesh an un-
quenched spirit survived. He felt it with his hand on
the Lord's brow; something in Hyrim still resisted the
fever. Through the long watch of the day, he nourished that spirit with treasure-berries and boiled,
brackish water. And in the evening the Lord rallied.
Some of the dry flush left his face; he began to sweat.
As his chills faded, his breathing became easier. By
nightfall he was sleeping quietly.

But it appeared that he had begun to recover too
late. Deep in the dark night, the grip of the mud bore
the raft into an open flat devoid of trees. There the
current eddied, turned back on itself, formed a slow

whirlpool just broad enough to catch all four sides of the raft and start sucking it down.

And the Bloodguard could do nothing. Here all strength and fidelity lost their worth; here no Vow had meaning. The mission was in Lord Hyrim's hands, and he was weak.

But when Korik wakened him, the Lord's eyes were lucid. He listened as Korik told him of the mission's plight. Then after a time he said, "How far must we go to escape?"

"A league, Lord." Korik indicated the direction with a nod.

"So far? Friend Korik, someday you must tell me how we came to these straits." Sighing, he pulled himself close to the fire and began eating the mission's store of *aliantha*. He made no attempt to rise until he had eaten it all.

Then, with Sill's help, he climbed to his feet on the slowly revolving raft, and moved into position. Bracing himself against the Bloodguard, he thrust his staff between the logs into the mud.

A snatch of song broke through his teeth; the staff began to pulse in his hands.

For a time, his exertions had no effect. Power mounted in his staff, grew higher at the command of his uncertain strength, but the raft still sank deeper into the Swamp. The stench of decay and death thickened. Lord Hyrim groaned at the strain, and summoned more of his strength. He began to sing aloud.

Blue sparks burst from the wood of his staff, ran down into the muck. With a loud sucking noise, the raft pulled free of the eddy, lumbered away. Swinging around the whirlpool, it started northward.

For a long time, Lord Hyrim kept the raft moving. Then he reached the marshwaders on the north side of the eddy. There the Bloodguard threw out *clingor* lines to the trees ahead, used the ropes to pull the raft along. At once, Hyrim dropped his power and slumped forward. Sill bore him back to the center of the raft. As soon as he lay down by the embers of the fire, he was asleep.

But now the Bloodguard no longer needed his help.

They cast out the *clingor* ropes and heaved on them, hauled the raft between the trees. Their progress was slow, but they did not falter. And when the mud became so thick that their ropes broke under the strain, they strung lines between the trees and left the raft. Sill carried Lord Hyrim lashed to his back, and moved through the mire by pulling himself along the lines while the other Bloodguard strung new ropes ahead and released the ones behind. Then, at last, in the light of dawn, the mud changed to soft wet clay, the trees gave way to stands of cane and marshgrass, and the Bloodguard began to feel solid ground with their bare toes.

Thus they came out into the wide belt of marsh that bordered Lifeswallower.

In the distance ahead, they could see the steep hills which formed the southern edge of Seareach.

The mission had lost three days.

Yet the Bloodguard did not begrudge Lord Hyrim the time to cook a hot meal from the last supplies. The Lord was worn and wasted; his once-round face had become as lean as a wolf's. He needed food and rest. And the mission would make good speed across Seareach toward *Coercri*. If necessary, the Bloodguard could carry Lord Hyrim.

When he had eaten, the Lord groaned to his feet, and started toward the hills. He set a slow pace; he was forced to rest long and often. The Bloodguard soon saw that at this rate they would need all day to cross the five leagues to the hills. But the Lord refused their offer of aid. "Haste?" he said. "I have no heart for haste." And his voice had a bitterness which surprised them until Korik reminded them of what they had heard from Warhaft Hoerkin, and of what the Lord's response had been. Hyrim apparently believed Hoerkin's prophecy concerning the downfall of the Giants.

Yet the Lord labored throughout the day to reach the hills, and the next day he strove to climb the hills as if he had changed during the night, recovered his sense of urgency. Rolling his eyes at the arduous slope, he pushed himself, labored upward at the limit of his returning strength.

When at last he crested the hill, he and all the Bloodguard paused to look at Seareach.

The land which the Old Lords had given to the Giants for a home was wide and fair. Enclosed by hills on the south, mountains on the west, and the Sunbirth Sea on the east, it was a green haven for the shipwrecked voyagers. But although they used the Land—cultivated the rolling countryside with crops of all kinds, planted immense vineyards, grew whole forests of the special redwood and teak trees from which they crafted their huge ships—they did not people it. They were lovers of the sea, and preferred to make their dwelling places in the cliffs of the rocky coast, forty leagues east from where the mission now stood.

During the age of Damelon Giantfriend, when the Unhomed were more numerous, they had spread out along the coast, building homes and villages across the whole eastern side of Seareach. But their numbers had slowly declined, until now they were only a third of what they had once been. Yet they were a long-lived, story-loving, gay people and the lack of children hurt them cruelly. Out of slow loneliness, they had left their scattered homes in the north and south of Seareach, and had formed one community—a sea-cliff city where they could share their few children and their songs and their long tales. Despite their ancient custom of long names—names which told the tale of the thing named—they called their city simply *Coercri*, The Grieve. There they had lived since High Lord Kevin's youth.

Looking out over the land of the Giants, Lord Hyrim gave a low cry. "Korik! Pray that Hoerkin lied! Pray that his message was a lie! Ah, my heart!" He clutched at his chest with both hands, and started down the soft slope into Seareach at a run.

Korik and Sill caught him swiftly, placed a hand under each of his arms. They bore him up between them so that he could move more easily. Thus the mission began its journey toward The Grieve.

Lord Hyrim ran that way for the rest of the day, resting only at moments when the pain in his chest became unendurable. And the Bloodguard knew that he had good reason. Lord Mhoram had said, *Twenty days*. This was the twentieth day of the mission.

The next dawn, when Lord Hyrim arose from his exhausted sleep, he spurned Korik and Sill, and ran alone.

His pace soon brought the mission to the westmost of the Giants' vineyards. Korik sent Doar and Shull through the rows, searching for some sign. But they reported that the Giants who had been working this vineyard had left it together in haste. The matter was clear. Giantish hoes and rakes as tall as men lay scattered among the vines with their blades and teeth still in the marks of their work, and several of the leather sacks in which the Giants usually carried their food and belongings had been thrown to the ground and abandoned. Apparently, the Unhomed had received some kind of signal, and had dropped their work at once to answer it.

Their footprints in the open earth of the vineyard ran in the direction of *Coercri*.

That day, the mission passed through vineyards, teak stands, fields. In all of them, the scattered tools and supplies told the same tale. But the next day came a rain which effaced the footprints and work signs. The Bloodguard were able to gain no more knowledge from such things.

During the night, the rain ended. In the slow breeze, the Bloodguard could smell sea salt. The clear sky appeared to promise a clear day, but the dawn of the twenty-third day had a red cast scored at moments with baleful glints of green, and it gave the Lord no relief. After he had eaten the treasure-berries Sill offered him, he did not arise. Rather, he wrapped his arms around his knees and bowed his head as if he were cowering.

For the sake of the mission, Korik spoke. "Lord, we must go. The Grieve is near."

The Lord did not raise his head. His voice was muffled between his knees. "Are you impervious to fear? Do you not know what we will find? Or does it not touch you?"

"We are the Bloodguard," Korik replied.

"Yes," Lord Hyrim sighed. "The Bloodguard. And I am Hyrim son of Hoole, Lord of the Council of Revelstone. I am sworn to the services of the Land. I should have died in Shetra's place. If I had her strength."

Abruptly, he sprang to his feet. Spreading his arms, he cried in the words of the old ritual, " 'We are the new preservers of the Land—votaries of the Earthpower. Sworn and dedicate—dedicate— We will not rest—' " But he could not complete it. *"Melenkurion!"* he moaned, clutching his black robe at his chest. *"Melenkurion* Skyweir! Help me!"

Korik was loath to speak, but the mission compelled him. "If the Giants are to be aided, we must do it."

"Aided?" Lord Hyrim gasped. "There is no aid for them!" He stooped, snatched up his staff. For several shuddering breaths, he held it, gripped it as if to wrest courage from it. "But there are other things. We must learn— The High Lord must be told what power performed this abomination!" His eyes had a shadow across them, and their lids were red as if with panic. Trembling, he turned and started toward *Coercri.*

Now the mission did not hasten. It moved cautiously toward the Sea, warding against an ambush. Yet the morning passed swiftly. Before noon, the Bloodguard and the Lord reached the high lighthouse of The Grieve.

The lighthouse was a tall spire of open stonework that stood on the last and highest hill before the cliffs of the coast. The Giants had built it to guide their roving ships, and someone was always there to tend the focused light beam of the signal fire.

But as the Bloodguard crept up the hill toward the foot of the spire, they could see that the fire was dead. No gleam of light or wisp of smoke came from the cupola atop the tower.

They found blood on the steps of a lighthouse. It was dry and black, old enough to resist the washing of the rain.

At a command from Korik, Vale ran up the steep steps into the spire. The rest of the Bloodguard waited, looking out over *Coercri* and the Sunbirth Sea.

In the noon sun under a clear sky, the Sea was bright with dazzles, and out of sight below the rim of the cliff the waves made muffled thunder against the piers and levees of The Grieve.

There, like a honeycomb in the cliff, was the city of the Giants. All its homes and halls and passages, all its entrances and battlements, had been delved into the rock of the coast. And it was immense. It had halls where five hundred Giants could gather for their Giantclaves and their stories which consumed days in the telling; it had docks for eight or ten of the mighty Giant ships; it had hearths and homes enough for all the remnant of the Unhomed.

Yet it showed no sign of habitation. The back of The Grieve, the side facing inland, looked abandoned. Above it, an occasional gull screamed. And below, the Sea beat. But it revealed no life.

However, *Coercri* had been built to face the Sea. Still the Bloodguard hoped to find Giants there.

Then Vale came down out of the lighthouse. He spoke directly to Lord Hyrim. "One Giant is there." He indicated the cupola of the spire with a jerk of his head. "She is dead." After a moment, he said, "She was killed. Her face and the top of her head are gone. Her brain is gone. Consumed."

All the Bloodguard looked at Lord Hyrim.

He was staring at Vale with red in his eyes. His lean face was twisted. In his throat, he made a confused noise like a snarl. His knuckles were white on his staff. Without a word, he turned and started down toward the main entrance of The Grieve.

Then Korik gave his commands. Of the eleven Bloodguard, Vale, Doar, Shull, and two others he instructed to remain at the lighthouse, to watch, and to give warning if necessary, and to carry out the mission if the others fell. Three he sent northward to begin exploring *Coercri* from that end. And with Tull and Sill, he followed Lord Hyrim. These three took the Lord away from the main entrance toward the south of the city.

Together, the four crept into The Grieve on its southern side.

The entrance they chose was a tunnel that led straight through the cliff, sloping slightly downward. They passed along it to its end, where it opened into a roofless rampart overhanging the Sea. From this vantage, they could see much of the city's cliff front. Ramparts like the one on which they stood alternately projected and receded along the wall of rock for several levels below them, giving the face of the city a knuckled appearance. They could see into many of the projections until the whole city passed out of sight north of them behind a bulge in the cliff. Down at sea level, just south of this bulge, was a wide levee between two long stone piers.

The levee and the piers were deserted. Nothing moved on any of the ramparts. Except for the noise of the Sea, the city was still.

But when Lord Hyrim opened a high stone door and entered the apartments beyond it, he found two Giants lying cold in a pool of dried blood. Both their skulls were broken asunder and empty, as if the bones had been blasted apart from within.

In the next set of rooms were three more Giants, and in the next set three more, one of them a child—all dead. They lay among pools of their blood, and the blood was spattered around as if someone had stamped through the pools while they were still fresh. All including the child had been slain by having their heads rent open.

But they were not decayed. They had not been long dead—not above three days.

"Three days," Korik said.

And Lord Hyrim said bitterly, "Three days."

They went on with the search.

They looked into every apartment along the rampart until they were directly above the levee. In each set of rooms, they found one or two or three Giants, all slaughtered in the same way. And none but the youngest children showed any sign of resistance, of struggle.

The few youngest bodies were contorted and frantic; all the rest lay as if they had been simply struck dead where they stood or sat.

When the searchers entered one round meeting hall, they discovered that it was empty. And the huge kitchen beyond it was also empty. The stove fires had fallen into ash, but the cooks had not been killed there.

The sight dismayed Lord Hyrim. Groaning, he said, "They went to their homes to die! They knew their danger—and went to their homes to await it. They did not fight—or flee—or send for help. *Melenkurion abatha!* Only the children— What horror came upon them?"

The Bloodguard had no answer. They knew of no wrong potent enough to commit such a slaughter unresisted.

As he left the hall, Lord Hyrim wept openly.

From that rampart, he and the Bloodguard worked downward through the levels of *Coercri*. They took a crooked stairway which descended back into the cliff, then toward the Sea again. At the next level, they again went to look into the rooms. Here also all the Giants were dead.

Everywhere it was the same. The Unhomed had gone to their private dwellings to die.

Then an urgency came upon the Bloodguard and the Lord. They began to hasten. The Lord leaped down the high stairs, ran along the ramparts to inspect the apartments. In their black garb, the four flew downward like the ravens of midnight, taking the tale of shed blood and blasted skulls.

When they were more than halfway down The Grieve, Korik stopped them. He had noticed a change in the air of the city. But the difference was subtle; for a moment, he could not identify it. Then he ran into the nearest apartment, hastened to the lone Giant dead in one of the back rooms, touched the pool of blood.

This Giant had been slain more recently; a few spots of the pool were still damp.

Perhaps the slayer was still in the city, stalking its last victims.

At once, Lord Hyrim whispered, "We must reach the lowest level swiftly. If any Giants yet live, they will be there."

Korik nodded. Tull sprinted to scout ahead as the others ran to the stairs and started down them. On each level, they stopped long enough to find one dead Giant, test the condition of the blood. Then they raced on downward.

The blood grew steadily damper. Two levels above the piers, they found a child whose flesh still retained a vestige of warmth.

They explored the next level more carefully. And in one room they discovered a Giant with the last blood still dripping from her riven skull.

With great caution, they crept down the final stairs.

The stairway opened on a broad expanse of rock, the base of the two piers and the head of the levee between them. The tide was low and quiet—the waves broke far down the levee—but still the sound filled the air. Even here, the Bloodguard and the Lord could not see beyond the great cliff-bulge just north of the piers. This bulge, and the outward bend of *Coercri*'s southern tip, formed a shallow cove around the levee. The flat base of the city lay in the afternoon shadow of the cliff, and the unwarmed rock was damp with spray.

No one moved on the piers, or along the walkway which traversed the city from its southern end northward around the curve of the cliff.

Cut into the base of the cliff behind the walkway and the headrock of the piers were many openings. All had heavy stone doors to keep out the Sea in storms. But most of the doors were open. They led into workshops—high chambers where the Giants formed the planks and hawsers of their ships. Like the meeting halls and kitchens, these places were deserted. But, unlike the western vineyards and fields, the workshops had not been abandoned suddenly. All the tools hung in their racks on the walls; the tables and benches were free of work; even the floors were clean. The Giants laboring there had taken the time to put their shops in order before they went home to die.

But one smaller door near the south end of the headrock was tightly closed. Lord Hyrim tried to open it, but it had no handle, and he could not grip the smooth stone.

Korik and Tull approached it together. Forcing their fingers into one crack of the door, they heaved at it. With a scraping noise like a gasp of pain, it swung outward, admitting shadow light to the chamber beyond.

The single room was bare; it contained nothing but a low bed against one side wall. It was lightless, and the air in it smelled stale.

On the floor against the back wall sat a Giant.

Even crouched with his knees drawn up before him, he was as tall as the Bloodguard. His staring eyes caught the light and gleamed.

He was alive. A shallow breath stirred his chest, and a thin trail of saliva ran from the corner of his mouth into his grizzled beard.

But he made no move as the four entered the cell. No blink or flicker of his eyes acknowledged them.

Lord Hyrim rushed toward him gladly, then stopped when he saw the look of horror on the Giant's face.

Korik approached the Giant, touched one of the bare arms which gripped his knees. The Giant was not cold; he was not another Hoerkin.

Korik shook the Giant's arm, but the Giant did not respond. He sat gaping blindly out the doorway. Korik looked a question at the Lord. When Hyrim nodded, Korik struck the Giant across the face.

His head lurched under the blow, but it did not penetrate him. Without blinking, he raised his head again, resumed his stare. Korik prepared to strike again with more force, but Lord Hyrim stopped him. "Do him no injury, Korik. He is closed to us."

"We must reach him," Korik said.

"Yes," said Hyrim. "Yes, we must." He moved close to the Giant, and called, "Rockbrother! Hear me! I am Hyrim son of Hoole, Lord of the Council of Revelstone. You must hear me. In the name of all the Unhomed—in the name of friendship and the Land —I adjure you! Open your ears to me!"

The Giant made no reply. The slow rate of his breathing did not vary; his white gaze did not falter.

Lord Hyrim stepped back, studied the Giant. Then he said to Korik, "Free one of his hands." He rubbed one heel of his staff, and when he took his hand away a blue flame sprang up on the metal. "I will attempt the *caamora*—the fire of grief."

Korik understood. The *caamora* was a ritual by which the Giants purged themselves of grief and rage. They were impervious to any ordinary fire, but the flames hurt them, and they used that pain at need to help them master themselves. Swiftly, Korik pried the Giant's right hand loose from its grip, pulled the arm back so that its hand was extended toward Lord Hyrim.

Moaning softly, "Stone and Sea, Rockbrother! Stone and Sea!" the Lord increased the strength of his Lordsfire. He placed the flame directly under the Giant's hand, enveloped the fingers in fire.

At first, nothing happened; the ritual had no effect. The Giant's fingers hung motionless in the flame, and the flame did not consume them. But then they twitched, groped, clenched. The Giant pushed his hand farther into the fire, though his fingers were writhing in pain.

Abruptly, he drew a deep shuddering breath. His head snapped back, thudded against the wall, dropped forward onto his knees. Yet still he did not withdraw his hand. When he raised his head again, his eyes were full of tears.

Trembling, panting, he pulled back his hand. It was undamaged.

At once, Lord Hyrim extinguished his fire. "Rockbrother," he cried softly. "Rockbrother. Forgive me."

The Giant stared at his hand. Time passed as he became slowly aware of his situation. At last he recognized the Lord and the Bloodguard. Suddenly he flinched, jerked both hands to the sides of his head, gasped, "Alive?" Before Lord Hyrim could answer, he went on, "What of the others? My people?"

Lord Hyrim clutched his staff for support. "All dead."

"Ah!" the Giant groaned. His hands dropped to his knees, and he leaned his head back against the wall. "Oh, my people!" The tears streamed down his cheeks like blood.

The Lord and the Bloodguard watched him in silence, waited for him. At last his grief eased, and his tears ceased. When he brought his head forward from the wall, he murmured as if in defeat, "He has left me to the last."

With a visible effort, Lord Hyrim forced himself to ask, "Who is he?"

The Giant answered in misery, "He came soon—he came soon after we had learned the fate of the three brothers—the brothers of one birth—Damelon Rockbrother's omen of the end. This spring—ah, was it so recent? It needs more time. There should be years given to it. There—ah, my people! This spring—this—we knew at last that the old slumbering ill of the Sarangrave was awake. We thought to send word to brave Lord's Keep—" For a moment, he choked on the grief in his throat. "Then we lost the brothers. Lost them. We arose to one sunrise, and they were gone.

"We did not send to the Lords. How could we bear to tell them that our hope was lost? No. Rather, we searched. From the Northron Climbs to the Spoiled Plains and beyond, we searched. We searched—through all the summer. Nothing. In despair, the searchers returned to The Grieve, *Coercri,* last home of the Unhomed.

"Then the last searcher returned—Wavenhair Haleall, whose womb bore the three. Because she was their mother, she searched when all others had given up the search, and she was the last to return. She had journeyed to the Shattered Hills themselves. She called all the people together, and told us the fate of the three before she died. The wounds of the search—"

He groaned again. "Now I am the last. Ah, my people!" As he cried out, he moved, shoved himself to his feet, stood erect against the wall. Towering over his hearers, he put back his head and began to sing the old song of the Unhomed.

Now we are Unhomed,
    bereft of root and kith and kin.
From other mysteries of delight,
    we set our sails to resail our track;
    but the winds of life blew not the way
      we chose,
and the land beyond the Sea was lost.

It was long, like all Giantish songs. But he sang only a fragment of it. Soon he fell silent, and his chin dropped to his breast.

Again Lord Hyrim asked, "Who is he?"

The Giant answered by resuming his tale. "Then he came. Omen of the end and Home turned to misery and gall. Then we knew the truth. We had seen it before—in lighter times, when the knowledge might have been of some use—but we had denied it. We had seen our evil, and had denied it, thinking that we might find our way Home and escape it. Fools! When we saw him, we knew the truth. Through folly and withering seed and passion and impatience for Home, we had become the thing we hate. We saw the truth in him. Our hearts were turned to ashes, and we went to our dwellings—these small rooms which we called homes in vain."

"Why did you not flee?"

"Some did—some four or five who did not know the long name of despair—or did not hear it. Or they were too much like him to judge. The ill of the Sarangrave took them—they are no more."

Compelled by the ancient passion of the Bloodguard, Korik asked, "Why did you not fight?"

"We had become the thing we hate. We are better dead."

"Nevertheless!" Korik said. "Is this the fealty of the Giants? Does all promised faithfulness come to this? By the Vow, Giant! You destroy yourselves, and let the evil live! Even Kevin Landwaster was not so weak."

In his emotion, he forgot caution, and all the Bloodguard were taken unaware. The sudden voice behind them was cold with contempt; it cut through

them like a gale of winter. Turning, they found that
another Giant stood in the doorway. He was much
younger than the Giant within, but he resembled the
older Giant. The chief difference lay in the contempt
that filled his face, raged in his eyes, twisted his mouth
as if he were about to spit.

In his right hand, he clenched a hot green stone. It
blazed with an emerald strength that shone through
his fingers. As he gripped it, it steamed thickly.

He stank of fresh blood; he was spattered with it
from head to foot. And within him, clinging to his
bones, was a powerful presence that did not fit his
form. It slavered from behind his eyes with a great
force of malice and wrong.

"Hmm," he said in a despising tone, "a Lord and
three Bloodguard. I am pleased. I had thought that
my friend in the Sarangrave would take all like you—
but I see I shall have that pleasure myself. Ah, but
you are not entirely scatheless, are you? Black becomes you. Did you lose friends to my friend?" He
laughed with a grating sound, like the noise of boulders being crushed together.

Lord Hyrim stepped forward, planted his staff, said
bravely, "Come no closer, *turiya* Raver. I am Hyrim,
Lord of the Council of Revelstone. *Melenkurion
abatha! Duroc minas mill khabaal!* I will not let you
pass."

The Giant winced as Lord Hyrim uttered the
Words of power. But then he laughed again. "Hah!
Little Lord! Is that the limit of your lore? Can you
come no closer than that to the Seven Words? You
pronounce them badly. But I must admit—you have
recognized me. I am *turiya* Herem. But we have new
names now, my brothers and I. There is Fleshharrower, and Satansfist. And I am named Kinslaughterer."

At this, the older Giant groaned heavily. The Raver
glanced into the back of the cell, and said in a tone
of satisfaction, "Ah, there he is. Little Lord, I see that
you have been speaking with Sparlimb Keelsetter. Did
he tell you that he is my father? Father, why do you
not welcome your son?"

The Bloodguard did not look at the older Giant. But they heard Keelsetter's pain, and understood it. Something within the Giant was breaking. Suddenly, he gave a savage roar. Leaping past the four, he attacked Kinslaughterer.

His fingers caught the Raver's throat. He drove him back out of the doorway onto the headrock of the piers.

Kinslaughterer made no attempt to break his father's hold. He resisted the impetus until his feet were braced. Then he raised the green stone, moved it toward Keelsetter's forehead.

Both fist and stone passed through the older Giant's skull into his brain.

Keelsetter screamed. His hands dropped, his body went limp. He hung from the point of power which impaled his head.

Grinning ravenously, the Raver held his father there for a long moment. Then he tightened his fist. Deep emerald flashed; the stone blasted the front of Keelsetter's skull. He fell dead, pouring blood over the headrock.

Kinslaughterer stamped his feet in the spreading pool.

He appeared oblivious to the four, but he was not. As Korik and Tull started forward to attack him, he swung his arm, hurled a bolt of power at them. It would have slain them before they reached the doorway, but Lord Hyrim lunged, thrust up his staff between them. The end of his staff caught the bolt. It detonated with such force that it broke the staff in two, and flung the four humans against the back of the cell.

The impact made them unconscious.

Thus even the Vow could not preserve the Bloodguard from the extremity of their need.

Korik was the first to reawaken. Hearing returned before sight or touch, and he began to listen. In his ears, the noise of the Sea grew, became violent. But the sound was not the sound of waves in storm; it was more erratic, more vicious. When his sight was restored, he was surprised to find that he could see. He had expected the darkness of clouds.

But early starlight shone through the doorway from a clear night sky. Outside, the Sea thrashed and heaved across the piers and up the levee as if goaded by rowels. And along the sky lightning leaped, followed by such thunder that he felt the bursting in his chest. Through the spray a high wind howled. And still the sky was clear.

There was a bayamo upon the Sea.

Then a different lightning struck upward into the heavens—a bolt as green as blazing emerald. It came from the levee. Looking through the darkness, Korik discerned the form of the Raver, Kinslaughterer. He stood down in the levee, so close to the tide that the waves broke against his knees. With his stone, he hurled green blasts into the sky, and shook his arms as if the windstorm were his to command.

On the levee behind him were three dead forms— the three Bloodguard whom Korik had sent to the northern end of the city.

For a time, Korik did not comprehend what Kinslaughterer was doing. But then he perceived that the seas out beyond the piers moved in consonance with Kinslaughterer's arms. As the Giant-Raver waved and gestured, they heaved and reared and broke and piled themselves together.

Farther away, the situation was worse. Slowly, with great pitchings and shudders, a massive wall of water rose out of the ocean. Kinslaughterer's green lightning glared across the face of it as it mounted, tossed its crest higher and higher. And as it grew, it moved toward the cliff.

The Raver was summoning a tsunami.

Korik turned to rouse his companions.

Sill and Tull were soon conscious and alert. But Lord Hyrim lay still, and blood trickled from the corner of his mouth. Swiftly, Sill ran his hands over the Lord's body, reported that Hyrim had several broken ribs, but no other injuries. Together, Korik and Sill chafed his wrists, slapped his neck. At last, his eyelids fluttered, and he awakened.

He was dazed. At first, he could not grasp Korik's tidings. But when he looked out into the night, he understood. Already, the mounting tidal wave appeared half as high as the cliff, and its writhing had a dark, ill cast. There was enough hatred concentrated in it to shatter The Grieve. When Lord Hyrim turned from it, his face was taut with terrible purpose.

He had to shout to make himself heard over the roar of waves and wind and thunder. "We must stop him! He violates the Sea! If he succeeds—if he bends the Sea to his will—the Law that preserves it will be broken. It will serve the Despiser like another Raver!"

Korik answered, "Yes!" There was a fury in the Bloodguard. They would have disobeyed any other decision.

Yet Sill remembered caution enough to say, "He has the Illearth Stone."

"No!" Lord Hyrim searched the floor for the pieces of his staff. When he found them, he called for *clingor*. Tull gave him a length of line. He used it to lash the two pieces of his staff together, metal heels joined. Clutching this unwieldly instrument, he said, "That is only a fragment of the Stone! The Illearth Stone itself —is much larger! But in our worst dreams we did not guess that the Despiser would dare cut pieces of the Stone for his servants. His mastery of it must—must be very great. Thus he is able to subdue Giants—the Ravers and the Stone together, the Stone empowering the Raver, and the Raver using the stone! And the others—Fleshharrower, Satansfist—they also must possess fragments of the Stone. Do you hear, Korik?"

"I hear," Korik replied. "The High Lord will be warned."

Lord Hyrim nodded. The pain in his ribs made him wince. But he thrust his way out of the cell into the howling wind. Korik, Sill, and Tull followed at once.

Ahead of them, Kinslaughterer labored in an ecstasy of power. Though it was still some distance from the piers, the tsunami towered over him, dwarfed his stolen form. Now he was chanting to it, invoking it. His words cut through the tumult of the storm.

> Come, Sea!
> Obey me!
> Raise high!
> crash down!
> Break rock!
> break stone:
> crush heart:
> grind soul:
> rend flesh:
> crack whole!
> Eat dead
> for bread!
> Come, Sea!
> Obey me!

And the seas answered, piled still higher. Now the wave's crest frothed and lashed level with the upper ramparts of *Coercri*.

The Bloodguard wished to attack instantly, but Lord Hyrim held them back. So that he would not be heard by Kinslaughterer, he mouthed the words, "I must strike the first blow." Then he moved over the headrock as fast as his damaged chest permitted.

When the four started into the levee, the huge wall of water already appeared to be leaning over them. Only the might of Kinslaughterer's Stone kept it erect. As they approached, he was too consumed by the spectacle of his own power to sense them. But in the last moment, some instinct warned him. He spun suddenly, found Lord Hyrim within a few yards of him.

Roaring savagely, he raised his glowing fist to hurl a blast at the Lord.

But while the Raver cocked his arm, Lord Hyrim leaped the last distance toward him. With the lashed fragments of his staff, the Lord struck upward.

The metal heels hit Kinslaughterer's hand before his bolt was ready.

The two powers clashed in a blaze of green and

blue. Kinslaughterer's greater force drove his might like lightning down the length of Lord Hyrim's arms into his head and body. The green fire burned within him, burned his brain and heart. When the flame ceased, he collapsed.

But the clash scorched Kinslaughterer's hand, and its recoil knocked his arm back. He lost the Stone. It fell, rolled away from him across the headrock.

At once, the three Bloodguard sprang; together they struck the Raver with all their strength. And in that assault their Vow at last found utterance. The Giant-Raver was dead before his form fell into the water.

Yet still for a long moment the Bloodguard hurled blows at him, driven by the excess of their rage and abomination. Then the splashing of saltwater cooled them, and they perceived that the storm had begun to fade.

Without the compulsion of the Stone, the wind failed. The lightning stopped. After a few last rolls, the thunder fell away.

The tidal wave made a sound like an avalanche as it fell backward into the Sea. Its spray wet the faces of the Bloodguard, and its waves broke over their thighs. Then it was gone.

Together, the three hastened back to Lord Hyrim. He still clung to life, but he was almost at an end; the Raver's blast had burned him deeply. His eye sockets were empty, and from between his hollow lids a thin green smoke rose up into the starlight. As Sill lifted him into a sitting position, his hands groped about him as if they were searching for his staff, and he said weakly, "Do not—do not touch—take—"

He could not speak it. The effort burst his heart. With a groan, he died in Sill's arms.

For a time, the Bloodguard stood over him in silence, gave him what respect they could. But they had no words to say. Soon Korik went and took up Kinslaughterer's fragment of the Illearth Stone. Without a will to drive it, it was dull; it showed only fitful gleams in its core. But it hurt his hand with a deep and fiery cold. He clenched it in his fist.

"We will take it to the High Lord," he said. "Per-

haps the other Ravers have such power. The High
Lord may use this power to defeat them."

Sill and Tull nodded. In the ruin of the mission,
there was no other hope left to them.

"Then we sent homeward the bodies of our fallen
comrades," Tull said softly. "There was no need for
haste—we knew that their Ranyhyn could find a way
in safety north of the Sarangrave. And when that task
was done, we returned to the five who stood watch
at the lighthouse. Two of them Korik charged to return to Lord's Keep with all possible speed, so that
Revelstone might be warned. And because he judged
that the war had already begun—that the High Lord
would be marching in the South Plains with the Warward—I was charged, and Shull and Vale with me,
to bear these tidings southward, the way I have come.
With Sill and Doar, Korik undertook the burden of
the Illearth Stone, so that it might be taken in safety
to Revelstone for the Lords."

At last the Bloodguard fell silent. For a long time,
Troy sat gazing sightlessly at the stone before him. He
felt deaf and numb—too shocked to hear the low
breeze blowing around Kevin's Watch, too stunned to
feel the chill of the mountain air. Dead? he asked
silently. All dead? But it seemed to him that he felt
nothing. In him there was a pain so deep that he was
not conscious of it.

But in time he recollected himself enough to raise
his head, look over at Lord Mhoram. He could see
the Lord dimly. His forehead was tight with pain, and
his eyes bled tears.

With an effort, Troy found his voice. It was husky
with emotion as he asked, "Is this what you saw—
last night? Is this it?"

"No." Mhoram's reply was abrupt. But it was not
abrupt with anger; it was abrupt with the exertion of
suppressing his sobs. "I saw Bloodguard fighting in the
service of the Despiser."

There was a long and heartrending pause before
Tull said through his teeth, "That is impossible."

"They should not have touched the Stone," the Lord breathed weakly. "They should not—!"

Troy wanted to question Mhoram, ask him what he meant. But then suddenly he realized that he was seeing more clearly. His fog was lifting.

At once, he rose to his knees, turned, braced his chest on the edge of the parapet. Instinctively, he tightened his sunglasses on his face.

Along the rim of the eastern horizon dawn had already begun.

EIGHTEEN: Doom's Retreat

IMMEDIATELY, Troy jumped erect to face the sun.

His companions stood with him in tense silence, as if they intended to share what he would see. But he knew that even the Bloodguard could not match his mental sight. He paid no attention to them. All his awareness was consumed by the gradual revelations of the dawn.

At first, he could see only a fading gray and purple blankness. But then the direct rays of the sun caught the platform, and his surroundings began to lift their heads out of the mist. Above the long fall into shadow, he received his first visual sense of the wide open air in which Kevin's Watch stood as if on the tip of a dark finger accusing the heavens. In the west, across a distance too great for any sight but his, he saw sunlight touch the thin snowcaps of the mountain wedge which separated the South Plains from Garroting Deep. And as the sun climbed higher, he made out the long curve of peaks running south and then west from the valley of Mithil Stonedown to Doom's Retreat.

Then the light reached down to the hills which formed the eastern border of the Plains between Kevin's Watch and Andelain. Now he could follow the whole course of the Mithil River northwest and then north until it joined the Black. He felt strangely elevated and mighty. His gaze had never comprehended so much before, and he understood how High Lord Kevin must have felt. Standing on the Watch was like being on the pinnacle of the Earth.

But the sun kept rising. Like a tide of illumination, it flooded across the Plains, washing away the last of his blindness.

What he saw staggered him where he stood. Horror filled his eyes like the rush of an avalanche. It was worse than anything he could have imagined.

He made out the Warward first. His army had just begun to march; it crept south along the mountain wedge. He saw it as hardly more than a smudge in the foothills, but he could gauge its speed. It was still two days from Doom's Retreat.

Hiltmark Quaan's force was closer to him, and farther from the Retreat. But the horsemen were moving faster. He estimated their numbers instinctively, instantly; he knew at once that they had been decimated. More than a third of the two hundred Bloodguard were gone, and of Quaan's twelve Eoward less than six remained. They hurried raggedly, almost at a dead rout.

Raging at their heels came a vast horde of *kresh*— at least ten thousand of the savage yellow wolves. The mightiest of them, the most powerful two thousand, bore black riders—ur-viles. The ridden *kresh* ran in tight wedges, and the ur-vile loremasters at the wedge tips threw torrents of dark force at every rider who fell within their reach.

In an effort to control the pace, restrain it from utter flight, Eoman turned at intervals. Twenty or forty warriors threw themselves together at the yellow wall to slow the charge of the *kresh*. Troy could see flashes of blue fire in these sorties; Callindrill and Verement were alive. But two Lords were not enough. The riders were hopelessly outnumbered. And they were already well beyond the Mithil River in their race toward Doom's Retreat. Even if they ran no faster, they would reach the Retreat before the marching Warward.

Quaan had been unable to gain the last day that the marchers needed.

Yet even that was not the most crushing sight. Behind the wolves came the main body of Lord Foul's army. This body was closer than the others to Kevin's Watch, and Troy could see it with appalling clarity.

The Giant striding at its head was the least of its horrors. At the Giant's back marched immense ranks of Cavewights—at least twenty thousand of the strong, ungainly rock delvers. Behind them hurried an equal number of ur-viles, loping on all fours for better speed. Through their ranks, hundreds of fearsome, lionlike *griffins* alternately trotted and flew. And after the Demondim-spawn came a seething, grim army so huge that Troy could not even guess its numbers: humans, wolves, Waynhim, forest animals, creatures of the Flat, all radiating the fathomless blood-hunger which coerced them—many myriad of warped, rabid creatures, the perverted handiwork of Lord Foul and the Illearth Stone.

Most of this prodigious army had already crossed the Mithil in pursuit of Hiltmark Quaan and his command. It moved with such febrile speed that it was little more than three days from Doom's Retreat. And it was so mighty that no ambush, however well conceived, could hope to stand against it.

But there would be no ambush. The Warward did not know its peril, and would not reach the Retreat in time.

Like jagged hunks of rock, these facts beat Warmark Troy to his knees. "Dear God!" he breathed in anguish. "What have I done?" The avalanche of revelations battered him down. "Dear God. Dear God. What have I done?"

Behind him, Lord Mhoram insisted with mounting urgency, "What is it? What do you see? Warmark, what do you see?" But Troy could not answer. His world was reeling around him. Through the vertigo of his perceptions, his clutching mind could grasp only one thought: this was his fault, all of it was his fault. The futility of Korik's mission, the end of the Giants, the inevitable slaughter of the Warward—everything was on his head. He had been in command. And when the debacle of his command was over, the Land would be defenseless. He had served the Despiser from the start without knowing it, and what Atiaran Trellmate had given her life for was worse than nothing.

"Worse," he gasped. He had condemned his warriors to death. And they were only the beginning of the toll Lord Foul would exact for his misjudgment. "Dear God." He wanted to howl, but his chest was too full of horror; it had no room for outcries.

He did not understand how the Despiser's army could be so *big*. It surpassed his most terrible nightmares.

Wildly, he surged to his feet. He tore at his breast, trying to wrest enough air from his unbreathable failure for just one cry. But he could not get it; his lungs were clogged with ruin. A sudden loud helplessness roared in his ears, and he pitched forward.

He did not realize that he had tried to jump until Terrel and Ruel caught his legs and hauled him back over the parapet.

Then he felt a burning in his cheeks. Lord Mhoram was slapping him. When he flinched, the Lord pulled close to him, shouted into his eyeless face, "Warmark! Hile Troy! Hear me! I understand—the Despiser's army is great. And the Warward will not reach Doom's Retreat in time. I can help!"

Dumbly, instinctively, Troy tried to straighten his sunglasses on his face, and found that they were gone. He had lost them over the edge of Kevin's Watch.

"Hear me!" Mhoram cried. "I can send word. If either Callindrill or Verement lives, I can be heard. They can warn Amorine." He grabbed Troy's shoulders, and his fingers dug in, trying to gain a hold on Troy's bones. "Hear! I am able. But I must have reason, hope. I cannot—if it is useless. Answer!" he demanded through clenched teeth. "You are the Warmark. Find hope! Do not leave your warriors to die!"

"No," Troy whispered. He tried to break away from Mhoram's grip, but the Lord's fingers were too strong. "There's no way. Foul's army is too big."

He wanted to weep, but Mhoram did not let him. "Discover a way!" the Lord raged. "They will be slain! You must save them!"

"I can't!" Troy shouted in sudden anger. The stark impossibility of Mhoram's demand touched a hidden resource in him, and he yelled, "Foul's army is too goddamn big! Our forces are going to get there too late! The only way they can stay alive just a little longer is to run straight through the Retreat and keep going until they drop! There's nothing out there—just Wastes, and Desert, and a clump of ruins, and—!"

Abruptly, his heart lurched. Kevin's Watch seemed to tilt under him, and he grabbed at Mhoram's wrists to steady himself. "Sweet Jesus!" he whispered. "There is one chance."

"Speak it!"

"There's one chance," Troy repeated in a tone of wonder. "Jesus." With an effort, he forced his attention into focus on Mhoram. "But you'll have to do it."

"Then I will do it. Tell me what must be done."

For a moment longer, the sweet sense of reprieve amazed Troy, outweighing the need to act, almost dumbfounding him. "It's going to be rough," he murmured to himself. "God! It's going to be rough." But Mhoram's insistent grip held him. Speaking slowly to help himself collect his thoughts, he said, "You're going to have to do it. There's no other way. But first you've got to get through to Callindrill or Verement."

Lord Mhoram's piercing gaze probed Troy. Then Mhoram helped the Warmark to his feet. Quietly, the Lord asked, "Do Callindrill and Verement live?"

"Yes. I saw their fire. Can you reach them? They don't have any of that High Wood."

Mhoram smiled grimly. "What message shall I give?"

Now Troy studied Mhoram. He felt oddly vulnerable without his sunglasses, as if he were exposed to reproach, even to abhorrence, but he could see Mhoram acutely. What he saw reassured him. The

Lord's eyes gleamed with hazardous potentials, and the bones of his skull had an indomitable hue. The contrast to his own weakness humbled Troy. He turned away to look out over the Plains again. The ponderous movement of Lord Foul's hordes continued as before, and at the sight he felt a resurgence of panic. But he held onto his power of command, gripped it to keep his shame at bay. Finally, he said, "All right. Let's get going. Tull, you'd better go back to the Stonedown. Have the Ranyhyn brought as far up the trail as possible. We've got a long run ahead of us."

"Yes, Warmark," Tull left the Watch soundlessly.

"Now, Mhoram. You had the right idea. Amorine has got to be warned. She has got to get to the Retreat ahead of Quaan." It occurred to him that Quaan might not be alive, but he forced that fear down. "I don't care how she does it. She's got to have that ambush ready when the riders arrive. If she doesn't—" He had to lock his jaw to keep his voice from shaking. "Can you communicate that?" He shuddered to think of the warriors' plight. After a twenty-five-day march, they would have to run the last fifty miles— only to learn that their ordeal was not done. Pushing himself around to face Mhoram, he demanded, "Well?"

Mhoram had already taken the *lomillialor* rod from his robe, and was lashing it across his staff with a *clingor* thong. As he secured the rod, he said, "My friend, you should leave the Watch. You will be safer below."

Troy acquiesced without question. He gazed at the armies once more to be sure that he had gauged their relative speeds accurately, then wished Lord Mhoram good luck, and started the descent. The stairs felt slippery under his hands and feet, but he was reassured by Ruel's presence right below him. Soon he stood on the ledge at the base of the Watch, and stared up into the blue sky toward Lord Mhoram.

After a pause that seemed unduly long to Troy's quickening sense of urgency, he heard snatches of song from atop the shaft. The song mounted into the air, then abruptly fell silent. At once, flame erupted around Lord Mhoram. It engulfed the whole platform of the Watch, and it filled the air with an impression of reverberation, as if the cliff face echoed a protracted and inaudible shriek. The noiseless ululation made Troy's ears burn, made him ache to cover them and hide his head, but he forced himself to withstand it. He did not take his gaze off the Watch.

The echoing was mercifully brief. Moments after its last vibration had faded, Terrel came down the stair, half carrying Mhoram.

Troy was afraid that the Lord had damaged himself. But Mhoram only suffered from a sudden exhaustion —the price of his exertion. All his movements were weak, unsteady, and his face dripped with sweat, but he managed a faint smile for Troy. "I would not care to be Callindrill's foe," he said wanly. "He is strong. He sends riders to Amorine."

"Good." Troy's voice was gruff with affection and relief. "But if we don't get to Doom's Retreat before midafternoon tomorrow, it'll be wasted."

Mhoram nodded. He braced himself on Terrel's shoulder, and stumbled away along the ledge with Troy and Ruel behind him.

They made slow progress at first because of Mhoram's fatigue, but before long they reached a small, pine-girdled valley plentifully grown with *aliantha*. A breakfast of treasure-berries rejuvenated Lord Mhoram, and after that he moved more swiftly.

Behind Mhoram and Terrel, with Ruel at his back, Troy traveled on an urgent wind, a pressure for haste, that threatened to become a gale. He was eager to reach the Ranyhyn. When they met Tull and the other Bloodguard on their way up the trail, he mounted Mehryl at once, and hurried the Ranyhyn into a brisk trot back toward Mithil Stonedown.

He intended to ride straight past the village to the Plains, where the Ranyhyn could run. However, as he and his companions approached the Stonedown, he saw the Circle of elders waiting beside the trail. Reluctantly, he stopped and saluted them.

"Hail, Warmark Troy," Terass Slen-mate replied.

"Hail, Lord Mhoram. We have heard some of the tidings of war, and know that you must make haste. But Triock son of Thuler would speak with you."

As Terass introduced him, Triock stepped forward.

"Hail, elders of Mithil Stonedown," Mhoram responded. "Our thanks again for your hospitality. Triock son of Thuler, we will hear you. But speak swiftly—time presses heavily upon us."

"It is no great matter," said Triock stiffly. "I wish only to seek pardon for my earlier conduct. I have reason for distress, as you know. But I kept my Oath of Peace at Atiaran Trell-mate's behest, at a time when I sorely wished to break it. I have no wish to dishonor her courage now.

"It was my hope that Trell Gravelingas would stay with the High Lord—to protect her." He said this defiantly, as if he expected Mhoram to reprimand him. "Now he is not with her—and I am not with her. My heart fears this. But if it were possible, I would take back my harshness to you."

"There is no need for pardon," Mhoram answered. "My own weak faith provoked you. But I must tell you that I believe Thomas Covenant to be a friend of the Land. The burden of his crime hurts him. I believe he will seek atonement at the High Lord's side."

He paused, and Triock bowed in a way that said he accepted the Lord's words without being convinced. Then Mhoram went on, "Triock son of Thuler, please accept a gift from me—in the name of the High Lord, who is loved by all the Land." Reaching into his robe, he brought out his *lomillialor* rod. "This is High Wood, Triock. You have been in the Loresraat, and will know some of its uses. I will not use it again." He said this with a resolution that surprised Troy. "And you will have need of it. I am called seer and oracle—I speak from knowledge, though the need itself is closed to me. Please accept it—for the sake of the love we share—and as expiation for my doubt."

Triock's eyes widened, and the twisting of his face relaxed briefly. Troy caught a glimpse of what Triock might have looked like if his life had not been blighted.

In silence, he accepted the rod from Lord Mhoram's hands. But when he held the High Wood, his old bitterness gripped his features again, and he said dourly, "I may find a use which will surprise you." Then he bowed, and the other elders bowed with him, freeing Mhoram and Troy to be on their way.

Troy threw them a salute, and took his opportunity. He had no time to spare for Mhoram's strange gift, or for Triock's brooding promises. Instead, he clapped Mehryl with his heels, and led his companions out of the valley of Mithil Stonedown at a gallop.

In a short time, they rounded the western spur of the mountains, and swung out into the Plains. As Troy scanned his companions, he was surprised to see that Tull's mount could keep up the pace. This Ranyhyn had been ridden through danger at cruel speeds for the past eight days, and the strain had wounded its gait. But it was a Ranyhyn; its head was up, its eyes were proud, and its matted mane jumped on its neck like a flag gallantly struggling to unfurl. For a moment, Troy understood why the Ramen did not ride. But he made no concessions to the Ranyhyn's fatigue. Throughout the day, he kept his company running like rapid thunder into the west.

He ached to join his warriors, to share the fight and the desperation with them, to show them the one way in which they might be able to steal a victory out of the teeth of Lord Foul's army. Only an exigent need for sleep forced him to stop during part of the night.

Ruel awakened him before dawn, and he rode on again along the base of the Southron Range. When daylight returned his vision to him, he could see the cliffs near Doom's Retreat ahead. Now his direct route to the Retreat would take him angling rapidly closer to the vanguard of Lord Foul's army. But he kept his heading. Near that horde of *kresh* and ur-viles, he would find whatever was left of the mounted Eoward.

He caught sight of Quaan's force sooner than he had expected. The Hiltmark must have taken his riders on a southward curve toward the Retreat to keep their pursuers as far as possible from the march of the Warward. Shortly after noon, Troy and his com-

panions crested a high foothill which enabled them to
look some distance north into the Plains. And there,
only a league away, they saw the tattered, fleeing remnant of Quaan's command.

At first, Troy felt a thrill of relief. He could see
Hiltmark Quaan riding beside his standard-bearer
among the warriors. At least sixscore Bloodguard galloped among the Eoward. And the blue robes of
Callindrill and Verement were clearly visible through
the dark surge of the retreat.

But then Troy perceived how the riders were moving. They were almost completely routed. In a tight
mass like a swath of panic on the Plains, they pushed
and jostled against each other, threw frantic glances
behind them in ways that unbalanced their mounts,
bristled with angry and fearful cries. Some of them
whipped their horses.

Behind them, the *kresh* ran like a yellow gale
scored with black.

Nevertheless, the distance between the warriors and
the wolves remained constant. After a moment, Troy
understood. Quaan's Eoward were struggling to match
exactly the hunting pace of the *kresh*. The wolves
themselves could not maintain a dead run. They were
forced by the weight of their riders, and by the long
distance of the chase, to travel at the swift, loping gait
of a hunting pack. And Quaan's warriors fought to
keep their flight almost directly under the noses of the
wolves. In this way, they lured the *kresh* onward.
With prey so near, the wolves could neither rest nor
turn aside.

Quaan's strategy was cunning—cunning and fatal.
The warriors also could not rest. They were vulnerable to every spurt of speed from the *kresh*. And any
warrior who was unseated for any reason was instantly torn to pieces. Another Eoward had already
been lost this way. But if Quaan could maintain these
tactics, the marching Eoward would have until late
afternoon to reach their positions in Doom's Retreat.

The Warmark did not bother to calculate the
odds. He urged Mehryl ahead. At full stretch, the
Ranyhyn raced to join Quaan.

When they saw Troy and Lord Mhoram, the warriors gave a raw, dry cheer. Quaan, Callindrill, and Verement dashed out toward the Warmark. But there was little joy in their reunion. The plight of the Eoward was desperate. When he drew close to them, Troy saw that most of the horses were virtually prostrate on their feet; only their fear of the wolves kept them up and running. And the warriors were in no better condition. They had ridden for days without proper food or sleep. None of them lacked injuries. The dust of the Plains clung to their faces and clotted their wounds, making the cuts and rents look like premature scars. Troy had to tear his aching gaze from them to salute the Hiltmark.

Through the thunder of the hooves, Quaan shouted, "Hail, Warmark! Well met!" As Troy swung Mehryl into place beside him, he added, "Not eight days, I fear!"

"Did you send word to Amorine?" Troy yelled.

"Yes!"

"Then it's all right! Seven will be enough!" He clapped the Hiltmark's shoulder, then slowed Mehryl, and dropped back among the warriors.

Immediately, dust and fear and tension swirled around him like the hot breath of the *kresh*. Now he could hear the hunting snarl of the wolves, and the roynish barking of the ur-viles. He felt their presence as if they were his fault—as if they had been created by his folly. Yet he forced himself to smile at his warriors, shout encouragement through the din. He could not afford self-recrimination. The burden of saving the Warward was on his shoulders now.

Moments later, a surge ran through the barking commands of the ur-viles. Troy guessed that the pursuers were about to attempt another spurt.

He looked ahead quickly toward the sheer cliffs of Doom's Retreat. They were no more than two leagues away. There the western tip of the Southron Range swung northward to meet the southeast corner of the mountain wedge which separated the South Plains from Garroting Deep, and between these two ranges was the defile of Doom's Retreat. The narrow canyon lay like a gash through the rock, and its crooked length provided the Land's only access to the Wastes and the Gray Desert.

Troy's gaze sprang to the mouth of the canyon.

The last marching Eoward were still arriving at the Retreat.

If they were not given more time, they would be caught outside the canyon by the *kresh*. Their ambush would fail.

The Warmark was moving too swiftly for hesitation. When he was sure that the Warward had been Quaan's riders, he pushed Mehryl ahead, away from the *kresh*, and caught the Hiltmarks' attention with a wave of his arm. Then he gave Quaan a hand signal which ordered the Eoward to turn and attack.

Quaan did not falter; he understood the need for the order. Despite the maimed condition of his command, he sent up a shrill, piercing whistle which drew the eyes of his officers toward him. With hand signals, he gave the Hafts and Warhafts their instructions.

Almost at once, the riders responded. The outer Eoward peeled back, and the warriors in the center tried to turn where they were. Frantically, they fought their horses around to face the wolves.

Disaster struck the maneuver immediately. As soon as the riders stopped fleeing, *kresh* crashed in among them. The whole trailing edge of Quaan's command went down under the onslaught; and the ur-vile loremasters whirled their iron staves, throwing acid power gleefully over the fallen humans and horses. The screaming of the horses shot through the tumult of snarls and cries. Instantly, a wide swath of gray-green bracken turned blood-red.

But the abrupt profusion of corpses broke the charge of the *kresh*. Their leaders stopped to kill and tear and eat, and this threw the following wolves into confusion. Only the ur-vile wedges drove straight ahead, into the milling heart of the Eoward.

Bloodguard raced to the aid of the warriors. The three Lords threw themselves at the nearest ur-viles. Other warriors rallied and struck. And through the center of the fight Warmark Troy charged like a madman, hacking at every wolf within reach.

For a time, the *kresh* were held. The warriors fought with a desperate fury, and the cool Bloodguard broke wolves in all directions. Working together, the Lords blasted one ur-vile wedge apart, then another. But that accounted for only a tenth of the mounted ur-viles. The others regrouped, began to restore order, coordination, to the *kresh*. Some of the horses lost their footing on the slick ground. Others went out of control with fear, threw their riders, and lost themselves in futile plunges among the wolves.

Troy saw that if any of the warriors were to survive this fight they would have to flee soon.

He battled his way toward the Lords. But suddenly a whole pack of *kresh* swirled about him. Mehryl spun, dodging the fangs and kicking. Troy fought as best he could, but Mehryl's whirling unbalanced him. Twice he almost lost his seat. A wolf leaped up at him, and he barely saved himself by jabbing his sword into its belly.

Then Ruel brought other Bloodguard to his aid. In a concerted charge, ten of them hammered into the pack, shattered it. Troy righted himself, tried uselessly to straighten his missing sunglasses, then cursed himself and sent Mehryl toward the Lords again.

As he moved, he snapped a glance at the Retreat. The last of the marchers were just disappearing down the canyon.

"Do something!" he howled when he neared Lord Mhoram. "We're being slaughtered!"

Mhoram spun and shouted to Callindrill and Verement, then returned to the Warmark. "On my signal!" he yelled over the din. "Flee on my signal!" Without waiting for a reply, he pushed his Ranyhyn into a gallop and dashed toward the Retreat with the other Lords.

In a hundred yards, they separated. Verement stopped directly between the conflict and the Retreat, while Mhoram raced straight north and Callindrill ran south. When they were in position, they formed a long line across the approach to Doom's Retreat.

They dismounted. Lord Verement held his staff upright on the ground in the center as Mhoram and
Callindrill whirled their staffs and shouted strange invocations through the noise of battle. While they prepared, Troy fought his way to Quaan's side, told him
what Mhoram had said. The Hiltmark accepted it
without pausing. They separated, battled away toward
the flanks of the struggle, spreading the command.

Troy feared that Mhoram's call would come too
late. The power of ninetyscore ur-viles rapidly organized the turbulent *kresh*. As the Eoward gathered
themselves to flee, the ur-viles wrenched the *kresh*
away from the tearing of carcasses, bunched them
again into fighting wedges, and hurled them at the
warriors.

In that instant, Lord Mhoram signaled with his
staff.

The riders sent their horses running straight toward
Doom's Retreat. They seemed to rush out from under
the piled spring of the wolves. Once again, the trailing
warriors crashed to the ground under a massive
breaker of *kresh*. But this time the remaining riders
did not fight back. They gave free rein to the fear of
their horses, and fled.

The suddenness of their flight opened a gap between them and the wolves, and the gap widened
slowly as the horses at last found release for all their
accumulated dread. In moments, Troy and Quaan
with the last three Eoward and little more than a
hundred Bloodguard flashed by on either side of Lord
Verement. As they passed him, he took his staff from
where he had planted it in the line between Mhoram
and Callindrill, caught it by one end with both hands,
and cocked it behind his head.

Then the last rider had crossed the line.

Verement swung his staff and struck the ground of
the line with all his might.

Instantly, a shimmering wall of force sprang up between Mhoram and Callindrill. When the first *kresh*
charged it, it flared into brilliant blue flame, and
hurled them back.

Seeing that the wall held, Lord Mhoram leaped onto the Ranyhyn, and sprinted after the warriors. Lord Verement followed as swiftly as his sturdy mustang could carry him. When they neared Troy and Quaan, Mhoram shouted, "Make haste! The forbidding cannot hold! The ur-viles will break it! Flee!"

The warriors needed no urging, and Quaan dashed after them, stridently herding them toward the Retreat. Troy went with him. For a moment, Mhoram and Verement were right behind them. But suddenly the Lords stopped. At the same time, all the Bloodguard wheeled their Ranyhyn, and pounded back toward the forbidding.

Cursing in dismay, Troy turned to see what had happened.

Lord Callindrill was on the ground near the wall. Several badly wounded warriors had fallen from their mounts within yards of the blue fire, and Callindrill was trying to help them. Rapidly, he tore their clothing into strips, made tourniquets and bandages.

He did not look up to see his danger.

Already the ur-viles were preparing to fight the wall. They sent most of the riderless *kresh* running to pass around the ends of the fire. Three ur-vile wedges moved forward to attack. The rest retreated a short distance and began re-forming themselves into a huge, single wedge.

Troy kicked Mehryl into a gallop, and joined the Bloodguard following Mhoram and Verement.

Lord Mhoram was twenty yards ahead of Troy, but he could not reach Callindrill in time. The three ur-vile wedges near the fire attacked. They did not try to break the Lords' wall. Instead, the loremasters concentrated all their power in one place. With a harsh clang, they struck their iron staves together. A great spew of liquid force gushed from the impact, splashed into the forbidding fire, and passed through it.

In black, burning gouts, the corrosive fluid dropped toward Callindrill. It fell just short of him, did not touch him. But it hit the ground with a concussion that flung him and the injured warriors into the air like limp bundles.

When they flopped down again, they lay still.

At once, the three wedges hurried aside, and the new, single, massed wedge started lumbering toward the wall.

Simultaneously, the first *kresh* rounded both ends of the fire.

The next instant, Lord Mhoram threw himself from his Ranyhyn's back, landed beside Callindrill. A quick glance told him that the warriors were dead; the force of the concussion had killed them. He concentrated on Callindrill. Touching the Lord's chest with his hands, he confirmed what his eyes told him; life still flickered in Callindrill, but his heart was not beating.

Then Troy reached Mhoram's side, and the Bloodguard poised themselves to defend the Lords. On horseback, Verement worked at the wall of forbidding, tightened it against the assault of the wedge. But it could not withstand fifteen hundred ur-viles. The wedge moved slowly, but it was hardly twenty yards from the fire. And *kresh* poured around the ends of the wall now, pelting toward the Bloodguard and Lords. The Bloodguard moved out to meet the wolves, but a hundred Bloodguard could not hold back five thousand *kresh* for long.

"Flee!" Mhoram yelled. "Go! Save yourselves! We must not all die here!"

But he did not wait to observe that no one obeyed him. Instead, he bent over the fallen Lord again. Holding his lower lip in his teeth, he massaged Callindrill's chest, hoping to renew his pulse. But his heart remained motionless.

Mhoram drew a sudden sharp breath, raised his fist, and hammered once with all his might on Callindrill's chest.

The blow jolted the Lord's heart. It lurched, stumbled, then broke into a limping beat.

Mhoram shouted for Morril. At once, the Bloodguard leaped down from his Ranyhyn, caught Callindrill in his arms, and sprang up again. Seeing this, Lord Verement broke away from the forbidding wall, started back toward Doom's Retreat. Mhoram and Troy mounted, surged away from the wall after him.

The Bloodguard followed in a protective ring around the Lords.

A moment later, the massed ur-vile wedge hit the wall and tore it. Dark, liquid power shredded the blue flame, ripped it into fragments and scattered it. Instantly, the rest of the *kresh* flooded after the escaping Ranyhyn. And the wolves pouring around the ends of the wall changed direction to intercept the riders.

But the Ranyhyn outdistanced them. The great horses of Ra pulled past Verement and thundered toward Doom's Retreat.

Ahead, under the late afternoon shadow of the cliffs, Hiltmark Quaan was urging the last of his warriors into the canyon.

Maddened by the escape of so many prey, the *kresh* howled with rage, and swung to converge on Lord Verement.

His mustang ran hard and bravely. But it was already exhausted; slowly the *kresh* gained on it. Before it had covered half the distance to the Retreat, Troy could see that it would lose the race.

He called for help, but the Bloodguard did not respond. Only Thomin, the Bloodguard personally responsible for Verement, remained behind. Incensed, Troy started to go back himself, but Mhoram stopped him by shouting, "There is no need!"

Thomin waited until the last possible moment—until the *kresh* were raging at the heels of the mustang. Then he pulled the Lord onto his own Ranyhyn, and carried him away toward the Retreat.

Almost at once, the mustang fell screaming under an avalanche of wolves.

For an instant, the haze of the cliff shadow turned sickly red in Troy's sight. But then Mehryls' taut run bore him beyond the scream, took him straight toward the gap in the cliffs. He flashed into the deeper gloom of the defile. Except for the slit of light ahead, he could see nothing. The sharp change made him feel that he was foundering. The rumble of hooves pounded back at him from the cliffs, and behind the echo came the shrill croaking derision of the ravens. He felt waters of darkness closing over his head. When he broke

out the end of the Retreat into the dim, late light of
day, he was almost dazzled with relief.

As he passed, First Haft Amorine gave a piercing
shout, and thousands of warriors dashed away from
the cliffs on either side of the gap. Despite the long
fatigue which radiated from them, they ran with precision, took positions, formed an arc over the end of
the canyon, sealing the trap.

Moments later, the first *kresh* came howling out of
the Retreat and sprang at them. The whole arc of
warriors staggered under the shock of impact. But
Amorine had eighteen Eoward braced to meet the onslaught. The arc gave ground, but did not break.

With an effort, Troy brought himself under control.
Over to one side, he could hear Lord Verement barking, "Release me! Am I a child, that I must be carried?" Troy grinned grimly, then drew Mehryl up
behind the arc so that he would be ready to help his
warriors if the wolves outweighed them. He ached to
see the outcome of the trap, but the darkness of the
Retreat foiled his sight.

Soon, however, he could hear the sounds of combat
echoing out of the defile. Over the noise of the embat-
tled arc, he made out a sudden raw howl as the *kresh*
in the Retreat found themselves attacked from above
by twenty Eoward hidden in the canyon walls. At
first, the howl contained surprise and ferocity, but no
fear; the wolves did not understand their danger.

The ur-viles were wiser. Their commands cut stridently through the rage of the wolves. And soon the
howling changed. To their dismay, the *kresh* began to
understand the glee of the ravens. And the yammering of the ur-viles became fiercer, more desperate. In
the narrow defile, they could not make effective use of
their fighting wedges, and without that focus of power,
they were vulnerable to arrows and spears and rockfalls. Caught in a seething, confused mass of wolves,
the wedges began to collapse.

As the wedges crumbled, fear and uncertainty penetrated the wolves' fury for blood. In tattered bunches,
the *kresh* broke away, tried to flee through the canyon. But the cramped panic of their numbers only

hampered them, and made the ur-viles more vulnerable. And death rained down on them through the jeering of the ravens. In mad frenzy, wild to fight an enemy they could not reach, the *kresh* started to attack the ur-viles.

No wolves or ur-viles escaped. When the battle was done, the entire vanguard of Fleshharrower's army lay dead in Doom's Retreat.

For one moment, a hush fell over the battleground; even the ravens were silent. Then a hoarse cheer came echoing from the canyon. The Eoward sealing the end of the Retreat responded loudly. And the ravens began sailing down to the defile's floor, where they feasted on Demondim-spawn and *kresh*.

Slowly, Troy became aware that First Haft Amorine was at his side. When he turned to her, he felt that he was grinning insanely, but even without his sunglasses he did not care. "Congratulations, Amorine," he said. "You've done well." The evening fog on his sight was already so bad that he had to ask her about casualties.

"We have lost few warriors," she replied with dour satisfaction. "Your battle plan is a good one."

But her praise only reminded him of the rest of Lord Foul's army, and of the ordeal still before the Warward. He shook his head. "Not good enough." But then, rather than explain what he meant, he said to her, "First Haft, give my thanks to the warriors. Get them fed and settled for the night—there won't be any more fighting today. When they're taken care of, we'll have a council."

Amorine's gaze showed that she did not understand his attitude, but she saluted without question, and moved away to carry out his orders. His blank mist swallowed her at once. Darkness blew about him as if it rode on the wind of the Warward's shouting. He called for Ruel, and asked the Bloodguard to guide him to Lord Mhoram.

They found Mhoram beside a small campfire under the lee of the westward mountains. He was tending Lord Callindrill. Callindrill had regained consciousness, but his skin was as pale as alabaster, and he looked weak. Mhoram cooked some broth over the campfire, and massaged Callindrill while the broth heated.

Lord Callindrill greeted the Warmark faintly, and Troy replied with pleasure. He was glad to see that Callindrill was not mortally injured; he was going to need the Lord. He was going to need every help or power that he could find.

But he had other things to consider before he began to think about his need for help. When he had assured himself that Lord Callindrill was on the way to recovery, he drew Mhoram away for a private talk.

He waited until they were beyond earshot of the Warward's camp. Then he sighed wearily, "Mhoram, we're not finished. We can't stop here." Without transition, as if he had not changed subjects, he went on, "What are we going to do about Lord Verement? One of us has got to tell him—about Shetra. I'll do it if you want. I probably deserve it."

"I will do it," Mhoram murmured distantly.

"All right." Troy felt acutely relieved to be free of that responsibility. "Now, what about this—what Tull told us? I don't like the idea of telling everyone that—that the mission—" He could not bring himself to say the words, *The Giants are dead.* "I don't think the warriors will survive what's ahead if they know what happened to the mission. It's too much. Having three Giants taken over by Ravers is bad enough. And I'll have to tell them worse things than that myself."

Softly, Mhoram breathed, "They deserve to know the truth."

"Deserve?" Troy's deep feeling of culpability flooded into anger. "What they deserve is victory. By God, don't tell me what they deserve! It's a little late for you to start worrying about what they know or don't know. You've seen fit to keep secrets from me all along. God knows how many horrors you still haven't told me. Keep your mouth shut about this."

"That choice was made by the Council. No one person has the right to withhold knowledge from another. No one is wise enough." Mhoram spoke as if he were wrestling with himself.

"It's too late for that. If you want to talk about

rights—you don't have the right to destroy my army."

"My friend, have you—have you suffered—has the withholding of knowledge harmed you?"

"How should I know? Maybe if you had told me the truth—about Atiaran—we wouldn't be here now. Maybe I would have been afraid of the risk. You tell me if that's good or bad." Then his anger softened. "Mhoram," he pleaded, "they're right on the edge. I've already pushed them right to the edge. And we're not done. I just want to spare them something that will hurt so bad—"

"Very well," Mhoram sighed in a tone of defeat. "I will not speak of the Giants."

"Thank you," Troy said intensely.

Mhoram gazed at him searchingly, but through his darkness he could not read the Lord's expression. For a moment, he feared that Mhoram was about to tell him something, reveal the last mysteries of Trell and Elena and Covenant. He did not want to hear such things—not now, when he was already so overburdened. But finally the Lord turned silently and started back toward Callindrill.

Troy followed him. But on the way he paused to speak with Terrel, who was the ranking Bloodguard. "Terrel, I want you to send scouts out to the South Plains. I don't expect Foul's army before midday tomorrow, but we shouldn't take any chances—and the warriors are too tired. But there's one thing. If Foul or Fleshharrower or whoever is in command sends any scouts this way, make sure they know we're here. I don't want them to have any doubt about where to find us."

"Yes, Warmark," Terrel said, and stepped away to make the arrangements. Troy and Mhoram went on to their campfire.

They found Lord Verement feeding Callindrill. As he spooned the broth to Callindrill's lips, the hawk-faced Lord talked steadily in a low, exasperated tone, as if his pride were offended; but his movements were gentle, and he did not abandon the task to Mhoram. He hovered over Callindrill until the warm broth had restored a touch of color to his pale cheeks. Then

Verement stood up and rasped, "You would be less foolhardy were you not Ranyhyn-borne. A lesser mount would teach you the limits of your own strength."

This inverted repetition of Verement's old accusation against himself momentarily overcame Lord Mhoram. A moan escaped through his teeth, and his eyes filled with tears. For that moment, his courage seemed to fail him, and he reached toward Verement as if he were groping through blind grief. But then he caught himself, smiled crookedly at the rough look of surprise and concern on Verement's face. "Come, my brother," he murmured. "I must speak with you." Together, they walked away into the night, leaving Troy to watch over Callindrill.

In a wan voice, Callindrill asked, "What has happened? What disturbs Mhoram?"

Sighing heavily, Troy seated himself beside the Lord. He was full of all the evil he had caused. He had to swallow several times before he could find his voice to say, "Runnik came back from Korik's mission. Lord Shetra died in the Sarangrave."

Then he was grateful that Callindrill did not speak. He did not think he could stand the reprimand of any more pain. They sat together in silence until Lord Mhoram returned alone.

Mhoram carried himself sorely, as if he had just been beaten with clubs. The flesh around his eyes was red and swollen, sorrowful. But his eyes themselves wielded a hot peril, and his glances were like spears. He said nothing about Lord Verement. Words were unnecessary; Mhoram's expression revealed how Verement took the news of his wife's death.

To steady himself, Mhoram set about preparing food for Troy and himself. Their meal passed under a shroud of gloom, but as he ate Lord Mhoram slowly mastered himself, relaxed the pain in his face. To match him, Warmark Troy grappled inwardly for the tone of confidence he would need when the council started. He did not want his doubt to show; he did not intend to make his army pay for his personal dilemmas and inadequacies. When Hiltmark Quaan approached the fire and announced that all the Hafts were ready, both Troy and Mhoram answered him resolutely, calmly.

The Lord threw a large pile of wood onto the fire while Quaan brought his officers into a wide circle around it. But despite the bright blaze of the fire, the Hafts looked hazy and insubstantial to Troy. For an irrational instant, he feared that they would break into illusions and disappear when he told them what they had to do. But he braced himself. Hiltmark Quaan and First Haft Amorine stood near him like pillars on one side, and Lord Mhoram watched him from the other. Clearing his throat, he opened the council.

"Well, we're here. In spite of everything, we've accomplished something that any of us would have said was impossible. Before we get into what's ahead, I want to thank you all for what you've done. I'm proud of you—more than I'll ever be able to say."

As he spoke, he had to resist a temptation to duck his head, as if he were ashamed of his uncovered eyelessness. Painfully, he wondered what effect this view of him would have on the Hafts. But he forced himself to hold his head up as he continued. "But I have to tell you plainly—we haven't come near winning this war yet. We've made a good start, but it's only a start. Things are going to get worse—" He lost his voice for a moment, and had to clench himself to recover it. "It's not going to work out the way I planned. Hiltmark Quaan—First Haft Amorine— you've done everything you could do—everything I asked. But it's not going to work out the way I told you it would.

"But—first things first. We've got reports to make. Hiltmark, will you go first?"

Quaan bowed, and stepped forward into the circle. His square, white-haired visage was streaked with grime and blood and fatigue, but his open gaze did not falter. In blunt, unaffected language, he described all that had happened to his command since he had left Revelstone—the raft ride and run to the Mithil valley, the blockade there, the progression of the battle as Fleshharrower, the corrupted Giant of whom

Manethrall Rue had spoken, organized successive efforts to break the hold of the defenders. For five days, the Bloodguard, the warriors, and the two Lords withstood Cavewights, *kresh,* warped manlike creations of the Illearth Stone, ur-viles.

"But on the sixth day," Quaan continued, "Fleshharrower came against us himself." Now his voice expressed the weariness of long fighting and lost warriors. "With a power that I do not name, he called a great storm against us. Abominable creatures like those of which Manethrall Rue spoke fell upon us from the sky. They cast fear among our mounts, and we were driven back. Then Fleshharrower broke the forbidding, and sent *kresh* and ur-viles to pursue us. Time and again, we turned to fight, so that the enemy might be delayed—and time and again we were overmastered. Often we sent riders ahead to bear warning, but every messenger was slain—flocks of savage cormorants assailed them from the sky, and destroyed them all, though some of them were Bloodguard.

"Still we fought," he concluded. "At last we are here. But half the Bloodguard and eight of the Eoward were slain. And the horses have passed the end of their strength. Many will never bear riders again, and all need long days of rest. The battle which remains must be met afoot."

When he finished, he returned to his place in the circle. His courage was evident, but as he moved, his square shoulders seemed already to be carrying all the weight they could bear. And because Troy could find no words for his respect and gratitude, he said nothing. Silently, he nodded to First Haft Amorine.

She described briefly the last few days of the Warward's march, then she reported on the present condition of the army. "Water and *aliantha* are not plentiful here, beyond Doom's Retreat. The Warward carries food which may be stretched for five days or six—no more. The warriors themselves are sorely damaged by their march. Even the uninjured are crippled by exhaustion. Great numbers have wounds about their feet and shoulders—wounds which do not heal. Threescore of the weakest died during our last run to the Retreat. Many more will die if the War-ward does not rest now."

Her words made Troy groan inwardly; they were full of unintended reproaches. He was the Warmark. He had promised victory again and again to people who trusted him. And now— He felt a sharp desire to berate himself, tell the Hafts just how badly he had miscalculated. But before he could begin, Lord Callindrill spoke. The wounded Lord was supported by two Bloodguard, but he was able to make his weak voice heard.

"I must speak of the power which Hiltmark Quaan did not name. I still do not comprehend how the Despiser gained mastery over a Giant—it surpasses my understanding. But Fleshharrower is in truth a Giant, and he is possessed of a great power. He bears with him a fragment of the Illearth Stone."

Lord Mhoram nodded painfully. "Alas, my friends," he said, "this is a dark time for all the Land. Danger and death beset us on every hand, and ill defies all defense. Hear me. I know how this Giant—this Flesh-harrower—has been turned against us. It is accomplished through the combined might of the Stone and the Ravers. Either alone would not suffice—the Giants are strong and sure. But together—! Who in the Land could hope to endure? Therefore the Giant carries a fragment of the Illearth Stone, so that the Despiser's power will remain upon him, and the Raver will possess an added weapon. *Melenkurion abatha!* This is a great evil."

For a moment, he stood silent as if in dismay, and distress filled the Hafts as they tasted the magnitude of the ill he described. But then he drew himself up, and his eyes flashed around the circle. "Yet it is always thus with the Despiser. Let not the knowledge of this evil blind you or weaken you. Lord Foul seeks to turn all the good of the Land to harm and corruption. Our task is clear. We must find the strength to turn harm and corruption to good. For that reason we fight. If we falter now, we become like Fleshharrower —unwilling enemies of the Land."

His stern words steadied the Hafts, helped them to

recover their resolve. However, before he or Troy could continue, Lord Verement said harshly, "What of the Giants, Mhoram? What of the mission? How many other souls have already been lost to the Despiser?"

Verement had entered the circle across from Troy while Lord Callindrill had been speaking. The clouds on Troy's sight prevented him from seeing Verement's expression, but when the Lord spoke his voice was raw with bitterness. "Answer, Mhoram. Seer and oracle! Is Hyrim dead also? Do any Giants yet live?"

Troy felt Verement's bitterness as an attack on the Warward, and he used words like whips to strike back. "That isn't our concern. There's nothing we can do about it. We're stuck here—we're going to live or die here! It doesn't matter what's happening anywhere else." In his heart, he felt that he was betraying the Giants, but he had no choice. "All we can do is fight! Do you hear me?"

"I hear you." Lord Verement fell silent as if he understood Troy's vehemence, and the Warmark seized his chance to change the subject.

"All right," he said to the whole circle. "At least now we know where we stand. Now I'll tell you what we're going to do about it. I have a plan, and with Lord Mhoram's help I'm going to make it work."

Bracing himself, he said bluntly, "We're going to leave here. Fleshharrower and his army probably won't arrive before midday tomorrow. By that time, we will be long gone."

The Hafts gaped and blinked momentarily as they realized that he was ordering another march. Then several of them groaned aloud, and others recoiled as if he had struck them. Even Quaan winced openly. Troy wanted to rush into explanations, but he contained himself until Amorine stepped forward and protested, "Warmark, why will your former plan not suffice? The warriors have given their utmost to gain Doom's Retreat as you commanded. Why must we leave?"

"Because Foul's army is too goddamn big!" He did not want to shout, but for a while he could not stop himself. "We've killed ten thousand *kresh* and a couple thousand ur-viles. But the rest of that army is still out there! It's not three times bigger than we are—or even five times bigger! Fleshharrower has twenty times our numbers, twenty! I've seen them." With an effort, he caught hold of his pointless fury, jerked it down. "My old plan was a good one while it lasted," he went on. "But it just didn't take into account that Foul's army might be so big. Now there's only two things that can happen. If that Giant sends his army in here just ten or twenty thousand at a time, the fight is going to last for weeks. But we've only got food for six days—we'll starve to death in here. And if he cuts through in one big blast, he'll get control of both ends of the Retreat. Then we'll be trapped, and he can pick us off in his own good time.

"Now listen to me!" he shouted again at the chagrined Hafts. "I'm not going to let us get slaughtered as long as there is anything I can do to stop it—anything at all! And there is one thing, just one! I've got one more trick to play in this game, and I'm going to play it if I have to carry every one of you on my back!"

He glared around the circle, trying to fill his eyeless stare with authority, command, some kind of power that would make the Warward obey him. "We will march at dawn tomorrow."

Darkness shrouded his sight, but in the firelight he could see Quaan's face. The old veteran was wrestling with himself, struggling to find the strength for this new demand. He closed his eyes briefly, and all the Hafts waited for him as if he had their courage in his hands, to uphold or deny as he saw fit. When he opened his eyes, his face seemed to sag with fatigue. But his voice was steady.

"Warmark, where will we march?"

"West for now," Troy replied quickly, "toward those old ruins. It won't be too bad. If we handle things right, we can go slower than we have so far."

"Will you tell us your plan?"

"No." Troy was tempted to say, If I tell you, you'll be so horrified that you'll never follow me. But instead he added, "I want to keep it to myself for a while—get it ready. You'll just have to trust me." He sounded to himself like a man falling out of a tree, shouting to the people above him as he fell that he would catch them.

"Warmark," Quaan said stiffly, "you know that I will always trust you. We all trust you."

"Yes, I know," Troy sighed. A sudden weariness flooded over him, and he could barely hear his own voice. He had already fallen a long way since he had left Revelstone. Miscalculations denuded his ideas of all their vitality, divested them of their power to save. He wondered how many other things he would have torn from him before this war was done. A long moment passed before he could find enough energy to say, "There's one more thing. It's got to be done—we don't have any choice anymore. We've got to leave some people behind. To try to hold the Retreat—make Fleshharrower think we're still here—slow him down. It'll be suicide, so we'll need volunteers. Two or three Eoward should be enough to make it work."

Quaan and Amorine took this stolidly; they were warriors, familiar with this kind of thinking. But before Troy could say anything else, Lord Verement sprang into the circle. "No!" he barked, striking the ground with his staff. "None will be left behind. I forbid it!"

Now Troy could see him clearly. His lean face looked as sharp as if it had been taken to a grindstone, and his eyes flamed keenly. Troy's throat felt abruptly bone-dry. With difficulty, he said, "Lord Verement, I'm sorry. I've got no choice. This march'll kill the warriors unless they can go more slowly. So somebody has got to gain them time."

"Then I will do it!" Verement's tone was raw. "I will hold Doom's Retreat. It is a fit place for me."

"You can't," Troy objected, almost stammering. "I can't let you. I'll need you with me." Unable to bear the force of Verement's gaze, he turned to Lord Mhoram for help.

"Warmark Troy speaks truly," Mhoram said carefully. "Death will not heal your grief. And you will be sorely needed in the days ahead. You must come with us."

"By the Seven!" Verement cried. "Do you not hear me? I have said that I will remain! Shetra my wife is lost! She whom I loved with all my strength, and yet did not love enough. *Melenkurion!* Do not speak to me of cannot or must! I will remain. No warriors will be left behind."

Mhoram cut in, "Lord Verement, do you believe that you are able to defeat Fleshharrower?"

But Verement did not reply to that question. "Heal Callindrill," he said harshly. "I will require you both. And call the Bloodguard from the Plains. I start at dawn." Then he swung away, and stalked out of the circle into the night.

His departure left Troy bewildered and exhausted. He felt that the burden of the Warward already clung to his shoulders, bent his back so that he moved as if he were decrepit. His confused fatigue made him unfit for speeches, and he dismissed the Hafts abruptly. As he did so, he felt that he was failing them—that they needed him to lead them, give them a strong figure around which they could rally. But he had no strength. He went to his blankets as if he hoped that some kind of fortitude would come to him in a dream.

He sank at once into exhaustion, and slept until sleep was no longer possible for him—until the sunrise above the mountains filled his brain with shapes and colors. When he arose, he discovered that he had slept through all the noise of the Warward as it broke camp and began its march. Already the last Eoward were shambling away from Doom's Retreat. They trudged as if they were maimed into the dry, heat-pale land of the Southron Wastes.

Cursing dully at his weakness, he grabbed a few bites of the food Ruel offered him, then hurried away toward the Retreat.

There he found Callindrill and Mhoram, with a small group of Bloodguard. On either side of the defile's southern end, the Lords had climbed as high as they could up the scree into the jumbled boulders piled against the canyon walls. From these positions, they plied their staffs in a way that cast a haze across the air between them.

Beyond them, in Doom's Retreat itself, Lord Verement clambered over the rocks and fallen shale. As he moved, he waved the fire of his staff like a torch against the darkness of the cliffs. Only Thomin accompanied him.

Troy looked closely at Callindrill. The wounded Lord looked wan and tired, and sweat glistened on his pale forehead, but he stood on his own, and wielded his staff firmly. Troy saluted him, then climbed the scree on the other side to join Lord Mhoram.

When he reached Mhoram, he sat and watched while the haze moved and took shape. It appeared to revolve slowly like a large wheel standing in the end of the Retreat. Its circumference fitted just within the scree and stone, so that it effectively blocked the canyon floor, and it turned as if it were hanging on a pivot between Mhoram and Callindrill. Beyond it, Troy could see only the empty Retreat—the raven-cleaned bones of the ur-viles and wolves—and the lone Lord struggling up and down the sides of the canyon with his flame bobbing like a will-o'-the-wisp.

Soon, however, both Mhoram and Callindrill ended their exertions. They planted their staffs like anchors in the edges of the haze, and leaned back to rest. Lord Mhoram greeted Troy tiredly.

After a moment's hesitation, Troy nodded toward Verement. "What's he doing?"

Mhoram closed his eyes, and said as if he were answering Troy, "We have made a Word of Warning."

While he was thinking of ways to rephrase his question, Troy asked, "What does it do?"

"It seals Doom's Retreat."

"How will it work? I can see it. It won't take Fleshharrower by surprise."

"Your sight is keen in some ways. I cannot see the Word."

Awkwardly, Troy asked, "Is there anyone still out there—besides Verement?"

"No. All the warriors have left. The scouts have

been recalled. None may pass this way now without encountering the Word."

"So he's committed himself—he's stuck out there."

"Yes." Mhoram bit at the word angrily.

Troy returned to his first question. "What does he hope to gain? It's suicide."

Mhoram opened his eyes, and Troy felt the force of the Lord's gaze. "We will gain time," Mhoram said. "You spoke of a need for time." Then he sighed and looked away down the canyon. "And Lord Verement Shetra-mate will gain an end to anguish."

Numbly, Troy watched Verement. The hawkish Lord did not look like a man in search of relief. He threw himself up and down in the tumbled edges of the defile, kicked his way through the shale and the fleshless bones and the watchful silence of the ravens, as if he were possessed. And he was exhausting himself. Already his stride was unsteady, and he had fallen several times. Yet he had covered less than a third of Doom's Retreat with the invisible skein of his fire. But some power, some relentless coercion of will, kept him going. Throughout the morning, he continued his weird progress along the canyon, stopping only at rare moments to accept water and treasure-berries from Thomin. By midmorning, he was half done.

Now, however, he could no longer keep up his pace. He had to lean on Thomin as he stumbled up into the rocks and down again, and his staff's fire guttered and smoked. A few ravens dropped out of their high nests and sailed around him as if to see how much longer he would endure. But he went on; the force which blazed in him did not waver.

In the end, he was compelled to leave the last yards of the Retreat unwoven. Thomin pointed out to him the rising dust of Fleshharrower's approach. Shortly, the leading wave of yellow wolves came into view. Lord Verement dropped his task, straightened his shoulders; he gave Thomin one final order. Then he walked out of Doom's Retreat to meet the army of the Despiser.

The wide front of wolves rushed toward him, suddenly eager for prey. But at the last they hesitated, halted. The unflinching challenge of his stance threw them into confusion. Though they snapped and snarled fiercely, they did not attack. They encircled the two men, and ran howling around them while the rest of the army made its approach.

Fleshharrower's army marched out of the northeast until the dark line of it filled the horizon, and the tramping of its myriad feet shook the ground. The Despiser's hordes seemed to cover the whole Plains, and their tremendous numbers dwarfed Lord Verement like an ocean. When the Giant came forward, kicked his way through the wolves to confront the Lord and the Bloodguard, his size alone made the two men appear puny and insignificant.

But when the Giant was within ten yards of him, Verement made a forbidding gesture. "Come no closer, *moksha* Raver!" he shouted hoarsely. "I know you, Jehannum Fleshharrower! Go back! Back to the evil which made you. I deny you passage—I, Verement Shetra-mate, Lord of the Council of Revelstone! You may not pass here!"

Fleshharrower stopped. "Ah, a Lord," he said, peering down at Verement as if the Lord were too tiny to be seen easily. "I am amazed." His face was twisted, and his leer gave him an expression of acute pain, as if his flesh could not disguise the hurt of the rabid presence within it. But his voice seemed to suck and cling in the air like quicksand. It held only derision and lust as he continued, "Have you come to welcome me to the slaughter of your army? But of course you know it is too small to be called an army. I have fought and followed you from Andelain, but do not think that you have outwitted me. I know you seek to meet me in Doom's Retreat because your army is too weak to fight elsewhere. Perhaps you have come to surrender—to join me."

"You speak like a fool," Verement barked. "No friend of the Land will ever surrender to you, or join you. Admit the truth, and go. Go, I say! *Melenkurion abatha!*" Abruptly, he caught his staff in both hands and raised it over his head. *"Duroc minas mill khabaal!* With all the names of the Earthpower, I command you! There is no victory for the Despiser here!"

As Verement shouted his Words, the Raver flinched. To defend himself, he thrust his hand into his leather jerkin, snatched out a smooth green stone that filled his fist. A lambent emerald flame played in its depths, and it steamed like boiling ice. He clenched it, made it steam more viciously, and exclaimed, "Verement Shetra-mate, for a hundred leagues I have driven two Lords before me like ants! Why do you believe that you can resist me now?"

"Because you have killed Shetra my wife!" the Lord cried in rage. "Because I have been unworthy of her all my life! Because I do not fear you, Raver! I am free of all restraint! No fear or love limits my strength! I match you hate for hate, *moksha* Raver! *Melenkurion abatha!*"

His staff whirled about his head, and a livid blue bolt of power sprang from the wood at Fleshharrower. Simultaneously, Thomin rushed forward with his fingers crooked like claws, threw himself at the Giant's throat.

Fleshharrower met the attack easily, disdainfully. He caught Verement's bolt on his Stone and held it burning there like a censer. Almost at once, the blue flame turned deep dazzling green, blazed up higher. And with his other hand, the Giant dealt Thomin a blow which sent him sprawling behind Verement.

Then Fleshharrower flung the fire back.

The Lord's fury never winced. Swinging his staff, he jabbed its metal end like a lance into the gout of power. Savage cracking noises came from the wood as it bucked and bent—but the staff held. Verement shouted mighty words over the flame, compelled it to his will again. Slowly the green burned blue on his staff. When he had mastered it, he hurled it again at the Raver.

Fleshharrower began to laugh. Verement's attack, multiplied by some of the Giant's own power, caught on the Stone as if the green rock were its wick. There it grew hungrily until the column of emerald fire reached high into the air.

Laughing, the Raver shot this fire toward Verement. It splintered his staff, flash-burned the pieces to cinders, deluged him. But then the flame bent itself to his form, gripped him, clung and crawled all over him like a corona. His arms dropped, his head fell forward until his chin touched his chest, his eyes closed; he hung in the fire as if he had been nailed there.

Triumphantly, Fleshharrower cried, "Now, Verement Shetra-mate! Where is your defiance now?" For a moment, his derision scaled upward, echoed off the cliffs. Then he went on: "Defeated, I see. But harken to me, puppet. It may be that I will let you live. Of course, to gain life you must change your allegiance. Repeat these words— 'I worship Lord Foul the Despiser. He is the one word of truth.' "

Lord Verement's lips remained clamped shut. Within the paralyzing fire, his cheek muscles bulged as he set his jaws.

"Speak it!" Fleshharrower roared. With a jerk of the Stone, he tightened the corona around Verement. A gasp of agony tore the Lord's lips apart. He began to speak.

"I—worship—"

He went no further. Behind him, Thomin jumped up to carry out his last duty. With one kick, the Bloodguard broke Lord Verement's back. Instantly, the Lord fell dead.

Thomin's face was taut with murder as he sprang again at Fleshharrower's throat.

This time, the Bloodguard's attack was so swift and ruthless that it broke past the Raver's defenses. He caught Fleshharrower, dug his fingers into the Giant's neck. For a moment, the Giant could not tear him away. He ground his fingers into that thick throat with such passion that Fleshharrower could not break his hold.

But then the Raver brought the Stone to his aid. With one blast, he burned Thomin's bones to ash with-

in him. The Bloodguard collapsed in a heap of struc-
tureless flesh.

Then for a time Fleshharrower seemed to go mad.
Roaring like a cataclysm, he jumped and stamped on
Thomin's form until the Bloodguard's bloody remains
were crushed into the grass. And after that, he sent
the vast hordes of his wolves howling into the gullet
of Doom's Retreat. Driven by his fury, they ran blindly
down the canyon, and hurtled into the Word of Warning.

The first wolf to touch the Word triggered it. In
that instant, the piled rock within the walls seemed to
blow apart. The power which Verement had placed
there threw down the sloped sides of the defile. A
deadly rain of boulders and shale fell into the canyon,
crushing thousands of wolves so swiftly that the pack
had time for only one yowl of terror.

When the dust blew clear, Fleshharrower could see
that the Retreat was now blocked, crowded with
crumbled rock and scree. An army might spend days
struggling through the rubble.

The setback appeared to calm him. The hunger for
vengeance did not leave his eyes, but his voice was
steady as he shouted his commands. He called forward
the *griffins*. Flying heavily with ur-viles on their backs,
they went into the Retreat to fight Verement's Word.
And behind them Fleshharrower sent his rock-wise
Cavewights to clear the way for the rest of the army.

Compelled by his power, the creatures worked with
headlong desperation. Many of the *griffins* were destroyed because they flew mindlessly against the Word.
Scores of Cavewights killed each other in their frenzy
to clear the debris from the canyon floor. But lore-wise
ur-viles finally tore down the Word of Warning. And
the Cavewights accomplished prodigious feats. Given
sufficient time and numbers, they had the strength and
skill to move mountains. Now they heaved and tore at
the rubble. They worked through the night, and by
dawn they had cleared a path ten yards wide down
the center of the Retreat.

Holding the Stone high, Fleshharrower led his army
through the canyon. At the south end of the Retreat,

he found the Warward gone. The last of his enemies
—a small band of riders including two Lords—were
galloping away out of reach. He howled imprecations
after them, vowing that he would pursue them to the
death.

But then his farseeing Giantish eyes made out the
Warward, seven or eight leagues beyond the riders.
He marked the direction of their march—saw where
they were headed. And he began to laugh again. Peals
of sarcasm and triumph echoed off the blank cliffs of
Doom's Retreat.

The Warward marched toward Garroting Deep.

NINETEEN: The Ruins of the Southron Wastes

By the time Warmark Troy rode away from
Doom's Retreat with the Lords Mhoram and Callindrill and a group of Bloodguard, he had put aside his
enervation, his half-conscious yearning to hide his
head. Gone, too, was the sense of horror which had
paralyzed him when Lord Verement died. He had
pushed these things down during the dark night, while
Mhoram and Callindrill fought to maintain the Word
of Warning. Now he felt strangely cauterized. He was
the Warmark, and he had returned to his work. He
was thinking—measuring distances, gauging relative
speeds, forecasting the Warward's attrition rate. He
was in command.

He could see his army's need for leadership as
clearly as if it were in some way atrocious. Ahead of
him, the Warward had swung slightly south to avoid
the immediate foothills of the mountains, and across
this easier ground it moved at a pace which would
cover no more than seven leagues a day. But still the
conditions of the march were horrendous. His army

was traveling into the dry half-desert of the Southron Wastes.

No vestige or hint of autumn ameliorated the arid breeze which blew northward off the parched, lifeless Gray Desert. Most of the grass had already failed, and the few rills and rivulets which ran down out of the mountains evaporated before they reached five leagues into the Wastes. And even south of the foot-hills the terrain was difficult—eroded and rasped and cut by long ages of sterile wind into jagged hills, gullies, arroyos. The result was a stark, heat-pale land possessed by a weird and unfriendly beauty. The War-ward had to march over packed ground that felt as hard and hostile as rock underfoot, and yet sent up thick dust as if the soil were nothing but powder.

Within three leagues of the Retreat, Troy and his companions found the first dead warrior. The Wood-helvennin corpse lay contorted on the ground like a torture victim. Exhaustion blackened its lips and tongue, and its staring eyes were full of dust. Troy had a mad impulse to stop and bury the warrior. But he was sure of his calculations; in this acrid heat, the losses of the Warward would probably double every day. None of the living could afford the time or strength to care for the dead.

By the time the Warmark caught up with his army, he had counted ten more fallen warriors. Numbers thronged in his brain: eleven dead the first day, twenty-two the second, forty-four the third—six hundred and ninety-three human beings killed by the cruel demands of the march before he reached his destination. And God alone knew how many more— He found himself wondering if he would ever be able to sleep again.

But he forced himself to pay attention as Quaan and Amorine reported on their efforts to keep the warriors alive. Food was rationed; all water jugs were refilled at every stream, however small; every Haft and Warhaft moved on foot, so that their horses could carry the weakest men and women; Quaan's remaining riders also walked, and their damaged mounts bore packs and collapsed warriors; all scouting and water

gathering were done by the Bloodguard. And every
warrior who could go no farther was supplied with
food, and ordered to seek safety in the mountains.

There was nothing else the commanders could do.

All this filled Troy with pain. But then Quaan described to him how very few warriors chose to leave
the march and hide in the hills. That news steadied
Troy; he felt it was both terrible and wonderful that
so many men and women were willing to follow him
to the utter end of his ideas. He mustered his confidence to answer Quaan's and Amorine's inevitable
questions.

Quaan went bluntly to the immediate problem.
"Does Fleshharrower pursue us?"

"Yes," Troy replied. "Lord Verement gained us
about a day. But that Giant is coming after us now—
he's coming fast."

Quaan did not need to ask what had happened to
Lord Verement. Instead, he said, "Fleshharrower will
move swiftly. When will he overtake us?"

"Sometime tomorrow afternoon. Tomorrow evening
at the latest."

"Then we are lost," said Amorine, and her voice
shook. "We can march no faster. The warriors are too
weary to turn and fight. Warmark," she implored,
"take this matter from me. Give the First Haft's place
to another. I cannot bear—I cannot give these commands."

He tried to comfort her with his confidence. "Don't
worry. We're not beaten yet." But to himself he
sounded more hysterical than confident. He had a
sudden desire to scream. "We won't have to march
any faster than this. We're just going to turn south a
fraction more, so that we'll reach that old ruined city
—'Doriendor Corishev,' Mhoram calls it. We should
get there before noon tomorrow."

He felt that he was speaking too quickly. He forced
himself to slow down while he explained his intentions. Then he was relieved to see dour approval
in the faces of his officers. First Haft Amorine took a
deep, shuddering breath as she caught hold of her
courage again, and Quaan's eyes glinted with bloody

promises for the enemy. Shortly, he asked, "Who will command the Eoward which must remain?"

"Permit me," Amorine said. "I am at the end of my strength for this marching. I wish to fight."

The Hiltmark opened his mouth to answer her, but Troy stopped them both with a gesture. For a moment, he juggled burdens mentally, seeking a point of balance. Then he said to Quaan, "The Lords and I will stay behind with First Haft Amorine. We'll need eight Eoward of volunteers, and every horse that can still stand. The Bloodguard will probably stay with us. If we handle it right, most of us will survive."

Quaan frowned at the decision. But his acceptance was as candid as his dislike. To Amorine, he said, "We must find those who are willing, and prepare them today, so that tomorrow no time will be lost."

In answer, the First Haft saluted both Quaan and Troy, then rode away among the Warward. She carried herself straighter than she had for several days, and her alacrity demonstrated to Troy that he had made the correct choice. He nodded after her, sardonically congratulating himself for having done something right.

But Quaan still had questions. Shortly, he said, "I ask your pardon, Warmark—but we have been friends, and I must speak of this. Will you not explain to me why we march now? If Doom's Retreat is not the battleground you desire, perhaps Doriendor Corishev will serve. Why must this terrible march continue?"

"No, I'm not going to explain. Not yet." Troy kept his final plan to himself as if by silence and secrecy he could contain its terrors. "And Doriendor Corishev won't serve. We could fight there for a day or two. But after that, Fleshharrower would surround us and just squeeze. We've got to do better than that."

The Hiltmark nodded morosely. Troy's refusal saddened him like an expression of distrust. But he managed a wry smile as he said, "Warmark, is there no end to your plans?"

"Yes," Troy sighed. "Yes, there is. And we're go-

ing to get there. After that, Mhoram is going to have
to save us. He promised—"

Because he could not bear to face Quaan with his
inadequacies, he turned away. Clapping Mehryl with
his heels, he went in search of the Lords. He wanted
to explain his intentions for Doriendor Corishev, and
to find out what additional help Mhoram or Callindrill
could give the Warward.

During the rest of that day and the next morning,
he received regular reports from the Bloodguard on
Fleshharrower's progress. The Giant-Raver's army
was large and unwieldy; it had covered only nine
leagues during the day after it traversed Doom's Retreat. But it did not halt during the dark night, and
took only one short rest before dawn. Troy judged
that the Giant would reach Doriendor Corishev by
mid-afternoon.

That knowledge made him ache to drive the Warward faster. But he could not. Too many warriors left
the army or died that night and the next morning. To
his dismay, the attrition tripled. A litany of numbers
ran through his brain: eleven, thirty-three, ninety-nine
—at that rate, the march itself would claim four thousand four victims by the end of six days. And lives
would be lost in Doriendor Corishev. He needed complex equations to measure the plight of his army. He
did not try to hurry it.

As a result, the warriors were only a league ahead
of Fleshharrower when they started up the long slope
toward the ruins of Doriendor Corishev. The ancient
city sat atop a high hill under the perpetual frown of
the mountains, and the hill itself crested a south-
running ridge. The ruins were elevated on a line that
separated, hid from each other, the east and west sides
of the Southron Wastes. In past ages, when the city
lived and thrived, it had commanded perfectly the
northern edge of that region, and now the low, massive remains of fortifications testified that the inhabitants of the city had known the value of their position.
According to the legends which had been preserved in
Kevin's Lore, these people had been warlike; they had
needed their strategic location. Lord Callindrill trans-

lated the name as "masterplace" or "desolation of enemies."

The legends said that for centuries Doriendor Corishev had been the capital of the nation which gave birth to Berek Halfhand.

That was the age of the One Forest's dominion in the Land. Then there were no Wastes south of the mountains; the region was green and populous. But in time it became too populous. Groups of people from this southern country slowly moved up into the Land, and began to attack the Forest. At first, they only wanted timber for the civilization of Doriendor Corishev. Then they wanted fields for crops. Then they wanted homes. With the unconscious aid of other immigrants from the north, they eventually accomplished the maiming of the One Forest.

But that injury had many ramifications. On the one hand, the felling of the trees unbound the interdict which the Colossus of the Fall had held over the Lower Land. The Ravers were unleashed—a release which led with deft inevitability to the destruction of Doriendor Corishev's monarchy in the great war of Berek Halfhand. And on the other hand, the loss of perhaps a hundred thousand square leagues of Forest altered the natural balances of the Earth. Every falling tree hammered home an ineluctable doom for the masterplace. As the trees died, the southern lands lost the watershed which had preserved them from the Gray Desert. Centuries after the ravage of the One Forest became irreversible, these lands turned to dry ruin.

But the city had been deserted since the time of Berek, the first Lord. Now, after millennia of wind and dust, nothing remained of the masterplace except the standing shards of its walls and buildings, a kind of ground map formed by the bloodless stumps of its grandeur. Warmark Troy could have hidden his whole army in its labyrinthian spaces and ways. Behind fragmentary walls that reached meaninglessly into the sky, the warriors could have fought guerrilla war for days against an army of comparable size.

Troy trusted that Fleshharrower knew this. His

plans relied heavily on his ability to convince the Giant that the Warward chose to make its last stand in Doriendor Corishev, rather than under the certain death of Garroting Deep. He marched his army straight up the long hillside, and into the toothless gate of the masterplace. Then he took the warriors through the city and out its western side, where they were hidden from Fleshharrower by the ridge on which the city stood.

There he gave Quaan all the instructions and encouragement he could. Then he saluted the Hiltmark, and watched as the main body of the Warward marched away down the slope. When it was gone, he and his volunteers returned to the city with the two Lords, First Haft Amorine, all the Bloodguard, and every horse still strong enough to bear a rider.

Within the ruined walls, he addressed the eight Eoward that had offered to buy the Warward's escape from Doriendor Corishev. He had a taut, dry feeling in his throat as he began, "You're all volunteers, so I'm not going to apologize for what we're doing. But I want to be sure you know why we're doing it. I have two main reasons. First, we're going to give the rest of the warriors a chance to put some distance between them and Fleshharrower. Second, we're going to help squeeze out a victory in this war. I'm preparing a little surprise for Foul's army, and we're going to help make it work. Parts of that army move faster than others—but if they get too spread out, they won't all fall into my trap. So we're going to pull them together here."

He paused to look over the warriors. They stood squarely before him with expressions colored by every hue of grimness and fatigue and determination, and their very bones seemed to radiate mortality. At the sight, he began to understand Mhoram's statement that they deserved to know the truth; they were serving his commands with their souls. Roughly, he went on, "But there's one more thing. Fleshharrower may be planning a surprise or two for us. Many of you were with Hiltmark Quaan during that storm—you know what I'm talking about. That Giant has power, and he intends to use it. We're going to give him a chance. We're going to be a target, so that whatever he does will hit us instead of the rest of the Warward. I think we can survive it—if we do things right. But it's not going to be easy."

Abruptly, he turned to Amorine, and ordered her to deploy the Eoward in strategic positions throughout the east side of the masterplace. "Make sure of your lines of retreat. I don't want people getting lost in this maze when it's time for us to pull out." Then he spoke to the Bloodguard, asked them to scout beyond the city along the ridge. "I've got to know right away if Fleshharrower tries to surround us."

Terrel nodded, and a few of the Bloodguard rode away.

First Haft Amorine took her Eoward back across Doriendor Corishev. They left all their horses, including the Ranyhyn, at the west gate under the care of several Bloodguard.

Accompanied by the rest of the Bloodguard, Troy and the two Lords made their way on foot to the east wall.

While they passed through the ruins, Lord Mhoram asked, "Warmark, do you believe that Fleshharrower will not attempt to surround us? Why would he do otherwise?"

"Instinct," Troy replied curtly. "I think he'll be very careful to let us escape on the west side. You heard him laugh—back at Doom's Retreat—when he saw where we were going. I think that what he really wants is to trap us against Garroting Deep. He's a Raver. He probably thinks the idea of using that Forest against us is hilarious."

Then he was grateful that Mhoram refrained from asking him what his own ideas about Garroting Deep were. He did not want to think about that. Instead, he tried to concentrate on the layout of the city, so that he could find his way through it at night if necessary. But his heart was not in the task. Too many other anxieties occupied him.

When he reached the east wall, and climbed up on

some rubble to peer over it, he saw Fleshharrower's army.

It approached like a great discoloration, a dark bruise, on the pale ground of the Wastes. Its front stretched away both north and south of the ruins. It was less than a league away.

And it was immense beyond comprehension. Troy could not imagine how Lord Foul had been able to create such an army.

It came forward until it reached the foot of the hill upon which Doriendor Corishev stood.

As he watched, Troy gripped the handle of his sword as if it were the only thing that kept him from panic. Several times, he reached up to adjust the sunglasses he no longer possessed. The movement was like an involuntary prayer or appeal. But neither of the Lords observed him. Their faces were set toward Fleshharrower.

Troy almost shouted with elation when the Giant-Raver stopped his army at the foot of the hill. The halt ran through his hordes like a shock, as if the force which drove them had struck a wall. The wolves smelled prey; they sent up a howl of frustration at the halt. Ur-viles barked furiously. Warped humans groaned, and Cavewights hopped hungrily from foot to foot. But Fleshharrower's command mastered them all. They spread out until they formed a ready arc around the entire eastern side of the hill, then set themselves to wait.

When he was satisfied with the position of his army, the Raver took a few steps up the hill, placed his fists on his hips, and shouted sardonically, "Lords! Warriors! I know you hear me! Listen to my words! Surrender! You cannot escape—you are ensnared between the Desert and the Deep. I can eradicate you from the Earth with only a tenth of my strength. Surrender! If you join me, I may be merciful." At the word *merciful,* a yammer of protest and hunger went up from his army. He waited for the outcry to pass before he continued: "If not, I will destroy you! I will burn and blast your homes. I will make Revelwood a charnal, and use Revelstone for an offal ground. I will wreck and ravage the Land until Time itself breaks! Hear me and despair! Surrender or die!"

At this, an irresistible impulse caught hold of the Warmark; frustration and rage boiled up in him. Without warning, he leaped onto the wall. He braced his feet to steady himself, and raised his fists defiantly. "Fleshharrower!" he shouted. "Vermin! I am Warmark Hile Troy! I command here! I spit in your face, Raver! You're only a slave! And your master is only a slave! He's a slave to hunger, and he gnaws his worthlessness like an old bone. Go back! Leave the Land! We're free people. Despair has no power over us. But I'll teach you despair if you dare to fight me!"

Fleshharrower snapped an order. A dozen bow-strings thrummed; shafts flew past Troy's head as Ruel snatched him down from the wall. Troy stumbled as he landed, but Ruel upheld him. When the War-mark regained his balance, Mhoram said, "You took a grave risk. What have you gained?"

"I've made him mad," Troy replied unsteadily. "This has got to be done right, and I'm going to do it. The madder he gets, the better off we are."

"Are you so certain of what he will do?"

"Yes." Troy felt an odd confidence, a conviction that he would not be proved wrong until the end. "He's already doing it—he's stopped. If he's mad enough, he'll attack us first himself. His army will stay stopped. That's what we want."

"Then I believe that you have succeeded," Lord Callindrill inserted quietly. He was gazing over the wall as he spoke. Mhoram and Troy joined him, and saw what he meant.

Fleshharrower had retreated until there was a flat space of ground between himself and the hill. Around him, the army shifted. Several thousand ur-viles moved to form wedges with their loremasters poised on both sides of the space. There they waited while the Giant-Raver marked out a wide circle in the dirt, using the tip of one of the loremaster's staves. Then Fleshharrower ordered all but the ur-viles away from the circle.

When the space was cleared, the loremasters began
their work.

Chanting in arhythmic unison like a mesmerized
chorus of dogs, the ur-viles bent their might forward,
into the hands of their loremasters. The loremasters
thrust the points of their staves into the rim of Fleshharrower's circle, and began to rock the irons slowly
back and forth.

A low buzzing noise became audible. The ur-viles
were singing in their own roynish tongue, and their
song made the flat, hard ground vibrate. Slowly, the
buzz scaled upward, as if a swarm of huge, mad bees
were emprisoned in the dirt. And the earth in the circle began to pulse visibly. A change like an increase
of heat came over the rock and soil; hot, red gleams
played through the circle erratically, and its surface
seethed. The buzz became fiercer, sharper.

The process was slow, but its horrible fascination
made it seem swift to the onlookers. As daylight
started to fall out of the stricken sky, the buzz replaced it like a cry of pain from the ground itself. The
Raver's circle throbbed and boiled as if the dirt within
it were molten.

The sound tormented Troy; it clawed at his ears,
crawled like lice over his flesh. Sweat slicked his eyeless brows. For a time, he feared that he would be
compelled to scream. But at last the cry scaled past
the range of his senses. He was able to turn away, rest
briefly.

When he looked back toward the circle, he found
that the ur-viles had withdrawn from it. Fleshharrower stood there alone. A demonic look clenched his
face as he stared into the hot, red, boiling soil.

In his hands, he held one of the loremasters. It
gibbered fearfully, clung to its stave, but it could not
break his grip.

Laughing, Fleshharrower lifted the loremaster over
his head and hurled it into the circle. As it hit the
ground, its scream died in a flash of fire. Only its stave
remained, slowly melting on the surface.

As the sun set, Fleshharrower began using his fragment of the Stone to reshape the molten iron, forge it into something new.

Softly, as if he feared that the Giant-Raver might hear him, Troy asked the Lords, "What's this for? What's he doing?"

"He makes a tool," Mhoram whispered, "some means to increase or concentrate his power."

The implications of that gave Troy a feeling of grim gratification. His strategy was justified at least to the extent that the main body of the Warward would be spared this particular attack. But he knew that such justification was not enough. His final play lay like a dead weight in his stomach. He expected to lose command of the Warward as soon as he revealed it; it would appall the warriors so much that they would rebel. After all his promises of victory, he felt like a false prophet. Yet his plan was the Warward's only hope, the Land's only hope.

He prayed that Lord Mhoram would be equal to it.

With the sunset, his sight failed. He was forced to rely on Mhoram to report the Raver's progress. In the darkness, he felt trapped, bereft of command. All that he could see was the amorphous, dull glow of the liquid earth. Occasionally, he made out flares and flashes of lurid green across the red, but they meant nothing to him. His only consolation lay in the fact that Fleshharrower's preparations were consuming time.

Along the wall on both sides of him, First Haft Amorine's Eoward kept watch over the Raver's labors. No one slept; the poised threat of Fleshharrower's army transfixed everyone. Moonrise did not ease the blackness; the dark of the moon was only three nights away. But the Raver's forge-work was bright enough to pale the stars.

During the whole long watch, Fleshharrower never left his molten circle. Sometime after midnight, he retrieved his newly made scepter, and cooled it by waving it in a shower of sparks over his head. Then he affixed his fragment of the Stone to its end. But when that was done, he remained by the circle. As night waned toward day, he gestured and sang over

the molten stone, weaving incantations out of its hot
power. It lit his movements luridly, and the Stone
flashed across it at intervals, giving green glimpses of
his malice.

But this was indistinct to Troy. He clung to his
hope. In the darkness, his calculations were the only
reality left to him, and he recited them like counters
against the night. When the first slit of dawn touched
him from the east, he felt a kind of elation.

Softly, he asked for Amorine.

"Warmark." She was right beside him.

"Amorine, listen. That monster has made his mistake—he's wasted too much time. Now we're going to
make him pay for it. Get the warriors out of here.
Send them after the Warward. Whatever happens,
that Giant won't get as many of us as he thinks. Just
keep one warrior for every good horse we have."

"Perhaps all should depart now," she replied, "before the Raver attacks."

Troy grinned at the idea. He could imagine Fleshharrower's fury if the Giant's attack found Doriendor
Corishev empty. But he knew that he had not yet
gained enough time. He answered, "I want to squeeze
another half day out of him. With the Bloodguard and
a couple hundred warriors, we'll be able to do it.
Now get going."

"Yes, Warmark." She left his side at once, and soon
he could hear most of the warriors withdrawing. He
gripped the wall again, and stared away into the
sunrise, waiting for sight.

Shortly, he became aware that the dry breeze out of
the south was stiffening.

Then the haze faded from his mind. First he became able to see the ruined wall, then the hillside;
finally he caught sight of the waiting army.

It had not moved during the night.

It did not need to move.

Fleshharrower still stood beside his circle. The fire
in the ground had died, but before it failed, he had
used it to wrap himself in a shimmering, translucent
cocoon of power. Within the power, he was as erect
as an icon. He held his scepter rigidly above his head;

he did not move; he made no sound. But when the sunlight touched him, the wind leaped suddenly into a hard blow like a violent exhalation through the teeth of the Desert. And it increased in ragged gusts like the leading edge of a sirocco.

Then a low cry from one of the warriors pulled Troy's attention away from Fleshharrower. Turning his head, he looked down the throat of the mounting gale.

From the southeast, where the Southron Range met the Gray Desert, a tornado came rushing toward Doriendor Corishev. Its undulating shaft plowed straight across the Wastes.

It conveyed such an impression of might that several moments passed before Troy realized it was not the kind of whirlwind he understood.

It brought no rain or clouds with it; it was as dry as the Desert. And it carried no dust or sand; it was as clean as empty air. It should not have been visible at all. But its sheer force made it palpable to Troy's sight. He could feel it coming. It was so vivid to him that at first he could not grasp the fact that the tornado was not moving with the wind.

The gale blew straight out of the south, tearing dust savagely from the ground as it came. And the tornado cut diagonally across it, ignored the wind to howl straight toward Doriendor Corishev.

Troy stared at it. Dust clogged his mouth, but he did not know this until he tried to shout something. Then, coughing convulsively, he wrenched himself away from the sight. At once, the sirocco hit him. When he stopped looking at the tornado, the force of the wind sent him reeling. Ruel caught him. He pivoted around the Bloodguard, and threw himself toward Lord Mhoram.

When he reached Mhoram, he shouted, "What is it?"

"Creator preserve us!" Mhoram replied. The yowling wind whipped his voice from his lips, and Troy barely heard him. "It is a vortex of trepidation."

Troy tried to thrust his words past the wind to Mhoram's ears. "What will it do?"

Shouting squarely into Troy's face, Mhoram answered, "It will make us afraid!"

The next moment, he pulled at Troy's arm, and pointed upward, toward the top of the tornado. There a score of dark creatures flew, riding the upper reaches of the vortex.

The tornado had already covered more than half the distance to Doriendor Corishev, and Troy saw the creatures vividly. They were birds as large as *kresh*. They had clenched satanic faces like bats, wide eagle-wings, and massive barbed claws. As they flew, they called to each other, showing double rows of hooked teeth. Their wings beat with lust.

They were the most fearsome creatures Troy had ever seen. As he stared, he tried to rally himself against them—judge their speed, calculate the time left before their arrival, plan a defense. But they staggered his mind; he could not comprehend an existence which permitted them.

He struggled to move, regain his balance enough to tell himself that he was already tasting the vortex of trepidation. But he was paralyzed. Voices shouted around him. He had a vague impression that Flesh-harrower's hordes greeted the vortex with glee—or were they afraid of it, too? He could not tell.

Then Ruel grabbed his arm, snatched him away from the wall, shouted into his ear, "Warmark, come! We must make a defense!"

Troy could not remember ever having heard a Bloodguard shout before. But even now Ruel's voice did not sound like panic. Troy felt that there was something terrible in such immunity. He tried to look around him, but the wind lashed so much dust across the ruins that all details were lost. Both Lords were gone. Warriors ran in all directions, stumbling against the wind. Bloodguard bobbed in and out of view like ghouls.

Ruel shouted at him again. "We must save the horses! They will go mad with fear!"

For one lorn moment, Troy wished High Lord Elena were with him, so that he could tell her this was not his fault. Then, abruptly, he realized that he had made another mistake. If he were killed, no one would know how to save the Warward. His final plan would die with him, and every man and woman of his army would be butchered as a result.

The realization seemed to push him over an edge. He plunged to his knees. The sirocco and the dust were strangling him.

Ruel shouted, "Warmark! Corruption attacks!"

At the word *Corruption,* a complete lucidity came over Troy. Fear filled all his thoughts with crystalline incisiveness. At once, he perceived that the Bloodguard was trying to undo him; Ruel's impenetrable fidelity was a deliberate assault upon his fitness for command.

The understanding made him reel, but he reacted lucidly, adroitly. He took one last look around him, saw one or two figures still surging back and forth through the livid anguish of the dust. Ruel was moving to capture him. Overhead, the dark birds dropped toward the ruins. Troy picked up a rock and climbed to his feet. When Ruel touched him, he suddenly gestured away behind the Bloodguard. Ruel turned to look. Troy hit him on the back of the skull with the rock.

Then the Warmark ran. He could not make progress against the wind, so he worked across it. The walls of buildings loomed out of the dust at him. He started toward a door.

Without warning, he stumbled into First Haft Amorine.

She caught at him, buffeted him with cries like fear. But she, too, was someone faithful, someone who threatened him. He lunged at her with his shoulder, sent her sprawling. Immediately, he dodged into the maze of the masterplace.

He fell several times as the wind sprang at him through unexpected gaps in the walls. But he forced himself ahead. The clarity of his terror was complete; he knew what he had to do.

After a swift, chaotic battle, he found what he needed. With a rush, he lurched out into the center of a large, open space—the remains of one of Doriendor

Corishev's meeting halls. In this unsheltered expanse, the force of the wind belabored him venomously. He welcomed it. He felt a paradoxical glee of fear; his own terror delighted him. He stood like an exalted fanatic in the open space, and looked up to see how long he would have to wait.

When he glanced behind him, his heart leaped. One of the birds glided effortlessly toward him, as if it were in total command of the wind. It had a clear approach to him. The ease of its movement thrilled him, and he poised himself to jump into its jaws.

But as it neared him, he saw that it carried Ruel's crumpled body in its mighty talons. He could see Ruel's flat, dispassionate features. The Bloodguard looked as if he had been betrayed.

A convulsion shook Troy. As the bird swooped toward him, he remembered who he was. The strength of terror galvanized his muscles; he snatched out his sword and struck.

His blow split the bird's skull. Its weight bowled him over. Green blood spewed from it over his head and shoulders. The hot blood burned him like a corrosive, and it smelled so thickly of attar that it asphyxiated him. With a choked cry, he clawed at his forehead, trying to tear the pain away. But the acid fire consumed his headband, burned through his skull into his brain. He lost consciousness.

He awoke to silence and the darkness of night.

After a long lapse of time like an interminable scream, he raised his head. The wind had piled dust over him, and his movement disturbed it. It filled his throat and mouth and lungs. But he bit back a spasm of coughing, and listened to the darkness.

All around him, Doriendor Corishev was as still as a cairn. The wind and the vortex were gone, leaving only midnight dust and death to mark their path. Silence lay over the ruins like a bane.

Then he had to cough. Gasping, retching, he pushed himself to his knees. He sounded explosively loud to himself. He tried to control the violence of his coughing, but he was helpless until the spasm passed.

As it released him, he realized that he was still clutching his sword. Instinctively, he tightened his grip on it. He cursed his night blindness, then told himself that the darkness was his only hope.

His face throbbed painfully, but he ignored it.

He kept himself still while he thought.

This long after the vortex, he reasoned, all his allies were either dead or gone. If the vortex and the birds had not killed them, they had been swept from the ruins by Fleshharrower's army. So they could not help him. He did not know how much of that army had stayed behind in the masterplace.

And he could not see. He was vulnerable until daylight. Only the darkness protected him; he could not defend himself.

His first reaction was to remain where he was, and pray that he was not discovered. But he recognized the futility of that plan. At best, it would only postpone his death. When dawn came, he would still be alone against an unknown number of enemies. No, his one chance was to sneak out of the city now and lose himself in the Wastes. There he might find a gully or hole in which to hide.

That escape was possible, barely possible, because he had one advantage; none of Fleshharrower's creatures except the ur-viles could move through the ruins at night as well as he. And the Raver would not have left ur-viles behind. They were too valuable. If Troy could remember his former skills—his sense of ambience, his memory for terrain—he would be able to navigate the city.

He would have to rely on his hearing to warn him of enemies.

He began by sliding his sword quietly into its scabbard. Then he started groping his way over the hot sand. He needed to verify where he was, and knew only one way to do it.

Nearby, his hands found a patch of ground that felt burned. The dirt which stuck to his fingers reeked of attar. And in the patch, he located Ruel's twisted body. His sense of touch told him that Ruel was badly charred. The dark bird must have caught fire when it died, and burned away, leaving the Bloodguard's corpse behind.

The touch of that place nauseated him, and he backed away from it. He was sweating heavily. Sweat stung his burns. The night was hot; sunset had brought no relief to the ruins. Folding his arms over his stomach, he climbed to his feet.

Standing unsteadily in the open, he tried to clear his mind of Ruel and the bird. He needed to remember how to deal with blindness, how to orient himself in the ruins. But he could not determine which way he had come into this open place. Waving his arms before him, he went in search of a wall.

His feet distrusted the ground—he could not put them down securely—and he moved awkwardly. His sense of balance had deserted him. His face felt raw, and sweat seared his eye sockets. But he clenched his concentration, and measured the distance.

In twenty yards, he reached a wall. He touched it at an angle, promptly squared himself to it, then moved along it. He needed a gap which would permit him to touch both sides of the wall. Any discrepancy in temperature between the sides would tell him his directions.

After twenty more yards, he arrived in a corner. Turning at right angles, he followed this new wall. He kept himself parallel to it by brushing the stone with his fingers. Shortly, he stumbled into some rubble, and found an entryway.

The wall here was thick, but he could touch its opposite sides without stretching his arms. Both sides felt very warm, but he thought he discerned a slightly higher temperature on the side facing back into the open space. That direction was west, he reasoned; the afternoon sun would have heated the west side of a wall.

Now he had to decide which way to go.

If he went east, he would be less likely to meet enemies. Since they had not already found him, they might be past him, and their search would move from east to west after the Warward. But if any chance of help from his friends or Mehryl remained, it would be on the west side.

The dilemma seemed to have no solution. He found himself shaking his head and moaning through his teeth. At once, he stuffed his throat with silence. He decided to move west toward Mehryl. The added risk was preferable to a safe escape eastward—an escape which would leave him alone in the Southron Wastes, without food or water or a mount.

He leaned against the unnatural heat of the wall for a few moments, breathing deeply to steady himself. Then he stood up, grasped his sense of direction with all the concentration he could muster, and started walking straight out into the ruined hall.

His progress was slow. The uncertainty of his steps made him stagger repeatedly away from a true westward line. But he corrected the variations as best he could, and kept going. Without the support of a wall, his balance grew worse at every stride. Before he had covered thirty yards, the floor reeled around him, and he dropped to his knees. He had to clamp his throat shut to keep from whimpering.

When he regained his feet, he heard quiet laughter —first one voice, then several. It had a cruel sound, as if it were directed at him. It resonated slightly off the walls, so that he could not locate it, but it seemed to come from somewhere ahead.

He froze where he stood. Helplessly, he prayed that the darkness would cover him.

But a voice shattered that hope. "Look here, brothers," it said. "A man—alone." Its utterance was awkward, thick with slavering, but Troy could understand it. He could hear the malice in the low chorus of laughter which answered it.

Other voices spoke.

"A man, yes. Slayer take him!"

"Look. Such pretty clothes. An enemy."

"Ha! Look again, fool. That is no man."

"He has no eyes."

"Is it an ur-vile?"

"No—a man, I say. A man with no eyes! Here is some sport, brothers."

All the voices laughed again.

Troy did not stop to wonder how the speakers could see him. He turned, started to run back the way he had come.

At once, they gave pursuit. He could hear the slap of bare feet on stone, the sharp breathing. They overtook him swiftly. Something veered close to him, tripped him. As he fell, the running feet surrounded him.

"Go gently, brothers. No quick kill. He will be sport for us all."

"Do not kill him."

"Not kill? I want to kill. Kill and eat."

"The Giant will want this one."

"After we sport."

"Why tell the Giant, brothers? He is greedy."

"He takes our meat."

"Keep this one for ourselves, yes."

"Slayer take the Giant."

"His precious ur-viles. When there is danger, men must go first."

"Yes! Brothers, we will eat this meat."

Troy heaved himself to his feet. Through the rapid chatter of the voices, he heard, *go first,* and almost fell again. If these creatures were the first of Fleshharrower's army to enter the masterplace—! But he pushed down the implications of that thought, and snatched out his sword.

"A sword? Ho ho!"

"Look, brothers. The man with no eyes wants to play."

"Play!"

Troy heard the lash of a whip; cord flicked around his wrist. It caught and jerked, hauled him from his feet. Strong hands took his sword. Something kicked him in the chest, knocked him backward. But his breastplate protected him.

One of the voices cried, "Slayer! My foot!"

"Fool!" came the answer. There was laughter.

"Kill him!"

A metallic weapon clattered against his breastplate, fell to the ground. He scrambled for it in the dust, but sudden hands shoved him away. He recoiled and got to his feet again.

He heard the whistle of the whip, and its cord lashed at his ankles. But this time he did not go down.

"Do not kill him yet. Where is the sport?"

"Make him play."

"Yes, brothers. Play."

"Play for us, man with no eyes."

The whip burned around his neck. He staggered under the blow. The bewildering crossfire of voices went on.

"Play, Slayer take you!"

"Sport for us!"

"Why sport? I want meat. Blood-wet meat."

"The Giant feeds us sand."

"Play, I say! Are you blind, man with no eyes? Does the sun dazzle you?"

This gibe was met with loud laughter. But Troy stood still in his dismay. *The sun?* he thought numbly. Then he had chosen the wrong direction, east instead of west; he had walked right into these creatures. He wanted to scream. But he was past screaming. He could feel the light of his life going out. His hands shook as he tried to straighten his sunglasses.

"Dear God," he groaned.

Numbly, as if he did not know what he was doing, he put his fingers to his lips and gave a shrill whistle.

The whip coiled around his waist and whirled him to the ground.

"Play!" the voices shouted raggedly together.

But when he stumbled to his feet again, he heard the sound of hooves. And a moment later, Mehryl's whinny cut through the gibbering voices. It touched Troy's heart like the call of a trumpet. He jerked up his head, and his ears searched, trying to locate the Ranyhyn.

The voices changed to shouts of hunger as the hooves charged.

"Ranyhyn!"

"Kill it!"

"Meat!"

Hands grabbed Troy. He grappled with a fist that

held a knife. But then the noise of hooves rushed close to him. An impact flung his assailant away. He turned, tried to leap onto Mehryl's back. But he only put himself in Mehryl's path. The shoulder of the Ranyhyn struck him, knocked him down.

Then he could hear bare feet leaping to the attack. The whip cracked, knives swished. Mehryl was forced away from him. Hooves skittered on the stone as the Ranyhyn retreated. Howling triumphantly, the creatures gave chase. The sounds receded.

Troy pushed himself to his feet. His heart thudded in his chest; pain throbbed sharply in his face. The noises of pursuit seemed to indicate that he was being left alone. But he did not move. Concentrating all his attention, he tried to hear over the beat of his pain.

For a long moment, the open space around him sounded empty, still. He waved his arms, and touched nothing.

But then he heard a sharp intake of breath.

He was trembling violently. He wanted to turn and run. But he forced himself to hold his ground. He concentrated, bent all his alertness toward the sound. In the distance, the other creatures had lost Mehryl. They were returning; he could hear them.

But the near voice hissed, "I kill you. You hurt my foot. Slayer take them! You are my meat."

Troy could sense the creature's approach. It loomed out of the blankness like a faint pressure on his face. The rasp of its breathing grew louder. With every step, he felt its ambience more acutely.

The tension was excruciating, but he held himself still. He waited. Interminable time passed.

Suddenly, he felt the creature bunching to spring.

He snatched Manethrall Rue's cord from his belt, looped it around the neck of his attacker, and jerked as the creature hit him. He put all his strength into the pull. The creature's leap toppled him, but he clung to the cord, heaved on it. The creature landed on top of him. He threw his weight around, got himself onto the creature. He kept pulling. Now he could feel the limpness of the body under him. But he did not release his hold. Straining on the cord, he banged the creature's head repeatedly against the stone.

He was gasping for breath. Dimly, he could hear the other creatures charging him.

He did not release his hold.

Then power crackled through the air. Flame burst around him. He heard shouts, and the clash of swords. Bowstrings thrummed. Creatures screamed, ran, fell heavily.

A moment later, hands lifted Troy. Rue's cord was taken from his rigid fingers. First Haft Amorine cried, "Warmark! Warmark! Praise the Creator, you are safe!" She was weeping with relief. People moved around him. He heard Lord Mhoram say, "My friend, you have led us a merry chase. Without Mehryl's aid, we would not have found you in time." The voice came disembodied out of the blankness.

At first, Troy could not speak. His heart struggled through a crisis. It made him gasp so hard that he could barely stand. He sounded as if he were trying to sob.

"Warmark," Amorine said, "what has happened to you?"

"Sun," he panted, "is—the sun—shining?" The effort of articulation seemed to impale his heart.

"Warmark? Ah, Warmark! What has been done to you?"

"The sun!" he retched out. He was desperate to insist, but he could only stamp his foot uselessly.

"The sun stands overhead," Mhoram answered. "We have survived the vortex and its creatures. But now Fleshharrower's army enters Doriendor Corishev. We must depart swiftly."

"Mhoram," Troy coughed hoarsely. "Mhoram." Stumbling forward, he fell into the Lord's arms.

Mhoram held him in a comforting grip. Without a word, the Lord supported him until some of his pain passed, and he began to breathe more easily. Then Mhoram said quietly, "I see that you slew one of the Despiser's birds. You have done well, my friend. Lord Callindrill and I remain. Perhaps seventy of the Bloodguard survive. First Haft Amorine has preserved a handful of her warriors. After the passing of the vortex, all the Ranyhyn returned. They saved many horses. My friend, we must go."

Some of Mhoram's steadiness reached Troy, and he began to regain control of himself. He did not want to be a burden to the Lord. Slowly, he drew back, stood on his own. Covering his burned forehead with his hands as if he were trying to hide his eyelessness, he said, "I've got to tell you the rest of my plan."

"May it wait? We must depart at once."

"Mhoram," Troy moaned brokenly, "I can't see."

TWENTY: Garroting Deep

Two days later—shortly after noon on the day before the dark of the moon—Lord Mhoram led the Warward to Cravenhaw, the southmost edge of Garroting Deep. In noon heat, the army had swung stumbling and lurching like a dying man around the foothills, and had marched northward to a quivering halt before the very lips of the fatal Deep. The warriors stood on a wide, grassy plain—the first healthy green they had seen since leaving the South Plains. Ahead was the Forest. Perhaps half a league away on either side, east and west, were mountains, steep and forbidding peaks like the jaws of the Deep. And behind was the army of *moksha* Fleshharrower.

The Giant-Raver drove his forces savagely. Despite the delay at Doriendor Corishev, he was now no more than two leagues away.

That knowledge tightened Lord Mhoram's cold, weary dread. He had so little time in which to attempt Warmark Troy's plan. From this position, there were no escapes and no hopes except the one Troy had envisioned. If Mhoram were not successful—successful soon!—the Warward would be crushed between the Raver and Garroting Deep.

Yet he doubted that he could succeed at all, regardless of the time at his disposal. In a year or a score of years, he might still fail. The demand was so great— Even the vortex of trepidation had not made him feel so helpless.

Yet he shuddered when he thought of the vortex. Although Troy had saved virtually all the Warward, the men and women who had remained in the masterplace had paid heavily for their survival. Something in Lord Callindrill had been damaged by Fleshharrower's attack. The strain of combat against bitter ill had humiliated him in some way, taught him a deep distrust of himself. He had not been able to resist the fear. Now his clear soft eyes were clouded, pained. When he melded his thoughts with Lord Mhoram, he shared knowledge and concern, but not strength; he no longer believed in his strength.

In her own way, First Haft Amorine suffered similarly. During the Raver's onslaught, she had held the collapsing remains of her command together by the simple force of her courage. She had taken the terror of her warriors upon herself. Every time one of them fell under the power of the vortex, or died in the talons of the birds, she had tightened her grip on the survivors. And after that, when the sirocco had passed, she began a frantic search for Warmark Troy. The perverted, manlike creatures that rushed into the ruins —some with claws for fingers, others with cleft faces and limbs covered with suckers, still others with extra eyes or arms, all of them warped in some way by the power of the Stone—steadily brought more and more of the city under their control. But she fought her way through them as if they were mere shades to haunt her while she hunted. The idea of following Mehryl was hers.

But the Warmark's blindness was too much for her. The cause of it was clear. The slain bird's corrosive blood had ravaged his face, and that burning had undone the Land's gift of sight. Neither of the Lords had any hurtloam, *rillinlure,* or other arts of healing with which to counteract the hurt. When she understood Troy's plight, she appeared to lose herself; independent will deserted her. Until she rejoined the Warward, she followed Lord Mhoram's requests and instructions blankly, like a puppet from which all authority had evaporated. And when she saw Hiltmark Quaan again, she transferred herself to him. As she told him of Troy's plan, she was so numb that she did not even falter.

The Warmark himself had said nothing more after describing his final strategy. He wrapped himself in his blindness and allowed Mhoram to place him on Mehryl's back. He did not ask about Fleshharrower's army, though only the speed of the Ranyhyn saved him and his companions from being trapped in the city. Despite the scream of frustration which roared after the riders, he carried himself like an invalid who had turned his face to the wall.

And Lord Mhoram also suffered. After the battle of the masterplace, fatigue and dread had forced tenacious fingers into the crevices and crannies of his soul, so that he could not shake them off. Yet he helped the First Haft and Lord Callindrill as best he could. He knew that only time and victory could heal their wounds; but he absorbed those parts of their burdens which came within his reach, and gave back to them all the consolation he possessed.

There was nothing he could do to ease the shock which Amorine's report of the Warmark's final plan gave Quaan. As she spoke, the Hiltmark's concern for her gave way to a livid horror on behalf of the warriors. His expression flared, and he erupted, "Madness! Every man and woman will be slain! Troy, what has become of you? By the Seven! Troy—Warmark!"— he hesitated awkwardly before uttering his thought— "Do you rave? My friend," he breathed gripping Troy's shoulders, "how can you meditate such folly?"

Troy spoke for the first time since he had left Doriendor Corishev. "I'm blind," he said in a hollow voice, as if that explained everything. "I can't help it." He pulled himself out of Quaan's grasp, sat down near the fire. Locating the flames by their heat, he hunched toward them like a man studying secrets in the coals.

Quaan turned to Mhoram. "Lord, do you accept this madness? It will mean death for us all—and destruction for the Land."

Quaan's protest made the Lord's heart ache. But before he could find words for any answer, Troy spoke suddenly.

"No, he doesn't," the Warmark said. "He doesn't actually think I'm a Raver." Inner pain made his voice harsh. "He thinks Foul had a hand in summoning me—interfered with Atiaran somehow so that I showed up, instead of somebody else who might have *looked* less friendly." He stressed the word *looked,* as if sight itself were inherently untrustworthy. "Foul wanted the Lords to trust me because he knew what kind of man I am. Dear God! It doesn't matter how much I hate him. He knew I'm the kind of man who backs into corners where just being fallible is the same thing as treachery.

"But you forget that it isn't up to me anymore. I've done my part—I've put you where you haven't got any choice. Now Mhoram has got to save you. It's on his head."

Quaan appeared torn between dismay for the Warward and concern for Troy. "Even a Lord may be defeated," he replied gruffly.

"I'm not talking about a Lord," Troy rasped. "I'm talking about Mhoram."

In his weariness, Lord Mhoram ached to deny this, to refuse the burden. He said, "Warmark, of course I will do all that lies within my strength. But if Lord Foul has chosen you for the work of our destruction—ah, then, my friend, all aid will not avail. The burden of this plan will return to you at the last."

"No." Troy kept his face toward the fire, as if here reliving the acid burn which had blinded him. "You've given your whole life to the Land, and you're going to give it now."

"The Despiser knows me well," Mhoram breathed. "He ridicules me in my dreams." He could hear echoes of that belittling mirth, but he held them at a distance. "Do not mistake me, Warmark. I do not flinch this burden. I accept it. On Kevin's Watch I made my promise—and you dared this plan because of that promise. You have not done ill. But I must speak what is in my heart. You are the Warmark. I believe that the command of this fate must finally return to you."

"I'm blind. There's nothing more I can do. Even Foul can't ask any more of me." The heat of the fire made the burn marks on his face lurid. He held his hands clasped together, and his knuckles were white.

In distress, Quaan gazed at Mhoram with eyes that asked if he had been wrong to trust Troy.

"No," Lord Mhoram answered. "Do not pass judgment upon this mystery until it is complete. Until that time, we must keep faith."

"Very well," Quaan sighed heavily. "If we have been betrayed, we have no recourse now. To flee into the Desert will accomplish only death. And Cravenhaw is a place to fight and die like any other. The Warward must not turn against itself when the last battle is near. I will stand with Warmark Troy." Then he went to his blankets to search for sleep among his fears. Amorine followed his example dumbly, leaving Callindrill and Mhoram with Troy.

Callindrill soon dropped into slumber. And Mhoram was too worn to remain awake. But Troy sat up by the embers of the campfire. As the Lord's eyes closed, Troy was still huddled toward the flames like a cold cipher seeking some kind of remission for its frigidity.

Apparently, the Warmark found an answer during the long watch. When Lord Mhoram awoke the next morning, he found Troy erect, standing with his arms folded across his breastplate. The Lord studied him closely, but could not discern what kind of answer Troy had discovered. Gently, he greeted the blind man.

At the sound of Mhoram's voice, Troy turned. He held his head with a slight sideward tilt, as if that position helped him focus his hearing. The old halfsmile which he had habitually worn during his years in Revelstone was gone, effaced from his lips. "Call Quaan," he said flatly. "I want to talk to him."

Quaan was nearby; he heard Troy, and approached at once.

Fixing the Hiltmark with his hearing, Troy said, "Guide me. I'm going to review the Warward."

"Troy, my friend," Quaan murmured, "do not torment yourself."

Troy stood stiffly, rigid with exigency. "I'm the Warmark. I want to show my warriors that blindness isn't going to stop me."

Mhoram felt a hot premonition of tears, but he held them back. He smiled crookedly at Quaan, nodded his answer to the old veteran's question. Quaan saluted Troy, bravely ignoring the Warmark's inability to see him. Then he took Troy's arm, and led him away to the Eoward.

Lord Mhoram watched their progress among the warriors—watched Quaan's respectful pain guiding Troy's erect helplessness from Eoman to Eoman. He endured the sight as best he could, and blinked down his own heart hurt. Fortunately, the ordeal did not last long; Fleshharrower's pursuit did not allow Troy time for a full review of the Warward. Soon Mhoram was mounted on his Ranyhyn, Drinny son of Hynaril, and riding on toward Cravenhaw.

He spent most of that day watching over the Warmark. But the next morning, while the Warward made its final approach to Garroting Deep, he was forced to turn his attention to his task. He had to plan some way in which to keep his promise. He melded his thoughts with Lord Callindrill, and together they searched through their combined knowledges and intuitions for some key to Mhoram's dilemma. In his dread, he hoped to gain courage from the melding, but the ache of Callindrill's self-distrust denied him. Instead of receiving strength, Mhoram gave it.

With Callindrill's help, he prepared an approach to his task, arranged a series of possible answers according to their peril and likelihood of success. But by noon, he had found nothing definitive. Then he ran out of time. The Warward staggered to a halt at the very brink of Garroting Deep.

There, face-to-face with the One Forest's last remaining consciousness, Lord Mhoram began to taste the full gall of his inadequacy. The Deep's dark, atavistic rage left him effectless; he felt like a man with no fingers. The first trees were within a dozen yards of him. Like irregular columns, they appeared suddenly out of the ground, with no shrubs or bushes leading up to them, and no underbrush cluttering the greensward on which they stood. They were sparse at first. As far back as he could see, they did not grow thickly enough to close out the sunlight. Yet a shadow deepened on them; mounting dimness spurned the sunlight. In the distance, the benighted will of the Forest became an almost tangible refusal of passage. He felt that he was peering into a chasm. The idea that any bargain could be made with such a place seemed to be madness, vanity woven of dream stuff. For a long time, he only stood before the Deep and stared, with a groan of cold dread on his soul.

But Troy showed no hesitation. When Quaan told him where he was, he swung Mehryl around and began issuing orders. "All right, Hiltmark," he barked, "let's get ready for it. Food for everyone. Finish off the supplies, but make it fast. After that, move the warriors back beyond bowshot, and form an arc around Lord Mhoram. Make it as wide as possible, but keep it thick—I don't want Fleshharrower to break through. Lord Callindrill, I think you should fight with the Warward. And Quaan—I'll speak to the warriors while they're eating. I'll explain it all."

"Very well, Warmark." Quaan sounded distant, withdrawn into the recessed stronghold of his courage; and the lines of his face were taut with resolution. He returned Troy's blind salute, then turned and gave his own orders to Amorine. Together, they went to make the Warward's final preparations.

Troy pulled Mehryl around again. He tried to face Mhoram, but missed by several feet. "Maybe you'd better get started," he said. "You haven't got much time."

"I will wait until you have spoken to the Warward." Sadly, Mhoram saw Troy grimace with vexation at the discovery that he had misjudged the Lord's position. "I need strength. I must seek it awhile."

Troy nodded brusquely, and turned away as if he meant to watch the Warward's preparations.

Together, they waited for Quaan's signal. Lord Callindrill remained with them long enough to say, "Mhoram, the High Lord had no doubt of your fitness for the burden of these times. She is no ordinary judge of persons. My brother, your faith will suffice." His voice was gentle, but it implicitly expressed his belief that his own faith did not suffice. When he walked away from the Deep to take his stand with the warriors, he left Mhoram wrestling with insistent tears.

A short time later, Quaan reported that the Warward was ready to hear Troy. The Warmark asked Quaan to guide him to a place from which he could speak, and they trotted away together. Lord Mhoram walked after them. He wished to hear the Warmark's speech.

Troy stopped within the wide-seated arc of warriors. He did not need to ask for silence. Except for the noises of eating, the warriors were still, too exhausted to talk. They had marched and ached in blank silence for the last three days, and now they chewed their food with a kind of aghast lifelessness, ate as if compelled by an old habit unassoiled by any remaining endurance, desire. Moving their jaws, staring out of moistureless eyes, they looked like dusty skeletons, bare, dry bones animated by some obsession not their own.

Mhoram could not hold back his tears. They ran down his jaw and spattered like warm pain on his hands where he held his staff.

Yet he was glad that Troy could not see what his plans had done to the Warward.

Warmark Hile Troy faced the warriors squarely, held up his head as if he were offering his burns for inspection. Sitting on Mehryl's back, he was stiff with discipline—a rigid refusal of his own abjection. As he began to speak, his voice was hoarse with conflicting impulses, but he grew steadier as he continued.

"Warriors!" he said abruptly. "We are here. For

victory or defeat, this is the end. Today the outcome of this war will be decided.

"Our position is desperate—but you know that. Fleshharrower is only a league away by now. We're caught between his army and Garroting Deep. I want you to know that this is not an accident. We didn't panic and run here out of fear. We didn't come here because Fleshharrower forced us. You aren't victims. We came here on my order. I made the decision. When I was on Kevin's Watch, I saw how big Fleshharrower's army is. It's so big that we wouldn't have had a chance in Doom's Retreat. So I made the decision. I brought us here.

"I believe we're going to win today. We are going to cause the destruction of that horde—I believe it. I brought you here because I believe it. Now let me tell you how we're going to do it."

He paused for a moment, and became even stiffer, more erect, as he braced himself for what he had to say. Then he went on, "We are going to fight that army here for one reason. Lord Mhoram needs time. He's going to make this plan of mine work—and we have to keep him safe until he's ready.

"When he's ready"—Troy seemed to clench himself—"we're going to run like hell into Garroting Deep."

If he expected an outcry, he was surprised; the warriors were too weak to protest. But a rustle of anguish passed among them, and Mhoram could see horror on many faces.

Troy went on promptly, "I know how bad that sounds. No one has ever survived the Deep—no one has ever returned. I know all that. But Foul is hard to beat. Our only chance is something that seems impossible. I believe we won't be killed.

"While we fight, Lord Mhoram is going to summon Caerroil Wildwood, the Forestal. And Caerroil Wildwood is going to help us. He's going to give us free passage through Garroting Deep. He's going to defeat Fleshharrower's army.

"I believe this. I want you to believe it. It will work. The Forestal has no reason to hate us—you know that. And he has every reason to hate Fleshharrower. That Giant is a Raver. But the only way Caerroil Wildwood can get at Fleshharrower is to give us free passage. If we run into Garroting Deep, and Fleshharrower sees that we aren't harmed—then he'll follow us. He hates us and he hates the Deep too much to pass up a chance like this. It will work. The only problem is to summon the Forestal. And that is up to Lord Mhoram."

He paused again, weighing his words before he said, "Many of you have known Lord Mhoram longer than I have. You know what kind of man he is. He'll succeed. You know that.

"Until he succeeds, the only thing we have to do is fight—keep him alive while he works. That's all. I know how tough it's going to be for you. I—I hear how tired you are. But you are warriors. You will find the strength. I believe it. Whatever happens, I'll be proud to fight with you. And I won't be afraid to lead you into Garroting Deep. You are the true preservers of the Land."

He stopped, waiting for some kind of answer.

The warriors gave no cheers or shouts or cries; the extravagant grip of their exhaustion kept them silent. But together they heaved themselves to their feet. Twelve thousand men and women stood to salute the Warmark.

He seemed to hear their movement and understand it. He saluted them once, rigidly. Then he turned his proud Ranyhyn, and went trotting back toward where he had left Lord Mhoram.

He caught Mhoram by surprise, and the Lord failed to intercept him. He moved as if he were held erect by the stiffness of extreme need; his voice rocked as he said to the empty air where Mhoram had been, "I hope you understand what'll happen if you fail. We won't have any choice. We'll still have to go into the Deep. And pray the Forestal doesn't kill us until Fleshharrower follows. We'll all die that way, but maybe the Raver will, too."

Mhoram hastened toward Troy. But Terrel was closer to the Warmark, and he spoke before Mhoram could stop him. "That we will not permit," he said dispassionately. "It is suicide. We do not speak of the Warward. But we are the Bloodguard. We will not permit the Lords to enact their own death. We failed to prevent High Lord Kevin's self-destruction. We will not fail again."

"I hear you," Mhoram replied sharply. "But that moment has not yet come. First I must work." Turning to Troy, he said, "My friend, will you remain with me while I make this attempt. I need—I have need of support."

Troy seemed to totter on Mehryl's back. But he caught hold of the Ranyhyn's mane, steadied himself. "Just tell me if there's anything I can do." He reached out his hand, and when Mhoram clasped it, he slipped down from Mehryl's back.

Mhoram gripped his hand for a moment, then released him. The Lord looked over at the Warward, saw that it was preparing to meet Fleshharrower's charge. He turned his attention to the Deep. Dread constricted his heart. He was afraid that Caerroil Wildwood would simply strike him where he stood for the affront of his call—strike all the army. But he was still his own master. He stepped forward, raised his staff high over his head, and began the ritual appeal to the woods.

"Hail, Garroting Deep! Forest of the One Forest! Enemy of our enemies! Garroting Deep, hail! We are the Lords—foes to your enemies, and learners of the *lillianrill* lore. We must pass through!

"Harken, Caerroil Wildwood! We hate the ax and flame which hurt you. Your enemies are our enemies. Never have we brought edge of ax or flame of fire to touch you—nor ever shall. Forestal, harken! Let us pass!"

There was no answer. His voice fell echoless on the trees and grass; nothing moved or replied in the dark depths. He strained his senses to listen and look for any sign, but none came. When he was sure of the silence, he repeated the ritual. Again there was no reply. After a third appeal, the silent gloom of the Deep seemed to increase, to grow more profound and ominous, as he beseeched it.

Through the Forest's unresponsiveness, he heard the first gleeful shout of Fleshharrower's army as it caught sight of the Warward. The hungry cry multiplied his dread; his knuckles whitened as he resisted it. Planting his staff firmly on the grass, he tried another approach.

While the sun arced through the middle of the afternoon, Lord Mhoram strove to make himself heard in the heart of Garroting Deep. He used every Forestal name which had been preserved in the lore of the Land. He wove appeals and chants out of every invocation or summoning known to the Loresraat. He bent familiar forms away from their accustomed usage, hoping that they would unlock the silence. He even took the Summoning Song which had called Covenant to the Land, altered it to fit his need, and sang it into the Deep. It had no effect. The Forest remained impenetrable, answerless.

And behind him the last battle of the Warward began. As Fleshharrower's hordes rushed at them, the warriors raised one tattered cheer like a brief pennant of defiance. But then they fell silent, saved the vestiges of their strength for combat. With their weapons ready, they faced the ravening that charged toward them out of the Wastes.

The Raver's army crashed murderously into them. Firing their arrows at close range, they attempted to crack the momentum of the charge. But the horde's sheer numbers swept over slain ur-viles and Cavewights and other creatures, trampled them underfoot, drove into the Warward.

Its front lines crumbled at the onslaught; thousands of ill beasts broke into its core. But Hiltmark Quaan rallied one flank, and First Haft Amorine shored up the other. For the first time since she had left Doriendor Corishev, she seemed to remember herself. Throwing off her enervation of will, she brought her Eoward to the aid of the front lines. And Lord Callindrill held his ground in the army's center. Whirling his staff about his head, he rained blue fiery force in all directions. The creatures gave way before him; scores of unorganized ur-viles fell under his fire.

Then Quaan and Amorine reached him from either side.

From a place deep within them, beyond their most bereft exhaustion, the men and women of the Land brought up the strength to fight back. Faced with the raw malevolence of Lord Foul's perverse creations, the warriors found that they could still resist. Bone-deep love and abhorrence exalted them. Passionately, they hurled themselves at the enemy. Hundreds of them fell in swaths across the ground, but they threw back the Raver's first assault.

Fleshharrower roared his orders; the creatures drew back to regroup. Ur-viles hurried to form a wedge against Lord Callindrill, and the rest of the army shifted, brought Cavewights forward to bear the brunt of the next charge.

In an effort to disrupt these preparations, Quaan launched an attack of his own. Warriors leaped after the retreating beasts. Lord Callindrill and one Eoward ran to prevent the formation of the ur-vile wedge. For several furious moments, they threw the black Demondim-spawn into chaos.

But then the Giant-Raver struck, used his Stone to support the ur-viles. Several blasts of emerald fire forced Callindrill to give ground. At once, the wedge pulled itself together. The Eoward had to retreat.

It was a grim and silent struggle. After the first hungry yell of the attack, Fleshharrower's army fought with dumb, maniacal ferocity. And the warriors had no strength for shouts or cries. Only the tumult of feet, and the clash of weapons, and the moans of the maimed and dying, and the barking of orders, punctuated the mute engagement. Yet Lord Mhoram felt these clenched sounds like a deafening din; they seemed to echo off his dread. The effort to ignore the battle and concentrate on his work squeezed sweat out out of his bones, made his pulse hammer like a prisoner against his temples.

When traditional names and invocations failed to bring the Forestal, he began using signs and arcane symbols. He drew pentacles and circles on the grass with his staff, set fires burning within them, waved eldritch gestures over them. He murmured labyrinthian chants under his breath.

All were useless. The silence of the Deep's gloom sounded like laughter in his ears.

Yet the sounds of killing came steadily nearer. All the valiance of the warriors was not enough; they were driven back.

Troy heard the retreat also. At last he could no longer contain himself. "Dear God, Mhoram!" he whispered urgently. "They are being butchered."

Mhoram spun on Troy, raging, "Do you think I am unaware?" But when he beheld the Warmark, he stopped. He could see Troy's torment. The sting of sweat made the Warmark's burns flame garishly; they throbbed with pain. His hands groped aimlessly about him, as if he were lost. He was blind. For all his power to plan and conceive, he was helpless to execute even the simplest of his ideas.

Lord Mhoram wrenched his anger into another channel. With its strength, he made his decision.

"Very well, my friend," he breathed heavily. "There are other attempts to be made, but perhaps only one is perilous enough to have some hope of success. Stand ready. You must take my place if I fall. Legends say that the song I mean to sing is fatal."

As he strode forward, he felt a new calm. Confronting his dread, he could see that it was only fear. He had met and mastered its kindred when a Raver had laid hands on him. And the knowledge he had gained then could save the Warward now. With peril in his eyes, he went toward the Deep until he was among the first trees. There he ignited his staff and raised it over his head, carefully holding it away from any of the branches. Then he began to sing.

The words came awkwardly to his lips, and the accents of the melody seemed to miss their beats. He was singing a song to which no former Lord had ever given utterance. It was one of the dark mysteries of the Land, forbidden because of the hazard it carried. Yet the words of the song were clear and simple. Their peril lay elsewhere. According to Kevin's Lore, they belonged like cherished treasure to the Forestals of the One Forest. The forestals slew all mortals who profaned those words.

Nevertheless, Lord Mhoram lifted up his voice and sang them boldly.

> Branches spread and tree trunks grow
> Through rain and heat and snow and cold:
> Though wide world's winds untimely blow,
> And earthquakes rock and cliff unseal,
>
> My leaves grow green and seedlings bloom.
> Since days before the Earth was old
> And Time began its walk to doom,
> The Forests world's bare rock anneal,
>
> Forbidding dusty waste and death.
> I am the Land's Creator's hold:
> I inhale all expiring breath,
> And breathe out life to bind and heal.

As his singing faded into the distance, he heard the reply. Its music far surpassed his own. It seemed to fall from the branches like leaves bedewed with rare melody—to fall and flutter around him, so that he stared as if he were dazzled. The voice had a light, high, clear sound, like a splashing brook, but the power it implied filled him with awe.

> But ax and fire leave me dead.
> I know the hate of hands grown bold.
> Depart to save your heart-sap's red:
> My hate knows neither rest nor weal.

A shimmer of music rippled his sight. When it cleared, he saw Caerroil Wildwood walking toward him across the greensward.

The Forestal was a tall man with a long white beard and flowing white hair. He wore a robe of purest samite, and carried a gnarled wooden rod like a scepter in the crook of one arm. A garland of purple and

white orchids about his neck only heightened his austere dignity. He appeared out of the gloaming of the
Deep as if he had stepped from behind a veil, and he
moved like a monarch between the trees. They nodded
to him as he passed. With every step, he scattered
droplets of melody about him as if his whole person
were drenched in song. His sparkling voice softened
the severity of his mien. But his eyes were not soft.
From under his thick white brows, a silver light shone
from orbs without pupil or iris, and his glances had
the force of physical impact.

Still humming the refrain of his song, he approached Lord Mhoram. His gaze held the Lord motionless until they were almost within arm's reach of
each other. Mhoram felt himself being probed. The
sound of music continued, and some time passed before he realized that the Forestal was speaking to him,
asking him, "Who dares taint my song?"

With an effort, Lord Mhoram set aside his awe to
answer, "Caerroil Wildwood, Forestal and servant of
the Tree-soul, please pardon my presumption. I intend no offense or taint. But my need is urgent, surpassing both fear and caution. I am Mhoram son of
Variol, Lord of the Council of Revelstone, and a de-
fender of the Land in tree and rock. I seek a boon,
Caerroil Wildwood."

"A boon?" the Forestal mused musically. "You
bring a fire among my trees, and then ask a boon?
You are a fool, Mhoram son of Variol. I make no
bargains with men. I grant no boons to any creature
with knowledge of blade or flame. Begone." He did
not raise his voice or sharpen his song, but the might
of his command made Mhoram stagger.

"Forestal, hear me." Mhoram strove to keep his
voice calm. "I have used this fire only to gain your
notice." Extinguishing his staff, he lowered it to the
ground and gripped it as a brace against the Forestal's
refusal. "I am a Lord, a servant of the Earthpower.
Since the Lords began, all have sworn all their might
to the preservation of Land and Forest. We love and
honor the wood of the world. I have done no harm to

these trees—and never shall, though you refuse my boon and condemn the Land to fire and death."

Humming as if to himself, Caerroil Wildwood said, "I know nothing of Lords. They are nothing to me. But I know men, mortals. The Ritual of Desecration is not forgotten in the Deep."

"Yet hear me, Caerroil Wildwood." Mhoram could feel the sounds of battle beating against his back. But he remembered what he had learned of the history of the One Forest, and remained steady, serene. "I do not ask a boon for which I can make no return. Forestal, I offer you a Raver."

At the word *Raver,* Caerroil Wildwood changed. The dewy, glistening aura of his music took on an inflection of anger. His eyes darkened; their silver light gave way to thunderheads. Mist spread from his orbs, and drifted upward through his eyebrows. But he said nothing, and Mhoram continued.

"The people of the Land fight a war against the Despiser, the ancient tree ravager. His great army has driven us here, and the last battle now rages in Cravenhaw. Without your aid, we will surely be destroyed. But with our death, the Land becomes defenseless. Then the tree ravager will make war upon all the Forest—upon the trees in beautiful Andelain, upon slumbering Grimmerdhore and restless Morinmoss. In the end, he will attack the Deep and you. He must be defeated now."

The Forestal appeared unmoved by this appeal. Instead of replying to it, he hummed darkly, "You spoke of a Raver."

"The army which destroys us even now is commanded by a Raver, one of the three decimators of the One Forest."

"Give me a token that you speak the truth."

Lord Mhoram did not dare hesitate. Though the ground he trod was completely trackless, unmapped by any lore but his own intuition, he answered promptly, "He is *moksha* Raver, also named Jehannum and Fleshharrower. In ages long past, he and *turiya* his brother taught the despising of trees to the once-friendly Demondim. *Samadhi* his brother guided the

monarch of Doriendor Corishev when that mad king
sought to master the life and death of the One Forest."

"*Moksha* Raver," Caerroil Wildwood trilled lightly,
dangerously. "I have a particular hunger for Ravers."

"Their might is greatly increased now. They share
the unnatural power of the Illearth Stone."

"I care nothing for that," the Forestal replied almost brusquely. "But you offered a Raver to me. How
can that be done, when he defeats you even now?"

The sounds of battle came inexorably nearer as the
Warward was driven back. Lord Mhoram heard less
combat and more slaughter with every passing moment. And he could feel Warmark Troy panting behind him. With all his hard-won serenity, he answered,
"That is the boon I ask, Caerroil Wildwood. I ask safe
passage for all my people through Garroting Deep.
This boon will deliver *moksha* Raver into your hands.
He and all his army, all his ur-viles and Cavewights
and creatures, will be yours. When the Raver sees that
we flee into the Deep and are not destroyed, he will
follow. He will believe that you are weak—or that
you have passed away. His hatred for us, and for the
trees, will drive him and all his force into your
demesne."

A moment that throbbed urgently in Mhoram's ears
passed while Caerroil Wildwood considered. The battle noise seemed to say that soon there would be
nothing of the Warward left to save. But Mhoram
faced the Forestal, and waited.

At last, the Forestal nodded. "It is a worthy bargain," he sang slowly. "The trees are eager to fight
again. I am prepared. But there is a small price to be
paid for my help—and for the tainting of my song."

The upsurge of Mhoram's hope suddenly gave way
to fear, and he spun to try to stop Warmark Troy.
But before he could shout a warning, Troy said
fervidly, "Then I'll pay it! I'll pay anything. My army
is being slaughtered."

Mhoram winced at the irrevocable promise, tried to
protest. But the Forestal sang keenly, "Very well. I

accept your payment. Bring your army cautiously among the trees."

Troy reacted instantly; he whirled, leaped for Mehryl's back. Some instinct guided him; he landed astride the Ranyhyn as securely as if he could see. At once, he went galloping toward the battle, yelling with all his strength, "Quaan! Retreat! Retreat!"

The Warward was collapsing as he shouted. The ranks of the warriors were broken, and Fleshharrower's creatures ranged bloodily among them. More than two-thirds of the Eoward had already fallen. But something in Troy's command galvanized the warriors for a final exertion. Breaking away, they turned and ran.

Their sudden flight opened a brief gap between them and Fleshharrower's army. At once, Lord Callindrill set himself to widen the gap. Protected by a circle of Bloodguard, he unleashed a lightning fire that caught in the grass and crackled across the front of the foe. His blast did little damage, but it caused the Raver's forces to hesitate one instant in their pursuit. Using that instant, he followed the warriors. Together the survivors—hardly more than ten Eoward —ran straight toward Mhoram.

When he saw them coming, Lord Mhoram went out to meet Troy. He pulled the Warmark from Mehryl's back—it was not safe to ride under the branches of the Deep—took his arm, and guided him toward the trees. The fleeing warriors were almost on their heels when Mhoram and Troy strode into Garroting Deep.

Caerroil Wildwood had vanished, but his song remained. It seemed to resonate lightly off every leaf in the Forest. Mhoram could feel it piloting him, and he followed it implicitly. Behind him, he heard the warriors consummating their exhaustion in a last rush toward sanctuary or death. He heard Quaan shouting as if from a great distance that all survivors were now among the trees. But he did not look back. The Forestal's song exercised a fascination over him. Gripping Troy's arm and peering steadily ahead into the gloom, he moved at a brisk walk along the path of the melody.

With Callindrill, Troy, Quaan, Amorine, twoscore Bloodguard, all the Ranyhn, and more than four thousand warriors, Lord Mhoram passed for a time out of the world of humankind.

Slowly, the music transmuted his conscious alertness, drew him into a kind of trance. He felt that he was still aware of everything, but that now nothing touched him. He could see the onset of evening in the altered dimness of the Deep, but he felt no passage of time. In openings between the trees, he could see the Westron Mountains. By the changing positions of the peaks, he could gauge his speed. He appeared to be moving faster than a galloping Ranyhn. But he felt no exertion or strain of travel. The breath of the song wafted him ahead, as if he and his companions were being inhaled by the Deep. It was a weird, dreamy passage, a soul journey, full of speed he could not experience and events he could not feel.

Night came—the moon was completely dark—but he did not lose sight of his way. Some hint of light in the grass and leaves and song made his path clear to him, and he went on confidently, untouched by any need for rest. The Forestal's song released him from mortality, wrapped him in careless peace.

Sometime during the darkness, he heard the change of the song. The alteration had no effect on him, but he understood its meaning. Though the Forest swallowed every other sound, so that no howls or screams or cries reached his ears, he knew that Fleshharrower's army was being destroyed. The song described ages of waiting hate, of grief over vast tracts of kindred lost, ages of slow rage which climbed through the sap of the woods until every limb and leaf shared it, lived it, ached to act. And through that melodic narration came whispers of death as roots and boughs and trunks moved together to crush and rend.

Against the immense Deep, even Fleshharrower's army was small and defenseless—a paltry insult hurled against an ocean. The trees brushed aside the power of the ur-viles and the strength of the Cavewights and the mad, cornered, desperate fear of all the other creatures. Led by Caerroil Wildwood's song, they simply throttled the invaders. Flames were stamped out, blade wielders were slain, lore and force were overwhelmed. Then the trees drank the blood and ate the bodies—eradicated every trace of the enemy in an apotheosis of ancient and exquisite fury.

When the song resumed its former placid wafting, it seemed to breathe grim satisfaction and victory.

Soon after that—Mhoram thought it was soon—a rumble like thunder passed over the woods. At first, he thought that he was hearing Fleshharrower's death struggle. But then he saw that the sound had an entirely different source. Far ahead and to the west, some terrible violence occurred in the mountains. Red fires spouted from one part of the range. After every eruption, a concussion rolled over the Deep, and a coruscating exhaust paled the night sky. But Mhoram was immune to it. He watched it with interest, but the song wrapped him in its enchantments and preserved him from all care.

And he felt no concern when he realized that the Warward was no longer behind him. Except for Lord Callindrill, Troy, Amorine, Hiltmark Quaan, and two Bloodguard, Terrel and Morril, he was alone. But he was not anxious; the song assuaged him with peace and trust. It led him onward and still onward through a measureless night into the dawn of a new day.

With the return of light, he found that he was moving through a woodland profuse with purple and white orchids. Their soft, pure colors fell in with the music as if they were the notes Caerroil Wildwood sang. They folded Mhoram closely in the consolation of the melody. With a wide, unconscious smile he let himself go as if the current which carried him were an anodyne for all his hurts.

His strange speed was more apparent now. Already through gaps in the overhanging foliage, he could see the paired spires of *Melenkurion* Skyweir, the tallest peaks in the Westron Mountains. He could see the high, sheer plateau of Rivenrock as the struggle it concealed continued. Eruptions and muffled booms came echoing from the depths of the mountain, and red bursts of force struck the sky at irregular intervals. But still he was untouched. His speed, his exhilarating, easy swiftness, filled his heart with gay glee. He had covered thirty or forty leagues since entering the Deep. He felt ready to walk that way forever.

But the day passed with the same timeless evanescence that had borne him through the night. Soon the sun was close to setting, yet he had no sense of duration, no weary or hungry physical impression that he had traveled all day.

Then the song changed again. Gradually, it no longer floated him forward. The end of his wafting filled him with quiet sadness, but he accepted it. The thunders and eruptions of Rivenrock were now almost due southwest of him. He judged that he and his companions were nearing the Black River.

The song led him straight through the Forest to a high bald hill that stood up out of the woodland like a wen of barrenness. Beyond it, he could hear a rush of water—the Black River—but the hill itself caught his attention, restored some measure of his self-awareness. The soil of the hill was completely lifeless, as if in past ages it had been drenched with too much death ever to bloom again. And just below its crown on the near side stood two rigid trees like sentinels, witnesses, ten yards or more apart. They were as dead as the hill—blackened, bereft of limbs and leaves, sapless. Each dead trunk had only one bough left. Fifty feet above the ground, the trees reached toward each other, and their limbs interwove to form a crossbar between them.

This was Gallows Howe, the ancient slaying place of the Forestals. Here, according to the legends of the Land, Caerroil Wildwood and his brethren had held their assizes in the long-past ages when the One Forest still struggled for survival. Here the Ravers who had come within the Forestals' grasp had been executed.

Now *moksha* Fleshharrower hung from the gibbet. Black fury congested his face, his swollen tongue protruded like contempt between his teeth, and his eyes stared emptily. A rictus of hate strained and stretched all his muscles. His dying frenzy had been so

extravagant that many of his blood vessels had ruptured, staining his skin with dark hemorrhages.

As Lord Mhoram gazed upward through the thick-
ening dusk, he felt suddenly tired and thirsty. Several
moments passed before he noticed that Caerroil Wildwood was nearby. The Forestal stood to one side of
the hill, singing quietly, and his eyes shone with a red
and silver light.

At Mhoram's side, Warmark Troy stirred as if he
were awakening, and asked dimly, "What is it? What
do you see?"

Mhoram had to swallow several times before he
could find his voice. "It is Fleshharrower. The Forestal
has slain him."

A sharp intensity crossed Troy's face, as if he were
straining to see. Then he smiled. "Thank God."

"It is a worthy bargain," Caerroil Wildwood sang.
"I know that I cannot slay the spirit of a Raver. But
it is a great satisfaction to kill the flesh. He is
garroted." His eyes flared redly for a moment, then
faded toward silver again. "Therefore do not think
that I have rescinded my word. Your people are unharmed. The presence of so many faithless mortals
disturbed the trees. To shorten their discomfort, I
have sent your people out of Garroting Deep to the
north. But because of the bargain, and the price yet
to be paid, I have brought you here. Behold the retribution of the Forest."

Something in his high clear voice made Mhoram
shudder. But he remembered himself enough to ask,
"What has become of the Raver's Stone?"

"It was a great evil," the Forestal hummed severely.
"I have destroyed it."

Quietly, Lord Mhoram nodded. "That is well."
Then he tried to focus his attention on the matter of
Caerroil Wildwood's price. He wanted to argue that
Troy should not be held to the bargain; the Warmark
had not understood what was being asked of him.
But while Mhoram was still searching for words, Terrel
distracted him. Silently, the Bloodguard pointed away
upriver.

The night was almost complete; only open starlight

and the glow of Caerroil Wildwood's eyes illumined Gallows Howe. But when the Lord followed Terrel's indication, he saw two different lights. Far in the distance, Rivenrock's fiery holocaust was visible. The violence there seemed to be approaching its climacteric. The fires spouted furiously, and dark thunder rolled over the Deep as if great cliffs were cracking. The other light was much closer. A small, grave, white gleam shone through the trees between Mhoram and the river. As he looked at it, it moved out of sight beyond the Howe.

Someone was traveling through Garroting Deep along the Black River.

An intuition clutched Lord Mhoram, and at once he found he was afraid. Glimpses and visions which he had forgotten during the past days returned to him. Quickly, he turned to the Forestal. "Who comes? Have you made other bargains?"

"If I have," sang the Forestal, "they are no concern of yours. But these two pass on sufferance. They have not spoken to me. I allow them because the light they bear presents no peril to the trees—and because they hold a power which I must respect. I am bound by the Law of creation."

"*Melenkurion!*" Mhoram breathed. "Creator preserve us!" Catching hold of Troy's arm, he started up the bald hill. His companions hastened after him. He passed the gibbet, gained the crest of the Howe, and looked down beyond it at the river.

Two men climbed the hill toward him from the riverbank. One of them held a shining stone in his right hand, and supported his comrade with his left arm. They moved painfully, as if they ascended against a weight of barrenness. When they were near the hilltop, in full view of all Mhoram's company, they stopped.

Slowly, Bannor held up the *orcrest* so that it lighted the crest of the Howe. With a nod, he acknowledged the Lords.

When Thomas Covenant realized that all the people on the hill were watching him, he pushed away from Bannor's support, stood on his own. The exertion cost him a sharp effort. As he stood, he wavered unsteadily. In the *orcrest* light, his forehead gleamed atrociously. His eyes held a sightless stare—a stare without object, and yet of such intensity that his eyes appeared to be crossed, as if he were so conscious of his own duplicities that he could not see singly. His hands clenched each other against his chest. But then a fierce blast from Rivenrock struck him, and he almost lost his balance. He was forced to reach his half-hand toward Bannor. The movement bared his left fist.

On his wedding finger, the argent ring throbbed hotly.

PART III

The Blood
of the Earth

TWENTY-ONE: Lena's Daughter

TROY had called Thomas Covenant's Unbelief a bluff. But Covenant was not playing a mental game. He was a leper. He was fighting for his life.

Unbelief was his only defense against the Land, his only way to control the intensity, the potential suicide, of his response to the Land. He felt that he had lost every other form of self-protection. And without self-protection he would end up like the old man he had met in the leprosarium—crippled and fetid beyond all endurance. Even madness would be preferable. If he went mad, he would at least be insulated from knowing what was happening to him, blind and deaf and numb to the vulturine disease that gnawed his flesh.

Yet as he rode westward away from Revelwood with High Lord Elena, Amok, and the two Bloodguard, in quest of Kevin Landwaster's Seventh Ward, he knew that he was changing. By fits and starts, his ground shifted under him; some potent, subtle Earthpower altered his personal terrain. Unstable footing shrugged him toward a precipice. And he felt helpless to do anything about it.

The most threatening aspect of his immediate situation was Elena. Her nameless inner force, her ancestry, and her strange irrefusability both disturbed and attracted him. As they left the Valley of Two Rivers, he was already cursing himself for accepting her invitation. And yet she had the power to sway him. She tangled his emotions, and pulled unexpected strands of assent out of the knot.

This was not like his other acquiescences. When Lord Mhoram had asked him to go with the Warward, he had agreed because he completely lacked alterna-

401

tives. He urgently needed to keep moving, keep
searching for an escape. No similar reasoning vindi-
cated him when the High Lord had asked him to accompany her. He felt that he was riding away from
the crux of his dilemma, the battle against Lord Foul
—evading it like a coward. But in the moment of decision he had not even considered refusing. And he
sensed that she could draw him farther. Hopelessly,
without one jot or tittle of belief to his name, he
could be made to follow her, even if she went to attack the Despiser himself. Her beauty, her physical
presence, her treatment of him, ate away portions of
his armor, exposing his vulnerable flesh.

Traveling through the crisp autumn of Trothgard,
he watched her alertly, timorously.

High and proud on the back of Myrha, her Ranyhyn, she looked like a crowned vestal, somehow both
powerful and fragile—as if she could have shattered
his bones with a glance, and yet would have fallen
from her seat at the touch of a single hurled handful
of mud. She daunted him.

When Amok appeared beside her as if concretized
abruptly out of blank air, she turned to speak with
him. They exchanged greetings, and bantered pleas-
antly like old friends while Revelwood fell into the
distance behind them. Amok's reticence on the subject
of his Ward did not prevent him from gay prolixity
in other matters. Soon he was singing and talking happily as if his sole function were to entertain the High
Lord.

As Amok whiled away the morning, Covenant
gazed over the countryside around him.

The party of the quest rode easily up out of the lowlands of Trothgard. They traveled a few points south
of westward, roughly paralleling the course of the Rill
River toward the Westron Mountains. The western
edge of Trothgard, still sixty or sixty-five leagues
away, was at least three thousand feet higher than the
Valley of Two Rivers, and the whole region slowly
climbed toward the mountains. Already the High
Lord's party moved into the gradual uprise. Covenant
could feel their relaxed ascent as they rode through

woodlands anademed in autumn, ablaze with orange, yellow, gold, red leaf-flames, and over lush grassy hillsides, where the scars of Stricken Stone's ancient wars had been effaced by thick heather and timothy like healthy new flesh over the wounds, green with healing.

He was barely able to sense the last hints of Trothgard's convalescence. Under the mantling growth of grass and trees, all the injuries of Kevin's last war had not been undone. From time to time, the riders passed near festering barren patches which still refused all repair, and some of the hills seemed to lie awkwardly, like broken bones imperfectly set. But the Lords had labored to good effect. The air of Trothgard was tangy, animate, vital. Very few of the trees showed that their roots ran down into once-desecrated soil. The new Council of Lords had found a worthy way to spend their lives.

Because of what it had suffered, Trothgard touched Covenant's heart. He found that he liked it, trusted it. At times as the day passed into afternoon, he wished that he was not going anywhere. He wanted to roam Trothgard—destinationless, preferably alone—without any thought of Wards or rings or wars. He would have welcomed the rest.

Amok seemed a fit guide for such sojourns. The bearer of the Seventh Ward moved with a sprightly, boyish stride which disguised the fact that the pace he set was not a lazy one. And his good spirits bubbled irrepressibly. He sang long songs which he claimed to have learned from the faery *Elohim*—songs so alien that Covenant could distinguish neither words nor sentences, and yet so curiously suggestive, so like moonlight in a forest, that they half entranced him. And Amok told intimate tales of the stars and heavens, describing merrily the sky dance as if he had pranced in it himself. His happy voice complemented the clear, keen evening air and the sunset conflagration of the trees, interwove his listeners like an incantation, a mesmerism.

Yet in the twilight of Trothgard, he disappeared

suddenly, gestured himself out of visibility, leaving the High Lords' party alone.

Covenant was startled out of his reverie. "Where—?"

"Amok will return," answered Elena. In the gloaming, he could not tell if she were looking at him or through him or into him or in spite of him. "He has only left us for the night. Come, ur-Lord," she said as she dropped lightly down from Myrha's back. "Let us rest."

Covenant followed her example, released his mount to Bannor's care. Myrha and the other two Ranyhyn galloped away, stretching their legs after a day's walking. Then Morin went to the Rill for water while Elena began to make camp. She produced a small urn of graveling, and used the fire-stones to cook a frugal meal for herself and Covenant. Her face followed the motion of her hands, but her vision's strange otherness was far distant, as if in the earthy light she read of events on the opposite edge of the Land.

Covenant watched her; in the performance of even the simplest chores she fascinated him. But as he studied her lithe form, her sure movements, her bifurcated gaze, he was trying to regain a grip on himself, trying to recover some sense of where he stood with her. She was a mystery to him. Out of all the strong and knowledgeable people of the Land, she had chosen him to accompany her. He had raped her mother —and still she had chosen him. In Glimmermere she had kissed— The memory made his heart hurt. She had chosen him. But not out of anger or desire for retribution—not for any reason that Trell would have approved. He could see in her smiles, hear in her voice, feel in her ambience that she intended him no harm. Then why? From what secret forgetfulness or passion did her desire for his company spring? He needed to know. And yet he was half afraid of the answer.

After supper, when he sat drinking his ration of springwine across the pot of graveling from Elena, he mustered his courage to question her. Both Bloodguard had withdrawn from the campsite, and he was

relieved that he did not have to contend with them.
Rubbing his fingers through his beard, remembering
the peril of physical sensations, he began by asking her
if she had learned anything from Amok.

She shook her head unconcernedly, and her hair
haloed her head in the graveling light. "We are surely
several days from the location of the Seventh Ward.
There will be time enough for the questioning of
Amok."

He accepted this, but it did not meet his need.
Tightening his hold on himself, he asked her why she
had chosen him.

She gazed at him or through him for several moments before she replied. "Thomas Covenant, you
know that I did not choose you. No Lord of Revelstone chose you. Drool Rockworm performed your
first summoning, and he was guided by the Despiser.
In that way, we are your victims, just as you are his.
It may be as Lord Mhoram believes—perhaps the
Land's Creator also chose. Or perhaps the dead Lords
—perhaps High Lord Kevin himself wields some influence from beyond his lost grave. But I made no
choice." Then her tone changed, and she went on,
"Yet had I chosen—"

Covenant interrupted her. "That isn't what I meant.
I know why this is happening to me. It's because I'm a
leper. A normal person would just laugh— No, what I
meant is, why did you ask me to come with you—
looking for the Seventh Ward? Surely there were other
people you could have chosen."

Gently, she returned, "I do not understand this disease which causes you to be a—leper. You describe
a world in which the innocent are tormented. Why are
such things done? Why are they permitted?"

"Things aren't so different here. Or what did you
think it was that happened to Kevin? But you're
changing the subject. I want to know why you picked
me." He winced at the memory of Troy's chagrin
when the High Lord had announced her choice.

"Very well, ur-Lord," she said with a tone of re-
luctance. "If this question must be answered, I will

answer it. There are many reasons for my choice. Will you hear them?"

"Go ahead."

"Ah, Unbeliever. At times I think that Warmark Troy is not so blind. The truth—you evade the truth. But I will give you my reasons. First, I prepare for the chances of the future. If at the last you should come to desire the use of your white gold, with the Staff of Law I am better able to aid you than any other. I do not know the wild magic's secret—but there is no more discerning tool than the Staff. And if at the last you should turn against the Land, with the Staff I will be able to resist you. We possess nothing else which can hope to stand against the power of white gold.

"But I seek other goals also. You are no warrior—and the Warward will meet great peril, where only power and skill in combat may hope to preserve life. I do not wish to risk your death. You must be given time to find your own reply to yourself. And for myself I seek companionship. Neither Warmark Troy nor Lord Mhoram can be spared from the war. Do you desire more explanation?"

He sensed the incompleteness of her response, and forced himself to pursue it despite his fear. With a grimace of distaste for the pervasive irrectitude of his conduct in the Land, he said deliberately, "Companionship? After all I've done. You're remarkably tolerant."

"I am not tolerant. I do not make choices without consulting my own heart."

For a moment, he faced squarely the implications of what she said. It was what he had both wanted and feared to hear. But then a complex unwillingness, composed of sympathy and dread and self-judgment, deflected him. It made his voice rough as he said, "You're breaking Trell's heart. And your mother's."

Her face stiffened. "Do you accuse me of Trell's pain?"

"I don't know. He would be following us if he had any hope left. Now he knows for sure that you're not even thinking about punishing me."

He stopped, but the sight of the pain he had given her made him speak again, rush to answer replies, counteraccusations, that she had not uttered. "As for your mother—I've got no right to talk. I don't mean about what I did to her. That's something I can at least understand. I was in such—penury—and she seemed so rich.

"No, I mean about the Ranyhyn—those Ranyhyn that went to Mithil Stonedown every year. I made a bargain with them. I was trying to find some solution —some way to keep myself from going completely insane. And they hated me. They were just like the Land—they were big and powerful and superior— and they loathed me." He rasped that word *loathed*, as if he were echoing, *Leper outcast unclean!* "But they reared to me—a hundred of them. They were driven—

"So I made a bargain with them. I promised that I wouldn't ride—wouldn't force one of them to carry me. And I made them promise— I was trying to find some way to keep all that size and power and health and fidelity from driving me crazy. I made them promise to answer if I ever called them. And I made them promise to visit your mother."

"Their promise remains." She said this as if it gave her a deep pride.

He sighed. "That's what Rue said. But that's not the point. Do you see? I was trying to give her something, make it up to her somehow. But that doesn't work. When you've hurt someone that badly, you can't go around giving them gifts. That's arrogant and cruel." His mouth twisted at the bitter taste of what he had done. "I was really just trying to make myself feel better.

"Anyway, it didn't work. Foul can pervert anything. By the time I got to the end of the Quest for the Staff of Law, things were so bad that no bargain could have saved me."

Abruptly, he ran out of words. He wanted to tell Elena that he did not accuse her, could not accuse her —and at the same time a part of him did accuse her.

That part of him felt that Lena's pain deserved more loyalty.

But the High Lord seemed to understand this. Though her elsewhere gaze did not touch him, she replied to his thought. "Thomas Covenant, you do not altogether comprehend Lena my mother. I am a woman—human like any other. And I have chosen you to be my companion on this quest. Surely my choice reveals my mother's heart as well as my own. I am her daughter. From birth I lived in her care, and she taught me. Unbeliever, she did not teach me any anger or bitterness toward you."

"No!" Covenant breathed. "No." No! Not her, too! A vision of blood darkened his sight—the blood on Lena's loins. He could not bear to think that she had forgiven him, she!

He turned away. He felt Elena watching him, felt her presence reaching toward him in an effort to draw him back. But he could not face her. He was afraid of the emotions that motivated her; he did not even name them to himself. He lay down in his blankets with his back to her until she banked the graveling for the night and settled herself to sleep.

The next morning, shortly after dawn, Morin and Bannor reappeared. They brought Myrha and Covenant's mount with them. He roused himself, and joined Elena in a meal while the Bloodguard packed their blankets. And soon after they had started westward again, Amok became visible at the High Lord's side.

Covenant was in no mood for any more of Amok's spellbinding. And he had made a decision during the night. There was a risk he had to take—a dangerous gesture that he hoped might help him recover some kind of integrity. Before the youth could begin, Covenant clenched himself to contain the sudden hammering of his heart, and asked Amok what he knew about white gold.

"Much and little, Bearer," Amok answered with a laugh and a bow. "It is said that white gold articulates the wild magic which destroys peace. But who is able to describe peace?"

Covenant frowned. "You're playing word games. I asked you a straight question. What do you know about it?"

"Know, Bearer? That is a small word—it conceals the magnitude of its meaning. I have heard what I have been told, and have seen what my eyes have beheld, but only you bear the white gold. Do you call this knowledge?"

"Amok," Elena came to Covenant's aid, "is white gold in some way interwoven with the Seventh Ward? Is white gold the subject or key of that Ward?"

"Ah, High Lord, all things are interwoven." The youth seemed to relish his ability to dodge questions. "The Seventh Ward may ignore white gold, and the master of white gold may have no use for the Seventh Ward—yet both are power, forms and faces of the one Power of life. But the Bearer is not my master. He shadows but does not darken me. I respect that which he bears, but my purpose remains."

Elena's response was firm. "Then there is no need to evade his questions. Speak of what you have heard and learned concerning white gold."

"I speak after my fashion, High Lord. Bearer, I have heard much and learned little concerning white gold. It is the girding paradox of the arch of Time, the undisciplined restraint of the Earth's creation, the absent bone of the Earthpower, the rigidness of water and the flux of rock. It articulates the wild magic which destroys peace. It is spoken of softly by the *Bhrathair,* and named in awe by the *Elohim,* though they have never seen it. Great *Kelenbhrabanal* dreams of it in his grave, and grim Sandgorgons writhe in voiceless nightmare at the touch of its name. In his last days, High Lord Kevin yearned for it in vain. It is the abyss and the peak of destiny."

Covenant sighed to himself. He had feared that he would receive this kind of answer. Now he would have to go further, push his question right to the edge of his dread. In vexation and anxiety he rasped, "That's enough—spare me. Just tell me how white gold—" For an instant he faltered. But the memory of Lena compelled him. "—how to use this bloody ring."

"Ah, Bearer," Amok laughed, "ask the Sunbirth Sea or *Melenkurion* Skyweir. Question the fires of Gorak Krembal, or the tinder heart of Garroting Deep. All the Earth knows. White gold is brought into use like any other power—through passion and mystery, the honest subterfuge of the heart."

"Hellfire," Covenant growled in an effort to disguise his relief. He did not like to admit to himself how glad he was to remain ignorant on this subject. But that ignorance was vital to his self-defense. As long as he did not know how to use the wild magic, he could not be blamed for the fate of the Land. In a secret and perfidious part of his heart, he had risked his question only because he trusted Amok to give him an unrevealing answer. Now he felt like a liar. Even his attempts at integrity were flawed. But his relief was greater than his self-distaste.

That relief enabled him to change the subject, attempt a normal conversation with the High Lord. He felt as awkward as a cripple; he had not conversed casually with another person since before the onset of his leprosy. But Elena responded willingly, even gladly; she welcomed his attention. Soon he no longer had to search for leading questions.

For some time, their talk floated on the ambience of Trothgard. As they climbed westward through the hills and woodlands and moors, the autumn air grew crisper. Birds roved the countryside in deft flits and soars. The cheerful sunlight stretched as if it might burst at any moment into sparkles and gleams. In it, the fall colors became dazzling. And the riders began to see more animals—rabbits and squirrels, plump badgers, occasional foxes. The whole atmosphere seemed to suit High Lord Elena. Gradually, Covenant came to understand this aspect of Lordship. Elena was at home in Trothgard. The healing of Kurash Plenethor became her.

In the course of his questions, she avoided only one subject—her childhood experiences with the Ranyhyn. Something about her young rides and initiations was too private to be treated under the open sky. But on other topics she replied without constraint. She allowed herself to be led into talk of her years in the Loresraat, of Revelwood and Trothgard, of Revelstone and Lordship and power. He sensed that she was helping him, allowing him, cooperating, and he was grateful. In time, he no longer felt maimed during the pauses in their conversation.

The next day passed similarly. But the day after that, this unthreatened mood eluded him. He lost his facility. His tongue grew stiff with remembered loneliness, and his beard itched irritably, like a reminder of peril. It's impossible, he thought. None of this is happening to me. Deliberately, driven by his illness, and by all the survival disciplines he had lost, he raised the question of High Lord Kevin.

"I am fascinated by him," she said, and the core of stillness in her voice sounded oddly like the calm in the eye of a storm. "He was the highest of all Berek Heartthew's great line—the Lord most full of dominion in all the Land's known or legended history. His fidelity to the Land and the Earthpower knew neither taint nor flaw. His friendship with the Giants was a matter for a fine song. The Ranyhyn adored him, and the Bloodguard wove their Vow because of him. If he had a fault, it was in excessive trust—yet how can trust be counted for blame? At the first, it was to his honor that the Despiser could gain Lordship from him—Lordship, and access to his heart. Was not Fangthane witnessed and approved by the *orcrest* and *lomillialor* tests of truth? Innocence is glorified by its vulnerability.

"And he was not blind. In the awful secret of his doubt, he refused the summons which would have taken him to his death in Treacher's Gorge. In his heart-wrung foresight or prophecy, he made decisions which preserved the Land's future. He prepared his Wards. He provided for the survival of the Giants and the Ranyhyn and the Bloodguard. He warned the people. And then with his own hand he destroyed—

"Thomas Covenant, there are some who believe that the Ritual of Desecration expressed High Lord

Kevin's highest wisdom. They are few, but eloquent. The common understanding holds that Kevin strove to achieve that paradox of purity through destruction—and failed, for he and all the works of the Lords were undone, yet the Despiser endured. But these few argue that the final despair or madness with which Kevin invoked the Ritual was a necessary sacrifice, a price to make possible ultimate victory. They argue that his preparations and then the Ritual—forcing both health and ill to begin their work anew—were enacted to provide us with Fangthane's defeat. In this argument, Kevin foresaw the need which would compel the Despiser to summon white gold to the Land."

"He must have been sicker than I thought," Covenant muttered. "Or maybe he just liked desecrations."

"Neither, I think," she replied tartly, sternly. "He was a brave and worthy man driven to extremity. Any mortal or unguarded heart may be brought to despair—for this reason we cling to the Oath of Peace. And for this same reason High Lord Kevin fascinates me. He avowed the Land, and defiled it—in the same breath affirmed and denounced." Her voice rose on the inner wind of her emotion. "How great must have been his grief? And how great his power had he only survived that last consuming moment—if, after beholding the Desecration, and hearing the Despiser's glee, he had lived to strike one more blow!

"Thomas Covenant, I believe that there is immeasurable strength in the consummation of despair—strength beyond all conceiving by an unholocausted soul. I believe that if High Lord Kevin could speak from beyond the grave, he would utter a word which would unmarrow the very bones of Lord Foul's Despite."

"That's madness!" Covenant gasped thickly. Elena's gaze wavered on the edge of focus, and he could not bear to look at her. "Do you think that some existence after death is going to vindicate you after you've simply extirpated life from the Earth? That was exactly Kevin's mistake. I tell you, he is roasting in hell!"

"Perhaps," she said softly. To his surprise, the

storm implied in her voice was gone. "We will never possess such knowledge—and should not need it to live our lives. But I find a danger in Lord Mhoram's belief that the Earth's Creator has chosen you to defend the Land. It is in my heart that this does not account for you.

"However, I have thought at times that perhaps our dead live in your world. Perhaps High Lord Kevin now restlessly walks your Earth, searching a voice which may utter his word here."

Covenant groaned; Elena's suggestion dismayed him. He heard the connection she drew between Kevin Landwaster and himself. And the implications of that kinship made his heart totter as if it were assailed by potent gusts of foreboding. As they rode onward, the new silence between them glistened like white eyes of fear.

This mood grew stronger through that day and the next. The magnitude of the issues at stake numbed Covenant; he did not have the hands to juggle them. He withdrew into silence as if it were a chrysalis, an armor for some special vulnerability or metamorphosis. An obscure impulse like a memory of his former days with Atiaran prompted him to drop away from Elena's side and ride behind her. At her back, he followed Amok into the upper reaches of Trothgard.

Then, on the sixth day, the thirteenth since he had left Revelstone, he came to himself again after a fashion. Scowling thunderously, he raised his head, and saw the Westron Mountains ranging above him. High Lord Elena's party was nearing the southwest corner of Trothgard, where the Rill River climbed up into the mountains; and already the crags and snows of the range filled the whole western sky. Trothgard lay unrolled behind him like the Lords' work exposed for review; it beamed in the sunlight as if it were confident of approbation. Covenant frowned at it still more darkly, and turned his attention elsewhere.

The riders moved near the rim of the canyon of the Rill. The low, incessant rush of its waters, unseen below the edge of the canyon, gave Trothgard a dimension of sound like a subliminal humming made by the mountains and hills. All the views had a new suggestiveness, a timbre of implication. It reminded Covenant that he was climbing into one of the high places of the Land—and he did not like high places. But he clenched his frown to anchor the involuntary reactions of his face, and returned to Elena's side. She gave him a smile which he could not return, and they rode on together toward the mountains.

Late that afternoon, they stopped, made camp beside a small pool near the edge of the canyon. Water came splashing out of the mountainside directly before them, and collected in a rocky basin before pouring over the rim toward the Rill. That pool could have served as a corner marker for Trothgard. Immediately south of it was the Rill's canyon; on the west, the mountains seemed to spring abruptly out of the ground, like a frozen instant of ambuscade; and Kurash Plenethor lay draped northeastward across the descending terrain. The aggressive imminence of the mountains contrasted vividly with the quiet panoply of Trothgard—and that contrast, multiplied by the lambent sound of the unseen Rill, gave the whole setting a look of surprise, an aspect or impression of suddenness. The atmosphere around the pool carried an almost tangible sense of boundary.

Covenant did not like it. The air contained too much crepuscular lurking. It made him feel exposed. And the riders were not forced to stop there; enough daylight remained for more traveling. But the High Lord had decided to camp beside the pool. She dismissed Amok, sent the two Bloodguard away with the Ranyhyn and Covenant's horse, then set her pot of graveling on a flat rock near the pool, and asked Covenant to leave her alone so that she could bathe.

Snorting as if the very air vexed him, he stalked off into the lee of a boulder where he was out of sight of the pool. He sat with his back to the stone, hugged his knees, and gazed down over Trothgard. He found the woodland hills particularly attractive as the mountain shadow began to fall across them. The peaks seemed to exude an austere dimness which by slow degrees submerged Trothgard's luster. Through simple size and grandeur, they exercised precedence. But he preferred Trothgard. It was lower and more human.

Then the High Lord interrupted his reverie. She had left her robe and the Staff of Law on the grass by her graveling. Wrapped only in a blanket, and drying her hair with one corner of it, she came to join him. Though the blanket hung about her thickly, revealing even less of her supple figure than did her robe, her presence felt more urgent than ever. The simple movement of her limbs as she seated herself at his side exerted an unsettling influence over him. She demanded responses. He found that his chest hurt again, as it had at Glimmermere.

Striving to defend himself against an impossible tenderness, he flung away from the boulder, walked rapidly toward the pool. The itching of his beard reminded him that he also needed a bath. The High Lord remained out of sight; Bannor and Morin were nowhere around. He dropped his clothes by the graveling pot, and went to the pool.

The water was as cold as snow, but he thrust himself into it like a man exacting penance, and began to scrub at his flesh as if it were stained. He attacked his scalp and cheeks until his fingertips tingled, then submerged himself until his lungs burned. But when he pulled himself out of the water and went to the graveling for warmth, he found that he had only aggravated his difficulties. He felt whetted, more voracious, but no cleaner.

He could not understand Elena's power over him, could not control his response. She was an illusion, a figment; he should not be so attracted to her. And she should not be so willing to attract him. He was already responsible for her; his one potent act in the Land had doomed him to that. How could she not blame him?

Moving with an intemperate jerkiness, he dried himself on one of the blankets, then draped it by the pot to dry, and began to dress. He put on his clothes fiercely, as if he were girding for battle—laced and hauled and zipped and buckled himself into his sturdy boots, his T-shirt, his tough, protective jeans. He checked to be sure that he still carried his penknife and Hearthrall Tohrm's *orcrest* in his pockets.

When he was properly caparisoned, he went back through the twilight toward the High Lord. He stamped his feet to warn her of his approach, but the grass absorbed his obscure vehemence, and he made no more noise than an indignant specter.

He found her standing a short distance downhill from the boulder. She was gazing out over Trothgard with her arms folded across her chest, and did not turn toward him as he drew near. For a time, he stood two steps behind her. The sky was still too sun-pale for stars, but Trothgard lay under the premature gloaming of the mountains. In the twilight, the face of the Lords' promise to the Land was veiled and dark.

Covenant twisted his ring, wound it on his finger as if he were tightening it to the pitch of some outbreak. Water from his wet hair dripped into his eyes. When he spoke, his voice was harsh with a frustration that he could neither relieve nor repress.

"Hellfire, Elena! I'm your father!"

She gave no sign that she had heard him, but after a moment she said in a low, musing tone, "Triock son of Thuler would believe that you have been honored. He would not utter it kindly—but his heart would speak those words, or hold that thought. Had you not been summoned to the Land, he might have wed Lena my mother. And he would not have taken himself to the Loresraat, for he had no yearning for knowledge—the stewardship of Stonedownor life would have sufficed for him. But had he and Lena my mother borne a child who grew to become High Lord of the Council of Revelstone, he would have felt honored—both elevated and humbled by his part in his daughter.

"Hear me, Thomas Covenant. Triock Thuler-son of Mithil Stonedown is my true father—the parent of my heart, though he is not the sire of my blood. Lena my mother did not wed him, though he begged her to share her life with him. She desired no other sharing —the life of your child satisfied her. But though she would not share her life, he shared his. He provided for her and for me. He took the place of a son with Trell Lena's father and Atiaran her mother.

"Ah, he was a dour parent. His heart's love ran in broken channels—yearning and grief and, yes, rage against you were diminishless for him, finding new paths when the old were turned or dammed. But he gave to Lena my mother and to me all a father's tenderness and devotion. Judge of him by me, Thomas Covenant. When dreaming of you took Lena's thoughts from me—when Atiaran lost in torment her capacity to care for me, and called to herself all Trell her husband's attention—then Triock son of Thuler stood beside me. He is my father."

Covenant tried to efface his emotions with acid. "He should have killed me when he had the chance."

She went on as if she had not heard him. "He shielded my heart from unjust demands. He taught me that the anguishes and furies of my parents and their parents need not wrack or enrage me—that I was neither the cause nor the cure of their pain. He taught me that my life is my own—that I could share in the care and consolation of wounds without sharing the wounds, without striving to be the master of lives other than my own. He taught me this—he who gave his own life to Lena my mother.

"He abhors you, Thomas Covenant. And yet without him as my father I also would abhor you."

"Are you through?" Covenant grated through the clench of his teeth. "How much more do you think I can stand?"

She did not answer aloud. Instead, she turned toward him. Tears streaked her cheeks. She was silhouetted against the darkening vista of Trothgard as she stepped up to him, slipped her arms about his neck, and kissed him.

He gasped, and her breath was snatched into his lungs. He was stunned. A black mist filled his sight as her lips caressed his.

Then for a moment he lost control. He repulsed her as if her breath carried infection. Crying, "Bastard!" he swung, backhanded her face with all his force.

The blow staggered her.

He pounced after her. His fingers clawed her blanket, tore it from her shoulders.

But his violence did not daunt her. She caught her balance, did not flinch or recoil. She made no effort to cover herself. With her head high, she held herself erect and calm; naked, she stood before him as if she were invulnerable.

It was Covenant who flinched. He quailed away from her as if she appalled him. "Haven't I committed enough crimes?" he panted hoarsely. "Aren't you satisfied?"

Her answer seemed to spring clean and clear out of the strange otherness of her gaze. "You cannot ravish me, Thomas Covenant. There is no crime here. I am willing. I have chosen you."

"Don't!" he groaned. "Don't say that!" He flung his arms about his chest as if to conceal a hole in his armor. "You're just trying to give me gifts again. You're trying to bribe me."

"No. I have chosen you. I wish to share life with you."

"Don't!" he repeated. "You don't know what you're doing. Don't you understand how desperately I— I—?"

But he could not say the words, *need you.* He choked on them. He wanted her, wanted what she offered him more than anything. But he could not say it. A passion more fundamental than desire restrained him.

She made no move toward him, but her voice reached out. "How can my love harm you?"

"Hellfire!" In frustration, he spread his arms wide like a man baring an ugly secret. "I'm a leper! Don't you see that?" But he knew immediately that she did not see, could not see because she lacked the knowledge or the bitterness to perceive the thing he called *leprosy.* He hurried to try to explain before she stepped closer to him and he was lost. "Look. Look!" He pointed at his chest with one accusing finger. "Don't you understand what I'm afraid of? Don't you comprehend the danger here? I'm afraid I'll become another Kevin! First I'll start loving you, and then I'll learn how to use the wild magic or whatever, and then Foul will trap me into despair, and then I'll be destroyed. *Everything* will be destroyed. That's been his plan all along. Once I start loving you or the Land or anything, he can just sit back and laugh! Bloody hell, Elena! Don't you see it?"

Now she moved. When she was within arm's reach, she stopped, and stretched out her hand. With the tips of her fingers, she touched his forehead as if to smooth away the darkness there. "Ah, Thomas Covenant," she breathed gently, "I cannot bear to see you frown so. Do not fear, beloved. You will not suffer Kevin Landwaster's fate. I will preserve you."

At her touch, something within him broke. The pure tenderness of her gesture overcame him. But it was not his restraint which broke; it was his frustration. An answering tenderness washed through him. He could see her mother in her, and at the sight he suddenly perceived that it was not anger which made him violent toward her, not anger which so darkened his love, but rather grief and self-despite. The hurt he had done her mother was only a complex way of hurting himself—an expression of his leprosy. He did not have to repeat that act.

It was all impossible, everything was impossible, she did not even exist. But at that moment he did not care. She was his daughter. Tenderly, he stooped, retrieved her blanket, wrapped it around her shoulders. Tenderly, he held her face in his hands, touched her sweet face with the impossible aliveness of his fingers. He stroked away the salt pain of her tears with his thumbs, and kissed her forehead tenderly.

TWENTY-TWO:
Anundivian Yajña

THE next morning, they left Trothgard, and rode into the unfamiliar terrain of the mountains. Half a league into the range, Amok brought them to a bridge of native stone which spanned the narrowing river-gorge of the Rill. To ameliorate his own dread of heights as well as to steady his mount, Covenant led his horse across. The bridge was wide, and the Bloodguard bracketed him with their Ranyhyn; he had no difficulty.

From there, Amok guided the High Lord's party up into the recesses of the peaks.

Beyond the foothills, his path became abruptly demanding—precipitous, rugged, and slow. He was reduced to a more careful pace as he led the riders along valleys as littered and wracked as wrecks—up treacherous slides and scree falls which lay against cliffs and cols and coombs as if regurgitated out of the mountain gut-rock—down ledges which traversed weathered stone fronts like scars. But he left no doubt that he knew his way. Time and again he walked directly to the only possible exit from a closed valley, or found the only horse-worthy trail through a rockfall, or trotted without hesitation into a crevice which bypassed a blank peak. Through the rough-hewn bulk and jumble of the mountains, he led the High Lord with the obliqueness of a man threading an accustomed maze.

For the first day or so, his goal seemed to be simply to gain elevation. He took the riders scrambling upward until the cold appeared to pour down on them from the ice tips of the tallest peaks. Thinner air gave

Covenant visions of scaling some inaccessible and remorseless mountain, and he accepted a thick half-robe from Bannor with a shiver which was not caused by the chill alone.

But then Amok changed directions. As if he were finally satisfied by the icy air and the pitch of the mountain-scapes, he sought no more altitude. Instead, he began to follow the private amazement of his trail southward. Rather than plunging deeper into the Westron Mountains, he moved parallel to their eastern borders. By day, he guided his companions along his unmarked way, and at night he left them in sheltered glens and coombs and gorges, where there were unexpected patches of grass for the mounts, to deal as they saw fit with the exhilarating or cruel cold.

He did not seem to feel the cold himself. With his thin apparel fluttering against his limbs, he strode ahead in unwearied cheerfulness, as if he were impervious to fatigue and ice. Often he had to hold himself back so that the Ranyhyn and Covenant's mustang could keep pace with him.

The two Bloodguard were like him—unaffected by cold or altitude. But they were *Haruchai,* born to these mountains. Their nostrils distended at the vapory breath of dawn or dusk. Their eyes roamed searchingly over the sunward crags, the valleys occasionally bedizened with azure tarns, the hoary glaciers crouching in the highest cols, the snow-fed streams. Though they wore nothing but short robes, they never shivered or gasped at the cold. Their wide foreheads and flat cheeks and confident poise betrayed no heart upsurge, no visceral excitement. Yet there was something clear and passionate in their alacrity as they watched over Elena and Covenant and Amok.

Elena and Covenant were not so immune to the cold. Their susceptibility clung to them, made them eager for each new day's progress toward warmer southern air. But their blankets and extra robes were warm. The High Lord did not appear to suffer. And as long as she did not suffer, Covenant felt no pain. Discomfort he could ignore. He was more at peace than he had been for a long time.

Since they had left Trothgard—since he had made the discovery which enabled him to love her without despising himself—he had put everything else out of his mind and concentrated on his daughter. Lord Foul, the Warward, even this quest itself, were insubstantial to him. He watched Elena, listened to her, felt her presence at all times. When she was in the mood to talk, he questioned her readily, and when she was not he gave her silence. And in every mood he was grateful to her, poignantly moved by the offer she had made—the offer he had refused.

He could not help being conscious of the fact that she was not equally content. She had not made her offer lightly, and seemed unwilling to understand his refusal. But the sorrow of having given her pain only sharpened his attentiveness toward her. He concentrated on her as only a man deeply familiar with loneliness could. And she was not blind to this. After the first few days of their mountain trek, she again relaxed in his company, and her smiles expressed a frankness of affection which she had not permitted herself before. Then he felt that he was in harmony with her, and he traveled with her gladly. At times he chirruped to his horse as if he enjoyed riding it.

But in the days that followed, a change slowly came over her—a change that had nothing to do with him. As time passed—as they journeyed nearer to the secret location of the Seventh Ward—she became increasingly occupied by the purpose of her quest. She questioned Amok more often, interrogated him more tensely. At times, Covenant could see in the elsewhere stare of her eyes that she was thinking of the war—a duty from which she had turned aside—and there were occasional flashes of urgency in her voice as she strove to ask the questions that would unlock Amok's mysterious knowledge.

This was a burden that Covenant could not help her bear. He knew none of the crucial facts himself. The days passed; the moon expanded to its full, then declined toward its last quarter, but she made no progress. Finally, his desire to assist her in some way led him to speak to Bannor.

In a curious way, he felt unsafe with the Blood-guard—not physically, but emotionally. There was a tension of disparity between himself and Bannor. The *Haruchai*'s stony gaze had the magisterial air of a man who did not deign to utter his judgment of his companions. And Covenant had other reasons to feel uncomfortable with Bannor. More than once, he had made Bannor bear the brunt of his own bootless outrage. But he had nowhere else to turn. He was entirely useless to Elena.

Since his days in Revelstone, he had been alert to a fine shade of discrepancy in the Bloodguard's attitude toward Amok—a discrepancy which had been verified but not explained in Revelwood. However, he did not know how to approach the subject. Extracting information from Bannor was difficult; the Bloodguard's habitual reserve baffled inquiry. And Covenant was determined to say nothing which might sound like an offense to Bannor's integrity. Bannor had already proved his fidelity in the Wightwarrens under Mount Thunder.

Covenant began by trying to find out why the Bloodguard had seen fit to send only Bannor and Morin to protect the High Lord on her quest. He was acutely aware of his infacility as he remarked, "I gather you don't think we're in any great danger on this trip."

"Danger, ur-Lord?" The repressed lilt of Bannor's pronunciation seemed to imply that anyone protected by the Bloodguard did not need to think of danger.

"Danger," Covenant repeated with a touch of his old asperity. "It's a common word these days."

Bannor considered for a moment, then said, "These are mountains. There is always danger."

"Such as?"

"Rocks may fall. Storms may come. Tigers roam these low heights. Great eagles hunt here. Mountains"—Covenant seemed to hear a hint of satisfaction in Bannor's tone—"are perilous."

"Then why— Bannor, I would really like to know why there are only two of your Bloodguard here."

"Is there need for more?"

"If we're attacked—by tigers, or whatever? Or what if there's an avalanche? Are two of you enough?"

"We know mountains," Bannor replied flatly. "We suffice."

This assertion was not one that Covenant could contradict. He made an effort to approach what he wanted to know in another way, though the attempt took him onto sensitive ground—terrain he would rather have avoided. "Bannor, I feel as if I'm slowly getting to know you Bloodguard. I can't claim that I understand—but I can at least recognize your devotion. I know what it looks like. Now I get the feeling that something is going on here—something—inconsistent. Something I don't recognize.

"Here we are climbing through the mountains, where anything could happen. We're following Amok who knows where, even though we've got next to no idea what he's doing, never mind why he's doing it. And you're satisfied that the High Lord is safe when she's only got two Bloodguard to protect her. Didn't you learn anything from Kevin?"

"We are the Bloodguard," answered Bannor stolidly. "She is safe—as safe as may be."

"Safe?" Covenant protested.

"A score or a hundredscore Bloodguard would not make her more safe."

"I admire your confidence."

Covenant winced at his own sarcasm, paused for a moment to reconsider his questions. Then he lowered his head as if he meant to batter Bannor's resistance down with his forehead, and said bluntly, "Do you trust Amok?"

"Trust him, ur-Lord?" Bannor's tone hinted that the question was inane in some way. "He has not led us into hazard. He has chosen a good way through the mountains. The High Lord elects to follow him. We do not ask for more."

Still Covenant felt the lurking presence of something unexplained. "I tell you, it doesn't fit," he rasped in irritation. "Listen. It's a little late in the day for these inconsistencies. I've sort of given up—they don't do me any good anymore. If it's all the same to you, I'd rather hear something that makes sense.

"Bannor, you— Bear with me. I can't help noticing it. First there was something I don't understand, something—out of pitch—about the way you Bloodguard reacted to Amok when he came to Revelstone. You— I don't know what it was. Anyway, at Revelwood you didn't exactly jump to help Troy when he caught Amok. And after that—only two Bloodguard! Bannor, it doesn't make sense."

Bannor was unmoved. "She is the High Lord. She holds the Staff of Law. She is easily defended."

That answer foiled Covenant. It did not satisfy him, but he could think of no way around it. He did not know what he was groping for. His intuition told him that his questions were significant, but he could not articulate or justify them in any utile way. And he reacted to Bannor's trenchant blankness as if it were some kind of touchstone, a paradoxically private and unavoidable criterion of rectitude. Bannor made him aware that there was something not altogether honest about his own accompaniment of the High Lord.

So he withdrew from Bannor, returned his attention to Elena. She had had no better luck with Amok, and her air of escape as she turned toward Covenant matched his. They rode on together, hiding their various anxieties behind light talk of mutual commiseration.

Then, during the eleventh evening of their sojourn in the mountains, she expressed an opinion to him. As if the guess were hazardous, she said, "Amok leads us to *Melenkurion* Skyweir. The Seventh Ward is hidden there." And the next day—the eighteenth since they had left Revelwood, and the twenty-fifth since the War Council of the Lords—the rhythm of their trek was broken.

The day dawned cold and dull, as if the sunlight were clogged with gray cerements. A troubled smell shrouded the air. Torn fragments of wind flapped back and forth across the camp as Elena and Covenant ate their breakfast, and far away they could hear a flat, detonating sound like the retort of balked canvas on unlashed spars. Covenant predicted a storm. But the First Mark shook his head in flat denial, and Elena said, "This is not the weather of storms." She glanced warily up at the peaks as she spoke. "There is pain in the air. The Earth is afflicted."

"What's happening?" A burst of wind scattered Covenant's voice, and he had to repeat his question at a shout to make himself heard. "Is Foul going to hit us here?"

The wind shifted and lapsed; she was able to answer normally. "Some ill has been performed. The Earth has been assaulted. We feel its revulsion. But the distance is very great, and time has passed. I feel no peril directed toward us. Perhaps the Despiser does not know what we do." In the next breath, her voice hardened. "But he has used the Illearth Stone. Smell the air! There has been malice at work in the Land."

Covenant began to sense what she meant. Whatever amassed these clouds and roiled this wind was not the impassive natural violence of a storm. The air seemed to carry inaudible shrieks and hints of rot, as if it were blowing through the aftermath of an atrocity. And on a subliminal level, almost indiscernible, the high bluff crags seemed to be shuddering.

The atmosphere made him feel a need for haste. But though her face was set in grim lines, the High Lord did not hurry. She finished her meal, then carefully packed the food and graveling away before calling to Myrha. When she mounted, she summoned Amok.

He appeared before her almost at once, and gave her a cheerful bow. After acknowledging him with a nod, she asked him if he could explain the ill in the air.

He shook his head, and said, "High Lord, I am no oracle." But his eyes revealed his sensitivity to the atmosphere; they were bright, and a sharp gleam lurking behind them showed for the first time that he was capable of anger. A moment later, however, he turned his face away, as if he did not wish to expose any private part of himself. With a flourishing gesture, he beckoned for the High Lord to follow him.

Covenant swung into his mount's *clingor* saddle, and tried to ignore the brooding ambience around him. But he could not resist the impression that the ground under him was quivering. Despite all his recent experience, he was still not a confident rider—he could not shed his nagging distrust of horses—and he worried that he might fulfill the prophecy of his height fear by falling off his mount.

Fortunately, he was spared cliff ledges and exposed trails. For some time, Amok's path ran along the spine of a crooked rift between looming mountain walls. The enclosed valley did not challenge Covenant's uncertain horsemanship. But the muffled booming in the air continued to grow. As morning passed, the sound became clearer, echoed like brittle groans off the sheer walls.

Early in the afternoon, Amok led the riders around a final bend. Beyond it, they found an immense landslide. Great, scalloped wounds stood opposite each other high in the walls, and the jumbled mass of rock and scree which had fallen from both sides was piled up several hundred feet above the valley floor.

It completely blocked the valley.

This was the source of the detonations. There was no movement in the huge fall; it had an old look, as if its formation had been forgotten long ago by the mountains. But tortured creaks and cracks came from within it as if its bones were breaking.

Amok walked forward, but the riders halted. Morin studied the blockage for a moment, then said, "It is impassable. It breaks. Perhaps on foot we might attempt it at its edges. But the weight of the Ranyhyn will begin a new fall." Amok reached the foot of the slide, and beckoned, but Morin said absolutely, "We must find another passage."

Covenant looked around the valley. "How long will that take?"

"Two days. Perhaps three."

"That bad? You would think this trip wasn't long enough already. Are you sure that isn't safe? Amok hasn't made any mistakes yet."

"We are the Bloodguard," Morin said.

And Bannor explained, "This fall is younger than Amok."

"Meaning it wasn't here when he learned his trail? Damnation!" Covenant muttered. The landslide made his desire for haste keener.

Amok came back to them with a shade of seriousness in his face. "We must pass here," he said tolerantly, as if he were explaining something to a recalcitrant child.

Morin said, "The way is unsafe."

"That is true," Amok replied. "There is no other." Turning to the High Lord, he repeated, "We must pass here."

While her companions had been speaking, Elena had gazed speculatively up and down the landfall. When Amok addressed her directly, she nodded her head, and responded, "We will."

Morin protested impassively, "High Lord."

"I have chosen," she answered, then added, "It may be that the Staff of Law can hold the fall until we have passed it."

Morin accepted this with an emotionless nod. He took his mount trotting back away from the slide, so that the High Lord would have room in which to work. Bannor and Covenant followed. After a moment, Amok joined them. The four men watched her from a short distance.

She made no complex or strenuous preparations. Raising the Staff, she sat erect and tall on Myrha's back for a moment, faced the slide. From Covenant's point of view, her blue robe and the Ranyhyn's glossy coat met against the mottled gray background of scree and rubble. She and Myrha looked small in the deep sheer valley, but the conjunction of their colors and forms gave them a potent iconic appearance. Then she moved.

Singing a low song, she advanced to the foot of the slide. There she gripped the Staff by one end, and lowered the other to the ground. It appeared to pulse as she rode along the slide's front, drawing a line in the dirt parallel to the fall. She walked Myrha to one wall, then back to the other. Still touching the ground with the Staff, she returned to the center.

When she faced the slide again, she lifted the Staff, and rapped once on the line she had drawn.

A rippling skein of verdigris sparks flowed up the fall from her line. They gleamed like interstices of power on every line or bulge of rock that protruded from the slope. After an instant, they disappeared, leaving an indefinite smell like the aroma of orchids in the air.

The muffled groaning of the fall faded somewhat.

"Come," the High Lord said. "We must climb at once. This Word will not endure."

Briskly, Morin and Bannor started forward. Amok loped beside them. He easily kept pace with the Ranyhyn.

As he looked upward, Covenant felt nausea like a presage in his guts. His jaw muscles knotted apprehensively. But he slapped his mount with his heels, and rode at the moaning fall.

He caught up with the Bloodguard. They took positions on either side of him, followed Elena and Amok onto the slope.

The High Lord's party angled back and forth up the slide. Their climbing balanced the danger of delay against the hazard of a direct attack on the slope. Covenant's mustang labored strenuously, and its struggles contrasted with the smooth power of the Ranyhyn. Their hooves kicked scuds of shale and scree down the fall, but their footing was secure, confident. There were no mishaps. Before long, Covenant stood on the rounded *V* atop the slide.

He was not prepared for what lay beyond the blockage. Automatically, he had expected the south end of the valley to resemble the north. But from the ridge of the landslide, he could see that the huge scalloped wounds above him were too big to be explained by the slide as it appeared from the north.

Somewhere buried directly below him, the valley floor plunged dramatically. The two avalanches had interred a precipice. The south face of the slide was three or four times longer than the north. Far below him, the valley widened into a grassy bottom featured by stands of pine and a stream springing from one of the walls. But to reach that alluring sight, he had to descend more than a thousand feet down the detonating undulation of the slide.

He swallowed thickly. "Bloody hell. Can you hold that?"

"No," Elena said bluntly. "But what I have done will steady it. And I can take other action—if the need arises."

With a sharp nod, she started Amok down the slope.

Bannor told Covenant to stay close behind him, then eased his Ranyhyn over the edge after Amok. For a moment, Covenant felt too paralyzed by prophetic trepidation to move. His dry, constricted throat and awkward tongue could not form words. Hellfire, he muttered silently. Hellfire.

He abandoned himself, pushed his mustang after Bannor.

Part of him knew that Morin and then Elena followed him, but he paid no attention to them. He locked his eyes on Bannor's back and tried to cling there for the duration of the descent.

Before he had gone a hundred feet, the skittishness of his mount drove everything else from his mind. Its ears flinched as if it were about to shy at every new groan within the fall. He heaved and sawed at the reins in an effort to control the horse, but he only aggravated its distress. Faintly, he could hear himself mumbling, "Help. Help."

Then a loud boom like the crushing of a boulder shivered the air. A swath of slide jumped and shifted. The rubble under Covenant began to slip.

His mount tried to spring away from the shift. It shied sideways, and started straight down the slope.

Its lunge only precipitated the slide. Almost at once, the mustang was plunging in scree that poured over its knees.

It struggled to escape downward. Each heave increased the weight of rubble piling against it.

Covenant clung frantically to the *clingor* saddle. He

fought to pull the horse's head aside, make his mount angle out of the slide's main force. But the mustang had its teeth on the bit now. He could not turn it.

Its next plunge buried it to its haunches in the quickening rush of rubble. Covenant could hear Elena shouting stridently. As she yelled, Bannor's Ranyhyn sprang in front of him. Plowing through the scree, it threw its weight against his mount. The impact almost unseated him, but it deflected his horse. Guided by Bannor, the Ranyhyn shoved against the horse, forced it to fight toward the cliff.

But the avalanche was already moving too heavily. A small boulder struck the mustang's rump; the horse fell. Covenant sprawled down the slope out of Bannor's reach. The rubble tumbled him over and over, but for a moment he managed to stay above it. He got his feet under him, tried to move across the slide.

Through the gathering roar of the fall, he heard Morin shout, "High Lord!" The next instant, she flashed by him, riding Myrha straight down the outer edge of the slide. Fifty feet below him, she swung into the avalanche. With a wild cry, she whirled the Staff of Law and struck the fall.

Fire blazed up through the slide. Like a suddenly clenched fist, the rubble around Covenant stopped moving. His own momentum knocked him backward, but he jumped up again in time to meet Bannor as the Bloodguard landed his Ranyhyn on the small patch of steady ground. Bannor caught Covenant with one hand, swung him across the Ranyhyn's back, charged away out of the slide.

When they reached the relatively still ground against the cliff wall, Covenant saw that Elena had saved him at the risk of herself. The stasis which she had applied to the slipping tons of the avalanche was not large enough to include her own position. And an instant later, that stasis broke. An extra breaker of rubble dropped toward her.

She had no second chance to wield the Staff. Almost at once, the wave of scree crashed over her and Myrha.

An instant later, she appeared downhill from Myrha.

The Ranyhyn's great strength momentarily sheltered her.

But the fall piled against Myrha's chest. And Covenant's mustang, still madly fighting the slide, hurtled toward the Ranyhyn. Instinctively, Covenant tried to run back into the avalanche to help Elena. But Bannor held him back with one hand.

He started to struggle, then stopped as a long *clingor* rope flicked out over the slide and caught the High Lord's wrist. With his Ranyhyn braced against the wall below Covenant and Bannor, First Mark Morin flung out his line, and the adhesive leather snared Elena. She reacted immediately. "Flee!" she yelled to Myrha, then clutched the Staff and heaved against the waist-deep flow of scree as Morin pulled her to safety.

Though the great mare was battered and bleeding, she had other intentions. With a tremendous exertion, she lunged out of the mustang's path. As the screaming horse tumbled past, she turned and caught its reins in her teeth.

For one intense moment, she held the mustang, hauled it to its feet, swung it in the direction of the wall.

Then the avalanche swept them down a steep bulge. The sudden plunge sank her. With a rushing cry, the weight of the landslide poured over her.

Somehow, the mustang kept its feet, struggled on down the slope. But Myrha did not reappear.

Covenant hugged his stomach as if he were about to retch. Below him, Elena cried, "Myrha! Ranyhyn!" The passion in her voice appalled him. Several moments passed before he realized that his rescue had carried his companions more than two-thirds of the way down the slide.

"Come," Bannor said flatly. "The balance has broken. There will be more falls. We are imperiled here." His efforts had not even quickened his breathing.

Numbly, Covenant sat behind Bannor as his Ranyhyn picked its way along the wall to the High Lord and Morin. Elena looked stricken, astonished with grief. Covenant wanted to throw his arms around her, but the Bloodguard gave him no chance. Bannor took him on down the slope, and Morin followed with the High Lord riding emptily at his back.

They found Amok awaiting them on the grass at the bottom of the valley. His eyes held something that resembled concern as he approached the High Lord and helped her to dismount. "Pardon me," he said quietly. "I have brought you pain. What could I do? I was not made to be of use in such needs."

"Then begone," Elena replied harshly. "I have no more use for you this day."

Amok's gaze constricted as if the High Lord had hurt him. But he obeyed her promptly. With a bow and a wave, he wiped himself out of sight.

Dismissing him with a grimace, Elena turned toward the landslide. The piled rubble creaked and retorted more fiercely now, promising other slides at any moment, but she ignored the hazard to kneel at the foot of the scree. She bent forward as if she were presenting her back to a whip, and tears streaked her voice as she moaned, "Alas, Ranyhyn! Alas, Myrha! My failure has slain you."

Covenant hurried to her. He ached to throw his arms around her, but her grief restrained him. With an effort, he said, "It's my fault. Don't blame yourself. I should know how to ride better." Hesitantly, he reached out and stroked her neck.

His touch seemed to turn her pain to anger. She did not move, but she screamed at him, "Let me be! This is indeed your doing. You should not have sent the Ranyhyn to Lena my mother."

He recoiled as if she had struck him. At once, his own instinctive ire flamed. The panic of his fall had filled his veins with a tinder that burned suddenly. Her quick recrimination changed him in an instant. It was as if the peace of his past days had been transformed abruptly into umbrage and leper's vehemence. He was mute with outrage. Trembling, he turned and stalked away.

Neither Bannor nor Morin followed him. Already they were busy tending the cuts and abrasions of their Ranyhyn and his mustang. He strode past them, went on down the valley like a scrap of frail ire fluttering helplessly along the breeze.

After a while, the dull detonations of the landslide began to fade behind him. He kept on walking. The smell of the grass tried to beguile him, and within the pine stands a consoling susurrous and gloom, a soft, quiet, sweet rest, beckoned him. He ignored them, paced by with a jerky, mechanical stride. Thick anger roiled his brain, drove him forward. Again! he cried to himself. Every woman he loved—! How could such a thing happen twice in the same life?

He went on until he had covered almost a league. Then he found himself beside a trilling stream. Here the bottom of the valley was uneven on both sides of the brook. He searched along it until he found a grass-matted gully from which he could see nothing of the valley's northward reach. There he threw himself down on his stomach to gnaw the old bone of his outrage.

Time passed. Soon shadows crossed the valley as the sun moved toward evening. Twilight began as if it were seeping out of the ground between the cliffs. Covenant rolled over on his back. At first, he watched with a kind of dour satisfaction as darkness climbed the east wall. He felt ready for the isolation of night and loss.

But then the memory of Joan returned with redoubled force. It stung him into a sitting position. Once again, he found himself gaping at the cruelty of his delusion, the malice which tore him away from Joan—for what? Hellfire! he gasped. The gloaming made him feel that he was going blind with anger. When he saw Elena walking into the gully toward him, she seemed to move through a haze of leprosy.

He looked away from her, tried to steady his sight against the failing light on the eastern cliff; and while his face was averted, she approached, seated herself on the grass by his feet. He could feel her presence vividly. At first she did not speak. But when he still refused to meet her gaze, she said softly, "Beloved. I have made a sculpture for you."

With an effort, he turned his head. He saw her bent forward, with a hopeful smile on her lips. Both her hands extended toward him a white object that appeared to be made of bone. He paid no attention to it; his eyes slapped at her face as if that were his enemy.

In a tone of entreaty, she continued, "I formed it for you from Myrha's bones. I cremated her—to do her what honor I could. Then from her bones I formed this. For you, beloved. Please accept it."

He glanced at the sculpture. It caught his unwilling interest. It was a bust. Initially, it appeared too thick to have been made from any horse's bone. But then he saw that four bones had been in some way fused together and molded. He took the work from her hands to view it more closely. The face interested him. Its outlines were less blunt than in other marrowmeld work he had seen. It was lean and gaunt and impenetrable —a prophetic face, taut with purpose. It expressed someone he knew, but a moment passed before he recognized the countenance. Then, gingerly, as if he feared to be wrong, he said, "It's Bannor. Or one of the other Bloodguard."

"You tease me," she replied. "I am not so poor a crafter." There was a peculiar hunger in her smile. "Beloved, I have sculpted you."

Slowly, his ire faded. After all, she was his daughter, not his wife. She was entitled to any reproach that seemed fit to her. He could not remain angry with her. Carefully, he placed the bust on the grass, then reached out toward her and took her into his arms as the sun set.

She entered his embrace eagerly, and for a time she clung to him as if she were simply glad to put their anger behind them. But gradually he felt the tension of her body change. Her affection seemed to become grim, almost urgent. Something taut made her limbs hard, made her fingers grip him like claws. In a voice that shook with passion, she said, "This also Fangthane would destroy."

He lifted his cheek from her hair, moved her so that he could see her face.

That sight chilled him. Despite the dimness of the light, her gaze shocked him like an immersion in polar seas.

The otherness of her sight, the elsewhere dimension

of its power, had focused, concentrated until it became the crux of something savage and illimitable. A terrible might raved out of her orbs. Though her gaze was not directed at him, it bored through him like an auger. When it was gone, it left a bloody weal across him.

It was a look of apocalypse.

He could not think of any other name for it but *hate*.

TWENTY-THREE: Knowledge

THE sight sent him stumbling up the gully away from her. He had trouble keeping himself erect; he listed as if a gale had left him aground somewhere. He heard her low cry, "Beloved!" but he could not turn back. The vision made his heart smoke like dry ice, and he needed to find a place where he could huddle over the pain and gasp alone.

For a time, smoke obscured his self-awareness. He ran into Bannor, and fell back as if he had smashed against a boulder. The impact surprised him. Bannor's flat mien had the force of a denunciation. Instinctively, he recoiled. "Don't touch me!" He lurched off in another direction, stumbled through the night until he had placed a steep hill between himself and the Bloodguard. There he sat down on the grass, wrapped his arms around his chest, and made a deliberate effort to weep.

He could not do it. His weakness, his perpetual leprosy, dammed that emotional channel; he had spent too long unlearning the release of grief. And the frustration of failure made him savage. He brimmed with old, unresolved rage. Even in delusion, he could not escape the trap of his illness. Leaping to his feet, he shook his fists at the sky like a reefed and lonely galleon firing its guns in bootless defiance of the invulnerable ocean. Damnation!

But then his self-consciousness returned. His anger became bitterly cold as he bit off his shout, clamped shut that outlet for his fury. He felt that he was waking up after a blind sleep. Snarling extremely between his teeth, he stalked away toward the stream.

He did not bother to take off his clothes. Fiercely, he dropped flat on his face in the water as if he were diving for some kind of cauterization or release in the glacial frigidity of the brook.

He could not endure the cold for more than a moment; it burned over all his flesh, seized his heart like a convulsion. Gasping, he sprang up and stood shuddering on the rocky streambed. The water and the breeze sent a ravenous ache through his bones, as if cold consumed their marrow. He left the stream.

The next instant, he saw Elena's gaze again, felt it sear his memory. He halted. A sudden idea threw back the chill. It sprang practically full-grown into view as if it had been maturing for days in the darkness of his mind, waiting until he was ready.

He realized that he had access to a new kind of bargain—an arrangement or compromise distantly similar, but far superior, to the one which he had formed with the Ranyhyn. They were too limited; they could not meet his terms, fulfill the contract he had made for his survival. But the person with whom he could now bargain was almost ideally suited to help him.

It was just possible that he could buy his salvation from the High Lord.

He saw the difficulties at once. He did not know what the Seventh Ward contained. He would have to steer Elena's apocalyptic impulse through an unpredictable future toward an uncertain goal. But that impulse was something he could use. It made her personally powerful—powerful and vulnerable, blinded by obsession—and she held the Staff of Law. He might be able to induce her to take his place, assume his position at the onus of Lord Foul's machinations. He might be able to lead her extravagant passion to replace his white gold at the crux of the Land's doom. If he could get her to undertake the bitter responsibility which had been so ineluctably aimed at him, he would be free. That would remove his head from the chopping block of this delusion. And all he had to do in return was to place himself at Elena's service in any way which would focus rather than dissipate her inner drives—keep her under control until the proper moment.

It was a more expensive bargain than the one he had made with the Ranyhyn. It did not allow him to remain passive; it required him to help her, manipulate her. But it was justified. During the Quest for the Staff of Law, he had been fighting merely to survive an impossibly compelling dream. Now he understood his true peril more clearly.

So much time had passed since he had thought freedom possible that his heart almost stopped at the thrill of the conception. But after its first excitement, he found that he was shivering violently. His clothes were completely soaked.

Aching with every move, he started back toward the gully and the High Lord.

He found her sitting despondent and thoughtful beside a bright campfire. She wore one blanket over her robe; the others were spread out by the blaze for warmth. When he entered the gully, she looked up eagerly. He could not meet her eyes. But she did not appear to notice the chagrin behind his blue lips and taut forehead. Snatching up a warm blanket for him, she drew him close to the fire. Her few low comments were full of concern, but she asked him nothing until the flames had beaten back his worst shivers. Then, shyly, as if she were inquiring where she stood in relation to him, she reached up and kissed him.

He returned the caress of her lips, and the movement seemed to carry him over an inner hurdle. He found that he could look at her now. She smiled softly; the voracious power of her gaze was lost again in its elsewhere otherness. She appeared to accept his kiss at its surface valuation. She hugged him, then seated herself beside him. After a moment, she asked, "Did it surprise you to learn that I am so vehement?"

He tried to excuse himself. "I'm not used to such things. You didn't give me fair warning."

"Pardon me, beloved," she said contritely. Then she went on. "Were you very dismayed—by what you have beheld in me?"

He thought for a while before he said, "I think if you ever looked at me that way I would be as good as dead."

"You are safe," she assured him warmly.

"What if you change your mind?"

"Your doubt chastises me. Beloved, you are part of my life and breath. Do you believe that I could set you aside?"

"I don't know what to believe." His tone expressed vexation, but he hugged her again to counteract it. "Dreaming is like—it's like being a slave. Your dreams come out of all the parts of you that you don't have any control over. That's why—that's why madness is the only danger."

He was grateful that she did not attempt to argue with him. When the shivering was driven from his bones, he became incontestably drowsy. As she put him to bed, wrapped him snugly in his blankets by the campfire, the only thing which kept him from trusting her completely was the conviction that his bargain contained something dishonest.

For the most part, he forgot that conviction during the next three days. His attention was clouded by a low fever which he seemed to have caught from his plunge in the stream. Febrile patches appeared on his obdurately pale cheeks; his forehead felt clammy with sweat and cold; and his eyes glittered as if he were in the grip of a secret excitement. From time to time, he dozed on the back of his battered mount, and awoke to find himself babbling deliriously. He could not always remember what he had said, but at least once he had insisted maniacally that the only way to stay well was to be perpetually awake. No antiseptic could cleanse the wounds inflicted in dreams. The innocent did not dream.

When he was not mumbling in half-sleep, he was occupied with the trek itself.

The High Lord's party was nearing some kind of destination.

The morning after the landslide had dawned into crisp sunshine—a clear vividness like an atonement for the previous day's distress. When Amok had appeared to lead the High Lord onward, Elena had whistled as if she were calling Myrha, and another Ranyhyn had answered the summons. Covenant had watched it gallop up the valley with amazement in his face. The fidelity of the Ranyhyn toward their own choices went beyond all his conceptions of pride or loyalty. The sight had reminded him of his previous bargain—a bargain which both Elena and Rue had said was still kept among the great horses. But then he had struggled up on his mustang, and other matters had intruded on his fever-tinged thoughts. He had retained barely enough awareness to place Elena's marrowmeld gift in Bannor's care.

After the riders had followed Amok out of the valley, Covenant caught his first glimpse of *Melenkurion* Skyweir. Though it was still many leagues almost due southeast of him, the high mountain lifted its twin, ice-bound peaks above the range's rugged horizon, and its glaciers gleamed blue in the sunlight as if the sky's azure feet were planted there. Elena's guess seemed correct: Amok's ragged, oblique trail tended consistently toward the towering Skyweir. It vanished almost immediately as Amok led the riders into the lee of another cliff, but it reappeared with increasing frequency as the day passed. By the following noon, it dominated the southeastern horizon.

But at night Covenant did not have the mountains veering around him. He could not see *Melenkurion* Skyweir. And after the evening meal, his fever abated somewhat. Freed from these demands and drains upon his weakened concentration, he came to some vague terms with his bargain.

It did not need her consent; he knew this, and berated himself for it. Once the thrill of hope had faded into fever and anxiety, he ached to tell her what he had been thinking. And her attentiveness to him made him ache worse. She cooked special healing broths and stews for him; she went out of her way to supply him with *aliantha*. But his emotions toward her had changed. There was cunning and flattery in his responses to her tenderness. He was afraid of what would happen if he told her his thoughts.

When he lay awake late at night, shivering feverishly, he had a bad taste of rationalization in his mouth. Then it was not embarrassment or trust which kept him from explaining himself. His jaws were locked by his clinging need for survival, his rage against his own death.

Finally, his fever broke. Late in the afternoon of the third day—the twenty-first since the High Lord's party had left Revelwood—a sudden rush of sweat poured over him, and a tight inner cord seemed to snap. He felt himself relaxing at last. That night, he fell asleep while Elena was still discussing the ignorance or failure of comprehension which kept her from learning anything from Amok.

A long, sound sleep restored his sense of health, and the next morning he was able to pay better attention to his situation. Riding at Elena's side, he scrutinized *Melenkurion* Skyweir. It stood over him like an aegis, shutting out the whole southeastern dawn. With a low surge of apprehension, he judged that the High Lord's party would probably arrive there before this day was done. Carefully, he asked her about the Skyweir.

"I can tell you little," she replied. "It is the tallest mountain known to the Land, and its name shares one of the Seven Words. But Kevin's Lore reveals little of it. Perhaps there is other knowledge in the other Wards, but the First and Second contain few hints or references. And in our age the Lords have gained nothing of their own concerning this place. None have come so close to the Skyweir since people returned to the Land after the Ritual of Desecration.

"It is in my heart that these great peaks mark a place of power—a place surpassing even Gravin Threndor. But I have no evidence for this belief apart from the strange silence of Kevin's Lore. *Melenkurion* Skyweir is one of the high places of the Land—and yet the First and Second Wards contain no knowledge of it beyond a few old maps, a fragment of one song, and

two unexplained sentences which, if their translation
is not faulty, speak of *command* and *blood*. So," she
said wryly, "my failure to unlock Amok is not altogether surprising."

This brought her back to a contemplation of her ignorance, and she lapsed into silence. Covenant tried to
think of a way to help her. But the effort was like trying to see through a wall of stone; he had even less of
the requisite knowledge. If he intended to keep his side
of the bargain, he would have to do so in some other
way.

He believed intuitively that his chance would come.

In the meantime, he settled himself to wait for Amok
to bring them to the mountain.

Their final approach came sooner than he had expected. Amok took them down a long col between two
blunt peaks, then into a crooked ravine that continued
to descend while it shifted toward the east. By noon
they had lost more than two thousand feet of elevation.
There the ravine ended, leaving them on a wide, flat,
barren plateau which clung to the slopes of the great
mountain. The plateau ran east and south as far as
Covenant could see around *Melenkurion* Skyweir. The
flat ground looked like a setting, a base for the fifteen
or twenty thousand feet of its matched spires. And east
of the plateau were no mountains at all.

The Ranyhyn were eager for a run after long days
of constricted climbing, and they cantered out onto the
flat rock. With surprising fleetness, Amok kept ahead
of them. He laughed as he ran, and even increased his
pace. The Ranyhyn stretched into full stride, began to
gallop in earnest, leaving Covenant's mustang behind.
But still Amok's prancing step outran them. Gaily, he
led the riders east and then south down the center of
the plateau.

Covenant followed at a more leisurely gait. Soon he
was passing along the face of the first peak. The plateau here was several hundred yards wide, and it extended southward until it curved west out of sight
beyond the base of the second peak. The spires joined
each other a few thousand feet above the plateau, but
the line of juncture between them remained clear, as if

the two sides differed in texture. At the place where this line touched the plateau, a cleft appeared in the flat rock. This crevice ran straight across the plateau to its eastern edge.

Ahead of Covenant, the Ranyhyn had ended their gallop near the rim of the crevice. Now Elena trotted down its length toward the outer edge of the plateau. Covenant swung his mustang in that direction, and joined her there.

Together, they dismounted, and he lay down on his stomach to peer over the precipice. Four thousand feet below the sheer cliff, a dark, knotted forest spread out as far as he could see. The woods brooded over its rumpled terrain—a thick-grown old blanket of trees which draped the foot of the Westron Mountains as if to conceal, provide the solace of privacy for, a rigid and immediate anguish. And northeastward across this covered expanse ran the red-black line of the river which spewed from the base of the cleft. Inaudible in the distance, it came moiling out of the rock and slashed away through the heart of the forest. The river looked like a weal in the woods, a cut across the glowering green countenance. This scar gave the hurt, rigid face an expression of ferocity, as if it dreamed of rending limb from limb the enemy which had scored it.

Elena explained the view to Covenant. "That is the Black River," she said reverently. She was the first new Lord ever to see this sight. "From this place, it flows a hundred fifty leagues and more to join the Mithil on its way toward Andelain. Its spring is said to lie deep under *Melenkurion* Skyweir. We stand on Rivenrock, the eastern porch or portal of the great mountain. And below us is Garroting Deep, the last forest in the Land where a Forestal still walks—where the maimed consciousness of the One Forest still holds communion with itself." For a moment, she breathed the brisk air. Then she added, "Beloved, I believe that we are not far from the Seventh Ward."

Pushing himself back from the edge, he climbed unsteadily to his feet. The breeze seemed to carry vertigo up at him from the precipice. He waited until he was several strides from the edge before he replied, "I hope so. For all we know, that war could be over by now. If Troy's plans didn't work, Foul might be halfway to Revelstone."

"Yes. I, too, have felt that fear. But my belief remains that the Land's future will not be won in war. And that battle is not in our hands. We have other work."

Covenant studied the distance of her eyes, measuring the risk of offending her, then said, "Has it occurred to you that you might not be able to unlock Amok?"

"Of course," she returned sharply. "I am not blind."

"Then what will you do, if he doesn't talk?"

"I hold the Staff of Law. It is a potent key. When Amok has guided us to the Seventh Ward, I will not be helpless."

Covenant looked away with a sour expression on his face. He did not believe that it would be that easy.

At Elena's side, he walked back along the crevice toward the two Bloodguard and Amok. The afternoon was not far gone, but already *Melenkurion* Skyweir's shadow stretched across Rivenrock. The shadow thickened the natural gloom of the cleft, so that it lay like a fault of darkness across the plateau. At its widest, it was no more than twenty feet broad, but it seemed immeasurably deep, as if it went straight down to the buried roots of the mountain. On an impulse, Covenant tossed a small rock into the cleft. It bounced from wall to wall on its way down; he counted twenty-two heartbeats before it fell beyond hearing. Instinctively, he kept himself a safe distance from the crevice as he went on toward Bannor and Morin.

The two Bloodguard had unpacked the food, and Covenant and Elena made a light meal for themselves. Covenant ate slowly, as if he were trying to postpone the next phase of the quest. He foresaw only three alternatives—up the mountain, down the crevice, across the cleft—and they all looked bad to him. He did not want to do any kind of climbing or jumping; the simple proximity of precipices made him nervous. But when he saw that the High Lord was waiting for him, he recollected the terms of his bargain. He finished what he

was eating, and tried to brace himself for whatever
Amok had in mind.

Gripping the Staff of Law firmly, Elena turned to her
guide. "Amok, we are ready. What should be done
with the Ranyhyn? Will you have us ride or walk?"

"That is your choice, High Lord," said Amok with a
grin. "If the Ranyhyn remain, they will not be needed.
If they depart, you will be forced to resummon them."

"Then we must walk to follow you now?"

"Follow me? I have said nothing of leaving this
place."

"Is the Seventh Ward here?" she asked quickly.

"No."

"Then it is elsewhere."

"Yes, High Lord."

"If it is elsewhere, we must go to it."

"That is true. The Seventh Ward cannot be brought
to you."

"To go to it, we must walk or ride."

"That also is true."

"Which?"

As he listened to this exchange, Covenant felt a quiet
admiration for the way in which Elena tackled Amok's
vagueness. Her past experience appeared to have
taught her how to corner the youth. But with his next
answer he eluded her.

"That is your choice," he repeated. "Decide and go."

"Do you not lead us?"

"No."

"Why not?"

"I act according to my nature. I do what I have been
created to do."

"Amok, are you not the way and the door of the
Seventh Ward?"

"Yes, High Lord."

"Then you must guide us."

"No."

"Why not?" she demanded again. "Are you capri-
cious?" Covenant heard a hint of desperation in her
tone.

Amok replied in mild reproof, "High Lord, I have

been created for the purpose I serve. If I appear willful, you must ask my maker to explain me."

"In other words," Covenant interjected heavily, "we're stuck without the other four Wards. This is Kevin's way of protecting—whatever it is. Without the clues he planted with such cleverness in the other Wards, we're up against a blank wall."

"The *krill* of Loric came to life," said Amok. "That is the appointed word. And the Land is in peril. Therefore I have made myself accessible. I can do no more. I must serve my purpose."

The High Lord searched him for a moment, then said sternly, "Amok, are my companions unsuitable to your purpose in some way?"

"Your companions must suit themselves. I am the way and the door. I do not judge those who seek."

"Amok"—she hung fire, and her lips moved silently as if she were reciting a list of choices—"are there conditions to be met—before you can guide us onward?"

Amok bowed in recognition of her question, and answered with a chuckle, "Yes, High Lord."

"Will you guide us to the Seventh Ward when the conditions are met?"

"That is the purpose of my creation."

"What are your conditions?"

"There is only one. If you desire more, you must conceive them without my aid."

"What is your condition, Amok?"

The youth gazed impishly askance at Elena. "High Lord," he said in a tone of soaring glee, "you must name the power of the Seventh Ward."

She gaped at him for an instant, then exclaimed, *"Melenkurion!* You know I lack that knowledge."

He was unmoved. "Then perhaps it is well that the Ranyhyn have not departed. They can bear you to Revelstone. If you gain wisdom there, you may return. You will find me here." With a bow of infuriating insouciance, he waved his arms and vanished.

She stared after him and clenched the Staff as if she meant to strike the empty air of his absence. Her back was to Covenant; he could not see what was happening in her face, but the tension of her shoulders made him fear that her eyes were drawing into focus. At that thought, blood pounded in his temples. He reached out, tried to interrupt or distract her.

His touch caused her to swing around toward him. Her face looked emaciated—her flesh was tight over the pale intensity of her skull—and she seemed astonished, as if she had just discovered her capacity for panic. But she did not move into his arms. She halted, deliberately closed her eyes. The bones of her jaw and cheeks and forehead concentrated on him.

He felt an abyss opening in his mind.

He did not comprehend the black, yawning sensation. Elena stood before him in the shadow of *Melenkurion* Skyweir like an icon of gleaming bone robed in blue; but behind her, behind the solid stone of Rivenrock, darkness widened like a crack across the cistern of his thoughts. The rift sucked at him; he was losing himself.

The sensation came from Elena.

Suddenly, he understood. She was attempting to meld her mind with his.

A glare of fear shot through the sable vertigo which drained him. It illuminated his peril; if he abandoned himself to the melding, she would learn the truth about him. He could not afford such a plunge, could never have afforded it. Crying, No! he recoiled, staggered back away from her within himself.

The pressure eased. He found that his body was also retreating. With an effort, he stopped, raised his head.

Elena's eyes were wide with disappointment and grief, and she leaned painfully on the Staff of Law. "Pardon me, beloved," she breathed. "I have asked for more than you are ready to give." For a moment, she remained still, gave him a chance to respond. Then she groaned, "I must think," and turned away. Supporting herself with the Staff, she moved slowly along the cleft toward the outer edge of the plateau.

Shaken, Covenant sat straight down on the rock, and caught his head in his hands. Conflicting emotions tore at him. He was dismayed by his narrow escape, and angry at his weakness. To save himself, he had hurt Elena. He thought that he should go to her, but something in the focused isolation of her figure warned him not to intrude. For a time, he gazed at her with an ache in his heart. Then he climbed to his feet, muttering at the needless air, "He could've had the decency to tell us—at least before she lost her Ranyhyn."

To his surprise, the First Mark answered, "Amok acts according to the law of his creation. He cannot break that law merely to avoid pain."

Covenant threw up his hands in disgust. Fulminating uselessly, he stalked away across the plateau.

He spent the remainder of the afternoon roving restlessly from place to place across Rivenrock, searching for some clue to the continuation of Amok's trail. After a while, he calmed down enough to understand Morin's comment on Amok. Morin and Bannor were the prisoners of their Vow; they could speak with authority about the exigencies of an implacable law. But if the Bloodguard sympathized with Amok, that was just one more coffin nail in the doom of the High Lord's quest.

Covenant's effectlessness was another such nail. He could hear the inflated fatuity of his bargain mocking him now. How could he help Elena? He did not even know enough to grasp the issues Amok raised. Though his disconsolate hiking covered a wide section of the plateau, he learned nothing of any significance. The barren stone was like his inefficacy—irreducible and binding. While the last sunlight turned to dust in the sky, he bent his steps toward the graveling glow which marked the High Lord's camp. He was brooding on the familiar idea that futility governed his very existence.

He found Elena beside her pot of graveling. She looked both worn and whetted, as if the pressure on her ground down her individuality, fitted her to the pattern of her Lord's duty. Resolution gleamed in the honed patina of her bones. She had accepted all the implications of her burden.

Covenant cleared his throat awkwardly. "What have you got? Have you figured it out?"

In a distant voice, she asked, "How great is your knowledge of Warmark Troy's battle plan?"

"I know generally what he's trying to do—nothing specific."

"If his plan did not fail, the battle began yesterday."

He considered for a moment, then inquired carefully, "Where does that leave us?"

"We must meet Amok's condition."

He gestured his incomprehension. "How?"

"I do not know. But I believe that it may be done."

"You're missing four Wards."

"Yes," she sighed. "Kevin clearly intended that we should gain the Seventh Ward only after mastering the first Six. But Amok has already violated that intent. Knowing that we have not comprehended Loric's *krill*, he still returned to us. He saw the Land's peril, and returned. This shows some freedom—some discretion. He is not explicitly bound by his law at all points."

She paused, and after a moment Covenant said, "Offhand, I would say that makes him dangerous. Why would he drag us all the way out here when he knew we would get stuck—unless he was trying to distract you from the war?"

"Amok intends no betrayal. I hear no malice in him."

To penetrate her abstraction, he snapped, "You can be fooled. Or are you forgetting that Kevin even accepted Foul as a Lord?"

Steadily, Elena replied, "Perhaps the first Six Wards do not contain the name of this power. Perhaps they teach only the way in which Amok may be brought to speak its name himself."

"In that case—"

"Amok guided us here because in some way it is possible for us to meet his condition."

"But can you find the right questions?"

"I must. What other choice exists for me? I cannot rejoin the Warward now."

Her voice had a dull finality, as if she were passing sentence on herself. Early the next morning, she called Amok.

He appeared, grinning boyishly. She gripped the Staff of Law in both hands and braced it on the rock before her.

In the dawn under *Melenkurion* Skyweir, they began to duel for access to the Seventh Ward.

For two days, High Lord Elena strove to wrest the prerequisite name from Amok. During the second day, a massive storm brooded on the southeastern horizon, but it did not approach Rivenrock, and everyone ignored it. While Covenant sat twisting his ring around his finger, or paced restlessly beside the combatants, or wandered muttering away at intervals to escape the strain, she probed Amok with every question she could devise. At times, she worked methodically; at others, intuitively. She elaborated ideas for his assent or denial. She forced him to recite his answers at greater and greater length. She led him through painstaking rehearsals of known ground, and launched him with all her accuracy toward the unknown. She built traps of logic for him, tried to fence him into contradictions. She sought to meld her mind with his.

It was like dueling with a pool of water. Every slash and counter of her questions touched him as if she had slapped a pond with the flat of her blade. His answers splashed at every inquiry. But when she strove to catch him on her need's point, she passed through him and left no mark. Occasionally he allowed himself a laughing riposte, but for the most part he parried her questions with his accustomed cheerful evasiveness. Her toil earned no success. By sunset, she was trembling with frustration and suppressed fury and psychic starvation. The very solidity of Rivenrock seemed to jeer at her.

In the evenings, Covenant comforted her according to the terms of his bargain. He said nothing of his own fears and doubts, his helplessness, his growing conviction that Amok was impenetrable; he said nothing about himself at all. Instead, he gave her his best attention, concentrated on her with every resource he possessed.

But all his efforts could not touch the core of her distress. She was learning that she did not suffice to meet the Land's need, and that was a grief for which there was no consolation. Late at night, she made muffled grating noises, as if she ground her teeth to keep herself from weeping. And in the morning of the third day—the thirty-second since she had left Revelstone—she neared the end of her endurance. Her gaze was starved and hollow, and it had an angle of farewell.

Thickly, Covenant asked her what she was going to do.

"I will appeal." Her voice had a raw, flagellated sound. She looked as frail as a skeleton—mere brave, fragile bones standing in the path of someone who, for all his boyish gaiety, was as unmanageable as an avalanche. A presage like an alarm in his head told Covenant that her crisis was at hand. If Amok did not respond to her appeals, she might turn to the last resort of her strange inner force.

The violence of that possibility frightened him. He caught himself on the verge of asking her to stop, give up the attempt. But he remembered his bargain; his brain raced after alternatives.

He accepted her argument that the answer to Amok's condition must be accessible. But he believed that she would not find it; she was approaching the problem from the wrong side. Yet it seemed to be the only side. Kicking at the rubbish which clogged his mind, he tried to imagine other approaches.

While his thoughts scrambled for some kind of saving intuition, High Lord Elena took her stance, and summoned Amok. The youth appeared at once. He greeted her with a florid bow, and said, "High Lord, what is your will today? Shall we set aside our sparring, and sing glad songs together?"

"Amok, hear me." Her voice grated. Covenant could hear depths of self-punishment in her. "I will play no more games of inquiry with you." Her tone expressed both dignity and desperation. "The need of the Land will permit no more delay. Already, there is war in the distance—bloodshed and death. The Despiser marches against all that High Lord Kevin sought to preserve when he created his Wards. This insisting upon conditions is false loyalty to his intent. Amok, I appeal. In the name of the Land, guide us to the Seventh Ward."

Her supplication seemed to touch him, and his reply

was inordinately grave. "High Lord, I cannot. I am as I was made to be. Should I make the attempt, I would cease to exist."

"Then teach us the way, so that we may follow it alone."

Amok shook his head. "Then also I would cease to exist."

For a moment, she paused as if she were defeated. But in the silence, her shoulders straightened. Abruptly, she lifted the Staff of Law, held it horizontally before her like a weapon. "Amok," she commanded, "place your hands upon the Staff."

The youth looked without flinching into the authority of her face. Slowly, he obeyed. His hands rested lightly between hers on the rune-carved wood.

She gave a high, strange cry. At once, fire blossomed along the Staff; viridian flames opened from all the wood. The blaze swept over her hands and Amok's; it intensified as if it were feeding on their fingers. It hummed with deep power, and radiated a sharp aroma like the smell of duress.

"Kevin-born Amok!" she exclaimed through the hum. "Way and door to the Seventh Ward! By the power of the Staff of Law—in the name of High Lord Kevin son of Loric who made you—I adjure you. Tell me the name of the Seventh Ward's power!"

Covenant felt the force of her command. Though it was not leveled at him—though he was not touching the Staff—he gagged over the effort to utter a name he did not know.

But Amok met her without blinking, and his voice cut clearly through the flame of the Staff. "No, High Lord. I am impervious to compulsion. You cannot touch me."

"By the Seven!" she shouted. "I will not be denied!" She raged as if she were using fury to hold back a scream. *"Melenkurion abatha! Tell me the name!"*

"No," Amok repeated.

Savagely, she tore the Staff out of his hands. Its flame gathered, mounted, then sprang loudly into the sky like a bolt of thunder.

He gave a shrug, and disappeared.

For a long, shocked moment, the High Lord stood frozen, staring at Amok's absence. Then a shudder ran through her, and she turned toward Covenant as if she had the weight of a mountain on her shoulders. Her face looked like a wilderland. She took two tottering steps, and stopped to brace herself on the Staff. Her gaze was blank; all her force was focused inward, against herself.

"Failed," she gasped. "Doomed." Anguish twisted her mouth. "I have doomed the Land."

Covenant could not stand the sight. Forgetting all his issueless thoughts, he hurried to say, "There's got to be something else we can do."

She replied with an appalling softness. Tenderly, almost caressingly, she said, "Do you believe in the white gold? Can you use it to meet Amok's condition?" Her voice had a sound of madness. But the next instant, her passion flared outward. With all her strength, she pounded the Staff against Rivenrock, and cried, "Then do so!"

The power she unleashed caused a wide section of the plateau to lurch like a stricken raft. The rock bucked and plunged; seamless waves of force rolled through it from the Staff.

The heaving knocked Covenant off his feet. He stumbled, fell toward the cleft.

Almost at once, Elena regained control over herself. She snatched back the Staff's power, shouted to the Bloodguard. But Bannor's reflexes were swifter. While the rock still pitched, he bounded surefootedly across it and caught Covenant's arm.

For a moment, Covenant was too stunned to do anything but hang limply in Bannor's grip. The High Lord's violence flooded through him, sweeping everything else out of his awareness. But then he noticed the pain of Bannor's grasp on his arm. He could feel something prophetic in the ancient strength with which Bannor clenched him, kept him alive. The Bloodguard had an iron grip, surer than the stone of Rivenrock. When he heard Elena moan, "Beloved! Have I harmed you?" he was already muttering half aloud, "Wait. Hold on. I've got it."

His eyes were closed. He opened them, and discovered that Bannor was holding him erect. Elena was nearby; she flung her arms around him and hid her face in his shoulder. He said, "I've got it." She ignored him, started to mumble contrition into his shoulder. To stop her, he said sharply, "Forget it. I must be losing my mind. I should have figured this out days ago."

Finally she heard him. She released him and stepped back. Her ravaged face stiffened. She caught her breath between her teeth, pushed a hand through her hair. Slowly, she became a Lord again. Her voice was unsteady but lucid as she said, "What have you learned?"

Bannor released Covenant also, and the Unbeliever stood wavering on his own. His feet distrusted the stone, but he locked his knees, and tried to disregard the sensation. The problem was in his brain; all his preconceptions had shifted. He wanted to speak quickly, ease Elena's urgent distress. But he had missed too many clues. He needed to approach his intuition slowly, so that he could pull all its strands together.

He tried to clear his head by shaking it. Elena winced as if he were reminding her of her outburst. He made a placating gesture toward her, and turned to confront the Bloodguard. Intently, he scrutinized the blank metal of their faces, searched them for some flicker or hue of duplicity, ulterior purpose, which would verify his intuition. But their ancient, sleepless eyes seemed to conceal nothing, reveal nothing. He felt an instant of panic at the idea that he might be wrong, but he pushed it down, and asked as calmly as he could, "Bannor, how old are you?"

"We are the Bloodguard," Bannor replied. "Our Vow was sworn in the youth of Kevin's High Lordship."

"Before the Desecration?"

"Yes, ur-Lord."

"Before Kevin found out that Foul was really an enemy?"

"Yes."

"And you personally, Bannor? How old are you?"

"I was among the first *Haruchai* who entered the Land. I shared in the first swearing of the Vow."

"That was centuries ago." Covenant paused before he asked, "How well do you remember Kevin?"

"Step softly," Elena cautioned. "Do not mock the Bloodguard."

Bannor did not acknowledge her concern. He answered the Unbeliever inflexibly, "We do not forget."

"I suppose not," Covenant sighed. "What a hell of a way to live." For a moment, he gazed away toward the mountain, looking for courage. Then, with sudden harshness, he went on, "You knew Kevin when he made his Wards. You knew him and you remember. You were with him when he gave the First Ward to the Giants. You were with him when he hid the Second in those bloody catacombs under Mount Thunder. How many times did you come here with him, Bannor?"

The Bloodguard cocked one eyebrow fractionally. "High Lord Kevin made no sojourns to Rivenrock or *Melenkurion* Skyweir."

That answer rocked Covenant. "None?" His protest burst out before he could stop it. "Are you telling me you've never been here before?"

"We are the first Bloodguard to stand on Rivenrock," Bannor replied flatly.

"Then how—? Wait. Hold on." Covenant stared dizzily, then hit his forehead with the heel of his hand. "Right. If the Ward is some kind of natural phenomenon—like the Illearth Stone—if it isn't something he put here—Kevin wouldn't have to come here to know about it. Loric or somebody could have told him. Loric could have told anybody."

He took a deep breath to steady himself. "But everybody who might have known about it died in the Desecration. Except you."

Bannor blinked at Covenant as if his words had no meaning.

"Listen to me, Bannor," he went on. "A lot of things are finally starting to make sense. You reacted strangely—when Amok turned up at Revelstone that first time. You reacted strangely when he turned up at

Revelwood. And you let the High Lord herself follow him into the mountains with just two Bloodguard to protect her. Just two, Bannor! And when we end up stuck here on this godforsaken rock, Morin has the actual gall to apologize for Amok. Hellfire! Bannor, you should have at least told the High Lord what you know about this Ward. What kind of loyal do you think you are?"

Elena cautioned Covenant again. But her tone had changed; his thinking intrigued her.

"We are the Bloodguard," Bannor said. "You cannot raise doubt against us. We do not *know* Amok's intent."

Covenant heard the slight stress which Bannor placed on the word *know*. To his own surprise, he felt a sudden desire to take Bannor at his word, leave what the Bloodguard *knew* alone. But he forced himself to ask, "Know, Bannor? How can you not know? You've trusted him too much for that."

Bannor countered as he had previously, "We do not trust him. The High Lord chooses to follow him. We do not ask for more."

"The hell you don't." His effort of self-compulsion made him brutal. "And stop giving me that blank look. You people came to the Land, and you swore a Vow to protect Kevin. You swore to preserve him or at least give your lives for him and the Lords and Revelstone until Time itself came to an end if not forever, or why are you bereft even of the simple decency of sleep? But that poor desperate man outsmarted you. He actively saved you when he destroyed himself and everything else he merely believed in. So there you were, hanging from your Vow in empty space as if all the reasons in the world had suddenly disappeared.

"And then! Then you get a second chance to do your Vow right when the new Lords come along. But what happens? Amok turns up out of nowhere, and there's a war on against Foul himself—and what do you do? You let this creation of Kevin's lead the High Lord away as if it were safe and she didn't have anything better to do.

"Let me tell you something, Bannor. Maybe you

don't positively know Amok. You must have learned
some kind of distrust from Kevin. But you sure as hell
understand what Amok is doing. And you *approve!*"
The abrupt ferocity of his own yell stopped him for an
instant. He felt shaken by the moral judgments he saw
in Bannor. Thickly, he continued, "Or why are you
risking her for the sake of something created by the
only man who has ever succeeded in casting doubt on
your incorruptibility?"

Without warning, Amok appeared. The youth's arrival startled Covenant, but he took it as a sign that
he was on the right track. With a heavy sigh, he said,
"Why in the name of your Vow or at least simple
friendship didn't you tell the High Lord about Amok
when he first showed up?"

Bannor's gaze did not waver. In his familiar, awkward, atonal inflection, he replied, "Ur-Lord, we have
seen the Desecration. We have seen the fruit of perilous lore. Lore is not knowledge. Lore is a weapon, a
sword or spear. The Bloodguard have no use for weapons. Any knife may turn and wound the hand which
wields it. Yet the Lords desire lore. They do work of
value with it. Therefore we do not resist it, though we
do not touch it or serve it or save it.

"High Lord Kevin made his Wards to preserve his
lore—and to lessen the peril that his weapons might
fall into unready hands. This we approve. We are the
Bloodguard. We do not speak of lore. We speak only
of what we know."

Covenant could not go on. He felt that he had al-
ready multiplied his offenses against Bannor too much.
And he was moved by what Bannor said, despite the
Bloodguard's flat tone.

But Elena had learned enough to pursue his reasoning. Her voice was both quiet and authoritative as
she said, "First Mark—Bannor—the Bloodguard must
make a decision now. Hear me. I am Elena, High
Lord by the choice of the Council. This is a question of
loyalty. Will you serve dead Kevin's wisdom, or will
you serve me? In the past, you have served two causes,
the dead and the living. You have served both well.
But here you must choose. In the Land's need, there

is no longer any middle way. There will be blood and
blame upon us all if we allow Corruption to prevail."

Slowly, Bannor turned toward the First Mark. They
regarded each other in silence for a long moment.
Then Morin faced the High Lord with a magisterial
look in his eyes. "High Lord," he said, "we do not
know the name of the Seventh Ward's power. We have
heard many names—some false, others dead. But one
name we have heard only uttered in whispers by High
Lord Kevin and his Council.

"That name is the *Power of Command*."

When Amok heard the name, he nodded until his
hair seemed to dance with glee.

TWENTY-FOUR: Descent to Earthroot

COVENANT found that he was sweating. Despite the chill breeze, his forehead was damp. Moisture itched in his beard, and cold perspiration ran
down his spine. Morin's submission left him feeling
curiously depleted. For a moment, he looked up at the
sun as if to ask it why it did not warm him.

Melenkurion's spires reached into the morning like
fingers straining to bracket the sun. Their glaciered tips
caught the light brilliantly; the reflected dazzle made
Covenant's eyes water. The massive stone of the peaks
intimidated him. Blinking rapidly, he forced his gaze
back to High Lord Elena.

Through his sun blindness, he seemed to see only
her brown, blond-raddled hair. The lighter tresses
gleamed as if they were burnished. But as he blinked,
his vision cleared. He made out her face. She was
vivid with smiles. A new thrill of life lit her countenance with recovered hope. She did not speak, but her
lips formed the one word, *Beloved*.

Covenant felt that he had betrayed her.

Morin and Bannor stood almost shoulder to shoulder behind her. Nothing in the alert poise of their balance, or in the relaxed readiness of their arms, expressed any surprise or regret at the decision they had made. Yet Covenant knew they had fundamentally alerted the character of their service to the Lords. He had exacted that from them. He wished he could apologize in some way which would have meaning to the Bloodguard.

But there was nothing he could say to them. They were too absolute to accept any gesture of contrition. Their solitary communion with their Vow left him no way in which to approach them. No apology was sufficient.

"The Power of Command," he breathed weakly. "Have mercy on me." Unable to bear the sight of Elena's relieved, triumphant, grateful smile, or of Amok's grin, he turned away and walked wearily out across the plateau toward Rivenrock's edge as if his feet were trying to learn again the solidity of the stone.

He moved parallel to the cleft, but stayed a safe distance from it. As soon as he could see a substantial swath of Garroting Deep beyond the cliff edge, he stopped. There he remained, hoping both that Elena would come to him and that she would not.

The prevailing breeze from the Forest blew into his face, and for the first time in many days he was able to distinguish the tang of the season. He found that the autumn of the Land had turned its corner, traveled its annual round from joy to sorrow. The air no longer gleamed with abundance and fruition, with ripeness either glad or grim. Now the breeze tasted like the leading edge of winter—a sere augury, promising long nights and barrenness and cold.

As he smelled the air, he realized that Garroting Deep had no fall color change. He could make out stark black stands where the trees had already lost their leaves, but no blazonry palliated the Deep's darkness. It went without transition or adornment from summer to winter. He sensed the reason with his eyes and nose; the old Forest's angry clench of consciousness consumed all its strength and will, left it with neither the ability nor the desire to spend itself in mere displays of splendor.

Then he heard footsteps behind him, and recognized Elena's tread. To forestall whatever she wanted to tell him or ask him, he said, "You know, where I come from, the people who did this to a forest would be called pioneers—a very special breed of heroes, since instead of killing other human beings they concentrate on slaughtering nature itself. In fact, I know people who claim that all our social discomfort comes from the mere fact that we've got nothing left to pioneer."

"Beloved," she said softly, "you are not well. What is amiss?"

"Amiss?" He could not bring himself to look at her. His mouth was full of his bargain, and he had to swallow hard before he could say, "Don't mind me. I'm like that Forest down there. Sometimes I can't seem to help remembering."

In the silence, he sensed how little this answer satisfied her. She cared about him, wanted to understand him. But the rebirth of hope had restored the urgency of her duty. He knew that she could not spare the time to explore him now. He nodded morosely as she said, "I must go—the Land's need bears heavily upon me." Then she added, "Will you remain here —await my return?"

At last, he found the strength to turn and face her. He met the solemn set of her face, the displaced otherness of her gaze, and said gruffly, "Stay behind? And miss risking my neck again? Nonsense. I haven't had a chance like this since I was in Mount Thunder."

His sarcasm was sharper than he had intended, but she seemed to accept it. She smiled, touched him lightly on the arm with the fingers of one hand. "Come, then, beloved," she said. "The Bloodguard are prepared. We must depart before Amok places other obstacles in our way."

He tried to smile in return, but the uncertain muscles of his face treated the attempt like a grimace. Muttering at his failure, he went with her back toward the Bloodguard and Amok. As they walked, he watched her sidelong, assessed her covertly. The strain of the past three days had been pushed into the background; her forthright stride and resolute features expressed new purpose, strength. The resurgence of hope enabled her to discount mere exhaustion. But her knuckles were tense as she gripped the Staff, and her head was thrust forward at a hungry angle. She made Covenant's bargain lie unquiet in him, as if he were an inadequate and unbinding grave.

In his mind, he could still feel Rivenrock heaving. He needed steadier footing; nothing would save him if he could not keep his balance.

Vaguely, he observed that the First Mark and Bannor were indeed ready to travel. They had bound all the supplies into bundles, and had tied these to their backs with *clingor* thongs. And Amok sparkled with eagerness; visions seemed to caper in his gay hair. The three of them gave Covenant an acute pang of unpreparedness. He did not feel equal to whatever lay ahead of the High Lord's party. A pulse of anxiety began to run through his weary mood. There was something that he needed to do; he needed to try to recover his integrity in some way. But he did not know how.

He watched as the High Lord bade farewell to the Ranyhyn. They greeted her gladly, stamping their feet and nickering in pleasure at the prospect of activity after three days of patient waiting. She embraced each of the great horses, then stepped back, gripping the Staff, and saluted them in the Ramen fashion.

The Ranyhyn responded by tossing their manes. They regarded her with proud, laughing eyes as she addressed them.

"Brave Ranyhyn—first love of my life—I thank you for your service. We have been honored. But now we must go on foot for a time. If we survive our path, we will call upon you to carry us back to Revelstone—in victory or defeat, we will need the broad backs of your strength.

"For the present, be free. Roam the lands your hearts and hooves desire. And if it should come to pass that we do not call—if you return unsummoned to the Plains of Ra—then, brave Ranyhyn, tell all your kindred of Myrha. She saved my life in the landslide, and gave her own for a lesser horse. Tell all the Ranyhyn that Elena daughter of Lena, High Lord by the choice of the Council, and holder of the Staff of Law, is proud of your friendship. You are the Tail of the Sky, Mane of the World."

Raising the Staff, she cried, "Ranyhyn! Hail!"

The great horses answered with a whinny that echoed off the face of *Melenkurion* Skyweir. Then they wheeled and galloped away, taking with them Covenant's mustang. Their hooves clattered like a roll of fire on the stone as they swept northward and out of sight around the curve of the mountain.

When Elena turned back toward her companions, her sense of loss showed clearly in her face. In a sad voice, she said, "Come. If we must travel without the Ranyhyn, then let us at least travel swiftly."

At once, she turned expectantly to Amok. The ancient youth responded with an ornate bow, and started walking jauntily toward the place where the Skyweir's cliff joined the cleft of the plateau.

Covenant tugged at his beard, and watched hopelessly as Elena and Morin followed Amok.

Then, as abruptly as gasping, he exclaimed, "Wait!" The fingers of his right hand tingled in his beard. "Hang on." The High Lord looked questioningly at him. He said, "I need a knife. And some water. And a mirror, if you've got one—I don't want to cut my throat."

Elena said evenly, "Ur-Lord, we must go. We have lost so much time—and the Land is in need."

"It's important," he snapped. "Have you got a knife? The blade of my penknife isn't long enough."

For a moment, she studied him as if his conduct were a mystery. Then, slowly, she nodded to Morin. The First Mark unslung his bundle, opened it, and took out a stone knife, a leather waterskin, and a shallow bowl. These he handed to the Unbeliever. At once, Covenant sat down on the stone, filled the bowl, and began to wet his beard.

He could feel the High Lord's presence as she stood directly before him—he could almost taste the tension with which she held the Staff—but he concentrated on scrubbing water into his whiskers. His heart raced as if he were engaged in something dangerous. He had a vivid sense of what he was giving up. But he was impelled by the sudden conviction that his bargain was false because it had not cost him enough. When he picked up the knife, he did so to seal his compromise with his fate.

Elena stopped him. In a low, harsh voice, she said, "Thomas Covenant."

The way she said his name forced him to raise his head.

"Where is the urgency in this?" She controlled her harshness by speaking quietly, but her indignation was tangible in her voice. "We have spent three days in delay and ignorance. Do you now mock the Land's need? Is it your deliberate wish to prevent this quest from success?"

An angry rejoinder leaped to his lips. But the terms of his bargain required him to repress it. He bent his head again, splashed more water into his beard. "Sit down. I'll try to explain."

The High Lord seated herself cross-legged before him.

He could not comfortably meet her gaze. And he did not want to look at *Melenkurion* Skyweir; it stood too austerely, coldly, behind her. Instead, he watched his hands as they toyed with the stone knife.

"All right," he said awkwardly. "I'm not the kind of person who grows beards. They itch. And they make me look like a fanatic. They— So I've been letting this one grow for a reason. It's a way of proving—a way to demonstrate so that even somebody as thick-headed and generally incoherent as I am can see it— when I wake up in the real world and find that I don't have this beard I've been growing, then I'll know for sure that all this is a delusion. It's proof. Forty or fifty days' worth of beard doesn't just vanish. Unless it was never really there."

She continued to stare at him. But her tone changed.

She recognized the importance of his self-revelation. "Then why do you now wish to cut it away?"

He trembled to think of the risks he was taking. But he needed freedom, and his bargain promised to provide it. Striving to keep the fear of discovery out of his voice, he told her as much of the truth as he could afford.

"I've made another deal—like the one I made with the Ranyhyn. I'm not trying to prove that the Land isn't real anymore." In the back of his mind, he pleaded, Please don't ask me anything else. I don't want to lie to you.

She probed him with her eyes. "Do you believe, then —do you accept the Land?"

In his relief, he almost sighed aloud. He could look at her squarely to answer this. "No. But I'm willing to stop fighting about it. You've done so much for me."

"Ah, beloved!" she breathed with sudden intensity. "I have done nothing—I have only followed my heart. Within my Lord's duty, I would do anything for you."

He seemed to see her affection for him in the very hue of her skin. He wanted to lean forward, touch her, kiss her, but the presence of the Bloodguard restrained him. Instead, he handed her the knife.

He was abdicating himself to her, and she knew it. A glow of pleasure filled her face as she took the knife. "Do not fear, beloved," she whispered. "I will preserve you."

Carefully, as if she were performing a rite, she drew close to him and began to cut his beard.

He winced instinctively when the blade first touched him. But he gritted himself into stillness, locked his jaw, told himself that he was safer in her hands than in his own. He could feel the deadliness of the keen edge as it passed over his flesh—it conjured up images of festering wounds and gangrene—but he closed his eyes, and remained motionless.

The knife tugged at his beard, but the sharpness of the blade kept the pull from becoming painful. And soon her fingers found his knotted jaw muscles. She stroked his clenching to reassure him. With an effort, he opened his eyes. She met his gaze as if she were smiling through a mist of love. Gently, she tilted back his head, and cleaned the beard away from his neck with smooth, confident strokes.

Then she was done. His bared flesh felt vivid in the air, and he rubbed his face with his hands, relishing the fresh texture of his cheeks and neck. Again, he wanted to kiss Elena. To answer her smile, he stood up and said, "Now I'm ready. Let's go."

She grasped the Staff of Law, sprang lightly to her feet. In a tone of high gaiety, she said to Amok, "Will you now lead us to the Seventh Ward?"

Amok beckoned brightly, as if he were inviting her to a game, and started once more toward the place where the cleft of Rivenrock vanished under *Melenkurion* Skyweir. Morin quickly repacked his bundle, and placed himself behind Amok; Elena and Covenant followed the First Mark; and Bannor brought up the rear.

In this formation, they began the last phase of their quest for the Power of Command.

They crossed the plateau briskly. Amok soon reached the juncture of cliff and cleft. There he waved to his companions, grinned happily, and jumped into the crevice.

Covenant gasped in spite of himself, and hurried with Elena to the edge. When they peered into the narrow blackness of the chasm, they saw Amok standing on a ledge in the opposite wall. The ledge began fifteen or twenty feet below and a few feet under the overhang of the mountain. It was not clearly visible. The blank stone and shadowed dimness of the cleft formed a featureless abyss. Amok seemed to be standing on darkness which led to darkness.

"Hellfire!" Covenant groaned as he looked down. He felt dizzy already. "Forget it. Just forget I ever mentioned it."

"Come!" said Amok cheerfully. "Follow!" His voice sounded over the distant, subterreanean gush of the river. With an insouciant stride, he moved away into the mountain. At once, the gloom swallowed him completely.

Morin glanced at the High Lord. When she nodded,

he leaped into the cleft, landed where Amok had been standing a moment before. He took one step to the side, and waited.

"Don't be ridiculous," Covenant muttered as if he were talking to the dank, chill breeze which blew out of the crevice. "I'm no Bloodguard. I'm just ordinary flesh and blood. I get dizzy when I stand on a chair. Sometimes I get dizzy when I just stand."

The High Lord was not listening to him. She murmured a few old words to the Staff, and watched intently as it burst ino flame. Then she stepped out into the darkness. Morin caught her as her feet touched the ledge. She moved past him, and positioned herself so that the light of the Staff illuminated the jump for Covenant.

The Unbeliever found Bannor looking at him speculatively.

"Go on ahead," said Covenant. "Give me time to get up my courage. I'll catch up with you in a year or two." He was sweating again, and his perspiration stung the scraped skin of his cheeks and neck. He looked up at the mountain to steady himself, efface the effects of the chasm from his mind.

Without warning, Bannor caught him from behind, lifted him, and carried him to the cleft.

"Don't touch me!" Covenant sputtered. He tried to break free, but Bannor's grip was too strong. "By hell! I—!" His voice scaled into a yell as Bannor threw him over the edge.

Morin caught him deftly, and placed him, wide-eyed and trembling, on the ledge at Elena's side.

A moment later, Bannor made the jump, and the First Mark passed Covenant and Elena to stand between her and Amok. Covenant watched their movements through a stunned fog. Numbly, he pressed his back against the solid stone, and stared into the chasm as if it were a tomb. Some time seemed to pass before he noticed the High Lord's reassuring hold on his arm.

"Don't touch me," he repeated aimlessly. "Don't touch me."

When she moved away, he followed her automatically, turning his back on the sunlight and open sky above the cleft.

He rubbed his left shoulder against the stone wall, and kept close to Elena, stayed near her light. The Staff's incandescence cast a viridian aura over the High Lord's party, and reflected garishly off the dark, flat facets of the stone. It illuminated Amok's path without penetrating the gloom ahead. The ledge— never more than three feet wide—moved steadily downward. Above it, the ceiling of the cleft slowly expanded, took on the dimensions of a cavern. And the cleft itself widened as if it ran toward a prodigious hollow in the core of *Melenkurion* Skyweir.

Covenant felt the yawning rent in the mountain rock as if it were beckoning to him, urging him seductively to accept the drowsy abandon of vertigo, trust the chasm's depths. He pressed himself harder against the stone, and clung to Elena's back with his eyes. Around him, darkness and massed weight squeezed the edges of the Staff's light. And at his back, he could hear the hovering vulture wings of his private doom. Gradually, he understood that he was walking into a crisis.

Underground! he rasped harshly at his improvidence. He could not forget how he had fallen into a crevice under Mount Thunder. That experience had brought him face-to-face with the failure of his old compromise, his bargain with the Ranyhyn. Hellfire! He felt he had done nothing to ready himself for an ordeal of caves.

Ahead of him, the High Lord followed Morin and Amok. They adjusted themselves to her pace, and she moved as fast as she safely could on the narrow ledge. Covenant was hard pressed to keep up with her. Her speed increased his apprehension; it made him feel that the rift was spreading its jaws beside him. He labored fearfully down the ledge. It demanded all his concentration.

He had no way to measure duration or distance— had nothing with which to judge time except the accumulation of his fear and strain and weariness—but gradually the character of the cavern's ceiling changed. It spread out like a dome. After a while, Elena's fire lit only one small arc of the stone. Around it, spectral shapes peopled the darkness. Then the rough curve of rock within the Staff's light became gnarled and pitted, like the slow clenching of a frown on the cave's forehead. And finally the frown gave way to stalactites. Then the upper air bristled with crooked old shafts and spikes—poised spears and misdriven nails—pending lamias—slow, writhed excrescences of the mountain's inner sweat. Some of these had flat facets which reflected the Staff's fire in fragments, casting it like a chiaroscuro into the recessed groins of the cavern. And others leaned toward the ledge as if they were straining ponderously to strike the heads of the human interlopers.

For some distance, the stalactites grew thicker, longer, more intricate, until they filled the dome of the cavern. When Covenant mustered enough fortitude to look out over the crevice, he seemed to be gazing into a blue-lit, black, inverted forest—a packed stand of gnarled and ominous old trees with their roots in the ceiling. They created the impression that it was possible, on the sole trail of the ledge, for him to lose his way.

The sensation excoriated his stumbling fear. When Elena came abruptly to a stop, he almost flung his arms around her.

Beyond her in the Staff's velure light, he saw that a massive stalactite had angled downward and attached itself to the lip of the ledge. The stalactite hit there as if it had been violently slammed into place. Despite its ancientness, it seemed to quiver with the force of impact. Only a strait passage remained between the stalactite and the wall.

Amok halted before this narrow gap. He waited until his companions were close behind him. Then, speaking over his shoulder in an almost reverential tone, he said, "Behold Damelon's Door—entryway to the Power of Command. For this reason among others, none may approach the Power in my absence. The knowledge of this unlocking is contained in none of High Lord Kevin's Wards. And any who dare Damelon's Door without this unlocking will not find the

' Power. They will wander forever lorn and pathless in the wilderness beyond. Now hear me. Pass swiftly through the entryway when it is opened. It will not remain open long."

Elena nodded intently. Behind her, Covenant braced himself on her shoulder with his right hand. He had a sudden inchoate feeling that this was his last chance to turn back, to recant or undo the decisions which had brought him here. But the chance—if it was a chance—passed as quickly as it had come. Amok approached the Door.

With slow solemnity, the youth extended his right hand, touched the blank plane of the gap with his index finger. In silence he held his finger at that point, level with his chest.

A fine yellow filigree network began to grow in the air. Starting from Amok's fingertip, the delicate web of light spread outward in the plane of the gap. Like a skein slowly crystallizing into visibility, it expanded until it filled the whole Door.

Amok commanded, "Come," and stepped briskly through the web.

He did not break the delicate strands of light. Rather, he disappeared as he touched them. Covenant could see no trace of him on the ledge beyond the Door.

Morin followed Amok. He, too, vanished as he came in contact with the yellow web.

Then the High Lord started forward. Covenant stayed with her. He kept his grip on her shoulder; he was afraid of being separated from her. Boldly, she stepped into the gap. He held her and followed. When he touched the glistening network, he winced, but he felt no pain. A swift tingling like an instant of ants passed over his flesh as he crossed the gap. He could feel Bannor close behind him.

He found himself standing in a place different from the one he had expected.

As he looked around him, the web faded, vanished. But the Staff of Law continued to burn. Back through the gap, he could see the ledge and the stalactites and the chasm. But no chasm existed on this side of Damelon's Door. Instead there stretched a wide stone floor in which stalactites and stalagmites stood like awkward colonnades, and a mottled ceiling hunched over the open spaces. Hushed stillness filled the air; a moment passed before Covenant realized that he could no longer hear the low background rumble of *Melenkurion* Skyweir's river.

With an encompassing gesture, Amok said formally, "Behold the Audience Hall of Earthroot. Here in ages long forgotten the sunless lake would rise in season to meet those who sought its waters. Now, as the Earth-power fades from mortal knowledge, the Audience Hall is unwet. Yet it retains a power of mazement, to foil those who are unready in heart and mind. All who enter here without the proper unlocking of Damelon's Door will be forever lost to life and use and name."

Grinning, he turned to Elena. "High Lord, brighten the Staff for a moment."

She seemed to guess his intention. She straightened as if she anticipated awe; eagerness seemed to gleam on her forehead. Murmuring ritualistically, she struck the Staff's heel on the stone. The Staff flared, and a burst of flame sprang toward the ceiling.

The result staggered Covenant. The surge of flame sparked a reaction in all the stalactites and stalagmites. They became instantly glittering and reflective. Light ignited on every column, resonated, rang in dazzling peals back and forth across the cave. It burned into his eyes from every side until he felt that he was caught on the clapper of an immense bell of light. He tried to cover his eyes, but the clangor went on in his mind. Gasping, searching blindly for support, he began to founder.

Then Elena silenced the Staff. The clamoring light faded away, echoed into the distance like the aftermath of a clarion. Covenant found that he was on his knees with his hands clamped over his ears. Hesitantly, he looked up. All the reflections were gone; the columns had returned to their former rough illuster. As Elena helped him to his feet, he was muttering weakly, "By hell. By hell." Even her fond face, and the flat, unamazed countenances of the Bloodguard, could not counteract his feeling that he no longer knew where he was. And when Amok led the High Lord's party onward, Covenant kept stumbling as if he could not find his footing on the stone.

After they left the perilous cavern, time and distance passed confusedly for him. His retinas retained a capering dazzle which disoriented him. He could see that the High Lord and Amok descended a slope which spread out beyond the range of the Staff's light like a protracted shore, a colonnaded beach left dry by the recession of a subterreanean sea. But his feet could not follow their path. His eyes told him that Amok led them directly down the slope, but his sense of balance registered alterations in direction, changes in the pitch and angle of descent. Whenever he closed his eyes, he lost all impression of straightness; he reeled on the uneven surface of a crooked trail.

He did not know where or how far he had traveled when Elena stopped for a brief meal. He did not know how long the halt lasted, or what distance he walked when it was over. All his senses were out of joint. When the High Lord halted again, and told him to rest, he sank down against a stalagmite and went to sleep without question.

In dreams he wandered like one of the lorn who had improvidently braved Damelon's Door in search of Earthroot—he could hear shrill, stricken wails of loss as if he were crying for his companions, crying for himself—and he awoke to a complete confusion. The darkness made him think that someone had pulled the fuses of his house while he lay bleeding and helpless on the floor beside his coffee table. Numbly, he groped for the receiver of the telephone, hoping that Joan had not yet hung up on him. But then his fumbling fingers recognized the texture of stone. With a choked groan, he sprang to his feet in the midnight under *Melenkurion* Skyweir.

Almost at once, the Staff flamed. In the blue light, Elena arose to catch him with her free arm and clasp him tightly. "Beloved!" she murmured. "Ah, beloved. Hold fast. I am here." He hugged her achingly, pressed his face into her sweet hair until he could still his pain, regain his self-command. Then he slowly released her. He strove to express his thanks with a smile, but it broke and fell into pieces in his face. In a raw, rasping voice, he said, "Where are we?"

Behind him, Amok fluted, "We stand in the Aisle of Approach. Soon we will gain Earthrootstair."

"What"—Covenant tried to clear his head—"what time is it?"

"Time has no measure under *Melenkurion* Skyweir," the youth replied imperviously.

"Oh, bloody hell." Covenant groaned at the echo he heard in Amok's answer. He had been told too often that white gold was the crux of the arch of Time.

Elena came to his relief. "The sun has risen to midmorning," she said. "This is the thirty-third day of our journey from Revelstone." As an afterthought, she added, "Tonight is the dark of the moon."

The dark of the moon, he muttered mordantly to himself. Have mercy— Terrible things happened when the moon was dark. The Wraiths of Andelain had been attacked by ur-viles— Atiaran had never forgiven him for that.

The High Lord seemed to see his thoughts in his face. "Beloved," she said calmly, "do not be so convinced of doom." Then she turned away and started to prepare a spare meal.

Watching her—seeing her resolution and personal force implicit even in the way she performed this simple task—Covenant clenched his teeth, and kept the silence of his bargain.

He could hardly eat the food she handed to him. The effort of silence made him feel ill; holding down his passive lie seemed to knot his guts, make sustenance unpalatable. Yet he felt that he was starving. To ease his inanition, he forced down a little of the dry bread and cured meat and cheese. The rest he returned to Elena. He felt almost relieved when she followed Amok again into the darkness.

He went dumbly after her.

Sometime during the previous day, the High Lord's party had left behind the Audience Hall. Now they traveled a wide, featureless tunnel like a road through the stone. Elena's light easily reached the ceiling and walls. Their surfaces were oddly smooth, as if they had been rubbed for long ages by the movement of something rough and powerful. This smoothness made the tunnel seem like a conduit or artery. Covenant distrusted it; he half expected thick, laval ichor to come rushing up through it. As he moved, he played nervously with his ring, as if that small circle were the binding of his self-control.

Elena quickened her steps. He could see in her back that she was impelled by her mounting eagerness for the Power of Command.

At last, the tunnel changed. Its floor swung in a tight curve to the left, and its right wall broke off, opening into another crevice. This rift immediately became a substantial gulf. The stone shelf of the road narrowed until it was barely ten feet wide, then divided into rude steep stairs as it curved downward. In moments, the High Lord's party was on a stairway which spiraled around a central shaft into the chasm.

Many hundreds of feet below them, a fiery red glow lit the bottom of the gulf. Covenant felt that he was peering into an inferno.

He remembered where he had seen such light before. It was rocklight—radiated stone-shine like that which the Cavewights used under Mount Thunder.

The descent affected him like vertigo. Within three rounds of the shaft, his head was reeling. Only Elena's unwavering light, and his acute concentration as he negotiated the uneven steps, saved him from pitching headlong over the edge. But he was grimly determined not to ask either Elena or Bannor for help. He could afford no more indebtedness; it would nullify his bargain, tip the scales of payment against him. No! he muttered to himself as he lurched down the steps. No. No more. Don't be so bloody helpless. Save something to bargain with. Keep going. Distantly, he heard himself panting, "Don't touch me. Don't touch me."

A spur of nausea roweled him. His muscles bunched as if they were bracing for a fall. But he hugged his chest, and clung to Elena's light for support. Her flame bobbed above her like a tongue of courage.

Slowly its blue illumination took on a red tinge as she worked down toward the gulf's glow.

He made the descent grimly, mechanically, like a volitionless puppet stalking down the irregular steps of his designated end. Round by round, he approached the source of the rocklight. Soon the red illumination made the Staff's flame unnecessary, and High Lord Elena extinguished it. Ahead of her, Amok began to move more swiftly, as if he were impatient, jealous of all delays which postponed the resolution of his existence. But Covenant followed at his own pace, effectively unconscious of anything but the spiraling stairs and his imperious dizziness. He went down the last distance through a high wash of rocklight as numbly as if he were sleepwalking.

When he reached the flat bottom, he took a few wooden steps toward the lake, then stopped, covered his eyes against the deep, fiery, red light, and shuddered as if his nerves jangled on the edge of hysteria.

Ahead of him, Amok crowed jubilantly, "Behold, High Lord! The sunless lake of Earthroot! Unheavened sap and nectar of great *Melenkurion* Skyweir, the sire of mountains! Ah, behold it. The long years of my purpose are nearly done." His words echoed clearly away, as if they were seconded by scores of light crystal voices.

Drawing a tremulous breath, Covenant opened his eyes. He was standing on the gradual shore of a still lake which spread out before him as far as he could see. Its stone roof was high, hidden in shadows, but the lake was lit everywhere by rocklight burning in the immense pillars which stood up like columns through the lake—or like roots of the mountain reaching down to the water. These columns or roots were evenly spaced along and across the cavern; they were repeated regularly into the vast distance. Their rocklight, and the vibrant stillness of the lake, gave the whole place a cloistral air, despite its size. Earthroot was a place to make mere mortals humble and devout.

It made Covenant feel like a sacrilege in the sanctified and august temple of the mountains.

The lake was so still—it conveyed such an impression of weight, massiveness—that it looked more like fluid bronze than water, a liquid cover for the unfathomable abysses of the Earth. The rocklight gleamed on it as if it were burnished.

"Is this—?" Covenant croaked, then caught himself as his question ran echoing lightly over the water, restating itself without diminishment into the distance. He could not bring himself to go on. Even the low shuffling of his boots on the stone echoed as if it carried some kind of prophetic significance.

But Amok took up the question gaily. "Is the Power of Command here, in Earthroot?" The echoes laughed as he laughed. "No. Earthroot but partakes. The heart of the Seventh Ward lies beyond. We must cross over."

High Lord Elena asked the next question carefully, as if she, too, were timid in the face of the awesome lake. "How?"

"High Lord, a way will be provided. I am the way and the door—I have not brought you to a pathless end. But the use of the way will be in your hands. This is the last test. Only one word am I permitted to say: do not touch the water. Earthroot is strong and stern. It will take no account of mortal flesh."

"What must we do now?" she inquired softly to minimize the echoes.

"Now?" Amok chuckled. "Only wait, High Lord. The time will not be long. Behold! Already the way approaches."

He was standing with his back to the lake, but as he spoke he gestured behind him with one arm. As if in answer to this signal, a boat came into sight around a pillar some distance from the shore.

The boat was empty. It was a narrow wooden craft, pointed at both ends. Except for a line of bright reflective gilt along its gunwales and thwarts, it was unadorned—a clean, simple work smoothly formed of light brown wood, and easily long enough to seat five people. But it was unoccupied; no one rowed or steered it. Without making a ripple, it swung gracefully around the pillar, and glided shoreward. Yet in

Earthroot's sacramental air, it did not seem strange; it was a proper and natural adjunct of the bronze lake. Covenant was not surprised to see that it carried no oars.

He watched its approach as if it were an instrument of dread. It made his wedding ring itch on his finger. He glanced quickly at his hand, half expecting to see that the band glowed or changed color. The argent metal looked peculiarly vivid in the rocklight; it weighed heavily on his hand, tingled against his skin. But it revealed nothing. "Have mercy," he breathed as if he were speaking directly to the white gold. Then he winced as his voice tripped away in light echoes, spread by a multitude of crystal repetitions.

Amok laughed at him, and clear peals of glee joined the mimicry.

High Lord Elena was now too enrapt in Earthroot to attend Covenant. She stood on the shore as if she could already smell the Power of Command, and waited like an acolyte for the empty boat.

Soon the craft reached her. Silently, it slid its prow up the dry slope, and stopped as if it were ready, expectant.

Amok greeted it with a deep obeisance, then leaped lithely aboard. His feet made no sound as they struck the planks. He moved to the far end of the craft, turned, and seated himself with his arms on the gunwales, grinning like a monarch.

First Mark Morin followed Amok. Next, High Lord Elena entered the craft, and placed herself on a seat board near its middle. She held the Staff of Law across her knees. Covenant saw that his turn had come. Trembling, he walked down the shore to the wooden prow. Apprehension beat in his temples, but he repressed it. He clutched the gunwales with both hands, climbed into the craft. His boots thudded and echoed on the planks. As he sat down, he seemed to be surrounded by the clatter of unseemly burdens.

Bannor shoved the boat into the lake, and sprang immediately aboard. But by the time he had taken his seat, the boat had glided to a halt. It rested as if it were fused to the burnished water a few feet from shore.

For a moment, no one moved or spoke. They sat bated and hushed, waiting for the same force which had brought the boat to carry it away again. But the craft remained motionless—fixed like a censer in the red, still surface of the lake.

The pulse in Covenant's head grew sharper. Harshly, he defied the echoes. "Now what do we do?"

To his surprise, the boat slid forward a few feet. But it stopped again when the repetitions of his voice died. Once again, the High Lord's party was held, trapped.

He stared about him in astonishment. No one spoke. He could see thoughts concentrate the muscles of Elena's back. He looked at Amok once, but the youth's happy grin so dismayed him that he tore his gaze away. The ache of his suspense began to seem unendurable.

Bannor's unexpected movement startled him. Turning, he saw that the Bloodguard had risen to his feet. He lifted his seat board from its slots.

For an oar! Covenant thought. He felt a sudden upsurge of excitement.

Bannor held the board in both hands, braced himself against the side of the boat, and prepared to paddle.

As the end of the board touched the water, some power grabbed it, wrenched it instantly from his grasp. It was snatched straight down into the lake. There was no splash or ripple, but the board vanished like a stone hurled into the depths.

Bannor gazed after it, and cocked one eyebrow as if he were speculating abstractly on the kind of strength which could so easily tear something away from a Bloodguard. But Covenant was not so calm. He gaped weakly, "Hellfire."

Again the boat moved forward. It coasted for several yards until the echoes of Covenant's amazement disappeared. Then it stopped, resumed its reverent stasis.

Covenant faced Elena, but he did not need to voice

his question. Her face glowed with comprehension. "Yes, beloved," she breathed in relief and triumph. "I see." And as the boat once more began to glide over the lake, she continued, "It is the sound of our voices which causes the boat to move. That is the use of Amok's way. The craft will seek its own destination. But to carry us it must ride upon our echoes."

The truth of her perception was immediately apparent. While her clear voice cast replies like ripples over Earthroot, the boat slid easily through the water. It steered itself between the pillars as if it were pursuing the lodestone of its purpose. Soon it had passed out of sight of Earthrootstair. But when she stopped speaking—when the delicate echoes had chimed themselves into silence—the craft halted again.

Covenant groaned inwardly. He was suddenly afraid that he would be asked to talk, help propel the boat. He feared that he would give his bargain away if he were forced into any kind of extended speech. In self-defense, he turned the demand around before it could be directed at him. "Well, say something," he growled at Elena.

A light, ambiguous smile touched her lips—a response, not to him, but to some satisfying inner prospect. "Beloved," she replied softly, "we will have no difficulty. There is much which has not been said between us. There are secrets and mysteries and sources of power in you which I perceive but dimly. And in some ways I have not yet spoken of myself. This is a fit place for the opening of hearts. I will tell you of that Ranyhyn-ride which took the young daughter of Lena from Mithil Stonedown into the Southron Range, and there at the great secret horse-rite of the Ranyhyn taught her—taught her many things."

With a stately movement, she rose to her feet facing Covenant. She set the Staff of Law firmly on the planks, and lifted her head to the ceiling of Earthroot's cavern. "Ur-Lord Thomas Covenant," she said, and the echoes spread about her like a skein of gleaming rocklight, interweaving the burnished water, "Unbeliever and white gold wielder, Ringthane—beloved

—I must tell you of this. You have known Myrha. In her youth, she came to Lena my mother, according to the promise of the Ranyhyn. She carried me away to the great event of my girlhood. Thus you were the unknowing cause. Before this war reaches its end for good or ill, I must tell you what your promises have wrought."

Have mercy on me! he cried again in the obdurate incapacity of his heart. But he was too numb, too intimidated by the lake and the echoes, to stop her. He sat in mute dread, and listened as Elena told him the tale of her experience with the Ranyhyn. And all the time, the craft bore them on an oblique, intimate course between the lake pillars, floated them on the resonances of her voice as if it were ferrying them to a terrible shore.

Her adventure had occurred the third time that Lena her mother had allowed her to ride a Ranyhyn. During the two previous annual visits to Mithil Stonedown, dictated by the Ranyhyn promise to Covenant Ringthane, the old horse from the Plains of Ra had rolled his eyes strangely at the little girl as Trell her grandfather had boosted her onto its broad back. And the next year young Myrha took the old stallion's place. The mare gazed at Elena with that look of deliberate intention which characterized all the Ranyhyn —and Elena, sensing the Ranyhyn's offer without understanding it, gladly gave herself up to Myrha. She did not look back as the mare carried her far away from Mithil Stonedown into the mountains of the Southron Range.

For a day and a night, Myrha galloped, bearing Elena far south along mountain trails and over passes unknown to the people of the Land. At the end of that time, they gained a high valley, a grassy glen folded between sheer cliffs, with a rugged, spring-fed tarn near its center. This small lake was mysterious, for its dark waters did not reflect the sunlight. And the valley itself was wondrous to behold, for it contained hundreds of Ranyhyn—hundreds of proud, glossy, star-browed stallions and mares—gathered together for a rare and secret ritual of horses.

But Elena's wonder quickly turned to fear. Amid a chorus of wild, whinnied greetings, Myrha carried the little girl toward the lake, then shrugged her to the ground and dashed away in a flurry of hooves. And the rest of the Ranyhyn began to run around the valley. At first they trotted in all directions, jostling each other and sweeping by the child as if they were barely able to avoid crushing her. But gradually their pace mounted. Several Ranyhyn left the pounding mob to drink at the tarn, then burst back into the throng as if the dark waters roiled furiously in their veins. While the sun passed overhead, the great horses sprinted and bucked, drank at the tarn, rushed away to run again in the unappeasable frenzy of a dance of madness. And Elena stood among them, imperiled for her life by the savage flash and flare of hooves—frozen with terror. In her fear, she thought that if she so much as flinched she would be instantly trampled to death.

Standing there—engulfed in heat and thunder and abysmal fear as final as the end of life—she lost consciousness for a time. She was still standing when her eyes began to see again; she was erect and petrified in the last glow of evening. But the Ranyhyn were no longer running. They had surrounded her; they faced her, studied her with a force of compulsion in their eyes. Some were so close to her that she inhaled their hot, damp breath. They wanted her to do something—she could feel the insistence of their wills battering at her immobile fear. Slowly, woodenly, choicelessly, she began to move.

She went to the tarn and drank.

Abruptly, the High Lord dropped her narration, and began to sing—a vibrant, angry, and anguished song which cast ripples of passion across the air of Earthroot. For reasons at which Covenant could only guess instinctively, she broke into Lord Kevin's Lament as if it were her own private and immedicable threnody.

> Where is the Power that protects
> beauty from the decay of life?
> preserves truth pure of falsehood?

secures fealty from that slow stain of chaos
which corrupts?
How are we so rendered small by Despite?
Why will the very rocks not erupt
for their own cleansing,
or crumble into dust for shame?

While echoes of the song's grief ran over the lake,
she met Covenant's gaze for the first time since she
had begun her tale.

"Beloved," she said in a low, thrilling voice, "I was
transformed—restored to life. At the touch of those
waters, the blindness or ignorance of my heart fell
away. My fear melted, and I was joined to the communion of the Ranyhyn. In an instant of vision, I
understood—everything. I saw that in honor of your
promise I had been brought to the horserite of
Kelenbhrabanal, Father of Horses—a Ranyhyn ritual
enacted once each generation to pass on and perpe-
tuate their great legend, the tale of mighty *Kelenbhrabanal's* death in the jaws of Fangthane the Render. I
saw that the turmoiled running of the Ranyhyn was
their shared grief and rage and frenzy at the Father's
end.

"For *Kelenbhrabanal* was the Father of Horses,
Stallion of the First Herd. The Plains of Ra were his
demesne and protectorate. He led the Ranyhyn in
their great war against the wolves of Fangthane.

"But the war continued without issue, and the
stench of shed blood and rent flesh became a sickness
in the Stallion's nostrils. Therefore he made his way
to Fangthane. He stood before the Render, and said,
'Let this war end. I smell your hate—I know that you
must have victims, else in your passion you will consume yourself. I will be your victim. Slaughter me, and
let my people live in peace. Appease your hate on
me, and end this war.' And Fangthane agreed. So
Kelenbhrabanal bared his throat to the Render's
teeth, and soaked the earth with his sacrifice.

"But Fangthane did not keep his word—the wolves
attacked again. The Ranyhyn were leaderless, heart-
stricken. They could not fight well. The remnant of

the Ranyhyn was compelled to flee into the mountains. They could not return to their beloved Plains until they had gained the service of the Ramen, and with that aid had driven the wolves away.

"Thus each generation of the Ranyhyn holds its horserite to preserve the tale of the Stallion—to hold pure in memory all their pride at his self-sacrifice, and all their grief at his death, and all their rage at the Despite which betrayed him. Thus they drink of the mind-uniting waters, and hammer out against the ground the extremity of their passion for one day and one night. And thus, when I had tasted the water of the tarn, I ran and wept and raged with them throughout the long exaltation of that night. Heart and mind and soul and all, I gave myself to a dream of Fangthane's death."

Listening to her, clinging to her face with his eyes, Covenant felt himself knotted by the clench of unreleasable grief. She was the woman who had offered herself to him. He understood her passion now, understood the danger she was in. And her elsewhere glance was drawing into focus; already he could feel conflagrations blazing at the corners of her vision.

His dread of that focus gave him the impetus to speak. With his voice rent between fear and love, he wrenched out hoarsely, "What I don't understand is what Foul gets out of all this."

TWENTY-FIVE: The Seventh Ward

FOR a long moment, High Lord Elena gripped the Staff of Law and glared down at him. Focus crackled on the verge of her gaze; it was about to lash out and scourge him. But then she seemed to recollect who he was. Slowly, the passion dimmed in her face, went behind in inward veil. She lowered herself to her seat in the boat. Quietly, dangerously, she asked, "All this? Do you ask what Lord Foul gains from what I have told you?"

He answered her with quivering promptitude. Careless now of the illimitable range of implications with which the echoes multiplied his voice, he hastened to explain himself, ameliorate at least in this way the falseness of his position.

"That, too. You said it yourself—that old, unsufferable bargain I made with the Ranyhyn put you—where you are. Never mind what I did to your mother. That, too. But it's really this time I'm thinking about. You summoned me, and we're on our way to the Seventh Ward—and I want to know what Foul gets out of it. He wouldn't waste a chance like this."

"This is no part of his intent," she replied coldly. "The choice to summon you was mine, not his."

"Right. That's the way he works. But what made you decide to summon me?—I mean aside from the fact that you were going to call me anyway at some time or other because I have the simple misfortune to wear a white gold wedding ring and have two fingers missing. What made you decide then—when you did?"

"*Dukkha* Waynhim gave us new knowledge of Fangthane's power."

"New knowledge, by hell!" Covenant croaked. "Do you think that was an accident? Foul released him." He shouted the word *released*, and its echoes jabbered about him like dire significances. "He released that poor suffering devil because he knew exactly what you would do about it. And he wanted me to be in the Land then, at that precise time, not sooner or later."

The importance of what he was saying penetrated her; she began to hear him seriously. But her voice remained noncommittal as she asked, "Why? How are his purposes served?"

For a moment, he shied away from what he was thinking. "How should I know? If I knew, I might be able to fight it somehow. Aside from the idea that I'm supposed to destroy the Land—" But Elena's grave attention stopped him. For her sake, he mustered his courage. "Well, look at what's happened because of me. I did something to Loric's *krill*—therefore Amok showed up—therefore you're going to try to unlock the Seventh Ward. It's as neat as clockwork. If you'd summoned me sooner, then when we got to this point you wouldn't be under such pressure to use lore you don't understand. And if all this had happened later, you wouldn't have come here at all—you would have been too busy fighting the war.

"As for me"—he swallowed and looked away for an instant, then took a step closer to the root of his bargain—"this is the only way I can possibly get off the hook. If things had gone differently, there would have been a lot more pressure on me—from everywhere—to learn how to use this ring. And Joan— But this way you've been distracted—you're thinking about the Seventh Ward instead of wild magic or whatever. And Foul doesn't want me to learn what white gold is good for. I might use it against him.

"Don't you see it? Foul put us right where we are. He released *dukkha* so that we would be right here now. He must have a reason. He likes to destroy people through the things that make them hope. That way he can get them to desecrate— No wonder this is the dark of the moon." He was poignantly conscious of the way in which he endangered his own cause as he concluded softly, "Elena, the Seventh Ward might be the worst thing that has happened yet."

But she had her answer ready. "No, beloved. I do not believe it. High Lord Kevin formed his Wards in a time before his wisdom fell into despair. Fangthane's hand is not in them. It may be that the Power of Command is perilous—but it is not ill."

Her statement did not convince him. But he did not have the heart to protest. The echoes placed too much stress on even his simplest words. Instead, he sat gazing morosely at her feet while he scratched at the itch of his wedding band. As the echoes died—as the boat slid gently to a stop in the water—he felt that he had missed a chance for rectitude.

For a time, no voice arose to move the boat.

Covenant and Elena sat in silence, studying their private thoughts. But then she spoke again. Softly, reverently, she recited the words of Lord Kevin's Lament. The boat glided onward again.

Shortly the craft rounded another column, and Covenant found himself staring at a high, sparkling, silent waterfall ahead. Its upper reaches disappeared into the shadows of the cavern's ceiling. But the torrents which poured noiselessly down its ragged surface caught the fiery rocklight at thousands of bright points, so that the falls looked like a cascade of hot, rich, red gems.

The boat flowed smoothly on Elena's recitation toward a rock levee at one side of the waterfall, and slid up into place. At once, Amok leaped from the craft, and stood waiting for his companions on the edge of Earthroot. But for a moment they did not follow him. They sat spellbound by the splendor and silence of the falls.

"Come, High Lord," the youth said. "The Seventh Ward is nigh. I must bring my being to an end." His tone matched the unwonted seriousness of his countenance.

Elena shook her head vaguely, as if she were remembering her limitations, her weariness and lack of knowledge. And Covenant covered his eyes to block out the disconcerting noiseless tumble and glitter of the falls. But then Morin stepped up onto the levee, and Elena followed him with a sigh. Gripping the gunwales with both hands, Covenant climbed out of the craft. When Bannor joined them, the High Lord's party was complete.

Amok regarded them soberly. He seemed to have aged during the boat ride. The cheeriness had faded from his face, leaving his ancient bones uncontradicted. His lips moved as if he wished to speak. But he said nothing. Like a man looking for support, he gazed briefly at each of his companions. Then he turned away, went with an oddly heavy step toward the waterfall. When he reached the first wet rocks, he scrambled up them, and stepped into the plunging water.

With his legs widely braced against the weight of the falls, he looked back toward his companions. "Do not fear," he said through the silent torrent. "This is merely water as you have known it. Earthroot's potency springs from another source. Come." With a beckoning gesture, he disappeared under the falls.

At this, Elena stiffened. The nearness of the Seventh Ward filled her face. Discarding her fatigue, she hastened behind Morin toward the waterfall.

Covenant followed her. Wracked, weary, full of uncomprehending dread, he nevertheless could not hang back now. As Elena pushed through the cascade and passed out of sight, he thrust himself up the wet jumble of rocks, began to crouch toward the falls. Spray dashed into his face. The rocks were too slick for him; he was forced to crawl. But he kept moving to evade Bannor's help. Holding his breath, he burrowed into the water as if it were an avalanche.

It almost flattened him; it pounded him like the accumulated weight of his delusion. But as he propped himself up against it—as the falls drenched him, filled his eyes and mouth and ears—he felt some of its vitality. It attacked him like an involuntary ablution, a cleansing performed as the last prerequisite of the Power of Command. It scrubbed at him as if it meant to peel his bones. But the water force missed his face and chest. It laid bare all his nerves, but failed to purify the marrow of his unfitness. A moment later, he crawled raw and untransmogrified into the darkness beyond the waterfall.

Quivering, he shook his head, blew the water out of his mouth and nose. His hands told him that he was on flat stone, but it felt strange, both dry and slippery. It resisted solid contact with his palms. And he could see nothing, hear no scuffles or whispers from his companions. But his sense of smell reacted violently. He found himself in an air so laden with force that it submerged every other odor of his life. It swamped him like the stink of gangrene, burned him like the reek of brimstone, but it bore no resemblance to these or any other smells he knew. It was like the polished, massive expanse of Earthroot—like the immensity of the rocklit cavern—like the continual, adumbrated weight of the waterfall—like the echoes—like the deathless stability of *Melenkurion* Skyweir. It reduced his restless consciousness to the scale of mere brief flesh.

It was the smell of Earthpower.

He could not stand it. He was on his knees before it, with his forehead pressed against the cold stone and his hands clasped over the back of his neck.

Then he heard a low, flaring noise as Elena lit the Staff of Law. Slowly, he raised his head. The sting of the air filled his eyes with tears, but he blinked at them, and looked about him.

He was in a tunnel which ran straight and lightless away from the falls. Down its center—out of the distance and into the falls—flowed a small stream less than a yard wide. Even in the Staff's blue light, the fluid of this stream was as red as fresh blood. This was the source of the smell—the source of Earthroot's dangerous potency. He could see its concentrated might.

He pushed to his feet, scrambled toward the tunnel wall; he wanted to get as far as possible from the stream. His boots slipped on the black stone floor as if it were glazed with ice. He had to struggle to keep his balance. But he reached the wall, pressed himself against it. Then he looked toward Elena.

She was gazing as if with bated breath down the tunnel. A rapt, exultant expression filled her face, and she seemed taller, elevated in stature by her grasp on the Staff of Law—as if the Staff's flame fed a fire within her, a blaze like a vision of victory. She looked like a priestess, an enactor of hallowed and effective rites, approaching the occult ground of her strength. The very gaps of her elsewhere gaze were crowded with exalted and savage possibilities. They made Covenant forget the uncomfortable power of the air, forget the tears which ran from his eyes like weeping, and step forward to warn her.

At once, he lost his footing, barely managed to avoid a fall. Before he could try again, he heard Amok say, "Come. The end is at hand." The youth's speech sounded as spectral as an invocation of the dead, and High Lord Elena started down the tunnel in answer to his summons. Quickly Covenant looked around, found Bannor behind him. He caught hold of Bannor's arm as if he meant to demand, Stop her! Don't you see what she's going to do? But he could not say it; he had made a bargain. Instead, he thrust away, tried to hurry after Elena.

He could find no purchase for his feet. His boots skidded off the stone; he seemed to have lost his sense of balance. But he scrabbled grimly onward. With an intense effort of will, he relaxed the force of his strides, pushed less sharply against the ground. As a result, he gained some control over his movements, contrived to keep pace with the High Lord.

But he could not catch her. And he could not watch where she was going; his steps required too much concentration. He did not look up until the assailing odor took a leap which almost reduced him to his knees again. Tears flooded his eyes so heavily that they felt irretrievably blurred, bereft of focus. But the smell told him that he had reached the spring of the red stream.

Through his tears, he could see Elena's flame guttering.

He squeezed the water out of his eyes, gained a moment in which to make out his surroundings. He stood behind Elena in a wider cave at the tunnel's end. Before him, set into the black stone end-wall like an exposed lode-facet, was a rough, sloping plane of wet rock. This whole plane shimmered; its emanations distorted his ineffectual vision, gave him the impression that he was staring at a mirage, a wavering in the solid stuff of existence. It confronted him like a porous membrane in the foundation of time and space. From top to bottom, it bled moisture which dripped down the slope, collected in a rude trough, and flowed away along the center of the tunnel.

"Behold," Amok said quietly. "Behold the Blood of the Earth. Here I fulfill the purpose of my creation. I am the Seventh Ward of High Lord Kevin's Lore. The power to which I am the way and the door is here."

As he spoke, his voice deepened and emptied, grew older. The weary burden of his years bent his shoulders. When he continued, he seemed conscious of a need for haste, a need to speak before his old immunity to time ran out.

"High Lord, attend. The air of this place unbinds me. I must complete my purpose now."

"Then speak, Amok," she replied. "I hear you."

"Ah, hear," said Amok in a sad, musing tone, as if her answer had dropped him into a reverie. "Where is the good of hearing, if it is not done wisely?" Then he recollected himself. In a stronger voice, he said, "But hear, then, for good or ill. I fulfill the law of my creation. My maker can require no more of me.

"High Lord, behold the Blood of the Earth. This is the passionate and essential ichor of the mountain rock—the Earthpower which raises and holds peaks high. It bleeds here—perhaps because the great weight of *Melenkurion* Skyweir squeezes it from the dense rock—or perhaps because the mountain is willing to lay bare its heart's-blood for those who need and can find it. Whatever the cause, its result remains. Any soul who drinks of the EarthBlood gains the Power of Command."

He met her intense gaze, and went on, "This Power is rare and potent—and full of hazard. Once it has been taken in from the Blood, it must be used swiftly —lest its strength destroy the drinker. And none can endure more than a single draft—no mortal thew and bone can endure more than a single swallow of the Blood. It is too rare a fluid for any cup of flesh to hold.

"Yet such hazards do not explain why High Lord Kevin himself did not essay the Power of Command. For this Power is the power to achieve any desired act—to issue any command to the stone and soil and grass and wood and water and flesh of life, and see that command fulfilled. If any drinker were to say to *Melenkurion* Skyweir, 'Crumble and fall,' the great peaks would instantly obey. If any drinker were to say to the Fire-Lions of Mount Thunder, 'Leave your bare slopes, attack and lay waste Ridjeck Thome,' they would at once strive with all their strength to obey. This Power can achieve anything which lies within the scope of the commanded. Yet High Lord Kevin did not avail himself of it.

"I do not know all the purposes which guided his heart when he chose to leave the EarthBlood untasted. But I must explain if I can the deeper hazards of the Power of Command."

Amok spoke in a tone of deepening, spectral hollowness, and Covenant listened desperately, as if he were clinging with raw, bruised fingers to the precipice of Amok's words. Hot things hammered in his veins, and tears like rivulets of fire ran unstanchably down his sweating cheeks. He felt that he was suffocating on the smell of EarthBlood. His ring itched horribly. He could not keep his balance; his footing constantly oozed from under him. Yet his perceptions went beyond all this. His flooded senses stretched as if they were at last thrusting their heads above water. As Amok spoke of deeper hazards, Covenant became aware of a new implication in the cave.

Through the brunt of the Blood, he began to smell something wrong, something ill. It crept insidiously across the whelming odor like an oblique defiance which seemed to succeed in spite of the immense force which it opposed, undercut, betrayed. But he could not locate its source. Either the Power of Command itself was in some way false, or the wrong was elsewhere, making itself apparent slowly through the dense air. He could not tell which.

No one else appeared to notice the subtle reek of ill. After a short, tired pause, Amok continued his explication.

"The first of these hazards—first, but perhaps not foremost—is the one great limit of the Power. It holds no sway over anything which is not a natural part of the Earth's creation. Thus it is not possible to Command the Despiser to cease his warring. It is not possible to Command his death. He lived before the arch of Time was forged—the Power cannot compel him.

"This alone might have given Kevin pause. Perhaps he did not drink of the Blood because he could not

conceive how to levy any Command against the Despiser. But there is another and subtler hazard. Here
any soul with the courage to drink may give a Command—but there are few who can foresee the outcome of what they have enacted. When such
immeasurable force is unleashed upon the Earth, any
accomplishment may recoil upon its accomplisher. If
a drinker were to Command the destruction of the
Illearth Stone, perhaps the Stone's evil would survive
uncontained to blight the whole Land. Here the
drinker who is not also a prophet risks self-betrayal.
Here are possibilities of Desecration which even High
Lord Kevin in his despair left slumbering and untouched."

The stench of wrong grew in Covenant's nostrils,
but still he could not identify it. And he could not
concentrate on it; he had a question which he fevered
to ask Amok. But the tenebrous atmosphere clogged
his throat, stifled him.

While Covenant struggled for breath, something
happened to Amok. During his speech, his tone had
become older and more cadaverous. And now, in the
pause after his last sentence, he suddenly lurched as
if some taut cord within him snapped. He staggered a
step toward the trough of Blood. A moment passed
before he could straighten his stance, raise his head
again.

A look of fear or pain or grief widened his eyes,
and around them lines of age spread visibly, as if his
skin were being crumpled. The soft flesh of his cheeks
eroded; gray ran through his hair. Like a dry sponge,
he soaked up his natural measure of years. When
he spoke again, his voice was weak and empty. "I
can say no more. My time is ended. Farewell, High
Lord. Do not fail the Land."

Convulsively, Covenant gasped out his question.
"What about the white gold?"

Amok answered across a great gulf of age, "White
gold exists beyond the arch of Time. It cannot be
Commanded."

Another inward snapping shook him; he jerked
closer to the trough.

"Help him!" croaked Covenant. But Elena only raised the Staff of Law in a mute, fiery salute.

With an age-palsied exertion, Amok thrust himself erect. Tears ran through the wrinkled lattice of his cheeks as he lifted his face toward the roof of the cave, and cried in a stricken voice, "Ah, Kevin! Life is sweet, and I have lived so short a time! Must I pass away?"

A third snapping shuddered him like an answer to his appeal. He stumbled as if his bones were falling apart, and tumbled into the trough. In one swift instant, the Blood dissolved his flesh, and he was gone.

Covenant groaned helplessly, "Amok!" Through the blur of his own ineffectual tears, he gaped at the red, flowing rill of EarthBlood. Imbalance poured into him from the stone, mounted in his muscles like vertigo. He lost all sense of where he was. To steady himself, he reached out to grasp Elena's shoulder.

Her shoulder was so hard and intense, so full of rigid purpose, that it felt like naked bone under the fabric of her robe. She was poised on the verge of her own climax; her passion was tangible to his touch.

It appalled him. Despite the dizziness which unanchored his mind, he located the source of the nameless reek of wrong.

The ill was in Elena, in the High Lord herself.

She seemed unconscious of it. In a tone of barely controlled excitement, she said, "Amok is gone—his purpose is accomplished. Now there must be no more delay. For the sake of all the Earth, I must drink and Command." To Covenant's ears, she sounded rife with hungry conclusions—so packed with needs and duties and intents that she was about to shatter.

The realization caught him like a damp hand on the back of his neck, forced him inwardly to his knees. When she stepped out of his grasp, moved toward the trough of Blood, he felt that she had torn away his last defense. Elena! he wailed silently, Elena! His cries were cries of abjection.

For a moment, he knelt within himself as if he were in the grip of a vision. Dizzily, he saw all the manifest ways in which he was responsible for Elena—all the ways in which he had caused her to be who and what and where she was. His duplicity was the cause—his violence, his futility, his need. And he remembered the apocalypse hidden in her gaze. That was the ill. It made him shudder in anguish. He watched her through his blur of tears. When he saw her bend toward the trough, all of him leaped up in defiance of the slick rock, and he cried out hoarsely, "Elena! Don't! Don't do it!"

The High Lord stopped. But she did not turn. The whole rigor of her back condensed into one question: *Why?*

"Don't you see it?" he gasped. "This is all some plot of Foul's. We're being manipulated—*you're* being manipulated. Something terrible is going to happen."

For a time, she remained silent while he ached. Then, in a tone of austere conviction, she said, "I cannot let pass this chance to serve the Land. I am forewarned. If this is Fangthane's best ploy to defeat us, it is also our best means to strike at him. I do not fear to measure my will against his. And I hold the Staff of Law. Have you not learned that the Staff is unsuited to his hands? He would not have delivered it to us if it were in any way adept for his uses. No. The Staff warrants me. Lord Foul cannot contrive my vision."

"Your vision!" Covenant extended his hands in pleading toward her. "Don't you see what that is? Don't you see where that comes from? It comes from me—from that unholy bargain I made with the Ranyhyn. A bargain that failed, Elena!"

"Yet it would appear that you bargained better than you knew. The Ranyhyn kept their promise—they gave in return more than you could either foresee or control." Her answer seemed to block his throat, and into his silence she said, "What has altered you, Unbeliever? Without your help, we would not have gained this place. On Rivenrock you gave aid without stint or price, though my own anger imperiled you. Yet now you delay me. Thomas Covenant, you are not so craven."

"Craven? Hellfire! I'm a bloody coward!" Some of

his rage returned to him, and he sputtered through the sweat and tears that ran into his mouth, "All lepers are cowards. We have to be!"

At last, she turned toward him, faced him with the focus, the blazing holocaust, of her gaze. Its force ripped his balance away from him, and he sprawled in fragments on the stone. But he pushed himself up again. Driven by his fear of her and for her, he dared to confront her power. He stood tenuously, and abandoned himself, took his plunge.

"Manipulation, Elena," he rasped. "I'm talking about manipulation. Do you understand what that means? It means using people. Twisting them to suit purposes they haven't chosen for themselves. Manipulation. Not Foul's—mine! I've been manipulating you, using you. I told you I'd made another bargain—but I didn't tell you what it is. I've been using—using you to get myself off the hook. I promised myself that I would do everything I could to help you find this Ward. And in return I promised myself that I would do everything I could to make you take my responsibility. I watched you and helped you so that when you got here you would look exactly like that—so you would challenge Foul yourself without stopping to think about what you're doing—so that whatever happens to the Land would be your fault instead of mine. So that I could escape! Hell and blood, Elena! Do you hear me? Foul is going to get us for sure!"

She seemed to hear only part of what he said. She bent her searing focus straight into him, and said, "Was there ever a time when you loved me?"

In an agony of protest, he half screamed, "Of course I loved you!" Then he mastered himself, put all his strength back into his appeal. "It never even occurred to me that I might be able to use you until —until after the landslide. When I began to understand what you're capable of. I loved you before that. I love you now. I'm just an unconscionable bastard, and I used you, that's all. Now I regret it." With all the resources of his voice, he beseeched her, "Elena, please don't drink that stuff. Forget the Power of

Command and go back to Revelstone. Let the Council decide what to do about all this."

But the way in which her gaze left his face and burned around the walls of the cave told him that he had not reached her. When she spoke, she only confirmed his failure.

"I would be unworthy of Lordship if I failed to act now. Amok offered us the Seventh Ward because he perceived that the Land's urgent need surpassed the conditions of his creation. Fangthane is upon the Land now—he wages war now—Land and life and all are endangered now. While any power or weapon lies within my grasp, I will not permit him!" Her voice softened as she added, "And if you have loved me, how can I fail to strive for your escape? You need not have bargained in secret. I love you. I wish to serve you. Your regret only strengthens what I must do."

Swinging back toward the trough, she raised the Staff's guttering flame high over her head, and shouted like a war cry, *"Melenkurion abatha! Ward yourself well, Fangthane! I seek to destroy you!"*

Then she stooped to the EarthBlood.

Covenant struggled frantically in her direction, but his feet scattered out from under him again, and he went down with a crash like a shock of incapacity. As she lowered her face to the trough, he shouted, "That's not a good answer! What happens to the Oath of Peace?"

But his cry did not penetrate her exaltation. Without hesitation, she took one steady sip of the Blood, and swallowed it.

At once, she leaped to her feet, stood erect and rigid as if she were possessed. She appeared to swell, expand like a distended icon. The fire of the Staff ran down the wood to her hands. Instantly, her whole form burst into flame.

"Elena!" Covenant crawled toward her. But the might of her blue, crackling blaze threw him back like a hard wind. He struck the tears from his eyes to see her more clearly. Within her enveloping fire, she was unharmed and savage.

While the flame burned about her, enfolded her from head to foot in fiery cerements, she raised her arms, lifted her face. For one fierce moment she stood motionless, trapped in conflagration. Then she spoke as if she were uttering words of flame.

"Come! I have tasted the EarthBlood! You must obey my will. The walls of death do not prevail. Kevin son of Loric! Come!"

No! howled Covenant, No! Don't! But even his inner cry was swamped by a great voice which shivered and groaned in the air so hugely that he seemed to hear it, not with his ears, but with the whole surface of his body.

"Fool! Desist!" Staggering waves of anguish poured from the voice. "Do not do this!"

"Kevin, hear me!" Elena shouted back in a transported tone. "You cannot refuse! The Blood of the Earth compels you. I have chosen you to meet my Command. Kevin, come!"

The great voice repeated, "Fool! You know not what you do!"

But an instant later, the ambience of the cave changed violently, as if a tomb had opened into it. Breakers of agony rolled through the air. Covenant winced at every surge. He braced himself where he knelt, and looked up.

The specter of Kevin Landwaster stood outlined in pale light before Elena.

He dwarfed her—dwarfed the cave itself. Monumentally upright and desolate, he was visible through the stone rather than within the cave. He towered over Elena as if he were part of the very mountain rock. He had a mouth like a cut, eyes full of the effects of Desecration, and on his forehead was a bandage which seemed to cover some mortal wound. "Release me!" he groaned. "I have done harm enough for one soul."

"Then serve me!" she cried ecstatically up to him. "I offer you a Command to redeem that harm. You are Kevin son of Loric, the waster of the Land. You have known despair to its dregs—you have tasted the full cup of gall. That is knowledge and strength which no one living can equal.

"High Lord Kevin, I Command you to battle and defeat Lord Foul the Despiser! Destroy Fangthane! By the Power of the EarthBlood, I Command you."

The specter stared aghast at her, and raised his fists as if he meant to strike her. "Fool!" he repeated terribly.

The next instant, a concussion like the slamming of a crypt shook the cave. One last pulse of anguish pummeled the High Lord's party; Elena's flame was blown out like a weak candle; darkness flooded the cave.

Then Kevin was gone.

A long time passed. When Covenant regained consciousness, he rested wearily for a while on his hands and knees, glad of the darkness, and the reduced scale of the cave, and the specter's absence. But eventually he remembered Elena. Pushing himself to his feet, he reached toward her with his voice. "Elena? Come on. Elena? Let's get out of here."

At first, he received no response. Then blue fire flared as Elena lit the Staff. She was sitting like a wreck on the floor. When she turned her wan, spent face toward him, he saw that her crisis was over. All her exaltation had been consumed by the act of Command. He went to her, helped her gently to her feet. "Come on," he said again. "Let's go."

She shook her head vaguely, and said in an exhausted voice, "He called me a fool. What have I done?"

"I hope we never find out." A rough edge of sympathy made him sound harsh. He wanted to care for her, and did not know how. To give her time and privacy to gather her strength, he stepped away. As he glanced dully around the cave, he noticed Bannor, noticed the faint look of surprise in Bannor's face. Something in that unfamiliar expression gave Covenant a twist of apprehension. It seemed to be directed at him. He probed for an explanation by asking, "That was Kevin, wasn't it?"

Bannor nodded; the speculative surprise remained on his face.

"Well, at least it wasn't that beggar— At least now we know it wasn't Kevin who picked me for this."

Still Bannor's gaze did not change. It made Covenant feel uncomfortably exposed, as if there were something indecent about himself that he did not realize.

Confused, he turned back to the High Lord.

Suddenly, a silent blast like a howl of stone jolted the cave, made it tremble and jump like an earthquake. Covenant and Elena lost their footing, slapped against the floor. Morin's warning shout echoed flatly:

"Kevin returns!"

Then the buried tomb of the air opened again; Kevin's presence resonated against Covenant's skin. But this time the specter brought with him a ghastly reek of rotten flesh and attar, and in the background of his presence was the deep rumble of rock being crushed. When Covenant raised his head from the bucking floor, he saw Kevin within the stone— furiously poised, fists cocked. Hot green filled the orbs of his eyes, sent rank steam curling up his forehead; and he dripped with emerald light as if he had just struggled out of a quagmire.

"Fool!" he cried in a paroxysm of anguish. "Damned betrayer! You have broken the Law of Death to summon me—you have unleashed measureless opportunities for evil upon the Earth—and the Despiser mastered me as easily as if I were a child! The Illearth Stone consumes me. Fight, fool! I am Commanded to destroy you!"

Roaring like a multitude of fiends, he reached down and clutched at Elena.

She did not move. She was aghast, frozen by the result of her great dare.

But Morin reacted instantly. Crying, "Kevin! Hold!" he sprang to her aid.

The specter seemed to hear Morin—hear and recognize who he was. An old memory touched Kevin, and he hesitated. That hesitation gave Morin time to reach Elena, thrust her behind him. When Kevin threw off his uncertainty, his fingers closed around Morin instead of the High Lord.

He gripped the Bloodguard and heaved him into the air.

Kevin's arm passed easily through the rock, but Morin could not. He crashed against the ceiling with tremendous force. The impact tore him from Kevin's grasp. But that impact was sufficient. The First Mark fell dead like a broken twig.

The sight roused Elena. At once, she realized her danger. She whirled the Staff swiftly about her head. Its flame sprang into brilliance, and a hot blue bolt lashed straight at Kevin.

The blast struck him like a physical blow, drove him back a step through the stone. But he shrugged off its effects. With a deep snarl of pain, he moved forward, snatched at her again.

Shouting frantically, *"Melenkurion abatha!"* she met his attack with the Staff. Its fiery heel seared his palm.

Again he recoiled, gripping his scorched fingers and groaning.

In that momentary reprieve, she cried strange invocations to the Staff, and swung its blaze around her three times, surrounding herself with a shield of power. When the specter grabbed for her once more, he could not gain a hold on her. He squeezed her shield, and his fingers dripped with emerald ill, but he could not touch her. Whenever he dented her defense, she healed it with the Staff's might.

Yelling in frustration and pain, he changed his tactics. He reared back, clasped his fists together, and hammered them at the floor of the cave. The stone jumped fiercely. The lurch knocked Covenant down, threw Bannor against the opposite wall.

A gasping shudder like a convulsion of torment shot through the mountain. The cave walls heaved; rumblings of broken stone filled the air; power blared.

A crack appeared in the floor directly under Elena. Even before she was aware of it, it started to open. Then, like ravenous jaws, it jerked wide.

High Lord Elena dropped into the chasm.

Kevin pounced after her, and vanished from sight.

His howls echoed out of the cleft like the shrieking of a madman.

But even as they disappeared, their battle went on. Lords-fire spouted hotly up into the cave. The thunder of tortured stone pounded along the tunnel, and the cave pitched from side to side like a nausea in the guts of *Melenkurion* Skyweir. In his horror, Covenant thought that the whole edifice of the mountain was about to tumble.

Then he was snatched to his feet, hauled erect by Bannor. The Bloodguard gripped him with compelling fingers, and shouted at him through the tumult, "Save her!"

"I can't!" The pain of his reply made him yell. Bannor's demand rubbed so much salt into the wound of his essential futility that he could hardly bear it. "I cannot!"

"You must!" Bannor's grasp allowed no alternatives.

"How?" Waving his empty hands in Bannor's face, he cried, "With these?"

"Yes!" The Bloodguard caught Covenant's left hand, forced him to look at it.

On his wedding finger, his ring throbbed ferally, pulsed with power and light like a potent instrument panting to be used.

For an instant, he gaped at the argent band as if it had betrayed him. Then forgetting escape, forgetting himself, forgetting even that he did not know how to exert wild magic, he pulled despairingly away from Bannor and stumbled toward the crevice. Like a man battering himself in armless impotence against a blank doom, he leaped after the High Lord.

TWENTY-SIX: Gallows Howe

BUT he failed before he began. He did not know how to brace himself for the kind of battle which raged below him. As he passed the rim of the crevice, he was hit by a blast of force like an eruption from within the rift. He was defenseless against it; it snuffed out his consciousness like a frail flame.

Then for a time he rolled in darkness—ran in a blind, caterwauling void which pitched and broke over him until he staggered like a ship with sprung timbers. He was aware of nothing but the force which thrashed him. But something caught his hand, anchored him. At first he thought that the grip on his hand was Elena's—that she held him now as she had held him and kept him during the night after his summoning. But when he shook clear of the darkness, he saw Bannor. The Bloodguard was pulling him out of the crevice.

That sight—that perception of his failure—undid him. When Bannor set him on his feet, he stood listing amid the riot of battle—detonations, deep, groaning creaks of tormented stone, loud rockfalls—like an empty hulk, a cargoless hull sucking in death through a wound below its waterline. He did not resist or question as Bannor half carried him from the cave of the EarthBlood.

The tunnel was unlit except by the reflected glares of combat, but Bannor moved surely over the black rock. In moments, he brought his shambling charge to the waterfall. There he lifted the Unbeliever in his arms, and bore him like a child through the weight of the falls.

In the rocklight of Earthroot, Bannor moved even

501

more urgently. He hastened to the waiting boat, installed Covenant on one of the seats, then leaped aboard as he shoved out into the burnished lake. Without hesitation, he began to recite something in the native tongue of the *Haruchai*. Smoothly, the boat made its way among the cloistral columns.

But his efforts did not carry the craft far. Within a few hundred yards, its prow began to tug against its intended direction. He stopped speaking, and at once the boat swung off to one side. Gradually, it gained speed.

It was in the grip of a current. Standing in the center of Covenant's sightless gaze, Bannor cocked one eyebrow slightly, as if he perceived an ordeal ahead. For long moments, he waited for the slow increase of the current to reveal its destination.

Then in the distance he saw what caused the current. Far ahead of the craft, rocklight flared along a line in the lake like a cleft which stretched out of sight on both sides. Into this cleft Earthroot rushed and poured in silent cataracts.

He reacted with smooth efficiency, as if he had been preparing for this test throughout the long centuries of his service. First he snatched a coil of *clingor* from his pack; with it, he lashed Covenant to the boat. In answer to the vague question in Covenant's face, he replied, "The battle of Kevin and the High Lord has opened a crevice in the floor of Earthroot. We must ride the water down, and seek an outlet below." He did not wait for a response. Turning, he braced his feet, gripped one of the gilt gunwales, and tore it loose. With this long, curved piece of wood balanced in his hands for a steering pole, he swung around to gauge the boat's distance from the cataract.

The hot line of the crevice was less than a hundred yards away now, and the boat slipped rapidly toward it, caught in the mounting suction. But Bannor made one more preparation. Bending toward Covenant, he said quietly, "Ur-Lord, you must use the *orcrest*." His voice echoed with authority through the silence.

Covenant stared at him without comprehension.

"You must. It is in your pocket. Bring it out."

For a moment, Covenant continued to stare. But at last the Bloodguard's command reached through his numbness. Slowly, he dug into his pocket, pulled out the smooth lucid stone. He held it awkwardly in his right hand, as if he could not properly grip it with only two fingers and a thumb.

The cataract loomed directly before the boat now, but Bannor spoke calmly, firmly. "Hold the stone in your left hand. Hold it above your head, so that it will light our way."

As Covenant placed the *orcrest* in contact with his troubled ring, a piercing silver light burst from the core of the stone. It flared along the gunwale in Bannor's hands, paled the surrounding rocklight. When Covenant numbly raised his fist, held the stone up like a torch, the Bloodguard nodded his approval. His face wore a look of satisfaction, as if all the conditions of his Vow had been fulfilled.

Then the prow of the boat dropped. Bannor and Covenant rode the torrent of Earthroot into the dark depths.

The water boiled and heaved wildly. But one end of the crevice opened into other caverns. The cataracts turned as they fell, and thrashed through the crevice as if it were an immense chute or channel. By the *orcrest* light, Bannor saw in time which way the water poured. He poled the boat so that it shot downward along the torrent.

After that, the craft hurtled down the frenetic watercourse in a long nightmare of tumult, jagged rocks, narrows, sudden, heart-stopping falls, close death. The current tumbled, thundered, raced from cavern to cavern through labyrinthian gaps and tunnels and clefts in the fathomless bowels of *Melenkurion* Skyweir. Many times the craft disappeared under the fierce roil of the rush, but each time its potent wood—wood capable of withstanding Earthroot—bore it to the surface again. And many times Bannor and Covenant foundered in cascades that crashed onto them from above, but the water did not harm them—either it had lost its strength in the fall, or it was already diluted by other buried springs and lakes.

Through it all, Covenant held his *orcrest* high. Some last unconscious capacity for endurance kept his fingers locked and his arm raised. And the stone's unfaltering fire lighted the boat's way, so that, even in the sharpest hysteria of the current, Bannor was able to steer, avoid rocks and backwaters, fend around curves—preserve himself and the Unbeliever. The torrent's violence soon splintered his pole, but he replaced it with the other gunwale. When that was gone, he used a seat board as a rudder.

Straining and undaunted, he brought the voyage through to its final crisis.

Without warning, the boat shot down a huge flow into a cavern that showed no exit. The water frothed viciously, seeking release, and the air pressure mounted, became more savage every instant. A swift eddy caught the craft, swung it around and under the massive pour of water.

Helplessly, the boat was driven down.

Bannor clawed his way to Covenant. He wrapped his legs around Covenant's waist, snatched the *orcrest* from him. Clutching the stone as if to sustain himself with it, Bannor clamped his other hand over Covenant's nose and mouth.

He held that position as the boat sank.

The plunging weight of water thrust them straight under. Pressure squeezed them until Bannor's eyes pounded in their sockets, and his ears yowled as if they were about to rupture. He could feel Covenant screaming in his grasp. But he held his grip in the extremity of the last faithfulness—clung to the bright strength of the *orcrest* with one hand, and kept Covenant from breathing with the other.

Then they were sucked into a side tunnel, an outlet. Immediately, all the pressure of the trapped air and water hurled them upward. Covenant went limp; Bannor's lungs burned. But he retained enough alertness to swing himself upright as the water burst free. In a high, arching spout, it carried the two men into the cleft of Rivenrock, and sent them shooting out into the open morning of the Black River and Garroting Deep.

For a moment, sunshine and free sky and forest

reeled around Bannor, and flares of released pressure staggered across his sight. Then the fortitude of his Vow returned. Wrapping both arms around Covenant, he gave one sharp jerk which started the Unbeliever's lungs working again.

With a violent gasp, Covenant began breathing rapidly, feverishly. Some time passed before he showed any signs of consciousness, yet all the while his ring throbbed as if it were sustaining him. Finally, he opened his eyes, and looked at Bannor.

At once, he started to struggle weakly in his *clingor* bonds. Bannor appeared to him like one of the djinn who watches over the accursed. But then he lapsed. He recognized where he was—how he had arrived there—what he had left behind. He went on staring nakedly while Bannor untied the lines which lashed him to the boat.

Over the Bloodguard's shoulder, he could see the great cliff of Rivenrock—and behind it *Melenkurion Skyweir*—shrinking as the boat scudded downriver. From the cleft, turgid black smoke broke upward in gouts sporadically emphasized by battle flashes deep within the mountain. Muffled blasts of anguish rent the gut-rock, wreaking havoc in the very grave of the ages. Covenant felt he was floating away on a wave of ravage and destruction.

Fearfully, he looked down at his ring. To his dismay, he found that it still throbbed like an exclamation of purpose. Instinctively, he clasped his right hand over it, concealed it. Then he faced forward in the boat, turned away from Bannor and Rivenrock as if to protect his shame from scrutiny.

He sat huddled there, weak and staring dismally, throughout the swift progress of the day. He did not speak to Bannor, did not help him bail out the boat, did not look back. The current spewing from Rivenrock raised the Black River to near-flood levels, and the light Earthroot craft rode the rush intrepidly between glowering walls of forest. The morning sun glittered and danced off the dark water into Covenant's eyes—but he stared at it without blinking, as if even the protective reflex of his eyelids were exhausted.

And after that, nothing interfered with his sightless vision. The sodden food which Bannor offered to him he ate automatically, with his left hand concealed between his thighs. Midday and afternoon passed unrecognized, and when evening came he remained crouched on his seat, clenching his ring against his chest as if to protect himself from some final stab of realization.

Then, as dusk thickened about him, he became aware of the music. The air of the Deep was full of humming, of voiceless song—an eldritch melody which seemed to arise like passion from the faint throats of all the leaves. It contrasted sharply with the distant, storming `climacteric of *Melenkurion* Skyweir, the song of violence which beat and shivered out of Rivenrock. Gradually, he raised his head to listen. The Deep song had an inflection of sufferance, as if it were deliberately restraining a potent melodic rage, sparing him.

In the light of the *orcrest,* he saw that Bannor was guiding the boat toward a high, treeless hill which rose against the night sky close to the south bank. The hill was desolate, bereft of life, as if its capacity to nourish even the hardiest plants had been irremediably scalded out of it. Yet it seemed to be the source of the Deep's song. The melody which wafted riverward from the hill sounded like a host of gratified furies.

He regarded the hill incuriously. He had no strength left to care about such places. All his waning sanity was focused on the sounds of battle from *Melenkurion* Skyweir—and on the grip which concealed his ring. When Bannor secured the boat, and took hold of his right elbow to help him ashore, Covenant leaned on the Bloodguard and followed his guidance woodenly.

Bannor went to the barren hill. Without question, Covenant began to struggle up it.

Despite his weariness, the hill impinged upon his awareness. He could feel its deadness with his feet as if he were shambling up a corpse. Yet it was eager death; its atmosphere was thick with the slaughter of enemies. Its incarnate hatred made his joints ache as he climbed it. He began to sweat and tremble as if he were carrying the weight of an atrocity on his shoulders.

Then, near the hilltop, Bannor stopped him. The Bloodguard lifted the *orcrest*. In its light, Covenant saw the gibbet beyond the crest of the hill. A Giant dangled from it. And between him and the gibbet—staring at him as if he were a concentrated nightmare—were people, people whom he knew.

Lord Mhoram stood there erect in his battle-grimed robe. He clasped his staff in his left hand, and his lean face was taut with vision. Behind him were Lord Callindrill and two Bloodguard. The Lord had a dark look of failure in his soft eyes. Quaan and Amorine were with him. And on Mhoram's right, supported by the Lord's right hand, was Hile Troy.

Troy had lost his sunglasses and headband. The eyeless skin of his skull was knotted as if he were straining to see. He cocked his head, moved it from side to side to focus his hearing. Covenant understood intuitively that Troy had lost his Land-born sight.

With these people was one man whom Covenant did not know. He was the singer—a tall, white-haired man with glowing silver eyes, who hummed to himself as if he were dewing the ground with melody. Covenant guessed without thinking that he was Caerroil Wildwood, the Forestal of Garroting Deep.

Something in the singer's gaze—something severe, yet oddly respectful—recalled the Unbeliever to himself. At last he perceived the fear in the faces watching him. He pushed himself away from Bannor's support, took the weight of all his burdens on his own shoulders. For a moment, he met the trepidation before him with a glare so intense that it made his forehead throb. But then, as he was about to speak, a fierce detonation from Rivenrock shook his bones, knocked him off balance. When he reached toward Bannor, he exposed the shame of his ring.

Facing Mhoram and Troy as squarely as he could, he groaned, "She's lost. I lost her." But his face twisted, and the words came brokenly between his lips, like fragments of his heart.

His utterance seemed to pale the music, making the muffled clamor from Rivenrock louder. He felt every blast of the battle like an internal blow. But the deadness under his feet became more and more vivid to him. And the gibbeted Giant hung before him with an immediacy he could not ignore. He began to realize that he was facing people who had survived ordeals of their own. He flinched, but did not fall, when their protests began—when Troy gave a strangled cry, "Lost? Lost?" and Mhoram asked in a stricken voice, "What has happened?"

Under the night sky on the lifeless hilltop—lit by the stars, and the twin gleams of Caerroil Wildwood's eyes, and the *orcrest* fire—Covenant stood braced on Bannor like a crippled witness against himself, and described in stumbling sentences High Lord Elena's plight. He made no mention of the focus of her gaze, her consuming passion. But he told all the rest—his bargain, Amok's end, the summoning of Kevin Landwaster, Elena's solitary fall. When he was done, he was answered by an aghast silence that echoed in his ears like a denunciation.

"I'm sorry," he concluded into the stillness. Forcing himself to drink the bitter dregs of his personal inefficacy, he added, "I loved her. I would have saved her if I could."

"Loved her?" Troy murmured. "Alone?" His voice was too disjointed to register the degree of his pain.

Lord Mhoram abruptly covered his eyes, bowed his head.

Quaan, Amorine, and Callindrill stood together as if they could not endure what they had heard alone.

Another blast from Rivenrock shivered the air. It snatched Mhoram's head up, and he faced Covenant with tears streaming down his cheeks. "It is as I have said," he breathed achingly. "Madness is not the only danger in dreams."

At this, Covenant's face twisted again. But he had nothing more to say; even the release of assent was denied him. However, Bannor seemed to hear something different in the Lord's tone. As if to correct an injustice, he went to Mhoram. As he moved, he took from his pack Covenant's marrowmeld sculpture.

He handed the work to Mhoram. "The High Lord gave it to him as a gift."

Lord Mhoram gripped the bone sculpture tightly, and his eyes shone with sudden comprehension. He understood the bond between Elena and the Ranyhyn; he understood what the giving of such a gift to Covenant meant. A gasp of weeping swept over his face. But when it passed, it left his self-mastery intact. His crooked lips took on their old humane angle. When he turned to Covenant again, he said gently, "It is a precious gift."

Bannor's unexpected support, and Mhoram's gesture of conciliation, touched Covenant. But he had no strength to spare for either of them. His gaze was fixed on Hile Troy.

The Warmark winced eyelessly under repeated blows of realization, and within him a gale brewed. He seemed to see Elena in his mind—remember her, taste her beauty, savor all the power of sight which she had taught him. He seemed to see her useless, solitary end. "Lost?" he panted as his fury grew. "Lost? Alone?"

All at once, he erupted. With a livid howl, he raged at Covenant, "Do you call that love?! Leper! Unbeliever!"—he spat the words as if they were the most damning curses he knew—"This is all just a game for you! Mental tricks. Excuses. You're a leper! A moral leper! You're too selfish to love anyone but yourself. You have the power for everything, and you won't use it. You just turned your back on her when she needed you. You—despicable—leper! Leper!" He shouted with such force that the muscles of his neck corded. The veins in his temples bulged and throbbed as if he were about to burst with execration.

Covenant felt the truth of the accusation. His bargain exposed him to such charges, and Troy hit the heart of his vulnerability as if some prophetic insight guided his blindness. Covenant's right hand twitched in a futile fending motion. But his left clung to his chest as if to localize his shame in that one place.

When Troy paused to gather himself for another assault, Covenant said weakly, "Unbelief has got nothing to do with it. She was my daughter."

"What?!"

"My daughter." Covenant pronounced it like an indictment. "I raped Trell's child. Elena was his granddaughter."

"Your daughter." Troy was too stunned to shout. Implications like glimpses of depravity rocked him. He groaned as if Covenant's crimes were so multitudinous that he could not hold them all in his mind at one time.

Mhoram spoke to him carefully. "My friend—this is the knowledge which I have withheld from you. The withholding gave you unintended pain. Please pardon me. The Council feared that this knowledge would cause you to abominate the Unbeliever."

"Damn right," Troy panted. "Damn right."

Suddenly, his accumulated passion burst into action. Guided by a sure instinct, he reached out swiftly, snatched away Lord Mhoram's staff. He spun once to gain momentum, and leveled a crushing blow with the staff at Covenant's head.

The unexpectedness of the attack surpassed even Bannor. But he recovered, sprang after Troy, jolted him enough to unbalance his swing. As a result, only the heel of the staff clipped Covenant's forehead. But that sent him tumbling backward down the hill.

He caught himself, got to his knees. When he raised a hand to his head, he found that he was bleeding profusely from a wound in the center of his forehead.

He could feel old hate and death seeping into him from the blasted earth. Blood ran down his cheeks like spittle.

The next moment, Mhoram and Quaan reached Troy. Mhoram tore the staff from his grasp; Quaan pinned his arms. "Fool!" the Lord rasped. "You forget the Oath of Peace. Loyalty is due!"

Troy struggled against Quaan. Rage and anguish mottled his face. "I haven't sworn any Oath! Let go of me!"

"You are the Warmark of the Warward," said Mhoram dangerously. "The Oath of Peace binds. But if you cannot refrain from murder for that reason, refrain because the Despiser's army is destroyed. Fleshharrower hangs dead on the gibbet of Gallows Howe."

"Do you call that victory? We've been decimated! What good is a victory that costs so much?" Troy's fury rose like weeping. "It would have been better if we'd lost! Then it wouldn't have been such a waste!" The passion in his throat made him gasp for air as if he were asphyxiating on the reek of Covenant's perfidy.

But Lord Mhoram was unmoved. He caught Troy by the breastplate and shook him. "Then refrain because the High Lord is not dead."

"Not?" Troy panted. "Not dead?"

"We hear her battle even now. Do you not comprehend the sound? Even as we listen, she struggles against dead Kevin. The Staff sustains her—and he has not the might she believed of him. But the proof of her endurance is here, in the Unbeliever himself. She is his summoner—he will remain in the Land until her death. So it was when Drool Rockworm first called him."

"She's still fighting?" Troy gaped at the idea. He seemed to regard it as the conclusive evidence of Covenant's treachery. But then he turned to Mhoram and cried, "We've got to help her!"

At this, Mhoram flinched. A wave of pain broke through his face. In a constricted voice, he asked, "How?"

"How?" Troy fumed. "Don't ask me how. *You're* the Lord! We have got to help her!"

The Lord pulled himself erect, clenched his staff for support. "We are fifty leagues from Rivenrock. A night and a day would pass before any Ranyhyn could carry us to the foot of the cliff. Then Bannor would be required to guide us into the mountain in search of the battle. Perhaps the effects of the battle have destroyed all approaches to it. Perhaps they would destroy us. Yet if we gained the High Lord, we would have nothing to offer her but the frail strength of two Lords. With the Staff of Law, she far surpasses us. How can we help her?"

They faced each other as if they met mind to mind across Troy's eyelessness. Mhoram did not falter under the Warmark's rage. The hurt of his inadequacy showed clearly in his face, but he neither denied nor cursed at his weakness.

Though Troy trembled with urgency, he had to take his demand elsewhere.

He swung toward Covenant. "You!" he shouted stridently. "If you're too much of a coward to do anything yourself, at least give me a chance to help her! Give me your ring!—I can feel it from here. Give it to me! Come on, you bastard. It's her only chance."

Kneeling on the dead, sabulous dirt of the Howe, Covenant looked up at Troy through the blood in his eyes. For a time, he was unable to answer. Troy's adjuration seemed to drop on him like a rockfall. It swept away his last defense, and left bare his final shame. He should have been able to save Elena. He had the power; it pulsed like a wound on his wedding finger. But he had not used it. Ignorance was no excuse. His claim of futility no longer covered him.

The barren atmosphere of the Howe ached in his chest as he climbed to his feet. Though he could hardly see where he was going, he started up the hill. The exertion made his head hurt as if there were splinters of bone jabbing his brain, and his heart quivered. A silent voice cried out to him, No! No! But he ignored it. With his halfhand, he fumbled at the ring. It seemed to resist him—he had trouble gripping it— but as he reached Troy he finally tore it from his finger. In a wet voice, as if his mouth were full of blood, he said, "Take it. Save her." He put the band in Troy's hand.

The touch of the pulsing ring exalted Troy. Clenching his fingers around it, he turned, ran fearlessly to the hillcrest. He searched quickly with his ears, located the direction of Rivenrock, faced the battle. Like a titan, he swung his fist at the heavens; power flamed from the white gold as if it were answering his passion. In a livid voice, he cried, "Elena! Elena!"

Then the tall white singer was at his side. The music took on a forbidding note that spread involuntary stasis like a mist over the hilltop. Everyone froze, lost the power of movement.

In the stillness, Caerroil Wildwood lifted his gnarled scepter. "No," he trilled, "I cannot permit this. It is a breaking of Law. And you forget the price that is owed to me. Perhaps when you have gained an incondign mastery over the wild magic, you will use it to recant the price." With his scepter, he touched Troy's upraised fist; the ring dropped to the ground. As it fell, all the heat and surge of its power faded. It looked like mere metal as it struck the lifeless earth, rolled lightly along the music, and stopped near Covenant's feet.

"I will not permit it," the singer continued. "The promise is irrevocable. In the names of the One Tree and the One Forest—in the name of the unforgiving Deep—I claim the price of my aid." With a solemn gesture like the sound of distant horns, he touched his scepter to Troy's head. "Eyeless one, you have promised payment. I claim your life."

Lord Mhoram strove to protest. But the singer's stasis held him. He could do nothing but watch as Troy began to change.

"I claim you to be my disciple," the singer hummed. "You shall be Caer-Caveral, my help and hold. From me you shall learn the work of a Forestal, root and branch, seed and sap and leaf and all. Together we will walk the Deep, and I will teach you the songs of the trees, and the names of all the old, brave, wakeful woods, and the ancient forestry of thought and mood. While trees remain, we will steward together, cherishing each new sprout, and wreaking wood's revenge on each hated human intrusion. Forget your foolish friend. You cannot succor her. Caer-Caveral, remain and serve!"

The song molded Troy's form. Slowly, his legs grew together. His feet began to send roots into the soil. His apparel turned to thick dark moss. He became an old

stump with one last limb upraised. From his fist green
leaves uncurled.

Softly, the singer concluded, "Together we will restore life to Gallows Howe." Then he turned toward
the Lords and Covenant. The silver brilliance of his
eyes increased, dimming even the *orcrest* fire; and he
sang in a tone of dewy freshness:

> Ax and fire leave me dead.
>   I know the hate of hands grown bold.
> Depart to save your heart-sap's red:
>   My hate knows neither rest nor weal.

As the words fluted through them, he disappeared into
the music as if he had wrapped it about him and
passed beyond the range of sight. But the warning melody lingered behind him like an echo in the air, repeating his command and repeating it until it could not
be forgotten.

Gradually, like figures lumbering stiffly out of a
dream, the people on the hilltop began to move again.
Quaan and Amorine hastened to the mossy stump.
Grief filled their faces. But they had endured too
much, struggled too hard, in their long ordeal. They
had no strength left for horror or protest. Amorine
stared as if she could not comprehend what had happened, and tears glistened in Quaan's old eyes. He
called, "Hail, Warmark!" But his voice sounded weak
and dim on the Howe, and he said no more.

Behind them, Lord Mhoram sagged. His hands
trembled as he held up his staff in mute farewell. Lord
Callindrill joined him, and they stood together as if
they were leaning on each other.

Covenant dropped numbly to his knees to pick up
his ring.

He reached for it like an acolyte bending his forehead to the ground, and when his fingers closed on it,
he slid it into place on his wedding finger. Then, with
both hands, he tried to wipe the blood out of his eyes.

But as he made the attempt, a blast from Rivenrock

staggered the air. The mountain groaned as if it were grievously wounded. The concussion threw him on his face in the dirt. Blackness filled the remains of his sight as if it were flooding into him from the barren Howe. And behind it he heard the blast howling like the livid triumph of fiends.

A long tremor passed through the Deep, and after it came an extended shattering sound, as if the whole cliff of Rivenrock were crumbling. People moved; voices called back and forth. But Covenant could not hear them clearly. His ears were deluged by tumult, a yammering, multitudinous yell of glee. And the sound came closer. It became louder and more immediate until it overwhelmed his eardrums, passed beyond the range of physical perception and shrieked directly into his brain.

After that, voices reached him obscurely, registered somehow through his overdriven hearing.

Bannor said, "Rivenrock bursts. There will be a great flood."

Lord Callindrill said, "Some good will come of it. It will do much to cleanse the Wightwarrens under Mount Thunder."

Lord Mhoram said, "Behold—the Unbeliever departs. The High Lord has fallen."

But these things surpassed him; he could not hold onto them. The black dirt of Gallows Howe loomed in his face like an incarnation of midnight. And around it, encompassing it, consuming both it and him, the fiendish scream scaled upward, filling his skull and chest and limbs as if it were grinding his very bones to powder. The howl overcame him, and he answered with a cry that made no sound.

TWENTY-SEVEN: Leper

THE shriek climbed, became louder as it grew more urgent and damaging. He could feel it breaking down the barriers of his comprehension, altering the terrain of his existence. Finally he seemed to shatter against it; he fell against it from a great height, so that he broke on its remorseless surface. He jerked at the force of the impact. When he lay still again, he could feel the hardness pressing coldly against his face and chest.

Gradually he realized that the surface was damp, sticky. It smelled like clotting blood.

That perception carried him across a frontier. He found that he could distinguish between the flat, bitter, insulting shriek outside and the ragged hurt inside his head. With an agonizing effort, he moved one hand to rub the caked blood out of his eyes. Then, tortuously, he opened them.

His vision swam into focus like a badly smeared lens, but after a while he began to make out pieces of where he was. There was plenty of soulless yellow light. The legs of the sofa stood a few feet away across the thick defensive carpet. He was lying prostrate on the floor beside the coffee table as if he had fallen off a catafalque. With his left hand, he clutched something hard to his ear, something that shrieked brutally.

When he shifted his hand, he discovered that he was holding the receiver of the telephone. From it came the shriek—the piercing wail of a phone left off its hook. The phone itself lay on the floor just out of reach.

A long, dumb moment passed before he regained

enough of himself to wonder how long ago Joan had hung up on him.

Groaning, he rolled to one side and looked up at a wall clock. He could not read it; his eyes were still too blurred. But through one window he could see the first light of an uncomfortable dawn. He had been unconscious for half the night.

He started to his feet, then slumped down again while pain rang in his head. He feared that he would lose consciousness once more. But after a while, the noise cleared, faded into the general scream of the phone. He was able to get to his knees.

He rested there, looking about him at the controlled orderliness of his living room. Joan's picture and his cup of coffee stood just where he had left them on the table. The jolt of his head on the table edge had not even spilled the coffee.

The sanctuary of the familiar place gave him no consolation. When he tried to concentrate on the room's premeditated neatness, his gaze kept sliding back to the blood—dry, almost black—which crusted the carpet. That stain violated his safety like a chancre. To get away from it, he gripped himself and climbed to his feet.

The room reeled as if he had fallen into vertigo, but he steadied himself on the padded arm of the sofa, and after a moment he regained most of his balance. Carefully, as if he were afraid of disturbing a demon, he placed the receiver back on its hook, then sighed deeply as the shriek was chopped out of the air. Its echo continued to ring in his left ear. It disturbed his equilibrium, but he ignored it as best he could. He began to move through the house like a blind man, working his way from support to support—sofa to doorframe to kitchen counter. Then he had to take several unbraced steps to reach the bathroom, but he managed to cross the distance without falling.

He propped himself on the sink, and rested again. When he had caught his breath, he automatically ran water and lathered his hands—the first step in his rite of cleansing, a vital part of his defense against a relapse. For a time, he scrubbed his hands without raising his head. But at last he looked into the mirror.

The sight of his own visage stopped him. He gazed at himself out of raw, self-inflicted eyes, and recognized the face that Elena had sculpted. She had not placed a wound on the forehead of her carving, but his cut only completed the image she had formed of him. He could see a gleam of bone through the caked black blood which darkened his forehead and cheeks, spread down around his eyes, emphasizing them, shadowing them with terrible purposes. The wound and the blood on his gray, gaunt face made him look like a false prophet, a traitor to his own best dreams.

Elena! he cried thickly. What have I done?

Unable to bear the sight of himself, he turned away and glanced numbly around the bathroom. In the fluorescent lighting, the porcelain of the tub and the chromed metal of its dangerous fixtures glinted as if they had nothing whatever to do with weeping. Their blank superficiality seemed to insist that grief and loss were unreal, irrelevant.

He stared at them for a long time, measuring their blankness. Then he limped out of the bathroom. Grimly, deliberately, he left his forehead uncleaned, untouched. He did not choose to repudiate the accusation written there.

Glossary

Acence: a Stonedownor, sister of Atiaran
ahamkara: Hoerkin, "the Door"
Ahanna: painter, daughter of Hanna
aliantha: treasure-berries
amanibhavam: horse-healing grass, poisonous to men
Amatin: a Lord, daughter of Matin
Amok: mysterious guide and servant to ancient Lore
Amorine: First Haft, later Hiltmark
anundivian yajña: "lost" Ramen craft of bone-sculpting
Asuraka: Staff-Elder of the Loresraat
Atiaran Trell-mate: a Stonedownor, mother of Lena
aussat Befylam: child-form of the *jheherrin*

Banas Nimoram: the Celebration of Spring
Bann: a Bloodguard, assigned to Lord Trevor
Bannor: a Bloodguard, assigned to Thomas Covenant
Baradakas: a Hirebrand of Soaring Woodhelven
Berek Halfhand: Heartthew, founder of the Line of
    Lords, first of the Old Lords
Bhrathair: a people met by the wandering Giants
Birinair: a Hirebrand; later a Hearthrall of Lord's Keep
Bloodguard: the defenders of the Lords
bone-sculpting: ancient Ramen craft, marrowmeld
Borillar: a Hirebrand and Hearthrall of Lord's Keep
Brabha: a Ranyhyn, Korik's mount

caamora: Giantish ordeal of grief by fire
Caer-Caveral: apprentice Forestal of Morinmoss For-
    est

Caerroil Wildwood: Forestal of Garroting Deep
Callindrill Faer-mate: a Lord
Cavewights: evil creatures existing under Mount Thunder
Celebration of Spring: the Dance of the Wraiths of Andelain on the dark of the moon in the middle night of spring
Cerrin: a Bloodguard, assigned to Lord Shetra
Circle of elders: Stonedown leaders
clingor: adhesive leather
Close, the: council chamber of Lord's Keep
Colossus, the: ancient stone figure guarding the Upper Land
Cord: second Ramen rank
Cording: ceremony of becoming a Cord
Corimini: Eldest of the Loresraat
Corruption: Bloodguard name for Lord Foul
Creator, the: legendary Timelord and Landsire, enemy of Lord Foul
Crowl: a Bloodguard

Damelon Giantfriend: Old High Lord, son of Berek Halfhand
Dance of the Wraiths: Celebration of Spring
Demondim: spawners of ur-viles and Waynhim
Desolation, the: era of ruin in the Land, after the Ritual of Desecration
Despiser, the: Lord Foul
Despite: Power of Evil
dharmakshetra: "to brave the enemy," Waynhim name
diamondraught: Giantish liquor
Doar: a Bloodguard
Drinishok: Sword-Elder of the Loresraat
Drinny: a Ranyhyn, Lord Mhoram's mount, foal of Hynaril
Drool Rockworm: a Cavewight, later leader of the Cavewights, finder of the Staff of Law
dukkha: "victim," Waynhim name
Dura Fairflank: a mustang, Thomas Covenant's mount

Earthfriend: title first given to Berek Halfhand
Earthpower, the: the source of all power in the Land

Elena: High Lord during first attack by Lord Foul; daughter of Lena
Elohim: people met by the wandering Giants
Eoman: twenty warriors plus a Warhaft
Eoward: twenty Eoman plus a Haft

fael Befylam: serpent-form of the *jheherrin*
Faer: mate of Lord Callindrill
Fangthane the Render: Ramen name for Lord Foul
Fire-Lions: fire-flow of Mount Thunder
fire-stones: graveling
First Haft: third-in-command of the Warward
First Mark: the Bloodguard commander
First Ward of Kevin's Lore: primary knowledge left by Lord Kevin
Fleshharrower: a Giant-Raver, Jehannum, *moksha*
Forbidding: a repelling force, a wall of power
Forestal: a protector of the Forests of the Land
Foul's Creche: the Despiser's home
Furl Falls: waterfall at Revelstone
Furl's Fire: warning fire at Revelstone

Gallows Howe: place of execution in Garroting Deep
Garth: Warmark of the Warward of Lord's Keep
Gay: a Winhome of the Ramen
Giantclave: Giantish conference
Giants: the Unhomed, ancient friends of the Lords
Gilden: a maplelike tree with golden leaves
Gildenlode: a power-wood formed from Gilden trees
Glimmermere: a lake on the upland above Revelstone
Gorak Krembal: Hotash Slay
Grace: a Cord of the Ramen
graveling: fire-stones, made to glow by stone-lore
Gravelingas: a master of stone-lore
Gravin Threndor: Mount Thunder
Gray Slayer: plains name for Lord Foul
Grieve, The: *Coerci,* Giant city
griffin: lionlike beast with wings

Haft: commander of an Eoward
Haruchai, the: original race of the Bloodguard
Healer: a physician

Hearthrall of Lord's Keep: a steward responsible for light, warmth, and hospitality
Heart of Thunder: cave of power in Mount Thunder
Heartthew: Berek Halfhand
heartwood chamber: Woodhelven meeting place
Heer: leader of a Woodhelven
Herem: a Raver, Kinslaughterer, *turiya*
High Lord: leader of the Council of Lords
High Lord's Furl: banner of the High Lord
High Wood: *lomillialor,* offspring of the One Tree
Hile Troy: Warmark of High Lord Elena's Warward
Hiltmark: second-in-command of the Warward
Hirebrand: a master of wood-lore
Hoerkin: a Warhaft
Home: original homeland of the Giants
Howor: a Bloodguard, assigned to Lord Loerya
Hurn: a Cord of the Ramen
hurtloam: a healing mud
Huryn: a Ranyhyn, Terrel's mount
Hynaril: a Ranyhyn, mount of Tamarantha and Mhoram
Hyrim: a Lord, son of Hoole

Illearth Stone: stone found under Mount Thunder, source of evil power
Imoiran Tomal-mate: a Stonedownor
Irin: a warrior of the Third Eoman of the Warward

Jain: a Manethrall of the Ramen
Jehannum: a Raver, Fleshharrower, *moksha*
jheherrin: soft ones, living by-products of Foul's misshaping

Kam: a Manethrall of the Ramen
Kelenbhrabanal: Father of Horses in Ranyhyn legends
Kevin Landwaster: son of Loric Vilesilencer, last High Lord of the Old Lords
Kevin's Lore: knowledge of power left by Kevin in the Seven Wards
Kinslaughterer: a Giant-Raver, Herem, *turiya*
Kiril Threndor: chamber of power deep under Mount Thunder, Heart of Thunder

Koral: a Bloodguard, assigned to Lord Amatin

Korik: a Bloodguard, a commander of the original *Haruchai* army

kresh: savage, giant, yellow wolves

krill, **the:** enchanted sword of Loric, a mystery to the New Lords, wakened to power by Thomas Covenant

Kurash Plenethor: region once called Stricken Stone and later Trothgard

Kurash Qwellinir: the Shattered Hills

Lal: a Cord of the Ramen

Land, the: generally, area found on the Map

Law of Death, the: the separation of the living and the dead

Lena: a Stonedownor, daughter of Atiaran and Trell; mother of Elena

Lifeswallower: the Great Swamp

lillianrill: wood-lore, or masters of wood-lore

Lithe: a Manethrall of the Ramen

Llaura: Heer of Soaring Woodhelven

Loerya Trevor-mate: a Lord

lomillialor: High Wood, a wood of power

Lord: master of the Sword and Staff parts of Kevin's Lore

Lord-Fatherer: Berek Halfhand

Lord Foul: the enemy of the Land

"Lord Mhoram's Victory": a painting by Ahanna

Lords-fire: staff fire used by the Lords

Lord's Keep: Revelstone

loremaster: ur-vile leader

Loresraat: Trothgard school at Revelwood where Kevin's Lore is studied

Lorewarden: teacher at the Loresraat

loreworks: Demondim power laboratory

Loric Vilesilencer: Old High Lord, son of Damelon Giantfriend

lor-liarill: Gildenlode

Lower Land, the: land east of Landsdrop

Maker, the: *jheherrin* name for Lord Foul

Maker-place: Foul's Creche

Malliner: Woodhelven Heer, son of Veinnin
Mane: a Ranyhyn
Maneing: ceremony of becoming a Manethrall
Manethrall: highest Ramen rank
Manhome: main dwelling place of the Ramen
Marny: a Ranyhyn, Tuvor's mount
marrowmeld: bone-sculpting
Mehryl: a Ranyhyn, Hile Troy's mount
Melenkurion abatha: phrase of invocation or power
Mhoram: a Lord, later High Lord, son of Variol
moksha: a Raver, Jehannum, Fleshharrower
Morin: First Mark of the Bloodguard, commander in
    original *Haruchai* army
Morril: a Bloodguard, assigned to Lord Callindrill
Murrin Odona-mate: a Stonedownor
Myrha: a Ranyhyn, Elena's mount

Oath of Peace: oath by the people of the Land against
    needless violence
Odona Murrin-mate: a Stonedownor
Old Lords: Lords prior to the Ritual of Desecration
Omournil: Woodhelven Heer, daughter of Mournil
One Forest, the: ancient forest which covered most of
    the Land
One Tree, the: mystic tree from which the Staff of Law
    was made
orcrest: a stone of power
Osondrea: a Lord, later High Lord, daughter of
    Sondrea

Padrias: Woodhelven Heer, son of Mill
Peak of the Fire-Lions: Mount Thunder
Pietten: Woodhelven child damaged by Lord Foul's
    minions, son of Soranal
Porib: a Bloodguard
Power of Command: Seventh Ward of Kevin's Lore
Pren: a Bloodguard
Prothall: High Lord, son of Dwillian
Puhl: a Cord of the Ramen

Quaan: Warhaft of the Third Eoman of the Warward,
    later Hiltmark, then Warmark

Quest, the: the search to rescue the Staff of Law
Quirrel: a Stonedownor, companion of Triock

Ramen: people who serve the Ranyhyn
Ranyhyn: the great, free horses of the Plains of Ra
Ravers: Lord Foul's three ancient servants
Revelstone: Lord's Keep, mountain city of the Lords
Revelwood: seat of the Loresraat
rhadhamaerl: stone-lore or masters of stone-lore
Ridjeck Thome: Foul's Creche
rillinlure: healing wood dust
Ringthane: Ramen name for Thomas Covenant
Rites of Unfettering: the ceremony of becoming Un-
    fettered
Ritual of Desecration: act of despair by which High
    Lord Kevin destroyed the Old Lords and ruined
    most of the Land
Rockbrother, Rocksister: terms of affection between
    men and Giants
roge Befylam: Cavewight-form of the *jheherrin*
Rue: a Manethrall, formerly named Gay
Ruel: a Bloodguard, assigned to Hile Troy
Runnik: a Bloodguard
Rustah: a Cord of the Ramen

sacred enclosure: Vespers hall at Revelstone
Saltheart Foamfollower: a Giant, friend of Thomas
    Covenant
samadhi: a Raver, Sheol, Satansfist
Sandgorgons: monsters described by the Giants
Satansfist: a Giant-Raver, Sheol, *samadhi*
Satansheart Soulcrusher: Giantish name for Lord Foul
Seven Wards, the: collection of knowledge left by Lord
    Kevin
Seven Words, the: power-words
Sheol: a Raver, Satansfist, *samadhi*
Shetra Verement-mate: a Lord
Shull: a Bloodguard
Sill: a Bloodguard, assigned to Lord Hyrim
Slen Terass-mate: a Stonedownor
Soranal: Woodhelven Heer, son of Thiller
Soulcrusher: Giantish name for Lord Foul

Sparlimb Keelsetter: a Giant, father of triplets
springwine: a mild, refreshing liquor
Staff, the: a branch of Kevin's Lore studied at the Loresraat
Staff of Law, the: formed by Berek from the One Tree
Stonedown: a stone-village
Stonedownor: one who lives in a stone-village
Stricken Stone: region of Trothgard before renovation
suru-pa-maerl: a stone craft
Sword, the: a branch of Kevin's Lore studied at the Loresraat
Sword-Elder: chief Lorewarden of the Sword at the Loresraat

Tamarantha Variol-mate: a Lord, daughter of Enesta
Terass Slen-mate: an elder of Mithil Stonedown, daughter of Annoria
Terrel: a Bloodguard, assigned to Lord Mhoram, a commander of the original *Haruchai* army
test of truth, the: test of veracity by *lomillialor* or *orcrest*
Thew: a Cord of the Ramen
Thomin: a Bloodguard, assigned to Lord Verement
Tohrm: a Gravelingas and Hearthrall of Lord's Keep
Tomal: a Stonedownor craftmaster
treasure-berries: *aliantha,* nourishing fruit found throughout the Land
Trell Atiaran-mate: Gravelingas of Mithil Stonedown, father of Lena
Trevor Loerya-mate: a Lord
Triock: a Stonedownor, son of Thuler
Tull: a Bloodguard
turiya: a Raver, Herem, Kinslaughterer
Tuvor: First Mark of the Bloodguard, a commander of the original *Haruchai* army

Unbeliever, the: Thomas Covenant
Unfettered, the: lore-students freed from conventional responsibilities
Unhomed, the: the Giants
upland: plateau above Revelstone

Upper Land: land west of Landsdrop
ur-Lord: title given to Thomas Covenant
ur-viles: Demondim-spawn, evil creatures of power

Vailant: former High Lord
Vale: a Bloodguard
Valley of Two Rivers: site of Revelwood
Variol Farseer Tamarantha-mate: a Lord, later High Lord, son of Pentil, father of Mhoram
Verement Shetra-mate: a Lord
viancome: meeting place at Revelwood
Viles: sires of the Demondim
Vow, the: Bloodguard oath of service to the Lords

Ward: a unit of Kevin's Lore
Warhaft: commander of an Eoman
Warlore: "Sword" knowledge in Kevin's Lore
Warmark: commander of the Warward
Warrenbridge: entrance to the catacombs under Mount Thunder
Warward, the: army of Lord's Keep
Wavenhair Haleall: a Giant, wife of Sparlimb Keelsetter, mother of triplets
Waynhim: tenders of the Waymeets, Demondim-spawn but opponents of the ur-viles
Whane: a Cord of the Ramen
Wightwarren: home of the Cavewights under Mount Thunder
Winhome: lowest Ramen rank
Woodhelven: wood-village
Woodhelvennin: inhabitants of a wood-village
Word of Warning: a powerful, destructive forbidding
Wraiths of Andelain: creatures of living light that perform the Dance at the Celebration of Spring

Yeurquin: a Stonedownor, companion of Triock
Yolenid: daughter of Loerya

About the Author

Born in 1947 in Cleveland, Ohio, **Stephen R. Donaldson**
makes his publishing debut with The Covenant Trilogy.
From ages three to sixteen, he lived in India, where his
father, an orthopedic surgeon, worked extensively with
lepers. (It was after hearing one of his father's speeches
on the subject of leprosy that he conceived the character
of Thomas Covenant as protagonist for an epic fantasy.)
He graduated from the College of Wooster (Ohio) in 1968,
served two years as a conscientious objector doing hospital
work in Akron, then attended Kent State University,
where he received his M.A. in English in 1971. He now
lives in Albuquerque, New Mexico.